THOMAS MANN

Doctor Faustus

TRANSLATED FROM THE GERMAN
BY JOHN E. WOODS

Alfred A. Knopf   New York   1997

THIS IS A BORZOI BOOK
PUBLISHED BY ALFRED A. KNOPF, INC.

Copyright © 1997 by Alfred A. Knopf, Inc.
All rights reserved under International and Pan-American
Copyright Conventions. Published in the United States by
Alfred A. Knopf, Inc., New York, and simultaneo
Canada by Random House of Canada Limited.
Distributed by Random House, Inc., I

http://www.random

Originally published in German by Bermann-Fischer Ve
Stoc
Copyright © 1947 by Thoma

Library of Congress Cataloging-in-Public
Mann, Thomas,
[Doktor Faust
Doctor Faustus : the life of the German comp
Leverkühn as told by a friend / by Thomas Mann ; t
by John E. Woods.—1st
p.   cm.
ISBN 0-375-40054-0
1. Germany—History—1789–1900—Fiction.
2. Germany—History—20th century—Fiction.
I. Woods, John E. (John Edwin)   II. Title
PT2625.A44D63   1997
833'.912—dc21   97-2818   CIP

Manufactured in the United States of America
First Edition

Frontispiece: Thomas Mann, 1944, by E. E. Gottlieb,
courtesy of S. Fischer Verlag GmbH

DOCTOR FAUSTUS

*The Life
of the
German Composer
Adrian Leverkühn
As Told
by a Friend*

DOCTOR FAUSTUS

ALSO BY THOMAS MANN

Buddenbrooks

The Magic Mountain

Death in Venice and Seven Other Stories

Joseph and His Brothers

The Transposed Heads

Lo giorno se n'andava, e l'aer bruno
toglieva gli animai che sono in terra
dalle fatiche loro, ed io sol uno
m'apparechiava a sostener la guerra
sì del cammino e sì della pietate,
che ritrarrà la mente che non erra.
O Muse, o alto ingegno, or m'aiutate,
o mente che scrivesti ciò ch'io vidi,
qui si parrà la tua nobilitate.

Dante, *Inferno*, Canto II

I

WITH UTMOST EMPHASIS I wish to assert that it is not out of any desire to thrust my own person into the foreground that I offer a few words about myself and my circumstances in preface to this account of the life of the late Adrian Leverkühn, to this first and certainly very provisional biography of a musical genius, a revered man sorely tried by fate, which both raised him up and cast him down. I offer such words solely under the presumption that the reader—or better, future reader, since at the moment there is still not the slightest prospect that my manuscript will ever see the light of public day, unless, that is, by some miracle it were to leave our beleaguered Fortress Europe and share the whispered secrets of our isolation with those outside—but, please, allow me to begin anew: Only because I assume that someone might wish in passing to be informed as to who and what the writer is, do I preface these disclosures with a few remarks concerning my person, though not without real apprehension that in so doing I may move the reader to doubt whether he finds himself in the right hands, which is to say: whether, given all that I am, I am the right man for a task to which I am drawn more by my heart, perhaps, than by any legitimizing affinity.

Reading back over these preceding lines, I cannot help noticing a certain uneasiness, a labored breathing, only too characteristic of the state of mind in which I find myself here today (in Freising on the Isar, on 23 May 1943, two years after Leverkühn's death, which is to say, two years since he passed from the depth of night into deepest night), as I sit down in my little study of so many years to commence my description of the life of my unfortunate friend, resting now (oh, may it be so!) with God—characteristic, I say, of a state of mind that is the most onerous combination of a heart-pounding need to speak and a deep reticence before my own inadequacy.

I am a thoroughly even-tempered man, indeed, if I may say so, a healthy, humanely tempered man with a mind given to things harmonious and reasonable, a scholar and *conjuratus* of the "Latin host," not without ties to the fine arts (I play the viola d'amore), but a son of the muses in the academic sense of the term, who gladly regards himself a descendant of the German humanists associated with *Letters of the Obscure Men,* an heir to Reuchlin, Crotus of Dornheim, Mutianus, and Eoban Hesse. Though scarcely presuming to deny the influence of the demonic on human life, I have always found it a force totally foreign to my nature and have instinctively excluded it from my worldview, having never felt the slightest inclination boldly to seek out the intimacy of those nether powers, or worse, wantonly to challenge them, or to give them so much as my little finger when they have approached me with temptation. This attitude has meant sacrifices, both in ideal terms and as regards my physical wellbeing, for once it became apparent that my views could not be reconciled with the spirit and claims of our historical developments, I did not hesitate prematurely to retire from the teaching profession I loved. In that respect, I am at peace with myself. But this same firmness or, if you like, narrowness of my ethical position can only reinforce my doubts as to whether I ought truly to feel called to the task I have taken on.

I had barely put my pen to paper when a word flowed from it that is already the source of some personal discomfiture: the word "genius," I spoke of my late friend's musical genius. Now the word "genius," though in some sense extravagant, nonetheless has a noble, harmonious, and humanely healthy character and ring, and someone such as myself—to the extent that he makes no claim that his own person has any share in that exalted region or has ever been graced with *divinis influxibus ex alto*—should see no reasonable argument for shying from it, no point in not speaking of it and dealing with it, while casting a cordial upward glance of reverent familiarity. So it seems. And yet it cannot be, nor has it ever been denied that the demonic and irrational have a disquieting share in that radiant sphere, that there is always a faint, sinister connection between it and the nether world, and for that very reason those reassuring epithets I sought to attribute to genius—"noble," "humanely healthy," and "harmonious"—do not quite fit, not even when (and it is rather painful for me to make this distinction) not even when it is a matter of a pure and authentic genius, bestowed or perhaps inflicted by God, rather than an acquired and destructive genius, a sinful and morbid necrosis of natural talents, the fruition of some horrible pact. . . .

Here I break off, stung by the humiliation of my own artistic inadequacies and lack of control. Adrian himself would surely never—in, let us say, a symphony—have announced such a theme so prematurely, would at most have let it insinuate itself from afar in some subtly concealed and almost impalpable fashion. Though, for that matter, what I have let slip may strike the reader as merely an obscure, dubious allusion, and only I see myself as having indiscreetly and clumsily blurted everything out at once. For a person like myself, when dealing with a subject as dear to the heart, as searingly urgent as this, it is very difficult, indeed it verges on impudence, to assume the standpoint of the composer and to treat the matter with an artist's playful equanimity. Which was the reason for my overhasty differentiation between pure and impure genius, a distinction whose existence I acknowledge, only immediately to ask if it has a right to exist. Indeed experience has forced me to ponder that question so intensely, so earnestly, that at times I have been frightened by the notion that in so doing I am being carried beyond an appropriate and wholesome level of thought and am myself experiencing an "impure" enhancement of my natural talents. . . .

And I break off anew, because I now recall that I broached the topic of genius and what is surely the influence of the demonic upon it solely to illustrate my doubts as to whether I possess the necessary affinity for my task. And so may whatever I now bring to account against my scruples of conscience serve to offset them. It was my lot in life to spend many years in intimate proximity with a man of genius, the hero of these pages, to know him from childhood on, to witness his growth, and his fate, and to play a modest supporting role in his work. The libretto adapted from Shakespeare's comedy *Love's Labour's Lost*, Leverkühn's mischievous youthful composition, comes from me; I was also permitted some influence on the preparation of the texts for both the grotesque opera suite *Gesta Romanorum* and the oratorio *The Revelation of St. John the Divine*. That is one factor, or perhaps several. I am, moreover, in possession of papers, of priceless manuscripts, which the deceased bequeathed to me, and to no one else, in a will written during a period of health or, if I may not put it that way, during a period of comparative and legal sanity, papers I shall use to document my presentation—indeed, I plan to select certain of them for direct inclusion in it. But firstly and lastly, and this justification has always carried the greatest validity, if not before man, then before God: I loved him—with terror and tenderness, with indulgence and doting admiration, seldom asking whether he in any way returned my feelings.

Which he did not, oh no. In the testamentary document transferring his compositional sketches and journals, one finds expression of a friendly, businesslike, I might almost say, a gracious trust in my conscientiousness, fidelity, and rectitude that certainly does me honor. But love? Whom could this man have loved? A woman at one time—perhaps. A child toward the end—that may be. And a lightweight dandy, a winner of every heart in every season, whom, presumably just because he was fond of him, Adrian sent away—to his death. To whom might he have opened his heart, whom would he ever have let into his life? That was not Adrian's way. He accepted others' devotion—I could almost swear often without even realizing it. His indifference was so vast that he hardly ever noticed what was happening around him, in whose company he might be, and the fact that he very rarely addressed by name the person with whom he was speaking leads me to believe that he did not know it, though the addressee had every right to assume so. I might compare his isolation to an abyss into which the feelings others expressed for him vanished soundlessly without a trace. All around him lay coldness—and what an odd sensation it is to use the very word that he himself once recorded in a horrendous context! Life and experience can lend individual words a certain accent that estranges them entirely from their everyday meaning and lends them an aura of dread that no one who has not met them in their most horrifying context can ever understand.

MY NAME IS Dr. Serenus Zeitblom, Ph.D. I am unhappy myself with this odd delay in the presentation of my calling card, but as things turned out, the literary current of my disclosures constantly held me back until this moment. I am sixty years of age, having been born in A.D. 1883, the eldest of four children, in Kaisersaschern on the Saale, district of Merseburg, the same town in which Leverkühn also spent his school days—which means I can postpone a detailed characterization of them until the appropriate time. Since the course of my own life is interlaced at many points with that of the *meister,* it will be best if I recount both lives jointly and thus avoid the error of getting ahead of my story, which one is always inclined to do when one's heart is full.

For now, let it suffice to say that I was born into a modest, semiprofessional, middle-class world; my father, Wolgemut Zeitblom, was a druggist—the more important of the two in town, by the way, since the other pharmacy had trouble holding its own and never enjoyed the same public trust shown Blessed Messengers, as the Zeitblom establishment was called. Our family belonged to the town's small Catholic parish, whereas the majority of the population, of course, was of the Lutheran persuasion; and my mother in particular was a pious daughter of the Church and conscientiously discharged her religious obligations, whereas my father, presumably for want of time, was laxer in such matters, though he never disavowed the sort of open solidarity with his fellow believers that carried a certain political impact. Remarkably enough, both our pastor, the Reverend Rector Zwilling and the town's rabbi, Dr. Carlebach by name, were occasional guests in our parlor above the shop and laboratory, something that could not easily have occurred in Protestant homes. The man of the Roman church was the better looking of the two. But my abiding impression, primarily based on my father's remarks perhaps, is that the short man of the Talmud, with his long beard and decorative skullcap, far exceeded his colleague of the other creed in erudition and religious subtlety. It may be due to that youthful experience, but also to the keen-eared receptivity of Jewish circles for Leverkühn's work, that I was never able to agree fully with our Führer and his paladins on precisely the issue of the Jews and their treatment—nor did that fact fail to have an influence on my resignation from the teaching profession. To be sure, my path has also been crossed by other specimens of the race, and here I need only think of Breisacher, an independent scholar in Munich—on whose bafflingly unsympathetic character I hope to shed some light in the appropriate place.

As for my Catholic background, most assuredly it molded and influenced my inner self; which is not to say, however, that from that tonality of life there could ever arise any dissonance with my humanistic worldview, with my love for "the finest arts and sciences," as people used to say. Between these two elements of my personality there has always reigned a perfect accord, which is probably not difficult to maintain if one grew up, as I did, in the setting of an old town where memories and monuments extend back to pre-schismatic days, to a world of Christian unity. Kaisersaschern lies, to be sure, in the middle of the homeland of the Reformation, in the heart of Luther country, with which one associates names of towns like Eisleben, Wittenberg, Quedlinburg, but also Grimma, Wolfenbüttel, and Eisenach—which, in turn, helps explain the inner life of Leverkühn, the Lutheran, and also ties into his original course of study, theology. But I like to compare the Reformation to a bridge that leads not only out of the scholastic period into our world of freer thinking, but at the same time deep into the Middle Ages as well—perhaps even deeper than the Catholic Christian tradition of calm devotion to learning that was left untouched by the break-up of the Church. For my part I feel very much at home in that golden sphere where the Holy Virgin was called *"Jovis alma parens."*

As for further mandatory items in my vita, I can record that my parents made it possible for me to attend our local secondary school—the same one where, two grades below me, Adrian received his lessons—which had been founded in the second half of the fifteenth century and had, until only shortly before, borne the name School of the Brethren of the Common Life. That name was discarded merely out of a certain embarrassment at its sounding both excessively historical and rather odd to modern ears, and the school now called itself St. Boniface Gymnasium, after the nearby church. Upon graduation at the beginning of the current century, I turned without hesitation to the study of classical languages, in which even as a high-school pupil I had excelled to some extent and to which I devoted myself at the Universities of Giessen, Jena, Leipzig, and, between 1904 and 1905, Halle—at the same time, then, and not by mere chance, that Leverkühn was a student there.

And here in passing, as so often, I cannot help savoring that inner and almost mysterious bond between my interest in classical philology and a lively and loving eye for man's beauty and the dignity of his reason—a bond made manifest in the very name we give the study of ancient languages, the "humanities," whereby the psychological connection between linguistic and human passion is crowned by the idea of pedagogy, so that the call to be an educator of the young proceeds almost as a matter of course from one's vocation as a scholar of language. The man of the exact sciences can, of course, become a teacher, but never a pedagogue in the sense and to the degree that the disciple of *bonae litterae* can. And it seems to me that that other, perhaps even more internal and yet strangely inarticulate language, the language of tones (if one may call music that) cannot be included, either, in the pedagogic, humanistic sphere, though I am well aware that music played an ancillary role in Greek education and in the public life of the *polis* generally. It seems to me, however, that despite the logical, moral rigor music may appear to display, it belongs to a world of spirits, for whose absolute reliability in matters of human reason and dignity I would not exactly want to put my hand in the fire. That I am nevertheless devoted to it with all my heart is one of those contradictions which, whether a cause for joy or regret, are inseparable from human nature.

All this as an aside to my topic. Or again, not, since the question of whether one can draw a clear and secure line between the noble, pedagogical world of the human spirit and a world of spirits approached at one's own peril is very much, indeed all too much, part of my topic. What sphere of human life, be it the most sterling and worthily benevolent, can ever be totally inaccessible to the influence of forces from below—indeed, one must add, free of any need to come into fruitful contact with them? This latter thought, which is not improper even for someone who personally finds all things demonic quite alien, has stayed with me from certain moments of a trip to Italy and Greece, where, after passing my state exams, I spent almost a year and a half on a study tour made possible by my good parents. As I gazed out from the Acropolis across to the Sacred Way, along which initiates to the mysteries had processed—adorned with the saffron band, the name of Iacchus on their lips—and then, upon arriving at the place of initiation itself, as I stood in the enclosure of Eubouleus under the overhanging rocks beside the cleft of Pluto, there and then I sensed something of the abundant feeling for life that found expression in the initiatory rites by which Olympic Greece honored the divinities of the deep; and later, behind my lectern, I often explained to my senior students how culture is actually the reverent, orderly, I may even say, propitiatory inclusion of the nocturnal and monstrous in the cult of the gods.

At age twenty-six, upon returning home from that trip, I found employment at a secondary school of my hometown, the same school where I had received my educational training, and where for several years I provided elementary instruction in Latin and Greek, as well as some history—until, that is, in the fourteenth year of the century, I transferred to Freising in Bavaria, my permanent residence ever since, where for over two decades I had the satisfaction of teaching those same subjects as a professor at the local high school, and also as an instructor at the theological seminary.

Very early on, indeed soon after my appointment in Kaisersaschern, I became engaged to be married—a need for order in my life and a desire to conform to ethical standards led me to take this step. Helene, née Ölhafen, my splendid wife, who even now in my declining years still looks after me, was the daughter of an older classicist colleague in Zwickau in the Kingdom of Saxony, and at the risk of bringing a smile to the reader's face, I will admit that the glowing young lady's first name, Helene—such precious syllables—played a not insignificant role in my choice as well. Such a name implies a consecration, the pure magic of which is not to be denied, even should the appearance of her who bears it satisfy its lofty claims only in a modest, middle-class fashion—and then only fleetingly, for the charms of youth are quick to fade. We likewise gave the name Helene to our daughter, who long ago wed a fine man, the manager of the Regensburg branch of the Bavarian Security and Exchange. In addition to her, my dear wife has given me two sons, so that I have experienced all due joys and worries of fatherhood, if within modest limits. There was never, I will admit, a bewitching charm about any of my children. They were no competition for the childhood beauty of little Nepomuk Schneidewein, Adrian's nephew and the apple of his eye late in life—I would be the last person to claim that. Both my sons now serve their Führer, one as a civil servant, the other in the armed forces, and just as my estrangement from my nation's authorities has left a certain void around me, so, too, one can only describe the ties of these young men to their quiet parental home as loose.

III

THE LEVERKÜHNS CAME from a stock of better-off craftsmen and farmers who flourished partly in and around Schmalkald, partly along the Saale River in provincial Saxony. Adrian's immediate family had settled several generations before at Buchel, a farmstead attached to the village of Oberweiler not far from Weissenfels—a forty-five minute train ride from Kaisersaschern—where a wagon met you at the station, but only by prearrangement. Buchel was large enough to lend its owner the title of freeholder or yeoman and comprised a good eighty acres of fields and meadows, a share in some cooperatively managed woodland, and a very comfortable timberwork house set on a stone foundation. Together with its barns and stalls it formed an open square, in the middle of which stood a massive old linden tree enclosed at its base by a green wooden bench and covered in June with marvelously fragrant blossoms. This beautiful tree, fixed forever in my memory, was somewhat in the way of the wagons maneuvering in the courtyard, I suppose, and I have heard that as a young man each heir would argue with his father that common sense required its removal, only later, then, as owner of the farm, to defend the tree against the same demands from his own son.

How often must that linden tree have lent its shade to the childhood games and naps of little Adrian; and it was in full bloom when, in 1885, he was born upstairs at Buchel, the second son of Jonathan and Elsbeth Leverkühn. His brother, Georg, who surely runs the farm up there nowadays, was his senior by five years. A sister, Ursel, followed later at the same interval. Since my parents were in the Leverkühn's circle of

friends and acquaintances in Kaisersaschern (indeed the two families
had been on especially cordial terms for years), in seasons of good
weather we spent many a Sunday afternoon at the farm, where as city
dwellers we gratefully partook of the hearty country fare with which
Frau Leverkühn regaled us: robust brown bread and sweet butter,
golden honey in the comb, luscious strawberries in cream, curdled
milk served in blue bowls and strewn with dark bread crumbs and
sugar. In the days when Adrian—or Adri as they called him—was still
very young, his retired grandparents lived there as well, although the
farm was completely in the hands of the younger generation and the
old man's only contribution (listened to with respect, by the by) came
at the supper table, where he would sit grumbling toothlessly. I have
few memories of those forebears, who soon died, both at about the
same time. All the more clearly, then, can I see their children, Jonathan
and Elsbeth Leverkühn, though in the course of my boyhood, high-
school, and student years their image shifted and changed, gliding,
with that efficient imperceptibility time manages so well, from youthful adulthood to wearier phases.

Jonathan Leverkühn was a man of finest German stamp, the kind
one scarcely ever sees now in our cities and certainly not one of those
who, with what is often overbearing bluster, represent our version of
the human race nowadays—a physiognomy somehow marked by the
past, preserved out in the country, so to speak, and brought in from a
Germany predating the Thirty Years' War. That was my notion of him,
when as an adolescent I came to view him with at least semi-educated
eyes. Ash-blond hair in need of a comb fell over the prominent brow—
dividing it neatly into two halves, each with a swollen vein at the temple—hung unfashionably long, thick, and ragged over the nape of the
neck, and merged beside the small, well-formed ears into a curly blond
beard that covered cheeks, chin, and the hollow below the lip. From
beneath the short, slightly drooping moustache, the lower lip jutted
out in a rather bold curve to form a smile of extraordinary charm,
which nicely matched rather intense but nonetheless half-smiling blue
eyes wrapt in gentle shyness. The bridge of the nose was thin, its curve
delicate; the cheeks above the beard were set back in the shadow of the
cheekbones and seemed even a bit gaunt. He left his sinewy throat exposed and was no friend of standard city attire, which did not do anything for his looks, and especially not for his hands—a strong, tanned,
parched, and lightly freckled hand whose grip completely covered the
head of his cane whenever he set out for a council meeting in the village.

A physician might have read a certain veiled tension in the eyes, a

certain sensitivity about the temples, as a tendency to migraine headaches, to which Jonathan indeed was susceptible, but only moderately,
no more than once a month and just for a day, with almost no interruption in work. He loved his pipe, a half-length porcelain affair with
a lid and a distinctive tobacco odor that hung in the air of the downstairs rooms and was far more pleasant than stale cigar or cigarette
smoke. He loved to smoke it with a good jug of Merseburg beer as a
nightcap. On winter evenings, when his land and legacy lay beneath
snow outside, you would see him reading, usually a mammoth family
Bible bound in smooth pigskin and secured with leather clasps, which
had been printed around 1700 under license of the Duke of Braunschweig and not only included the "wise and spiritual" prefaces and
marginal notes of Dr. Martin Luther, but also all kinds of compendia,
locos parallelos, and a historical-moral poem by one Herr David von
Schweinitz explaining each chapter. A legend came with the book, or
better, a specific claim had been handed down with it, that it had belonged to the Princess of Braunschweig-Wolfenbüttel who had married the son of Peter the Great. Later then, she had faked her own
death, even arranged her own burial, whereas in reality she had fled to
Martinique and married a Frenchman there. And how often Adrian,
with his thirst for the comic, would later laugh with me at this tale and
at how his father would raise gentle, deep eyes from the book to tell it,
and then, apparently quite undisturbed by the somewhat scandalous
provenance of his Holy Writ, return to Herr von Schweinitz's verse
commentaries or the "Wisdom of Solomon to the Tyrants."

Parallel to this spiritual bias in his reading, however, was another
trend that in certain ages might have been characterized as a desire to
"speculate the elements." That is, on a modest scale and with modest
means, he pursued studies in the natural sciences—biology, and even
chemistry and physics, too, with occasional assistance from my father,
who would provide items from his laboratory. I chose an obsolete
and not unprejudicial term for such endeavors, however, because there
was evident in them a certain trace of mysticism, which at one time
would have been suspect as an interest in sorcery. I wish to add, moreover, that I have always completely understood this mistrust felt by
an epoch of religious spirituality toward any nascent passion to explore the secrets of nature. Those who fear God must regard that
passion as a libertine intimacy with what is forbidden—despite any
contradiction some might find in a view that sees God's creation,
nature and life itself, as morally murky territory. On her own, nature
produces such a plethora of things that have a puzzling way of spilling

over into the realm of magic—ambiguous moods, half-concealed allusions that insinuate some eerie uncertainty—that a piety of self-
imposed decency could not help seeing any association with such
things as a bold transgression.

There were many times of an evening when Adrian's father would
open his books with colorful illustrations of exotic moths and sea creatures, and we all—his sons and I, and on occasion Frau Leverkühn as
well—would gather to gaze from over the back of his leather wing
chair; and he would point with his forefinger at the splendors and oddities pictured there: the papilios and morphos of the tropics, flitting
along, somber and radiant, in all the colors of the palette, configured
and patterned with the most exquisite taste any artisan could ever in-
vent—insects that in their fantastically exaggerated beauty eke out an
ephemeral life and some of which native peoples consider to be evil
spirits that bear malaria. The most glorious hue that they flaunted, an
azure of dreamlike beauty, was, so Jonathan explained, not a real or
genuine color, but was produced by delicate grooves and other variations on the scaly surface of their wings, a device in miniature that
could exclude most of the light rays and bend others so that only the
most radiant blue light reached our eyes.

"Look at that," I can still hear Frau Leverkühn say, "so it's a sham?"

"Do you call the blue of the sky a sham?" her husband replied, leaning back to look up at her. "You can't tell me what pigment produces
it, either."

And indeed, as I write this, it is as if I were standing with Frau Elsbeth, with Georg and Adrian behind their father's chair, and following
his finger across those images. There were illustrated clearwings with
no scales on their wings, which resemble delicate glass threaded with a
net of darker veins. One such butterfly, whose transparent nakedness
makes it a lover of dusky, leafy shade, is called *Hetaera esmeralda,* its
wings smudged with just a dark splash of violet and pink, so that in
flight, with nothing else visible, it imitates a windblown petal. There
was also the leaf butterfly, whose wings flaunt a triad of vivid color
above, but whose underside counterfeits a leaf with bizarre precision,
not just in shape and veining, but also by duplicating little impurities—
mimicked water drops, warty fungal growths, and such. When this
cunning creature lands amid foliage and folds up its wings, it vanishes,
so totally assimilated to its environment that even its most voracious
enemy cannot make it out.

Jonathan shared with some success his own enthusiasm for a defensive mimicry shrewd enough to include flaws of detail. "How did the

animal manage it?" he might ask. "How does nature accomplish it through the animal? For it is impossible to ascribe the trick to the animal's calculated observation. Yes, yes, nature knows her leaf precisely, not just in its perfection, but with all its little everyday blemishes and defects, and she obligingly, mischievously repeats its external appearance in another realm, on the underside of the wings of this butterfly of hers, in order to delude her other creatures. But why give a devious advantage to this one in particular? And though, to be sure, it serves the butterfly's purpose when at rest to resemble a leaf to a T, what is that purpose from the viewpoint of its hungry pursuers—the lizards, birds, and spiders that are supposed to feed on it, but, whenever it likes, cannot make it out no matter how keen an eye they have? I'm asking you why so that you don't ask me."

And if this butterfly could become invisible to defend itself, you needed only to page ahead in the book to make the acquaintance of those that achieved the same results by being as conspicuously, indeed gaudily, sweepingly visible as possible. They were not only especially large, but also colored and patterned in splendid flamboyance, and as Father Leverkühn noted, they flew in their seemingly defiant garb at an ostentatiously leisurely pace—not that anyone might call them brazen, for there was something mournful about how they moved along, never trying to hide, and yet without a single animal—be it ape, bird, or lizard—ever casting them a glance. Why? Because they tasted disgusting. And because their striking beauty, and the slowness of their flight, advertised that fact. Their juices had such a repulsive odor and taste that if a predator erred and mistakenly attacked in hopes of a fine meal, it immediately spat the morsel out again with every sign of nausea. Their inedibility is known throughout the natural world, however, and they are secure—sadly secure. We at least, there behind Jonathan's chair, asked ourselves if there could be happiness in such security, or if there was not something rather dishonorable about it. And what was the result? Other species of butterflies trickily decked themselves out in the same ominous gaudy attire and then floated along in that same slow flight, untouchably secure and mournful, despite their edibility.

Such information would make Adrian laugh till he literally shook and tears came to his eyes, and his amusement was catching, so that I, too, had to laugh heartily. But Father Leverkühn would reprimand us with a "Hush!" because he believed all these things should be regarded with meek reverence—the same dark reverence, for instance, with which he regarded the indecipherable hieroglyphics on the shells of certain mussels, usually with the aid of a large, square magnifying glass, which he would then let us use as well. To be sure, these creatures, the marine snails and shellfish, were likewise an extraordinary sight, at least when you paged through illustrations of them under Jonathan's tutelage. To think that all those spirals and vaults (each executed with such marvelous self-assurance, the elegance of form as bold as it was delicate) with their pinkish entryways, their splendid, iridescent glazes, their multiform chambers, were the work of their own gelatinous inhabitants—at least if one held to the notion that nature does her own work and did not call upon the Creator, for there is something so strange about imagining Him as the inventive craftsman and ambitious artist of this glazed pottery that one is never more tempted than here to interpose a supervisory divinity, the Demiurge— I was about to say: to imagine these exquisite dwellings as the product of the mollusks they defend, that was the most astonishing thought.

"You," Jonathan said to us, "have a rigid structure that was formed inside you as you grew—as you can easily prove by pinching your elbows, your ribs—a skeleton that provides your flesh, your muscles, their stability and that you carry around inside you, though it might be better to say: it carries you around. But here it is just the opposite. These creatures have fixed their rigidity on the outside, not as a framework, but as a house, and the fact that it is external and not internal must be the reason for such beauty."

We boys, Adrian and I, probably looked at each with a dumbfounded, half-suppressed smile at a paternal remark like this about the vanity of the visible.

It could be malicious at times, this aesthetic of externality; because certain conical snails—charmingly asymmetric specimens, dipped in veined pale pink or honey-brown speckled with white—were infamous for their poisonous sting; and, on the whole, to hear the master of Buchel Farm tell it, there was no denying a certain murkiness or fantastic ambiguity about this entire curious segment of life. A peculiar ambivalence in regard to these showy creatures had always been manifest in the very disparate uses to which they were put. In the Middle Ages they had been part of the standing inventory of witches' kitchens and alchemists' cellars and were considered the proper vessels for poisons and love potions. On the other hand they had concurrently seen service in the Church as tabernacles for the host and as reliquaries, even as Communion chalices. As in so many things, there was a meeting here—of poison and beauty, poison and sorcery, but of sorcery and liturgy as well. And if we did not think such things on our own, Jonathan Leverkühn's commentary was sure to make us vaguely aware of them.

As for those hieroglyphics that gave him no moment's peace, they were to be found on the shell of a medium-sized conch from New Caledonia, set in pale reddish-brown against an off-white background. The characters, as if drawn with a brush, blended into purely decorative lines toward the edge, but over large sections of the curved surface their meticulous complexity gave every appearance of intending to communicate something. As I recall, they displayed a strong resemblance to early Oriental scripts, much like the stroke of Old Aramaic; and indeed my father had to borrow from the quite respectable holdings of the Kaisersaschern town library to provide his friend archaeological volumes that gave him an opportunity for study and comparison. Needless to say, these researches led to nothing, or rather only to a confusion and contradiction that came to nothing. With considerable melancholy, Jonathan admitted as much when he would show us the puzzling illustration. "It has been proved," he said, "that it is impossible to get to the bottom of these symbols. Unfortunate, but true, my lads. They elude our understanding and, it pains me to say, probably always will. But when I say they 'elude' us, that is really only the opposite of 'reveal,' for the idea that nature has painted this code, for which we lack the key, purely for ornament's sake on the shell of one of her creatures—no one can convince me of that. Ornament and meaning have always run side by side, and the ancient scripts served simultaneously for decoration and communication. Let no one tell me nothing is being communicated here! For the message to be inaccessible, and for one to immerse oneself in that contradiction—that also has its pleasure."

Did he consider that, were this really a written code, nature would surely have to command her own self-generated, organized language? For from among those invented by man, which should she choose to express herself? Even as a boy I understood quite clearly, however, that nature, being outside of man, is fundamentally illiterate—which in my eyes is precisely what makes her eerie.

Yes, Father Leverkühn was a speculator and a brooder, and as I have noted, his interest in research—if one can speak of research, since it was actually a matter of mere dreamy contemplation—always moved along one particular path, that is the mystical or intuitive semi-mystical, down which, it seems to me, human thought is almost inevitably led when in pursuit of the natural world. Every collaborative venture with nature, every attempt to tease phenomena out of her, to "tempt" her by exposing her workings through experiment—it all comes very close to sorcery, indeed is already within its realm and is the work of the "Tempter," or so earlier epochs were convinced, and a very respectable view it is, if you ask me. I would like to know with what eyes those epochs would have regarded the man from Wittenberg who, as we learned from Jonathan, some hundred and more years previously had conceived an experiment for making music visible, which we indeed saw demonstrated on occasion. Among what little laboratory apparatus Adrian's father had at his disposal was a freely rotating glass disk resting only on a peg through its center, and on its surface the miracle came to pass. The disk, you see, was strewn with fine sand, and then he would take an old cello bow and in a descending motion stroke the rim of the disk, setting up vibrations that caused the agitated sand to shift and order itself into astonishingly precise and diverse figures and arabesques. These visual acoustics, in which clarity and mystery, the legitimate and the miraculous, converged with ample charms, delighted us boys, and we often asked for a demonstration, not least because the experimenter enjoyed performing it.

He took similar pleasure in the work of Jack Frost, and on winter days when precipitated crystals would fill the little windows of the Buchel farmhouse, he could sit for a good half-hour examining their structure with both the naked eye and his magnifying glass. I would say: Everything would have been fine and he could have moved on to other things, if what was generated there had kept, as it ought, to symmetry and pattern, to strict mathematics and regularities. But for it to mimic plant life with impudent legerdemain, to fake the prettiest fern fronds and grasses, the chalices and stars of flowers, for it to play the icy dilettante in the organic world—that was what Jonathan could not get over, what set him shaking and shaking his head in something like disapproval, but also in admiration. Were these phantasmagorias an imitation of plant life, or were they the pattern for it?—that was his question. Neither, he presumably replied to himself; they were parallel formations. Nature in her creative dreaming, dreamt the same thing both here and there, and if one spoke of imitation, then certainly it had to be reciprocal. Should one take the children of the soil as models because they possessed the depth of organic reality, whereas the ice flowers were mere external phenomena? But as phenomena, they were the result of an interplay of matter no less complex than that found in plants. If I understood our friendly host correctly, what concerned him was the unity of animate and so-called inanimate nature, the idea that we sin against the latter if the boundary we draw between the two spheres is too rigid, when in reality it is porous, since there is no elementary capability that is reserved exclusively for living creatures or that the biologist could not likewise study on inanimate models.

And just how confusing the interaction is between these two realms we learned from the "devouring drop," to which more than once Father Leverkühn fed a meal before our very eyes. A drop of whatever it was—paraffin, or some volatile oil, I don't recall specifically, though I believe it was chloroform—a drop, I say, is not an animal, not even a primitive one, not even an amoeba; one does not assume that it has an appetite, seeks nourishment, knows to retain what is digestible and refuse what is not. But that is precisely what our drop did. It was swimming by itself in a glass of water into which Jonathan had introduced it, probably with a pipette. And what he now did was this: With a pair of pincers he picked up a tiny glass rod, actually a thread of glass coated with shellac, and placed it in the vicinity of the drop. That was all that he did, the drop did the rest. It formed a little convexity on its surface, a sort of mount of conception, through which it then ingested the rod lengthwise. Meanwhile it extended itself, took on a pear shape so as to encompass its prey entirely and not leave either end sticking out; and as it gradually reassumed its spherical shape, more ovoid at first, it began, I give you my word, to dine on the shellac that coated the glass rod and to distribute it throughout its own body. When it had finished and had resumed its globular form, it pushed the utensil, now neatly licked clean, back across to the periphery and out into the surrounding water.

I cannot claim that I liked to watch, but I do admit that I was spellbound, and so, too, was Adrian, although such exhibitions always greatly tempted him to break into laughter, which he suppressed only out of respect for his father's seriousness. Perhaps one could find humor in the devouring drop; but that was certainly not how I felt when it came to certain incredible and eerie natural products that Adrian's father managed to breed from some bizarre culture, and which he likewise permitted us to observe. I will never forget the sight. The crystallization vessel in which this transpired was filled to three-quarters with a slightly mucilaginous liquid, diluted sodium silicate to be precise, and from the sandy bottom up rose a grotesque miniature landscape of different colored growths—a muddle of vegetation, sprouting blue, green, and brown and reminiscent of algae, fungi, rooted polyps, of mosses, too, but also of mussels, fleshy flower spikes, tiny trees or twigs, and here and there even of human limbs—the most remarkable thing my eyes had ever beheld, remarkable not so much because of their very odd and perplexing appearance, however, but because of their deeply melancholy nature. And when Father Leverkühn would ask us what we thought they were, and we hesitantly answered that they might be plants, he would reply, "No, that they're not, they only pretend to be. But don't think less of them for it! The fact that they give their best to pretense deserves all due respect."

It turned out that these growths were of purely inorganic origin and arose with the aid of chemicals that came from Blessed Messengers pharmacy. Before pouring in the sodium silicate solution, Jonathan had sown the sand on the bottom of the vessel with various crystals—with, if I am not mistaken, potassium dichromate and copper sulfate; and as the result of a physical process called "osmotic pressure," these seeds had produced their pitiable crop, for which their custodian immediately tried all the harder to solicit our sympathy. He showed us, you see, that these woeful imitators of life were eager for light, or "heliotropic" as science says of life-forms. To prove it to us, he exposed his aquarium to sunlight, while shading it on three sides; and behold, within a very short time the whole dubious crew—mushrooms, phallic polyps, tiny trees, and algae meadows, plus those half-formed limbs—bent toward the pane of glass through which the light was falling, pressing forward with such longing for warmth and joy that they literally clung to the pane and stuck fast there.

"Even though they're dead," Jonathan said, and tears came to his eyes—whereas Adrian, as I could well see, was shaking with suppressed laughter.

For my part I leave it to the reader whether such things deserve laughter or tears. I have only this to say: Phantasms of this sort are exclusively the concern of nature, and in particular of nature when she is willfully tempted by man. In the worthy realm of the humanities one is safe from all such spooks.

IV

SINCE THE PRECEDING SECTION has swelled to excess as it is, it
is best I commence a new one so that I may also pay honor in a few
words to the image of the mistress of Buchel, to Adrian's dear mother.
It may well be that the gratitude one feels for childhood—and all those
tasty snacks she served us—lends special radiancy to that image, but I
must say that no more engaging woman has ever entered my life than
Elsbeth Leverkühn, and I speak of her simple, intellectually quite
unassuming person out of a respect that flows from the conviction that
her son's genius owed much to her vital, solid character.

And if I enjoyed observing the handsome old German head of her
spouse, I took no less pleasure in letting my eyes linger on her figure—
for how thoroughly pleasant, singularly sturdy, clearly proportioned it
was. Born in the vicinity of Apolda, she was a brunette, a coloring frequent enough in German regions that one need not immediately assume that the accessible genealogy will reveal Roman blood. Her dark
complexion, her almost black hair, and the quiet, friendly cast of her
eyes might have led one to take her for an Italian, had that not been
contradicted by a certain Germanic coarseness to the features of the
face. It formed a shortened oval, her face did, with a chin that was
rather pointed, a nose that was not quite regular, but slightly flattened
and upturned at the end, and a demure mouth whose lines were neither
sharp nor voluptuous. That dark hair I mentioned half-covered the
ears, and as I grew older slowly turned silver; she wore it pulled back
so tight that it shimmered and the part in it exposed white skin above
her forehead. Nevertheless, stray locks might hang charmingly in front

of the ears—but not always and so probably not intentionally. She wore her braid, still quite thick when we were children, wound around the back of her head in country fashion, often entwining it with a colorful embroidered ribbon on holidays.

She was no more given to city clothes than was her husband; ladylike attire did not suit her, whereas she looked splendid in the semi-folkloric peasant costume we knew her in: the heavy, home-sewn (as we put it) skirt and a kind of trimmed bodice with a square neckline exposing her somewhat short, thick neck and the upper part of the breast, upon which lay a simple, light, gold pendant. The brownish hands, with the wedding ring on the right, were accustomed to work, but no more rough than they were carefully manicured, and were, I must say, a pleasure to behold—they had something so humanely right and dependable about them—but so, too, were her well-turned feet, which were neither too large nor too little; and she would set them down firmly in their comfortable flat-heeled shoes and green or gray woolen stockings that fit snugly around her trim ankles. All of that was pleasant. But the loveliest thing about her was her voice, a warm mezzo-soprano, and when she employed it for speech, colored with a touch of a Thuringian accent, it was extraordinarily winning. I did not say "ingratiating," because that would imply intention and awareness. The charm of her voice came from an inner musicality, which otherwise remained latent, for Elsbeth did not concern herself with music, did not espouse it, so to speak. It might happen that for no special reason she would reach for the old guitar decorating the living-room wall and strum a few cords or even hum a tag of a verse from a song; but she did not go in for actual singing, although I would bet that the most splendid material lay waiting to be developed.

In any case, never have I heard anyone speak more sweetly, although what she said was always very simple, very down-to-earth; and in my opinion it is significant that from Adrian's first hour his ear was maternally caressed by such natural, instinctively tasteful euphony. For me, it helps to explain the incredible sensitivity to tone-color that manifests itself in his work, although the objection lies at hand that his brother, Georg, enjoyed the same advantage without its having had any influence whatever in shaping his life. He looked more like his father, by the way, whereas Adrian was physically more like his mother—which, however, does not seem to fit with the fact that it was Adrian, and not Georg, who inherited his father's tendency to migraine. But the general makeup of my late friend, including many details—the dark complexion, the cut of the eyes, the shape of the mouth and chin—it all came from his mother's side, which was especially obvious as long as he was clean-shaven, that is before he grew that very off-putting imperial; but that didn't happen until later years. The pitch-black of his mother's eyes and the azure of his father's had fused in Adrian into shadowy blue-gray-green irises sprinkled with metallic flecks and pupils circled by a rust-hued ring; and it has always been an inner certainty of mine that it was the contradiction of those parental eyes blended in his own that caused him to waver in his own preference in this matter, so that his whole life long he could never decide which eyes, black or blue, he found more beautiful in others. But it was always one of the extremes, the sheen of pitch or the flash of blue between the lashes, that captivated him.

Frau Elsbeth had a truly fine influence on the hired hands at Buchel—really just a few during off-season, who were then augmented only at harvest by workers from the area—and if I saw things correctly, her authority among those people was even greater than her husband's. I can still picture some of them: the figure of Thomas the stableboy, for example, the same fellow who would meet us at the station in Weissenfels and drive us back as well—a one-eyed man, and though exceptionally bony and tall, afflicted with a humpback that sat very high, on which he would frequently let little Adrian ride; it had been, so the *meister* often later assured me, a very practical and comfortable seat. I recall, moreover, a milkmaid named Hanne, with a floppy bosom and bare, eternally dungcaked feet, with whom Adrian (for a reason to be spelled out later) likewise maintained a closer friendship as a lad; and a Frau Luder, the woman in charge of the dairy, who wore a widow's cap and an unusually dignified expression, which was in part her way of protesting against her wanton last name and in part could be traced to the fact that she was renowned for the excellent caraway cheese she made. If the mistress of Buchel did not tend to us in the dairy barn, home of beneficial treats, Frau Luder would, holding out glasses to catch the lukewarm, foaming milk, still redolent of the useful animal releasing it under the strokes of the milkmaid squatting on a stool.

I would certainly not get caught up in detailed reminiscences of this bucolic childhood world, this simple setting of field and wood, pond and hill, if it were not the very world—parental home and native landscape—that enfolded Adrian's early years (until he turned ten) and brought the two of us together so often. Our use of familiar pronouns is rooted in those years, and he must have addressed me by my first name back then, too—I can no longer hear it, but it is unthinkable that as a six- or eight-year-old he did not call me Serenus, or simply Seren, just as I called him Adri. It must have been during our early years at school, though the exact moment cannot be determined, when he ceased to grant me that intimacy and, if he addressed me at all, began to use my last name—whereas it would have seemed to me impossibly harsh to reply in like fashion. It was so—though far be it from me for it to appear as if I wished to complain. It simply seemed worth mentioning that I called him Adrian, whereas he, when not evading use of a name entirely, called me Zeitblom. And having established that curious fact, to which I had grown perfectly accustomed, let us return to Buchel.

He had a friend, and so did I, in the farm's dog Suso—that indeed was his somewhat peculiar name—a rather scruffy spaniel, whose face broke into a wide grin when he was brought his meal, but who could prove more than a little dangerous to strangers and led an unconventional life, for he was chained to his house next to his bowls during the day and set free to range the courtyard only in the still of the night. Together we two would peer into the jostling filth of the pigsty, well aware of the old wives' tale about how these slovenly, cunning domesticated beasts with their white-lashed blue eyes and gross flesh-colored bodies sometimes ate little boys; we forced our vocal chords to mimic the oink-oink of their underground language and watched the pink roiling litter of piglets at the teats of the mother sow. We laughed together at the colony of hens behind chicken wire, at their pedantic bustlings accompanied by dignified, measured discourse that only occasionally broke into hysteria; and we paid visits to the bees' lodgings behind the house—cautious visits, since we were acquainted with the throbbing, though not unbearable pain that ensued if one of these nectar gatherers landed by mistake on your nose and foolishly felt obliged to sting.

I think of currant bushes in the kitchen-garden and how we slid clusters of berries through our lips, of meadow sorrel we nibbled, of certain blossoms and how we had learned to suck a trace of fine nectar from their throats, of acorns we chewed lying on our backs in the woods, of purple sun-warmed blackberries gleaned from bushes along the roadside and how their tart juice quenched our childish thirst. And we were children—but I am moved to look back not out of nostalgia, but for his sake and at the thought of his fate, which ordained that he ascend from that valley of innocence to inhospitable, indeed terrifying heights. His was an artist's life; and because it was granted to me, an ordinary man, to view it from so close-up, all the feelings of my soul for human life and fate have coalesced around this exceptional form of human existence. For me, thanks to my friendship with Adrian, the artist's life functions as the paradigm for how fate shapes all our lives, as the classic example of how we are deeply moved by what we call becoming, development, destiny—and it probably is so in reality, too. For although his whole life long the artist may remain nearer, if not to say, more faithful to his childhood than the man who specializes in practical reality, although one can say that, unlike the latter, he abides in the dreamlike, purely human, and playful state of the child, nevertheless the artist's journey from those pristine early years to the late, unforeseen stages of his development is endlessly longer, wilder, stranger—and more disturbing for those who watch—than that of the everyday person, for whom the thought that he, too, was once a child is cause for not half so many tears.

I urgently request the reader, by the way, to credit what I have said here with such feeling to my authorial account and not to believe it represents Leverkühn's thoughts. I am an old-fashioned man, stuck in certain romantic views dear to me, among which is the heightened drama of an antithesis between the artist and the bourgeois. Adrian would have coolly contradicted any statement like the foregoing—that is, if he had found it worth his trouble to contradict. For he had extremely level-headed—and in response to others, often caustic—opinions about art and being an artist, and was so averse to the "Romantic fuss" the world at one time enjoyed making about such matters that he did not even like to hear the words "art" and "artist," as was evident from the face he would make when someone spoke them. It was the same with the word "inspiration," which one definitely had to avoid in his company—if need be, by substituting a phrase like "fresh idea." He hated and scorned the word—and I cannot help lifting my hand from the blotter surrounding my page to cover my eyes when I think of that hate and that scorn. Ah, both were too tortured to be merely the impersonal result of intellectual changes that came with the times. Those, to be sure, had their effect, and I can recall that even as a student he once said to me that the nineteenth century must have been an uncommonly cozy period, since never had it been more painful for humanity to separate itself from the views and customs of the previous epoch than it was for the present generation.

I mentioned in passing the pond, which lay only ten minutes from the farmhouse. Circled by willows, it was called the Cattle Trough—probably because of its oblong shape and because the cows liked to stroll down to the banks for a drink—and its water was, I cannot say why, so exceptionally cold that only in late afternoon, after it had been in the sun for hours, did we dare swim in it. As for the hill, it was about a half-hour's walk away—a walk gladly undertaken. The knoll was called Mount Zion (a quite inappropriate, but surely age-old designation) and was good for sledding in winter, though the season seldom found me there. In summer the "peak," with its wreath of shady maples and a bench purchased by the village, offered a breezy spot with a fine view, which I would often enjoy with the Leverkühn family on Sunday afternoons before supper.

And here I feel constrained to mention the following: The framework of landscape and house where Adrian later established his life as a mature man—that is, when he settled for good with the Schweigestills in Pfeiffering near Waldshut in Upper Bavaria—very strangely resembled, even replicated, the framework of his childhood; or put another way, the setting of his later years curiously imitated that of his youth. Not only in the environs of Pfeiffering (or Pfeffering, the spelling could indeed vary) was there a communal bench set atop a hill—not, however, called Mount Zion, but the Rohmbühel; not only was there a pond like the Cattle Trough—here named Klammer Pool—about the same distance from the farm and likewise with very cold water. No, even the house, the courtyard, and the family circumstances also bore a striking correspondence to those at Buchel. In the courtyard was a tree—also somewhat in the way and yet left standing for sentimental reasons—not a linden, but an elm. Granted there were distinctive differences between the architecture of the Schweigestill house and that of Adrian's parents, since the former was part of an old cloister with thick walls, windows set in deep vaults, and somewhat musty corridors. But the pungent tobacco of the owner's pipe permeated the air in the downstairs rooms here as it had there; and the owner and his wife, Frau Schweigestill, were "parental"—that is, they were a long-faced, rather laconic, sensible, placid farmer and his perhaps somewhat imposing, but nicely proportioned wife, with hair drawn back tight and well-formed hands and feet, a woman also well along in years, but alert and eager to do her part. They had, by the way, an heir in their grown son, Gereon (not Georg) by name, a young man given to new machines and very progressive ideas when it came to farming; also a somewhat younger daughter named Clementina. The dog at the farm in Pfeiffering could grin as well, even though it was not called Suso, but bore the name Kaschperl, or at least had borne it originally. The farm's paying guest had other ideas about that "originally," you see; and I myself was witness to the process by which, under his influence, the name Kaschperl gradually became a mere memory, and the dog itself finally preferred to answer to Suso. There was no second son, which, however, enhanced the duplication more than it might have lessened it—for who ought this second son to have been?

I never spoke with Adrian about the whole compelling parallelism; I did not do so early on and for that very reason did not wish to do so later; but the phenomenon never pleased me. His choosing a residence that reproduced his earliest world, his hiding in the oldest level of a bygone life—his childhood—or at least in its external circumstances, may attest to a certain fidelity, but it also says something unsettling about a man's inner life. In Leverkühn's case it was all the more startling since I never observed his ties to his parental home to be marked by any special intimacy or emotion, and he broke them early on without discernible pain. Was this artificial "return" mere playacting? I cannot believe it. It reminds me, rather, of a man of my acquaintance who, although externally robust and sporting a beard, was so high-strung that whenever he fell ill—and he tended to be sickly—he would allow only a pediatrician to treat him. Moreover, the doctor into whose care he put himself, was so short that he, quite literally, could never have measured up to medical practice with adults and could only have specialized in children.

It seems advisable to remark on my own that this anecdote about the man with the pediatrician is a digression, insofar as neither of them will ever appear again in this account. If that is an error, and if it was already a manifest error for me to succumb to my tendency to get ahead of myself and start in now about Pfeiffering and the Schweigestills, I beg the reader will attribute such irregularities to the agitated state in which I have found myself ever since beginning this biographical enterprise—and not just during the hours spent writing it. I have been working on these pages for a series of days, but the reader should not be misled into thinking that, although I am trying to give some balance to my sentences and adequate expression to my thoughts, I am not in a permanently agitated state, which is evidenced by shakiness in my normally still quite steady handwriting. It is my belief, by the way, not only that those who read me will, in time, come to understand my inner turmoil, but also that in the long run it will not be foreign to them, either.

I forgot to mention that at the Schweigestill's farm, Adrian's later residence, there was also—which should come as no surprise—a milkmaid with a wobbly bosom and hard-working, dungcaked bare feet, who resembled Hanne from Buchel about as much as one milkmaid resembles another and who in replicated form was called Waltpurgis. I'll not speak of her here, but of her prototype, with whom little Adrian was on friendly terms because she loved to sing and used to arrange little singing lessons for us children. And strangely enough, whereas Elsbeth Leverkühn, with her lovely voice, abstained from singing out of some kind of chaste modesty, this creature still smelling of her animals would go at it with abandon. Her voice was raucous but her ear was good, and of an evening on the bench beneath the linden tree she would sing for us all sorts of folk songs, army tunes, and street ballads, most of them either maudlin or gruesome, whose words and melodies we quickly made our own. If we then sang along, she would drop to the third, move as needed down to the fifth or sixth, and leaving the treble to us, ostentatiously and ear-splittingly hold to her harmony. Meanwhile, apparently as an added inducement for our proper appreciation of this harmonious pleasure, a grin would spread over her face as broad as Suso managed when served his supper.

By "us" I mean Adrian, myself, and Georg, who was already thirteen when his brother and I were eight and ten years old. Little Ursel was always too small to participate in these exercises; but even with four singers one was already superfluous, so to speak, for the kind of vocal music to which barnyard Hanne was able to elevate our lusty voices raised in song. She taught us to sing rounds, you see—the ones children always sing, of course: "Row, row, row your boat," "Are you sleeping," and the one about the cuckoo and the jackass; and those twilight hours we enjoyed together have remained a fixed, important memory—or rather, the memory of them later took on enhanced meaning because they were, in terms of any evidence I can provide, what first brought my friend into contact with "music" that flowed with somewhat more artistic organization than is found in mere unison singing of songs. Here was a temporal intertwining with imitative entrances, to which one was prodded by a poke in the ribs from barnyard Hanne once the song was already underway, its melody having moved ahead to a certain point, but still before it had come to an end. Here melodic components were present in various layers without producing chaos; instead, the first phrase, as repeated note for note by a second singer, very pleasantly augmented its continuation being sung by the first voice. But once the first voice, forging ahead, had arrived—presuming the piece is, say, "Are you sleeping"—at the repeated "ringing bells" and begun their illustrative "ding-dong-ding," this provided the moving bass not only for the "morning bells" phrase to which the second voice had now advanced, but also for the opening "Are you sleeping," at which, after a new poke in the ribs, the third singer had entered musical time, only to be relieved again then by the first voice beginning anew, after having yielded the onomatopoetic ding-dong foundation to the second—and so forth. The fourth voice in our group was inevitably paired with one of the others, though whenever possible the attempt was made to enliven this duplication by growling it one octave lower; or it would begin even before the first voice, before dawn so to speak, either with the foundation of tolling bells or with the first line of melody warbled in variation as a *la-la-la*, and persevere with that for the whole duration of the song.

And so, although we were always separated from one another in time, each melodic present kept delightful company with all the others, and what we produced formed a charming weft, an ensemble sound, that "simultaneous" singing could never form—a structure whose vocal pattern we happily enjoyed without inquiring further about its nature and cause. At age eight or nine, Adrian probably did not do so either. Or was that brief burst of laughter—which he would release, more in mockery than amazement, after the last "ding-dong" echo had died away on the evening breeze and which I would know so well later, too—was it meant to say that he could see through the little song's construct, which is simply that the start of the melody is pitched in sequence by the second voice, so that the third part can serve as the bass for both? None of us was aware that under the direction of a milkmaid we were already moving on a comparatively high plane of musical culture, a branch of imitative polyphony, which had first had to be discovered in the fifteenth century before it could provide us with amusement. But in recalling Adrian's burst of laughter, I find in retrospect that within it lay knowledge and the initiate's sneer. That laugh stayed with him; I often heard it later when, sitting by my side at a concert or in the theater, he would be struck by some fine psychological allusion in the dialogue of a drama or by some trick of art, some ingenious event deep within the musical structure, of which the audience had no comprehension. At the time that laugh did not suit his young years at all, for it was the very same one he would laugh as an adult. It was a gentle thrust of air through the mouth and nose, and a simultaneous tossing back of the head, curt, cool, yes, contemptuous—or at best, it was as if he wished to say "Good job, droll, curious, amusing!" But at the same time his eyes, seeking out the distance, registered a special look, and the dusk of their metallic flecks would retreat deeper into shadow.

V

THE SECTION JUST CONCLUDED also swelled much too much for my taste, and it would seem only too advisable for me to ask myself whether the reader's patience is holding out. Every word I write here is of searing interest to me, but I must be very much on guard against thinking that that is any guarantee of sympathy on the part of the uninvolved reader! Although I should not forget, either, that I am writing not for the moment, nor for readers who as yet know nothing at all about Leverkühn and so could have no desire to learn more about him, but that I am preparing this account for a time when conditions for public response will be quite different—and with certainty one can say much more favorable—when the demand for details of this disturbing life, however adeptly or unadeptly presented, will be both less selective and more urgent.

That time will have come when our prison, which though extensive is nonetheless cramped and filled with suffocatingly stale air, has opened—that is, when the war raging at present has come to an end, one way or the other. And how that "or the other" sets me in terror—of both myself and the awful straits into which fate has squeezed the German heart! For in fact I have only "the other" in mind; I am relying on it, counting solely on it, against my conscience as a citizen. After all, never-failing public indoctrination has made sure that we are profoundly aware of the crushing consequences, in all their irrevocable horror, of a German defeat, so that we cannot help fearing it more than anything else in the world. And yet there is something that some of us fear—at certain moments that seem criminal even to ourselves, whereas others fear it quite frankly and permanently—fear more than a German defeat, and that is a German victory. I hardly dare ask myself to which of these two persuasions I belong. Perhaps to a third, in which one yearns for defeat constantly and consciously, but with unrelenting agony of conscience. My wishes and hopes are compelled to resist the victory of German arms, because my friend's work would be buried beneath it, covered with the curse of proscription and forgetfulness for perhaps a hundred years, thus missing its own age and receiving historical honor only in a later one. That is the special motive for my criminal deed, and I share that motive with a scattered number of people who are easily counted on the fingers of both hands. But my mental state is only a special variation on an outlook that has become the fate of our whole nation, always excepting cases of oversize stupidity and base self-interest; and I am not free from a tendency to see in this fate some special, unparalleled tragedy, although I know that other peoples have had to bear the burden of wishing the defeat of their nation for its own good and for the sake of a shared future. Yet given the German character, with its sincerity and gullibility, its need for loyalty and devotion, I would truly like to think that in our case the exacerbation of the dilemma is unique, nor can I help feeling profound rage against those who have brought such good people to a mental state that I am convinced weighs more heavily upon them than it would upon any other, hopelessly estranging them from themselves. What if by some unfortunate accident my sons were to find out about these papers and, with Spartan denial of every tender consideration, feel compelled to report me to the Gestapo—I need only imagine it in order to fathom, indeed with a kind of patriotic pride, the abysmal nature of the conflict in which we have landed.

I am perfectly aware that with the foregoing paragraph I have seriously compromised this new section as well, which I really had hoped to keep shorter, though I cannot suppress a psychological conjecture that I am actually seeking out delays and digressions, or at least am secretly eager to use any opportunity for them, because I fear what is yet to come. As proof of my honesty, I submit to the reader my entertaining the supposition that I am making difficulties because in my heart I am terrified by the task that duty and love have prompted me to undertake. But nothing, not even my own weakness, shall prevent me from continuing its execution—by picking up again now at my remark that it was our singing of rounds with barnyard Hanne that, as far as I know, first brought Adrian into contact with the sphere of music. To be sure, I am also aware that as he grew older he attended Sunday ser-

vices with his parents in the village church at Oberweiler, for which
a young music student used to come over from Weissenfels to play
the little organ, providing preludes, accompaniment for the hymns,
and solemnly tentative improvisations for the worshipers to exit the
church by. But I was almost never present for that, since we normally
arrived at Buchel only after services were over, and I can only say that
I never heard Adrian speak one word that would lead me to conclude
that his young mind had been affected in any way by the offerings of
that journeyman, or, if that is scarcely probable, that he had taken any
special note of the phenomenon of music in and of itself. As far as I can
see, he failed to pay it any attention back then, or indeed for years afterward, and kept the idea hidden, even from himself, that he might
have anything to do with the world of sound. I see it as subconscious
caution on his part; but one can probably draw on a physiological explanation as well, since it was in fact at the age of fourteen, with the onset of puberty and the emergence from the state of childish innocence,
that he began to experiment on his own with music on a keyboard in
his uncle's house in Kaisersaschern. It was at this same time, by the
way, that his inherited migraine began to give him bad days.

His brother Georg's future had always been clear, since he was to in-
herit the farm, and from the very start he lived in perfect harmony with
his vocation. What was to become of their second-born remained for
the parents an open question that would have to be decided by inclina-
tions and abilities he might demonstrate; and it was remarkable, then,
how early the notion became firmly fixed in their and all our minds
that Adrian would have to be a scholar. What kind of scholar remained
undecided for a long time, but even as a boy his whole moral demeanor, the way he expressed himself, his formal decisiveness, even his
gaze, his facial expression, never left a doubt in my father's mind, for
example, that this branch on the Leverkühn family tree was called to
"something higher" and that he would be the first educated man in
his family.

The origin and confirmation for this idea was the, one might almost
say, phenomenal ease with which Adrian absorbed his grammar-school
lessons, which were taught him at home. Jonathan Leverkühn did not
send his children to the village common school. His decision, I think,
was rooted less in a sense of social superiority than in an earnest desire
to provide them a more rigorous education than they could have received sharing lessons with the children of the crofters of Oberweiler.
Every afternoon, having finished his official duties, the school-
teacher—a rather young and delicate man, who never stopped being

afraid of the dog Suso—would come over to give lessons at Buchel, though in winter Thomas fetched him with the sled; and he had already imparted to thirteen-year-old Georg almost all the knowledge the lad would require as a foundation for any further studies, when he took over the elementary education of Adrian, then age eight. And now he, schoolmaster Michelsen, was the very first to declare loudly and with a certain fervor that "for God's sake" the lad must go on to high school and university, for he, Michelsen, had never before come across such a clever and agile mind, and it would be a shame not to do everything to clear the path to the heights of learning for such a pupil. He stated his case in those or similar words—in teacher's college jargon at any rate— and even spoke of *ingenium,* in part, of course, to show off with the word, which sounded rather droll when applied to such rudimentary achievements, but it also had obviously come to him from an astounded heart.

I was in fact never present at these lessons and know about them only from hearsay, but I can easily imagine that my Adrian's behavior must have had something downright offensive about it at times, even to a still boyish tutor accustomed to drumming material with spurs of praise and blasts of desperation into lamely struggling and resistant heads. "If you already know everything," I hear the young man saying on occasion, "then I can leave." Naturally it was not true that his pupil "already knew everything." But his attitude implied it, simply because here was a case of that quick, strangely sovereign comprehension and assimilation, always one step ahead and as sure as it is effortless, which quickly cools a teacher's praise, because he senses that such a mind can jeopardize the modesty of the heart and easily lead it into arrogance. From alphabet to syntax and grammar, from counting and the four arithmetic operations to calculating ratios and simple proportions, from memorizing little poems (there really was no memorizing; the verses were grasped and mastered immediately and with great precision) to putting into writing his own thoughts on topics of geography or local history—it was always the same: Adrian cocked an ear, turned away, and assumed an air as if to say, "Yes, fine, that much is clear, enough, go on!" To the pedagogical temperament, that implies rebellion. Surely the young man was constantly tempted to shout "What do you think you're doing! Make an effort!" But how does one make an effort when there is obviously no necessity?

As I said, I never attended these lessons; but I cannot help imagining that my friend reacted to the scientific data conveyed to him by Herr Michelsen with basically the same, rather indefinable demeanor with which he had responded under the linden tree upon learning that nine bars of horizontal melody, when placed vertically above one another in a trio, can result in a harmonious grouping of voices. His teacher knew a little Latin, which he taught Adrian and then declared that the boy—now age ten—was ready if not for the second then certainly for the first grade of higher education. His work was done.

And so at Easter 1895 Adrian left his parents' home and came to town to attend our Boniface Gymnasium (actually, School of the Brethren of the Common Life). His uncle, Nikolaus Leverkühn, his father's brother and a respected citizen of Kaisersaschern, consented to take the boy in.

VI

As for my hometown on the Saale, it should be noted for non-Germans that it lies somewhat to the south of Halle, near the border to Thuringia. I almost said it lay—for being separated from it now for so long, I find it has slipped into the past for me. But its spires surely still rise in the same place as always, though I cannot say whether or not its architectural profile has suffered from the profligate destruction of the air war, which, given the town's historic charms, would be extremely regrettable. And I add that remark with some composure, for along with no small portion of our population, including those hardest hit and homeless now, I share the sense that we are only getting what we gave, and if our atonement should be more terrible than our sins, then let our ears ring with the dictum that he who sows the wind shall reap the whirlwind.

And so it is not very far to Halle itself, Handel's birthplace, or to Leipzig, the city where Bach was cantor at St. Thomas, or Weimar or even Dessau and Magdeburg; but Kaisersaschern is a major railroad junction and with its twenty-seven thousand inhabitants quite self-sufficient, regarding itself, as does every German town, as a cultural and intellectual center of special importance. It earns its livelihood from various industries (machine tools, leather, textiles, armatures, chemicals, and assorted mills); and the historical museum, which features a chamber with crude instruments of torture, contains a very excellent library of twenty-five thousand volumes and five thousand manuscripts, among them two alliterative magic charms that scholars consider older than those of Merseburg—and of quite harmless import by the way, conjuring nothing more than a little rain, in the dialect of Fulda. The town was a bishopric during the tenth century and then again from the twelfth to the fourteenth. It has a castle and a cathedral, where one is shown the tomb of Kaiser Otto III, Adelheid's grandson and Theophano's son, who called himself both Emperor of the Romans and Saxonicus, not because he wanted to be a Saxon, but in the same sense that Scipio took the name Africanus—that is, because he had defeated the Saxons. Having been driven from his beloved Rome, he died of sorrow in 1002; his remains were then brought to Germany and interred in the cathedral of Kaisersaschern—very much counter to his own preference, for he was a perfect model of German self-contempt and had been ashamed of being German all his life.

One can say of the town—and I really would rather speak in past tenses, since it is the Kaisersaschern we knew in our youth of which I speak—one can say of the town that it had preserved a strong sense of the medieval, not just in outward appearance, but also in atmosphere. The old churches; the faithfully preserved residences and storehouses, buildings with exposed timberwork and projecting upper stories; a city wall with round steepled towers; tree-lined squares paved with cobblestones; a town hall hovering architecturally between Gothic and Renaissance, its steep roof ornamented by a bell tower above, loggias below, and two more spires that formed bays continuing down the façade to the ground floor—all that establishes a sense of life unbroken in its continuity with the past, indeed it seems to bear *nunc stans,* the famous scholastic formula for timelessness, on its brow. The town maintains its identity, which was the same three hundred, nine hundred years ago, against the river of time sweeping over it and constantly effecting many changes, whereas other things, those that define its image, are left standing out of reverence, which is to say, out of a devout defiance of and pride in time—are left as keepers of memory and dignity.

So much for the look of the town. But there hung in the air something of the state of the human heart during the last decades of the fifteenth century, a hysteria out of the dying Middle Ages, something of a latent psychological epidemic—a strange thing to say about a sensibly practical, modern town. But it was not modern, it was old, and age is the past as the present, a past only veneered with the present; and this may sound bold, but one could imagine a Children's Crusade suddenly erupting there—a Saint Vitus' dance, some utopian communistic lunatic preaching a bonfire of vanities, miracles and visions of the Cross, and roving masses of mystic enthusiasts. That did not occur, of course—how could it have? In compliance with the times and regulations, the police would not have allowed it. And yet! what all haven't the police refrained from acting upon in our own day—again in compliance with the times, which certainly do permit such things again of late. Our own times are secretly inclined—or, rather, anything but secretly, very purposefully in fact, with a particularly smug sense of purpose that leaves one doubting life's genuineness and simplicity and produces perhaps a very false, ill-fated historicity—our times are inclined, I say, to return to such epochs and enthusiastically repeat symbolic actions that have something sinister about them, that strike in the face of modern understanding: burning books, for instance, and other deeds I would rather not put into words.

The mark of such a neurotic descent into the depths of antiquity, of the secret psychological state of such a town, is found in the many "characters," eccentrics and harmless, half-crazy souls who live inside its walls and are, like the buildings, more or less part of the local scenery. Their opposite is composed of children, the "kids" who trail after them, mocking them, only to turn and run in superstitious panic. In certain eras a certain type of "old woman" has always been immediately suspected of witchcraft—the simple result of a disagreeably odd appearance, which probably first required suspicion for it to assume full form and be properly perfected for popular fantasy: short, grizzled, humpbacked, with malevolent runny eyes, hooked nose, thin lips, a cane raised in threat; probably the owner of cats, an owl, a talking bird. Kaisersaschern always harbored several specimens of the sort, of whom the most popular, the most teased and feared, was "Cellar Liese," so called because she lived in cellar quarters on Klein Gelbgiesser Gang—an old woman whose behavior had adapted to public prejudice, until even a totally unbiased person, upon meeting her (especially if the kids were right behind her and she was driving them off in a tirade of curses), might feel an archaic shudder come over him, even though there was nothing wrong with her at all.

And here one bold word that comes from the experiences of our own time. For any friend of enlightenment, the word, the concept, of *volk* always carries some archaic apprehension, and he knows that one needs to address the crowd as the *volk* only if one wishes to lure them into some regressive evil. What all has not happened before our eyes—and not just before our eyes, either—in the name of the *volk* that could never have happened in the name of God, or of humanity, or of justice! The fact is, however, that the *volk* is always the *volk*, at least at a certain level of its being, the archaic level, and that people, neighbors from

Klein Gelbgiesser Gang, who voted the Social Democratic ticket at the polls, were capable at the same time of seeing something demonic in the poverty of a little old lady who could not afford rooms above-ground, capable of reaching for their children when she approached in order to defend them from the witch's evil eye. And if such a woman were to be burned, which, with only slight changes in pretext, is hardly outside the realm of the conceivable these days, they would stand behind the barriers set up by the town council and gape, but presumably not revolt. I am speaking of the *volk*, but that same ancient collective layer exists in each of us, and, to say precisely what I think, I do not consider religion the most effective means by which to keep it safely under lock and key. In my opinion, the only help comes from literature, the humanistic sciences, the ideal of the free and beautiful human being.

But to return to the eccentrics of Kaisersaschern—there was, for instance, a man of indeterminate age, who at any sudden shout would feel compelled to perform a kind of jerky dance with knees pulled high, and making a sad and ugly face, he would smile, as if to apologize to the urchins after him in yowling pursuit. There was also a woman named Mathilde Spiegel, who dressed in hopelessly out-of-date fashions, in a frilly dress with a long train and what was known as a *fladus* (an asinine word, a corruption of the French *flûte douce* that probably originally meant "something flattering," but in this case was applied to an outlandishly curly coiffure topped by a bonnet), and who wandered the town in snooty derangement, always heavily rouged—though she was far too fatuous to be even remotely immoral—and accompanied by pug dogs dressed in little velvet warmers. And finally, there was a gentleman of small but independent means, with a purple knobbly nose and a heavy signet ring on his forefinger, whose name was actually Schnalle but whom the children had dubbed "Toodeyloot," because he had the quirk of adding that pointless warble to everything he said. He loved to go to the train station and, as a freight train pulled out, to raise his signet-finger and warn the man facing backwards in the seat on the roof of the caboose, "Don't fall off, don't fall off, toodeyloot!"

I sense that there is something undignified about including these ludicrous reminiscences, but the individuals mentioned, all public institutions so to speak, were uncommonly characteristic of the psychological profile of our town, itself the backdrop for eight years of Adrian's young life—and mine as well, for I spent them at his side—until he departed for university. For although I was two years older than he, and so two grades ahead of him, we usually spent recess in the walled-in schoolyard together, away from our respective classmates, and saw each other most afternoons, too—whether he would come over to my study above Blessed Messengers pharmacy or I would visit him at his uncle's house, 15 Parochial Strasse, where the mezzanine was occupied by musical instruments, the famed inventory of the Leverkühn firm.

VII

THIS WAS A QUIET SPOT, near the cathedral and away from Kaisersaschern's business district along Markt Strasse and Grieskrämer Zeile, a crooked narrow way with no sidewalk, and among its houses Nikolaus Leverkühn's was the most imposing. Three stories tall, not counting rooms in an attic that was set back behind a projecting bay, it was a merchant's house that dated from the sixteenth century, having once belonged to the grandfather of its present owner, and had five windows across the façade of the second story, but only four shuttered ones on the third, where the actual living quarters were located and the exterior ornamental woodcarving first began, whereas everything below, including the entrance, was left plain and unpainted. Even the stairway inside grew wider only above the landing on the mezzanine, which stood rather high above the stone-paved entry hall, so that visitors and customers (many of whom came from out of town, from Halle, even Leipzig) had no easy climb to reach their desired goal, the stock of instruments—which, as I intend to show shortly, was well worth a steep set of stairs.

Until Adrian's arrival, Nikolaus, a widower—his wife had died young—had lived in the house alone with an old, long-time housekeeper, Frau Butze; a maid; and a young Italian from Brescia named Luca Cimabue (he did indeed carry the family name of that thirteenth-century painter of Madonnas), an apprentice who assisted in making violins—for Uncle Leverkühn was also a violin-maker. He was a man with straight-hanging, unkempt, ash-blond hair and a beardless face with agreeable features: very prominent cheekbones; a hooked, slightly drooping nose; a large, expressive mouth; and brown eyes whose gaze betrayed earnest kindness, and cleverness as well. At home he always wore an artisan's shirt of pleated fustian buttoned to the collar. I can well believe this childless man, with a house far too large for him, was delighted to take in a young relative. And I have also heard that although he let his brother in Buchel pay for the boy's tuition, he accepted nothing for room and board. He treated Adrian, on whom he had cast a vaguely expectant eye, very much like his own son and enjoyed having a family member round out his table, which had so long consisted of only the aforementioned Frau Butze and, by a patriarchal gesture, his apprentice Luca.

It might have seemed surprising that this young Italian lad, who spoke only pleasantly broken German and who surely could have found an excellent opportunity at home to train in his specialty, had found his way to Adrian's uncle in Kaisersaschern; but that was an indication of the commercial ties Nikolaus Leverkühn maintained in all directions, not just with German centers of instrument-making like Mainz, Braunschweig, Leipzig, or Barmen, but also with foreign firms in London, Lyons, Bologna, even New York. He had sources everywhere for the symphonic merchandise on which his reputation was built—because he not only sold wares of first-class quality, but also kept a dependably complete stock of items usually not found on demand anywhere else. And so no sooner would a Bach festival be planned somewhere in the German Reich—one that, for stylistic authenticity would require an oboe d'amore, a deeper-voice instrument that had long since vanished from orchestras—than the old house on Parochial Strasse would be visited by a customer, a musician who had made the long trip because he wanted things done right and could try out the elegiac instrument on the spot.

The warehouse occupying the rooms of the mezzanine, which often resounded with the most diverse tone-colors making practice runs through the octaves, offered a splendid, enticing, and—if I may put it that way—culturally bewitching sight that caused one's private acoustic fantasy to surge and roar. With the exception of pianos, which Adrian's foster-father left to the industry specializing in them, there lay spread out before one everything that chimes and sings, that twangs, brays, rumbles, rattles, and booms—even the keyboard instruments were always represented, too, by a celesta with its charming bell-like tones. The enchanting violins were hung behind glass or lay bedded in cases that, like mummy-coffins, took the shape of their occupants; some were lacquered more yellowish, some more brownish, and their slender bows fitted securely into the lid, with silver wire entwining the nut—Italian violins, whose purity of form would have told the expert that their origin was Cremona, but also violins from Tyrol, Holland, Saxony, Mittenwald, plus those from Leverkühn's own workshop. The cello, which owes its ultimate form and rich song to Antonio Stradivari, was present in row after row; but its predecessor, the six-stringed viola da gamba, which in older works is still given equal honor, was always to be found there, too, along with the viola and the violin's elder cousin, the viola alta—just as my own viola d'amore, on whose seven strings I have held forth my whole life long, comes from Parochial Strasse. It was a gift from my parents at my confirmation.

Leaning there were several specimens of the *violone,* the giant violin, the cumbersome double-bass, capable of majestic recitatives, whose pizzicato is more sonorous than the roll of a tuned kettledrum, and from which one would never expect the veiled magic of its flageolet-like tones. And likewise present in quantity was its counterpart among the woodwinds, the contrabassoon, its sixteen feet of tubing robustly augmenting the basses in tones an octave lower than the notes as written, in every dimension double the size of its little brother, the jesting bassoon—and I call it that, because it is a bass instrument without the power of a real bass, strangely weak in tone, a bleating caricature. What a pretty thing it was, nonetheless, with its crook of a mouthpiece, its flashing mechanism of keys and levers. What a charming sight in general, this army of reeds at such a highly developed stage of technology, a challenge to the virtuoso's instincts in each of its variations: as a bucolic oboe; as an English horn, adept at mournful airs; as a multi-keyed clarinet, which can sound so spookily gloomy in its deep chalumeau register, but can sparkle at higher ranges in a blossoming sheen of silvery sound; as basset horn and bass clarinet.

All of them, reposing in velvet, were included in Uncle Leverkühn's inventory, plus flutes of various styles and materials—beechwood, passionfruit wood, ebony—with head pieces of ivory or sterling silver, along with their shrill relatives, the piccolos, whose tones can pierce an orchestral tutti to hold the heights and dance like whirling will-o'-the-wisps in magic incandescence. And only now came the shimmering chorus of brass instruments—from the dapper trumpet, whose bright alarms, jaunty tunes, and melting cantabiles can be seen in its very form, via that darling of the Romantic period, the convoluted French horn; via the slender, powerful slide trombone and the valve cornet; to the fundamental gravity of the great bass tuba. Even rare museum pieces, such as bronze lurs turned deftly to the right and left like steer horns, were usually in stock. But when seen with a boy's eyes, as I do today in recalling it, the most splendid part was the extensive display of percussion instruments—because things that one has met early on as toys under the Christmas tree, that have been the fragile stuff of childhood dreams, were exhibited here in a dignified and very genuine form for adult use. The snare drum—how different this one here looked from that quickly broken trinket of painted wood, parchment, and twine that we banged on as six-year-olds. This one was not made for hanging around the neck. The bottom head was stretched tight with catgut and made suitable for orchestral use by having been screwed to a metal tripod at a functional slant, while the wooden drumsticks, likewise more elegant than ours had been, were stuck invitingly into rings at the sides. There was a glockenspiel, on a childish version of which we both had probably practiced tapping out "Twinkle twinkle little star"; here, however, the meticulously tuned metal plates, arranged to vibrate freely on pairs of crossbars, lay in neat rows in their elegant lockable case, waiting to have melody struck from them by dainty steel hammers kept inside the padded lid. The xylophone, constructed apparently so that the ear could imagine the graveyard dance of skeletons enjoying the midnight hour, was here with its full complement of chromatically scaled bars. The tarnished giant cylinder of the bass drum was here, whose head was set booming by a felt-covered mallet; and the copper kettledrum, sixteen of which Berlioz still required for his orchestra—he had not known them in the form Nikolaus Leverkühn stocked, with a tuning mechanism that allows the drummer to adjust for a change in key with a twist of the hand. How well I remember the boyish tricks we would try out on it, with either Adrian or me—no, it was more likely only me—keeping up a steady roll on the head with the mallets, while Luca modulated the key up and down, yielding the strangest rumbling glissando. And one must also add those remarkable cymbals that only the Chinese and Turks know how to make—for they guard their secret of how to hammer glowing bronze—and that when once they are struck are held high in triumph, their insides turned toward the auditorium; the booming gong, the Gypsy's tambourine, the triangle that has one open corner and chimes brightly at the touch of a steel rod; little hollow castanets, the modern version of cymbals, that clack in the hand. And one must picture, towering over all these serious amusements, the golden architectural splendor of the Érard pedal harp, and then one will comprehend the magic fascination that Adrian's uncle's commercial rooms had for us boys—it was a paradise of silence, but in a hundred forms that all heralded harmony.

For us? No, I'd do better to speak only of myself, of my enchantment, my delight—I scarcely dare include my friend when speaking of such reactions, for I don't know if he was trying to play the son of the house for whom this was all just everyday routine or wanted to show his general coolness of character, but he maintained an almost shrugging indifference before all that splendor and usually responded to my admiring exclamations with a curt laugh or a "yes, pretty" or "funny stuff" or "the ideas people get" or "better than selling sugar loaves." As I sat there in his garret with its charming view across the jumbled roofs of the town, the castle pond, the old water tower, I might express a wish—and I stress, it was always I—to go downstairs together for a not exactly authorized visit to the stockroom; and young Cimabue would sometimes join us, partly I presume to keep an eye on us, partly to play circerone, our guide and interpreter, in his pleasant fashion. From him we learned the history of the trumpet: how at one time it had had to be made of several straight pieces of metal tubing joined by little spheres—that was before the art of bending brass tubes without splitting them had been mastered, which was first done, you see, by casting them in pitch and resin, later on, however, in lead, which would then melt away in the fire. He also liked to discuss some sage authorities' claim that no matter what material an instrument was made of, be it metal or wood, it would sound the way its specific form, its instrumental voice, sounded, and so it was of no consequence if a flute was made of wood or ivory, a trumpet of brass or silver. His master, he said, Adrian's *zio*, who as a violin-maker knew something about the importance of materials, of woods and varnishes, disputed all that and swore that he most definitely could hear what a flute was made of—he, Luca, volunteered to do likewise. Then he was sure to take a flute in his well-formed Italian hands and show us the mechanism (which had undergone such great changes and improvements over the last hundred and fifty years—since Quantz, the famous virtuoso) of both the more powerful Bohemian cylinder flute and the older conical version, which sounds sweeter. He demonstrated for us the fingering on a clarinet and on a seven-holed bassoon, whose sound, with its twelve closed and four open keys, blends so nicely with that of the horns; he taught us about the range of the instruments, how they are played, and much more.

In retrospect, there can be no doubt that, back then, whether consciously or not, Adrian followed those demonstrations at least as attentively as I—and to greater advantage than I was ever meant to gain from them. But he did not let anyone notice, and no gesture carried any intimation that all this had, or would ever have, anything to do with him. He left it to me to put questions to Luca; indeed, he usually stepped away to look at something other than what was being discussed, leaving me alone with the apprentice. I do not wish to say that he was shamming, nor do I forget that for us at that point music had hardly any reality other than the purely physical form it took in Nikolaus Leverkühn's armory. True, we had passing acquaintance with chamber music—which was played every week or two at Adrian's uncle's house, sometimes in my presence, and certainly not always in Adrian's. The group consisted of our cathedral organist, Herr Wendell Kretzschmar, a stutterer who would become Adrian's teacher only a little later; the choral director of Boniface Gymnasium; and Uncle Nikolaus, who joined them for selected quartets by Haydn and Mozart, for which he played first violin, Luca Cimabue second, Herr Kretzschmar cello, and the choral director viola. These were manly amusements, for which a glass of beer stood on the floor beside each player, who probably had a cigar in his mouth as well, and which were frequently interrupted by comments—breaking into the language of tones with an especially dry and odd sound—or by the tapping of bows and the counting back of bars whenever things got out of sync, which was almost always the choral director's fault. We had never heard a real concert, a symphony orchestra; and whoever wishes to, may find that sufficient explanation for Adrian's patent indifference to the world of instruments. In any case, he was of the opinion that one should find it sufficient and saw it as such himself. What I am trying to say is: He hid himself behind it, hid himself from music. For a long time, with intuitive perseverance, the man hid himself from his own destiny.

For a long time, by the way, no one ever thought of making any sort of connection between the young Adrian and music. The idea that he was meant to be a scholar was fixed firmly in every head and was constantly confirmed by his brilliant accomplishments in high school, by his status as head of his class, which began to waver slightly only in the upper grades, from about his sophomore year, at age fifteen, and primarily because of his migraine, which had begun to develop and kept him from what little homework he needed to do. All the same, he mastered the demands of school with ease—though the word "mastered" is not well chosen, for it cost him nothing to satisfy them; and if his excellence as a student did not carry with it the tender affection of his teachers (and it did not, as I often observed; instead there was evidence of a certain irritability, indeed of a desire to arrange minor defeats), that was not so much because he might have been considered arrogant—or wait, he was considered that, but not because one had the impression he took excessive pride in his achievements; on the contrary, he was not proud enough of them, and that was the source of his condescension, for it was palpably directed at everything he accomplished with such effortlessness, at the curriculum itself, at its various branches of study, the transmittal of which constituted the dignity and livelihood of the faculty, who therefore did not wish to see them polished off with over-talented indolence.

As for me, I stood on much more cordial terms with those gentlemen—no wonder, since I was soon to join them professionally and had already seriously declared my intention to do so. I, too, might call myself a good student, but was one and could be one solely because of my reverent love for study itself, especially for ancient languages and their classical poets and writers; I called upon and stretched what talents I had, whereas he let it be made evident at every opportunity—which is to say, he made no secret of it to me, and I justifiably feared it was not hidden from his teachers, either—just how immaterial and secondary, so to speak, the whole educational enterprise was to him. This often alarmed me—not on account of his future career, which given his aptitude was never in peril, but because I asked myself what, then, was not immaterial, not secondary to him. I did not see the "main thing," and it was truly indiscernible. In those years, school life is life itself; it embodies life; its interests form the horizon that every life needs in order to develop values, however relative those may be, by which character and abilities prove themselves. But they can serve that humane purpose only if their relativity remains unrecognized. A belief in absolute values, however illusionary, remains for me a prerequisite of life. My friend's talents were measured against values whose relativity seemed clear to him, yet with no visible point of possible reference that could have impaired them as values. There are poor students enough. Adrian, however, presented the singular phenomenon of a poor student as head of the class. I say that it alarmed me; and yet how impressive, how attractive it seemed to me as well, how it intensified my devotion to him, which, of course, was mixed with—will one ever know why?—something like pain, like hopelessness.

I wish to make room for one exception to the rule of ironic disparagement with which he regarded the rewards and requirements of school. It was his obvious interest in a discipline in which I shone less brightly, in mathematics. My own weakness in the subject, for which I could more or less compensate with exuberant diligence in philology, made me first realize that superior achievement in any field is, as is only natural, conditioned by sympathy with the object of study, and so it truly did me good to see my friend likewise find fulfillment here at least. Mathematics, as applied logic, which nevertheless stays within pure and lofty abstraction, holds a curious intermediate position between the humanistic and the realistic sciences; and from the descriptions Adrian shared in conversation of the delight it gave him, it became evident that at the same time he experienced this intermediateness as something elevated, dominating, universal, or as he put it, "the true." It was a great joy to hear him call something "true"; it was an anchor, a stay—one no longer asked oneself quite in vain about the "main thing."

"You're a slouch not to like it," he said to me one day. "Studying ordered relationships is ultimately the best there is. Order is everything. Romans thirteen: 'For what is of God is ordered.'" He blushed, and I stared at him with wide eyes. It turned out that he was religious.

With him, everything had to "turn out"; you first had to spot, surprise, catch him at it all, to see his cards, as it were—and then he would blush, while you could have kicked yourself for not having seen it long before. That he was doing algebra problems beyond what was expected or demanded, that he enjoyed working with logarithms, that he was sitting over quadratic equations before ever being required to identify exponential unknowns—I discovered all that only by accident, and in each instance cited, he first gave mockery a try before owning up. Yet another disclosure, if not to say exposure, had preceded the rest—I have made reference to it already: that he had made his own autodidactic, secret explorations of the keyboard, of chord structures, the compass card of musical keys, the circle of fifths, and that without any knowledge of notation or fingering, he had used these harmonic discoveries for all sorts of exercises in modulation and to build vaguely rhythmic structures of melody. He was in his fifteenth year when I discovered it. One afternoon, after looking in vain for him in his room, I found him sitting at a little harmonium that stood in a neglected corner of a hallway in the living quarters. I stood at the door listening to him for perhaps a minute, but, reproaching myself for that, I entered and asked him what he was up to. He eased off the bellows, pulled his hands from the manuals, and laughed with a blush.

"Idleness," he said, "is the root of all vice. I'm bored. When I'm bored, I putter and diddle around in here sometimes. This old treadle box stands so forlorn, but humble as it is, it can do it all. Look, this is curious—I mean, naturally there's nothing curious about it, but when you figure it out for yourself the first time, it seems curious how it all hangs together and goes in circles."

And he struck a chord, all black keys—F-sharp–A-sharp–C-sharp—
then added an E and with that, the chord, which had looked like
F-sharp major, was unmasked as belonging to B major, that is, as its fifth
or dominant. "A chord like this," he proposed, "has no key as such. It's
all relationship, and the relations form a circle." The A, which demands a resolution to G-sharp, yielding the modulation from B major
to A major, led him on until he came by way of A, D, and G major, to
C major, and from there into the flatted keys, thus demonstrating for
me that one can build a major or minor scale by using any of the twelve
tones of the chromatic scale.

"That's old hat, by the way," he said. "I noticed it some time ago.
Just watch how it can be done more subtly!" And he began to show me
modulations between more distant keys, exploiting so-called tertian
harmony, the Neapolitan sixth.

Not that he could have given names to these things; but he repeated,
"It's all relationship. And if you want to give it a more exact name, then
call it 'ambiguity.'" To illustrate his point he had me listen to a chord
progression in no particular key, showed me how such a progression
hovers between C and G major if you leave out the F, which would become an F-sharp in G major; how, if you avoid the B, the ear is kept in
uncertainty whether it should hear the chord as C or F major, but
adding a diminished B makes it the latter.

"Do you know what I think?" he asked. "That music is ambiguity as
a system. Take this note or this one. You can understand it like this or,
again, like this, can perceive it as augmented from below or as diminished from above, and, being the sly fellow you are, you can make use
of its duplicity just as you like." In short, he proved that in principle he
was skilled at enharmonic transpositions and not unskilled at certain
tricks for using them to evade a key and recasting them as modulation.

Why was I more than surprised, indeed moved and not a little
shocked? His cheeks had taken on a flush they never had for school-
work, not even algebra.

To be sure, I asked him to fantasize a little more for me, but I felt
something like relief when he turned me down with a "Nonsense!
Nonsense!" What sort of relief was that? It might have served as a les-
son to me how proud I had been of his universal indifference and how
clearly I sensed that his "curious" was indifference merely set on as a
mask. I surmised a budding passion—Adrian had a passion! Should I
have been glad? Instead it was somehow embarrassing and scary.

And so I now knew that he was working at music whenever he
thought himself alone; given the exposed location of his instrument,
however, it could not long remain a secret.

One evening his foster-father said to him, "Well, nephew, from what I heard you playing today, that wasn't the first time you've practiced."

"What do you mean, Uncle Niko?"

"Don't act the innocent. You were in fact making music."

"What a way to put it!"

"It's been applied to more foolish things. The way you got from F to A major was very ingenious. Do you enjoy it?"

"Oh, Uncle."

"Well, apparently you do. I want to tell you something. We'll have that old crate—no one bothers with it in any case—brought up to your room. Then you'll have it handy whenever you get the urge."

"That's dreadfully kind, Uncle, but it's certainly not worth the trouble."

"It's so little trouble that perhaps the pleasure will be all the greater. One more thing, nephew. You ought to take piano lessons."

"Do you think so, Uncle Niko? Piano lessons? I don't know, it sounds so 'hifalutin' and girlish."

"It could be even 'higher' and have nothing girlish about it. And if you study with Kretzschmar, it will be. As an old friend, he won't charge us an arm and a leg, and you'll get a foundation under your castles in the air. I'll speak to him."

Adrian repeated this conversation verbatim for me in the school-yard. From then on he had lessons twice a week with Wendell Kretzschmar.

VIII

STILL YOUNG AT THE TIME, at most in his late twenties, Wendell Kretzschmar was born in Pennsylvania of German-American parents and had received his musical education in the country of his birth. But he had early felt the pull back to the Old World, from where his grandparents had once emigrated and where both his own roots and those of his art were to be found; and in the course of a nomadic life, whose stations and stopovers seldom lasted longer than one or two years, he had come to Kaisersaschern as our organist—it was only one episode that had been preceded by others (for he had previously been employed as a conductor at small municipal theaters in the German Reich and Switzerland) and would be followed by others. He also enjoyed some prominence as a composer of orchestral pieces and saw his opera, *The Marble Statue*, produced and warmly received on several stages.

Unprepossessing in appearance, a squat man with a round skull, short-clipped moustache, and brown eyes whose gaze was now musing, now frisky, but always given to smiling, he could truly have benefited the intellectual and cultural life of Kaisersaschern—had there been, that is, any life of that sort. His organ playing was accomplished and powerful, but you could count on the fingers of one hand those parishioners capable of appreciating it. Nonetheless his free afternoon concerts at the church attracted a good crowd, for whom he played the organ music of Schütz, Buxtehude, Froberger, and of course Sebastian Bach, plus all sorts of curious compositions typical of the epoch between Handel's and Haydn's flourishing; and Adrian and I attended regularly. In comparison, his lectures were a total failure, at least to all appearances; he delivered them resolutely for one entire season in the hall of the Society for Beneficial Community Endeavor, always accompanied by examples on the piano, as well as demonstrations on a chalkboard easel. They were unsuccessful first of all because our community had no use for lectures in general; secondly because his topics were hardly popular ones, indeed seemed rather capricious and odd choices; and thirdly because his unfortunate stutter made listening to him a hair-raising journey along the edge of high cliffs, producing both terror and laughter and tending to divert one's attention totally from the intellectual content and transform the experience into anxious, tense waiting for the next convulsive impasse.

His affliction was the model of a particularly heavy and well-developed stutter—how tragic, since he was a man with a great wealth of urgent ideas and a passionate desire to communicate them in speech. And his boat could sail swiftly and jauntily over the waves for whole stretches at a time, with an eerie ease that seemed to belie his condition and could almost make one forget it; but inevitably, every once in a while, just as everyone correctly expected all along, the moment of shipwreck would arrive, and straining under its agony, he would stand there with a red and swollen face—whether he was impeded by a sibilant, which, with his mouth tugged wide, he would extend as the sound of a locomotive letting off steam; whether in his struggles with a labial his cheeks would puff out, his lips given over to the popping rapid-fire of short, soundless explosions; or whether, finally and simply, his breath would end up in hopeless stammering disarray, his funnel-shaped mouth snapping for air like a fish out of water. It is true that his moist eyes were laughing all the while, and apparently he saw the situation from its humorous side, but that was no consolation for everyone else, and ultimately one could not blame the public for avoiding these lectures—and with such unanimity that indeed several times only about a half dozen listeners occupied some front seats, namely: my parents, Adrian's uncle, young Cimabue, and the two of us, plus a couple of pupils from the girls' academy, who never failed to titter during the speaker's faltering seizures.

He himself would have been prepared to defray out of pocket the costs for the hall and lights, which were in no way covered by the admission fees; but my father and Nikolaus Leverkühn, arguing that the lectures were culturally important and benefited the community, had convinced the society's board to make up the difference, or rather to waive the rent. This was an accommodating gesture, since any benefit to the community was debatable, if for no other reason than the community's failure to appear, which, however, could in part be traced, as noted, to the all too specific nature of the topics treated. Wendell Kretzschmar subscribed to the principle—one we repeatedly heard from lips first shaped around the English language—that it was not a matter of other people's interest, but of his own, and thus of exciting their interest, which could only happen, indeed was guaranteed to happen, if one had a fundamental interest in the subject oneself and so, when speaking of it, could not help involving others in that interest, infecting them with it, thereby creating an interest never extant, never even suspected before—all of which was worth a great deal more than catering to one that already existed.

It was most regrettable that the local public gave him almost no opportunity to prove his theory. For the few of us who sat at his feet on numbered chairs in the yawning void of the old hall, it stood the test perfectly, for he captivated us with things we would never have thought could so hold our attention, and in the end even his dreadful stutter seemed only an intriguingly spellbinding expression of his own zeal. Whenever that calamity occurred, we would frequently all nod in unison to console him, and one gentleman or other could be heard to utter a soothing "There, there," or "It's all right," or "Doesn't matter!" Then with a cheerful apologetic smile, the paralysis would loosen and things would move along for a while with equally uncanny briskness.

What did he speak about? Well, the man was capable of devoting one entire hour to the question, "Why didn't Beethoven write a third movement for his last piano sonata, Opus 111?"—a topic worth discussing, without doubt. But imagine an announcement posted outside Community Endeavor Hall or inserted in the Kaisersaschern *Railroad Gazette,* and then ask yourself what level of public curiosity it could arouse. People flat-out did not wish to know why Opus 111 has only two movements. Those of us who assembled for the discussion enjoyed an uncommonly enriching evening, to be sure, even if up till then we had been totally unfamiliar with the sonata at issue. We did get to know it by way of the lecture, however, and in very precise detail, since Kretzschmar provided us an admirable, if rumbling, rendition on the very inferior upright available to him (a baby grand having not been authorized), interrupted now and then with an incisive analysis of its psychological content, including descriptions of the circumstances under which it—along with two others—had been composed; he also dwelt at length with caustic wit on the master's own explanation of why he had dispensed here with a third movement corresponding to

the first. Beethoven's response to his famulus's question, you see, had
been that he had no time and had therefore decided to make the second
a little longer instead. No time! And he had said it quite "calmly" no
less. The questioner had apparently not noticed the insult contained in
such an answer—and indeed justified by such a question. And now the
lecturer described Beethoven's state in 1820, when his hearing, afflicted
by an incurable degeneration, had progressed to almost total loss, and
it had now become clear that he would no longer be capable of conducting performances of his own works. He told us about the rumor
claiming that the famous composer had written himself dry, had used
up all his creative energies, and being incapable of larger works, was
busying himself, as had the aged Haydn, simply with copying out
Scottish songs—and about how the story had gained increasing currency, since for several years, in fact, nothing of significance bearing his
name had appeared on the market. Except that in late autumn, returning to Vienna from Mödling, where he had spent the summer, the master had sat down and written these three compositions for the piano in
one swoop, without ever looking up from the page, so to speak, and
had reported the fact to his patron, Count Brunswick, in order to reas-
sure him about his mental state.

And then Kretzschmar spoke of the sonata in C minor, which, to be
sure, is not easily seen as a finished and psychologically ordered work
and which had given both contemporary critics and friends a hard aesthetic nut to crack; just as, so he said, these same friends and admirers,
who revered him, had been utterly unable to follow him beyond the
summit to which he had once led them in the mature period of his
symphonies, piano concertos, and classic string quartets, and when
confronted with the works of the last period had stood with heavy
hearts before a process of disintegration, of alienation, of an ascent into
what no longer felt familiar, but eerie—stood, that is, before a *plus ultra*, in which they had been incapable of seeing anything more than a
degeneration into tendencies that had always been present, into an excess of introspection and speculation, a surfeit of minutia and mere
musical science, applied at times to even simple material, such as the
arietta theme for the stupendous variations that comprised the second
movement of this sonata. Yes, just as that movement's theme, moving
through a hundred vicissitudes, a hundred worlds of rhythmic contrast, outgrows itself and finally loses itself in dizzying heights that
could be called otherworldly or abstract, so, too, Beethoven's own
artistry had outgrown itself, had left the snug regions of tradition, and,
as humanity gazed on in horror, climbed to spheres of the totally per-

sonal, the exclusively personal—an ego painfully isolated in its own absoluteness, and, with the demise of his hearing, isolated from the sensual world as well. He was the lonely prince over a ghostly realm, from which came emanations evoking only a strange shudder in even the most well-disposed of his contemporaries, terrifying messages to which they could have reconciled themselves only at rare, exceptional moments.

So far so good, Kretzschmar said. But actually only conditionally good, only in an inadequate way. For one associated the idea of the exclusively personal with that of a boundless subjectivity and a radical will to harmonic expression, as opposed to polyphonic objectivity (and he asked us to fix that differentiation in our minds: harmonic subjectivity, polyphonic detachment); and yet, as with the late masterpieces in general, that comparison, that antithesis did not work here. In fact, Beethoven had been far more subjective, if not to say, far more "personal," in his middle period than toward the end; at that earlier stage he had been much more intent on letting all conventions, formulas, and flourishes (of which music was full after all) be consumed by personal expression, on fusing all that with the subjective dynamic. Despite the uniqueness, even freakishness of its formal language, Beethoven's late work—the five last piano sonatas for instance—had a quite different, much more forgiving and amenable relation to convention. Untouched, untransformed by the subjective, the conventional often emerged in the late works with a baldness—as if blown wide open, so to speak—with an ego-abandonment that, in turn, had an effect more terrifyingly majestic than any personal indiscretion. In these structures, the lecturer said, the subjective entered into a new relationship with the conventional, a relationship defined by death.

And at that word, Kretzschmar began to stutter violently; holding on to its initial consonant, his tongue set up a kind of machine-gun fire against his palate, setting jaw and chin pulsing in sync, before they came to rest in the vowel that allowed one to surmise the rest. But once the word had been recognized, it did not seem appropriate for someone to relieve him of it, to do what we sometimes did and call it out to him in jovial helpfulness. He had to complete it all on his own, and he did so. Where greatness and death came together, he declared, there arose a sovereign objectivity amenable to convention and leaving arrogant subjectivity behind, because in it the exclusively personal—which after all had been the surmounting of a tradition carried to its peak—once again outgrew itself by entering, grand and ghostlike, into the mythic and collective.

He did not ask whether we understood this, nor did we ask ourselves. If he thought the main point was that we heard it—why, then,
we shared this opinion completely. And it was in the light of all this, he
went on, that one must regard the work about which he was speaking in particular, the sonata Opus 111. And then he sat down at the upright and played the whole composition from memory, both the first
and the stupendous second movement, but in such a manner that he
shouted out his commentary while he played, and to call our attention
to a lead theme he would enthusiastically sing along by way of demonstration—all of which, taken together, resulted in a partly enthralling,
partly comical spectacle, repeatedly greeted with amusement by the little audience. Since he had a very heavy touch and served up a powerful
forte, he had to yell extra loudly just to make himself halfway understood and to sing at the top of his voice whenever he vocally underscored what he was playing. His mouth imitated what his hands were
doing. *Boom, boom—voom, voom—throom, throom—*he struck the
grimly vehement opening accents of the first movement, and in a high
falsetto he sang along with passages of melodic sweetness, which, like
delicate glimpses of light, now and then illuminate the storm-tossed
skies of the piece. Finally he laid his hands in his lap, rested for a moment and said, "Here it comes." He began the variations movement,
the *adagio molto semplice e cantabile.*

The arietta theme, destined for adventures and vicissitudes for
which, in its idyllic innocence, it seems never to have been born, is immediately called up and for sixteen bars says its piece, reducible to a
motif that emerges toward the end of its first half, like a short, soulful
cry—just three notes, an eighth, a sixteenth, and a dotted quarter, that
can only be scanned as something like: "sky of blue" or "lover's pain"
or "fare-thee-well" or "come a day" or "meadow-land"—and that is all.
But what now becomes of this gentle statement, this pensively tranquil
figure, in terms of rhythm, harmony, counterpoint, what blessings its
master bestows upon it, what curses he heaps upon it, into what dark-
nesses and superilluminations, where cold and heat, serenity and ecstasy are one and the same, he hurls and elevates it—one may well call
it elaborate, miraculous, strange, and excessively grand without
thereby giving it a name, because in actuality it is nameless; and Kretzschmar played all these stupendous transformations for us with hard-
working hands, singing along very fiercely: *"Dimdada,"* and shouting
loudly over it all. "Chain of trills!" he yelled. *"Fioriture* and caden-
zas! Do you hear convention abandoned? Here—language—is—no
longer—purged of flourishes—rather flourishes—of the appearance—

of their subjective—self-composure—the appearance—of art is thrown off—for ultimately—art always throws off—the appearance of art. *Dim —dada!* Just listen, please, how here—the melody is overwhelmed —by the weight of the chords' joints! It becomes static, monotone— two Ds, three Ds, one after the other—the chords do that—*dim— dada!* And now pay close attention to what happens here—"

It was extraordinarily difficult to listen simultaneously to his shouts and to the highly complex music they punctuated. But we tried, bent forward, straining, hands between the knees, shifting our gaze alternately between his hands and mouth. The hallmark of the movement is, in fact, the wide separation between bass and treble, between the right and left hands, and a moment arrives, a situation of extremes, where the poor theme seems to hover lonely and forlorn above a dizzyingly gaping abyss—an event of pallid grandeur, and hard on its heels comes an anxious shrinking-to-almost-nothing, a moment of startled fear, as it were, that such a thing could happen. And a great deal more happens yet before it comes to an end. But when it does end, and in the very act of ending, there comes—after all this fury, tenacity, obsessiveness, and extravagance—something fully unexpected and touching in its very mildness and kindness. After all its ordeals, the motif, this D–G–G, undergoes a gentle transformation. As it takes its farewell and becomes in and of itself a farewell, a call and a wave of goodbye, it experiences a little melodic enhancement. After an initial C, it takes on a C-sharp before the D, so that it now no longer scans as "sky of blue" or "meadow-land," but as "O—thou sky of blue," "green-est meadowland," "fare-thee-well, for good"; and this added C-sharp is the most touching, comforting, poignantly forgiving act in the world. It is like a painfully loving caress of the hair, the cheek—a silent, deep gaze into the eyes for one last time. It blesses its object, its dreadful journeys now past, with overwhelming humanization, lays it on the hearer's heart as a farewell, forever, lays it so gently that tears well up. "Now for-get the pain!" it says. "God was — great in us." "All was — but a dream." "Hold my — memory dear." Then it breaks off. Fast, hard triplets scurry toward a convenient final phrase that could easily conclude many another piece.

After that, Kretzschmar did not return from his upright to the lectern. He remained seated on his revolving stool, turned toward us, hands between his knees, in a position the same as ours, and with a few words concluded his lecture on the question of why Beethoven had not written a third movement to Opus 111. We had needed only to hear the piece, he said, to be able to answer the question ourselves. A

third movement? A new beginning, after that farewell? A return—
after that parting? Impossible! What had happened was that the sonata
had found its ending in its second, enormous movement, had ended
never to return. And when he said, "the sonata," he did not mean just
this one, in C minor, but he meant the sonata *per se*, as a genre, as a
traditional artform—it had been brought to an end, to its end, had
fulfilled its destiny, reached a goal beyond which it could not go;
canceling and resolving itself, it had taken its farewell—the wave
of goodbye from the D–G–G motif, consoled melodically by the
C-sharp, was a farewell in that sense, too, a farewell as grand as the
work, a farewell from the sonata.

And with that Kretzschmar departed, accompanied by sparse, but
prolonged applause, and we departed as well, more than a little preoccupied, weighed down with new ideas. As we put on coats and hats and
left, most of us, as people are wont to do, dazedly hummed to ourselves the evening's chief impression, the motif that constitutes the
theme of the second movement, in both its original and its leave-taking
form; and as the audience scattered, for a good while yet one could
hear from more distant streets—the quiet, reverberant streets of a small
town at night—echoes of "Fare-thee-well," "Fare-thee-well, for good,"
"God was — great in us."

That was not the last time we heard the stutterer lecture on
Beethoven. He soon spoke again about him, this time under the title
"Beethoven and the Fugue." I can recall this topic very precisely as
well and can still see the announcement before me, perfectly aware that
it was no more likely than the others to produce a life-threatening
crush inside Community Endeavor Hall. But our little group most decidedly found enjoyment and profit in this evening as well. Those who
envied and opposed the audacious innovator had always claimed in
fact, so we were told, that Beethoven could not write a fugue. "He simply cannot do it," they had said, well aware of what that meant, since
at the time the venerable artform still stood in high honor, and no composer could either find mercy before the court of music or satisfy the
potentates and great lords who commissioned it, if he could not hold
his own perfectly at the fugue. Prince Esterházy, for example, had been
a special friend of this masterly art, but in the *Mass in C* that Beethoven
had written for him, the composer had managed no more than unsuccessful stabs at a fugue, which, purely socially, had been a bit of bad
manners and, artistically, an unforgivable failing; and his oratorio,
Christ on the Mount of Olives, lacked any sort of fugal passage, although it would have most definitely been in order there. And such a

feeble effort as the fugue in the third quartet of Opus 59 was not exactly calculated to refute the allegation that the great man was a poor
contrapuntist—in which opinion the authorities of the musical world
could only be bolstered by the funeral march in the *Eroica* and the al-
legretto of the Symphony in A Major. And then there was the final
movement of the Cello Sonata in D, Opus 102, designated *Allegro fu-
gato*! Great had been the screaming and shaking of fists, Kretzschmar
reported. The entire work had been denounced as murky to the point
of unpalatability, and for at least twenty bars, they had claimed, such
scandalous confusion reigned—primarily the result of excessively colored modulations—that after that one could calmly close the file on
the man's incompetence in this strict style.

I interrupt my paraphrase here only to point out that the lecturer
was speaking about issues, concerns, matters of art that had never entered into our field of vision and only now, by means of his constantly
imperiled speech, did they emerge as shadows at its periphery; and to
observe that we had no way of verifying what he said other than by
means of his own annotated presentations at the piano, which we
heard with the dimly excited fantasy of children listening to fairy tales
they do not understand, even while their tender minds are nonetheless
enriched and stimulated in some strangely dreamlike, intuitive fashion.
"Fugue," "counterpoint," *"Eroica,"* "confusion resulting from excessively colored modulations," "strict style"—all those were in essence
fairy-tale whispers for us, but we heard them as gladly and as big-eyed
as children listen to something incomprehensible, indeed quite inappropriate for them—and with much more delight than they get from
what lies close at hand, from what is fitting and proper. Might this be
considered the most intensive and proud, perhaps even the most beneficial kind of learning—anticipatory learning, learning that leaps vast
stretches of ignorance? As a pedagogue I should probably not speak on
its behalf, but I know for a fact that young people show extraordinary
preference for it, and I suspect that with time the space that has been
skipped fills up all on its own.

Beethoven, then, so we heard, had enjoyed the reputation of being
unable to write a fugue, and the question was, how close was this nasty
slander to the truth? Apparently he had attempted to refute it. Several
times he had inserted fugues into subsequent piano music, but in a
three-voiced form: both in the *Hammerklavier* sonata and in the one
that begins in A-flat major. In one case he added "With some liberties,"
a sign that he was well aware of the rules he had broken. Why he
slighted them, whether out of personal autarchy or because he could

not handle them, was a point of ongoing dispute; and it was also disputed whether these structures deserved the name of fugue in the strict sense—for they seemed all too sonatalike, too expressive in intent, too harmonically chordal in character, and so hardly calculated to clear their composer of the charge of contrapuntal weakness. But then, to be sure, had come the great fugue overture, Opus 124 and the majestic fugues in the Gloria and Credo of the *Missa Solemnis,* proof at last that in wrestling with this angel the great combatant had remained the victor here, too, though departing perhaps halting upon his thigh.

Kretzschmar told us a terrifying tale, imprinting on our minds a horribly indelible image of the sacred burden of this struggle and of the person of the obsessed creator. It was midsummer 1819, the period when Beethoven was working on the *Missa* at the Hafner house in Mödling, in despair that every section was turning out much longer than expected, so that the deadline for its completion—it was a date in March the next year, for the installation of Archduke Rudolf as archbishop of Olmütz—could not possibly be met. And it happened that two friends, both musicians, came to visit him one afternoon, and no sooner had they entered the house than they heard shocking news. Both the master's maids had bolted that same morning after a wild scene that had occurred the night before, around one o'clock, awakening the entire house from slumber. The master had worked all evening, well into the night, on the Credo, the Credo with its fugue, never giving a thought to his evening meal, which still stood on the stove, whereupon the serving girls, having waited long in vain, at last yielded to nature and went to bed. But when, between twelve and one, the master had demanded his meal, he had found the maids asleep, the food ruined and charred, and had broken into the most violent rage, paying still less heed to the sleeping household since he could not even hear the racket he was making. "Could ye not watch with me one hour?" he had thundered over and over. But it had been five, six hours—and so the aggrieved maids had absconded by the first light of day, leaving to his own devices so uncontrollable a master, who, having had no midday meal either, had not eaten a bite since yesterday noon. Instead he had labored in his room, on the Credo, the Credo with its fugue; his disciples could hear him working behind the closed door. The deaf man sang, howled, and stomped over that Credo—the sound of it so horrifyingly moving that the blood froze in the eavesdroppers' veins. Just as they were about to depart in great trepidation, the door was flung open, and there in the doorframe stood Beethoven—what a sight! What a horrifying sight! In disheveled clothes, his facial features

so distorted that they could inspire fear, his eyes listening and filled
with mad abstraction, he had stared at them, looking as if he had just
come from a life-and-death struggle with all the hostile spirits of counterpoint. He had first stammered something incoherent and then broken into complaints and curses about the mess in his household, about
how everyone had run off, how they were letting him starve. The two
attempted to calm him—one helped him to get properly dressed, the
other ran to an inn to order a cheering meal. . . . Not until three years
later was the mass completed.

We did not know the work, we only heard about it. But who would
deny that it can also be instructive just to hear of a great unfamiliar
work? To be sure, a lot depends on the way in which it is spoken about.
Returning home from Wendell Kretzschmar's lecture, we had the feeling that we had heard the *Missa,* and that illusion was not a little influenced by the picture he had impressed on our minds of the haggard and
hungry master there in the doorframe.

Nor were we familiar with the "Monster of All Quartets" (which
formed the next part of the lecture and was one of Beethoven's last five,
written in six movements and performed four years after the completion of the *Missa*), since it was far too difficult for them to have dared
it at Nikolaus Leverkühn's; and yet with pounding hearts we heard
Kretzschmar speak of it, were vaguely moved, in fact, by the disparity
between the high honor in which, as we knew, this work likewise
stood in our own time and the agony, the grief-stricken or embittered
bewilderment, into which it had plunged his contemporaries—even his
most loyal, most ardent believers. That their despair had been aroused
primarily, though certainly not exclusively, by the final fugue was the
reason why Kretzschmar came to speak of it in connection with his
topic. It had been dreadful listening for healthy ears of the day, which
resisted hearing what its author did not have to hear, but had made
bold to conceive only in a soundless form: a savage brawl between hell-
ishly dissonant instrumental voices, wandering lost in heights and
depths, clashing with one another in variant patterns at every irregular
turn, so that the performers, unsure of both themselves and the music,
had probably not played it all that cleanly, thereby consummating the
Babel of confusion. Staggering—that was the lecturer's word for the
way a defect in the senses had enhanced intellectual daring and dictated
the future of our sense of beauty. But, he suggested, only with a certain
sycophancy is it possible even for us nowadays to pretend to see in this
piece—which, by the way, at the demand of the publisher was separated from the work and replaced with a final movement in a freer

style—to pretend to see in it nothing but the clearest, most agreeable form. He would be bold himself, he declared, perhaps even stick his foot in it, by declaring that in such a treatment of the fugue one could see hatred and violation, a thoroughly unaccommodating and problematical relationship with the artform, a reflection of the relationship, or lack thereof, between the great man and one still greater—at least in the opinion of many—Johann Sebastian Bach. But Bach had almost been lost to the memory of the period, and particularly in Vienna people still had no wish to hear about Protestant music. For Beethoven, Handel had been the king of kings, though he also had a great fondness for Cherubini, whose Medea Overture (when he could still hear) he could not hear often enough. He had owned only a very few works by Bach: a couple of motets, *The Well-Tempered Clavier,* a toccata, and some odds and ends, all collected in one volume. Into that volume had been inserted a note, written in an unknown hand, with the dictum: "One cannot better examine the depth of a man's musical knowledge than by attempting to learn how far he has come in his admiration for the works of Bach." At both sides of this text, however, the owner had used his thickest musical quill to draw an emphatic, vehement question mark.

This was very interesting and also paradoxical, since one might well say that had the period been more familiar with Bach, Beethoven's muse would have had easier access to understanding among his contemporaries. Matters stood, however, as follows. In spirit, the fugue belonged to an age of liturgical music which already lay far in the past for Beethoven; he had been the grand master of a profane epoch of music, in which that art had emancipated itself from the cultic to the cultural. Presumably, however, that was always merely a temporary and never a final emancipation. In the nineteenth century, masses written for the concert hall, the symphonies of Bruckner, the sacred music of Brahms and of Wagner (at least in *Parsifal*), all clearly reveal those old, never fully dissolved ties to a cultic setting; and as for Beethoven, he had written, in a letter to the director of a Berlin choral society requesting they perform his *Missa Solemnis,* that the work could most definitely be sung *a cappella* throughout; and indeed one section, the Kyrie, was already written with no instrumental accompaniment—and for his part, he added, he was of the opinion that that style was to be regarded as the only true style for church music. It could not be determined whether he was thinking here of Palestrina or of the contrapuntal polyphonic vocal style of the Spanish Netherlands, in which Luther had seen his musical ideal, of Josquin des Prez perhaps, or of Adrian

Willaert, the founder of the Venetian school. In any case, those words had spoken of liberated music's never extinguished homesickness for origins still bound to the cult; and Beethoven's violent attempts at the fugue had been those of a great dynamic and emotional spirit wrestling with an ingeniously cool compositional form that upon its knees had praised God, the orderer of the cosmos and all its many rounds, yet all the while had been caught up in another world of passions—strict, highly abstract, ruled by numbers and a chiming relationship with time.

That was Kretzschmar on "Beethoven and the Fugue," and it truly gave us several things to talk about on the way home—things to be silent together about, too, and quietly, vaguely to reflect upon—distant, grand things spoken in words that, whether skipping along nimbly, or getting horribly stuck, had pierced deeply into our souls. I say, our souls, but of course it is only Adrian's that I have in mind. What I heard, what I took in, is totally irrelevant. But it is important for the reader to know, and keep in mind, that my friend was stirred, impressed by these issues and concerns at the time, and it is for that reason that I am reporting in such detail about Wendell Kretzschmar's lecture series.

However opinionated, perhaps even high-handed his presentations were, he was unquestionably an ingenious man—that was evident in the stimulating, thought-provoking effect his words had on a highly gifted young mind like Adri Leverkühn's. What had chiefly impressed him, as he revealed on the way home and the following day in the schoolyard, was the distinction Kretzschmar had made between cultic and cultural epochs and his observation that the secularization of art, its separation from worship, was of only a superficial and episodic nature. The high-school sophomore was manifestly moved by an idea that the lecturer had not even articulated, but that had caught fire in him: that the separation of art from any liturgical context, its liberation and elevation to the isolated and personal, to culture for culture's sake, had burdened it with a solemnity without any point of reference, an absolute seriousness, a pathos of suffering epitomized in Beethoven's terrible appearance in the doorway—but that that did not have to be its abiding destiny, its perpetual state of mind. Just listen to the young man! With almost no real, practical experience in the field of art, he was fantasizing in a void and in precocious words about art's apparently imminent retreat from its present-day role to a happier, more modest one in the service of a higher fellowship, which did not have to be, as at one time, the Church. What it would be, he could not say. But that culture as an idea was a historically transitory phenomenon, that it could lose itself again in some other idea, that the future did not necessarily belong to it—he had most definitely extracted that notion from Kretzschmar's lecture.

"But the alternative to culture, " I interjected, "is barbarism."

"Beg your pardon," he said, "but barbarism is the antithesis of culture only within a structure of thought that provides us the concept. Outside of that structure the antithesis may be something quite different or not even an antithesis at all."

I mimicked Luca Cimabue by crossing myself and saying, "Santa Maria!" He just gave a burst of laughter.

On another occasion he said, "For an age of culture, our own age talks a bit too much about culture, don't you think? I would like to know if epochs that had culture even knew the word at all, used it, blazoned it. Naiveté, a lack of awareness, everything as second nature— that seems to me to be the first criterion for a state deserving the word 'culture.' What we lack is precisely that, the naiveté, and that deficiency, if one may call it that, protects us from many a colorful barbarism that would be quite compatible with culture, with very high culture indeed. What I'm saying is: Our level is that of civilized behavior—a very praiseworthy state, no doubt, but neither can there be any doubt that we would have to become much more barbaric to be capable of culture once again. Technology and comfort—having those, people speak of culture, but do not have it. Would you prevent me from seeing our homophonic-melodic music as a state of civilized musical behavior— in contrast to the old contrapuntal polyphonic culture?"

Much of this talk, which was intended to tease and annoy me, simply echoed what other people said. But he had a way of appropriating and personalizing what he had picked up that relieved his borrowings of any sense of the ridiculous, if not of its boyish dependency. He also commented at length—or we commented in excited exchange—on a Kretzschmar lecture entitled "Music and the Eye," yet another presentation that would have deserved a larger audience. As the title says, our speaker spoke of his art insofar as it appeals to the sense of sight, or rather appeals to it as well, which it already does, so he explained, in that it is written out—that is, in musical notation, the alphabet of tones, which since the days of the old neumes (a fixed system of strokes and dots that more or less suggested the flow of sound) had been employed continually and with ever-increasing precision. And his proofs were very entertaining (and flattering, too, since they insinuated that we had a kind of apprentice's or bottle washer's intimacy with music), showing how many of the idioms of the musician's jargon are derived not from the auditory but from the visual world of written notes. People spoke, for instance, of *occhiali,* because broken murky basses—half notes whose necks are linked together by strokes—ended up looking like pairs of spectacles; or certain cheap melodic sequences, in which the same interval was repeated in successive stairsteps (he showed us examples on his blackboard), were called "cobbler's patches." He spoke of the purely optical effect of written music and as-sured us that one glance at the notation sufficed for an expert to gain a definitive impression of a composition's spirit and quality. It had once happened that some dilettante's concoction he had received lay open on his music stand just as a visiting colleague had entered the room and, while still at the door, called out, "For God's sake, what sort of trash is that you have there?" On the other hand, he described for us the ravishing joy that just the visual image of a Mozart score provides the practiced eye—the clarity of its disposition, the lovely allocation among instrumental groups, the clever command of the rich transfor-mations in the melodic line. A deaf man, he shouted, someone with no experience of sound, would surely have to take delight in such sweet visions. "To hear with eyes belongs to love's fine wit," he said, quoting a Shakespeare sonnet, and claimed composers in every age had tucked away some things in their notation that were meant more for the read-ing eye than for the ear. When the Flemish masters of polyphony, for instance, had shaped their endless devices for interweaving voices in contrapuntal relationship so that when read backwards one voice was exactly like the other, it had very little to do with how it sounded, and he would bet that only a very few would have noticed the joke with their ears and that it had been intended instead for the eye of the pro-fessional. For instance, in his *Marriage at Cana* Orlando di Lasso had used six voices for the six jugs of water, which one could count more easily by sight than by ear; and in Joachim à Burck's *St. John Passion,* the phrase about "one of the officers" who strikes Jesus is set to just one note, but the "two" in the later phrase "and two others with him" is given two notes.

He introduced several more such Pythagorean jokes, intended more for the eye than the ear, hoodwinking the ear so to speak, in which mu-sic had indulged ever and again, and disclosed that, in the final analy-sis, he attributed them to the art's inherent lack of sensuality, indeed to its anti-sensualism, to a secret bias toward asceticism. Indeed it was the most intellectual of all the arts, which was evident from the fact that in music, as in no other art, form and content were intertwined, were ab-

solutely one and the same. One might very well say, music "appeals to
the ear"; but it did so only in a qualified sense—that is, only in those
instances where hearing, like any other sense, acted as the conduit, the
receptive organ for the intellectual content. But in fact there existed
music that did not reckon at all with ever being heard. That was the
case with a six-voiced canon by J. B. Bach, in which he had reworked a
thematic idea by Frederick the Great. In it one had a piece that was intended for neither the human voice nor any known instrument, indeed
for no sense-based realization whatever, but that was music *per se,* music as pure abstraction. Perhaps, Kretzschmar said, it was music's deepest desire not to be heard at all, not even seen, not even felt, but, if that
were possible, to be perceived and viewed in some intellectually pure
fashion, in some realm beyond the senses, beyond the heart even. Except, being bound to the world of senses, it then must again strive for
its most intense, indeed bewitching sensual realization, like a Kundry
who does not wish to do what she does and yet flings soft arms of lust
around the neck of the fool. It found its most powerful, sensual realization in orchestral music, where, entering through the ear, it seemed
to affect all the senses, to act as an opiate, allowing the pleasures of the
realm of sound to melt with those of color and fragrance. Here indeed
it played the role of the penitent in the garb of the sorceress.

There was one instrument, however—that was to say, one medium
of musical realization—through which music was, to be sure, made audible, but in a way that was only semi-sensual, almost abstract, and
thus strangely consistent with its intellectual nature: that was the piano. And to end the evening, he expatiated on it, and very interestingly.
Such a decidedly instrumental musician as Berlioz, he said, ought not
to be blamed for having spoken unkindly about an instrument that
could neither sustain a tone nor let it swell or ebb and that was such a
bitter disappointment when rendering orchestral music. It leveled
everything out by means of abstraction, and since an orchestrated idea
was frequently the idea in and of itself, its very substance, there was often hardly anything left of instrumental music when played on the piano. And so it was merely a means for remembering things one first
had to have heard in their reality. And yet, in turn, this abstraction also
meant something lofty and noble—meant the nobility of music itself,
which was its intellectual content; and whoever listened to a piano, to
the great music written for it, and only it, would hear and see music in
its intellectual purity, without any sensual medium, as it were, or only
a minimum of one. It had been a great hero of the orchestra, a skilled
rabble-rouser, Kretzschmar explained, a theatrical musician—yes, well,

Richard Wagner—who, upon hearing the *Hammerklavier* sonata once again in old age and losing himself in it, had burst into raptures for these "pure spectra of existence" (that had been his locution), exclaiming in his Saxon accent: "That sort of thing is conceivable only on the piano! And to play it for the masses—pure nonsense!" What homage for a seasoned instrumental magician to pay to the piano and its music! It had been more than a little characteristic of the conflict between asceticism and world-devouring hunger that made up the drama of his nature.

So much, then, for today about an instrument that was not one, at least not in the sense others were, for it lacked any special quality. It could, like the others, be treated as a solo instrument, as a vehicle for virtuosity, but that was the exception and, when viewed very precisely, a misuse. Seen properly, the piano was the direct and sovereign representative of music *per se* in all its intellectuality, and that was why it ought to be learned. But piano lessons should not be—at least not essentially, not first and last—instruction in some special skill, but instruction in . . .

"Music!" a voice in the tiny audience cried, for the speaker could not manage the final word, which he had used so frequently till now, and was still stuck mumbling its initial consonant.

"Yes indeed!" he said and, now rescued, took a sip of water and departed.

And perhaps I will be forgiven for bringing him on-stage one more time. For I still need to deal with a fourth lecture that Wendell Kretzschmar offered us, and in fact I would better have disregarded one of the others, for—again, I am not speaking of myself—none of them made so deep an impression on Adrian as this one did.

I can no longer recall the title exactly. It was called "The Elemental in Music" or "Music and the Elemental" or "The Elements of Music" or maybe even something else. In any case, the idea of the elemental, the primitive, of primal beginnings, played a decisive role in it, as did the notion that of all the arts, music in particular (however highly complex, richly and subtly developed that marvelous structure created by history over the course of centuries might be) had never cast aside the devout habit of reverently recalling its first beginnings and solemnly conjuring them up—in short, of celebrating its elemental forces. And in doing so, he said, it celebrated its capacity for cosmic metaphor, since those elements were, so to speak, the world's first and simplest building blocks, a parallel that a philosophizing artist of recent memory—and again, it was Wagner of whom he spoke—had cleverly put to use in his cosmogonic myth, *The Ring of the Nibelung,* by equating the basic elements of music with those of the world itself. For him the beginning of all things had its music—it was the music of the beginning and likewise the beginning of music, the E-flat major triad of the surging depths of the Rhine, the seven primitive chords, like cyclopean stones hewn from primeval rock, out of which the fortress of the gods rose up. On a brilliantly grand scale he had provided the myth of music along with that of the world, and by binding music to things and letting things declare themselves in music, had created an apparatus of ingenious simultaneity, very grand and heavy with meaning, if in the end a little too clever, perhaps, in comparison with certain revelations of the elemental in the art of pure musicians, of Beethoven and Bach, in the latter's prelude to the cello suite, for example—likewise in E-flat major and built on primitive triads, with references to only the most closely related keys, while the cello's voice spoke only the most basic, fundamental, and simple truth with, one might also say, nascent innocence. In order to prove receptive for the utter and unprecedented uniqueness of this creation—the lecturer told us from the piano, which he used to verify his words—the heart needed to be, as Scripture says, "swept with the besom," to be brought to that state of perfect emptiness and readiness that mystic instruction says is a condition for receiving God. And he recalled Anton Bruckner, who loved to refresh himself at the organ or piano with simple, long series of triads. "Is there anything more heartfelt, more glorious," he had cried, "than such a sequence of basic triads? Is it not like a cleansing bath for the soul?" And this assertion, Kretzschmar suggested, was also thought-provoking evidence for music's tendency to plunge back into the elemental and admire itself in its earliest beginnings.

He moved on. He spoke about music in its precultural state, when song had been a howl across several pitches; about the birth of the tonal system from the chaos of unstandardized sounds; and about the monodic isolation that had definitely reigned in Western music throughout the first Christian millennium—a singleness of intent and of voice, of which our harmonically schooled ears could have no conception, since we involuntarily tied every tone we heard to a harmony, although back then a tone would never have required or have been capable of such harmony. Moreover, in that early period, musical performance had more or less totally done away with a regular and periodically subdivided rhythm; old notation indicated a positive indifference to such encumbrances and revealed that, instead, musical performance must have had a quality something like free recitation, improvisation. But if one closely examined music, and in particular its most recently achieved stage of development, one noticed the secret desire to return to those conditions. Yes, the lecturer cried, it lay in the nature of this singular art that at every moment it was able to begin all over again, out of nothing, absent any knowledge of the cultural history through which it had already passed, of its achievements over the centuries—to rediscover itself, to regenerate. But in doing so it passed once again through the same primitive stages that had marked its historical beginnings, and in a very short time and far from the great massif of its development, could attain marvelous peaks of the most peculiar and isolated beauty—and the world might never hear. And now he told us a story that fitted in a most whimsical and thought-provoking way into the framework of the evening's observations.

Around the middle of the eighteenth century, a community of pious German sectarians, practicing Anabaptists, had flourished in his home state of Pennsylvania. Their leading and spiritually most respected members lived celibate lives and were therefore honored with the name of Solitary Brothers and Sisters. The majority had learned how to pair the married state with an exemplarily pure and godly life full of self-discipline and abstinence and strictly regulated by hard work and a healthy diet. Their settlements were two in number: one named Ephrata, in Lancaster County; the other, in Franklin County, called Snowhill; and all of them had respectfully looked up to their leader, shepherd, spiritual father—to a man named Beissel, the founder of the sect, in whose character intense devotion to God was united with the qualities of a pastor of souls and master of men, and fanatic religiosity with gruff energy.

Johann Conrad Beissel had been born of very poor parents in Eberbach in the Palatinate, and was orphaned early on. He had learned the baker's trade and as a journeyman apprentice had joined up with Pietists, members of the New Baptist Brethren, who had awakened within him slumbering tendencies—a predilection for a peculiar service of the truth and independent convictions about God. And thus brought dangerously close to spheres deemed heretical in Germany, the thirty-year-old had decided to flee the intolerance of the Old World and to emigrate to America, where in various places—Germantown, Conestoga—he had exercised the weaver's craft. But then a new wave of religious emotion had swept over him, and he followed the inner call to lead the spare, totally isolated life of a hermit in the wilderness, thinking only of God. But as it often happens that the fugitive, in fleeing humankind, may find his life entwined with his fellow man, he, too, soon found himself surrounded by a host of admiring followers and imitators of his seclusion; and instead of being rid of the world he was promptly, on a moment's notice, made head of a community that quickly developed into an independent sect, the Seventh Day Baptists, whom he ruled all the more absolutely since, to his knowledge, he had never sought out leadership, but had been called to it against his wishes and intentions.

Beissel had never enjoyed an education worth the name, but once awakened, he had taught himself to master reading and writing; and since his heart surged with mystical feeling and ideas, he came to exercise his leadership primarily as a writer and poet, feeding the souls of his flock. From his pen flowed a stream of didactic prose and religious songs for the edification of the brothers and sisters in their quiet hours and for the enrichment of their worship services. His style was highflown and cryptic, laden with metaphors, dark allusions to passages of Scripture, and a kind of erotic symbolism. A tract on the Sabbath, *Mysterion Anomalias,* and a collection of ninety-nine *Mystical and Very Secret Sayings* were his first works. Hot on their heels came a series of hymns, to be sung to familiar European chorales, appearing in print under such titles as *Tones of Divine Love and Praise, Jacob's Place of Struggle and Knighthood,* and *Zion's Hill of Incense.* These were smaller collections, which a few years later, enlarged and improved, became the official hymnal of the Seventh Day Baptists of Ephrata, a collection with the sweetly mournful title, *The Song of the Lonely and Forlorn Turtledove, Namely the Christian Church.* Printed and reprinted, enriched by enthusiastic fellow members of the sect—men and even more women, both single and married—the standard work appeared under various titles and was once even called *The Wondrous Sport of Paradise.* Ultimately it contained no less than seven hundred seventy hymns, including some with a vast number of stanzas. The songs were meant to be sung, but lacked notes. They were new texts to old melodies, and the community went on using them that way for years. But then Johann Conrad Beissel was overcome by new promptings. The spirit demanded that he take on not just the role of poet and prophet, but of composer as well.

Recently arrived in Ephrata was a young man named Herr Ludwig, who was skilled in the art of music and held singing classes, and Beissel loved to sit in on his musical lessons. There he must have made the discovery that music offered possibilities for expanding and fulfilling his spiritual kingdom of which young Herr Ludwig could scarcely have dreamt. The remarkable man quickly came to a decision. No longer the youngest, already in his late fifties, he set about to work out his own music theory, one suited to his special purposes; he froze out the singing teacher and took matters firmly in hand—with such success that within a short time he had made music the most important element in the religious life of the settlement.

The majority of the chorale melodies imported from Europe seemed to him really very forced, all too complicated and artificial to be truly serviceable for his sheep. He wanted to begin anew, do things better, produce a kind of music more suited to the simplicity of their souls, music that would enable them when performing it to achieve their own, simple kind of perfection. A functional and useful theory of melody was boldly and quickly established. He decreed that there should be "masters" and "servants" in every scale. Since he had decided to treat the triad as the melodic center of every given key, he called the notes that belonged to that chord "masters" and all other notes on the scale "servants." Every accented syllable in a text, then, would always have to be represented by a master and the unaccented ones by a servant.

When it came to harmony, he resorted to a summary method. He set up a table of chords for every possible key, and with it in hand anyone could quite easily write out a four- or five-part arrangement for his own tunes—unleashing a veritable composing frenzy in the community. Soon there was not a Seventh Day Baptist, whether male or female, who had not imitated the master and applied his easy method to composition.

Rhythm was the one part of the theory left for the robust man to resolve. He did so with overwhelming success. He carefully made his music conform to the cadence of the words, simply by giving longer notes to the accented syllables, shorter to the unaccented. It never entered his mind to establish a fixed relation among the values given to notes, which is precisely what gave his meter considerable flexibility. Practically all the music of his day was written in tempos of recurring measures of equal length—that is, in bars—but he either did not know that or did not care. This ignorance or brashness proved more useful to him than all else, because the floating rhythm made some of his compositions, particularly those set to prose, exceptionally effective.

Once he had set foot upon the field of music, this man cultivated it with the same stubbornness with which he had followed every other goal. He put together his thoughts about his theory and added them as a foreword to the *Turtledove*. In unceasing labor, he set notes to the poems in the *Hill of Incense,* some of them two and three times, and composed music for all the hymns he had written himself, plus for a great many of those that came from his pupils, male and female. As if that were not enough, he wrote a series of sizable choral works with texts taken directly from the Bible. It appeared he was getting ready to set the entirety of Holy Writ to music written by his recipe; he was certainly the man to entertain such an idea. If it never came to that, it was only because he had to devote a large part of his time to the performance of what he had written, to recitals and singing lessons—and his achievements there were downright extraordinary.

The music of Ephrata, Kretzschmar told us, had been too unusual, too strangely unorthodox, to be adopted by the outside world, and it had therefore fallen into practical oblivion once the sect of German Seventh Day Baptists had ceased to flourish. But a memory of it had been passed like some faint legend down through the decades, so that one could more or less describe why it had been so exceptional and moving. The tones emanating from the chorus had imitated delicate instrumental music, evoking a sense of heavenly sweetness and gentleness in those who heard it. It had all been sung falsetto, the singers barely opening their mouths or moving their lips—a most marvelous acoustic effect. The sound, in fact, had been cast upward toward the fairly low ceiling of the meetinghouse, and it had seemed as if those tones—unlike anything known to man, unlike any known form of church music, at any rate—had descended from on high to float angelically above the heads of the congregation.

At Ephrata this style of singing had fallen into total disuse by 1830. But at Snowhill in Franklin County, where a branch of the sect had stayed alive, it had still been cultivated at that time, and even if it was but a weak echo of the chorus in Ephrata trained by Beissel himself, no one who had heard it would forget such singing for the rest of his life. His own father, Kretzschmar recounted, had still been able to hear those sounds frequently as a young man, and in his old age never told his family about it without tears in his eyes. He had spent a summer near Snowhill back then, and one Friday evening, the beginning of the Sabbath, he had ridden over just to play the onlooker outside these pious people's house of worship. But then he had returned again and again; every Friday as the sun dipped low, driven by an irresistible longing, he had saddled his horse and ridden three miles to hear them. It had been quite indescribable, there was no comparison to anything else in the world. He had, after all (as old man Kretzschmar himself put it) sat in English, French, and Italian opera houses—that had been music for the ear; Beissel's, however, sounded deep in the soul and was no more and no less than a foretaste of heaven.

"A great art," the lecturer concluded, "which, as if aloof from time and its own grand march through it, was able to develop a little special history of its own and to lead down lost byways to such extraordinary bliss!"

I can recall as if it were yesterday leaving the lecture and walking home with Adrian. Although we did not have much to say to one another, we did not want to say good night for a long time, and from his uncle's house, to which I had accompanied him, he escorted me to the pharmacy, and then I walked him back to Parochial Strasse. We often did this, by the way. We both were amused by this man Beissel, by this backwoods dictator and his ludicrous energetic will, and we agreed that his music reform was strongly reminiscent of the line in Terence that speaks of, "acting foolishly with reason." And yet Adrian's attitude toward that curious figure differed from mine in such a distinctive way that this soon occupied my mind more than the subject itself. Unlike me, he insisted on preserving the right to appreciate amidst the mockery, the right—if not to say, the privilege—to maintain a kind of distance that included within it, along with the ridicule and laughter, the possibility of sympathetic acceptance, of conditional approval, of semiadmiration. In general such a claim to ironic distance, to an objectivity that assuredly has less to do with the honor of the cause than with that of the detached person, has always seemed to me to be a sign of inordinate arrogance. And for as young a man as Adrian was at the time, this attitude, one must admit, has something disquieting and insolent about it and is very apt to arouse concern about the health of his soul. To be sure, it is likewise very impressive for a schoolmate of a simpler cast of mind, and since I loved him, I loved his arrogance, too—perhaps I loved him because of it. Yes, that is surely how it was, that his haughtiness was the principal motive for the terrified love that I cherished in my heart for him all my life.

"Leave me be," he said, as we walked back and forth between our respective houses, our hands in our coat pockets against the winter fog enveloping the gas lanterns, "leave me be with my odd duck, I've got a soft spot for him. At least he had a sense of order, and even foolish order is always better than none at all."

"You can't seriously be defending," I replied, "such absurdly decreed order, a piece of childish rationalism like his invention of masters and servants. Just imagine how those Beissel hymns sounded, if each accented syllable had to be sung on a tone from the triad!"

"Not sentimental at any rate," he retorted, "but rigidly following its rules, and that's what I praise. Console yourself with the notion that there was plenty of room for fantasy—which, of course, you place above the law—in the free use of servant notes."

He had to laugh at the term, bending over as he walked and laughing down at the wet sidewalk.

"That's funny, very funny," he said. "But you'll have to grant me one thing: The law, every law has a chilling effect, and music has so much warmth of its own—like a cow stall, bovine warmth, one might say— that it can use all sorts of lawful means for chilling things down—has itself always yearned for them, too."

"There may be some truth in that," I admitted. "But in the end our Beissel provides no compelling proof of it. You forget that his uncontrolled rhythm, which was entirely a matter of feeling, at least balanced out the rigor of his melody. And then he invented a style of singing— aimed at the ceiling, to float back down in seraphic falsetto—that must have been bewitching and surely restored to the music all the 'bovine warmth' that he had previously removed with his pedantic chilling-off."

"Ascetic, Kretzschmar would say," he replied, "with ascetic chilling-off. In that regard Father Beissel was quite authentic. Music always does prior penance for its sensual realization. The old Flemish masters inflicted music with the most confounded tricks, all to the glory of God, and it was a tough go for it, considering all the highly unsensual and purely arithmetical stuff they devised. But then they let their penitential atonements sing, gave them over to the resonating breath of the human voice, which probably has the most bovine warmth of any sounding board imaginable . . ."

"Do you think so?"

"Why should I think otherwise! When it comes to bovine warmth, there's no comparison with any inorganic instrumental sound. Abstract, that the human voice may be—the abstracted human being, if you like. But it is an abstraction in about the same way as the naked body is abstract—it's practically genitalia."

Amazed, I said nothing. My thoughts took me far back into our, into his past.

"There you have it," he said, "your music." (And I was annoyed at the way he put it, which shoved music off on me, as if it were more my concern than his.) "There you have it whole, just as it always was. Its rigor, or what you might call the moralism of its form, must serve as the excuse for the bewitchments of its actual sound."

For a brief moment I felt I was the older, the more mature.

"A gift of life," I responded, "if not to say, a gift of God, such as music, should not have the mocking charge of paradox leveled at it for things that are merely evidence of the fullness of its nature. One should love them."

"Do you believe love is the strongest emotion?" he asked.

"Do you know any stronger?"

"Yes, interest."

"By which you probably mean a love that has been deprived of its animal warmth, is that it?"

"Let's agree on that definition!" he said with a laugh. "Good night!"

We had arrived again at the Leverkühn house, and he opened his front door.

IX

I SHALL NOT GLANCE BACK—far be it from me to count how many pages have piled up between the last Roman numeral and the one I just wrote. A mishap—a totally unexpected mishap, to be sure— has occurred, and it would be pointless to indulge in self-accusation and apologies on its account. The rueful question of whether I could and should have avoided it simply by assigning each of Kretzschmar's lectures its special chapter can only be answered in the negative. Each separate unit of a work requires its special bulk, a certain mass of requisite significance for the whole, and that bulk, that significant mass, belongs to the lectures only in their totality (to the extent I have reported them), and not to each individually.

But why do I attribute such significance to them? Why did I feel persuaded to reproduce them at such length? I shall supply the reason, and not for the first time. It is simply that Adrian heard these things back then, that they challenged his intelligence, took shape in his temperament, and offered his imagination something one might call nourishment, or stimulants—to the imagination those are one and the same. It was necessary, therefore, to have the reader be a witness to it all; for one cannot write a biography, cannot describe the growing structure of an intellectual life without leading the person for whom one writes back to the state of the student, of the novice at life and art, listening, learning, gazing now at his present, now at some premonition of what lies ahead. And as for music in particular, I hoped and I strove to let the reader catch a glimpse of it in precisely the same manner, to put him in touch with it in precisely the same way as it happened to my late friend. And for that his teacher's lectures seemed to me a means that I ought not disdain, that indeed was indispensable.

And so I would jokingly suggest that those guilty of skipping and fudging in the—granted, monstrous—lecture chapter should be dealt with in the same way Laurence Sterne deals with an imaginary listener, who lets a comment slip that betrays the fact that she has not been listening and whom the author then sends back to a previous chapter to fill in the gaps in her epic knowledge. Later, then, and now better informed, the lady rejoins the narrative fellowship and is received with a hearty welcome.

That scene comes to mind because as a senior—that is, during a time when I had already left for the University of Giessen—Adrian learned English on his own and under the tutelage of Wendell Kretzschmar, since it is a subject that lies outside the humanistic curriculum; he read Sterne's books with great pleasure, but especially Shakespeare's works, which the organist knew intimately and admired passionately. Together, Shakespeare and Beethoven formed a binary star that outshone all else in his intellectual heavens, and he loved to show his student the remarkable affinities and correspondences in the creative principles and methods of those two giants—only one example of how far the stutterer's pedagogic influence on my friend extended beyond that of a mere piano teacher. As such he had to pass on to him childish beginner's basics; but, with strange incongruity and on the side, so to speak, he had at the same time brought Adrian into first contact with the greatest things, opening for him the realm of world literature, awakening his curiosity with presentations that lured him into the vast expanses of the Russian, English, and French novel, encouraging him to study the lyric poetry of Shelley and Keats, Hölderlin and Novalis, giving him Manzoni and Goethe, Schopenhauer and Meister Eckehart to read. In both his letters and his own reports when I came home during vacations, Adrian allowed me to participate in his accomplishments; and I will not deny that, despite what I knew to be his quickness and suppleness of mind, I was at times worried about the excessive strain that these surely rather premature explorations were putting on his young system. Doubtless they constituted a significant plus for his final exams, of which, to be sure, he spoke disdainfully, though he was in the midst of preparing for them. He looked pale—and not just on the days when his inherited migraine bore down with dulling pressure on him. It was obvious that he slept too little, for he used the hours of the night to read. I did not fail to express my concern to Kretzschmar and to ask if he did not agree with me in seeing

Adrian's nature as one that, intellectually, it would be better to restrain than to push. But the musician, although much older than I, revealed himself to be a partisan of youth impatient for knowledge and disregardful of itself, a man given on the whole to a certain idealistic discipline of the body and indifference toward "health," which he considered a downright philistine, if not to say cowardly value.

"Yes, my dear friend," he said (and I shall omit the episodes of impasse that detracted from his polemic), "if you are for health—then that truly has little to do with intellect and art, even stands at some odds with them, and in any case the one has never been very concerned about the other. To play the good family doctor who warns about reading something prematurely, simply because it would be premature for him his whole life long—I'm not the man for that. And I find nothing more tactless and brutal than constantly trying to nail talented youth down to its 'immaturity,' with every other sentence a 'that's nothing for you yet.' Let him be the judge of that! Let him keep an eye out for how he manages. It's only too understandable that time drags for him until he can hatch from the shell of this old-fashioned German backwater."

So there I had it—and there Kaisersaschern had it, too. I was annoyed, because my viewpoint was certainly not that of the family doctor. Besides which, I saw and understood quite well that it was not just that Kretzschmar was not content to be a piano teacher and an instructor in some special technique, but also that he found music—the goal of his instruction—to be a specialty that stunted people if pursued one-sidedly, with no connection to other fields of thought, of form, of knowledge.

And indeed, from everything Adrian told me, a good half of his piano lessons at Kretzschmar's antiquated official quarters near the cathedral were devoted to conversations about philosophy and poetry. Nevertheless, as long as I was still at school with him, I could follow his progress literally from day to day. His self-taught familiarity with the keyboard and musical keys expedited his first steps, of course. He was conscientious about practicing his scales, but as far as I know used no particular lesson-book; instead, Kretzschmar simply had him play chorale arrangements and—as strange as they might sound on the piano—four-part psalms by Palestrina, consisting of pure chords with a few harmonic tensions and cadences; somewhat later came little preludes and fughettas by Bach, as well as his two-voiced inventions, the Sonata Facile by Mozart, one-movement sonatas by Scarlatti. He could not resist writing little pieces of his own for Adrian, too—

marches and dances, some as solos, some for four hands, where the musical substance lay in the second part, while the first, intended for the student, was kept quite easy, giving him the satisfaction of playing what was the leading role in a production that on the whole moved at a higher level of technical competence than his own.

All in all, it had something of the education of a princeling about it, and I recall that I used that very term when teasing my friend, and also recall how he gave his peculiar curt laugh and turned his head aside, as if he would have preferred not to hear it. Without doubt he was grateful to his teacher for a style of instruction that took into account that his student, given his general state of intellectual development, did not belong on the childish level of study at which his having taken up the piano so late put him. Kretzschmar had nothing against—indeed he encouraged—his young pupil's racing on ahead musically and applying a mind vibrating with cleverness to things that a pedantic mentor would have scorned as tomfoolery. For no sooner had Adrian learned his notes than he began writing them out, experimenting with chords on paper. The mania he developed back then for constantly thinking up musical puzzles to be solved like chess problems could have been cause for alarm, for there was some danger that he imagined that by devising and solving technical difficulties he was already composing. And so he would spend hours trying to connect, within the smallest possible space, chords containing all the notes of the chromatic scale, while at the same time trying not to shift the chords chromatically or produce harsh progressions. Or he took pleasure in constructing a very fierce dissonance and then finding all its possible resolutions, which, however, since the chord contained so many contradictions, had nothing to do with one another, so that the mordant sound, like a wizard's cryptogram, forged relationships between the most distant notes and keys.

One day this novice in the basic theory of harmony brought his own personal discovery of double counterpoint to Kretzschmar, who was much amused. That is to say: Adrian gave him two simultaneous parts to read, each of which could be either the upper or the lower voice and so were interchangeable. "Once you have figured out triple," Kretzschmar said, "keep it to yourself. I don't want to know anything about your overhasty puddings."

He kept a great deal to himself, at most letting only me share in his speculations at more relaxed moments—particularly his absorption in the problem of the unity, interchangeability, and identity of the horizontal and vertical. In my eyes he soon possessed an uncanny knack for inventing melodic lines whose notes could be set one above the other and, when played simultaneously, folded up into complicated harmonies—and, vice versa, of establishing chords made up of many notes that could be spread out horizontally into melodies.

It was probably between Greek and trigonometry classes, as he leaned against an abutment of the glazed brick wall in the schoolyard, that he told me about these magical amusements of his leisure time: about the transformation of the intervals within a chord (which occupied him more than anything else), of the horizontal, that is, into the vertical, of the sequential into the simultaneous. Simultaneity, he claimed, was in fact the primary factor, for each note, with its closer and more distant overtones, was itself a chord, and the scale was merely sound spread out analytically in horizontal sequence.

"But the actual chord itself, made up of several notes—that's something quite different. A chord wants to be moved forward, and the moment you move it along, lead it into another, each of its constituent parts becomes a voice. Or more correctly, from the moment the chord itself is assembled, its individual notes become voices intended for horizontal development. 'Voice' is a very good word, for it reminds us that music was song long before it was anything else—first one voice and then many—and that the chord is the result of polyphonic singing; and that means counterpoint, means an interweaving of independent voices that, to a certain degree and according to changeable laws of tastes, show regard for each other. I think one should never see a chordal combination of notes as anything but the result of voices in motion and should honor the voice that lies within each note of the chord—not honor the chord, however, but despise it as subjectively arbitrary so long as it cannot prove it has arisen as a vocal line, that is, polyphonically. The chord is not a harmonic drug, but is rather polyphony in and of itself, and the notes that make it up are voices. I maintain, however, that the more voicelike and the more explicitly polyphonic the character of the chord, the more dissonant it is. Dissonance is the criterion of its polyphonic merit. The more strongly dissonant a chord—that is, the more notes it contains that stand out from one another in distinctively effective ways—the more polyphonic it is and the more each single note has the character of a voice within the simultaneity of the total sound."

I stared at him for a good while, nodding humorously, mischievously.

"You're going to do all right," I finally said.

"Me?" he replied, turning to one side in his typical way. "I'm speaking of music, not about me—that makes a little difference."

He certainly insisted on that difference and spoke of music as if of a foreign power, some marvelous phenomenon that did not, however, touch him personally, spoke of it from a critical and condescending distance—but speak about it he did and had all that much more to say, since it was during those years (the last one I spent with him at school and my first two semesters at university) that his musical experience, his knowledge of the world's musical literature expanded quickly, so that very soon indeed the gap between what he knew and what he could play lent a certain obviousness to that difference he was so emphatic about. For while as a pianist he was attempting such pieces as Schumann's *Scenes from Childhood* and the two little sonatas of Opus 49 by Beethoven and as a student of music was very obediently setting chorales to harmonies that kept the theme at the center of each chord, he was quite rapidly, indeed almost too hastily and taxingly, gaining a perhaps incoherent, but often intensely detailed general overview of preclassical, classical, romantic, and modern late-Romantic compositions (and not just those of German origin, but also Italian, French, Slavic)—naturally, all by way of Kretzschmar, who was himself too much in love with everything, absolutely everything that had been rendered in notes not to have burned to introduce a pupil who could hear as well as Adrian to the many forms of a world made inexhaustibly rich by national character, traditional values, and the charms of personality, by historical and individual changes rung on its ideal beauty. Needless to say, entire lessons (extended, of course, without a second thought) were spent with Kretzschmar playing it all for his pupil on the piano—losing himself ever deeper in details, moving from one thing to a thousand others, interjecting (as we know from his "community" lectures) shouted comments and characterizations. Indeed, one could not have been treated to music played more captivatingly, forcefully, instructively.

I need hardly note that opportunities to hear music were extraordinarily sparse for a resident of Kaisersaschern. Apart from the chamber music diversions at Nikolaus Leverkühn's and the organ concerts in the cathedral, we would have had practically no opportunity, for only very rarely did a touring virtuoso or an out-of-town orchestra and conductor stray into our little town. And here Kretzschmar sprang into the breach, and with his lively piano-playing he satisfied, if only by way of provisional intimation, my friend's partially unconscious, partially unconfessed longing for culture—so plentifully that I might speak of a tidal wave of musical experience that flooded his still young, receptive mind. Afterward came years of denial and dissimulation, when Adrian took in much less music than during those years, although far more favorable opportunities were available.

It all began quite naturally with his teacher demonstrating the structure of the sonata for him from works by Clementi, Mozart, and Haydn. But it was not long before he came by way of that to the orchestra's sonata, the symphony, and moved on now, using piano reductions, to introduce his listener—watching with brows knit and lips parted—to the various historical and personal variations on this richest manifestation of created absolute sound, which speaks in manifold ways to both senses and intellect; he played for him instrumental works by Brahms and Bruckner, Schubert, Robert Schumann, and by more recent, indeed most recent composers, too, including compositions by Borodin, Tchaikovsky, and Rimsky-Korsakov, by Antonín Dvořák, Berlioz, César Franck, and Chabrier—all amid loud explanations that constantly challenged his pupil's fantasy to animate the piano's shadows with orchestral sounds. "Cello cantilena!" he cried. "You have to imagine it sustained throughout! Oboe solo! And meanwhile the flute does these fiorituras! Drum roll! Those are the trombones! The violins enter here! Read it in the score yourself! This little trumpet fanfare—I'll leave that out, I have only two hands!"

He did what he could with those two hands and often added his singing voice, which despite its caws and crows was quite tolerable—indeed its inner musicality and enthusiastic accuracy of expression were charming. Digressing and combining, he went from one thing to a thousand others, first because he had endless things in his head and one thought inspired another, but more especially because he had a passion for comparing, discovering relationships, proving influences, laying bare the interwoven connections of culture. He enjoyed—and could spend hours—making clear to his pupil the influence the French had had on the Russians, the Italians on the Germans, the Germans on the French. He let him hear what Gounod had taken from Schumann, César Franck from Liszt, how Debussy leaned on Musorgsky, and where d'Indy and Chabrier were Wagnerizing. A demonstration of how simple contemporaneity could establish linkages between temperaments as different as Tchaikovsky and Brahms was also one of his entertaining lessons. He played for him passages in the works of one that could just as easily have been by the other. In the case of Brahms, for whom he had very high regard, he showed Adrian the allusions to archaic elements, to old church modes, and how this ascetic component opened an avenue onto somber riches and dark abundance. He called his student's attention to how in this sort of Romanticism, with its audible references to Bach, the principle of polyphony earnestly confronted that of colorful modulation and drove it back. But it was really a matter of harmonic instrumental music's somewhat illegitimate ambition to integrate into its sphere certain values and methods that actually belonged to the old vocal polyphony and were merely superimposed on essentially homophonic instrumental harmonics. Polyphony, contrapuntal methods, had been brought in to lend higher intrinsic value to the middle voice—which in the system of a figured bass was only stuffing, only a byproduct of the chord. But true independence of the voices, true polyphony it was not, had not even been for Bach, in whose work one does indeed find contrapuntal devices handed down from the vocal age, but who to his marrow had been a harmonist and nothing else—had been that as a player of the tempered clavier, the instrument that was the prerequisite for the more modern art of harmonic modulation; and his harmonic counterpoint had ultimately had no more to do with the old vocal polyphony than did Handel's alfresco chords.

It was precisely for such pronouncements that Adrian had an especially sharp ear. In conversations with me he would be sure to scoff at them.

"Bach's problem," he said, "was this: 'How can one create polyphony that is harmonically meaningful?' For the moderns the question presents itself somewhat differently. It is more like 'How can one create harmony that has the appearance of polyphony?' Strange, how it looks like a bad conscience—homophonic music's bad conscience in the presence of polyphony."

Needless to say, so much listening provided a lively incentive for him to read scores, some of which he borrowed from his teacher's private collection, some from the town library. I would often find him pursuing such studies or writing out instrumentations. For included in his lessons was knowledge of the size of the register of each instrument in the orchestra (information the foster-child of an instrument dealer scarcely needed, by the way); and Kretzschmar had begun giving him assignments to orchestrate short pieces from the classical period or a movement from a piano piece by Schubert or Beethoven and also to provide instrumentation for the piano accompaniment to songs—exercises whose weaknesses and errors he would then point out to Adrian and correct. In this same period, Adrian made his first acquaintance with the glorious culture of the German art song, which after a rather arid prelude erupts marvelously in Schubert, to celebrate then its totally incomparable national triumphs with Schumann, Robert Franz,

Brahms, Hugo Wolf, and Mahler. A splendid encounter! I was fortunate to be present for it, to be able to take part in it. A pearl, a miracle like Schumann's "Moonlit Night" and the lovely sensitivity of the seconds in the accompaniment; that same master's other settings of Eichendorff poems, like the piece that conjures up all the romantic dangers and threats to the soul, ending in the eerie moralistic warning "Beware! Stay alert and awake!"; a lucky find like Mendelssohn's "On the Wings of Song," the invention of a musician whom Adrian would extol highly to me, saying that metrically he was the richest of all— what fruitful topics for discussion! In Brahms, as a composer of lieder, what my friend valued above all else was the strange austerity and modern stylistic treatment of the setting of biblical texts in the *Four Serious Songs,* particularly the religious beauty of "O death, how bitter thou art." But above all he loved to seek out Schubert's always darksome genius, brushed by death—and precisely at those points where it gives highest expression to a certain only half-defined, but ineluctably bleak solitude, as in the grand eccentric poem "I come from the mountains" by Schmidt of Lübeck, and in "Why do I pass the highways by, that other travelers take" from the *Winterreise,* with that second stanza that cuts to the heart:

> I have surely done no wrong,
> that I should shun humankind.

I heard him speak those words, along with the next two lines,

> Why then do I madly long
> Barren wilderness to find?

—pointing out its melodic diction to me. And to my unforgettable amazement, I saw tears come to his eyes.

Naturally his own attempts at instrumentation suffered from a lack of auditory experience, and Kretzschmar made it a point to correct this. During vacations at Michaelmas and Christmas, he traveled with Adrian (having obtained his uncle's permission) to whatever operas and concerts were being performed in not too distant cities: to Merseburg, to Erfurt, even to Weimar, so that he might hear realized in sound what he had known in mere piano reductions or perhaps only scanned as a score. And so he was able to savor the childlike, solemn esotericism of *The Magic Flute;* the perilous charm of *Figaro;* the demonic depths of the clarinets in Weber's gloriously ennobled operetta *Der Freischütz;* comparable figures of gloomy and painful isolation like Hans Heiling or the Flying Dutchman; and finally the lofty humanity

and brotherhood of *Fidelio*, with its great overture in C played before
the final scene. It had, in fact, as one could clearly see, impressed and
occupied his young receptive mind more than anything else he heard.
For days after that evening out-of-town, he kept the score of Overture
No. 3 with him, and studied it wherever he happened to be or go.

"Dear friend," he said, "apparently no one has been waiting for me
to declare it, but this is a perfect piece of music! Classicism—yes; nothing sophisticated about any of it, but it is great. I did not say *because* it
is great—since there is also a sophisticated greatness, but it is fundamentally more bumptious. Tell me, what do you think of greatness? I
find there is something uncomfortable about standing eye-to-eye with
it; it is a test of courage—can one really endure that gaze? One doesn't
endure it, one clings to it. Let me tell you, I am increasingly inclined to
admit that there is something peculiar about your music. A manifestation of highest energetic will—in no way abstract, but lacking an object, energetic will in pure space, in the clear ether—and where does
that occur a second time in the universe! We Germans have acquired
the term *per se* from philosophy and use it every day without intending anything very metaphysical. But here you have it, music like this is
energetic will, energetic will *per se*—not as an idea, but in its reality. I
offer for your consideration that this is almost a definition of God.
Imitatio Dei—I'm amazed it's not forbidden. Perhaps it is forbidden.
At least it is suspect—by which I merely mean: 'worth thinking about.'
Look here: the most dynamic, thrilling sequence of variations, of
events, of movement, but all within time, consisting solely of time divided, filled up, organized—and only once given a vague push toward
the concrete action of the plot by the trumpet's repeated distant signal. It is all of highest nobility and grandeur, yet kept witty and rather
detached, even in its 'beautiful' passages—neither dazzling nor all too
majestic, nor very exciting in terms of color, and yet so masterly one
cannot describe it. The way everything is introduced and turned and
positioned; the way a theme is led up to and left behind, is dispersed,
and in the dispersion something new is prepared, making each transition fertile, leaving no empty or tepid space; the way rhythm shifts so
supplely, the way a crescendo begins, takes on tributaries from several
sides, swells to a torrent, breaks into raging triumph, triumph itself,
triumph *per se*. I don't want to call it beautiful; the word 'beauty' has
always half-disgusted me, it has such a stupid face, and when they say
it, people feel lewd and lazy. But it is good, extremely good; it could
not be better, perhaps it dared not be better—"

That was the way he spoke. And I found its mixture of intellectual self-control and slight feverishness indescribably touching—touching, because he heard the feverishness himself and was offended by it; and reluctantly noticing the tremolo in his still cracking boyish voice, he turned away with a blush.

A massive dose of musical knowledge—and his own excited participation in it—became part of his life in those days, only to come then for years to what at least appeared to be a total standstill.

X

DURING HIS LAST, his senior, year at school, Leverkühn began, along with everything else, to study Hebrew, a nonrequired course, which I had not taken—and with that revealed to me the direction in which his professional plans were moving. It "turned out"— and I am intentionally repeating the locution I used to describe the moment when, with a chance word, he disclosed to me his religious inner life—it turned out that he wanted to study theology. His imminent final exams demanded a decision, the choice of a field of study, and he declared he had made his choice—declared it in response to his uncle's inquiry, who raised his eyebrows and said, "Bravo!" declared it spontaneously to his parents at Buchel, whose reaction was even more favorable, and he had already informed me some time before, though implying that he saw these studies not as a preparation for practical pastoral service in the church, but for an academic career.

That was probably meant as a kind of reassurance for me, which it was, too, for I took no pleasure whatever in picturing him as a curate or vicar, or even as a consistory councilor or superintendent. If only he had been a Catholic like us! I would have viewed his easily imagined ascent up the rungs of the hierarchy, to become a prince of the Church, as a happier, more appropriate prospect. But his actual decision to become a theologian came as something of a shock for me, and I think I probably did blanch when he revealed it to me. Why? I could hardly have said what other profession he should have chosen. I regarded nothing as good enough for him, really. What I mean is: In my eyes, the bourgeois, empirical side of every occupation simply did not seem worthy of him, and I had been constantly searching with no success for one in which I could imagine him actually, professionally engaged. The ambition I harbored for him was absolute, and all the same I felt terror in my bones at the realization—the very clear realization—that for his part he had made his choice out of arrogance.

We had indeed occasionally agreed—or more accurately, we had seconded the commonly expressed opinion—that philosophy is the queen of the sciences. For us, we concluded, it assumed among the sciences about the same place as the organ did among instruments. It took all fields of research within its purview, summarized them intellectually, ordered and refined their conclusions into a worldview, into a preeminent and authoritative synthesis that revealed the meaning of life, into an observant determination of man's place in the cosmos. My musings about my friend's future, about a "profession" for him, had always led me to similar notions. Those diverse pursuits that had made me fear for his health, his thirst for experience, always accompanied by critical commentary, justified such dreams. The most universal life, that of a sovereign polyhistor and philosopher, seemed to me the right one for him, and . . . but my powers of imagination had taken me no farther than that. Now I had to learn that he had quietly gone farther all on his own, that in secret and, to be sure, without any visible sign of it—and he announced his decision in very calm, commonplace words—he had outbid and confounded my own friendly ambitions for him.

Indeed there is, if you like, a discipline in which Queen Philosophy herself becomes a handmaiden, an auxiliary science, or, in academic terms, a "minor subject"—and that discipline is theology. Where love of wisdom rises to a contemplation of the highest of beings, the fountainhead of existence, to the study of God and things divine—there, one might say, the peak of scientific values, the highest and loftiest sphere of knowledge, the summit of thought, is achieved, supplying the inspired intellect with its most sublime goal. Most sublime, because here the profane sciences (my own, for example, philology, along with history and the rest) become mere weaponry in the service of the comprehension of sacred matters—and likewise a goal to be pursued in deepest humility, because, as Scripture says, "it passeth all understanding," and the human mind enters here into a commitment more devout, more trusting than any required of it by other fields of learning.

All this passed through my mind as Adrian shared his decision with me. If he had made it out of a certain urge for spiritual self-discipline, that is, out of a desire to place his cool and ubiquitous intellect—which in grasping everything so easily was spoiled by its own superiority—

within the confines of religion and to submit to it, I would have approved. It would not only have calmed my constant, silently vigilant,
indefinite worries about him, but it would also have touched me
deeply; for the *sacrificium intellectus,* which contemplative knowledge
of the next world necessarily brings with it, must be all the more respected the greater the intellect that must make it. But I basically did
not believe in my friend's humility. I believed in his pride, of which I
for my part was also proud, and had no real doubt that pride had been
the source of his decision. From that came the mixture of joy and fear
that constituted the terror passing through me at his announcement.

He saw my turmoil and apparently attributed it to thoughts of a
third party, his music teacher.

"I'm sure you're thinking Kretzschmar will be disappointed," he
said. "I am well aware that he would like me to surrender myself entirely to Polyhymnia. Strange, how people always want to tug you
down their own path. You can't please everyone. But I will remind him
that through the liturgy and its history, music plays a considerable role
in theological affairs—a more practical and artistic role in fact than in
the areas of mathematics and physics, in acoustics, that is."

By announcing that he intended to say this to Kretzschmar, he was,
as I well knew, actually saying it to me, and once I was alone again I
mulled this over and over. Certainly, the arts and music in particular—
no less than the sciences—assumed a subservient, subsidiary role in relation to the study and worship of God; and that idea was associated
with certain discussions we had once had about art's destiny, about its
emancipation from the cult, its cultural secularization—which on the
one hand had proved beneficial, on the other gloomily onerous. It was
quite clear to me: His desire, motivated by both personal and professional prospects, to reduce music to the level it had once held within
the worshiping community during what he considered a happier age
had contributed to his choice of profession. He wanted to see not only
the profane disciplines of research, but music as well placed beneath
the sphere to which he would devote his talents. And before me there
now floated, all of its own, a kind of materialization of his opinion: a
baroque painting, a gigantic altarpiece, on which all the arts and sciences, in meekly sacrificial poses, were offering their homage to the
apotheosis of theology.

Adrian laughed at my vision when I told him about it. He was in excellent spirits at the time, primed for any joke—which was understandable. For is not that fledgling moment of dawning freedom, when
the school door closes behind us, when the shell of the town in which

we have grown up cracks open, and the world lies before us—is that moment not the happiest or at least the most excitingly expectant in all our lives? The musical excursions with Wendell Kretzschmar to larger neighboring towns had allowed Adrian a few first sips of the world outside; and now Kaisersaschern, the town of witches and eccentrics, with its stockpile of instruments and a Kaiser's tomb in its cathedral, was to release him at last, and he would walk its streets again only as a visitor, smiling like a man who knows other places.

Was that true? Did Kaisersaschern ever set him free? Did he not take it with him wherever he went, and was he not controlled by it whenever he thought himself in control? What is freedom? Only what is indifferent and detached is free. What is distinctive and characteristic is never free, it is formed, determined, and bound. Was it not "Kaisersaschern" that spoke in my friend's decision to study theology? Adrian Leverkühn plus the town—together that most definitely equaled theology. Looking back I ask myself what else I should have expected. He later took up composing. But even if it was very bold music that he wrote—was it in any sense "free" music, music for one and all? That it was not. It was the music of someone who had never escaped; it was—down to its most arcane, ingeniously whimsical intricacy, to every breath and echo of the crypt emerging from it, characteristic music—the music of Kaisersaschern.

He was, I say, in a very good mood at the time, and why not! Exempted from orals because his written exams had shown such maturity, he had said goodbye to his teachers, expressing his gratitude for their assistance, while they in turn, out of respect for the career he had chosen, had held in check the private vexation that his condescending lack of effort had always aroused in them. All the same, during their private farewell meeting, the dignified director of the Grammar School of the Brethren of the Common Life, a Pomeranian named Dr. Stoientin, who had been his professor in Greek, Middle High German, and Hebrew, went out of his way to offer a warning in that general direction.

"*Vale*," he had said, "and God be with you, Leverkühn! That blessing comes from my heart, and whether or not you may be of the same opinion, I feel that you can use it. You are a person of rich gifts, and you know it—how could you not know it? You also know that He who sits on high and from Whom everything comes has entrusted you with those gifts, since indeed you intend to offer them to Him. And you are right: Natural merits are God's merits on our behalf, and not our own. It is His adversary, having himself come to grief out of pride, who strives to make us forget. He makes a wicked guest and is a roaring lion who walketh about seeking whom he may devour. You are among those who have every reason to be on guard against his wiles. This is a compliment I am paying you—or rather, to what you are with God's help. Be that in all humility, my friend, not with strut and bluster; and always bear in mind that self-satisfaction is itself apostasy and ingratitude to the Spender of every mercy!"

The words of an intrepid schoolmaster, under whom I later saw service as a teacher. A smiling Adrian recounted the message during one of the many walks we took through the meadows and woods at Buchel Farm that Easter. For it was there that he spent several weeks of freedom after graduation, and his parents had invited me to join him. I remember well the conversation we had about Stoientin's warnings as we strolled along that day, particularly about "natural merits," a term he had used in that farewell handshake. Adrian noted that he had taken it from Goethe, who liked to use it, often speaking of "innate merits" as well—a paradoxical combination by which he sought to deprive the word "merit" of its moral character and, conversely, to raise what is natural and inborn to an aristocratic merit outside a moral context. That was why he had rebuffed the demand of modesty that always comes from the naturally disadvantaged and had declared: "Only scoundrels are modest." Director Stoientin, however, had used the Goethe quote much more in the spirit of Schiller, for whom everything was a matter of freedom, and who therefore made a moral distinction between talent and personal merit, sharply separating merit and good fortune, which Goethe saw as inextricably interwoven. And the director had followed Schiller in calling nature God and innate talents the merits of God on our behalf, which we were to bear in humility.

"Germans," the fledging university student said, a blade of grass in his mouth, "have two-tracked minds and a way of illegitimately combining ideas. They always want it to be both/and; they want it all. They are capable of boldly producing antithetical principles of thought and life in the form of great personalities. But then they muddle things up, use the formulations of one in the sense of the other, making a jumble of it all and thinking they can put freedom and aristocracy, idealism and the artlessness of a child of nature all into the same box. But presumably it can't be done."

"Germans simply have both within them," I replied, "otherwise they could not have produced it in those two. A rich nation."

"A confused nation," he insisted, "and a puzzle to others."

We seldom philosophized, by the way, during those carefree weeks in the country. On the whole he was more in the mood for laughter and foolishness than for metaphysical conversations. I earlier made note of his sense of the comic, his craving for it, his habit of laughing, laughing to the point of tears; and I have presented a very false picture should the reader be unable to combine that sense of fun with the rest of his character. I do not want to say "his sense of humor"; to my ears the words sound too cozy and moderate to fit him. His love of laughter seemed instead a kind of refuge, a mildly orgiastic release (of which I was not fond and that always left me feeling uneasy) from the rigors of life that result from extraordinary talent. His being able to look back now over the school years just completed, to recall droll schoolmates and teachers, provided him an opportunity to give free reign to his love of laughter—as did memories of more recent educational experiences, those small-town opera productions, encounters in which one could not help seeing elements of the burlesque, though with no detriment to the solemnity of the work represented. And so a potbellied and knock-kneed King Heinrich in *Lohengrin* had to serve as the butt of ridicule—with that round, black hole of a mouth in a doormat of a beard through which he let spill his rumbling bass. Adrian was almost convulsed with laughter over him—and that is only one example, perhaps all too concrete, of what could prompt his laughing binges. Often their object was much vaguer, some bit of pure foolishness, and I admit I always had some difficulty seconding him. I am not so very fond of laughter; and whenever he indulged in it, I was always forced to think of a story that I knew only from his having told it to me. It came from Augustine's *De Civitate Dei* and was about how Ham, the son of Noah and father of Zoroaster the Magician, had been the only man ever to laugh upon being born, which could have happened only with the help of the Devil. I was compelled to recall it on every such occasion; but it was probably only one ingredient among other inhibitions—for example, that my own introspective view of him was too serious and not free enough from anxiety for me to have been able to join truly in his high spirits. And quite simply, a certain dryness and stiffness in my own nature probably made me awkward at it.

He later found in Rüdiger Schildknapp, the writer and Anglophile whose acquaintance he made in Leipzig, a far better partner for such moods—which is why I have always been a little jealous of the man.

A T HALLE on the Saale, theological and philological-pedagogical traditions are interwoven at many points, especially in the historical figure of August Hermann Francke—the town's patron saint, so to speak—the pietistic educator who at the end of the seventeenth century, shortly after the founding of the university, established the famous Francke Foundation, comprised of schools and orphanages, and in his own person and activities combined godly interests with the humanities and philology. And does not the Canstein Bible Institute, the primary authority for the revision of Luther's Bible, represent a combination of religion and textual criticism? Also active in Halle at the time was the eminent Latin scholar, Heinrich Osiander, at whose feet I very much wanted to sit; and to cap it all, the course on church history given by Dr. Hans Kegel, D.D., included, as I learned from Adrian, an unusual amount of secular material, of which I hoped to make good use, since I regarded history as my minor.

There was solid intellectual justification, therefore, for my deciding, after two semesters at both Jena and Giessen, to suckle at the breast of *alma mater hallensis*—which, by the way, for anyone with a rich imagination has the advantage of being identical with the University of Wittenberg, since the two were joined upon their reopening at the end of the Napoleonic Wars. Leverkühn had matriculated there six months before I joined him; and of course I do not deny that the personal factor of his presence played a strong, indeed definitive role in my decision. Shortly after his arrival, evidently feeling somewhat lonely and forlorn, he had in fact requested that I join him in Halle, and although a few months would have to pass before I followed his call, I had nonetheless been immediately prepared to do so—indeed, it might not even have required his invitation. My own wish to be near him, to see how he was doing, what progress he was making, and how his talents were unfolding in an atmosphere of academic freedom; the wish to live in daily communication with him, to watch over him, to keep an eye on him from close by—that presumably would have sufficed to lead me to him. To which was added, as noted, practical reasons having to do with my own studies.

Needless to say, in dealing in these pages with those two youthful years I spent in Halle with my friend—their course interrupted by vacations in Kaisersaschern and on his father's farm—I can only offer the same sort of foreshortened image in which his school days were reflected. Were they happy years? Yes, as the core of a period in life when one is free to strive, to survey the world with fresh senses and gather in its harvest—and insofar as I spent them at the side of a childhood companion to whom I was devoted. Indeed, the question of his life, his very being and becoming, ultimately interested me more than that of my own, which was simple enough, requiring me to give it little thought, but merely to work diligently to create conditions for its predetermined solution. The question of his life, in some sense much more lofty and more enigmatic, was a problem that, given my few worries about my own progress, I always had plenty of time and emotional energy left to pursue. And if I hesitate to pronounce those years as "happy"—always a questionable adjective, by the way—it is because I was drawn much more strongly into the sphere of his studies than he into mine, and because theological air did not suit me, seemed uncanny, made it difficult for me to breathe easily, and presented me with a dilemma of conscience. I felt, living there in Halle, whose intellectual atmosphere had for centuries been full of religious controversy—that is, of those intellectual squabbles and clashes that are always so detrimental to humanistic cultural endeavors—I felt there a little like one of my learned forebears, Crotus Rubianus, who was a canon in Halle around 1530, and whom Luther called "Crotus the Epicurean" no less, or even "Dr. Kröte, the toad who licks plates for the Cardinal of Mainz." But he called even the pope "the devil's sow," and was an all-round insufferable lout—albeit a great man. I have always sympathized with the anguish that the Reformation brought to minds like Crotus, for they saw in it an incursion of subjective, arbitrary impulse into the objective dogmas and ordinances of the Church. And he possessed the scholar's love of peace, was ready and willing to make reasonable compromises, had no objection to the laity receiving the chalice—which, to be sure, put him in a most painfully awkward position as a result of the gruesome punishments that his superior, Archbishop Albrecht, placed upon partaking Holy Communion under both kinds, as was the practice in Halle.

Such is the fate of tolerance, of the love of culture and peace, as they pass between the fires of fanaticism. It was Halle that had the first Lutheran superintendent: Justus Jonas, who arrived in 1541 and was one of those who, like Melanchthon and Hutten, had changed camps from the humanists to the reformers—much to Erasmus's distress. But what the wise man of Rotterdam found even worse was the hatred that Luther and his followers had called down upon classical learning, of which Luther personally had little enough, but which was nevertheless regarded as the source of his intellectual rebellion. Yet what had happened in those days in the lap of the Church universal (that is, the revolt of subjective arbitrariness against objective ties) would repeat itself some hundred and more years later within Protestantism itself, as a revolution of pious feelings and inner heavenly joy against a petrified orthodoxy, from which, to be sure, not even a beggar would any longer have accepted a crust of bread—as Pietism, that is, which at the founding of the University of Halle had commanded the entire faculty. Just as Lutheranism had been in its day, Pietism, for which the city was long the citadel, was likewise a renewal of the Church, a revitalizing reform of an atrophying religion falling into general indifference. And people like myself may well ask whether these periodic rescues of something already headed for the grave should, from a cultural viewpoint, actually be welcomed; whether these reformers should not instead be regarded as throwbacks and emissaries of misfortune. There surely can be no doubt that humanity would have been spared endless bloodletting and the most horrible self-mutilation had Martin Luther not restored the Church.

I would be unhappy if, on the basis of what I have just said, I should be regarded as a thoroughly irreligious man. That I am not, but rather hold with Schleiermacher, likewise a divine from Halle, who defined religion as the "feeling and taste for the infinite" and called that a "factual state" existing in man. The science of religion, then, has nothing to do with philosophical theses, but with a psychological fact, a given within man. That is reminiscent of the ontological proof of God, which was always my favorite and which on the basis of the subjective idea of a Highest Being posits His objective existence. In most energetic words, Kant has demonstrated that this proof cannot stand up against reason any better than its fellows. Science, however, cannot dispense with reason, and the desire to make a science out of our sense of the infinite and its eternal riddle means forcing together two utterly alien spheres in a manner that, in my eyes, is both unfortunate and sure to plunge one into never-ending difficulty. Religious feeling, which I in no way view as foreign to my own heart, is surely something other than a formal and denominationally bound creed. Would it not have been better to have left the human feeling for the infinite to our sense of piety, to the fine arts, to free contemplation, indeed to exact research as well—which as cosmology, astronomy, theoretical physics is quite capable of fostering that same feeling with truly religious reverence for the mystery of creation—instead of making it an exclusive field of learning and developing dogmatic structures, for just one copulative verb of which adherents gladly draw blood?

Pietism, true to its own enthusiasms, wanted, of course, to draw a sharp line between piety and science and claimed that no movement, no change in the realm of science can have any influence whatever on faith. But that was an illusion, for in all ages theology has willy-nilly let itself be influenced by the scientific currents of its era, has always wanted to be a child of its own time, although the times have made that increasingly difficult for theology, pushing it off into an anachronistic corner. Is there another discipline at the mere mention of whose name we feel so set back into the past, into the sixteenth, the twelfth century? No accommodation, no concessions to scientific criticism can help. Instead, those create a hybrid, a half-and-half of science and belief in revelation that is well on the way to capitulation. In trying to prove the tenets of its faith reasonable, orthodoxy itself made the mistake of allowing reason into religion's precincts. Pressed by the Enlightenment, theology had almost no other task than that of defending itself against the intolerable contradictions pointed out to it; and in order to escape them it absorbed so much of the same antirevelatory spirit that it ended up abandoning the faith. It was the age of the "reasonable worship of God" and of a generation of theologians in whose name Wolff declared in Halle: "Everything must be tested against reason as against the philosopher's stone"—a generation that declared as obsolete everything in the Bible that did not serve "moral improvement" and announced that it saw only a comedy of errors in the history of the Church and its teachings. Since this was going a bit too far, there arose an intermediary theology that tried to hold a rather conservative middle position between orthodoxy and a liberalism whose reasonableness constantly tended to run away with it. Except that ever since, the life of the "science of religion" has been determined by the terms "save" and "abandon," both of which sound as if they are barely scraping by—and with them theology has eked out an existence.

In its conservative form, holding tight to revelation and traditional exegesis, it has attempted to "save" whatever elements of biblical religion could be saved; and on the other, liberal, side, theology has accepted the historical-critical methods of profane historical science and "abandoned" its most important beliefs—miracles, large portions of Christology, the physical resurrection of Jesus, and more besides—to scientific criticism. What sort of science is that, which has such a precarious, coerced relationship with reason and is threatened with ruin by the very compromises it makes with it? In my opinion "liberal theology" is "wooden iron," a *contradictio in adjecto.* In its affirmation of culture and ready compliance with the ideals of bourgeois society, it demotes religion to a function of man's humaneness and waters down the ecstatic and paradoxical elements inherent in religious genius to ethical progressiveness. But religion cannot be reduced to mere ethics, and thus it turns out that scientific and real theological thought must once again part company. And so, it is said, although the scientific superiority of liberal theology is incontestable, its theological position is weak, for its moralism and humanism lack any insight into the demonic character of human existence. It is cultured, but shallow, and—so this argument goes—ultimately the conservative tradition has preserved far more of a true understanding of human nature and the tragedy of life, and therefore also has a deeper, more meaningful relation to culture than progressive-bourgeois ideology.

Here one can clearly see the infiltration of theological thought by irrational currents within philosophy, in whose domain the nontheoretical, the vital, the will or instinct—in short, once again, the demonic—had long since become a major theoretical issue. At the same time one notices a revival of interest in medieval Catholic philosophy, a turning to neo-Scholasticism and neo-Thomism. And by such means, to be sure, pallid liberal theology can take on deeper and stronger, yes, more glowing colors; it can be truer to the aesthetically antiquated ideas one instinctively associates with the word "theology." The civilized human mind, however—one may call it bourgeois, or simply leave it at civilized—cannot shake off the sense of something uncanny. For by its very nature, theology, once it is linked with the spirit of Life Philosophy, with irrationalism, runs the risk of becoming demonology.

I say all this simply in order to explain what I meant by the uneasiness aroused in me at times by my stay in Halle, by my participation in Adrian's studies and in the lectures I audited at his side in order to hear what he heard. I found no sympathy on his part for these apprehensions, for although he truly loved to debate with me the theological

questions that had been touched on in lectures and discussed in semi-
nars, he skirted every conversation that might have gone to the root of
the matter and addressed theology's problematical place among the
sciences and so avoided exactly what, to my somewhat anxious mind,
should have preceded all else. And it was no different in lectures and in
the conversations of his fellow students, members of Winfried, the
Christian fraternity that he had joined for appearance' sake and whose
guest I was on occasion. More of that later perhaps. I wish only to say
here that these young people—some robust and peasantlike, some of
the wan seminarian sort, some more distinguished figures, too, who
bore the stamp of their origin in good academic circles—were simply
theologians and as such behaved with respectable and godly good
cheer. But how one can be a theologian, how, given the intellectual climate of the present day, one takes the notion to choose that profession
(unless one is simply obeying the mechanism of family tradition)—
about that they had nothing to say; and it would doubtless have been
tactless prying on my part to cross-examine them about it. At best such
a radical question would have been appropriate and had some prospect
of an answer during a drinking spree when alcohol had freed hearts
of inhibitions. But it goes without saying that the fraternity brothers
of Winfried had the virtue of disdaining not only duelling scars, but
"drinking bouts" as well, and so were always sober—meaning unapproachable when it came to basic critical questions that might stir
things up. They knew that the Church and the state needed ecclesiastical civil servants, and that was why they were preparing for this career.
Theology for them was a given—and to be sure, it is indeed something
of a historical given.

I had to get used to the fact that Adrian also accepted it as such, although it pained me that, despite a friendship rooted in childhood, a
more probing inquiry was no more permissible with him than with his
colleagues. That shows how he allowed no one to get very close to him
and how certain impassable limits were set to any intimacy with him.
But did I not say that I found his choice of profession significant and
characteristic? Did I not explain it with the name "Kaisersaschern"? I
would often call upon that same name when the problematic nature of
Adrian's course of study troubled me. I told myself that we both had
proved ourselves authentic children of the nook of German antiquity
in which we had been reared—I as a humanist, and he as a theologian. And when I looked about me in our new surroundings, I found
that though the stage had expanded somewhat, it had not essentially changed.

XII

HALLE WAS, if not a metropolis, then at least a large city of more than two hundred thousand inhabitants; but despite all its modern hurly-burly, it did not try to hide, at least in the heart of town where we lived, the stamp of dignified old age. It is after all a thousand years now since a citadel near valuable saltworks on the Saale was added to the newly founded archdiocese of Magdeburg and Otto II bestowed it a town charter. Here one likewise experienced how behind a contemporary façade the depths of time are constantly interposing in soft ghostly tones, and not without also confronting the eye with enduring architectural tokens and even picturesquely breaching the present now and again in historical masquerade, in the folk costume of Halle, in the garb of ancestral salt-workers. My "diggings," to use student jargon, were behind St. Moritz church on Hansa Strasse, a narrow lane that might just as easily have run its obscure way through Kaisersaschern. And in a traditional gabled house on the market square, Adrian had found a room with an alcove that for both years of his stay he rented from the elderly widow of a civil servant. The view looked out on the square, the medieval town hall, the Gothic walls of St. Mary's church, between whose domed towers there runs a kind of Bridge of Sighs, and also took in the free-standing "Red Tower" (a very peculiar edifice, likewise in Gothic style), the statue of Roland, and the bronze statue of Handel. The room was barely adequate, with some faint hint of bourgeois elegance in a sofa and the red plush cloth on the square table, where books lay piled and where he drank his morning café au lait. He had completed the furnishings with a borrowed upright piano, always buried under music, some of which he had written himself. Tacked to the wall above it was an arithmetical etching that he had found in some curio shop or other: a so-called magic square, like the one visible in Dürer's *Melancolia*—along with hour-glass, compass, balance scales, polyhedron, and other symbols. As in that case, the square was divided into sixteen fields inscribed with Arabic numbers, but so that the "1" was at the lower right, the "16" at the upper left; and the magic—or curiosity—lay in the fact that when added, whether from the top or bottom, horizontally or diagonally, the numbers always gave the sum of thirty-four. I could never figure out the ordering principle behind those magically regular results, but it attracted the eye again and again, simply because of the prominent place Adrian had given the poster above his piano; and I suppose I never visited his rooms without a quick glance to check—across, aslant, or just straight down—its annoying accuracy.

There was the same coming and going between his quarters and mine that there had once been between the Blessed Messengers and his uncle's house—both of an evening, whether returning from the theater, a concert, or the Winfried fraternity, and of a morning, when one would stop by for the other and we would compare notes before setting out for the university. Philosophy, the required course for the first theology exams, was the spot where our two schedules crossed all on their own; and we both had signed up for Kolonat Nonnenmacher, one of the University of Halle's shining lights at the time, who with great verve and acumen lectured on the pre-Socratics, the Ionian philosophers of nature, on Anaximander, and, most extensively, on Pythagoras, though with an infusion of a great deal of Aristotelian stuff, since we know about the Pythagorean explanation of the world almost exclusively by way of the Stagirite. And so taking notes and looking up from time to time into the professor's gently smiling face with its mane of white, we heard about the early cosmological conceptions of an austere and pious mind, who had elevated his fundamental passion—mathematics, abstract proportion, numbers—to the principle of the world's origin and duration and who, as an initiate and savant standing before All Nature, had been the first to address it in a grand gesture as "cosmos," as order and harmony, as the spheres sounding in a system of intervals beyond our hearing. Numbers *per se* and the relationship of numbers as the constitutive essence of being and moral values— it was very impressive how what is beautiful, exact, and moral had solemnly merged here into the idea of authority animating the Pythagorean order, an esoteric school of religious renewers of life, silently obedient and strictly subordinate to the "*Autòs épha.*" I must reproach myself for being tactless, because at such words I automatically glanced Adrian's way to read his expression—tactless, that is, because of the discomfort in his response, the annoyance he showed in blushing and turning aside. He had no love of personal glances, refused entirely to entertain them, to return them; and it is almost incomprehensible that I, although knowing this peculiarity, could not always resist checking on him. With it I forfeited the possibility of speaking later with him candidly and objectively about things to which my mute glances had lent a personal connection.

All the better, then, when I did resist temptation and exercised the discretion he expected. What fine discussions we then had on our way home from Nonnenmacher's class about the effective influence, over millennia now, of the immortal thinker to whom we owe our knowledge of the Pythagorean conception of the world. We were delighted by Aristotle's theory of content and form—with content as the potential, the possible, urgently seeking form in order to realize itself; and form as that which moves but is unmoved, which is intellect and soul, the soul of what exists striving for self-realization, self-perfection as phenomenon—and thus were also delighted by his theory of entelechy, which as a piece of eternity penetrates and animates the body, manifesting itself in and giving shape to the organic, guides the body's mechanism, knows its goal, watches over its fate. Nonnenmacher had spoken of these intuitions very beautifully and eloquently, and Adrian proved to be extraordinarily moved by the concept. "When," he said, "theology declares the soul is from God, that is philosophically correct, for as the principle that forms each individual manifestation it is a part of the pure form of being-in-general, arising out of the thought that eternally thinks itself, which we call 'God.' . . . I think I understand what Aristotle meant with his 'entelechy.' It is the angel of each single creature, the genius of its life, whose knowledgeable guidance it gladly trusts. What one calls prayer is actually that trust announcing itself in admonition and entreaty. It is properly called prayer, however, because ultimately it is God whom we thereby address."

I could only think: May your angel prove wise and faithful!

I gladly heard these lectures at Adrian's side. I found the classes in theology that I attended for his sake—though not regularly—a questionable pleasure, and I audited them only in order not to be cut off from what was occupying his mind. For the first years of theological study, the curriculum's emphasis is on exegetical and historical matters, that is, on biblical studies, on the history of the Church and dogma, on confessional history; the middle years are devoted to systematics, which is to say, philosophy of religion, dogmatics, ethics, and apologetics; toward the end come the practical disciplines, meaning liturgics, homiletics, catechetics, the care of souls, the study of church order and law. But academic freedom leaves a great deal of room for personal preference, and Adrian also made use of such license to cast aside that sequence by throwing himself into systematic theology from the start—out of the general intellectual interest that best receives its due in this subject, to be sure, but also because the professor teaching systematics, Ehrenfried Kumpf, was the "juiciest" lecturer in the whole school, and his lectures were generally the most crowded of all, attended by students from all years of study, even nontheologians. I have already noted that we heard church history from Kegel, but those were dry sessions in comparison, for the monotone Kegel was no competition whatever for Kumpf.

The man was very much what students called a "rugged personality," and although I could not rid myself of a certain admiration for his temperament, I did not love him and found it impossible to believe that Adrian was not often embarrassed by his rough vigor as well, although he did not openly ridicule him. He was "rugged" simply in terms of physique: a tall, massive, heavy man with well-padded hands, a booming voice, and a lower lip that protruded slightly from so much speaking and tended to spray saliva. It is true that Kumpf usually read his material from a printed textbook—of his own penning, by the way; but his fame rested in his so-called "ex-curses," which—thrusting his frock coat aside by jamming both fists into his vertical pants pockets and stomping back and forth across his wide platform—he would interpolate into the lecture and which were an extraordinary pleasure for his students thanks to their spontaneity, bluntness, and robust good cheer and also to his picturesquely archaic style of speech. To quote the man himself, it was his practice to say a thing "in plain German" or perhaps "in good old-fashioned German—no feignings, no pretense," meaning clearly and straightforwardly, and "to pick and choose his German proper." Instead of "gradually" he said "a little and a little"; instead of "I hope," it was "I have good hope"; and he never said anything but "Holy Writ" when referring to the Bible. He said "it's old craft" when he meant "something's wrong." Of a man who in his opinion was ensnared in scientific error, he would say "he's on the slippery slope"; of a man of loose morals, "he's living like a pig in the old Kaiser's sty"; and he truly loved adages like "You must set pins if you would bowl" or "No use killing nettles to grow docks." Exclamations like "'sblood!" "zounds!" "cod's eyes!" or even "God's bodykins!" were no rarities from his mouth, and this last would regularly unleash trampled applause.

Theologically speaking, Kumpf was an advocate of that intermediary conservatism with critical-liberal infusions that I mentioned before. In his youth he was, as he told us in his peripatetic extemporizations, a radiantly enthusiastic student of our classical poetry and philosophy and boasted of having learned by heart all the "more important" works of Schiller and Goethe. But then something had come over him, something connected with the revival movement of the middle of the previous century, and the Pauline message of sin and justification had estranged him from aesthetic humanism. One has to be born a theologian to be able rightly to appreciate such spiritual encounters and Damascus experiences. Kumpf had convinced himself that our thinking is also broken and in need of justifying grace, and this was the basis of his liberalism, for it led him to view dogmatism as the intellectual version of Pharisaism. He had, therefore, come to his critique of dogma by precisely the opposite path that Descartes had taken—for whom, on the contrary, the certainty of self-awareness, the *cogitare,* had seemed more legitimate than all scholastic authority. That is the difference between theological and philosophical liberation. Kumpf had accomplished his with good cheer and a healthy trust in God and now re-created it "in plain German" for us listeners. He was not only anti-Pharisaical, anti-dogmatic, but also anti-metaphysical, oriented entirely toward ethical and epistemological concerns; a proclaimer of an ideal of personality grounded in morality, he was mightily ill-disposed toward the pietistic separation of world and faith. Indeed, his piety was worldly, he was receptive to healthy gratifications, an affirmer of culture—especially of German culture, for at every turn he revealed himself to be a massive nationalist of the Lutheran variety and could say nothing more vehement of someone than that he thought and taught "like a giddy foreigner." His head red with rage, he might very well add, "And may the Devil shit on him, amen!"—which would be greeted with more loud stamping.

His liberalism—based not in the humanistic distrust of dogma, but in a religious distrust of the reliability of our thinking—did not in fact prevent him from a sturdy faith in revelation, or, what is more, from being on very intimate, though, of course, strained terms with the Devil. I cannot and will not investigate to what extent he believed in the personal existence of the Adversary, but I tell myself that wherever there is theology—and especially where it is joined to so juicy a per-

sonality as Ehrenfried Kumpf's—then the Devil is part of the picture
and asserts his complementary reality over against that of God. It is
easy to say that a modern theologian views him "symbolically." In my
opinion, theology cannot be modern at all—which one may well consider a great advantage; and as for symbolism, I do not understand why
hell should be taken more symbolically than heaven. The common
man at any rate has never done so. He has always felt closer to the
crude, obscenely comic figure of the Devil than to more exalted
majesty; and in his way Kumpf was a common man. When he spoke of
"hell's horrid hole," which he loved to do—in that old-fashioned
phrase, which, though it sounded funny, was at the same time more
convincing than if he had simply said "hell"—one certainly did not
have the impression that he was speaking symbolically, but rather that
he definitely meant it "in good old-fashioned German—no feignings,
no pretense." Nor was it any different with the Adversary himself. I already said that as a scholar, as a man of science, Kumpf made concessions to the rational critique of biblical faith and, at least by fits and
starts, would "abandon" some things in a tone of intellectual candor.
But ultimately he saw the Liar, the Evil Enemy, at work primarily in
reason itself and seldom spoke of it without adding *"Si Diabolus non
esset mendax et homicida!"* He was loathe to call the Deceiver by
name, and instead used circumlocutions and folksy corruptions like
"Debbil," "Dickens," or "Deuce." Yet these partly timid, partly jocular avoidances and mutations had in fact something of a malicious
recognition of reality about them. Moreover, he was master of a whole
collection of pithy and curious terms for him, such as "Old Clootie,"
"Old Scratch," "Master *Dicis-et-non-facis,*" and "Black Caspar," which
likewise gave expression to his robustly personal and hostile relationship with God's Enemy.

After Adrian and I had called on Kumpf at his home, we were invited on a few occasions to share a family supper with him, his wife,
and their two garishly red-checked daughters, whose dampened braids
had been plaited so tightly that they stood out at angles from their
skulls. One of them said grace while we discreetly bowed our heads
over our plates. And then the master of the house—amid a great variety of outpourings dealing with God and the world, the Church, politics, the university, and even art and the theater, all unmistakably in
imitation of Luther's table talk—went at his food and drink with a
vengeance, both as an example to all and in token of the fact that he
had nothing against the good things of this world and their healthy
civilized enjoyment; he also repeatedly admonished us to keep up

doughtily with him and not disdain the gifts of God, the leg of lamb, the light Moselle. With dessert ended, and to our horror, he took a guitar from the wall and, pushing back from the table, crossing one leg over the other, began to strum the strings and sing in a booming voice songs like "How the Miller Loves to Roam" and "Lützow's Wild and Reckless Hunt," the "Lorelei" and *"Gaudeaumus Igitur."* "Who loves not women, wine, and song, remains a fool his whole life long"—it had to come, and it did. He shouted it, grabbing his rotund wife around the waist right in front of our eyes. And then he pointed a well-padded forefinger at a shadowy corner of the dining room, where almost no ray of light from the shaded lamp dangling above the table could penetrate. "Behold!" he cried. "There in the corner, the Mocker, the Killjoy, the sad, sour spook, and will not suffer our hearts to rejoice in God with meat and song! But he shall not have the better of us, the Archvillain, with his sly, fiery darts! *Apage!*" he thundered, grabbed a hard roll, and hurled it into the dark corner. The struggle ended, he gave the strings a strum and sang, "He who roves so gay and free."

It all was something of a horror, and I had to assume that Adrian surely felt that way, too, although his pride did not allow him to betray his teacher. All the same, after the duel with that Devil he had one of his fits of laughter out on the street, and it subsided only slowly under the diversion of conversation.

XIII

I STILL HAVE to devote a few words, however, to the figure of another teacher, who, given his intriguing ambiguity, is stamped on my memory more strongly than all the others. He was a private lecturer, Eberhard Schleppfuss, who for two semesters exercised his *venia legendi* in Halle, only to vanish again from the scene—where to, I do not know. Schleppfuss was a scrawny man of less than average height who wore no coat, but wrapped himself in a black cape fastened with a metal chain at the neck. He also wore a floppy hat with the brim rolled up at both sides, very much like a Jesuit's hat, which, when we students greeted him on the street, he would doff with a long sweep of his hand and say, "Your very humble servant." In my opinion he actually did drag one foot somewhat, though others disputed this, and I could not verify it with certainty every time I watched him walk, so that I will not insist on it and will instead ascribe it to a subconscious association with his name—yet the assumption was to some extent encouraged by the nature of his two-hour class. I cannot recall exactly the name under which it had been listed in the lecture schedule. Judging from its content, which, to be sure, floated rather aimlessly about, it could have been called "Psychology of Religion"—which probably was its name, by the way. It was a rarefied topic, and certainly not required for exams, and only a handful of students of an intellectual and more or less revolutionary frame of mind—ten or twelve in all—attended. I was surprised, however, that there weren't more, for Schleppfuss's presentation was provocative enough to have aroused widespread curiosity. Yet the example merely shows that even the piquant can forfeit popularity if tied to something intellectual.

I have already said that by its very nature theology tends—and under certain conditions must always tend—to become demonology. Schleppfuss was an example of this, if of a rather far-advanced and intellectual sort, since his demonic concept of God and the world was illuminated by psychology, making it acceptable, indeed appealing to the modern, scientific mind. His lecture style, perfectly calculated to impress young people above all, contributed to this. He spoke quite extempore, distinctly, without effort or pause, in phrases tinged with light irony and as precise as the printed word—and not from a chair behind his lectern, but somewhere off to one side, half-sitting, half-leaning against a railing, the tips of his fingers lying interlaced in his lap with thumbs spread wide, while his small forked beard bobbed up and down, revealing the splinter-sharp teeth set between it and his tapered and twirled moustache. Professor Kumpf's crude but honest treatment of the Devil was child's play in comparison to the psychological reality with which Schleppfuss endowed the Destroyer, the personified apostasy from God. For in dialectic fashion, if I may put it that way, he assimilated the offensively blasphemous into the divine, hell into the empyrean, and declared wickedness a necessary correlative born together with the holy, and the holy an enduring Satanic temptation, an almost irresistible provocation to sacrilege.

He demonstrated this by examples from the inner life of the "classical" epoch of religious predominance—that is, of the Christian Middle Ages, and in particular of its closing centuries, a time when the spiritual judge and the offender, the inquisitor and the witch were in total agreement about the reality of the betrayal of God, of pacts with the Devil, of ghastly intercourse with demons. The essential element was the enticement to blaspheme arising from what is sacrosanct; that was the whole point, as was obvious in the name apostates gave to the Holy Virgin, "The Fat Lady," or in the exceedingly vulgar remarks and horrible obscenities that the Devil secretly urged them to blurt out during the sacrifice of the mass and that Dr. Schleppfuss supplied verbatim, with interlaced fingertips. And out of good taste I shall abstain from repeating them, though I do not fault him for not exercising it himself and giving science its due instead—but it was strange to watch students conscientiously entering them in their oilcloth-bound notebooks. According to him, all of this—evil, the Evil One himself—was a necessary outpouring and inevitable extension of the holy existence of God Himself; and in like fashion, vice did not consist of itself, but derived its appetite from the defilement of virtue, without which it would have no roots; or, put another way, vice consisted of the enjoyment of freedom, the possibility to sin, which was inherent in the very act of creation.

In this there was expressed a certain logical imperfection in the om-
nipotence and omniscience of God, for what He had been unable to do
was to furnish the creature—that which He released from Himself and
which was now outside Him—with the inability to sin. This would
have meant withholding from what was created the free will to turn
away from God—which would have been an imperfect creation, indeed not a creation of and an externality apart from God at all. God's
logical dilemma had consisted in His having been incapable of granting
His creature, man and the angels, both the independence of choice—
that is, free will—and at the same time the gift of being incapable of sin.
Piety and virtue therefore consisted of making good use of the freedom
God had had to permit His creature as such—meaning, making no use
of it—which, to be sure, when one heard Schleppfuss talk, came out
somewhat as if this non-use of freedom implied a certain existential
weakening of the creature outside of God, a lessening in the intensity
of its existence.

Freedom. How strange the word sounded in Schleppfuss's mouth!
Granted, it had a certain religious accent, he was speaking as a theologian, and he in no way spoke disparagingly of it—on the contrary, he
revealed the lofty significance that had to be attributed to the idea by
God, since He had preferred to have man and the angels compromised
by sin rather than to withhold freedom from them. Fine—freedom was
the opposite of innate sinlessness; freedom meant either keeping faith
with God voluntarily or carrying on with devils and being able to mutter horrible things at mass. That was one definition, as supplied by the
psychology of religion. But in the life of earth's peoples and in the
struggles of history, freedom has surely played yet another role, whose
meaning is perhaps less spiritual but certainly not devoid of enthusiasm. It does so even now as I write this description of a man's life—in
the war that rages at present and, last but not least (or so I would like
to believe here in my retreat), in the soul and the thoughts of our German people, who perhaps for the first time in their lives, under the rule
of the most brazen despotism, have some glimmer of the difference
freedom makes. But we had not yet come to that back then. During
our student years, the question of freedom was not, or appeared not to
be, a burning issue, and so Dr. Schleppfuss could give the word the
meaning suitable to it in his class and leave other meanings aside. If
only I had had the impression that he had left them aside and, being en-
grossed solely in the perspective of his psychology of religion, had
given them no thought. But he had given them thought—I could not
rid myself of that feeling; and his theological definition of freedom was

an apologetic polemic directed against "more modern" ideas—that is, the more banal and everyday ideas his audience might have associated with it. Behold, he seemed to want to say, we have the word as well, it stands at our disposal—do not believe that it exists solely in your dictionary and that your idea of it is the only one dictated by reason. Freedom is a very great thing, the prerequisite of creation that prevented God from shielding us against apostasy. Freedom is the freedom to sin, and piety consists in making no use of freedom out of love for God, Who had to grant it.

That is how it came out—somewhat tendentious, somewhat malicious, if I was not totally misled. In short, it bothered me. I do not like it when someone wants to have it all his way, takes the word right out of his opponent's mouth, twists it, and creates a general confusion of concepts. It is being done at present with the greatest brazenness, and that is the chief cause of my living in seclusion. Certain people should not speak of freedom, reason, humanity—they should abstain purely out of fastidiousness. But it was about humanity that Schleppfuss spoke, too—naturally in the sense of the classical centuries of faith, which provided the spiritual frame of reference for his psychological arguments. He was clearly anxious to have it understood that humanity was not some idea discovered by freethinkers, their exclusive possession, but that it had always existed and that, for example, the acts of the Inquisition had been inspired by the most touching humanity. He told about a woman who had been imprisoned during that classical period, tried, and burned to ashes for having had intercourse with an incubus for six whole years, three times a week, and particularly on holy days—even when lying beside her sleeping husband. She had pledged to the Devil that she would become his property, body and soul, after seven years. But good fortune had shone upon her, for just before her time was up, God in His love had allowed her to fall into the hands of the Inquisition; and placed under only the lightest form of interrogation, she had provided a full and touchingly contrite confession, so that she most probably had obtained pardon from God. Indeed she had willingly gone to her death expressly declaring that, even if she could escape, she would most definitely prefer the stake if only to evade the power of the Demon. Her enslavement to filthy sins had made life itself that repulsive to her. And what beautiful integration of an entire culture was expressed in the harmonious understanding between judge and wrongdoer, what warm humanity in the satisfaction of having employed fire to snatch this soul from the Devil at the last moment, thereby obtaining for her God's forgiveness.

Schleppfuss impressed this on our hearts and told us to observe not only what humanity could be, but what it actually was. It would have been quite pointless to use another word from the freethinker's vocabulary and to speak here of gloomy superstition. Schleppfuss could employ this word as well, in the name of the classical centuries, to which it was anything but unknown. That woman with her incubus, and no one else, had sunk to absurd superstition. For she had fallen away from God, fallen away from faith, and that was superstition. Superstition did not mean belief in demons and incubi, but meant, as if calling down the pest, to have intercourse with them and to expect from them what can be expected only from God. Superstition meant gullibility for the whisperings and incitements of the Enemy of the human race; the concept included all invocations, songs, and conjurings, all transgressions in the realms of magic, all vice and crime, the *flagellum haereticorum fascinariorum,* the *illusiones daemonum.* That was how the concept of "superstition" could be defined, that had been its definition—and was it not truly interesting the way man uses words and how he makes thoughts from them!

Naturally the dialectical connection between evil and what is good and sacred played a significant role in theodicy, the vindication of God in light of evil's presence in the world, which took up a large part of Schleppfuss's course. Evil contributed to the perfect wholeness of the universe, and without the former the latter would never have been whole, which was why God permitted evil, for He was perfection and must therefore want what is perfectly whole—not in the sense of perfect goodness, but in the sense of omniformity and the mutual reinforcement of existence. Evil was far more evil when there was good, and good far more beautiful when there was evil, yes, perhaps (there could be disagreement on this) evil would not be evil at all were there no good—and good not good at all were there no evil. Augustine at least had gone so far as to say that the function of the bad was to let the good emerge more clearly, making it all the more pleasing and thus praiseworthy when compared to the bad. Here, to be sure, Thomism had stepped in with its warning that it was dangerous to believe God wanted evil to occur. God neither wanted that nor did He want evil not to occur, but rather He allowed evil to hold sway without wanting or not wanting it, and that, to be sure, worked to the advantage of perfect wholeness. But it would be an error to claim that God allowed evil for the sake of the good; for nothing should be regarded as good except that which of itself, and not in its accidents, corresponded to the idea "good." All the same, Schleppfuss said, this opened up the problem of the absolutely good and beautiful, of the good and beautiful with no relation to the evil and ugly—the problem of quality without comparison. Where comparison was lacking, he said, any standard of measurement was lacking, and one could not speak even of heavy or light, of large or small. The good and beautiful would then be robbed of their nature, reduced to being that was lacking in qualities, which was very similar to nonbeing and perhaps not even preferable to it.

We wrote it down in our oilcloth-bound notebooks so that, more or less consoled, we could carry it home. The true vindication of God in view of Creation's misery, we added under Schleppfuss's dictation, consisted in His ability to bring good out of evil. This attribute definitely demanded, to God's glory, that it be put into practice and could not have been revealed had God not consigned His creature to sin. In that case the universe would have been deprived of the good that God knows how to create out of evil, out of sin, suffering, and vice, and so the angels would have had less cause for hymns of praise. To be sure, as history constantly teaches us, the contrary is also true and much evil arises out of the good, so that God, in order to prevent this, would have also had to hinder the good and not have allowed the world to be at all. This, however, would have contradicted His nature as Creator, and therefore He had created the world as it is, that is, interlarded with evil—that is, it had to be yielded up in part to demonic influences.

It was never fully clear if Schleppfuss was presenting his own doctrinal views or if his only concern was to familiarize us with the psychology of the classical centuries of faith. Surely he ought not to have been a theologian without feeling some sympathy, even to the point of agreement, with this psychology. But the reason I was surprised that more young people were not drawn to his lectures was this: Whenever the topic was the power of demons over human life, sexual matters always played a conspicuous role. How could it have been otherwise? The demonic character of that domain was a primary fixture of that classical psychology; for it, sexuality was the demons' favorite playground, the ideal starting point for God's Adversary, the Enemy and Destroyer. For God had granted him greater magical power over coitus than over any other human act, not simply because its commission was outwardly indecent, but above all because through it our first father's perdition had been passed on as original sin through the entire human race. The procreative act, marked by aesthetic hideousness, was both the expression and the vehicle of original sin—what wonder, then, that the Devil had been left an especially free hand in the matter? It was not for nothing that the angel had said to Tobias: "The demon hath power to overcome those who lust." For the power of demons lay in man's loins, and it was those that had been meant by the Evangelist when he said: "When a strong man armed keepeth his palace, his goods are in peace." Needless to say, that was to be interpreted sexually; that sort of meaning could always be heard in mysterious words, and piety in particular had the sharp ears to hear them.

The only amazing thing was how weak the angels' watch, in particular over the saints of God, had proved to be in every age, at least in the matter of "peace." The book of holy fathers was full of reports of those who, though they may have defied all fleshly lusts, had more than likely been tempted by desires for women. "There was given to me a thorn in the flesh, the messenger of Satan to buffet me." That was an admission made to the Corinthians, and although the writer of the epistle may perhaps have meant something different, epilepsy or the like, piety at any rate interpreted it in its own way—and was probably correct in the end, for piety's instinct surely did not err in seeing a dark connection between the mind's afflictions and the demon of sex. Resisted temptation was, to be sure, no sin, but merely a test of virtue. And yet it was hard to draw the line between temptation and sin, for was not the former already the raging of sin in our blood, and was there not considerable surrender to evil in the state of itching lust? And here again the dialectical unity of good and evil emerged, for holiness was unimaginable without temptation and was measured by the awfulness of the temptation, by a person's potential for sin.

But from whom did such temptation come? Who was to be condemned on its account? It came from the Devil, that was easy to say. He was its source—the curse, however, was intended for the object. The object, the *instrumentum* of the tempter, was the female. Granted, she was at the same time also the instrument of holiness, for it would not exist without the ragings of sinful lust. And yet one could offer her only bitter thanks for that. Instead, the remarkable and profoundly significant thing was that although humankind was a sexual creature in two different forms, and although it was more appropriate to localize the demonic in the loins of the male than the female, nonetheless the whole curse of the flesh and the enslavement to sexuality had been laid upon the female, until it had come to proverbs like: "As a jewel of gold in a swine's snout, so is a fair woman." And since ancient times how many things of that sort had not been said, and with deep emotion, about the female! But they were intended for the lusts of the flesh in general, which was equated with the female, so that the carnal desire of the male was also credited to the female. "And I find more bitter than death the woman, and even a good woman is subject to the lusts of the flesh."

One might well have asked: And the good man is not, perhaps? And the holy man perhaps not all the more so? Yes, but that was the work of the female, as the representative of all carnal desire upon earth. Sex was her domain, and how could she who was called *femina*—which came half from *fides,* half from *minus,* and so meant "lesser faith"—not have stood on wickedly intimate footing with the filthy spirits who populate that realm, not be most particularly suspected of intercourse with them, of witchcraft? An example of this was that married woman who, in the trusting, slumbering presence of her husband, had carried on with an incubus, for years. To be sure, there were not only incubi, but succubi as well, and indeed there had been a depraved young man in that classical age who had lived with an idol whose devilish jealousy he would come to know in the end. For after several years he had married a respectable woman, though more for material advantage than out of true affection, but had been prevented from knowing her, for the idol had always lain between them. Whereupon the wife, in just indignation, had left him, and he found himself under the restraint of his impatient idol for the rest of his life.

Far more characteristic of this psychological situation, however, so Schleppfuss suggested, was the restraint imposed upon another young man of that same era, for it had come upon him through no fault of his own, but through female sorcery, and the means by which he had rid himself of it proved quite tragic. In memory of the studies I shared with Adrian, I will here insert a short version of a story over which lecturer Schleppfuss very wittily lingered.

Toward the end of the fifteenth century, in Meersburg near Constance, there lived an honest lad, Heinz Klöpfgeissel by name and a cooper by trade, of handsome figure and good health. His deep affection for a girl named Bärbel, the only daughter of a widowed sexton, was returned, and he wanted to marry her; but the couple's wish met with resistance from the father, for Klöpfgeissel was a poor fellow, and the sexton demanded that he first achieve a worthy position in life, become a master in his trade, before he would give him his daughter. The attraction between the young people, however, had proved stronger than their patience, and the two prematurely became as one. And so every night, when the sexton had gone to ring his bells, Klöpfgeissel climbed in at his Bärbel's window, and in their embraces each found the other the most splendid creature on earth.

And so things stood, when one day the cooper went off with some other merry fellows to Constance, where there was a parish fair and where they spent a fine day. Feeling their oats by evening, they decided to go to a low dive for women. This was not to Klöpfgeissel's liking and he did not want to go along. But the lads made fun of him, called him a prudish milksop, taunting him shamefully about whether things might not be what they should with him and if he was even up to it; and since he could not bear this and had been no more sparing of strong beer than the others, he let himself be talked into it, said, "Oho, I know different," and joined the lot in the bawdyhouse.

But there he suffered such an awful embarrassment that he did know himself what face to put on. For against every expectation, once he was with his slattern, a Hungarian female, things were most definitely not what they should have been with him; he was definitely not up to her—which made him both exceedingly angry and fearful. For not only did the hussy laugh at him, but she also shook her head doubtfully and said that something smelled rotten here, something was wrong—a lad of his build who suddenly could not manage it must be a victim of the Devil, someone must have brewed him a potion, and a good many other such phrases. He gave her a good deal of money for her not to tell his companions and returned home despondent.

As soon as possible, though not without some worry, he arranged a tryst with Bärbel, and while the sexton was ringing his bells, they spent a most fulfilling hour with one another. And with that his young man's honor was restored, and he could have been content. He cared for no one else except for his first and only, so why should he have cared much about himself except with her? But ever since that failure an uneasiness had remained in his mind, boring ever deeper, telling him he should put himself to the test and once, and never again, play his dearest darling false. And so he secretly scouted for an occasion to test himself—himself, but her as well, for he could not distrust himself without soft, indeed tender, though fearful suspicion being cast back on the girl on whom his soul hung.

And so it happened that the landlord of a winehouse—a sickly, potbellied man—had called him to his cellar to hammer loosened hoops more tightly to the staves of two casks; and the landlord's wife, a woman still fresh and crisp, had come along down to watch him work. She stroked his arm, laid her own against it, comparing, and gave him such looks that it would have been impossible to deny her what his flesh, however willing the spirit, proved after all to be quite frustrated in accomplishing, until he had to tell her he was not in the mood, was in haste, that her husband would soon come down—and took to his heels, still hearing her embittered mocking laugh and owing her a debt that no stout lad ever owes.

He was deeply wounded, perplexed at himself and not just himself; for the suspicion that had crept into his soul after the first mishap now possessed him entirely, and for him there was no longer any doubt that he was indeed a victim of the Devil. And therefore, since the salvation of a poor soul and the honor of its flesh were at risk, he went to the priest and through the grating whispered it all into his ear: how he was bedeviled and that he was not able to manage it, but instead was frustrated, except with one woman, and how could that be, and if religion did not know some motherly remedy for such an injury.

At that particular time and place, however, the pest of witchcraft was wickedly spreading, accompanied by many symptoms of wantonness, sin, and vice, all prompted by the Enemy of the human race as an offense against the majesty of God, and shepherds of souls had therefore been given the duty of keeping a strict eye out. The priest, who was only too familiar with the form of mischief that casts a spell on men's best vigor, carried Klöpfgeissel's confession to a higher authority. The sexton's daughter, on being arrested and interrogated, confessed that, when approached by an old hag, a midwife by profession, she had in truth and in deed—out of a heartfelt fear for the lad's faithfulness and to prevent his being purloined from her before he had been made hers before God and man—accepted a *specificum*, a salve, which ostensibly had been prepared from the fat of a dead, unbaptized child and with which she had secretly rubbed her Heinz during an embrace, drawing on his back a prescribed figure that would bind him securely to her. The midwife was questioned as well, but she stubbornly denied it. She had to be handed over to secular authority, to whom was delegated the use of interrogation methods unbecoming to the Church; and with the application of some pressure, there came to light what had to be expected: The old hag did indeed have an agreement with the Devil, who had appeared to her in the form of a goat-footed monk and persuaded her to renounce the persons of the Trinity and the Christian faith amidst most hideous insults, for which he had provided her with instructions for preparing not only such love salves, but also other odious panaceas, among them a grease, smeared with which any stick of wood promptly rose into the air, bearing its witch with it. The circumstances under which the Evil One had sealed his pact with the old woman were brought forward only bit by bit under repeated pressure, and were hair-raising.

For the girl who had been indirectly seduced, everything depended on how far the salvation of her own soul had been compromised by the receipt and use of the sordid preparation. Unfortunately for the sexton's daughter, the old woman alleged that the Dragon had given her the task of making numerous proselytes, since for every person she brought to him with enticements to use his gifts, he would make her that much more resistant to the eternal fire, so that after diligent mustering of recruits she would be fitted with asbestos armor against the flames of hell. That was Bärbel's undoing. The necessity of saving her soul from eternal damnation, of snatching her from the claws of the Devil by sacrificing her body, was perfectly obvious. And since, moreover, given such widespread wickedness, there was sore need for an example to be set, the two witches, old and young, were publicly burned at adjacent stakes. In the crowd of spectators stood the object of the bewitchment—Heinz Klöpfgeissel, his head bared, muttering prayers. The screams of his beloved, sounding strange and hoarse from the suffocating smoke, seemed to him to be the croaking voice of the Demon reluctantly forced out of her. From that hour on, the vile restraint laid upon him was lifted, for no sooner had his love been reduced to ashes than free use of his manhood, so sinfully taken from him, was restored to him again.

I have never forgotten that repulsive story, so typical of the spirit of Schleppfuss's course—and have never been able to set my mind at rest about it. At the time it was a frequent topic of conversation both between Adrian and me and in discussions among the members of Winfried; but I did not manage to arouse either in him (he always remained reserved and laconic when it came to his teachers and their lectures) or in his theological comrades the measure of outrage that would have satisfied my own anger at this anecdote and at Klöpfgeissel in particular. Even now in my thoughts I flare up at him, snorting and calling him a murderous ass in the full sense of that term! What did the imbecile have to complain about? Why did he have to test the thing out on other women, when he had one that he loved, so much apparently that he was left cold and "impotent" with others? But what does "impotency" mean in this case, when he possessed love's potency with the one? Love is certainly a kind of noble pampering of sexuality, and if it is not natural for that activity to hold back when love is absent, it is truly nothing less than unnatural for it to do so in the presence of and face to face with love. To be sure, Bärbel had pinned her Heinz down and "restrained" him—not by some devilish elixir, however, but with her charms and the spell of her own will, with which she protected him against other temptations. That the power of that protection, its influence on the lad's nature, was psychologically strengthened by the magic salve and the girl's belief in it—I can accept that, although it seems to me easier and more correct to regard the matter from his side and to make the selective state in which love had put him responsible for the inhibition that so foolishly offended him. But even this viewpoint includes a recognition of a certain natural wonder-working power of the mind and its ability to regulate and alter the organic and corporeal—and this, if you will, magic side of the matter was what Schleppfuss deliberately emphasized, of course, in his commentary on the Klöpfgeissel case.

He did so in a quasi-humanistic sense, in order to highlight the lofty view these ostensibly dark ages had fostered for the exclusive status of the human body. They had regarded it as nobler than all other earthly combinations of matter, and in its mutability under the influence of the mind, they had seen an expression of its grandeur, its high rank in the hierarchy of bodies. The body turned cold and hot out of fear and anger; it wasted away with sorrow, flourished with joy; mere mental disgust could produce the physiological effect of spoiled food; the sight of a plate of strawberries could raise blisters on the skin of some-one allergic to them; indeed sickness and death could be seen as the re-sult of purely mental activities. But from this insight about the mind's ability to change its own, requisite bodily material, it was only one step, and a necessary step, to a conviction, supported by the rich expe-rience of humanity, that one mind knowingly and willingly—that is, by means of magic—had the power to alter some other person's bodily substance. In other words: The reality of magic, of demonic influence and bewitchment was thereby confirmed, and certain phenomena—like the evil eye, an empirical complex concentrated in the saga of the basilisk's deadly glance—were thus wrested from the realm of so-called superstition. It would have been inhuman, culpably inhuman, to deny that an impure soul could by a mere glance, whether intentional or not, produce physically harmful effects in another person, particu-larly small children, whose tender substance was especially susceptible to the poison of such an eye.

The words of Schleppfuss in his rarefied course—rarefied in both its intellectual and questionable content. "Questionable" is a splendid word; I have always attached a great philological value to it. It calls up a desire both to pursue and to avoid, or at any rate a very cautious pur-suit, and stands in the twofold light shed by what is noteworthy and notorious in a thing—or person.

When meeting Schleppfuss on the street or in the halls of the uni-versity, we lent our greetings all the respect that the high intellectual level of his lectures instilled in us hour after hour; in return, he would doff his hat with an even deeper sweep than we gave our own and say, "Your very humble servant."

XIV

Numerology is not for me, and it was always only with apprehension that I observed Adrian's interest in it, which had always
been tacitly but clearly evident. But I really must applaud the fact that
it just happened to be the previous chapter that was furnished the
number XIII, which generally is regarded with mistrust and considered unlucky—and I am almost tempted to take it for more than a mere
accident. But, rationally speaking, it was an accident all the same, and
that is because ultimately this whole complex of experiences at the
University of Halle (just as was the case with the earlier Kretzschmar
lectures) forms a natural unity, and because it is only out of consideration for the reader, who is always keeping an eye out for places to
pause, for caesuras and new beginnings, that I have divided into several
chapters what in my own conscientious authorial opinion can really
lay no claim to such segmentation. And so if it were up to me, we
would still be in Chapter XI, and only my proclivity for making concessions provided Dr. Schleppfuss his number XIII. I do not begrudge him it—indeed, what is more, I would not have begrudged the
number XIII to the whole batch of memories dealing with our student years in Halle, for as I said before, the atmosphere of the town, its
theological air, did not do me good, and my participation as an auditor
in Adrian's studies was a sacrifice I made to our friendship amidst
many a misgiving.

Our friendship? I would do better to say: mine; for he did not insist
that I be beside him while he listened to Kumpf or Schleppfuss, or indeed realize I was missing lectures in my courses to do so. I did it com-

pletely on my own, solely out of an undeniable desire to hear what he heard, to know what he was learning—in short, to look after him, for that seemed to me absolutely imperative, if futile. What an oddly, painfully mixed awareness I am describing: urgency and futility. It was clear to me that his was a life that one could indeed watch over, but not influence; and my need to keep a constant eye out, not to let my friend from my side, included something very like a premonition that one day I would be set the task of providing a biographical account of my impressions of his youth. For this much is surely clear, that I have not dwelt at length on the preceding primarily in order to explain why I did not feel particularly comfortable in Halle, but rather for the same reason that I went into such detail about Wendell Kretzschmar's lectures in Kaisersaschern: That is, because it is and must be my concern for the reader to be a witness to Adrian's intellectual experiences.

For that same reason I now want to invite the reader to accompany us young sons of the Muses on the long walks beyond Halle that we all enjoyed taking together in good weather. For as Adrian's intimate from his hometown and because, although a nontheologian, I appeared to take a decided interest in divine studies, I was a warmly welcomed guest in the circle of the Christian fraternity Winfried and was allowed to participate in the group's country excursions dedicated to the enjoyment of God's green Creation.

This occurred more often than we two joined in, for I need not say that Adrian was not a very zealous fraternity brother and his membership was more a matter of marking time than of regular participation and involvement. Out of courtesy and to prove his good will toward observing proprieties, he had let himself be won over to Winfried, but more often than not he avoided its meetings (held in lieu of drinking bouts), offering various excuses, usually his migraine; and after over a year he was still so little on *frère-et-cochon* footing with its seventy-odd members that in speaking with them even fraternal use of first names and informal pronouns was clearly unnatural for him, and he often misspoke himself. Nevertheless they respected him, and when (one must almost say: on those rare occasions when) he arrived for a meeting in the smoky room adjoining the bar in Mütze's Tavern, the shouted hello that greeted him might contain some gibes for his being such a loner, but expressed genuine good cheer as well. For they valued his participation in theological and philosophical debates, to which, though without leading them, he would often give an interesting turn with just an interjected remark; and they especially enjoyed his musical talents, which were very useful, since he knew how to provide their obligatory glee-club songs with a fuller and more enlivening accompaniment than other pianists, and also, at the request of Baworinski, their presiding officer—a tall, dark fellow whose eyes were usually concealed under gently lowered lids and who kept his mouth puckered as if for a whistle—he would delight the assembly with a solo, a Bach toccata or a movement from Beethoven or Schumann. But sometimes he might sit down unbidden at the assembly hall piano, whose dull tones were strongly reminiscent of the inadequate instrument on which Wendell Kretzschmar had offered us his lessons in Community Endeavor Hall, and then immerse himself in some experimental improvisation—especially before the opening of a meeting, while we waited for all the other fraternity members to arrive. He had a way of entering I shall never forget: Offering a casual greeting and sometimes not even taking off his hat and coat, he would walk straight to the piano, his face strained with concentration, as if this had been the real point of his having come, and then with a strong attack would sound knotted chords and, his eyebrows raised high as he emphasized each modulating note, try out the preparations and resolutions he might have been considering on his way there. But this rush for the piano also had about it something of a yearning to find some hold, some shelter, as if the room and those filling it frightened him and he were seeking refuge there—and in himself as well, really—from the confusing and alien world into which he had strayed.

If he then continued to play, pursuing some fixed idea, transforming and loosely shaping it, someone from among those standing around—short Probst, maybe, a seminarian type with greasy, longish blond hair—might ask:

"What is that?"

"Nothing," the pianist answered with a quick shake of his head, a gesture that looked more as if he were shooing a fly.

"How can it be nothing," someone retorted, "since you're playing it?"

"He's improvising, it's a fantasy," tall Baworinski explained sensibly.

"A fantasy?" Probst cried in genuine shock, and his watery blue eyes cast a sidelong glance at Adrian as if he expected him to be burning up with fever.

Everyone burst into laughter—even Adrian, who let his clenched hands rest on the keys and bent his head down over them.

"Oh, Probst, what a muttonhead you are!" Baworinski said. "He's improvising, don't you understand? He thought it up just now."

"How can he think up so many notes, left and right, all at once?"

Probst asked defensively. "And how can he say it's nothing, when it's something he's playing? You can't play what doesn't exist?"

"Oh, yes, you can," Baworinski said softly. "You can even play what doesn't yet exist."

And I can still hear how a certain Deutschlin, Konrad Deutschlin—a sturdy lad with stringy hair falling onto his forehead—added, "Everything, my good Probst, was once nothing that became something."

"I can assure you all," Adrian said, "that it was truly nothing, in every sense of the word."

He now had to sit back up from being bent over with laughter; and from his face one could read that this was not easy for him, that he felt compromised. I remember, however, that Deutschlin now led a rather long and not at all uninteresting debate about creativity, a discussion of how it was subject to the limitations of all sorts of preconditions, to culture, tradition, imitation, convention, routine, although, in the end, not without human creativity's having been regarded as coming from on high—as a distant reflection of the power of divine being, as an echo of the almighty summons into existence—and productive imagination's having been given theological recognition after all.

By the way, and quite incidentally, it pleased me that I, too, although a student of profane studies admitted into this circle, could occasionally contribute to the entertainment by playing my viola d'amore when asked. Music, after all, was held in high regard here, if only on principle and in a certain nebulous way; they saw in music a divine art with which one ought to have "a relationship," of a romantically devotional sort, just as with nature. Music, nature, and cheerful devotion, those were closely related and prescribed ideas in the Winfried fraternity, and when I spoke of the "sons of the Muses," the phrase, which to some perhaps might not seem to apply to theology students, had its justification in that combination of attitudes, in that spirit of unconstrained piety and bright-eyed regard for the beautiful that likewise characterized our hikes into nature—and I now return to them.

In the course of our four semesters at Halle, these were undertaken two or three times *in corpore*—that is, when Baworinski put out a call mustering all seventy men. Adrian and I never participated in these mass enterprises. But individual groups of members on more intimate terms would also be formed for hikes; and so, together with a couple of the better fellows, we both joined in on repeated occasions. There was the presiding officer himself, plus the sturdy Deutschlin, then a certain Dungersheim, a Carl von Teutleben, and a couple of young fellows named Hubmeyer, Matthäus Arzt, Schappeler. I recall the names and more or less the physiognomies of those who bore them, though it would be superfluous to describe them.

One can forgo the immediate environs of Halle, a sandy plain lacking charm as a landscape, but in a few hours the train carries one up the Saale into lovely Thuringia; and there, usually in Naumburg or Apolda (the region where Adrian's mother had been born), we left the train and continued our journey with our knapsacks and rain-capes, and as footloose lads on Shank's mare set out on all-day marches, taking our meals in village inns or often on a piece of level ground at the edge of a woods and spending many a night in the hayloft of a farm, only to rise at dawn and wash and refresh ourselves at the long trough beside a running spring. Such a temporary style of life, when a city-dweller who engages in intellectual pursuits becomes a stopover guest at some primitive rural spot of Mother Earth's, in the certainty after all that very soon he will have to (or better, be permitted to) return to his customary and "natural" sphere of bourgeois comfort—such a voluntary cutting back and simplification easily, almost necessarily, has something artificial, patronizing, dilettantish about it, a trace of the comic of which we were in no way all that unaware and which was also probably the source of the genial smirks that many a farmer bestowed on us when we approached asking for straw to sleep on. What lent those smirks some geniality, perhaps even approval, was our youth; and one can indeed say that youth is the only legitimate bridge between the bourgeois and the natural, a prebourgeois state from which all student and fraternity romanticism is derived—the genuinely romantic phase of life. It was Deutschlin, whose mind was always energetically at work, who described the problematical nature of our current life in just that way during a discussion launched in a barn before falling asleep by the dull light of a stall lantern burning in one corner of that night's quarters; although he did add that it was the height of poor taste for youth to explain youth: A form of life that discussed and investigated itself, he said, dissolved itself as a form in the process, and only being that is direct and unreflective could enjoy true existence.

That was now disputed; Hubmeyer and Schappeler disputed it, nor was Teutleben in agreement, either. Wouldn't that be lovely, they suggested, if only old age were permitted to judge youth, leaving it forever the object of outside observation, as if it had no share in objective thought. But it did share in it, even when dealing with itself, and had to be allowed to speak as youth about youth. There was, after all, something one could call a sense of life, which was the equivalent of self-awareness, and if a form of life could cancel itself by such means, then there could be no possibility of informed life. Mere being lived in brute unconsciousness, some ichthyosaur existence, that got you nowhere; and nowadays one had to take one's stand in self-awareness and affirm one's specific form of life with an articulated sense of self—it had taken long enough for youth even to be recognized as such.

"That recognition, however, came more out of pedagogics, that is, from the older generation," one heard Adrian say, "than from youth itself. It found itself one day given the designation of an independent form of life by an era that speaks of the century of the child and has invented the emancipation of women, a very indulgent era in general—and youth eagerly agreed to it, of course."

"No, Leverkühn," Hubmeyer and Schappeler said, and the others seconded them—he was wrong there, wrong at least in great measure. It had been youth's own sense of life that, with the help of a growing self-awareness, had prevailed against the world, even if the latter had not been totally disinclined to grant recognition.

"Not in the least," Adrian said, "not disinclined at all." One needed only to say to this era "I have a specific sense of life," and it immediately bowed deeply before it. For youth, it was like cutting through butter, so to speak. And anyway, there could be no objection if youth and its era were in agreement.

"Why so flippant, Leverkühn? Don't you think it's a good thing that youth today is coming into its rights in bourgeois society, and that those values peculiar to the developing person are recognized?"

"Oh certainly," Adrian said. "But the other gentlemen started, you fellows started, we started from the idea . . ."

He was interrupted by laughter at his initial failure to use informal pronouns. I believe it was Matthäus Arzt who said, "That was perfect, Leverkühn. First you called us 'gentlemen,' then you managed a 'you fellows,' and finally a 'we' that almost put your tongue in a knot—you had the hardest time spitting that one out, you hardboiled individualist."

Adrian refused to accept the term. It was dead wrong, he said, he was not an individualist, he certainly affirmed the community.

"Theoretically, perhaps," Arzt replied, "with the supercilious exception of Adrian Leverkühn." He had been speaking about youth superciliously, too, as if he were not part of it and quite incapable of including himself or fitting in. For when it came to humility, he certainly did not know all too much about that.

The issue had not been one of humility, Adrian parried, but on the contrary, of a self-aware sense of life. And now Deutschlin made the motion that Leverkühn be allowed to finish what he had to say.

"There wasn't anything more," he said. "The discussion started with the idea that youth has a closer relationship to nature than a man matured by bourgeois society—rather like a woman, for instance, who is said to have a greater affinity to nature in comparison with a man. But I cannot agree there. I don't think that youth stands on especially intimate footing with nature. Its attitude toward nature is much more likely to be shy and brittle, alien, really. It takes years for a human being to accustom himself to his natural side and slowly set his mind at ease about it. Youth in particular—I mean the better bred sort of youth—is much more inclined to be shocked by it, to despise it, to behave hostilely toward it. What do we call nature? Woods and meadows? Mountains, trees, and lakes, the beauty of a landscape? For that, in my opinion, youth has much less an eye than the older, settled person. The young person is not very disposed to seeing and enjoying nature. He is inward-looking, intellectually inclined, averse to sensual things, in my opinion."

"*Quod demonstramus*," someone said, possibly Dungersheim, "we wanderers lying here in the straw, who are off to climb through Thuringia's forests, to Eisenach and the Wartburg."

"You always say, 'in my opinion,'" someone else interjected. "You probably mean to say: 'from my experience.'"

"You fellows accuse me," Adrian riposted, "of speaking superciliously about youth and not including myself in it. And now, all of a sudden, I'm supposed to have substituted myself for it."

"Leverkühn," Deutschlin said in reply, "has his own thoughts about youth, but he also apparently regards it as a specific form of life to be respected as such, and that's decisive. I was speaking of youth discussing itself only insofar as that dissipates the immediacy of life. As self-awareness, however, it strengthens existence, and in that sense, or better, to that extent I call it a good thing. The concept of youth is a prerogative and privilege of our nation, of us Germans—others hardly know it. Youth as its own self-conception is as good as unknown to them; they are amazed at the demeanor of German youth, so emphatically itself and endorsed by those of more advanced years—are even amazed at its garb, its disregard for bourgeois dress. Well, let them. German youth represents, as youth, the spirit of the people, the German spirit itself, which is young and full of the future—immature, if you like, but what does that mean! German deeds have always been done out of a certain immaturity, and it is not for nothing that we are the people of the Reformation. That, too, was a work of immaturity after all. The citizen of Florence during the Renaissance, he was mature, he said to his wife as he set out for church: 'Well, let us pay our reverence to the popular error!' But Luther was immature enough, a man of the people, of the German people enough, to bring about the new, the purified faith. And where would the world be, if maturity were the final word! In our immaturity we shall yet present it with many a renewal, many a revolution."

After these words of Deutschlin's everyone was silent for a while. There in the dark each was evidently stirred in his own way by a sense of personal and national youthfulness fused into a single emotion. Most were surely flattered somewhat by the idea of "powerful immaturity."

"If I only knew," I can hear Adrian say, breaking the silence, "why we are actually so immature, so young, as you put it, I mean as a people. After all, we go back as far as the others, and maybe it's only our history, our having been a little late at coming together and forming a shared self-awareness, that beguiles us with some special youthfulness."

"It's surely not that," Deutschlin rejoined. "In its highest sense, youth has nothing at all to do with political history, or with history as such. It is a metaphysical gift, something essential, a structure and a vocation. Have you never heard about German growth, German wanderings, about the German soul on its endless march? The German is, if you will, the eternal student, the eternally striving student among the nations . . ."

"And his revolutions," Adrian interjected with a quick burst of laughter, "are the wild parties he throws for world history."

"Very clever, Leverkühn. But I really am surprised that your Protestantism allows you to be so witty. One can also take what I call youth more seriously, too, if need be. To be young means to be primordial, to have remained close to the wellspring of life, means being able to rise up and shake off the fetters of an outmoded civilization, to dare what others lack the vital courage to do—to plunge back into what is elemental. The courage of youth—that is the spirit of dying and becoming, the knowledge of death and rebirth."

"Is that so German?" Adrian asked. "Rebirth was once called *renascimento* and happened in Italy. And 'back to nature,' that was first recommended in French."

"The one was cultural repair work," Deutschlin retorted, "the other a sentimental pastoral romance."

"Out of that pastoral romance," Adrian insisted, "came the French Revolution, and Luther's Reformation was only an offshoot and ethical byway of the Renaissance, its application in religious matters."

"In religious matters, there you have it. And the religious is in every way something different from a little archaeological refurbishment or the crisis of a social upheaval. Religiosity, that is youth itself perhaps;

it is the directness, the courage, and the depth of one's personal life, the will and ability to experience and live out in its full vitality that natural and demonic element of existence of which Kierkegaard has again made us aware."

"Do you believe religiosity is a peculiarly German talent?" Adrian asked.

"In the way I defined it, as inner youth, as spontaneity, as faith in life, as a Düreresque ride between death and the Devil—yes I do."

"And France, the land of cathedrals, whose king was called His Most Christian Majesty, and which produced theologians like Bossuet, like Pascal?"

"That was a long time ago. For centuries now France has been chosen by history to fulfill the Antichrist's mission in Europe. For Germany, the opposite is true, and you would feel and know it, Leverkühn, if only you weren't Adrian Leverkühn—that is, too cool to be young and too clever to be religious. You may go far with cleverness in the Church, but hardly in religion."

"Many thanks, Deutschlin," Adrian said, laughing. "You've given it to me in good plain German, as Ehrenfried Kumpf would say, with no whitewashing. I suspect I shall not go very far in the Church, either, but it is certain that without the Church I would not have become a theologian. I'm aware that the most talented among you, who have read your Kierkegaard, locate truth, even ethical truth, entirely in subjectivity and reject with horror collective life in the herd. But I cannot join you in your radicalism—which as the license of students, by the way, won't last long—in your Kierkegaardian separation of Church and Christianity. I still see in the Church—even in her current state as a secularized creature of the bourgeoisie—a citadel of order, an institution for objective discipline, a system of ditches and dams for the religious life, which otherwise would run wild, deteriorate into subjectivistic, numinous chaos, to a world of fantastic eeriness, to a sea of the demonic. Separating the Church and religion means forfeiting the ability to separate religion and madness . . ."

"Now listen here! " several voices said.

But: "He's right!" declared Matthäus Arzt candidly, whom the others called "social Arzt," the "social doctor," because social concerns were his passion; he was a Christian Socialist, and often quoted Goethe's statement that Christianity had been a political revolution that, having failed, became a moral one. And, as he said now, it had to become political again, that is socialist—that was the true and sole means for disciplining the religious impulse, whose possible dangerous degenerations Leverkühn had not done a bad job of describing. Religious socialism, religiosity committed to social concerns, that was the thing, for it all depended on finding the right commitment, and the theonomous bond had to be joined to the social bond, to the task God had imposed on us to perfect society. "Believe me," he said, "everything depends on the development of a responsible industrial population, of an international industrial nation that can someday create a genuine and just European economic society. In it will be found the impulses—indeed their seeds are already found—for shaping not just the technical realization of a new economic organization, not just for a thoroughgoing cleansing of the natural interrelations of life, but also for the founding of new political orders."

I am reproducing the speeches of these young men just as they were given, along with the terms that were part of a learned jargon whose bombast they were not in the least aware of; rather they used it quite naturally, with total satisfaction and ease, flinging stilted, pretentious phrases at one another with unpretentious virtuosity. "Natural interrelations of life" and "theonomous bond" were typical affectations; one could have put it more simply, but then it would not have been the language of their theological science. They loved to put the "existential question," spoke of "sacral space" or "political space" or "academic space," of "structural principle," of "dialectic tension," of "ontological correspondences," and so forth. And so now, with hands clasped behind his head, Deutschlin put the existential question about the genetic origin of Arzt's economic society. It was really nothing other than common business sense, and nothing else could ever be represented in an economic society. "We really must be clear on this point, Matthäus," he said, "that the social ideal of an economic social organization arises from the Enlightenment's autonomous mode of thought, in short, from rationalism, which still has never been grasped by the powerful forces beyond or beneath reason. You believe that out of mere human insight and reason, that by equating 'just' and 'socially useful,' you can build a just order from which, you think, will come new political forms. Economic space, however, is totally different from political, and there is no direct access from ideas of economic usefulness to a political consciousness related to history. I do not understand how you can fail to see that. Political order is related to the state, which is a given form of power and control that is not based in utility and in which quite different qualities are represented than those known to the agents of industrialists or to secretaries of labor unions—honor and dignity for example. For such qualities, my good man, people in the economic space do not bring with them the necessary ontological correspondences."

"Ah, Deutschlin, what are you talking about," Arzt said. "As modern sociologists we know quite well that the state is likewise determined by its useful functions. There is the administration of justice, there is the maintenance of security. And just in general, we really do live in an economic age; the economic is simply the historical character of our age, and honor and dignity won't help the state one whit if it does not know on its own how to recognize and guide economic relationships correctly."

Deutschlin admitted as much. But he denied that utilitarian functions were the essential basis of the state. The state's legitimacy lay in its sovereignty, its authority, which was therefore independent of the value judgments of the individual, since—in contradistinction to the humbug of the *contrat social*—it preceded the individual. Connections above and beyond the individual had, in fact, as much existential primality as individuals, and an economist could therefore understand nothing about the state, since he understood nothing about its transcendent foundation.

To which von Teutleben said, "I am certainly not without sympathy for the social-religious bond that Arzt advocates; it is better than none at all, and Matthäus is only too right when he says that everything depends on finding the right bond. But to be right, to be concurrently religious and political, it must come from the people, and what I now ask myself is, whether a new national character can arise out of an economic society. Look at the Ruhr. There you have a reservoir of human beings but no new cells of national character. Take a train sometime from Leuna to Halle. You'll see workers sitting together who can speak quite well about the question of wages, but that they might have drawn any sort of national popular strength from their common activity—that is not evident in their conversations. In economics, more and more it is the nakedly finite that holds sway . . ."

"But nationality is finite, as well," someone else recalled, either Hubmeyer or Schappeler, I cannot say for certain. "Nationality as eternal—we can't accept that as theologians. A capacity for enthusiasm is very good and the need for faith very natural for youth, but it is also a temptation, and one must take a very close look at the substance of these new bonds offered up on all sides nowadays as liberalism dies off—whether a bond is genuine as well and whether the object establishing such a commitment is something real or perhaps merely the product of, let us say, structural romanticism, which creates ideologi-

cal objects by nominalistic, if not to say, fictional means. It is my opinion, or my fear, that the people as an idol and the state as a utopia are
just such nominalistic bonds, and to profess faith in them—faith in
Germany, shall we say—provides no real binding commitment because
it has nothing whatever to do with personal substance and qualitative
content. For *that* there is no demand whatever, and when someone
says 'Germany!' and declares it to be a bond of commitment, he need
not prove—and no one asks, not even he of himself—how much Germanness he actually realizes in the personal, that is, in the qualitative
sense and to what extent he is capable of serving the affirmation of a
German form of life in the world. That is what I call nominalism, or
better, making a fetish of a name, and it is, in my opinion, ideological
idolatry."

"Fine, Hubmeyer," Deutschlin said, "what you say is all quite correct, and in any case I will grant you that your critique has brought us
closer to the problem. I disputed Matthäus Arzt because the ascen-
dancy of the utilitarian principle in economic space is not to my liking;
but I will agree with him totally that the theonomous bond *per se,* that
is, religiosity in general, has something formalistic and insubstantive
about it, that it needs down-to-earth, empirical repletion or application or verification, some act of obedience to God. And so Arzt has
chosen socialism and Carl Teutleben nationalism. And those are the
commitments between which we have to choose at present. I deny that
we have a surplus of ideologies, now that the slogan of freedom no
longer washes. There are, in fact, only these two possibilities of religious obedience and religious attainment: the socialist and the nationalist. As bad luck will have it, however, they both entail questions and
dangers, and very serious ones. Hubmeyer spoke very cogently about
a certain nominalistic hollowness and personal insubstantiality frequently found in professions of nationalist faith, and one should add
that as a general principle it means nothing to side with life-enhancing
objectivism if that has no bearing on the shaping of one's personal life
but is intended merely for solemn occasions, among which I would
even include the frenzy of sacrificial death. Two constituent values and
qualitative components are required for genuine sacrifice: the cause,
and the object sacrificed. We know of cases, however, where the personal substance of, let us say, Germanness, was very great and quite
spontaneously objectivized itself as sacrifice, yet where not only was
there a total lack of a professed faith in the nationalist bond, but the
sacrifice also took place under the most violent negation of it, so that
the tragedy consisted precisely in the contradiction between one's be-

ing and one's professed faith. . . . But enough for this evening about the nationalist commitment. As for the socialist, the hitch there is that once everything is regulated as well as possible in economic space, the question of a meaningful fulfillment of existence and of a life worthily led will remain just as open as it is today. We shall one day have the universal economic administration of earth, the complete victory of collectivism—fine, and with it will vanish man's relative insecurity, which the capitalist system with its inherent social catastrophes lets stand. That means: The last memories of the perils of human life will have vanished and with them, the spiritual problem in general. One asks oneself, why go on living . . ."

"Do you want to retain the capitalist system, Deutschlin," Arzt asked, "because it keeps alive the memory of the perils of human life?"

"No, I don't want that, my dear Arzt," Deutschlin replied in annoyance. "But surely one can still point out the tragic antinomies of which life is full."

"Those really needn't be pointed out," Dungersheim sighed. "They are trouble enough, and as a religious man one has to ask oneself whether the world is truly the sole work of a benevolent God or if it is not perhaps a cooperative venture—I won't say with whom."

"What I'd like to know," von Teutleben remarked, "is whether the youth of other nations lie in the straw like this and torment themselves with problems and antinomies."

"Hardly," Deutschlin replied dismissively. "For them everything is intellectually much easier and cozier."

"One should make the exception," Arzt suggested, "of Russia's revolutionary youth. There you'll find, if I'm not mistaken, an untiring interest in discussion and one hell of a lot of dialectic tension."

"The Russians," Deutschlin said sententiously, "have depth, but no form. Those to our west have form, but no depth. Only we Germans have both together."

"Well, if that isn't a nationalist commitment!" Hubmeyer said with a laugh.

"It is merely the commitment to an idea," Deutschlin assured him. "It is the challenge of which I speak. Our responsibility is exceptional, certainly beyond any degree to which we now fulfill it. The gap between what should be and what is is far wider for us than for the others, because our 'should' has been set very high."

"One would do well to disregard the nationalistic element in all this," Dungersheim warned, "and regard this complex of problems as bound up with the existence of modern man in general. It is certainly the case that with the loss of direct existential trust, which in ages past was the result of being thrust into a preexistent unifying order—by which I mean arrangements impregnated with the sacred and having a certain intentionality toward revealed truth—that with deterioration of that trust and the establishment of modern society, our relationship to people and things has become subject to endless reflection and complication and presents only problems and uncertainty, so that any attempt to plot the truth threatens to end in resignation and despair. Amidst disintegration, the search for the rudiments of new ordering forces is universal, though one can also grant that it is especially serious and urgent for us Germans and that the others do not suffer so much under their historical destiny, either because they are stronger, or because they are denser . . ."

"Denser," von Teutleben declared.

"That's what you say, Teutleben. But if we ascribe our keen awareness of this historical-psychological problem to our national honor and identify the striving for a new unifying order with our Germanness, then we are well on our way to subscribing to a myth of dubious authenticity and indubitable arrogance—that is, to the nationalist myth, with its structural romanticizing of the warrior, which is nothing more than natural heathenism in Christian trimmings, with Christ designated 'Lord of the heavenly hosts.' That, however, is a position definitely vulnerable to demonic forces . . ."

"Well, so what?" Deutschlin asked. "In every vital movement there are demonic forces hidden alongside the ordering qualities."

"Let us call things by their name," Schappeler demanded; though it may also be that it was Hubmeyer. "The demonic, in German, that means the instinctual. And that's precisely the case nowadays when the instincts are used in propaganda offering all sorts of commitments—the instincts are incorporated, too, you see, and the old idealism is decked out with a psychology of the instincts, creating the alluring impression of a greater concentration of reality. But that is why those offers may well end up being a swindle . . ."

Here I can only say "and so forth," for it is time to bring the re-creation of that conversation—or one such conversation—to an end. In reality it had no end or at least (what with its "bipolar posture" and "historically conscious analysis," with its "supratemporal qualities" and "ontic naturalness," "logical dialectics" and "objective dialectics") went on long into the night—labored, learned, and boundless—only finally to drift off into nothing, or better, into sleep, to which Baworinski as presiding officer admonished us, since in the morning (though it was already almost morning) we wanted to begin our hike early. How commendable that kindly nature held sleep at the ready, into which it took up our conversation to rock it into forgetfulness, and Adrian, who had not said anything for a long time, expressed his thanks in a few words as we curled up.

"Yes, good night. Lucky we can say it. Discussions should be held only right before bed, with sleep waiting to cover your back. How embarrassing after some intellectual conversation to have to walk around with your mind wide awake."

"But that's an escapist attitude," came a final mutter. Then the first snores echoed in our barn, contented announcements of surrender to the vegetative state, of which only a couple of hours sufficed to restore to sweet youth the power to unite a grateful enjoyment of nature— taken in with deep breaths and long looks—with obligatory and almost unceasing theological and philosophical debates, characterized by mutual impressing and impugning, challenging and instructing. The middle of June, when the heavy fragrance of jasmine and black alder spilled from ravines in the wooded hills scattered along the Thuringian basin, provided delicious days for hiking across the fertile, gently favored countryside, almost totally lacking in industry but dotted by friendly, compact villages with their half-timbered houses; and leaving behind first the region of plowed fields and then one devoted primarily to dairy farming and following the upland path along the ridge lined with firs and beeches and offering views deep into the valley of the Werra— the storied "Rennsteig," which runs from the Franconian Forest as far as Eisenach, the city of the Venusburg—one enjoys a scene that grows ever more beautiful, remarkable, romantic; and neither what Adrian had said about youth's feeling shy before nature nor his remark about the advantage of finding recourse in sleep after intellectual disputes seemed to have any sort of actual relevance. And it had hardly any for him, either, for unless a migraine had silenced him, he was a lively contributor to the day's conversation; and although nature elicited from him no cries of enthusiasm and he gazed at her with a certain meditative reserve, I nonetheless have no doubt that her images, rhythms, and high-borne melodies entered more deeply into his soul than into those of the others, so that in later years many a fleeting passage of pure, unruffled beauty emerging from his intellectually taut work has made me think of those shared impressions.

Yes, those were stimulating hours, days, and weeks. The oxygen tonic of life in the open air, the impressions of the landscape and its history, exhilarated these young men and raised their spirits to those luxurious, freely experimental thoughts typical of student years, for which in their later, parched professional lives, they would, as good philistines (even if as philistines with some intellectual interests), no longer have any use whatever. I often watched them at their theological and philosophical debates and pictured how these Winfried years would later seem to many of them the grandest period of their lives. I watched them, and I watched Adrian—with the crystal-clear intuition that these years would definitely not seem that way to him. And if I, as a nontheologian, was a guest among them—then he, although a theologian, was one even more so. Why? I sensed, not without some anxiety, an abyss between his own life and the destinies of these striving, high-purposed young men; it was the difference between the curve described by a life of good, indeed excellent averageness, sure soon to follow the line from the condition of the vagabonding, testing undergraduate to the world of the bourgeois, and the curve of someone invisibly singled out, who would never leave the path of the intellect and its problems, who would follow it no one knew where, and whose gaze, whose demeanor that never relaxed entirely into the fraternal, whose inhibitions at saying "you fellows" or "we," all made me, and presumably the others, sense that he suspected this difference as well.

Already by the beginning of his fourth semester, I saw signs that my friend was thinking of cutting his theological study short, even before his first exams.

XV

ADRIAN'S RELATIONSHIP with Wendell Kretzschmar had never broken off or even flagged. During every vacation, when he would return to Kaisersaschern, the young student of divine sciences saw his high-school musical mentor, visited him, and conferred with him in the organist's apartment near the cathedral, saw him at his Uncle Leverkühn's home as well, and once or twice prevailed on his parents to invite him for a weekend at Buchel Farm, where Adrian took extended walks with him and talked Jonathan Leverkühn into showing his guest Chladni's sonorous figures and the devouring drop. Kretzschmar was on very good terms with his aging host at Buchel, but less at ease, though not in any way on truly strained terms, with Frau Elsbeth, perhaps because she was distressed by his stuttering, which for precisely that reason grew worse in her presence, particularly in direct conversation. It was remarkable—after all, in Germany music enjoys the same high popular regard accorded literature in France, and no one is surprised, intimidated, made uneasy, or provoked to disdain or scorn by the fact that someone is a musician. I am likewise convinced that Elsbeth Leverkühn had the fullest respect for the work of Adrian's older friend, who performed his duties in the service of—indeed as an appointed officer of—the Church. All the same, during two and a half days that I spent together with him and Adrian at Buchel, I noticed in her behavior toward the organist a certain forced quality that no friendliness could quite cover, a reserve, a disapproval, to which, as I have noted, the latter responded with intensified stuttering that a few times turned almost calamitous—difficult to say whether simply because he sensed her discomfort, her mistrust, or whatever one should call it, or because her personality quite spontaneously called up in him certain nervous, embarrassed inhibitions.

As for me, I had no doubt that the peculiar tension between Kretzschmar and Adrian's mother was related to her son, that he was its source; and since my own feelings held the middle ground in the silent dispute raging between the two, I could feel how I tended now to one side and now the other. What Kretzschmar wanted, what he spoke to Adrian about during those walks, was clear to me, and my own wishes secretly supported him. I thought he was right when, in conversations with me as well, he would emphatically, even urgently champion his pupil's calling to be a musician, a composer. "He has," he said, "the initiate's, the composer's eye for music, not that of some outsider finding vague enjoyment in it. The way he can uncover connections between motifs, which the latter never sees, can perceive the division of a short segment into question and answer, as it were, can see just in general and from inside how it's done—it all confirms me in my opinion. It is only to his credit that he has not yet written any music, has not yet revealed a productive impulse by naively launching into youthful compositions. It is a matter of pride that prevents him from generating second-rate imitations."

I could only concur with all of it. But from the bottom of my heart I could understand his mother's protective concern and often felt a solidarity with her that bordered on hostility for this recruiter. I shall never forget one scene in the living room of the farmhouse at Buchel, when all four of us—mother and son, Kretzschmar and I—happened to be sitting together, and in the midst of a conversation between Elsbeth and the musician, burbling and sputtering in his inhibited way, a simple chat in which Adrian was not at all the topic, she reached out to her son sitting beside her and drew his head to her in the strangest way. She looped her arm around him, so to speak, not around his shoulders, but around his head, her hand resting on his brow, and then with her black eyes directed at Kretzschmar and still speaking to him in her sweet, resonant voice, she rested Adrian's head on her breast.

What sustained the relationship between master and student, however, was not only these personal meetings, but also letters exchanged fairly frequently (every two weeks I believe) between Halle and Kaisersaschern, about which Adrian would report from time to time and a few of which I even got to see myself. As early as Michaelmas 1904, I learned that Kretzschmar was negotiating to take over a class in piano and organ at Hase's Private Conservatory in Leipzig, which at the time, along with the city's own famous music school, had begun to enjoy a growing prestige that continued to increase over the next ten years, until the death of that excellent pedagogue, Clemens Hase (although the conservatory has long since ceased to play any role at all, that is, if it still exists). With the start of the next year, then, Wendell Kretzschmar left Kaisersaschern to assume his new position, and so from that point on their correspondence passed between Halle and Leipzig: Kretzschmar's pages covered on just one side in scratches and splatters of large, stiff print; and Adrian's messages written on rough, yellowish paper in his regular, slightly old-fashioned, and somewhat ornate handwriting, obviously executed with a round-hand pen. He let me have a look at both a rough draft of one of them, written in a very cramped and codelike script and filled with minuscule interpolations and corrections (but I was familiar with his hand from very early on and could always read everything without difficulty)—at both his rough draft, then, and Kretzschmar's reply. He did it apparently so that I would not be all too surprised by the step he was planning to take, if he should indeed decide to take it. For he had not yet decided and even after self-examination was still unsure and very hesitant, as was obvious from his letter, and evidently hoped to obtain advice from me as well—God only knew whether in the way of warning or of encouragement.

There could be no question of surprise on my part, nor would there have been even if, without any preparation, I had one day been presented with a fait accompli. I knew what was brewing—whether it would be carried out was another question; but it was also clear to me that ever since Kretzschmar's move to Leipzig, the organist's chances of winning had significantly increased.

In his letter, which demonstrated a superior capacity for critical self-observation and which as a confession I found extraordinarily touching in its ironic contrition, Adrian laid out for his former mentor (who wished to assume that role again, and in an even more decisive way) the scruples that held him back from the decision to change professions and fling himself totally into the arms of music. He halfway admitted that theology had disappointed him as an empirical subject—the reasons for which, of course, were not to be sought in that venerable science itself, or in his academic teachers, but in himself. That was apparent from the fact that he certainly did not know what other, better, more suitable choice he should have made. At times in the last two years, when he had taken counsel with himself about the possibilities for a change in direction, he had thought of switching to mathematics, which in high school he had always found to be fine sport. (The expression "fine sport" is taken verbatim from his letter.) But with a kind of alarm at himself he saw that if he were to make this discipline his own, swear fealty to it, identify with it, the day would come when he would very quickly be disenchanted with it as well, be bored by it, be as weary and fed up with it as if he had been force-fed with iron ladles. (I also remember verbatim this Baroque turn of phrase in the letter.) "I cannot conceal from you, gentle sir," he wrote (for although he generally addressed Kretzschmar in an ordinary, though formal fashion, he would at times fall into such antiquated usages), "neither from you nor from myself, that there be something godforsaken queer about your *apprendista,* a thing not of the workaday, and I play not all-hid here, but a thing that sooner gives cause to misericord than that it makes the eye shine bright." God had given him, he said, the gift of a versatile wit, which from early childhood on had grasped with no special effort everything offered it by education—had probably grasped all things too easily in fact for any one thing to have achieved its due respect, too easily for either blood or brain ever to have been warmed properly by a subject and his labors over it. "Dear friend and master," he wrote, "I fear I am a mean fellow, for I have not warmth. It is written, of course, that they who are neither cold nor hot but lukewarm are to be cursed and spewed out of the mouth. I would not call myself lukewarm; I am decidedly cold—but in my judgment of myself I beg exemption from the tastes of that Power who dispenseth both blessing and curse."

He continued: "It is ridiculous to say so, but I did best at our gymnasium. I was more or less in the right place there, and that is because high school doles out various subjects, one after the other, with points of view changing from one forty-five-minute period to the next—in short, because there is not yet any profession. But even those forty-five minutes on one subject grew too long for me, were long on boredom— the coldest thing in the world. Within fifteen minutes at most, I had figured out what the good man chewed on for another thirty with those boys. When studying authors, I would read ahead, had already read ahead at home, and if I did not know an answer it was only because I had read ahead and was already in the next class; a quarter hour of the *Anabasis,* that was too much of one and the same thing for my patience, and in token thereof a headache would appear"—he meant his migraine of course—"never arising out of the weariness of effort, but from surfeit, from cold boredom, and, dear master and friend, now that I am no longer a bachelor lad leaping from matter to matter, but am wed to a profession, to a course of study, it has grown stronger along with me, indeed at times wickedly so.

"Good Lord, I would not have you believe I consider myself too good for any profession. On the contrary: I can but pity any that I would make my own, and in the case of music that pity would be es-

pecially great, in which you may see my devotion, my exceptional regard—indeed, my professed love—for it.

"You will ask 'And was it not a pity that you chose theology?' I took
shelter in it not so much because I saw in it the highest of the sciences—though for that reason as well—as because I wished to submit
myself to it, to humble myself, to discipline myself, to punish the arrogance of my coldness—in short, out of *contritio*. I longed for the haircloth shirt and the thorny girdle beneath. I did what men did of old
when they knocked at the cloister door of some strict order. It has its
absurd and ridiculous sides, this life in the scientific cloister; but can
you understand how a secret terror warns me not to give it up, not to
shove Holy Writ under the bench and escape into the art to which you
introduced me and which, were it my profession, could only be an object of exceptional pity?

"You believe I am called to this art and suggest it is no great 'step
outside the path.' My Lutheranism agrees with that, since it sees theology and music as neighboring spheres, as members of the same family;
moreover, for me personally, music has always seemed a magical union
of theology and the fine sport of mathematics. Item: There is about it a
great deal of the dogged pursuit and laboratory work of the alchemist
and sorcerer of ages past, which likewise stood under the sign of theology, but at the same time under that of emancipation and apostasy—
and it was apostasy, not from the faith, that was not possible, but rather
in the faith. Apostasy is an act of faith, and everything is and happens
in God—falling away from Him most especially."

My citations are almost verbatim, where they are not entirely so. I
can indeed depend on my good memory; moreover, right after reading
the draft I put several things to paper for myself, in particular the passage about apostasy.

He then excused himself for the digression (though it was hardly
that) and went on to practical questions about which sort of musical
activity he should envisage if he were to follow Kretzschmar's urgings.
He expostulated that it was obvious from that start that he was lost to
any career as a virtuoso soloist; for "No use killing nettles to grow
docks," he wrote, and he had come into contact with the instrument—
or even with the very notion of trying it out—much too late, in which
one could clearly see a lack of any instinctual drive in that direction.
He had found his way to the keyboard not out of any desire to set himself up as its master, but rather out of a secret curiosity about music
itself; and, besides, he completely lacked the gypsy blood of the
concertizing artist, who presents himself to the public through music,

using the occasion of music. For there were certain psychological pre-conditions, he said, that he could not fulfill: the desire for a love affair with the crowd, for wreaths, for groveling bows and kisses thrown amid crashing applause. He avoided the terms that would have put a name to the matter: To wit, that even if he had not come to it too late, he would have been too bashful, too proud, too brittle, too lonely to be a virtuoso.

These same objections, he continued, stood in the way of a career as a conductor. No more than he felt called to be an instrumental conjurer could he see himself as a prima donna in tails waving a baton at an orchestra, as music's interpretative ambassador on earth, its representative at galas. And here he let slip a word that belongs with those that only a moment ago I mentioned as helping to explain matters: He spoke of being a recluse. He called himself a "recluse" and did not intend it as any kind of praise. He declared it to be a condition that expressed his lack of warmth, of sympathy, of love—and it was very much a question whether such a person would ever be much of an artist, for that surely always implied being the world's lover and beloved. But if both those goals were excluded—of soloist and conductor—what remained? Well, to be sure, music as such, the pledge to and betrothal with her, the hermetic laboratory where gold is cooked: composing. Wonderful! "And you, gentle sir, Albertus Magnus, my friend, you will initiate me in its arcane theoretical teachings, and most certainly—for I feel it, I know it beforehand, just as I know it from my little previous experience—I shall not prove all too stupid an *adeptus.* I shall grasp all the tricks and twists, very readily in fact, because my mind speeds ahead to meet them; the soil has been prepared and holds within it many a harvest. I shall refine the *prima materia* by adding the *magisterium,* and thus with fire and spirit, through many a bottleneck and retort, I shall force it to purification. What glorious business! I know none more intriguing or mysterious, none higher, lower, better, none for which it would require less persuasion to win me.

"And yet, why does some inner voice warn me: '*O homo fuge*'? I cannot give a fully articulated answer to the question. I can only say this much: I am afraid of making promises to art, because I doubt whether my nature—quite apart from the issue of talent—is such that I can satisfy art, for I can lay no claim to that robust naiveté that, as far as I see, is one of those things, nor is it the least of them, that are part of being an artist. Instead of which, my portion has been a quickly sated intellect, of which I can well say, indeed I swear by heaven and hell, that I do not pride myself in it one whit; and that, along with an attendant fatigue and a propensity to nausea (accompanied by head-ache), is the reason for my reticence and worry—it will, it should induce me to abstain. You see, gentle sir and good master, as young as I am I have learned enough about art to know—nor would I be your pupil if I did not—that art goes far beyond any schematics, conventions, or traditions, far beyond what one man learns from another, far beyond the trick of 'how it is done'; and yet it is undeniable that those things also still have a great relevance to art, and I can see it coming (for anticipating the future unfortunately or luckily is also part of my nature) that when confronted with the banality that constitutes the supporting structure, the stabilizing element behind even a work of genius, when confronted with what is common property, with the part that is culture, with the customary usages for achieving the beautiful—that I will be embarrassed by it all, will blush, grow faint, end up with a headache, and in very short order.

"How foolish and pretentious it would be to ask: 'Do you understand that?' For how could you not! This, then, is how beauty happens: The cellos intone all by themselves a somber, pensive theme that questions the world's folly in a forthright and highly expressive philosophical 'why' addressed to our hustle and bustle, our hounding and harrying. The cellos enlarge on this for a while, shaking their wise heads in regret over this riddle, and at a given, carefully considered point in their comments, the wind instruments, after a preparatory deep breath that causes shoulders to rise and fall again, enter with a chorale, stirringly solemn, splendidly harmonized, and played with all the muted dignity and gently constrained power of brass. With that, the sonorous melody pushes forward, approaching its highpoint, but, in accordance with the law of economy, avoids it for now, dodges, leaves an opening, leaves it aside, recedes, lingers very beautifully right there, but then steps back and makes room for another theme, a simple folk tune, jesting and pompous, apparently coarse by nature, but as shrewd as they come, too, and, when subjected to a few seasoned devices of orchestral analysis and coloration, proves amazingly capable of interpretation and sublimation. There is now some clever and sweet dandling with the little tune for a while; it is taken apart, each of its segments observed and transformed, and one charming figure in the middle voices is lifted to most magical heights, to the spheres of the violins and flutes, is cradled there for a while yet, until, at its most flattering moment, the gentle brass again announces the chorale from before, steps into the foreground, avoiding the long preparation of its first statement and entering not at the beginning, but as if the melody had already been there for a while, and now moves solemnly toward that

same highpoint from which it wisely refrained the first time, so that the
'Ah!'-effect, the surge of emotion is all the greater, when, ascending
ruthlessly and supported by harmonic passing tones from the bass
tuba, the brass gloriously bestrides the theme and then, gazing back, so
to speak, with worthy satisfaction on what it has accomplished, sings
its way modestly to the end.

"Dear friend, why does this make me laugh? Can one use what tradition offers, can one sanctify old artifices with more genius? Can one
achieve the beautiful with defter emotion? And yet I, the outcast, must
laugh, especially at those supporting grunts from the bombardon—
boom, boom, boom—bang! I may perhaps have tears in my eyes, but at
the same time the urge to laugh is overwhelming. I have been damned
from the start with the need to laugh at the most mysterious and impressive spectacles, and I fled from my exaggerated sense of the comic
into theology, hoping it would soothe the tickle—only to find a lot of
things awfully comic there as well. Why must almost everything appear to me as its own parody? Why must it seem to me as if almost all,
no, all the means and contrivances of art nowadays are good only for
parody? Those are truly rhetorical questions—all that is lacking is for
me to expect an answer to them from you. But you regard such a desperate heart, such a cold-nosed rascal as 'talented' for music, do you?
And call me to it, to you, instead of letting me humbly stick it out with
the divine sciences?"

This then was Adrian's confession, his defense. Nor do I have the
documentation of Kretzschmar's reply, either. I did not find it among
Leverkühn's papers. He probably preserved it and kept it with him a
while, but then lost it during a change of residence, in his move to
Munich, or Italy, or Pfeiffering. But in any case, I remember it almost as
exactly as I do Adrian's statements, even though I made no notes of it
at the time. The stutterer persisted in his summons, his admonition and
enticement. Not one word in Adrian's letter, he wrote, could have dissuaded him for even a moment from his conviction that it was music to
which his correspondent had truly been predestined by fate, music for
which he longed, which longed for him, from which, half in cowardice,
half in coquetry, he was hiding behind half-true analyses of his own
character and constitution, just as he had hidden behind theology, his
first and absurd choice of profession. "Affectation, Adri—and an even
worse headache is your punishment." The sense of the comic of which
he had boasted, or of which he accused himself, would be far more
compatible with art than with his present, artificial pursuits, for unlike
them, art could make use of it, could in general make much better
use—than he believed, or pretended to believe by way of excuse—of

the unattractive traits of personality he ascribed to himself. He, Kretz-schmar, would leave open the question to what extent all this was self-vilification intended to excuse a corresponding vilification of art; for to present art as copulation with the mob, as thrown kisses and posturing at galas, as a bellows for emotional surges, was indeed a slight misread-ing, and a willful one at that. What he was doing was trying to excuse himself from a life in art with precisely those characteristics that art de-mands. Art nowadays needed people like himself, precisely such peo-ple—and the joke, the hypocritical, hide-and-seek joke was that Adrian knew that only too well. The coldness, the "quickly sated in-tellect," the awareness of banality, the tendency to be easily wearied and surfeited, the capacity for disgust—it was all constituted to elevate to a profession that same talent to which it was linked.

Why? Because it all belonged only in part to the private personality; the rest, however, came from something above the individual, was an expression of a collective sense that the means of art had turned stale and were exhausted by history, of being bored by all that, of striving for new paths. "Art advances," Kretzschmar wrote, "and does so by means of the personality, which is the product and tool of its times and in which objective and subjective motives are joined beyond differen-tiation, each assuming the form of the other. Art's vital need for revo-lutionary progress and achievement of the new depends on the vehicle of the strongest subjective sense for what is hackneyed, for what has nothing more to say, for those standard, normal means that have now become 'impossible'; and so art helps itself to apparently unvital ele-ments: personal weariness and intellectual boredom, the disgust that comes with perceiving 'how it's done,' the cursed proclivity to see things in light of their own parody, the 'sense of the comic'—what I am saying is: Art, in its will to live and progress, puts on the mask of these dull-hearted personal traits in order to manifest, objectivize, and fulfill itself in them. Is that too much metaphysics for you? But really it is only just enough, and just the truth—the truth you ultimately know yourself. Make haste, Adrian, and decide! I am waiting. You are al-ready twenty, and you still have to learn a good many tricks of the trade, of the sort difficult enough to intrigue you. It is better to get a headache from practicing canons, fugues, and counterpoint, than from rebutting Kant's rebuttal of the proofs for God's existence. Enough of this playing the theological virgin!

> Virginity, though fine, needs motherhood to hallow
> What else is but a sad and barren field left fallow."

The letter concluded with this quotation from Cherubini's *Wayfarer,* and looking up from it, my eyes met Adrian's mischievous smile.

"Not badly parried, don't you think?" he asked.

"Not in the least," I replied.

"He knows what he wants," he continued, "and it is rather embarrassing that I don't know precisely."

"I think you know as well," I said. For I had, in fact, never regarded his letter as an actual refusal—though, to be sure, I had not believed it was written out of "affectation." That is truly not the correct word for intentionally making some impending decision more difficult, for plunging it into doubts. That the decision would be made, I foresaw with some emotion, and the fact that it was already as good as made served as the basis for an ensuing conversation about both our immediate futures. Our paths were parting in any case. Despite my severe nearsightedness, I had been found fit for military service and planned to put in my year of service now by signing up with the Third Field-Artillery Regiment in Naumburg. For his part, Adrian, who for some reason—perhaps his short stature or his habitual headaches—had been excused from service indefinitely, intended to spend several weeks at Buchel Farm, in order, as he said, to consult with his parents about the question of his changing professions. He implied, however, that he intended to present it as merely a change of universities—to some extent he represented it that way to himself. He wanted, so he would tell them, to allow his pursuit of music "to come more to the fore" and so would be transferring to the city where the musical mentor of his school years was working. What he did not say, however, was that he was giving up theology. But in fact his intention was to register again at the university for lectures in philosophy and to get his doctorate in that field.

At the beginning of the winter semester 1905, Leverkühn moved to Leipzig.

XVI

Needless to say, our formal goodbye was cool and reserved. It scarcely amounted to exchanged looks or a handshake. In the course of our young lives we had parted and met again too often for handshakes to have become our usual practice. He left Halle a day earlier than I, and we had spent his final evening at the theater—just the two of us, without anyone from Winfried along; he would be leaving the next morning, and we parted there on the street as we had hundreds of times before—we simply went in different directions. I could not help accentuating my farewell with the mention of his name—his first name, as was natural for me. He did not mention mine. "So long," he said, nothing more—it was an English idiom he had learned from Kretzschmar and used merely as a kind of ironic quote, just as he generally had a pronounced taste for quotes, those verbal allusions that remind us of something or someone. He added a jest about the episode of martial life awaiting me, and went his way.

He was in fact right not to take the separation too seriously. Within a year at most, once my military service was complete, we would meet again somewhere or other. And yet it was in some sense a break, the end of one era and the beginning of another; and if he did not seem to notice that, I indeed took note of it with a certain edgy sadness. By joining him in Halle, I had, so to speak, prolonged our school days; we had not lived there much differently from how we had in Kaisersaschern. I could not even compare the change now taking place with the period when I was already a university student and he was still in high school. I had left him behind then within the familiar framework of our hometown and St. Boniface Gymnasium and had dropped in on him from time to time. Only now, so it seemed to me, were our lives disconnecting, was each of us beginning to stand on his own two feet, which meant the end of what had seemed to me so necessary (if futile), the end of what I can only once again describe with the same words I have used before: I was no longer to know what he was doing and experiencing, was no longer to be able to stay close to him, keeping an attentive, constant eye on him, but would have to leave his side now, when it seemed most highly desirable for me to observe his life, though certainly without being able to change it—now, at precisely the moment when he was abandoning his career as a scholar, "shoving Holy Writ under his bench," to use his own expression, and flinging himself totally into the arms of music.

This was a significant decision, which, as I saw it, was uniquely stamped with destiny and which in some sense both annulled the recent past and reconnected with our common life from long ago, with moments whose memory I bore in my heart: with the time when I had found the lad experimenting on his uncle's harmonium, and, still farther back, with our singing canons with barnyard Hanne under the linden tree. It was a decision that raised my heart high with joy—and at the same time compressed it with fear. I can compare the feeling only with how a child on a swing feels, with that blend of exaltation and anxiety as it tugs its body upward to fly higher and higher. That this step was legitimate, necessary, a rectification of a false one, and that theology had been an evasion, a dissimulation—that was all clear to me, and I was proud that my friend no longer scrupled to profess its truth. Persuasion, to be sure, had been required to bring him to that profession; but whatever extraordinary results I promised myself from it, it eased my mind, amid my joyful uneasiness, to be able to say to myself that I had taken no part in the persuasion—at most having lent assistance by a certain fatalistic demeanor, by words like "I think you know, yourself."

What now follows is a letter that I received from him two months after I entered the service in Naumburg and read with much the same emotions a mother might feel upon reading such disclosures from her child—except, of course, that propriety demands one withhold this sort of thing from one's mother. I had written him three weeks previously—in care of Herr Wendell Kretzschmar at the Hase Conservatory, since I still did not know Adrian's address—telling him about the new and coarse conditions of my life and asking him to please give me some picture, however sketchy, of how he was faring in the big city, whether it suited him, and how he had organized his studies. I shall preface his answer simply by saying that its antiquated prose is, of course, intended as a parody, an allusion to his own quaint experiences in Halle and to the linguistic deportment of Ehrenfried Kumpf—at the same time, however, it also expresses his personality; it is a self-stylization, a manifestation of his inner disposition and of a highly characteristic tendency to hide behind and find fulfillment in parody.

He wrote:

> Leipzig, the Friday after The Purification, 1905
> in Peter Strasse, House Number 27

To my honorable, erudite, esteemed, beneficent Master and Ballistier!

We are obliged and grateful for your perturbation and epistle and for having given us lively and most comical tidings of your present dapper, dull, and demanding state, of your caperings and curry-combings, your polishings and musketings. The which did bring us keen amusement, most especially the drill-sergeant who, though he buffet and drub you, yet holds you in great account for your schooling and learning and for whom, while sitting in the mess, you were made to map out all poesy's meters by feet and *morae,* inasmuch as he believes such knowledge to be the prick of the mind's ennoblement. And if time suffice and that you may also have cause for marvel and laughter, I would requite you with a desperate piece of waggery and buffoonery which befell me here. Yet first would I speak my cordiality and good will and do hope that you suffer such strokes of the rod almost gladly and cheerly, for over time they will assist you to step forth at the end in the buttons and braid of a reserve subaltern.

The good word here is "In God shalt thou believe, to land and people cleave, and no man shalt thou grieve." On the banks of the Pleisse, Parthe, and Elster, life is indubitably of another sort and pulse than beside the Saale, for indeed here is gathered a passable great throng of folk, more than seven hundred thousand, which straightway gives rise to a certain sympathy and tolerance, much as the prophet displays a knowing and indulgently understanding heart for the sins of Ninevah, when he says in its favour, "That great city, wherein are more than sixscore thousand persons." You may imagine, then, what forbearance be required amongst thirty-fivescore thousand, to which during one of its fairs, the autumnal variety of which I tasted as yet but newly arrived, is added a notable confluence from all parts of Europe, besides Persia, Armenia, and other Asiatic lands.

Not that this Ninevah specially pleases me; 'tis surely not my fatherland's fairest city; Kaisersaschern is fairer, though it may more readily be fair and worthy, since it need only be old and still, and has no pulse. It is resplendent built, my Leipzig, much as if from a box of costly toy bricks; moreover its people speak a most devilish vulgar tongue, so that one shrinks at every shop before entering to bargain. It is as if our sweetly drowsing Thuringian, upon being awakened, were to thrust its jaw forward for a mouthful of impudence and wickedness times seven hundred thousand—horrible, horrible, though God forbid, certainly with no evil intent and always mixed with a self-mockery that they can afford by virtue of their worldly pulse. *Centrum musicae,* center of the printer's trade and the bookman's dibble-dabble, and illustriously universitied—albeit with buildings scattered: The central edifice is on Augustus Platz, the library adjacent the Gewandhaus, and special collegial buildings are apportioned to the various faculties, such as the Red House to the philosophic on the Promenade, the *Collegium Beatae Virginis* to the juridical in my own Peter Strasse, where fresh from Central Station and taking the first thoroughfare into town, I promptly found suitable refuge and lodging. Arrived in early afternoon, left my baggage at the repository, found my way here as if guided, read the placard on the gutter spout, rang, and forthwith came to terms in regard of the two rooms on the ground floor with the fat landlady, who spoke her devilish tongue. The hour was still so early and I still in the first flush of arrival, that I took in almost the entire town that same day—truly guided this time by the very porter who fetched my valise from the station, the selfsame source of that jape and foolery of which I spoke and mayhap yet tell.

My fat landlady raised nary a protest to my clavicymbal; they are customed to such here. Nor do I batter her ears all that much with it, since at present I pursue harmony and the *punctum contra punctum* principally in theory, with books, pen, and paper and at my own devices, which is to say: under the oversight and discipline of *amicus* Kretzschmar, to whom every few days I bear my exercises and works for censure or approval. Rejoiced uncommonly, the man did at my coming, and took me in his arms, for I did not wish to betray his confidency. Nor will he hear of me and

a conservatory, neither the great one nor the Hasean, where he in-
structs; 'twould be, he says, no climate for me, but rather I should
do as did Papa Haydn, who had no preceptor anywhere, but
rather procured for himself the *Gradus ad Parnassum* by Fux and
other sundry music of the day, most particularly that of Bach of
Hamburg, and doughtily perfected his craft therefrom. Twixt you
and me, the study of harmony results in many a yawn, whereas I
am immediately quickened by counterpoint, cannot play enough
amusing pranks in that magic arena, solve its never-ceasing problems with lusty fervour, and have already cobbled a whole pile of
droll studies in the canon and fugue, thereby garnering some
praise from my master. It is productive work, arousing fantasy
and invention, for a domino game of chords which lacks all theme
is, methinks, fit for neither washing nor cooking. Were it not better for one to learn all that—suspension, passing tones, modulation, preparations, and resolutions—*in praxi,* from hearing, from
experience and self-discovery, rather than from some book? But
on the whole and *per aversionem,* it is a foolishness, this mechanical separation of counterpoint and harmony, inasmuch as they
are insolubly intermingled, until one cannot teach each of itself,
but only the whole, to wit: music—an it be instructible. Kretzschmar admits as much, too, and says himself that one must, from
the first, do justice to the role melody plays in the creation of
good couplings. Most dissonances, he says, have more likely come
into harmony by way of melody than through any harmonic
combination.

And thus am diligent, *zelo virtutis,* indeed almost overburdened
and overbusied with matters, for am still hearing lectures of higher
learning, history of philosophy from Lautensack and both logic
and encyclopaedie of philosophic science from the famous Bermeter.—*Vale. Iam satis est.* Committing you herewith to God, that
He may defend you and all innocent hearts.—"Your very humble
servant," as was said in Halle.—As for that jape and prank due to
which there be something afoot twixt Satan and myself, I have
made you far too curious: 'Twas nothing more than that as night
fell on that first day, said porter led me astray—a churl, a rope
round his gut, with red cap and brass badge, in a rain mantle, speaking the same devilish tongue as every man here, with jutting bris-
tled jaw, and by my lights looked somewhat like our Schleppfuss
by reason of his small beard, in truth looked right like him, when
I think on it, or may have grown more like in my remembering

since—albeit he was stouter and fatter from his ale. Presented himself as a guide and proved himself such with a brass badge and two or three scraps of English and French, devilishly pronounced, *peaudiful puilding* and *antiquidé exdrèmement indéressant.*

Item, we came to terms, and for two full hours the fellow did show it all, took me everywhere: to Paul's Church with its marvelous, strange chamfered cloister; to Thomas's Church, for the sake of Johann Sebastian; and to his grave in John's Church, where the Reformation monument also is; and to the new Gewandhaus. 'Twas merry in the streets, for, as I told before, the Autumn Fair was still in swing, and all sort of hangings and banners extolling furs and other wares were hung from the windows down over the houses; and a great crowd was in all the streets, specially in the town's centre, near the Old Town Hall, where the fellow showed me the palace and Auerbach's Inn and the tower that yet stands of Pleissenburg citadel—where Luther had his disputation with Eck. And then the press and hurly-burly in the narrow streets behind the Market, antique, with steep-pitched roofs, through covered courts and lanes, past warehouses and cellars, being connected crossways labyrinthian. And all stuffed full with merchandizes, and the people thronging there gaze upon you with exotic eyes and speak in tongues of which you ne'er have heard a sound before. Right stirring it was, and you feel the world's pulse within your own body.

By degrees it grew dark, lights came on, the streets emptied as well, and I was weary and hungry. I bid my guide as a final service that he show me to an inn for my meal. A good one? he asks and winks. A good one, say I, an it be not too dear. He leads me to a house in an alley behind the main street—next the stairs leading up to the door, a rail of brass shiny as the churl's badge and the lantern o'er the door the very red of his cap. When I have paid him, he wishes me a hearty appetite and turns tail. I ring, the door opens of itself, and through the entry a dame in gaudy dress approaches, with rosy-hued cheeks, a rosary of waxy-hued pearls across her bulk, and greets me with almost coy demeanour, piping high sweet pleasure and dallying with me as one long awaited, escorts me then through portières into a shimmering chamber with walls paneled in cloth, a crystal chandelier, sconces at mirrors, and silken couches, upon which there sit waiting for you the nymphs and daughters of the wilderness, six or seven—how shall I put it— morphos, clearwings, esmeraldas, scantly clad, transparently clad, in tulle, gossamer, and glister; their long hair falling free, hair with lovelocks; powdered demiglobes, arms with bracelets, and gazing at you with eyes expectant and asparkle with chandelier light.

Gazing at me, not you. That churl, that ale-knight Schleppfuss, had led me to a bawdyhouse! I stand up and hide my sentiment, behold opposite me a piano standing open—a friend—tread straightway cross the carpet and, still standing, strike two, three chords, and know well what they were, for that phenomenon of sound was in full possession of my thoughts. Modulation from B major to C major, a brightening by one half-step, as in the hermit's prayer in the finale of the *Freischütz,* when timpani, trumpets, and hautboys enter on the fourth and sixth intervals of C. Know that now, afterwards, though knew it not at the time, but simply struck the keys. There steps to my side a nut-brown lass, in Spanish jacket, with large mouth, stubbed nose, and almond eyes—Esmeralda, who strokes my cheek with her arm. I turn about, thrust the bench aside with my knee, and stride back across the carpet, through this hell-hole of lusts, past the vaunting bawdstrot, through the entry, and down the stairs into the street, never touching the rail of brass.

There you have the rag and tatter that befell me, drawn at length, in payment for that bellowing corporal whom you instruct in the *ars metrificandi.* To which amen and pray for me! To this date I have heard but one Gewandhaus concert with Schumann's Third as pièce de résistance. A critic of the day praised this music for its 'comprehensive world view,' which sounds like pointless babble of the sort that classicists ridiculed with a vengeance. Yet it makes a good point, for it indicates an elevation of state that both music and musicians owe to Romanticism. For it emancipated music from the sphere of parochial speciality with local pipings and brought it in contact with the larger world of the mind, with the general artistic and intellectual motion of the time—let that not be forgotten. All of which proceeds from the later Beethoven and his polyphony, and I find it extraordinarily significant that the foes of Romanticism—to wit: of art stepping forward out of mere musicality and into the realm of the general intellect—were likewise always foes and lamenters of Beethoven's later development. Have you ever considered how different, how much more anguishingly meaningful the individualization of the voice in his highest works appears in comparison with older music, where it is done more deftly? There are judgments that provide amusement by their crude truth, which itself compromises the judge. Handel said of Gluck: "My cook knows more about counterpoint than he"—a colleague's verdict that I hold dear. Around 1850 a French critic of some repute, an ardent admirer of Beethoven until the Ninth Symphony, declared that work to be under the sway of a wearied mind, the dark pedantry of an ungifted contrapuntist. Do you know with what a thrill of amusement such felicitous errors fill me? Nothing is truer than that in the fugue Beethoven never achieved the technical assurance, skill, or ease that Mozart commanded. Which is precisely why his polyphony possesses an intellectuality that both outgrows and expands its musicality.

Mendelssohn, for whom, as you know, I have a tender spot, took up, so to speak, with Beethoven's third period, i.e., with his multivoiced style—and at something else and more than an ambling gait. The only objection I would raise against him is that polyphony came too easily to him. He is, despite his elves and nixies, a classicist.

Am playing a lot of Chopin and reading about him. I love what is angelic in his figure, recalling Shelley, his eccentrically and mysteriously veiled, impenetrable, aloof, unadventuresome existence— his not-wanting-to-know, his rebuff to material experience, the sublime incest of his fantastically delicate and seductive art. How well it speaks for him, that deeply attentive friendship extended by Delacroix, who writes him, *"J'espère vous voir ce soir, mais ce moment est capable de me faire devinir fou."* All quite possible for the Wagner of painting! Yet there is not a little in Chopin that more than anticipates Wagner, indeed passes him by, not only harmonically, but in a general psychological sense. Take the Nocturne in C-sharp minor, Opus 27 No. 1, and the duet that begins after the enharmonic substitution of C-sharp major with D-flat major. In its desperate beauty, the sound surpasses all *Tristan* orgies—and that by way of the piano's intimacy, not as a great brawl of lusts, nor with a theatrical mystique, which like the bullfight is robust in its very depravity. But take, above all, his ironic relationship with tonality, how it vexes, desists, disavows, and hovers, its mockery of the key signature. He goes far, amusingly and touchingly far . . .

The letter ends with the cry of *"Ecce epistola!"* To which is added: "Needless to say, you shall destroy this at once." The signature is an initial, that of his last name, an *L*, not an *A*.

XVII

I DID NOT OBEY his categorical instruction to destroy the letter—and who would blame a friendship that may lay claim to the term "deeply attentive," coined to describe Delacroix's friendship for Chopin? I did not obey the unreasonable demand right off because I felt a need to read over and over a text I had simply raced through the first time—not only to read it, but also to study it critically for style and psychology; and as time passed, it seemed to me the moment to destroy it had passed as well. I learned to regard it as a document that included as an essential part this order to destroy, which canceled itself out, so to speak, by its documentary nature.

This much was certain from the beginning: The directive at the end was motivated not by the whole letter, but by only a portion of it, the so-called waggery and buffoonery, the experience with that dreadful porter. But again, that portion was the whole letter, was the reason it had been written—not to amuse me (the writer doubtlessly knew that his "jape" would contain nothing I would find amusing), but to unburden himself of an upsetting impression, for which I, his childhood friend, was indeed his only recourse. All the rest is trimmings, wrappings, pretense, delaying tactics—and, afterward, as if nothing has happened, it is all covered up again with the aperçus of a voluble music critic. Everything is steered toward the—to use a very objective word—anecdote; it is in the background from the start, announcing itself in the first lines, only to be deferred. Still unspoken, it plays a role in the jest about the great city of Ninevah and the quotation with the prophet's skeptical exoneration of it. The anecdote comes close to being told at the point where mention is first made of the porter—and vanishes anew. The letter is apparently brought to a close before it gets told—*"Iam satis est"*—and, as if the matter has almost slipped the writer's mind and has required the quote of Schleppfuss's greeting to prompt him, is now told "just in passing," as it were, with a bizarre reference to his father's study of butterflies; yet it dare not conclude the letter, to which are appended remarks about Schumann, Romanticism, and Chopin, evidently with the aim of lessening the weight of the anecdote, of returning it to oblivion—or more correctly, the writer, so as to keep his pride, gives those remarks the appearance of pursuing that aim, for I do not believe that his real intention was for me, the reader, to skim right past the core of the letter.

Already on the second reading, I found it quite remarkable that the style, this burlesque or personal adaptation of Kumpfian antiquated German, lasts only until the adventure is told and is afterward casually dropped, so that its color is bleached out of the concluding pages, which display a modern verbal character. Does it not seem as if the archaized tone had fulfilled its purpose as soon as the story of being led astray was put to paper, as if from then on the tone was abandoned not only because it did not fit the ruse of those final observations, but also because, starting with the dating, that tone had been introduced solely in order to tell the story in it, to give the tale its appropriate atmosphere? And what atmosphere is that? As little as the term I have in mind seems applicable to a farce, I will use it: It is a religious atmosphere. It was clear to me: The language of the Age of Reformation, with its historical affinity to religious matters, was chosen for a letter intended to tell me this story. Without that ploy, how could the sentence have been put to paper that longed to be put to paper: "Pray for me!"? There can be no better example of quotation as camouflage, of parody as pretense. And just before it there is another term that gave me a jar on the very first reading and that has nothing farcical about it, but bears an expressly mystical, indeed religious stamp: That term is "hell-hole of lusts."

The coolness of the analysis to which I subjected Adrian's letter both then and just now will mislead few people about my true feelings as I read and reread it. Analysis necessarily has an appearance of coolness, even when it is employed in a state of profound shock. And shocked I was—no, worse, I was beside myself. My rage at the obscene prank of that ale-knight Schleppfuss knew no bounds; not that the reader should see in that any characterization of my nature, any token of personal prudery, for I was never a prude, and had I been the object of that Leipzig bamboozlement, I would have known to put a good face on things—no, but rather the reader should find in my feelings a characterization of Adrian's nature and essence, for which the word "prude" would truly be most ludicrously inappropriate, but which nevertheless might very well have been imbued with a modest sensitivity to crudeness and a desire for protection and forbearance.

My feelings were influenced to no little extent by his having told me of the adventure at all—weeks after it had occurred—which implied a breaching of what had otherwise been a total reserve I had always respected. As strange as it may sound in light of our long years of comradeship, the subject of love, of sexuality, of the flesh had never been touched upon in our conversations in any personal or intimate fashion; the matter had entered into our exchanges always and only through the medium of art and literature, occasioned by manifestations of passion in the intellectual sphere that prompted remarks from him that were matter-of-factly knowledgeable but in which his own person played no role. How could such a mind, such a spirit not have encompassed that element as well! There was proof enough that it did so in his restatement of ideas adopted from Kretzschmar about how the sensual was not to be disdained in art, and not just in it—plus many of his remarks about Wagner and such spontaneous comments as the one about the nakedness of the human voice and how older vocal music had compensated for it intellectually with the most confounded artistic devices. There was nothing virginal about that sort of thing; it showed his free and unruffled way of looking directly at the world of desire. On the other hand, it was indicative yet again not of my nature, but of his, that every time a conversation took such a turn it came as a shock, was a cause for bewilderment that made something inside me flinch. It was, to put it forcefully, as if one were listening to an angel expatiate on sin, and even in that case, though one has no reason to expect any frivolity or sauciness, any banal witticisms in regard to the subject, one would still be offended—despite full acknowledgment of his intellectual right to speak—and be tempted to plead "Silence, dear one! Thy lips are too pure and austere for these things."

Adrian's distaste for lascivious crudities was in fact so pronounced as to be forbidding, and I knew perfectly that look of disdainful revulsion and dismissive detachment when anything of the sort even remotely threatened. In Halle, in the Winfried circle, he was fairly secure against such attacks on his sensibilities; clerical propriety—at least in regard to words—kept them at bay. Among the seminarians there was no talk of women or wenches, girlfriends or love affairs. I do not know how those young theologians, each for himself, did in fact behave, whether they all chastely saved themselves for Christian marriage. As for myself, I must admit that I had tasted of the apple, and that for some seven or eight months back then I had an affair with a lass from the common folk, a cooper's daughter—a relationship that it was hard enough to keep secret from Adrian (I truly do not think he was aware of it) and that I broke off again in due time and in a kindly way because the poor thing's lack of education bored me, and I had nothing to say to her except just the one thing. I entered into the liaison not so much out of hot-bloodedness as out of curiosity, vanity, and a desire to put into practice one of the theoretical convictions I held: that is, antiquity's candid behavior in sexual matters.

Precisely that element, however, that sense of intellectual diversion, which I at least pretended, if perhaps somewhat pedantically, was completely missing in Adrian's attitude to the sphere in question. It is not my wish to speak of Christian inhibition, nor would I apply the catchword "Kaisersaschern," thereby invoking both its petite bourgeois morality and its medieval dread of sin. That would serve the truth very inadequately and would not suffice to suggest the loving respect, the antipathy to every possible offense, that his stance instilled in me. If one was unable—and unwilling—to imagine him in any sort of "amorous" situation, that was the result of the purity, chastity, intellectual pride, and cool irony that he wore like a suit of armor and that I held sacred—sacred in a certain painful and secretly humiliating fashion. For how painful and humiliating (except perhaps to the wicked) is the realization that purity has not been granted to life in the flesh, that instinct has no fear of intellectual pride, and that the most unbending arrogance must pay its tribute to nature, so that one can only hope that this humiliating descent to our human state—and thus, by God's will, to the bestial state as well—may be consummated in a form that is most tenderly adorned, most spiritually elevated, and veiled in the devotion of love, of purifying sentiment.

Need I add that the least hope of any of that is found in cases like those of my friend? The tender adornment, the ennobling veil, of which I spoke is the work of the soul, an intermediary, mediating component, which is deeply infused with poetry and in which instinct and intellect interpenetrate and are reconciled in a certain illusionary fashion—that is to say, a thoroughly sentimental stratum of life, in which, I admit, my own humanity feels quite cozily at home, but which is not for those of the most exacting tastes. A nature like Adrian's does not have much "soul." It is a fact, taught me by the probing observation of friendship, that the proudest intellect stands in most immediate confrontation with what is bestial, is most abjectly at its mercy; and that is the reason for the apprehensive anxiety that persons such as I must endure in dealing with a nature like Adrian's—it is also the reason why I found that damnable adventure he wrote me about to be so terrifyingly symbolic.

I saw him standing on the threshold to that den of pleasure, gazing at those waiting daughters of the wilderness, but only slowly comprehending. Just as he had once passed through the alien world of Mütze's Tavern in Halle—and I could picture it so clearly—I saw him striding blindly to the piano and striking those chords for which he could account only after the fact. I saw the stubbed-nose girl beside him—*Hetaera esmeralda*—her powdered demiglobes in a Spanish bodice, saw her stroke his cheek with her bared arm. I felt an intense longing to be transported there, across space and back in time. I craved to thrust the witch away from him with my knee, just as he had thrust the bench away to clear a path to the outside. For days I felt the touch of her flesh on my own cheek and—in disgust, in terror—I knew that it had been burning on his ever since. Again, I can only beg it not be seen as characteristic of me, but rather of him, that I was incapable of seeing the incident from its cheerful side. There was absolutely nothing cheering about it. If I have even remotely succeeded in providing the reader with a portrait of my friend's nature, then he can only feel along with me the indescribable shame, the mocking degradation, the danger in that touch.

He had never "touched" a female until then—of that I was and am irrevocably certain. But now a female had touched him—and he had fled. There is not a trace of the comic in that flight—I can assure the reader of that, should he be inclined to find in it anything of the kind. The extrication was comic at best, in the bitterly tragic sense of its futility. In my eyes, Adrian had not escaped, and he himself, to be sure, had seen it as an escape only very temporarily. The arrogance of the intellect had suffered the trauma of an encounter with soulless instinct. Adrian would return to the spot where his deceiver had led him.

XVIII

IN LIGHT OF MY ACCOUNT, of my narrative, may not the reader ask how I can be familiar with such precise details, since I was not always present, not always at the side of the late hero of this biography. It is true that I repeatedly lived apart from him for extended periods: During my year in the military, for example, although after its completion I resumed my studies at the University of Leipzig and gained thorough knowledge of the scope of his life there; likewise for the period of my educational tour of the classical world, which took place in the years 1908 and 1909. Our reunion upon my return was quite brief, since he was already entertaining the idea of leaving Leipzig and moving to southern Germany. There followed, then, our very longest period of separation, the two years he spent in Italy—after a short stay in Munich—together with his friend Schildknapp, a Silesian by birth, during which time I first completed my probation as a teacher at St. Boniface Gymnasium in Kaisersaschern and then assumed a permanent position on the faculty there. It was not until 1913, when Adrian had taken up residence in Pfeiffering in Upper Bavaria and I moved to Freising, that I again found myself in close proximity to him; but from then on certainly, with no (or as good as no) interruption, I watched with my own eyes as his life—long since tinged with the colors of its fate and marked by increasingly intense work—was played out over the next seventeen years, until the catastrophe of 1930.

When he arrived in Leipzig and once again placed himself under the guidance, tutelage, and supervision of Wendell Kretzschmar, he had long since ceased to be a beginner in the study of music—of that strangely cabalistic, simultaneously playful and rigorous, ingenious and profound craft. Sparked by an intelligence that grasped things instantly and disrupted at most by his own anticipatory impatience, his rapid progress in those areas that could be taught him—compositional technique, formal structure, orchestration—proved that his two-year theological episode in Halle had not loosened his ties to music, had not meant any real interruption of his preoccupation with it. His letter had reported something of his eager and prolific exercises in counterpoint. Kretzschmar placed almost even greater importance on instrumentation and, just as in Kaisersaschern, had him orchestrate a great deal of piano music, movements from sonatas, and even string quartets, so that there could then be long conversations in which he would discuss, criticize, and correct what Adrian had produced. He went so far as to commission him to orchestrate the piano reductions of single acts from operas with which Adrian was unfamiliar; and the comparison between the efforts of his pupil (who had heard and read Berlioz, Debussy, and the late romantics of both Germany and Austria) and the operas that Grétry or Cherubini had themselves produced gave both master and student cause to laugh. At the time, Kretzschmar was working on his own piece for the stage, *The Marble Statue,* and he also gave *particella* scores of one scene or another to his apprentice to orchestrate and then showed him how he himself had done it, or was intending to do it—resulting in numerous debates, during which, it goes without saying, the master's considerably greater experience usually held the field, though on at least one occasion the novice's intuition triumphed. For a certain mix of sounds, which Kretzschmar had rejected at first glance as imprudent and awkward, gradually won him over as being more appropriate than what he himself had had in mind, and at their next meeting he declared that he wanted to adopt Adrian's idea.

The latter was less proud of this than one might think. Teacher and pupil were essentially quite far apart in matters of musical instinct and intent—indeed, any aspirant in the arts finds himself almost by necessity dependent on the guidance of a master of his craft from whom he is already half-estranged by a generation's difference. Things only go well if the master nevertheless surmises and understands these hidden tendencies—sees them ironically, if need be—but is careful not to stand in the way of their development. And so Kretzschmar lived in the self-evident, unuttered conviction that music had found its ultimate, highest manifestation and efficacy in orchestral works—something Adrian no longer believed. To his twenty-year-old mind, as was not the case for his elders, the idea that the most highly developed instrumental art is bound to a harmonic conception of music was more than a historical insight—as he saw it, it had become something like a mindset in which past and future had fused. His cool regard for the hypertrophied sound apparatus of the gigantic post-Romantic orchestra; the urge to condense and return it to the role of servant it had played in the age of preharmonic, polyphonic vocal music; his fondness for both that music and the oratorio as a genre, in which he would later achieve his highest and boldest creations, *The Revelation of St. John* and *Lamentation of Dr. Faustus*—all that emerged very early on in both word and attitude.

All of which made him no less zealous at orchestration under Kretzschmar's direction, for he agreed with his teacher that one must master what has already been accomplished even if one no longer considers it essential, and he once said to me: A composer who has had enough of orchestral impressionism and so no longer wants to learn instrumentation seemed to him like a dentist who no longer studies root-canal work and reverts to the role of a yanking barber, because it has recently been discovered that dead teeth can cause rheumatoid arthritis. This comparison, so oddly far-fetched and yet so characteristic of the intellectual atmosphere of the day, lived on as a catchword that we often used in critical comments; and so a "dead tooth" preserved by artificially embalming its root became a symbol of certain modern creations for the refined orchestral palette—including his own symphonic fantasy *Phosphorescence of the Sea,* which he wrote, still under Kretzschmar's eye, upon returning to Leipzig from a holiday on the North Sea with Rüdiger Schildknapp and a semi-public performance of which Kretzschmar arranged on one occasion. It is a piece of exquisite tonepainting that attests to an astounding feel for bewitching mixtures of sound, which on first hearing the ear can barely unpuzzle; and a welltrained audience saw in its young composer a highly talented successor to the line of Debussy and Ravel. That he was not—and his whole life long he would no more count this demonstration of talent for coloristic orchestration among his actual compositions than he did the calligraphic, wrist-loosening exercises over which he had previously labored for Kretzschmar: the six- to eight-voice choruses; the fugue with three themes for string quintet with piano accompaniment; the symphony, which he presented bit by bit in *particella* score to Kretzschmar, with whom he then discussed its instrumentation; the Cello Sonata in A Major, with that very lovely slow movement whose theme he would later reuse in one of his Brentano Songs. In my eyes, *Phosphorescence of the Sea,* though sparkling with sound, was a very remarkable example of how an artist can put his best efforts into a task in which he no longer believes and can persist in excelling in an artistic style which to his mind is already hovering on the verge of obsolescence. "It's the root-canal work I've learned to do," he told me. "I take no responsibility for any streptococcal infection." Every word he said proved that he considered the genre of "tone-painting," of setting "nature's moods" to music, to be dead for good and all.

But to be quite frank, this unbelieving masterpiece of orchestral coloristic brilliance already bore clandestine traits of parody, of a general attitude of intellectual irony toward art that would so often emerge like an eerie stroke of genius in Leverkühn's later work. Many found this chilling, indeed repulsive and shocking, and that was the judgment of the better sort of people, though not of the best. The very superficial sort called it merely witty and amusing. In truth the parodistic element here was a proud flight from the sterility with which a great talent was threatened by skepticism, intellectual reticence, and an awareness of banality's deadly and expanding realm. I hope I am putting this right. My uncertainty and my sense of responsibility are equally large, for I am trying to clothe thoughts in words that are not primarily my own, but have been instilled in me solely through my friendship with Adrian. I prefer not to speak of a lack of naiveté on his part, for ultimately naiveté is the basis of being itself, of all being, of even the most self-aware and complicated. There is an almost unresolvable conflict between the inhibitions and the productive drives born with genius, between chastity and passion—and that conflict is itself the naiveté from which such an artistic existence lives, the soil for its own arduously characteristic growth; and the unconscious striving to create for one's "talent," for one's productive impulse, the scant but necessary advantage over the restraints of mockery, of arrogance, of intellectual self-consciousness—that instinctive striving surely begins to stir and become determinative at the moment when the purely mechanical studies preparatory to creating art first begin to mingle with one's own efforts (even if still quite preliminary and preparatory) at giving shape to one's art.

XIX

I MENTION THAT MOMENT because I am about to speak—not without a shiver, not without a faltering of the heart—of the fateful event that occurred about a year after I received, while still in Naumburg, the letter from Adrian quoted above, a little more than a year after his arrival in Leipzig and his first tour of the city, about which he wrote me in that same letter—that is, not long before I was discharged from the military and joined him again, finding him externally unchanged, but in reality already a marked man pierced by the arrow of fate. I feel I should invoke Apollo and the Muses to inspire me with the purest, tenderest words for what I shall say—tender out of consideration for the sensitive reader, for the memory of my late friend, and not least out of consideration for myself, to whom the telling of all this seems much like a painful personal confession. But the direction in which such an invocation would be aimed reveals to me the contradiction between my own psychological state and the actual coloration of the story I must tell, for its hue comes from very different strata of tradition, quite foreign to the fair skies of classical learning. I began this entire account with an expression of doubt as to whether I was the right man for the task. I shall not repeat the arguments I presented against such doubt. It is sufficient that, supported and strengthened by them, I intend to remain true to my enterprise.

I said that Adrian returned to the spot to which an impudent porter had led him. As one can see, that did not happen all that soon—for a whole year his pride of spirit held its own against the wound it had received; and it has always been some solace to me that his surrender to naked instinct and its mocking touch was not lacking in every spiritual veil, every human ennoblement. I see such a thing, in fact, whenever those urges, however crude, are fixed upon one definite, individual goal; I find them in the impulse to choose, even if the choice be involuntary and brazenly provoked by its object. A trace of love's purification is evident the moment instinct wears a human face, even the most anonymous, the most despicable. Which is to say, that Adrian returned to that place on account of one particular person, the one whose touch still burned on his cheek, the "nut-brown lass" in the jacket and with the large mouth, who had approached him at the piano and whom he called Esmeralda. It was she whom he sought there—and did not find.

His fixation, though calamitous, resulted in his leaving that locale after his voluntary second visit the same man he was after his involuntary first one, but not without his having determined the address of the female who had touched him. It resulted also in his having to undertake a rather long journey, under a musical pretext, to reach the object of his desire. At that time, May 1906, the first Austrian performance of *Salome* was to take place in Graz, the capital of Styria, with the composer himself conducting—the same opera whose world premiere a few months earlier Adrian had traveled with Kretzschmar to Dresden to see; and he now told his teacher and the friends he had made by then in Leipzig that he wanted to participate in the gala occasion and hear once more this successfully revolutionary work—to whose aesthetic sphere he was not in the least drawn, but which of course interested him in its technical musical aspects, particularly the way prose dialogue had been set to music. He traveled alone, and it cannot be documented with certainty whether he carried out his ostensible intention of traveling from Graz to Pressburg, or possibly first to Pressburg and then on to Graz, or if he merely shammed the stay in Graz and limited his visit to Pressburg, or Poszony as the Hungarians call it. For, after having had to leave her former place of employment to undergo hospital treatment, the female whose touch he still bore had ended up in a house there; and instinct drew him to her new locale, where he found her.

My hand is indeed trembling as I write, but I will say what I know in calm, collected words—always consoled to some degree by the thought I welcomed before, the thought of choice, the thought that something resembling the bond of love reigned here, lending some shimmer of human soul to the union of this precious young man with that ill-fated creature. To be sure, this comforting thought is linked inseparably to another, all the more dreadful one: that here, once and for all, love and poison were joined as a single experience, as a mythological unity embodied in the arrow.

It would appear that the poor creature's heart had feelings that responded to those the young man extended to her. There is no doubt she recalled her transient visitor from a year before. Her approaching him to stroke his cheek with her bared arm may have been the vulgarly tender expression of her susceptibility for everything that set him apart from her usual clientele. She learned from his own lips that he had made this long journey for her sake, and she thanked him—by warning him against her body. I know this from Adrian himself: She warned him; and does not that imply a gratifying disparity between the creature's higher humanity and that physical part of her, the vile commodity of trade cast to the gutter? The hapless woman warned the man who desired her against "herself"—and that means an act of the soul freely elevating itself above her pitiful physical existence, a humane act of distancing herself from it, an act of compassion, an act, if I may be permitted the word, of love. And, good heavens, was it not love as well—or what was it, what obsession, what act of will recklessly tempting God, what impulse to incorporate the punishment in the sin, or finally, what most deeply secreted desire to receive and conceive the demonic, to unleash a deadly chemical change within his own body was it—that caused him, though warned, to spurn the warning and insist on possessing that flesh?

I have never been able to think of that encounter without a religious shudder—for in that embrace, one party forfeited his salvation, the other found hers. The traveler from afar refused to reject her no matter what the risk—and to the wretched girl that must have come as a purifying, justifying, elevating blessing; and it appears that she offered him all the sweetness of her womanhood in repayment for what he was risking for her. She saw to it that he would never forget her; but he, who would never see her again, never forgot her for her own sake, either, and her name—the one he had given her from the beginning—haunts his work like a rune, legible to no one but me. And though it may be taken as vanity on my part, I cannot refrain at this point from noting a discovery he would one day confirm, although by his silence. Leverkühn was not the first composer, nor will he have been the last, who loved to insert secret messages as formulas or logograms in his work, revealing music's innate predilection for superstitious rites and observances charged with mystic numbers and alphabetical symbols. And thus within my friend's tonal tapestry there is conspicuously frequent use of a figure, a sequence of five or six notes, that begins with an

H (which Anglo-Saxons call a B) and ends on an Es (known in the English-speaking world as E-flat), with E and A alternating in between—a basic motif with an oddly melancholy sound that pervades his music in a variety of harmonic and rhythmic disguises, assigned now to one voice, now to another, often in its inverted form, as if turned on its axis, with the intervals still the same, but with the notes in reverse sequence. It appears first in what is probably the most beautiful of the thirteen Brentano lieder, all composed while he was still in Leipzig, in the heart-wrenching song: "Oh sweet maiden, how bad you are," which is totally governed by the motif; and then in the late work, with its unique blend of boldness and despair, most especially in *Lamentation of Dr. Faustus,* which was written in Pfeiffering and displays to an even greater extent a tendency to present those melodic intervals in harmonic simultaneity.

And that encoded sound reads as: H–E–A–E–Es: *Hetaera esmeralda.*

RETURNING TO LEIPZIG, Adrian expressed his amused admiration for that powerful opera he claimed to have heard a second time, and possibly actually had heard. I can still hear him say about its composer: "What a talented shipmate! The revolutionary as a bonny lad, cocky and congenial. After that great show of provocation and dissonance, the way it's all turned into geniality and beer hall bonhomie, all put in apple-pie order, so to speak, reconciling the philistine and assuring him nothing nasty was intended . . . But a hit, a hit indeed . . ." Five weeks after resuming his musical and philosophical studies, he decided to seek medical treatment for a localized infection. The specialist he consulted, Dr. Erasmi by name (Adrian had found the address listed in a street directory) was a heavyset man with a red face and black goatee, who had a way of puffing air between his pouted lips and did so both when standing erect and bending over, which he apparently found especially difficult to do. This habit was presumably a token of some physical distress, but also expressed an airy indifference, much as when someone dismisses—or tries to dismiss—a problem with a "Pooh!" And so the doctor puffed away all during the examination and then, somewhat in contradiction to his pooh-poohing, declared that a radical and rather lengthy therapy was required, which he began at once. And continuing the treatments, Adrian returned on the next three days as well; then Dr. Erasmi ordered a three-day pause and asked him to return on day four. But when his patient—who was not at all ill, his general health being in no way affected—returned for his appointment at four that afternoon, he encountered something totally unexpected and horrifying.

Whereas until now, after first climbing three steep flights of stairs in a rather gloomy building in the old city, he had always had to ring at the apartment door and then be admitted by a maid, this time he found the door wide open, as was also the case with the doors inside the apartment: The door to the waiting room was open, and beyond it, that to the consulting room; but so, too, was the door to the living room straight ahead, a "parlor" with two windows. What was more, the windows were wide open and all four curtains, billowed and lifted by the breeze, were alternately thrust far out into the room and pulled back into their dormers. In the middle of the room, however, was Dr. Erasmi, dressed in a ruffled white shirt and lying—goatee at the vertical, eyelids closed—on a tasseled cushion in an open coffin set atop two trestles.

How this had come about—why the dead man was lying there so alone and exposed to the wind, where the maid and Frau Dr. Erasmi might be, whether the undertakers were still in the apartment and waiting to screw on the lid or if they had temporarily left—what had led the visitor here at that strange juncture never became clear. Once I had arrived in Leipzig, Adrian could only describe for me how he had descended the three flights of stairs bewildered by what he had seen. He does not appear to have investigated the doctor's sudden death any further, had no interest in the matter, it seemed. He suggested that the man's constant "poohing" had surely always been a bad sign.

And I must now report—with secret aversion and despite an irrational horror—that his second choice was made under a similarly unlucky star. It took him two days to recover from the shock. Having again consulted only a Leipzig street directory, he now sought treatment from a certain Dr. Zimbalist, who resided on one of the commercial streets that converge at Market Square. On the ground floor was a restaurant, above it was a piano warehouse, and a portion of the third floor was occupied by quarters leased by the doctor, whose name caught one's eye downstairs on a porcelain sign beside the main entrance. The dermatologist's two waiting rooms, with one reserved for female patients, were decorated with potted plants—palms and African hemp. Medical journals and reference books (an illustrated history of morals for example) were to be found in the room where Adrian waited on that first and, again, on a second occasion.

Dr. Zimbalist was a short man with horn-rimmed spectacles, an oval bald spot running from his brow to the back of his head and framed by reddish hair, and a tag of a moustache beneath his nostrils—a style popular in those days among the upper classes, and which would later become a hallmark of a face in world history. His patterns of speech were sloppy, peppered with manly quips and bad puns. He was fully capable of taking a term like the "falls on the Rhine" and by substituting "rind" for "Rhine" turn it into slips on a banana peel. One did not, however, have the impression that he felt all that good about the joke himself. A kind of tic that lifted one cheek and a corner of the mouth, while the eye joined in with a squint, gave him a problematic sour look, an uneasiness and touchiness that boded no good. That was how Adrian described him to me, and how I picture him.

And now what happened is this. Adrian had undergone two treatments with his second doctor, when he set off to see him a third time. As he was climbing the stairs between the second and third floors, he met the man he had come to see descending the stairs between two stocky fellows who wore their stiff hats set at the back of their heads. Dr. Zimbalist's eyes were lowered as if he were minding every step down he took. One of his wrists was linked by a bracelet and chain to the wrist of one of his escorts. Looking up and recognizing his patient, he gave a sour wince of his cheek, nodded, and said, "Some other time!" Thunderstruck, Adrian, who otherwise would have stood in their way, pressed his back to the wall to let them pass, watched them depart, and soon followed back down the stairs. He saw them climb into a waiting car, which then drove off at high speed.

And so, after the first interruption in Adrian's cure, its continuation with Dr. Zimbalist came to an end. I must add that he no more concerned himself with what lay behind this second aborted attempt than he had with the strange circumstances accompanying his first experience. Why it was that Zimbalist had been taken away, and at the very hour set for the appointment—he let the matter rest. But as if frightened off now, he did not resume the cure, did not seek out a third doctor. He had even less cause to do so since the localized infection healed quickly and vanished with no further treatment—and, as I can confirm and sustain against any professional doubts, no secondary symptoms whatever were manifested. On one occasion in Wendell Kretzschmar's apartment, just as Adrian was presenting a compositional study, he did suffer a bad dizzy spell that sent him reeling and forced him to lie down. It turned into a two-day migraine, which except perhaps in its severity was no different from earlier attacks. And when, having been returned to civilian life, I moved to Leipzig, I found my friend's nature and ways unaltered.

XX

OR WERE THEY? For if he had not become a different person during the year of our separation, then he had certainly become even more himself, and that sufficed to impress me, especially since I had probably forgotten a bit just how he was. I have described the coolness of our goodbye in Halle. Our reunion, to which I had been looking forward so intensely, lacked nothing of that same quality, so that I, although nonplused, equally heartened and saddened, had to swallow and suppress whatever emotions wanted to brim over within me. I had not expected him to meet me at the train station, had not even notified him of my exact time of arrival. I simply sought out his apartment, without even having secured lodgings of my own. His landlady announced me to him, and as I entered the room I called out his name in a bright voice.

He was sitting at his desk, an old-fashioned rolltop secretary with a cupboard set atop it, writing out music.

"Hello," he said, without looking up. "We can talk in a moment." And he continued to work for several minutes, leaving it to me whether I should remain standing or make myself comfortable. One ought not take this amiss any more than I did. It was proof of an old and sure intimacy, of a life together that could not possibly have been affected by a year apart. It was simply as if we had said our goodbyes only the evening before. Nevertheless I felt a little frosted by disappointment, though I was cheered at the same time, in the way that characteristic things can cheer us. I had long since taken a seat in an armless easy chair upholstered with tapestry fabric, when he at last screwed his fountain pen tight and walked over to me without ever looking directly at me.

"You've come at just the right time," he said and sat down at the other side of the table. "The Schaffgosch Quartet is playing Opus 132 this evening. You are coming along, aren't you?"

I knew he meant the late Beethoven work, the String Quartet in A Minor.

"Since I'm here," I replied, "I'll come along with you. It will be good after so long a time to hear again the Lydian movement, the 'Hymn of Thanksgiving upon Recovery.'"

"I drain that cup," he said, "at every feast. My eyes are brimming o'er with tears!" And he began to speak of the Church modes and the Ptolemaic, or "natural" system, whose six different modes were reduced to two scales, the major and minor, by tempered or "false" tuning and of the superiority of modulation in "pure" scales when compared to tempered ones. He called the latter a compromise for home use, just as the well-tempered piano was really meant for use in the home—a preliminary armistice, not yet a hundred and fifty years old, which had accomplished all sorts of remarkable things, oh, very remarkable, but which we ought not to imagine was a pact made for eternity. He expressed great pleasure in the fact that it had been an astronomer and mathematician, Claudius Ptolemaeus, a man from Upper Egypt living in Alexandria, who had produced the best of all known scales, the natural or pure scale. It proved anew, he said, the relationship between music and the study of the heavens, just as it had been proved before by Pythagoras's theory of cosmic harmony. From time to time he would return to the quartet and its third movement—that alien air, that lunar landscape—and the enormous difficulty of performing it.

"Ultimately," he said, "every one of the four must be a Paganini, a master not only of his own part, but of the other three as well—it's no go otherwise. Thank God one can depend on these Schaffgosch people. It can be done nowadays, but it's on the border of the playable, and simply wasn't playable in its time. I find one of the most amusing things to be how a man who has risen above it all can be so ruthlessly unconcerned about earthly technicalities. 'What do I care about your damned fiddle!' he said to some fellow who complained."

We laughed—and the only odd thing was that we had not greeted one another at all.

"And by the way," he said, "there is also the fourth movement, that incomparable finale with its short marchlike introduction and the recitative so proudly declaimed by the first violin, as fitting a preparation as possible for the actual theme. It really is annoying—that is, if you prefer not to call it delightful—that there are things in music, at least in this music, that cannot be characterized by an adjective, or a combination of adjectives, search as you will in the whole realm of language. I have been agonizing over the problem of late—you can find no adequate term for the spirit, the attitude, the gesture of that theme. For there is a great deal of gesture to it. Tragically bold? Defiant, emphatic—élan raised to the sublime? None of it is any good. And 'splendid!' is, of course, only foolish capitulation. In the end, one ends up back at its businesslike title, its name: Allegro appassionato. That's still the best."

I agreed. Perhaps, I suggested, something would come to us this evening.

"You have to see Kretzschmar soon," it occurred to him to say. "Where are you staying?"

I told him that I would find a hotel room for the night and look for something suitable the next day.

"I can understand," he said, "your not giving me the job of finding some place for you. You can't leave that to anybody else. I've told the people at Café Central about you and that you'd be coming," he added. "I'll have to introduce you there soon."

By "people" he meant a group of young intellectuals with whom he had become acquainted through Kretzschmar. I was sure he would treat them more or less the way he had treated his Winfried brothers in Halle, but when I remarked how pleased I was that he had quickly made some good connections in Leipzig, he simply replied, "Well, connections . . ."

Schildknapp, the poet and translator, he went on to say, was the most amiable of the lot. But his problem was his not exactly superior self-confidence, so that he always held back the moment he noticed that someone wanted something from him, needed him, was trying to enlist his services. A man with a very strong, or perhaps it was a rather weak, sense of independence, he said. But likable, amusing, although always so short of money that he really had to keep an eye out to get by.

Further conversation that evening revealed what he would have liked from Schildknapp, who as a translator was on intimate terms with the English language and in general was a warm admirer of all things English. I learned that Adrian was looking for a text for an opera, and that already, years before he seriously approached the task, he was considering *Love's Labour's Lost*. What he had wanted from

Schildknapp, who was also well-versed in music, was an adaptation of the text; but he would hear nothing of it, in part because he had his own work to do and also probably in part because Adrian could hardly have compensated him at the time. Well, I later rendered that service to my friend and like to think back to that evening and our first exploratory conversation on the subject. I discovered that he was increasingly preoccupied with an interest in music wedded to word, with its vocal articulation; he was engaged now almost exclusively in composing lieder, shorter and longer songs, even fragments of epics, taking his material from a collection of Mediterranean verse in a rather felicitous German translation, which included Provençal and Catalonian lyrics from the twelfth and thirteen centuries, Italian poetry, visionary highlights from the *Divina Commedia,* as well as some Spanish and Portuguese works. It was almost inevitable, given the musical times and his youthful apprenticeship, that the influence of Gustav Mahler would be felt here and there. But already a sound, an attitude, a view, a melody wandering alone, were trying to make themselves heard with a firm and strange insistence—and today we recognize in all that the master of the grotesque visions of his *Apocalypse.*

It announced itself most clearly in the songs of this series taken from the *Purgatorio* and *Paradiso* and chosen with a clever sense of their affinity with music—for instance, in the piece that especially fascinated me and that Kretzschmar had also declared to be very good, where by the light of Venus the poet beholds the lesser lights (which are the souls of the blessed) describing their circles, some more quickly, others more slowly, "each according to its contemplation of God," and compares the various sparks distinguishable in the flame, the voices audible in the larger song, "when the one entwines the other." I was amazed and enchanted by the rendering of the sparks in the fire, by those entwining voices. And yet I did not know whether I preferred these fantasies on light within light or the more brooding pieces that gazed within rather than without—the ones in which everything is an unanswered question, a struggle with the unfathomable, where "doubt grows at the foot of truth" and even the cherub gazing into God's deepest depths cannot measure the abyss of His eternal resolve. Adrian had chosen the dreadfully harsh sequence of verses that speak of the damnation of the innocent and unknowing and question the inscrutable justice that delivers over to hell those who are good and pure, but unbaptized or as yet unreached by the faith. He had found it in himself to put music to the thundering reply proclaiming the good creature's powerlessness before the Good, which as the source of all justice cannot forsake itself for anything our reason is tempted to call unjust. I was outraged by this denial of the humane in favor of an unapproachable, absolute predestination—just as, in general, I acknowledge Dante's poetical greatness, but have always been put off by his penchant for cruelty and scenes of torture—and I recall that I scolded Adrian for having decided to compose music for this almost unbearable episode. It was on this same occasion that I met a look in his eyes that I had not known before and of which I was thinking when I asked myself whether it would be quite correct to claim that I had found him unaltered after our year of separation. That glance—which would remain unique to him, though one was not subjected to it frequently, but only now and then, and sometimes for no apparent reason—was indeed something new: mute, veiled, so aloof as to be almost offensive, and yet musing and cold with sadness, always ending in a not unfriendly, yet mocking smile with closed lips and in that gesture of turning away, which, however, was an old, familiar one.

The effect was painful and, whether intentionally or not, it wounded. But I quickly forgot it as I continued to listen, taking in the poignant musical diction given to the man in a parable from the *Purgatorio,* who bears a light on his back at night, which does not shine for him, but brightens the path for those who come after. It brought tears to my eyes. But I was even more pleased by Adrian's total success in shaping the poet's nine-line address to his own allegorical song, whose words are so dark and difficult and whose hidden meaning has no chance of being understood by the world. Let the poem, so its creator enjoins upon it, ask people to perceive its beauty if not its profundity. "Behold at least how beautiful I am!" How the music strives upward out of the adversity, artificial confusion, and strange anguish of the first three lines toward the gentle light of that final cry, there to be touchingly redeemed within in it—I immediately found it admirable and made no secret of my delighted approval.

"All the better if it amounts to something already," he said; and in subsequent conversations it became clear that the "already" referred not to his youth, but rather to the fact that he regarded the composition of lieder, however great his devotion to each task, as merely a preliminary exercise to the large-scale work of words set to music that he had in mind and whose subject was that comedy by Shakespeare. He strove to lend theoretical glory to his attempted union of music and word and quoted a rough maxim of Søren Kierkegaard's, which that thinker expected even those who knew something about music to endorse: He did not have much use for the sublimer sort of music that thought it could do without the word, because it regarded itself as ranking higher than the word, whereas it ranked lower. In response to my laughing disagreement, he admitted that Kierkegaard must therefore have had little respect for our Opus 132, and that on the whole the man uttered a great deal of aesthetic nonsense. But the maxim fit his own productive work too well for him to want to surrender it. He spurned program music: It was the wishy-washy product of a rotten, bourgeois age, an aesthetic changeling. But music and speech, he insisted, belonged together, were ultimately one—language was music, music a language; when separated, each always stood in reference to the other, imitated the other, made use of the other's methods, always insinuated that it was the substitute for the other. He tried to demonstrate for me how music could be word at its inception, could be conceived and planned as words, in the fact that Beethoven had been observed to compose in words. "What is he writing there in his notebook?" people had asked. "He's composing." "But he's writing words, not notes." Yes, that was his way of doing things. He would normally sketch out the conceptual flow of a composition in words, with at most a few notes strewn here and there. And at this point Adrian paused, obviously taken with the idea. Artistic thought, he suggested, formed an intellectual category unique to itself, and yet a first sketch of a painting or a statue hardly ever consisted of words—which was evidence of the special bond between music and language. It was very natural that music should catch fire from words, that the word should burst from music, as happened at the end of the Ninth Symphony. And finally, it was surely true that the whole development of German music had striven toward Wagner's dramas of music and word, had found its goal in them.

"One goal," I said, pointing to Brahms and to the kind of absolute music that had emerged in Adrian's own "Light on His Back"; and he found it all the easier to admit the qualification since his long-range plan was as un-Wagnerian as possible, not even remotely akin to that mythic pathos and demonic natural world: a revival of *opera buffa*, in the spirit of artistic satire and as a satire on artificiality, a thing of the most playful preciosity, mocking both affected asceticism and the euphuistic fruit that classical studies bore in society. He spoke to me with enthusiasm about his chosen subject, which offered the opportunity to place spontaneous oafishness side by side with the comically sublime and to render each ridiculous in the other. Archaic heroics, a bygone era's bombastic etiquette, rose up again in the person of Don Armado, whom he quite rightly declared to be a perfect operatic character. And he quoted for me, in English, lines from the work, to which he was obviously deeply attached: the despair of the witty Berowne over his own perjured love for the lady with pitch-balls stuck in her face for eyes; his having to groan and grovel for a woman who "by Heaven, will do the deed though Argus were her eunuch and her guard." Then the judgment spoken against this very Berowne, condemning him to spend his wit on speechless, groaning wretches for a year, and his cry:

> It cannot be, it is impossible.
> Mirth cannot move a soul in agony.

And repeating the couplet, he declared that he would definitely set it to music someday—it and that incomparable conversation in the fifth act about the folly of the wise, about the helpless, blind, humiliating misuse of wit when adorned with the fool's cap of passion. Only on the heights of poetic genius, he said, did statements such as these two lines flourish:

> The blood of youth burns not with such excess
> as gravity's revolt to wantonness.

I was pleased by his admiration, his love for the material, although the choice itself did not suit me at all and I was always somewhat displeased by its mockery of humanism's excesses, which, after all, ends up making humanism itself an object of ridicule as well. But that did not prevent me later from furnishing him the libretto. What I immediately tried to talk him out of, however, was his peculiar and totally impractical plan of setting his music to the English text, because he considered only it to be true, worthy, authentic, and also because the antiquated plays on words and doggerel rhymes seemed to demand it. He would not accept my main objection that a text in a foreign language would block any chance of the work's ever being realized on a German opera stage, since on principle he refused to imagine a contemporary audience for his remote, exclusive, whimsical dreams. It was a baroque idea, but one deeply rooted in his nature—composed of arrogance, a recluse's shyness, the old-fashioned German provincialism of Kaisersaschern, and an explicit cosmopolitanism. It was not for nothing that he was a son of the town in which Otto III lay buried. His distaste for the Germanness that he embodied (a revulsion that had drawn him, by the way, to the Anglicist and Anglomaniac Schildknapp) appeared in two divergent forms: an eccentric reticence to deal with the world and an inner need for the wide world beyond—which was what led him to insist that he could demand a German concert-hall audience listen to songs in a foreign language, or more correctly, that he could conceal songs from them in a foreign language. And indeed, during my year in Leipzig, he produced compositions based on original poems by Verlaine and by his particular favorite, William Blake—yet these remained unsung for decades. Those by Verlaine I later heard in Switzerland. One of them is a wonderful poem whose final line is: "*C'est l'heure exquise*"; another is the equally magical "*Chanson d'automne*"; a third, fantastically melancholy and maddeningly melodic, has three stanzas that open with: "*Un grand sommeil noir—Tombe sur ma vie.*" There were also a couple of dissolutely madcap pieces from his *Fêtes galantes*, including "*Hé! bonsoir, la lune!*" and above all the macabre proposal, with answering giggles: "*Mourons ensemble, voulez-vous?*" As for Blake's singular poetry, he had composed music for the famous verses about the rose that grows sick from the dark love of the worm that has found its way to her crimson bed. And then the uncanny sixteen lines of "Poison Tree," in which the poet waters his wrath with tears, suns it with smiles and deceitful wiles, until its tree bears a bright apple that poisons the friend who steals it—and whom the hater is glad to see lying dead beneath the tree the next morning. The poem's wicked simplicity was perfectly recreated in the music. But I was even more deeply impressed, on the very first hearing, by a song based on words by Blake: the dream of a chapel all of gold before which people stand, weeping, mourning, worshiping, but not daring to enter in. There now rises up the figure of a serpent, who knows how to force and force and force his way into the shrine, who draws his slimy length along the jeweled pavement, until he reaches the altar, where he vomits his poison out on the bread and on the wine. "So," the poet concludes, with the desperate logic of therefore and thus, "I turned into a sty and laid me down among the swine." The fearful nightmare of that vision, its growing horror, its sickening defilement, and its final fierce renunciation of a humanity degraded by the very sight—it was all reproduced with amazing urgency in Adrian's music.

But those are matters from a later period, though they all belong in a chapter dealing with Leverkühn's years in Leipzig. On the evening of my arrival, then, together we heard the concert by the Schaffgosch Quartet and paid a visit the next day to Wendell Kretzschmar, who privately described Adrian's progress for me in a way that made me proud and happy. There was nothing he feared less, he said, than his ever having to regret calling Adrian to music. A man so self-controlled and fastidious about all that was banal or crowd-pleasing would surely have a hard go in life, in matters both external and internal; but that was perfectly in order here, for only art could lend real weight to a life that would otherwise be bored to death by its own facileness. I also signed up for lectures by Lautensack and the famous Bermeter, glad I no longer had to listen to theology for Adrian's sake; and I had him introduce me to the Café Central group, a kind of Bohemian club that had laid claim to a smoky side room of the tavern, where of an afternoon its members read newspapers, played chess, and discussed cultural affairs. There were conservatory students, painters, writers, young publishers, as well as up-and-coming lawyers with an interest in the arts, a couple of actors from the Leipzig Kammerspiele, a stage under very literary direction, and so forth. Rüdiger Schildknapp, the translator, who was considerably older than we, probably in his early thirties, was, as noted, a member of the same circle; and since he was the only one with whom Adrian was on closer terms, I too became better acquainted with him and spent many hours in the company of them both. That I kept a critical eye on the man whom Adrian had honored with his friendship will, I fear, be evident in the preliminary sketch I wish to make of his personality—although I shall endeavor, as I have always endeavored, to treat him fairly.

Schildknapp had been born in a medium-sized town in Silesia, the son of a postal official whose position was not of the lowest rank, but who had been unable to rise to any really higher administrative level, councilor or whatever, such posts being reserved for men with academic credentials. His job demanded no high-school diploma, no legal training; one needed only to spend a few years in preparatory service and pass the exam for head secretary. Such had been the path taken by Schildknapp the Elder; but since he was a well-bred and well-mannered man with some social ambition, and since the Prussian hierarchy either excluded him from the upper circles of the town or, when it did admit him by way of exception, gave him a good taste of humiliation, he bickered with his fate, became a disgruntled, sulky man who made his family pay for his failed career by fits of foul temper. Rüdiger, his son, described for us very vividly, and with more emphasis on comedy than filial respect, how his father's social embitterment had soured not only his life, but that of his mother and siblings as well—all the more grievously, since, as befitted a cultivated gentleman, it had been manifested not in crude quarrels, but in a refined knack for affliction and expressive self-pity. He might come to the table for instance and, with his first spoonful of fruit soup swimming with cherries, bite down hard on a stone, chipping the crown of a tooth. "There, you see," he would say in a quivering voice, his arms outspread, "that's how it is, that's what happens to me, it's just like me, it's in my nature, it's meant to be! I had been so looking forward to this meal, had something of an appetite, it's a warm day, and a cold soup promised some refreshment. And then this had to happen. Fine, as you can see, joy has not been granted to me. I shall refrain from the rest. I shall retire to my room. Enjoy your meal," he concluded in a faltering voice and left the table, knowing full well that they would definitely not enjoy it and spreading deep depression in his wake.

One can imagine Adrian's amusement at these woefully funny accounts of scenes experienced with all the intensity of youth, though we always had to curb our laughter somewhat and keep it within the bounds of empathy—it was the storyteller's father after all. Rüdiger assured us that the head of the family had shared his sense of social inferiority with all the members of the family, more or less; he himself had departed his parental home bearing it with him as a kind of psychological bruise; but the vexation he felt appeared to have been one of the reasons he would not give his father the satisfaction of seeing matters mended in the person of his son and had dashed any hope that his son might at least become a councilor in the civil service. It was arranged for Rüdiger to graduate from high school and be sent off to university. But he had not managed to get even as far as exams to become an assessor, and had devoted himself to literature instead, preferring to forgo any monetary help from home rather than satisfy his father's most fervent wishes, which only disgusted him. He wrote poetry in free verse, critical essays, and short stories in a tidy prose style. But then—partly out of economic necessity, partly, too, because his own production was not exactly gushing forth—he shifted the burden of his endeavors to translation, in particular from his favorite language, English, and he not only furnished several publishing houses with German versions of English and American popular belles-lettres, but also obtained a commission from a Munich publisher specializing in deluxe editions and literary curiosities to translate older English literature: Skelton's morality plays, a few pieces by Fletcher and Webster, some didactic poems by Pope, and supplied excellent German editions of Swift and Richardson as well. He provided these works with well-grounded introductions and was very conscientious about translating matters of style and taste, was almost obsessively concerned with accuracy, with the congruence of expression between languages, and grew increasingly addicted to the intriguing charms and tribulations of reproducing a text. This, however, brought with it a psychological state that, on a different level, resembled that of his father. For he felt himself born to be a productive writer and spoke bitterly of being driven by necessity to serve others' work, of being consumed by a task that brought scant recognition—and what little there was he found galling. He wanted to be a poet, was convinced that he was one, and the fact that he was forced to play the literary middleman for tediously earned daily bread made him critical of the contributions of others and had become a subject of constant complaint. "If only I had the time," he would say, "and could work instead of having to drudge, would I ever show them then!" Adrian was inclined to believe him; but I, judging too harshly perhaps, suspected that this impediment was in essence a welcome pretext, a means of deceiving himself about his own lack of a genuine and conclusive creative impulse.

Despite which, one ought not to imagine him as peevish; on the contrary, he was very funny, sometimes even foolish, gifted with a veritable Anglo-Saxon sense of humor and a personality that the English would surely call "boyish." He would immediately strike up an acquaintance with all the sons of Albion who came to Leipzig as tourists, as continental knockabouts, as music enthusiasts, had an "elective affinity" for their language and spoke it perfectly, talking nonsense with great gusto, and could also do a very comical imitation of their attempts at German—the accent, the formal precision that failed as colloquial speech, the foreigner's weakness for literary turns of phrase, so that they said: "View yonder sight!" when they merely wanted to say: "Look at that!" And he looked exactly like them, too—but I've not yet said a thing about his appearance. It was very good and, despite a threadbare outfit that his finances dictated always remain the same, he looked the elegant and sporty gentleman. His facial features were striking, their out-and-out distinguished character only slightly marred by a mouth that was both somewhat jagged and weak—a trait I've often noticed among Silesians. Tall, broad-shouldered, with small hips and long legs, he wore—day in, day out—the same rather shabby plaid breeches, long woolen socks, sturdy ocher shoes, a shirt of coarse linen with an open collar, and over that a kind of jacket of by now indeterminate color and with sleeves that were too short. His hands, however, were genteel and long-fingered, with beautifully shaped oval and convex nails; and the finished effect was so undeniably that of a gentleman that he could dare to wear his informal street clothes to affairs where evening dress was the rule—and at such receptions, women preferred him just as he was to his rivals in correct black and white, and one would see him surrounded by females whose admiration was undisguised.

And yet! All the same! Even though his shoddy exterior was excused by a tiresome lack of money and could not detract from his status as a gentleman and cavalier, which as nature's truth shone through and counteracted appearances, that same truth was partly a deception, and in this complicated sense Schildknapp was an imposter. That sporty look was misleading, for he took no part in sports, except to do a little skiing in Saxony's "Switzerland" with his Englishmen in the winter, which easily led to bouts of intestinal catarrh that were not all that harmless in my opinion; but despite a tanned face and broad shoulders, his health did not have the firmest of footings, and in younger years he had once experienced some pulmonary bleeding—meaning he tended to tuberculosis. His luck with women did not, from what I could see, correspond to any luck they had with him—at least not individually; for although he truly adored them in the aggregate, it was a wandering, all-inclusive adoration that was so directed to their sex *per se,* to the lucky possibilities offered by the wide world, that each individual woman found him lethargic, frugal, reserved. The fact that he could have had all the amorous adventures he wished seemed to suffice for him, and it was as if he shied away from every tie to reality because he saw it as robbing him of the potential. And potentiality was his domain, the boundless realm of the possible, his kingdom—in that sense and to that extent he was a poet. He concluded from his last name (German for "squire") that his ancestors had been the errant escorts of knights and princes; and although he had never sat on a horse, was not even interested in finding one to mount, he felt he was a born equestrian. He attributed his frequent dreams of riding to atavistic memory, to an inheritance in the blood, and was uncommonly convincing at demonstrating for us how natural it felt for him to hold the reins in his left hand and pat his nag's neck with his right. The most frequent phrase to pass his lips were the two words, "one ought." It was his melancholy formula for weighing possibilities whose realization was blocked by his inability to make decisions. One ought to do this or that, to be or have this or that. One ought to write a Leipzig novel of manners; one ought to take a trip around the world, even if only as a dishwasher; one ought to study physics, astronomy, to purchase a little farm and just turn the soil in the sweat of one's face. And if we bought some coffee and had it ground, as we were leaving the grocery, he was quite capable of saying with a thoughtful nod of his head: "One ought to run a grocery!"

I spoke before of Schildknapp's sense of independence. This had already expressed itself in his abhorrence of the civil service, in his choice

of a freelance career. And yet he was really the servant of many masters—and was something of a sponge. But then, given his straitened
circumstances, why should he not make use of his good looks and social popularity? He got himself invited out a lot, ate his midday meal
here and there at houses all over Leipzig, even at the tables of rich Jews,
although he had been heard to make anti-Semitic remarks. People who
feel they are held back and not given their due, and who at the same
time present a distinguished appearance, often seek redress in racist
self-assertion. The only thing special in his case was that he did not like
Germans either, was steeped in their sense of national inferiority, and
so explained it all by saying that he would rather, or might just as well,
associate with Jews. For their part, these wives of Jewish publishers
and bankers looked up to him with that profound admiration their
race has for German master blood and long legs, and took great pleasure in giving him presents—the sporty socks, belts, sweaters, and
scarves he wore were presents for the most part, and had come not always totally unprompted. When accompanying a lady shopping, he
might very well point to an object and say, "Well, I wouldn't actually
spend money on it. At most I'd accept it as a gift." And accept it as a
gift he did—with the look of someone who had indeed said he
wouldn't spend money on it. And for the rest, he proved his independence to himself and others by fundamentally refusing to be accommodating—which meant that when you needed him, he was definitely
not to be had. If a dinner table suddenly lacked a gentleman and he was
asked to fill in, without fail he would say no. If someone desired his
agreeable company on a trip to a spa for a cure prescribed by the doctor, his refusal was all the more certain the clearer it became that the
other party set store by his companionship. Thus he had also refused
Adrian's proposal that he furnish the libretto to *Love's Labour's Lost*.
Yet he loved Adrian very much, was truly devoted to him; and Adrian
did not hold the rebuff against him, and was generally quite tolerant of
his foibles—about which Schildknapp could laugh himself as well—
and was much too grateful for his genial conversation, his tales of
his father, and his English foolishness ever to want to hold a grudge
against him. I never saw him laugh so much, to the point of tears even,
as when he was together with Rüdiger Schildknapp, who, as a genuine
humorist, knew how to find momentarily overwhelming comedy in
the most trivial things. It is a fact that the act of chewing on crunchy
zwieback fills the chewer's ears with a deafening noise, cutting him off
from the outside world; and at tea one day Schildknapp demonstrated
how a group of zwieback eaters could not possibly understand one an-

other and would have to restrict their conversation to "Beg pardon?" "Did you say something?" "Just a moment, please!" And how Adrian could laugh when Schildknapp quarreled with his own reflection in the mirror. He was, in fact, vain—not in any banal way, but with a poet's eye to the world's endless lucky potentialities, for which, though they far exceeded his ability to make a decision, he wished to remain young and handsome, and he fretted over his face's propensity for wrinkles at so early an age, over its premature weatherbeaten look. And indeed there was something old-mannish about the mouth, and from that and from the somewhat sagging nose descending to it (although one still would gladly have been prepared to call it classic), one could already anticipate Rüdiger's physiognomy in old age. And then there were the furrows in the brow, the creases joining nose and mouth, and all sorts of crow's-feet besides. And so he would warily bring his countenance up close to the mirror, make a sour face, grab his chin between thumb and forefinger, stroke down across his cheeks in disgust, and then with a wave of his right hand dismiss his face so emphatically that we both, Adrian and I, would burst into loud laughter.

I have not yet mentioned that his eyes were exactly the same color as Adrian's. It was in fact a most remarkable common trait, for his eyes displayed the very same mixture of blue-gray-green as Adrian's—even an identical rust-hued ring around the pupils could be discerned in both. However strange it may sound, it always seemed to me (and it came as something of a relief) that Adrian's laughter-filled friendship with Schildknapp had something to do with the sameness of their eye color—which is much the same as saying that it was based on a fact whose inconsequence was as profound as it was blithe. I hardly need add that they addressed one another all the time by their last names and with formal pronouns. And if I did not know how to amuse Adrian as well as Schildknapp, I did have the advantage over the Silesian of the intimacy of pronouns Adrian and I had shared since childhood.

XXI

THIS MORNING, while Helene, my good wife, was preparing our
breakfast beverage and a fresh Upper Bavarian autumn day began
to emerge clearly out of the obligatory morning fog, I read in the paper about the auspicious revival of our submarine war, which within
twenty-four hours has claimed as its victims no fewer than twelve
ships—including two large passenger liners, an English and a Brazilian,
with five hundred passengers aboard. We owe this success to a new
torpedo with fabulous capabilities, a construct of skilled German technology; and I cannot suppress a certain satisfaction at our ever resourceful spirit of invention, at our nation's competence, which despite
so many reverses refuses to yield and is still totally at the disposal of
the regime that led us into this war and has indeed laid the entire continent at our feet, replacing the intellectual dream of a European Germany with the albeit rather terrifying, rather flawed, and as the world
sees it, so it would seem, quite intolerable reality of a German Europe.
That involuntary feeling of satisfaction always yields then to the
thought that such sporadic triumphs—like these recent sinkings or the
commando exploit of kidnapping the fallen Italian dictator (and taken
just in itself, it was a splendid coup)—can still serve only to awaken
false hopes and prolong a war that in the view of reasonable men can no
longer be won. This is also the opinion of Monsignor Hinterpförtner,
the head of our theological seminary in Freising, as he candidly admitted to me in private over an evening glass of wine—a man who in no
way resembles that passionate scholar around whom was centered the
student uprising in Munich, which was then quelled in a ghastly blood-

bath, but whose understanding of the world permits him no illusions, not even the illusion that clings to a difference between not-winning and losing this war and thus conceals from people the truth that we have played *va banque,* that the failure of our plans to conquer the world is of necessity equivalent to a national catastrophe of the first order.

I am saying all this to remind the reader of the historical circumstances under which this account of Leverkühn's life is being written, and to make him realize how the agitated state that is part of my work is constantly being fused beyond recognition with that caused by the convulsions of our day. I am not speaking of a distraction, for as best as I can see these events cannot actually divert me from my biographical intentions. All the same—and despite my personal security—I can indeed say that the times do not exactly favor steady progress in a task such as mine. Moreover, concurrent with the uprising and subsequent executions in Munich, fever and chills announced an attack of influenza that kept me in bed for ten days and continued to sap the intellectual and physical powers of my sixty-year-old body for some time; and so it is no wonder that since I put the first lines of this account to paper, spring and summer have now become late autumn. In the meantime we have experienced the destruction of our venerable cities from the air—an act that would scream to the heavens were not we who suffer it ourselves laden with guilt. But since we are, the scream dies in the air and, like King Claudius's prayer, can "never to heaven go." How strange that lament for culture, raised now against crimes that we called down upon ourselves, sounds in the mouths of those who entered the arena of history proclaiming themselves bearers of a barbarism that, while wallowing in ruthlessness, was to rejuvenate the world. This earth-shaking, plummeting havoc has come breathtakingly close to my refuge several times now. The dreadful bombardment of the city of Dürer and Willibald Pirckheimer was no longer some distant event; and as the Last Judgment fell upon Munich as well, I sat here in my study, turning ashen, shaking like the walls, doors, and windowpanes of my house—and writing this account of a man's life with a trembling hand. But since this hand has reason to tremble in any case because of my subject, I did not let it bother me that a familiar difficulty was augmented a bit by the terror outside.

As I said, with the sort of hope and pride that the unfolding of German power rouses in us, we watched our Wehrmacht storm forth against the Russian hordes, who in turn defended their inhospitable but apparently very beloved homeland—a German offensive that within a few weeks had become a Russian one and that has led ever since to an apparently unending, unstoppable loss of terrain, to speak only of terrain. With profound bewilderment we registered the landing of American and Canadian troops on the southern coast of Sicily, the fall of Syracuse, Catania, Messina, Taormina; and we learned—with a mixture of horror and envy, with an acute awareness that we would be incapable of such a deed, whether in a good or a bad sense—that a nation whose mentality still permits it to draw sober, common-sense consequences from a series of scandalous defeats and losses, had done away with its great man, in order that a short time later it might grant the world what the world also demands of us, but which, out of a profound misery that will be far too sacred and dear to us, we cannot accept: unconditional surrender. Yes, we are a completely different nation, one that is a contradiction to sobriety and common sense and whose soul is powerfully tragic; our love belongs to fate, any fate, if only it is one, even a doom that sets the heavens afire with the red twilight of the gods.

The advance of the Muscovites into our prospective granary, the Ukraine, and the elastic withdrawal of our troops to a line along the Dnieper has accompanied my work—or rather, the work has accompanied those events. In the past few days it has become apparent that even this defensive barrier will not hold, though our Führer, hastening into action, commanded a massive halt to the retreat, spoke aptly and reprovingly of a "Stalingrad psychosis," and ordered that the Dnepr line be held at any price. The price, that "any price," has been paid, but to no avail; and how far and to where the Red tide of which our newspapers speak will yet surge is left to our powers of imagination, which are given to wild excesses as it is. For it belongs to the realm of the fantastic and goes against all sense of order and every expectation that Germany itself could possibly become the arena of one of our wars. Twenty-five years ago, we were wise enough to prevent it at the very last moment, but our increasingly tragically heroic state of mind apparently will no longer allow us to forsake a lost cause before the unthinkable becomes reality. Thank God there are still wide expanses between the fields of home and the havoc pressing in from the east, and we may be prepared to accept some painful losses on that front first, in order to defend even more tenaciously our European *lebensraum* against the mortal enemies of German order in the west. The invasion of our lovely Sicily offered no proof whatever that the enemy could possibly gain a foothold on the Italian mainland. Unfortunately it did prove possible, and just last week a Communist uprising in support of the Allies broke out in Naples, in the wake of which the city no longer

seemed worthy of German troops, so that after conscientiously de-
stroying the library and depositing a time bomb in the main post office, we abandoned the place with heads held high. Meanwhile there
is talk of invasion exercises in the Channel, which they say is thick
with ships, and the citizen asks himself—without permission, to be
sure—whether what happened in Italy, and may well continue to happen all the way up the peninsula, might not also happen in France, or
wherever, despite all our mandated faith in the inviolability of Fortress
Europe.

Yes, Monsignor Hinterpförtner is right: We are lost. Which is to say:
The war is lost, and that means more than a lost campaign, it means
that *we* in fact are lost—lost, our cause and soul, our faith and our
history. Germany is done for, or will be done for. An unutterable
collapse—economic, political, moral, and spiritual—in short, an all-
embracing collapse looms ahead. Not that I would have wished for
what threatens us, for it is despair, it is madness. Not that I would have
wished it, because my pity, my forlorn compassion, is far too deep for
this unhappy nation; and when I think back ten years to its awakening
and blind fervor, to the uprising that broke forth to break open and
break down, to the new beginning that was to purify everything, to
our popular and national rebirth, to that specious holy ecstasy, in
which, to be sure, were mixed, as warning signs of its treachery, so
much savage brutality and hulking vulgarity, so much obscene lust to
violate, torture, humiliate, and which, as every sensible person knew,
already bore war, this entire war within it—when I think back to all
that, then my heart shrinks at the enormous investment of faith, enthusiasm, and historical high passion that will now explode in a bankruptcy without compare. No, I would not have wished it—and have
had to wish it nonetheless—and I know that I wished it, too, wish it
now and will welcome it: out of hatred for the wanton contempt for
reason, the sinful ignoring of truth, the vulgar voluptuous cult of a
trashy myth, the culpable confounding of something that has run to
seed with what it once was, the sordid abuse and cheap peddling of
what was old and genuine, faithful and familiar, of what was fundamentally German, from which liars and frauds then prepared a stupe-
fying poisonous home-brew. That wild intoxication—for constantly
yearning to be intoxicated, we drank freely, and under that illusory eu-
phoria we have for years committed a plethora of disgraceful deeds—
must now be paid for. And with what? I have already supplied the
word, in conjunction with the word "despair." I will not repeat it. One
does not prevail a second time over the horror I felt as I wrote it before,
the very letters skittering sadly out of control.

*

ASTERISKS, TOO, SERVE to refresh the reader's eye and mind—it does not always require a Roman numeral, which gives a new section even stronger definition; and I could not possibly have granted a chapter of its own to the foregoing excursus on a present that Adrian Leverkühn did not himself experience. Having organized the printed layout with a familiar device, I will complete this section with several more entries about Adrian's years in Leipzig, though I do not deceive myself that my procedure makes it look as if the material lacks unity as a chapter, as if it consists of quite heterogeneous parts—but, then, my failure to do any better thus far would surely have sufficed for that. In reading back over what has been recorded till now—Adrian's dramatic wishes and plans, his earliest songs, that painful look he had acquired during our separation, the intellectual fascination of Shakespeare's comedy, Leverkühn's settings for poems in foreign languages, and his shy cosmopolitanism; plus the Bohemian club at the Café Central, mention of which led to a portrait of Rüdiger Schildknapp so detailed as to be open to criticism—I quite rightly ask myself whether such a motley of elements can possibly form a unified chapter. And now this present section must employ asterisks to nudge the reader to accept its uniting a backlog of data about Leverkühn's stay in Leipzig with a digression on the almost impossible circumstances under which I write my little book. Good composition it is not. But do I not recall that from the start I had to reproach myself for the lack of any controlled or methodical structure for my work? And my excuse is still the same. I am too close to my subject. My age and the composure that age should, proverbially, bring do not suffice for me to master it with a firmer and steadier hand. What is generally and greatly lacking is contrast, the basic differentiation between the material and him who shapes it. Have I not said more than once that the life with which I am dealing was closer, dearer, more intriguing to me than my own? And what is closest and most intriguing, most truly my own, is not mere "material," it is the person himself—and so hardly suitable for artistic segmentation. Far be it from me to deny the seriousness of art; but when things get serious one scorns art and is no longer capable of it. I can only repeat that the paragraphs and asterisks in this book are simply a concession to the reader's eyes, and that if it were up to me, I would write the whole thing in one fell swoop, in one breath, without any divisions, indeed without paragraphs and indentations. I merely lack the courage to present so inconsiderate a printed text to the eyes of the reading public.

*

SINCE I REMAINED with Adrian in Leipzig for a year, I also know
how he spent the other four years of his stay there—my teacher was
the conservatism of his mode of life, which often looked like rigidity
and could appear somewhat oppressive to me. It was not for nothing
that in his letter he had expressed sympathy for Chopin's not-wanting-
to-know, his unadventuresomeness. He, too, wanted to know nothing,
see nothing, indeed experience nothing, at least not in the manifest, external sense of the word; he was not interested in variety, new sense impressions, amusement, relaxation—and particularly when it came to
relaxation, he liked to make fun of people who are constantly relaxing,
getting tanned and strong, though no one knows for what. "Relaxation," he said, "is for people for whom it does no good." He had little
use for traveling in order to see something, absorb a new experience,
"educate" himself. He disdained pleasures of the eye, and as sensitive
as his hearing was, he had always had almost no desire to school his eye
to forms in the visual arts. He approved of the differentiation made between eye-people and ear-people, claimed it to be incontrovertible,
and counted himself definitely among the latter. As for myself, I have
never considered the distinction to be truly practicable and never quite
believed that his own eye was so closed and recalcitrant. True, Goethe
also says that music is totally inborn, something within that needs no
great nourishment from without, no experience drawn from life. But
there is also an interior sight, a sense of vision that is different from and
includes more than mere seeing. It is, moreover, profoundly contradic-
tory for a man like Leverkühn, with his keen awareness of the human
eye, which, after all, sparkles only for someone else's eye, to actually
reject perception of the world through that organ. I need mention only
the names Marie Godeau, Rudi Schwerdtfeger, and Nepomuk Schneidewein to conjure up Adrian's sensitivity to, indeed his weakness for
the magic of eyes, black eyes, blue eyes—though of course it is perfectly clear to me that it is a mistake to bombard the reader with names
that mean absolutely nothing to him and whose incarnations are still a
good way off, a mistake whose crude blatancy may well call into question whether it was freely made. But, to speak freely, what does free really mean! I am well aware that I wrote those empty, premature names
under compulsion.

    Adrian's journey to Graz, hardly undertaken for travel's sake, was
an interruption in the regularity of his life. Another was the trip to the
shore that he took with Schildknapp, the fruit of which, one can say,

was the symphonic tone-painting in one movement. And that work, in turn, was bound up with the third of these exceptions: a trip to Basel in the company of his teacher, Kretzschmar, to attend performances of Baroque sacred music, which were to be presented in St. Martin's church by the Chamber Chorus of Basel and for which Kretzschmar was to be the organist. Among the works heard were Monteverdi's *Magnificat,* organ studies by Frescobaldi, an oratorio by Carissimi, and a Buxtehude cantata. The impression left on Leverkühn by this *musica reservata,* by a music of emotions that in reaction to the constructivism of the Spanish Netherlands handled biblical texts with amazing human freedom and boldness of declamatory expression, dressing them in an instrumental language of recklessly descriptive gestures—this impression was very strong and long-lasting. He wrote me at length about it and also spoke about the modernity of musical methods that had erupted with Monteverdi—about his images of action, his punctuated rhythms, sudden reversals of emphasis, stirring figures; about the way he had strengthened the musical line by parallels in thirds and sixths and varied his cadences rhythmically; about his crescendi, tightly woven imitations, widened intervals, thrilling grand pauses, insistent *ostinati,* and rhythmic repetitions. Afterward he spent a great deal of time in the Leipzig library, copying out Carissimi's *Jephta* and Schütz's *Psalms of David.* Who could fail to recognize the stylistic influence of this madrigalism in the quasireligious music of his later years, in the *Apocalypse* and *Dr. Faustus?* The will to take expression to its very extremes was always a dominant element in his music, alongside the intellectual passion for austere order, for the linear style of the Netherlands. In other words: Heat and cold reigned side by side in his work, and at times, at the moments of greatest genius, they interlocked, the *espressivo* grabbed hold of strict counterpoint, the objective blushed with emotion, so that one had the impression of an incandescent construct, which more than anything else drove home for me the idea of the demonic and always reminded me of the fiery sketch that legend says a certain Someone drew in the sand for the reluctant architect of Cologne cathedral.

The connection, however, between Adrian's first journey to Switzerland and his earlier one to Sylt was as follows. That little nation, with its lively and unbounded cultural life, had and still has a Composer's Society, among whose activities are so-called orchestral first-readings, *lectures d'orchestre*—which is to say, the society's board, acting as a jury, arranges for a Swiss symphony orchestra under its own

conductor to try out the works of young composers (but with the public excluded and only musicians present) in order to give them the opportunity to hear their creations, gain experience, and school the
imagination on the reality of its sound. Such a reading, played by the
Orchestre de la Suisse Romande, was being held in Geneva more or
less concurrently with the concert in Basel, and Wendell Kretzschmar
had used his connections and succeeded in having Adrian's *Phosphorescence of the Sea* (a work, by way of exception, of a young German)
included in the program. This came as a total surprise to Adrian; Kretzschmar was enjoying the fun of leaving Adrian in the dark, who still
suspected nothing even while underway with his teacher from Basel to
the try-out in Geneva. And then Herr Ansermet raised his baton and
Adrian heard his "root-canal work"—his sparkling impressionist nocturne, which he himself did not take seriously, had not taken seriously
even as he wrote it, but which left him sitting on pins and needles at its
critical performance. What an absurd torture for the artist to know
that an audience identifies him with a work that, within himself, he has
moved beyond and that was merely a game played with something in
which he does not believe. Thank God open expression of both approval and disapproval was out of the question at these performances.
In accepting private praise and criticism, good advice and censure of
his mistakes, in French and German, he no more contradicted the delighted listeners than he did the dissatisfied. Nor, by the way, did he
agree with anyone.

He remained with Kretzschmar in Geneva, Basel, and Zurich for
about a week or ten days and had some fleeting contact with artistic
circles in those cities. They could not have found much to like in him—
could not have known what to make of him, really, at least not if they
set great store by innocuousness, loquaciousness, collegial openness. A
few, here and there, may have understood and been touched by the
shyness, the loneliness that enfolded him, by the lofty rigor of his
life—indeed, I know that it did occur, and find the fact revealing. It has
been my experience that there is great deal of understanding for and
knowledge of suffering in Switzerland, and, what is more, it plays a
greater role in the bourgeois life of its old cities than it does in places
of overinflated culture, in intellectual Paris, for instance. This, then,
provided a hidden point of contact. On the other hand, the intro-
verted Swiss mistrust of citizens of the German Reich was confronted
here with a special case of German mistrust of the "world"—as strange
as it may sound to call our little, narrowly confined neighbor the
"world," in contrast to the wide and mighty German Reich with its

great cities. There is, however, something incontestably correct in the term. Switzerland—neutral, polyglot, influenced by the French, open to breezes from the West—is, despite its tiny format, far more the "world," a far more European space than the political colossus to its north, where the word "international" has long been spoken as a slur and where gloomy provincialism has fouled the air and turned it musty. I have spoken of Adrian's inner cosmopolitanism before. But a German's sense of being a citizen of the world has always been something very different from worldliness, and my friend was too much the soul of apprehension in the fashionable world ever to feel a part of it. Several days before Kretzschmar, Adrian returned to Leipzig, to a city that bore the world within it, true, but where worldliness was more a guest than a resident, to a city with a ridiculous dialect— and where desire had first touched his pride. That touch had come as a profound shock, an experience of depths of which he had never thought the world capable, and, if I see it all correctly, an experience that contributed not a little to making him a recluse in the world. It is certainly quite wrong and typical of the German bystander's arrogance to deny the world its depths. But worldly depths do indeed exist, and it is a fate like any other, a fate one must accept: to be born in the provincial—and therefore that much more uncanny—depths of Germany.

For the entire four and a half years he lived in Leipzig, Adrian never moved from the house on Peter Strasse near the *Collegium Beatae Virginis,* but kept the same two-room apartment, where he had once again tacked the "magic square" above his upright piano. He attended lectures in philosophy and music history, read at the library, taking extensive notes, and brought his compositional exercises to Kretzschmar for critique: piano pieces, a "concerto" for string orchestra, and a quartet for flute, clarinet, *corno di bassetto,* and bassoon. (I am listing those pieces that are known to me and that are still extant, even if never published.) What Kretzschmar did was to point out limp passages for him, recommending a change of tempo, suggesting that a somewhat stolid rhythm be enlivened or that a theme be highlighted. He would point out a middle voice that got bogged down, a bass line that simply lay there instead of moving. He might put his finger on a transition that held together only on the surface, but had no organization and jeopardized the natural flow of the composition. He merely told his pupil what Adrian's own artistic sense could have or already had told him. A teacher is the personification of the apprentice's own conscience, confirming his doubts, explaining his discontents, prodding his own urge to improve. A pupil like Adrian, however, ultimately does not need a corrector and master. He would intentionally bring unfinished work to Kretzschmar in order to be told what he already knew on his own—in order then to make fun of the artistic sense of his teacher, which corresponded, in fact, to his own: the artistic sense (with the emphasis on the second word) that is the real agent of the work-idea (not the idea of a work, but the idea that is the opus itself, the objective and harmonic structure at rest within itself), the true manager of its unity and organic wholeness, plastering over cracks, plugging holes, establishing the "natural flow" that was not there originally, and so is not natural at all, but rather a product of art—in short, it is only after the fact and as a mediator that this manager creates an impression of immediacy and organic wholeness. There is a great deal of illusion in a work of art; one could go farther and say that it is illusory in and of itself, as a "work." Its ambition is to make others believe that it was not made but rather simply arose, burst forth from Jupiter's head like Pallas Athena fully adorned in enchased armor. But that is only a pretense. No work has ever come into being that way. It is indeed work, artistic labor for the purpose of illusion—and now the question arises whether, given the current state of our consciousness, our comprehension, and our sense of truth, the game is still permissible, still intellectually possible, can still be taken seriously; whether the work as such, as a self-sufficient and harmonically self-contained structure, still stands in a legitimate relation to our problematical social condition, with its total insecurity and lack of harmony; whether all illusion, even the most beautiful, and especially the most beautiful, has not become a lie today.

The question arises, I say, by which I mean: I learned to ask myself that question through my association with Adrian, whose keen eye, or if I may use the term, "keen feeling" for these things was absolutely incorruptible. Certain insights that he would express, tossing them like aperçus into a conversation, were totally foreign to my native good nature, and they hurt—not because my good nature was wounded, but on his account; they pained me, worried and frightened me, because I saw in them dangerous impediments to his own existence, inhibitions that could cripple the unfolding of his talents.

I have heard him say: "The work! It's a sham, something the bourgeoisie wants to believe still exists. It is counter to truth and counter to all seriousness. Only the briefest, highly compact musical moment is genuine and serious . . ."

How could that not have worried me, since I knew, after all, that he himself aspired to a work, planned to compose an opera!

I have likewise heard him say "Illusion and games have art's conscience opposed to them nowadays. Art wants to stop being illusion and games; it wants to become comprehension."

But if something has ceased to conform to its definition, does it not cease to exist altogether? And how will art live as comprehension? I remembered how he had written to Kretzschmar from Halle about banality's expanding realm. The teacher had not let that shake his belief in his student's calling. But these new charges leveled against illusion and games—that is, against form itself—seemed to imply that the expanding realm of the banal, of what was no longer permissible, threatened to swallow art whole. Deeply worried, I asked myself what efforts, what intellectual tricks, detours, and ironies would be necessary to save art, to reconquer it and achieve a work that as a travesty of innocence could still confess the state of comprehension from which it would be wrested!

There came a day, or rather a night, when my poor friend heard about what I have suggested here in more precise detail—spoken by ghastly lips, by a terrible assistant. A record of that occasion exists, and I will present it in its proper place. The reason for the instinctive terror that Adrian's statements aroused in me first became clear to me, found its explanation only then. But what I just now termed the "travesty of innocence"—how often, from early on, it announced its peculiar presence in his compositions. In them one found (at a level of highest musical development, against a background of extreme tensions) "banalities," naturally not in the sentimental sense or as jaunty ingratiation, but banalities in the sense of a technical primitivism, naiveté, or pseudo-naiveté, which Meister Kretzschmar would let pass with a tolerant smile for his unconventional pupil—to be sure, not because he saw them as a naiveté of the first degree, if I may put it that way, but rather understood them as something beyond novelty or tastelessness, as audacity clad in the robes of the beginner. I was always reminded of what the stutterer had taught us about the tendency of music to celebrate its elemental forces. And I was reminded as well of the linden tree in Buchel, where we sang our childish rounds and barnyard Hanne bawled the "second voice" so pedantically to our childish descant. It is not easy to describe even the simplest things without resorting to musical notation, which would give this little work an all too scholarly, technical appearance. But, for example, right in the middle of a composition whose key was constantly held in hovering abeyance, an F-major chord with A as its highest note was struck, only to be dissolved by the entry of a D-flat (or C-sharp) and then, as the melody retreated

a half-step back to A-flat, was transformed into D major with the suspension of the dominant B-flat, whereupon a new passing-note F resolved the chord into A major. And this nothing, this bit of music from
a primer, stood out in such relief, the chromatic passing notes, the C-
sharp (or D-flat), the F in between, the D-major tonic, were all stamped
with such demonstrative significance that the figure seemed to be a simultaneous mockery and glorification of something fundamental, a
painful, ironic remembrance of tonality, of the tempered scale, of traditional music itself.

This sort of thing also occurs repeatedly in the thirteen Brentano
Songs, to which I would definitely like to devote a few words before
concluding this chapter—my example, in fact, was taken from the
admirable serenade, "Hark, again the flute is weeping," with its final
lines:

> Through the night that now envelops,
> Shines for me the light of tones.

Adrian was doubtlessly so zealous about composing lieder during his
Leipzig years because he regarded the lyric marriage of music and
word as preparation for the dramatic union he had in mind. Presumably it also had something to do with his intellectual scruples about the
fate of the autonomous work, about the historical situation of art *per
se.* He mistrusted form as mere illusion, as a game—and so the small
and lyric form of the lied may have remained for him the most acceptable, the most serious, the truest; it may have seemed to him the most
likely to fulfill the theoretical challenge of compact brevity. All the
same, not only are several of these songs (as, for instance, "Oh Sweet
Maiden" with its lettered symbol, or "Hymn," "The Merry Musicians," "The Hunter to the Shepherd," and others as well) quite
lengthy, but also Leverkühn always wanted them to be regarded and
treated as a whole, that is, as a "work" that had proceeded out of one
definite stylistic conception, one underlying tone, out of his having
touched a wondrously sublime and deeply dreamlike poetic spirit; and
he would never let them be performed as individual songs, but only as
a complete cycle—from the unutterably mad and chaotic "Opening"
with its eerie final lines

> Oh star and flower, mind and dress,
> Love, pain and time and everness!

to the bleak, enraged and powerful final piece: "One I know so well . . .
death his name is"—a rigorous limitation that proved an extraordinary

barrier to their public performance during his lifetime, especially since one of the songs, "The Merry Musicians," is written for a whole quintet of voices: mother, daughter, two brothers, and the little boy who "broke his leg so early on"; that is, for alto, soprano, baritone, tenor, and child soprano, who have to perform this No. 4 in the cycle partly as an ensemble, partly solo, and even as a duet (sung by the two brothers). It was the first of the songs that Adrian orchestrated—or more correctly, arranged from the start—for a small orchestra of strings, woodwinds, and percussion; for a great deal is said in this strange poem about how pipe and tambourine, bells and cymbals, and a fiddle's merry trills accompany the airs that the fantastic, woeful little troupe sings for lovers in their chamber, for drunken guests and the lonely maid, drawing them all into the spell they cast by night, "when there's no human eye to see." The spirit and mood of the piece—with music that, like some ghostly street-ballad, is both sweet and tortured—are unique. And yet I would hesitate to award it the palm from among the thirteen, several of which make more intrinsic demands of music and are more profoundly fulfilled in it than this one, where the words speak of music. "Grandmother Snakecook"—that is another one of the songs, with its "Maria, from whose parlor have you come now?", with its sevenfold "Oh, woe, good mother, what woe!", which with incredible artistic empathy conjures up the most cozily frightening and terrifying domains of the German folk song. For it is indeed the case that this astute, true, and super-clever music is constantly, painfully wooing the melody of folk song—a melody forever unrealized, both there and not there, appearing as fragmented sound and vanishing again within a musical style spiritually alien to it, but out of which it still constantly attempts to give birth. It is both artistically moving and nothing less than a cultural paradox to behold how the natural developmental process, by which what is intellectual and refined grows out of what is elemental, is here reversed, so that the former now plays the role of the primal element, out of which simplicity seeks to wrest itself:

> Star whispers drifting
> holy and free,
> all distance lifting,
> speak now to me.

There is another piece, where sound is almost lost in space, in a cosmic ozone, while spirits in golden barques ply the heavenly seas and the tinkling flow of glittering song falls in ringlets—surges upward:

All is by kindness, by goodness surrounded,
offering comfort, a hand grasps a hand;
even at night by its light we are bounded,
timelessly held by an innermost band.

Surely in all of literature, word and sound have only rarely found and confirmed one another as they do here. Music turns its eye upon itself here and gazes at its own being. The way each note offers a comforting, kindly hand to the other, the way all things are bound up together, entwined and transformed in their kinship—that is music, and Adrian Leverkühn is its youthful master.

Even before Kretzschmar left Leipzig to become the principal conductor of the Lübeck City Theater, he made sure that the Brentano Songs were published. Schott in Mainz took them on commission, which meant Adrian, with help from Kretzschmar and myself (we both shared in the costs), had to pay for the printing but remained sole owner, while promising a twenty-percent share in net receipts to the publisher. He very carefully supervised the piano reduction, demanding that it be printed on rough, unglossy paper, in quarto format with a wide margin, and that the notes not be crowded on the page. He also insisted on a prefatory note stating that all performances, whether in concert or by music societies, required the author's permission, which would be granted only if all thirteen pieces were offered as a whole. This led to accusations of pretentiousness, which, together with the audacity of the music, made it even more difficult for the songs to find a public. In 1922 they were performed—not in Adrian's presence, but in mine—in the Tonhalle in Zurich, under the baton of the excellent Dr. Volkmar Andreae and with the "Merry Musicians" role of the boy who "broke his leg so early on" sung by a lad who unfortunately really was crippled and used a crutch to walk—little Jakob Nägli, whose pure, bell-like voice had indescribable power to touch the heart.

Let me note just in passing, by the way, that the pretty first edition of Clemens Brentano's poems from which Adrian worked was a present from me, a little volume I had brought to Leipzig for him from Naumburg. It goes without saying that the choice of the thirteen songs was totally his own; I had not the slightest influence on it. But I may say that it corresponded to my own wishes and expectations almost piece for piece. An inconsistent gift, the reader will say, for how could I, as a cultivated, ethical man, have anything to do really with that Romantic poet's childish and folkloric dreams, with words that float up out of—if not to say, degenerate into—a spectral, ghostly world? I can only answer: It was the music that made the gift possible—the music of these verses, which lies in so light a slumber that it needed only the gentlest touch of an expert hand to awaken it.

XXII

WHEN LEVERKÜHN left Leipzig in September 1910, at a time, that is, when I had already begun to teach high school in Kaisersaschern, he likewise first returned home, to Buchel, to attend his sister's wedding, which was celebrated there and to which, along with my parents, I was invited as well. Ursula, now twenty years old, married Johannes Schneidewein, an optician from Langensalza, an admirable man, whose acquaintance she had made while visiting a girl friend in that charming little town near Erfurt. Some ten or twelve years older than his bride, Schneidewein was Swiss by birth, of Bernese peasant stock. He had learned the craft of grinding lenses in his homeland, but a certain sequence of events had landed him in this spot in the German Reich, where he had bought a shop stocked with spectacles and optical apparatus of all sorts—which he now ran with some success. He was a very good-looking fellow and had held on to his Swiss dialect—which is such a pleasure to listen to, is so deliberate and dignified, interspersed with vestiges of an older German, with strangely solemn-sounding expressions that Ursel Leverkühn had already begun to pick up from him. She, too, although not a beauty, was an attractive person, taking after her father in facial features, but more after her mother in manner—with brown eyes, a slender figure, and a naturally friendly way about her. The two made a couple on whom eyes lingered approvingly. In the years between 1911 and 1923 they had four children together: Rosa, Ezechiel, Raimund, and Nepomuk, handsome youngsters, every one. The youngest, however, Nepomuk, was an angel. More of that later—at almost the very end of my story.

The wedding party was not large: Oberweiler's pastor, teacher, and the chairman of its town council, each with his wife; from Kaisersaschern, besides us Zeitbloms, only Uncle Nikolaus; relatives of Frau Elsbeth from Apolda; a couple from Weissenfels with their daughter, friends of the Leverkühns; plus brother Georg, the agronomist, and Frau Luder, who managed the dairy—and that was all. Wendell Kretzschmar sent best wishes from Lübeck in a telegram that reached the house in Buchel during the midday meal. It was not an evening affair. Everyone had gathered rather early that morning; after the ceremony in the village church we all returned to the bride's home for a splendid breakfast in the dining room, hung full with lovely copper utensils. Shortly thereafter the newlyweds drove off with old Thomas to the station in Weissenfels, there to board a train for their trip to Dresden, while the wedding guests spent several hours together over Frau Luder's fine fruit liqueurs.

That afternoon Adrian and I took a walk around the Cattle Trough and up Mount Zion. We needed to talk about the adaptation of *Love's Labour's Lost,* which I had taken on and which had already occasioned much discussion and correspondence between us. While in Syracuse and Athens, I had been able to send him the scenario and parts of the German verse translation, which I had based on Tieck and Hertzberg; and at times, where condensation made it necessary, I had added something of my own in as felicitous a style as possible. I was determined, in fact, at least to offer him a German version of the libretto as well, although he still held to his intention of composing the opera in English.

He was obviously glad to escape from the wedding party into the outdoors. The veiled cast of his eyes revealed that he was suffering from a headache—and oddly enough, the same signs had been noticeable in his father, too, both in the church and at the table. That this nervous condition should appear on solemn occasions, under the influence of emotion and excitement, is understandable. It held true for the older man. In his son's case, the physical cause was probably based more in the fact that it was only with reluctance and under constraint that had he taken part in this feast of the sacrifice of a maidenhead— that of his own sister, no less. Though to be sure he clothed his discomfort in words of appreciation for the simplicity and tasteful restraint with which the affair had been handled in our case, for the omission of "dances and usages" as he put it. He praised the fact that it had been held in broad daylight, that the old pastor's wedding homily had been short and plain, and that there had been no unseemly speeches at the meal—no speeches at all, just to be on the safe side. If only the veil, the white shroud of virginity, and the satin shoes of the dead had been omitted, it would have been even better. He had especially favorable words for the impression Ursel's fiancé, now her husband, had made on him.

"Good eyes," he said, "good stock, an honest, sound, tidy gentleman. He was permitted to woo her, gaze upon her, covet her—covet to make a Christian wife of her, as we theologians say with justifiable pride at having smuggled the Devil out of this union of the flesh by making a sacrament of it, the sacrament of Christian marriage. Really very comical, how what is natural and sinful has been taken prisoner by the sacrosanct, simply by prefixing the word 'Christian' to it—which basically doesn't change a thing. But one must admit that the domestication of what is naturally evil, of sex, by Christian marriage was a clever makeshift."

"I don't like hearing you handing nature over to evil," I replied. "Humanism, both old and new, calls that slandering the wellspring of life."

"My dear fellow, there's not much to slander there."

"One ends up," I said undaunted, "in the role of the negator of the works of Creation, one becomes the advocate of nothing. Whoever believes in the Devil is already his."

He laughed a curt laugh.

"You never get the joke. I was speaking as a theologian and so necessarily sounded like one."

"That will do!" I said with a laugh as well. "You tend to take your jokes more seriously than your serious statements."

Our conversation took place on the community bench atop Mount Zion, its maple trees shading us from the afternoon autumn sun. The fact was that I had already gone courting myself, even though the wedding, indeed a public announcement of the engagement, would have to wait until I assumed a permanent position on the faculty; but I wanted to tell him about the step Helene and I planned to take. His remarks did not exactly make it easier for me.

"And shall be one flesh," he began again. "Is that not a curious blessing? Pastor Schröder did not bother with that verse, thank God. It is rather embarrassing to hear, with the bridal pair right there in front of you. Of course it is meant only too well, a perfect example of what I call domestication. The intent apparently is to conjure the element of sin, of sensuality, of evil lust right out of marriage—for lust exists surely only if the flesh is twofold, not one, which means that to say they are to be one flesh is mollifying nonsense. On the other hand, it is a source of endless wonder that one flesh lusts after another; it is indeed a phenomenon—yes, well, the perfectly exceptional phenomenon of love. Of course, there is no way to separate sensuality and love. One best acquits love of the charge of sensuality by reversing things and proving there is an element of love in sensuality. Lust for another person's flesh means one has to overcome the resistance already blocking it, which is based in the strangeness of the *I* and the *you,* of the self and the other. The flesh—to retain the Christian term—is normally repulsed by everything except itself. It wants nothing to do with strange flesh. But when another person suddenly becomes the object of lust and desire, the relation between the *I* and the *you* is so drastically changed that it makes 'sensuality' an empty word. One cannot do without the concept of love, even when ostensibly nothing spiritual is involved. Every sensual act implies tenderness, after all, is an act of giving even as lust is taking, is happiness in making another happy, a demonstration of love. Lovers have never been 'one flesh,' and such an injunction only wants to drive love from marriage along with lust."

I was strangely moved and bewildered by his words, and despite a temptation to do so, I took care not to turn and look at him. I have indicated once before how one felt whenever he spoke of sensual matters. But he had never opened up this much before, and it seemed to me as if there was an explicitness in what he said that was quite unlike him, a mild tactlessness in regard both to himself and to his hearer, that unsettled me—as did my awareness that he had said all this while his eyes were clouded by a migraine. And yet I was very much in sympathy with the sense of what he had said.

"Well roared, lion!" I said as buoyantly as possible. "I call that standing up for the works of creation. No, you have nothing to do with the Devil. But it is clear to you, isn't it, that you've spoken much more as a humanist than as a theologian?"

"Let us say, as a psychologist," he replied. "A neutral middle point. And they are, I think, the people who love truth the most."

"And how would it be," I suggested, "if we were to speak now on a quite simple, personal, bourgeois level? I wanted to tell you that I am about to . . ."

I told him what I was about to do, told him about Helene, how I had become acquainted with her, how we had met. And, I said, if it would make his congratulations all the more heartfelt, he could rest assured that I would grant him full dispensation beforehand from any "dances and usages" at my own wedding feast.

He was very elated.

"Wonderful!" he cried. "My good lad, so you wish to be joined in holy matrimony. What a righteous notion! That sort of thing always comes as a surprise, although there's nothing surprising about it. Receive my blessing! 'But, if thou marry, hang me by the neck, if horns that year miscarry!'"

"'Come, come, you talk greasily,'" I quoted from the same scene. "If you knew the girl and the spirit of our alliance, you would know that there is no need to fear for my peace of mind, but that on the contrary, everything is directed toward the establishment of tranquility and peace, of a sober and undisturbed happiness."

"I don't doubt it," he said, "nor do I doubt it will succeed."

It looked for a moment as if he was tempted to shake my hand but then refrained. There was a longer lull in the conversation, but then, as we started home, it turned back to its main topic, to our planned opera, in particular to Act Four and the scene whose text had just served for our jests and which was one of those I definitely wanted to delete. The verbal sparring was downright offensive, and yet it served no dramatic purpose. Cuts were inevitable in any case. A comedy cannot last four hours—which had been and still remained the major objection to the *Meistersinger*. But Adrian apparently intended to use precisely these "old sayings" of Rosaline and Boyet, their "Thou can'st not hit it, hit it, hit it," etc., for the counterpoint of the overture, and generally haggled with me over every episode, although he had to laugh when I said he reminded me of Kretzschmar's Beissel, with his naive enthusiasm for setting half the world to music. He denied by the way that he felt embarrassed by the comparison. Something of the humorous respect he had felt upon first being told about that strange lawgiver and renewer of music had always stayed with him, he said. It was absurd to say so, but he had never really ceased to think of him, and of late had been thinking of him more often than ever.

"You need only recall," he said, "how I defended the childish tyranny of his master and servant notes against your accusation of silly rationalism. What instinctively pleased me about it was itself something instinctive and naively consistent with the spirit of music: the will, which it suggested in its own comical way, to establish something like a strict style. We may well need someone like him, though on a less childish level, today, just as badly as his flock needed him back then— we could use a master of system, a schoolmaster of objectivity and organization, with enough genius to combine the elements of restoration, indeed of the archaic, with revolution. . . ."

He had to laugh.

"I'm sounding just like Schildknapp. One ought. What all ought one not!"

"Your notion of the archaic-revolutionary schoolmaster," I said, "has something very German about it."

"I assume," he replied, "that you do not mean that comment as praise, but only as a critical characterization, as is indeed proper. But the idea might also be an expression of something needed by the age, something that might promise a remedy in a time of ravaged conventions and the dissolution of all objective obligations—in short, of a freedom that has begun to coat talent like a mildew and is showing signs of sterility."

I was unnerved by what he had said. It is hard to say why, but spoken from his lips—indeed, merely by their association with him—these words made me somehow apprehensive, an emotion that was a curious mix of alarm and awe. It stemmed from the fact that in proximity to him, sterility, the threat of paralyzed and blocked creativity, could be thought of only as something almost positive and proud, only in connection with some higher and purer intellectual force.

"It would be tragic," I said, "if infertility should ever be the outcome of freedom. It is always with the hope of releasing productive energies that freedom is procured."

"True," he replied. "And for a while it achieves what one expected of it. But freedom is really another word for subjectivity, and there comes a day when it can no longer stand itself, despairs at some point of the possibility of being creative on its own, and seeks protection and security in objectivity. Freedom always has a propensity for dialectic reversal. It very quickly recognizes itself in restraint, finds fulfillment in subordinating itself to law, rule, coercion, system—finds fulfillment in them, but that does not mean it ceases to be freedom."

"In your opinion, that is," I said with a laugh. "As far as it can see! But in reality that is no longer freedom at all, no more than a dictatorship born of revolution is still freedom."

"Are you sure of that?" he asked. "Moreover, that's a political song. In art, in any case, the subjective and objective are intertwined beyond recognition; each proceeds from the other and assumes the character of the other, the subjective takes shape as the objective and is awakened to spontaneity again by genius—'dynamized,' as we say—and all of a sudden is speaking the language of subjectivity. The musical conventions being destroyed today have not always been so very objective, so fixed from without. They were consolidations of living experience and as such fulfilled a task of vital importance for a long time: the task of organization. Organization is everything. Nothing exists without it, and art least of all. But aesthetic subjectivity now took over that same task; it set about to organize the work of art out of itself, and in freedom."

"You're thinking of Beethoven."

"Of him and the technical principle by which imperious subjectivity took control of musical organization—that is, by development of a theme. Development had been a small part of the sonata, a modest refuge for subjective illumination and energy. With Beethoven it becomes universal, the center of the entire form, which, even where it remains a given of convention, is absorbed by the subjective and newly created in freedom. The variation, an archaic device, a mere residue, becomes the means by which the form itself is spontaneously created anew. Development by variation expands over the entire sonata. It does so in Brahms as well, as the working-out of a theme, but even more radically and comprehensively. Take him as the example of how subjectivity transforms itself into objectivity! With him, music disposes of all conventional flourishes, formulas, and tags and in each moment, so to speak, creates the unity of the work anew, out of freedom. But it is precisely in so doing that freedom becomes the principle of comprehensive economy, which allows music nothing accidental and develops the most extreme diversity out of materials that are always kept identical. Where there is nothing unthematic left, nothing that might not prove it has been derived from a single abiding constant, one can scarcely still speak of a free style of composition. . . ."

"But nothing of strict style in the old sense, either."

"Old or new, I will tell you what I understand by strict style. I mean the total integration of all musical dimensions, the neutrality of each over against the other by means of complete organization."

"I don't quite understand."

"Music grows wild," he said. "Its various elements—melody, harmony, counterpoint, form, and instrumentation—have developed over time independently of one another, without any plan. Whenever one isolated realm of material was advanced by history and given higher rank, others remained behind, defying, within the unity of the work, the developmental stage now asserted by whatever had moved ahead. Take for instance the role that counterpoint plays in Romanticism. There it is a mere adjunct to homophonic composition. Either it is an external combination of homophonically conceived themes or simply a harmonic chorale clad in the ornamental array of pseudo-voices. But true counterpoint demands the simultaneity of independent voices. Counterpoint designed as melodic harmony, such as that in late Romantic works, is none at all. . . . What I mean is: The farther each individual realm of material develops—some even being fused with others, such as instrumental timbre with harmony in Romantic music—the more attractive and imperative the idea of a rational total organization of all musical material becomes, one that would clear away anachronistic incongruities and prevent one element from being the mere function of another, the way melody became a function of harmony in the Romantic period. It would be a matter of developing all dimensions simultaneously and of generating them separately so that they then converge. It would depend on the universal unity behind all of music's dimensions. And finally, it would mean the abrogation of the antitheses between the style of the polyphonic fugue and the essence of the homophonic sonata."

"Do you see a way to do that?"

"Do you know," he asked in return, "where I came closest to a strict style?"

I waited. He spoke so low that one could only barely understand him, forcing words between his teeth, as he usually did when he had a headache.

"Just once, in the Brentano cycle," he said, "in the song 'Oh sweet maiden.' It all comes from one basic figure, from a row of intervals capable of multiple variation, taken from the five notes B–E–A–E–E-flat—both the horizontal and vertical lines are determined and governed by it, to the extent that is possible in a basic motif with such a limited number of notes. It is like a word, a key word that leaves its signature everywhere in the song and would like to determine it entirely. It is, however, too short a word, with too little flexibility. The tonal space it provides is too limited. One would have to proceed from here and build longer words from the twelve steps of the tempered semitone alphabet, words of twelve letters, specific combinations and interrelations of the twelve semitones, rows of notes—from which, then, the piece, a given movement, or a whole work of several movements would be strictly derived. Each tone in the entire composition, melodic and harmonic, would have to demonstrate its relation to this predetermined basic row. None would dare recur until all have first occurred. No note would dare appear that did not fulfill its motif function within the structure as a whole. Free notes would no longer exist. That is what I would call a strict style."

"A striking idea," I said. "One might call it wholesale rational organization. One would gain from it an extraordinarily self-contained, unified voice, a conformity to almost astronomical regularities. But, when I imagine it—the immutable playback of such a row of intervals, no matter how varied in texture and rhythm, surely that would inevitably result in an awful impoverishment and stagnation of music."

"Probably," he answered with a smile that showed he had been prepared for this objection. It was the smile that revealed his strong resemblance to his mother, but there was a strain to it that I knew well, for it was the best he could manage under the pressure of a migraine.

"It can't be done all that simply, either. One would have to build into the system all known techniques of variation, even those decried as artificial—the same method, that is, that once helped development gain control over the sonata. I ask myself why I practiced those old contrapuntal devices for so long under Kretzschmar, filling all that music paper with inverted fugues, crab canons, and inverted crab canons. Well, you see, it can all now be put to use for ingenious modification of the twelve-tone word. Besides building the basic row, a word could be stated with each interval replaced by its inversion. One could, moreover, begin the figure with its final note and end on its first, and then invert it in this form as well. There you have four modes, each of which, moreover, could then be transposed to all twelve different roots of the chromatic scale, so that the sequence is now available to the composition in forty-eight different forms. If that doesn't suffice for you, I propose forming derivatives from the row by symmetrically selecting certain notes, which would result in new rows that are both independent of and yet still based on the basic row. I propose subdividing rows into segments that would be related to one another and yet compress and combine the tonal relationships. A composition can use two or more rows of thematic material, just as a double or triple fugue does. The decisive thing is that each tone, without exception, retains its positional value in the row or in one of its derivatives. That would assure what I call the neutrality of harmony and melody."

"A magic square," I said. "But do you entertain any hope that people will also hear all that?"

"Hear?" he replied. "Do you recall a community lecture that we once attended and from which we learned that one certainly does not have to hear everything in music? If by 'hearing' you mean the precise, detailed awareness of the *methods* by which the highest and strictest order, like that of the stars, a cosmic order and regularity, is achieved— no, people will not hear that. But they will hear or would hear the order itself, and the perception of it would provide an unknown aesthetic satisfaction."

"Very remarkable," I said. "The way you describe the matter, it ends

up being a kind of composing prior to composing. The entire disposition and organization of the material would have to be finished before
the actual work could begin, and so the question then is: Which is the
actual work? For the preparation of the material would consist of variation, and the productive process of variation, which one could call the
actual composing, would then be transferred back to the material itself—along with the composer's freedom. When he set to work, he
would no longer be free."

"Bound by the self-imposed constraint of order, which means free."

"Well, yes, the dialectic of freedom is unfathomable. But whoever
shaped the harmony could hardly be called free. Would the building of
chords not be purely haphazard, something left to blind chance?"

"Say, instead: left to the constellation. The polyphonic value of each
tone building a chord would be assured by the larger constellation.
The historical results—the emancipation of dissonance from resolution, so that dissonance achieves absolute value, as can already be
found in some passages in late Wagner—would justify every cluster of
sound that can prove its legitimacy to the system."

"And when the constellation produces something banal: consonance, the harmony of the triad, the cliché, the diminished seventh?"

"It would mean the constellation has renewed what was worn-out."

"I see there is an element of restoration in your utopia. It is very radical, but it eases the prohibition that has in fact already been placed on
consonance. The return to old-fashioned forms of variation is a similar
feature."

"Life's interesting phenomena," he replied, "probably always have
this Janus face to both the past and the future, are probably always
progressive and regressive in one. They reveal the ambiguity of life
itself."

"Is that not a generalization?"

"Of what?"

"Of our domestic national experience?"

"Oh, no indiscretions, please. And let's not be self-congratulatory,
either! All I want to say is that your objections—if they are meant as
objections—would count for nothing against the fulfillment of the ancient desire to impose order on every sound and to resolve music's
magical essence into human reason."

"You're trying to get to me by way of my humanistic honor," I said.
"Human reason! Beg your pardon, but the whole time your every
other word has been 'constellation.' But it really belongs more to astrology. The rationalism you call for has a great deal of superstition

about it—of a belief in something impalpable and vaguely demonic that's more at home in games of chance, in laying cards and casting lots, in augury. Contrary to what you say, your system looks to me as if it's more apt to resolve human reason into magic."

He put a closed fist to his temple.

"Reason and magic," he said, "surely meet and become one in what is called wisdom, initiation, in a belief in the stars, in numbers . . ."

I said nothing in reply since I could see that he was in pain. Indeed it seemed to me that everything he had said bore the stamp of pain, stood under its sign, however brilliant and worthy of consideration it might be. He himself seemed to give no further thought to our conversation; his halfhearted sighs and humming as we strolled along indicated as much. I certainly did, of course, while inwardly shaking my baffled head, but also silently pondering how thoughts may very well be described as being bound up with pain, without that in any way detracting from them.

We said little the rest of the way home. I remember we stopped for a few moments beside the Cattle Trough; taking a step or two away from the lane, we stood gazing at the pond, the reflection of the now setting sun in our eyes. The water was clear; you could tell it was shallow only near the bank. It fell off into darkness a short way out. It was well known that the pond was very deep in the middle.

"Cold," Adrian said pointing with his head, "much too cold for swimming now. . . . Cold," he repeated a moment later, this time with a noticeable shudder, and then turned to leave.

My duties required that I return to Kaisersaschern that same evening. Adrian delayed his departure for Munich, where he had decided to settle, by several days. I can picture him shaking his father's hand in farewell—for the last time, though he did not know it—giving his mother a kiss and perhaps leaning his head on her shoulder the same way he did that day in the living room while she talked with Kretzschmar. He was never to return to her, did not wish to. She came to him.

XXIII

"NO SHOULDERING THE WHEEL, no budging the cart," he wrote a few weeks later from the capital of Bavaria, in a parody of Kumpfian style that was his way of announcing that he had begun composition of *Love's Labour's Lost* and of prodding me to bring the rest of the adaptation to a quick conclusion. He needed an overview, he wrote, and wanted to anticipate some later sections in order to establish certain musical links and relationships.

He was living on Ramberg Strasse, near the Academy, subletting from the widow of a former senator from Bremen, named Rodde, who along with her two daughters occupied the ground floor apartment of the still new house. The room assigned him—immediately to the right of the entrance and facing the quiet street—had appealed to him because it was tidy and practically but comfortably furnished, and he had quickly put it in perfect order with the addition of his personal belongings, his books and notes. On the wall to the left there hung a, granted, rather absurd piece of decor, the relic of some forgotten enthusiasm—an immense etching framed in walnut and picturing Giacomo Meyerbeer at the piano, striking a chord, inspired eyes lifted to the circle of characters from his operas hovering around him. Within a short time the young lodger had developed a kind of fondness for this apotheosis, and, besides, his back was to it whenever he sat in his wicker chair at the desk, a simple extension table covered in green. And so he had left it hanging in place.

A little harmonium, a reminder of former days perhaps, stood in his room and proved useful. But since the Frau Senator usually kept to her quarters at the rear, overlooking the little garden, and since the daughters were not to be seen of a morning, either, he also had at his disposal the grand piano in the salon, a soft-toned Bechstein that had seen a bit too much use. The salon was furnished with upholstered armchairs, bronze candelabra, gilt lattice-back chairs, a coffee table covered by a brocade cloth, and a richly framed oil painting from 1850, badly darkened by age and picturing the Golden Horn with a view of Galata—in short, with things that were obviously remnants of a once well-to-do bourgeois household. The room was frequently the stage for small social gatherings into which Adrian let himself be drawn, at first with reluctance and then by way of habit, and for which, as circumstance would have it, he finally came to play something of the role of the son of the house. It was an artistic or semi-artistic world that assembled there—housebroken Bohemians, so to speak, well-mannered, but free and easy, and amusing enough to fulfill the expectations that had prompted Frau Senator Rodde to move her residence from Bremen to this southern German capital.

It was easy to picture her life to this point. Dark eyes, brown hair that was daintily curled and graying only slightly, a ladylike carriage, an ivory complexion, and pleasant, still rather well-preserved facial features—they bespoke the role that she had played all her life as a celebrated member of a patrician society and manager of a household full of servants and duties. After the death of her husband (an earnest portrait of whom, dressed in official robes, likewise decorated the salon), with her circumstances sharply reduced and no longer permitting her to maintain quite the same position in her accustomed milieu, she had felt free to follow the wishes of an as yet barely tapped and presumably insatiable lust for life and had directed them toward an interesting postlude in warmer, more humane surroundings. Her social gatherings were held, so she wanted others to believe, for the sake of her daughters—but primarily, as was fairly clear, she wanted to enjoy them herself and to be courted. One amused her best with slightly off-color, but never vulgar remarks, with some innuendo about the cozy but harmless morals of this city of art or with anecdotes about waitresses, models, and painters—which would entice from behind closed lips a high and subtly sensuous laugh.

Her daughters, Inez and Clarissa, obviously did not love that laugh—they would cast one another cold, disapproving glances that fully revealed the irritation these grown children felt at the unfulfilled human part of their mother's nature. And yet the younger daughter, Clarissa, had always consciously, insistently seconded their having been uprooted from a bourgeois world. She was a tall blond with a large face made paler by cosmetics, a full lower lip, and a rather undeveloped chin, and was training for a dramatic career, studying with the lead actor in heroic and fatherly roles at the Hoftheater. She wore her golden yellow hair in a daring coiffure, was partial to hats big as wheels, and loved eccentric feather boas. Her imposing figure worked well with such things, by the way, and softened their ostentation. Her penchant for the whimsical and macabre amused the circle of gentlemen who paid her court. She owned a sulfurous yellow tomcat named Isaak, which she dressed in mourning for the dead pope by tying a black satin bow to its tail. A skull motif was part of her room's decor, repeated both in a real, tooth-baring skeletal version and in the form of a bronze paperweight that lay as a hollow-eyed symbol of transience and "convalescence" atop a folio volume, which bore the name of Hippocrates in Greek letters. The book itself was hollow, with a smooth underside attached by four small screws that could be removed only with very careful turns of a fine tool. When Clarissa later took her life by swallowing the poison locked within its hollow space, Frau Senator Rodde presented me the object as a memento, and I still have it.

Inez, the older sister, was likewise destined for a tragic deed. She represented—should I say, nonetheless?—the conservative element in the little family, lived in protest against its having been uprooted, against southern Germany, this city of artists and Bohemianism, against her mother's soirees, and made a point of looking back to the old paternal world of bourgeois dignity and rigor. And yet one had the impression that this conservatism was a self-defense against her own internal frustrations and threats, to which on an intellectual level, however, she did indeed give some weight. Her figure was more delicate than Clarissa's, with whom she was on very good terms, whereas she silently but clearly disapproved of her mother. Her thick, ash-blond hair weighed heavily on her head, which she carried at a tilt, her neck extended, her lips pursed into a smile. Her nose had something of a bump; the glance of her pale eyes, almost fully veiled by the lids, was subdued, soft, and mistrustful, a knowing and mournful glance, though not without sallies at roguishness. Her education had been nothing if not perfectly correct: She had spent two years at an elegant girls' boarding school in Karlsruhe that was patronized by the court. She did not occupy herself with any art or science, but instead attached great importance to her daughterly role of managing the household; she read a great deal, however, and wrote extraordinarily well-crafted letters "home"—to the past, to the headmistress of her boarding school, to former girl friends—and penned poetry in secret. One day her sister let me see one of her poems, entitled "The Miner," the first stanza of which I can still recall. It read:

> I mine the human soul's deep shaft by night,
> Descending boldly down the silent dark,
> Where sorrow's precious ore has left a mark
> That glistens reticent and yet so bright.

I have forgotten the rest. Only the last line has stuck with me:

> And long no more to rise to happiness.

So much for now about the daughters, Adrian's housemates, with whom he soon established friendly relations. They were both very fond of him and in time convinced their mother to value him as well, although she did not find him very artistic. As for the guests of the house, it was often the case that an ever-changing group of them, including Adrian (or as he was called, "our lodger, Herr Dr. Leverkühn"), would be chosen to join the Roddes beforehand for supper in the dining room, which was furnished with an ornately carved oaken sideboard far too monumental for the space; later around nine o'clock, the others would appear for house music, tea, and conversation. These were colleagues of Clarissa's, some fiery young man or other who rolled his *r*'s or young ladies with voices that sat nicely forward; a married couple by the name of Knöterich—the husband, Konrad Knöterich, indigenous to Munich and looking a perfect ancient Teuton, a Sugambrian or Ubian or the like (the only thing lacking was the twisted tuft of hair on top), who pursued a vaguely artistic occupation and, though he would actually have preferred to be a painter, was now a dilettante maker of instruments and a cello-player of considerable savagery and inaccuracy, snorting fiercely through his aquiline nose as he played; and his wife, Natalia, a brunette who wore earrings and long black curls that dangled down over her cheeks, with an exotic Spanish look about her, likewise a painter of some sort. Then there was a scholar, Dr. Kranich, a numismatist and curator of the local coin museum, whose words were always clear, firm, and cheerfully sensible, although his voice was that of a hoarse asthmatic; plus two painter friends, members of the *Sezession,* Leo Zink and Baptist Spengler—the former an Austrian, from near Botzen, and a jokester to judge from his social technique, an ingratiating clown with a gentle drawl who was constantly making fun of himself and his excessively long nose, a faunish fellow who, with just a truly comic glance of his round, close-set eyes, could set women laughing, and that is always good for an opener; and the other, Spengler, born in central Germany, a skeptical man of the world with a very thick blond moustache, wealthy, hypochondriacal, well-read, but not a hard worker, who always smiled and blinked rapidly during conversation. Inez Rodde held him in greatest distrust—for what reason she would not say, but she did tell Adrian that he was underhanded, a sneak. Adrian confessed that he always found something intelligently calming about Baptist Spengler and enjoyed talking with him—but he was much less susceptible to the confiding familiarity of another guest who attempted to break through his brittle shyness.

This was Rudolf Schwerdtfeger, a talented young violinist, who sat among the first violins of the Zapfenstösser Orchestra, which played a significant role in the city's musical life, second only to that of the Hofkapelle. Born in Dresden, although his heritage lay more in the coastal lowlands, a blond of medium, trim stature, he had the polish and winning urbanity of Saxon civilization and, being both genial and ever ready to please, was a zealous frequenter of salons, who spent every free evening attending at least one and more commonly two or three soirees, blissfully applying himself to flirting with the fair sex, from young girls to more mature women. Leo Zink and he were on cool, at times precarious terms—I have often noticed that charmers do not like one another much and that this applies equally to both male gallants and beautiful women. For my part, I had nothing against Schwerdtfeger, indeed I honestly liked him, and his early, tragic death—shrouded as it was for me in a special, uncanny horror—came as the profoundest shock to me. How clearly I can still see this young man before me, with his boyish manner, easing his jacket into place with a shrug of one shoulder and at the same time tugging a corner of his mouth down in a quick grimace; and with that other naive habit of his of gazing intently or, as it were, furiously at his partner in conversation—lips curled into a pout, steel-blue eyes burrowing into the other person's face, focusing now on one eye, now on another. And what a wealth of good qualities he had, too, quite apart from his talent, which one was inclined to count among his charms. Frankness, decency, impartiality, an artist's casual indifference toward money and possessions—in short, a certain purity was unique to him and shone from those, I repeat, beautiful steel-blue eyes, which were set in a, granted, somewhat bulldoggish or puggish, but nonetheless youthfully attractive face.

He would often play music with the senator's widow, who was not a bad pianist—though this meant he was poaching on Knöterich's preserve, who longed to saw away at his cello, even when the guests would much rather have heard Rudolf's offerings. His playing was clean and cultivated—the tone was not large, but fell sweetly on the ear, and the technique more than a little brilliant. Seldom had one heard certain pieces by Vivaldi, Vieuxtemps, and Spohr, or Grieg's C-minor Sonata, or even the Kreutzer Sonata and works by César Franck played more impeccably. All the same, he was a man of simple tastes, untouched by literature, and yet anxious to be well thought of by people of intellectual rank—not only out of vanity, but also because he seriously valued their company and wished to elevate himself, to perfect himself through them. He set his sights on Adrian at once, wooed him, to the point of practically neglecting the ladies, asked for his opinion, for his company (which Adrian always refused in those days), was eager to engage him in musical and extra-musical conversation, and was not to be daunted, disillusioned, or disposed of by coolness, reserve, distance—a sign of an uncommon lack of guile, but also of a happy-go-lucky sensibility and natural good manners. Once, when Adrian had declined the Frau Senator's invitation, remaining in his room because of a headache and a total aversion to society, Schwerdtfeger had suddenly appeared at his door, in a cutaway and black ascot, to persuade him, ostensibly on behalf of several or all the guests, to join their company after all. It was so boring without him. . . . Which was more than a little astounding, since Adrian was anything but the life of a party. Nor do I know whether he let himself be won over on that occasion. And yet, despite the surmise that he was merely the object of Rudolf's general need to appear winning, Adrian probably could not help feeling a certain happy amazement at such indestructible attentiveness.

And with that I have provided a more or less complete list of those persons associated with the Rodde salon, all of them figures whose acquaintance, along with that of many other members of Munich society, I later made as a professor in Freising. Plus one person added only a little later: Rüdiger Schildknapp, who, following Adrian's example, had discovered that one ought to live in Munich rather than in Leipzig, and who had summoned sufficient will for the decision to turn advisability into a deed. The publisher of his translations of older English literature was located here, after all, which was of some practical value for Rüdiger; and besides, he had truly missed Adrian's company, whom he immediately brought to laughter with the tales of his father and his "View

yonder sight!" He had taken a room on the fourth floor of a house on
Amalien Strasse, not far from where his friend lived, and there he now
sat at his desk, wrapped in a coat and blanket, beside an open window
all winter long—for by nature he had an exceptional need of fresh air—
and consumed in part by hatred, in part by passionate addiction, encompassed by difficulties, and puffing away at cigarettes, he struggled
for the precise German equivalent of English words, phrases, and
rhythms. He usually ate his midday meal with Adrian, in the Hoftheater restaurant or in one of the beer cellars in the center of town, but
very soon, putting his Leipzig connections to good use, he gained en-
trée to private homes and managed to have a table set here and there for
him at noontime (not to mention evening invitations)—after a shopping trip, perhaps, with the lady of the house, who found his gentle-
manly poverty fascinating. This was the case with his publisher, the
proprietor of the firm Radbruch & Co. on Fürsten Strasse; it was the
case with the Schlaginhaufens, an elderly, wealthy, and childless couple
(the husband a private scholar of Swabian origin, the wife from a Munich family), who resided in a gloomy, but grand apartment on Brienner Strasse. Their splendidly columned salon was the meeting place of
a society that included both artists and aristocrats, although the lady of
the house, née von Plausig, was most pleased when both elements were
united in one and the same person, as, for instance, in the general intendant of the Royal Playhouse, His Excellency von Riedesel, who frequented her salon. Schildknapp likewise dined with Herr Bullinger, a
rich industrialist, who manufactured paper and lived on Widenmayer
Strasse near the river, occupying the *bel étage* of an apartment house he
had built himself, and with the family of a director of Pschorr Brewery,
Inc., and in other houses, too.

Rüdiger had introduced the Schlaginhaufens to Adrian as well, who,
as a monosyllabic stranger, now had superficial, uneventful encounters with eminent painters already elevated to the nobility, with the
Wagnerian heroine Tanya Orlanda, likewise with Felix Mottl, with
ladies of the Bavarian court, with "Schiller's great-grandson," Herr von
Gleichen-Russwurm, who wrote books on cultural history, and with
writers who wrote nothing at all, but spent themselves entertaining society with literary small talk. Nonetheless, it was also here where he
first made the acquaintance of Jeannette Scheurl, a woman of peculiar
charm and trustworthiness, a good ten years his elder, the daughter of
a high-ranking, but deceased Bavarian civil servant and his Parisian
wife—a crippled old lady confined to a wheelchair, yet possessed of
considerable intellectual energy, who had never taken the trouble to

learn German, and rightly so, since by the luck of linguistic convention her fluent French was her railway ticket to both status and wealth. Madame Scheurl lived near the Botanical Gardens with her three daughters, of whom Jeannette was the eldest, in the quite confined quarters of an apartment in whose little salon, decorated to look thoroughly Parisian, she gave extraordinarily popular musical teas. Concert singers, both male and female, with even average voices could fill these small rooms to bursting. Blue coaches from the court often stood outside the modest house.

As for Jeannette, she was an author, a novelist. Having grown up between two languages, her private idiom was charmingly flawed, but she wrote ladylike and original novels of manners that were not lacking in psychological and musical charm and were most definitely serious literature. She had immediately taken notice of Adrian and became his advocate, and he in turn felt at ease in her presence, in conversation with her. Fashionably ugly, with an elegant sheeplike face that blended the peasant and the aristocrat, just as her speech was a mixture of elements of Bavarian dialect and French, she was extraordinarily intelligent and at the same time wrapped in the naively demanding innocence of the aging spinster. There was a fluttery, drolly confused quality to her mind that could evoke even her own heartiest laughter—not at all the laugh of a Leo Zink ingratiating himself by self-mockery, but rather that of a quite pure heart disposed to mirth. Added to which, she was very musical, a pianist, who was ardent in her love of Chopin, had made some stabs at writing about Schubert, and was a friend of more than one person who had made a name for himself in the realm of contemporary music. A satisfying exchange on the subject of Mozart's polyphony and its relation to Bach had been the first of many such conversations between herself and Adrian. He was and remained her trusting and devoted friend over many years.

No one should expect, by the way, that the city he had chosen for his residence actually took him into its atmosphere, ever made him one of its own. Its beauty—that of a monumental village with a mountain stream plunging through it and an Alpine sky of föhn-blown blue overhead—may have been a treat for his eye; its comfortable ways, which had something of the freedom of a permanent masked ball about them, may have made his life easier. But its spirit (*sit venia verbo!*), its foolishly innocuous view of life, the sensuously decorative, carnivalesque attitude toward art of this self-indulgent Capua had to remain foreign to the soul of such a deep and austere man. It was the perfect city to evoke that look in his eyes I had known for years—that veiled, cold, and musingly distant look, followed by a smile as he turned his head away.

The city of which I speak is Munich at the end of the Regency—with only four years left until a war that would change its cozy sociability into chronic depression, bringing forth one sad grotesquery after another—this capital of beautiful vistas, whose political problems were confined to a peevish antagonism between a semi-separatist popular Catholicism and a lusty liberalism whose loyalty to the Reich was of the true-blue sort: Munich with its concerts in the Feldherrnhalle for the changing of the guard, its art galleries, its palaces of interior decoration and seasonal exhibitions, its rustic balls during carnival, its drunken binges on March ale, its weeklong monster fair held on October Meadow, where a defiantly lusty folksiness, long since corrupted by modern mass-marketing, celebrated its saturnalias; Munich with its fusty Wagnerism and its esoteric coteries celebrating aesthetic galas just beyond the Victory Gate by night, with its utterly comfy Bohemianism bedded in public approval. Adrian saw all this, wandered amid it, sampled it during the nine months of his first stay in Upper Bavaria—an autumn, a winter, a spring. He attended artists' balls with Schildknapp, and there in the illusory twilight of a stylishly decorated hall, he would again encounter the members of the Rodde circle—the young actors, the Knöterichs, Dr. Kranich, Zink and Spengler, the daughters of the house themselves; he might be sitting at a table with Clarissa and Inez, along with Rüdiger, Spengler, and Kranich, perhaps even with Jeannette Scheurl, when Schwerdtfeger—dressed as a peasant lad or in the costume of a fifteenth-century Florentine that showed off his pretty legs and lent him more than a little resemblance to Botticelli's portrait of a young man in a red cap—would approach and, caught up in the gala mood, totally forgetting for the moment any need to elevate his mind, and "just to be nice," would fetch the Rodde girls to dance. "Just to be nice," was his favorite phrase; he insisted that everything be done nicely and that lapses that were not nice were to be avoided. He had many obligations and urgent flirtations in the ballroom, but it would not have seemed very nice to him to completely neglect the ladies from Ramberg Strasse, with whom his relationship was more of the fraternal sort. But his diligence at being nice was so evident in his fussy approach that Clarissa said haughtily:

"Good God, Rudolf, if only you wouldn't put on that beaming face of the rescuer the moment you arrive! I can assure you we have danced enough already and don't need you at all."

"Need?" he replied with merry outrage in his somewhat guttural voice. "And the needs of my heart, are they to count for nothing?"

"Not one whit," she said. "Besides, I'm too tall for you."

And then she would go with him—her receding chin, which lacked an indentation beneath the full lower lip, raised proudly. Or it might be Inez who was asked and who would follow him to the dance floor, her eyes veiled and lips pursed. Nor, by the way, was he nice only to the sisters. He kept a close eye out not to slight anyone. Suddenly, especially if the sisters had declined to dance, he would grow thoughtful and take a seat at the table beside Adrian and Baptist Spengler, who always wore a domino and drank red wine. Blinking rapidly, a dimple showing in his cheek just above his thick moustache, Spengler might be offering a quote from Goncourt's diary or the letters of Abbé Galiani—and with that look of his that was almost furious with attentiveness, Schwerdtfeger would bore his eyes into the speaker's face. He would chat with Adrian about the program of the next Zapfenstösser concert and, as if more urgent demands or obligations did not exist on every side, insist that Adrian explain or enlarge on something he had recently said at the Roddes' about music, about the state of the opera or whatever, and devote himself entirely to him. He would take Adrian's arm and stroll around the edge of the crowded hall, chatting, addressing him with the informal pronoun that carnival manners permit, oblivious to the fact that his informality was not returned. Jeannette Scheurl later told me that upon Adrian's return to the table from one such promenade, Inez Rodde had said to him:

"You should not do him the favor. He wants to have it all."

"Maybe Herr Leverkühn wants to have it all, too," Clarissa remarked, her chin propped in her hand.

Adrian shrugged.

"What he wants," he replied, "is for me to write him a violin concerto that will let him be heard in the provinces."

"Don't do it!" Clarissa said again. "You would think of nothing but pretty niceties if you composed with him in mind."

"You think too highly of my flexibility," he rejoined—and had Baptist Spengler's bleating laughter to second him.

But enough of Adrian's participation in Munich's highlife! By that winter, he already had begun to join Schildknapp, and usually at his insistence, on excursions out into the notoriously wonderful environs (though they have been compromised somewhat by mass tourism) and had spent days with him in the fiercely sparkling snow of Ettal, Oberammergau, and Mittenwald. As spring arrived, there were still more of these expeditions, with goals such as the famous lakes or the theatrical castles of the people's favorite madman; and they often rode their bikes—for Adrian loved the bicycle as a mode of independent travel— wherever the road might lead across the greening countryside and would spend the night in whatever lodging, grand or unpretentious, offered itself. I mention all this, because it was in this very fashion that Adrian early on made the acquaintance of the spot that he would one day choose as the framework for his personal life: Pfeiffering near Waldshut and the Schweigestill farm.

The little town of Waldshut, which lacks all charm or points of interest, by the way, is a town on the railroad line to Garmisch-Partenkirchen, about an hour from Munich, and the next station, Pfeiffering or Pfeffering, is only ten minutes farther, although express trains do not stop there. They disregard the onion-domed steeple of Pfeiffering's church, which rises up out of a landscape that is still rather unremarkable here. Adrian's and Rüdiger's visit to the spot was pure improvisation and very fleeting that first time. They did not even stay the night at the Schweigestills', for they both had work to do the next morning and wanted to take the train from Waldshut back to Munich before evening. They had eaten their midday meal at the inn on the little town square, and since the train schedule left them several hours yet, they rode off down the tree-lined country road to Pfeiffering, walked their bikes through the village, asked a child the name of the nearby pond—Klammer Pool, they were told—cast a glance at the tree-crowned hill, the Rohmbühel, and then came upon a farm, above whose gate stood a religious coat-of-arms and where a yelping dog chained in the yard was called "Kaschperl" by a barefoot dairymaid, from whom they now requested a glass of lemonade—less out of thirst than because the farm, a massive Baroque structure with a great deal of character, had at once caught their eyes.

I do not know to what extent Adrian "noticed" anything that day, whether he immediately or only gradually, in the afterthought of memory, recognized certain relationships, transposed here into a different but not too distant key. I am inclined to believe that he was not consciously aware of his discovery at first, and that only later, perhaps in a dream, did he stumble upon the surprise. In any case, he said not a word to Schildknapp, but then he never mentioned the strange correspondence to me, either. And of course I may be mistaken. The pond and the hill, the huge old tree in the courtyard—an elm, I admit—with a bench built around the trunk and painted green, and the other additional details may have struck him at first glance, no dream may have

been necessary to open his eyes—and that he said nothing certainly
does not prove a thing.

It was Else Schweigestill who now stepped imposingly through the
front gate to greet the visitors, lent them a friendly ear, and made
lemonade in tall glasses with long-handled spoons. She served it to
them in a parlor to the left of the entryway, a vaulted room that was almost a formal hall or rustic drawing room, with a massive table, window nooks that revealed how thick the walls were, and a plaster
Winged Victory of Samothrace set atop the colorfully painted hutch.
There was even a dark brown piano. The room was not used by the
family, Frau Schweigestill explained, as she sat down beside her guests,
since they spent their evenings in a smaller room diagonally opposite,
near the front entrance. The house had far too much extra space; farther down on this same side was a quite sizable chamber, the so-called
abbot's study, which probably was given that name because it had
served as the office of the superior of the Augustinian monks who had
once worked here. And in saying this she confirmed the fact that the
farm had once been a cloister. The Schweigestills had settled here three
generations before.

Adrian remarked that he had grown up in the country himself, although he had been living in cities for some time now, inquired about
the size of the farm, and learned that it had around thirty-five acres of
fields and meadows, as well as some woodland. And those low buildings with the chestnut trees in front, in the open space across from the
courtyard—they belonged to the property as well. At one time lay
brothers used to live in them, but now they were almost always empty
and were not really fixed up to be livable. The summer before last an
artist fellow from Munich had rented space there, wanted to paint
scenery roundabout, the Waldshuter Moor and so on, and some other
pretty views, too, though they had ended up a little mournful, all gray
on gray. Three of them had been exhibited at the Glass Palace, she had
seen them there again herself, and Director Stiglmayer from the Bavarian Exchange Bank had paid money for one. Might the gentlemen be
painters, too, perhaps?

She had probably only mentioned that previous renter in order to
put words to her own guess and find out more or less with whom she
was dealing. When she learned she was talking to a writer and a musician, she raised her brows in respect and remarked as how that was
rarer and more interesting. Painters were like daisies in May. But the
gentlemen had seemed very serious sorts to her right off, whereas
painters were usually a loose and carefree lot, without much sense of

life's seriousness—by that she didn't mean the practical problems, earning money and such things, but by serious she meant more the dark side of life, its tribulations. She didn't want to be unfair to painters as a whole, by the by, since her renter back then, for instance, had been an exception to that kind of gaiety right from the start and was a very quiet man, kept to himself, more the somber sort— which was how his pictures had looked, too, those moody moors and lonely foggy glades, yes, really made a body wonder why Director Stiglmayer had picked one out to buy, and the gloomiest of the bunch it was, must have a tinge of melancholy himself, even though he was a financial man.

There she sat with them in her checked house apron, an oval brooch at its rounded neckline, her back straight, her brown hair only slightly flecked with gray and pulled back tight and smooth, so that the part revealed the white skin of her head; her small, well-formed, competent hands, a plain wedding band on the right one, were neatly folded on the tabletop.

She was partial to artists, don't y' know, she went on, her lilting Bavarian speech colored by its special idioms, but refined for all that, because they were understanding people, and understanding was the best and most important thing in life—that cheerfulness painters showed probably had its roots there, too, because there was both a cheerful and a serious sort of understanding, and it still wasn't certain which should be thought the better of. Maybe what was most fitting was a third sort: a quiet understanding. Artists had to live in the city, of course, because that was where the sort of culture they had to do with went on; but actually they belonged more rightly with the farmers— who lived out in nature and so were closer to understanding—than they did with city folk, whose understanding was either stunted or they had to stifle it for the sake of what people thought was proper, but that ended up the same as being stunted. She certainly didn't want to be unfair to city folk, though, either; there were always exceptions, hidden exceptions maybe, and Director Stiglmayer, to take him again, had shown a lot of understanding, and she didn't mean just the artistic sort, when he bought that gloomy painting.

At this point she offered her guests coffee and pound cake, but Schildknapp and Adrian said that they would rather use the time left them to have a look at the house and courtyard, if she would be so kind as to show them.

"Glad to," she said. "What a shame my Max" (this was Herr Schweigestill) "is out in the fields with Gereon, that's our son. They wanted to try out a new manure-spreader that Gereon's bought. The gentlemen will just have to make do with me."

They certainly would not call that making-do, they replied, and followed her through the solidly built house, looked into the family living room at the front, where the pungent odor of pipe smoke noticeable everywhere was most firmly entrenched; and then on to the abbot's study, an agreeable room, not so very large, somewhat older in architectural style than the exterior of the house, its character more that of 1600 than 1700—wainscoted, with uncarpeted plank floors and stamped leather covering the walls beneath the beamed ceiling, and with pictures of saints in the low-vaulted embrasure and on squares of painted glass fitted into some of the ring-leaded windowpanes; a wardrobe with iron hinges and locks stood against one wall, which also had a nook where a copper water kettle was hung above a copper sink. There was a corner bench covered with leather cushions and, not far from the window, a heavy oaken table built almost like a chest, with deep drawers under a polished top that had a sunken middle section and a higher rim and upon which stood a carved reading desk. Dangling from the beamed ceiling was a huge chandelier with stubs of wax candles still stuck in it—a piece of Renaissance decoration, with horns, palm antlers, and other fantastic shapes projecting irregularly from all sides.

The visitors were sincere in their praise of the abbot's study. Thoughtfully nodding his head, Schildknapp even suggested that one ought to settle here, ought to live here, but Frau Schweigestill wondered if it might not be too lonely here for a writer, too far from life and culture. She also led her guests upstairs, to the second floor, to show them a couple of the numerous bedrooms set in a row along the whitewashed, musty corridor. They were furnished with beds and chests in the style of the painted hutch in the formal hall, but only a few of them had bedclothes, puffy featherbeds towered high in rustic fashion. "So many bedrooms!" they both said. Yes, most of them were almost always empty, their hostess replied. One or two might be occupied, but only temporarily. For two years, until last fall, a Baroness von Handschuchsheim had lived here and rambled about the house—a lady whose ideas, as Frau Schweigestill put it, had refused to match those of the rest of the world, and who had sought refuge here from that mismatch. She herself had got along with her quite well, had enjoyed talking with her, and sometimes had even succeeded in getting her to laugh at her peculiar notions. But unfortunately it had proved impossible either to rid her of them or even to keep them from growing, so that the good baroness finally had to be placed under appropriate care.

Frau Schweigestill finished this tale as they descended the stairs again and stepped out into the courtyard to have a look at the stalls as well. Another time, she said, before that, one of the many bedrooms had been occupied by a young lady from the best social circles, who brought her baby into the world here—and since she was speaking with artists, she could say things straight out, even if she couldn't name names. The young lady's father had been a high-ranking judge, up in Bayreuth, and had bought himself an electric automobile—that had been the start of all his troubles. Because he had also hired a chauffeur to drive him to his office, and that young man, nothing special except he looked awfully dapper in his braided livery, had done wrong by the young lady, making her lose her head. He put her in a family way and when that became clearly obvious, there were outbursts of rage and despair, with her parents wringing their hands and tearing their hair, with cursing, wailing, denouncing, the like of which you would hardly have thought possible. Understanding had not exactly prevailed, neither the country nor the artistic sort, but just the wild fear of townsfolk for their social standing, and the young lady had literally writhed there on the floor in front of her parents, pleading and sobbing, while they cursed and shook their fists, until finally she had fainted dead away along with her mother. The judge, however, had found his way here one day and spoken with her, Frau Schweigestill: a short man with a gray goatee and gold spectacles, all bent over for grief. They had arranged for the young lady to give birth here where it was nice and quiet and to stay a while afterward, under the pretext of anemia. And as the short, high-ranking judge was leaving, he turned around once more and with tears welling up behind his gold-rimmed spectacles, had shaken her hand again, adding the words: "I thank you, my dear woman, for your kind understanding." But what he meant was understanding for the parents bent low by their grief, not for the young lady.

Who arrived then, too, a poor thing, with her mouth always wide open, her eyebrows raised; and while she had waited for her time confided a great deal in her, in Frau Schweigestill, had been willing to confess her own guilt, with no pretending she had been seduced—on the contrary, Carl, the chauffeur, had even told her: "It's no good, miss, we'd better not!" But it had been stronger than she was, and she had always been ready to pay for it with death, would still be ready, and being ready for death made up for everything, it seemed to her. She had been very brave, too, when her time came and brought her baby, a little girl, into the world with the help of good Dr. Kürbis, the local district physician, who could care less how it was that a child got here, if only everything else was in order otherwise and he didn't have to deal with a breech birth. But the young lady had remained awfully weak after the delivery, despite country air and good care, and simply wouldn't stop holding her mouth open and raising her eyebrows, which only made her cheeks look even hollower, and when her short, high-ranking father came to fetch her after a while, the sight of her had once again made tears shine behind his gold spectacles. The baby had been given to the Gray Sisters in Bamberg, but from then on the mother had been nothing more than a gray young miss herself, and with her only company a canary bird and a turtle her parents had given her out of pity, she had withered away in her room from consumption—but, then, the seed of it had probably always been inside her. Finally they had sent her off to Davos, but that was the last straw it seemed, because she died there almost right away—just as she'd always wanted. And if she was right about how being ready for death settles accounts ahead of time, then she was square and had got paid in full.

While their hostess told all about the young lady that she had taken in, they visited the cow barn, took a look at the horses, and cast a glance at the pigsty. They even walked over to the chicken coop and out to the bee hives behind the house, and then the friends asked what they owed, and were told not a thing. They thanked her for everything and bicycled back to Waldshut to catch their train. They were both agreed that the day had not been wasted and that Pfeiffering was a remarkable spot.

Adrian preserved the image of this locale in his soul, but it did not influence his decisions for some time. He wanted to move on, but farther than just an hour's train ride in the direction of the mountains. He had begun *Love's Labour's Lost,* the piano sketch of its expository scenes was complete, but then work came to a standstill. Parody of artificiality was difficult to maintain as a style; it demanded a mood of constantly fresh eccentricity and aroused in him a wish for alien air, for more profoundly strange surroundings. Restlessness held him in its sway. He was weary of family life on Ramberg Strasse, weary of a room that offered only uncertain solitude, where someone could suddenly enter and invite him to join the others. "I am searching," he wrote me, "probing deeply in the world all around, listening for some word about a place where I might bury myself away from the world and engage in undisturbed conversation with my life, my fate . . ." Strange, ominous words! Should my hand not tremble as I write, should I not feel cold in the pit of my stomach, at the thought of the conversation, the meeting, the transaction for which he consciously or unconsciously was seeking a venue?

It was Italy on which he decided and for which he set out toward the end of June, just as summer had begun—an unusual time of year for a tourist. He had talked Rüdiger Schildknapp into coming along.

XXIV

IN 1912 I left Kaisersaschern, still my residence at the time, to spend the long vacation, in the company of my young wife, visiting Adrian and Schildknapp in a Sabine mountain hamlet, where the friends had chosen to spend their summer for the second time now. They had wintered in Rome, and in May, as the heat increased, had sought out the mountains and the same hospitable house where they had come to feel at home during a three months' stay the previous year.

The town was Palestrina, the birthplace of the composer—called Praeneste by the ancients and mentioned by Dante in Canto XXVII of the *Inferno* as Penestrino, the stronghold of the princes of Colonna— a picturesque settlement propped against its mountain and accessible from the church below only by a street of low steps that was not very tidy and lay under the shadow of houses. A breed of little black pigs ran free on these stairs, and an inattentive pedestrian could easily find himself pressed against a wall by the bulky packs of the heavily laden donkeys that likewise passed up and down them. Beyond the town, the road became a mountain path that led past a Capuchin monastery to the scant remains of an acropolis at the peak, next to which were also the ruins of an ancient theater. Helene and I climbed to these venerable relics several times during our short stay, whereas Adrian, who after all "wanted to see nothing," never once during those months got beyond his favorite spot, the shady garden of the Capuchins.

The Manardi house where Adrian and Rüdiger lodged was certainly the most imposing in town, and although it was home to a family of six, it easily provided accommodation for us arriving guests as well. Set on the street of stairs, it was a massive and stern building, almost a palazzo or castello, which I judged to be from the second third of the seventeenth century, with sparely trimmed cornices under a flat, slightly overhanging tile roof, small windows, and an entrance decorated in early Baroque style, but boarded over, with the actual door cut into the planks and equipped with a little jangling bell. Our friends had been ceded a truly extensive realm on the ground floor, including a living room the size of a salon, which had two windows and a stone floor (but so did all the other rooms in the house), was cool, shady, a little dark, and simply furnished with wicker chairs and horsehair sofas, but was indeed so large that two people could live there, separated from one another by considerable space, each pursuing his business undisturbed. Opening off this room lay bedrooms, rather spacious if likewise simply appointed, a third now being opened for us guests.

The family dining room was located upstairs and adjoined an even larger kitchen, where friends from the village were received and which had a vast, gloomy chimney and was hung full with ladles out of a fairy tale and carving knives and forks that could have belonged to an ogre, its shelves filled with copper utensils, saucepans, bowls, platters, terrines, and mortars, and was ruled over by Signora Manardi; called Nella by her family (I believe her name was Peronella), a stately matron of the Roman type, with an arched upper lip, kindly brown (but not dark brown, just chestnut) eyes and hair pulled smoothly and tightly back and flecked with silver; her full evenly proportioned figure was that of a competent and simple country woman—and one would often see her small, but work-roughened hands, a double widow's band on the right one, set akimbo on sturdy hips bound tightly by apron strings.

She had one young daughter left from her marriage—Amelia, a child of thirteen or fourteen and of somewhat simple wits, who had a habit of holding up her spoon or fork at meals, passing it back and forth before her eyes, and repeating over and over, with the raised intonation of a question, some word that had stuck in her mind. A year or so before, among the Manardis' lodgers had been an elegant Russian family, whose head, a count or prince, was given to seeing ghosts and from time to time would furnish the rest of the household a sleepless night by taking pistol shots at spirits haunting his bedroom. The understandably lively memory of the event explained why Amelia would often and insistently ask her spoon, "*Spiriti? Spiriti?*" But lesser things could leave a profound fixation as well. On one occasion a German tourist had treated the word *melone*, which in Italian takes the masculine article *il,* in the German fashion—that is, as a feminine noun; and now the child sat there wagging her head, following the motions of her spoon with mournful eyes, and muttering: *"La melona? La melona?"* Signora Peronella and her brothers disregarded, did not even hear what to them was everyday behavior, and if a guest seemed taken aback, they merely gave him a smile of apology—but of touching tenderness, too, indeed almost of happiness, as if it were all rather charming. Helene and I likewise quickly became accustomed to Amelia's muffled commentary at meals. Adrian and Schildknapp no longer noticed at all.

The brothers of whom I spoke and who were about equally older and younger than their middle sister, the mistress of the house, were: Ercolano Manardi, a lawyer, usually called by the gratifying nickname *l'avvocato,* the pride of this otherwise rustically simple and uneducated family, a man of sixty, with a bristly gray moustache and a hoarse, bawling voice that, like a donkey's, had trouble getting started; and Sor Alfonso, the younger, in his middle forties, affectionately addressed as "Alfo" by his family, a farmer, whom, as we returned from our afternoon walks in the *campagna,* we might see on his little jackass riding home from his fields—feet almost dragging, a sunshade in hand, blue sunglasses on his nose. To all appearances, the lawyer no longer practiced his profession, but merely read the newspaper—indeed, did so unremittingly, taking the liberty on hot days of sitting in his underwear and reading it in his room, with the door wide open. This incurred the censure of Sor Alfo, who felt that in so doing the jurist—*"quest' uomo,"* he would say on such occasions—was presuming a bit too much. He would rail (behind his brother's back) against such provocative license and could not be brought around by his sister's conciliatory words, who alleged that the lawyer suffered from an excess of blood, putting him in constant danger of an apoplectic stroke due to the heat and thus necessitating light apparel. Then *"quest' uomo"* should at least keep his door shut, Alfo retorted, instead of exposing himself in that excessively comfortable state to the eyes of his family and the *distinti forestieri.* Higher education did not justify such brazen carelessness. It was clear that under a, to be sure, well-chosen pretext, the *contadino* was here giving vent to a certain animosity toward the educated member of the family, even though—or perhaps because—in his heart of hearts Sor Alfo shared the admiration all Manardis felt for the lawyer, whom they regarded as a kind of statesman. The two brothers had widely divergent views on many issues, for the lawyer was of a more conservative, somberly pious temperament, whereas Alfonso was a critical free spirit, *libero pensatore,* hostile to church, monarchy, and *governo,* all of which he described as pervaded with scandalous corruption. *"Ha capito, che sacco di birbaccione?"*— "Do you see what a sackful of rascals it is?"—was how he would usually conclude his indictment, being far better at words than the lawyer, who would angrily withdraw behind his newspaper after a few braying attempts at protest.

Another relative, a brother of Frau Nella's dead husband, Dario Manardi, a gentle and gray-bearded man of peasant stock who walked with a cane, also lived in the family house with his nondescript and sickly wife. They, however, took their meals separately, while Signora Peronella fed the seven of us (her brothers, Amelia, the two permanent guests, and the visiting couple) from her romantic kitchen—with a liberality, with an inexhaustible bill of fare, quite out of proportion to the modest price of board and room. For after we had enjoyed a substantial meal of *minestra,* songbirds with polenta, scaloppini in Marsala, a lamb dish or wild boar with compote, and lots of salad, cheese, and fruits, and our friends had lit *regie*-cigarettes to go with their black coffee, she might ask, in a voice suggesting that the exciting notion had just come to her: *"Signori,* now—a little fish?" A purple country wine, which between brays the lawyer drank in great gulps like water, a vintage too torrid as a suitable beverage for two meals a day, but that it would have been a shame to water, served to quench our thirst. Our *padrona* admonished us to drink copiously of it, with the words: "Drink! Drink! *Fa sangue il vino."* Alfonso, however, scolded her for spreading superstition.

Afternoons found us taking lovely walks that rang with a great deal of hearty laughter at Rüdiger Schildknapp's Anglo-Saxon jokes and that led down into the valley, along paths lined with mulberry bushes, on across well-tended fields of olive trees and garlands of grape, the arable land divided into little farmsteads, each surrounded by a wall breached by a monumental entrance gate. Must I say how very much I was moved—quite apart from being with Adrian again—by the classical sky, in which not the smallest cloud appeared during the weeks of our stay, by the mood of antiquity that lay upon the land and that now and then would take shape in the rim of a well, in the picturesque figure of a shepherd, in the demonic Pan-like head of a goat? It goes without saying that Adrian shared in the raptures of my humanist's heart with only a nod and a smile that was not without irony. These artists pay little attention to an encircling present that bears no direct relation to the world of work in which they live, and they therefore see in it nothing more than an indifferent framework for life, either more or less favorable to production. As we turned back to the village, we watched the sun set, and I never have seen a splendor of the evening sky to match it. A layer of gold, a thick, sleek stroke of it set in carmine, floated above the western horizon—quite phenomenal and so beautiful that the sight could indeed fill the soul with a certain mirth. And yet I felt a gentle prod of disapproval when Schildknapp, pointing at this wonderful display, shouted his, "View yonder sight!" and Adrian broke into the grateful laughter Rüdiger's humorous remarks always evoked from him. For it seemed to me that he used the opportunity to laugh at both the natural phenomenon itself and the thrill it gave Helene and me.

I have already mentioned the cloister garden above the town, to which our friends, portfolios in hand, climbed every morning to work, each in his separate spot. They had applied to the monks for permission to linger there, and it had been kindly granted. We, too, would often accompany them up to this rather haphazard garden of spice-laden shade set within a crumbling wall and discreetly leaving them to their work, spend the increasingly hot morning to ourselves behind a screen of oleander, laurel, and broom, invisible to them both, just as they were invisible to one another—Helene with her crocheting and I with a book, content and alertly mindful that nearby Adrian was making progress on his opera.

Once—unfortunately only once—during our stay, he sat down at the badly out-of-tune square piano in our friends' living room and played for us characteristic passages and a few entire scene sequences from the completed score (which included even most of the instrumentation for a select orchestra) of the "pleasant, conceited comedic called, *Loues Labors Lost,*" as the piece had been titled in 1598: the first act, including the scene set in Armado's house, and parts of several later ones that he had worked ahead on—especially Berowne's monologues, on which he had always had designs, both the one in verse at the end of the third act and the rhythmically unstructured one in the fourth, which was musically more successful than the former in expressing that lord's unremittingly comic and grotesque and yet genuine and profound despair over his having fallen for the suspect black beauty— "They have pitch'd a toil, I am toiling in a pitch, pitch, that defiles"— and in capturing his angry outburst of self-mockery—"By the Lord, this love is as mad as Ajax: it kills sheep, it kills me, I a sheep." This had come about partly because the rapid and disconnected word-play of his prose ejaculations had inspired the composer to especially whimsical inventions of accent, but partly also because in music the repetition of what is significant and already familiar, a reminder that is witty or profound, always makes the greatest impression as speech, and because in the second monologue elements of the first are recalled in the most delicious way. That was particularly evident in his reviling of his own heart for its infatuation with the "whitely wanton with a velvet brow, with two pitch-balls stuck in her face for eyes," and again quite especially in the musical image of those damned, beloved pitch-ball eyes: a dark flash, a mixture of cellos and flutes, a half-lyrically passionate and half-grotesque *melisma,* that returns as a savage caricature in the prose of "O, but her eye,—by this light, for her eye I would not love her," whereby the eyes' darkness is deepened all the more by the low pitch, the flash of light within it, given this time, however, to the piccolo.

There can be no doubt that the peculiarly insistent and indeed unnecessary characterization of Rosaline as a wanton, faithless, dangerous female—a portrayal of her that is scarcely justified dramatically and found only in Berowne's speeches, whereas in the reality of the comedy she is merely saucy and witty—there can be no doubt that this characterization arises from the compulsive urge of a poet unconcerned with artistic consistency to incorporate his personal experiences and take poetic revenge for them, whether it fits or no. Rosaline, as her lover never wearies of portraying her, is the dark lady of the second sonnet series, Elizabeth's maid of honor, Shakespeare's beloved, who betrayed him for a handsome young friend; and the "part of my rhyme and here my melancholy" with which Berowne appears on the stage for his prose monologue, saying "well, she has one o' my sonnets already," is one of those that Shakespeare directed to his own fair black beauty. How does it happen, then, that Rosaline applies to Berowne, who in the play is sharp-tongued and downright merry, this bit of wisdom:

> The blood of youth burns not with such excess
> As gravity's revolt to wantonness?

He is young and not "grave" at all, and surely not the person who could be the cause of an observation about how sad it is when the wise become fools and apply all the power of their wit to prove worth in simplicity. In the mouth of Rosaline and her friends, Berowne falls completely out of his role; he is no longer Berowne, but Shakespeare in his unhappy affair with the dark lady; and Adrian, who always carried with him an English pocketbook edition of the sonnets—that intrinsically odd trio of poet, friend, and lover—had from the very start striven to give Berowne music that matched the Berowne of those passages of dialogue that he himself loved and that describe him—with due reference to the caricatural style of the whole—as "grave," a man of intellectual weight and truly the victim of a shameful passion.

It was beautiful, and I praised it highly. And indeed, there was in what he played for us more than enough reason besides for praise and joyful amazement! One could with all due gravity apply to him what the learned pedant Holofernes says of himself: "This is a gift that I have, simple, simple! a foolish extravagant spirit, full of forms, figures, shapes, objects, ideas, apprehensions, motions, revolutions. These are begot in the ventricle of memory, nourished in the womb of *pia mater,* and delivered upon the mellowing of occasion." Wonderful! For what is of itself a purely incidental, comical occasion, the poet here provides a consummately perfect description of the artistic spirit—and one automatically applied it to the mind laboring here to translate this satiric work of Shakespeare's youth to the sphere of music.

If only there had not been something in that sublime exercise of intellect that kept one in a state of constant anxiety. "He who seeketh hard things shall have it hard," it says in the Letter to the Hebrews—a verse that applies both honorably and troublingly to my friend and his productive efforts. I should probably have been happy that he had at last abandoned the idea of putting music only to an original-language version of my dramatic adaptation of the work. Instead, he had set it as his task to compose in both English and German at once, which is to say: He had undertaken to allow the melody to coincide with his harmonies in both languages, taking care that it kept its melodic profile and was correctly declaimed in each. He appeared to be prouder of this clever feat, a veritable tour de force, than of the actual musical inventions from which the work lived—and that restriction of their uninhibited blossoming left me a little concerned.

Should I likewise return to the sense of gentle affront or distress caused me personally by the subject itself, the mockery of the study of antiquity, which in the work appears as ascetic preciosity? The party guilty of this caricature of humanism was not Adrian, but Shakespeare, and from him, too, comes that twisted ordering of ideas, in which the terms "study" and "barbarism" play such a peculiar role. The former is intellectual monkishness, a learned refinement that profoundly despises life and nature, which indeed sees barbarism in life and nature, in immediacy, humanity, feeling. Even Berowne, who intercedes on behalf of the natural with those sworn to abide in this grove of academe, admits that he "for barbarism spoke more than for that angel knowledge." Granted, this angel is made to look ridiculous, but really only

by ridiculous means; for the "barbarism" to which the confederates re-
vert, the sonnet-drunk infatuation that is the punishment for their
sham alliance, is likewise a wittily stylized caricature, a lampooning of
love—and Adrian's sounds made only too sure that in the end feeling
is no better off than the presumptuous renunciation of it. And what
else but music, I thought, was by its very nature called to be the guide
that leads us out of the sphere of absurd artificiality into open air, into
the world of nature and humanity? Except that music abstained. What
Lord Berowne calls "barbarism"—that is, whatever is spontaneous
and natural—celebrates no triumphs in this music.

In terms of art, what my friend had woven here was most admirable.
Disdaining the bombast of numbers, he had originally intended to instrument the score for the classical orchestra of Beethoven, and it was
only for the sake of Armado, the comically pompous Spaniard, that he
had included a second pair of horns, three trombones, and a bass tuba
in his orchestra. But the style of the entire work was strictly that of
chamber music, a filigree handiwork, a clever grotesquery of notes, humorous and ingenious in its combinations and rich with the inventions
of a refined playfulness; and any lover of music who, weary of Romantic democracy and popular moralistic harangues, might have demanded an art or for art's sake, or for artists' and experts' sake, art with
no ambitions or rather with only the most exclusive ambitions, would
have had to be enraptured by this self-centered and perfectly cool esotericism—which in the esoteric spirit of the piece, however, at every
turn mocked and exaggerated itself as parody, mixing a drop of sadness, a grain of hopelessness into the rapture.

Yes, in the contemplation of this music, admiration and sadness mingled in the most peculiar way. "How beautiful!" one's heart said—or at
least mine said to itself—"and how sad!" For what one admired was a
wittily melancholy work of art, an intellectual feat worthy of the name
heroic, laconic anguish behaving like playful travesty—which I do not
know how to characterize other than to call it an unrelenting, tense,
breakneck game played by art at the very edge of impossibility. And
that was what made one sad. But admiration and sadness, admiration
and worry, is not that almost a definition of love? With painfully
strained love for him and all that was his—that was how I listened to
Adrian's performance. I was unable to say much; Schildknapp, always
a very good and receptive audience, was much more quick-witted and
clever than I in commenting on what had been offered us—whereas afterward I sat over *pranzo* at the Manardis' table, numb and preoccupied, still moved by those very feelings that the music we had just

heard had so totally excluded. *"Bevi! Bevi!"* the *padrona* said. *"Fa sangue il vino!"* And Amelia passed her spoon back and forth before her eyes, murmuring, *"Spiriti? . . . Spiriti? . . ."*

That evening was already one of the last that we, my good wife and I, spent in the uncommon framework our friends had given their lives. A few days later, after a stay of three weeks, we had to extricate ourselves again and begin the trip home to Germany, while for several months, well into autumn, they remained faithful to the idyllic regularity of their existence, with its cloister garden, family table, *campagna* rimmed with sleek gold, stony living room, and evenings of reading by lamplight. That was how they had spent the entire summer the previous year, nor had their life in the city during the winter been essentially different, either. They lived in the Via Torre Argentina, near the Teatro Constanzi and the Pantheon, three flights up, and had a landlady who prepared breakfast and a light supper. They took their main meal, paid for by the month, in a nearby trattoria. In Rome, the role of the cloister garden in Palestrina was played by the Villa Doria Pamphyli, where they pursued their work on warm spring and autumn days beside a beautifully constructed fountain, to which from time to time a cow or freely grazing horse might come to drink. Adrian seldom missed the municipal orchestra's afternoon concerts held on the Piazza Colonna. Occasional evenings might belong to the opera. As a rule they spent them in some quiet corner of a coffeehouse, playing dominoes over a glass of hot orange punch.

They associated with no one else—or as good as no one, their isolation in Rome being almost as total as in the country. They completely avoided the German element—Schildknapp would invariably take flight the moment a sound of his mother tongue struck his ear; he was perfectly capable of climbing right back off an omnibus or train if he encountered "Germans" there. But their solitary life, or double solitary life as it were, offered hardly any opportunity to strike up an acquaintance with the locals, either. Twice during the winter they were invited to the home of a patroness of art and artists, a lady of undetermined origins: Madame de Coniar, to whom Rüdiger Schildknapp had a letter of introduction from friends in Munich. In her apartment on the Corso, decorated with autographed photos framed in plush and silver, they met an international throng of artistic types—theater people, painters and musicians, Poles, Hungarians, Frenchmen, even Italians—each one of whom they just as quickly lost sight of again. At times, leaving Adrian behind and driven by his own sympathies into the arms of young Englishmen, Schildknapp would go off with them to drink

malmsey in bars or join them on an excursion to Tivoli or the Trappists
of Quattro Fontane, where he would drink eucalyptus schnapps, talk
nonsense, and recover from the ravaging difficulties of the art of
translation.

In short, both in the city and in their secluded mountain town, the
two lived the life of men who avoided the world and its people and
were concerned solely with the claims of their work. One can at least
put it that way. And shall I now say that for me personally, as loath as
I was, as always, to leave Adrian's side, the departure from the Manardi
house was likewise bound up with a certain secret sense of relief? But
in saying so I am duty-bound, as it were, to justify that feeling, and that
will be difficult to do without placing myself and others in a rather
ridiculous light. The truth is that in one certain point, *in puncto puncti,*
as young people like to say, I was a somewhat strange exception among
my housemates, was an incongruity, so to speak: that is, in my capacity and posture as a married man, who had paid his tribute to what—
half in apology, half in glorification—we call "nature." No one else did
so in the castello house on the street of stairs. Our splendid landlady,
Frau Peronella, had been a widow for years; her daughter Amelia was
a rather foolish child. The brothers Manardi, both lawyer and farmer,
appeared to be hardened bachelors—indeed one could easily imagine
that neither had ever touched a woman. There was Dario, the gray and
gentle brother-in-law, with his very tiny, sickly wife, whom one would
have favored with the term "married couple" surely in only its most
charitable sense. And then, finally, there were Adrian and Rüdiger
Schildknapp, who for month after month remained within the peacefully austere circle we had come to know, living a life no different
from that of the monks in the cloister up the hill. Ought there not be
something embarrassing and depressing about that for me, an ordinary man?

I spoke earlier of Schildknapp's special relationship to the wide
world of lucky possibilities and of his habitual stinginess with such a
treasure, expressed as stinginess with himself. I saw in it the key to his
mode of life; it served as an explanation for what was for me the more
inexplicable fact that he managed such things at all. It was different
with Adrian—although I was aware that their shared chastity was the
foundation of their friendship, or, if that is too sweeping a term,
of their life together. I presume that I have not succeeded in hiding
from the reader a certain jealousy of the Silesian's relationship with
Adrian—and so he may also understand that it was this shared factor,
this link of continence, that was the ultimate object of my jealousy.

If Schildknapp lived, if I may put it that way, as a roué of potentialities, Adrian now led—and this I could not doubt—the same life of a saint he had led before taking his trip to Graz, or better, to Pressburg. I now trembled, however, at the thought that since then—since that embrace, since his temporary illness and the loss of his doctors during its course—his chastity no longer arose from the ethos of purity, but rather from the tumult of impurity.

There had always been something of *"noli me tangere"* about his nature—I knew it well, was quite familiar with his distaste for any close physical proximity to people, for "breathing the same air" with them, for actually touching them. He was, in the true sense of the word, a man of "distaste," of evasion, of reserve, of aloofness. Physical displays of affection seemed inimical to his nature, even his handshakes were infrequent and performed with a certain haste. This peculiarity evidenced itself more clearly than ever during the weeks we had recently been together, and yet it seemed to me, I can scarcely say why, as if his "Don't touch me!", his "Back off three paces!", had changed its meaning in some sense, as if not only was some demand being rejected, but as if also he was shying from and avoiding some reverse demand on his own part—which, again, was apparently connected with his abstention from women.

Only a keenly observant friendship like mine could have felt or suspected such a shift in what these things meant, and God forbid that those perceptions might have detracted from my joy in being near Adrian! What was happening inside him could shock me, but never drive me from him. There are people with whom it is not easy to live, but whom it is impossible to leave.

XXV

THE DOCUMENT to which repeated reference has been made in these pages, Adrian's secret manuscript, in my possession since his demise and guarded like a precious, dreadful treasure—here it is, I shall confide it now. The biographical moment for its inclusion has come. Having now turned my back, as it were, on his refuge of choice, which he shared with his Silesian and where I visited him, I shall cease to speak, and the reader will hear Adrian's unmediated voice in this twenty-fifth chapter.

But is it only his? The document at hand is a dialogue, after all. Another, quite other, terrifyingly other voice, is indeed the principal speaker, and the scribe in his stony hall simply sets down what he has heard it say. A dialogue? Is it truly that? I would have to be mad to believe it. And neither can I believe that in the depths of his soul he considered what he saw and heard to be real, both while he heard and saw it and afterward as he put it on paper—despite the cynicisms with which his conversational partner attempted to convince him of his objective presence. But if he, the visitor, did not exist—and I am horrified to admit that such words allow, even if only conditionally and as a possibility, for his reality!—it is gruesome to think that the cynicism, the mockery, and the humbug likewise comes from his own stricken soul. . . .

It goes without saying that I do not intend to surrender Adrian's manuscript to the printer. With my own quill I shall transcribe it to my text, word for word, from music paper covered with the dark black strokes of the same script I described once before—a small, old-fashioned, ornate round-hand, a monkish hand one might say. He apparently used music paper because nothing else was available at the moment, or because the little shop down below on St. Agapitus square could supply him with no acceptable stationery. There are always two lines written in the upper five-line grid and two in the bass; but the white area in between is also filled with two lines of script throughout.

There is no determining precisely when it was written, for the document bears no date. If my own conviction is of any value, it definitely cannot have been composed after our visit to the little mountain town or during our stay there. Either it comes from an earlier period of the summer when we spent three weeks with the two friends, or it dates from the previous summer, when they first were guests of the Manardis. That the experience on which the manuscript is based already lay behind him when we arrived, that Adrian had already had the following conversation by then—of that I am certain; just as I am sure he put it in writing immediately after the encounter, the very next day presumably.

And so I shall transcribe it—and I fear no distant explosions rattling my study will be needed to make my hand tremble and send the letters skittering out of control as I write. . . .

—MUM, MUM'S THE WORD. And mum will I be, if but out of shame alone and to spare mankind, why! out of social consideration. I am of firm and stern resolve and would not slack the seemly reins of reason ere I close. Yet I did see Him, at last, at last; was with me here in the chamber, did search me out, all unexpected and yet long since expected, and spoke right copious words with Him and afterward have but one vexation, an uncertainty of what it was caused me to shake the whole time, whether 'twas the cold or He. Did I deceive myself mayhap, or He me, that it was cold, so that I might shake and by shaking gain certainty that it was He, in earnest, He in His own person? For as many a man knows, the fool does not shake at his phantasm, but feels at his ease instead and has intercourse with it sans disquiet and quivering. Would He perchance make a fool of me, and by the bitter cold deceive me to think I am no fool, and He no phantasm, in that I shook before Him in fear and infirmity? He is shrewd.

Mum's the word. So mum will I mum. I shall mum it all down on this music paper here, while my fellow *in eremo*, with whom I laugh, drudges some distance off in our chamber, translating the alien he dotes upon into the homely he detests. Thinks I write music, and if he

were to see 'tis words I write, would think that Beethoven surely did
so as well.

Afflicted creature that I am, had lain in the dark all the day with
tedious head ache, having often to retch and vomit, as comes with
severe visitations, but toward evening came bettering, all unhoped and
of a sudden. Could hold down the soup the mother brought me
(*"Poveretto!"*), afterward also cheerly drank a glass of the red (*"Bevi,
bevi!"*) and was at once so sturdy that I even paid me with a cigarette.
And could have gone out as well, as had been agreed the day before.
Dario M. wished to present us to his guild below, to make us acquaint
with Praeneste's better citizens, show us its precincts, its billiard and
reading rooms. Wishing to give the good man no offense, we gave our
promise—which fell to Sch. to keep alone, I being excused by my visitation. After *pranzo,* with mouth pulled sour and at Dario's side, he
trudged down to greet the grangers and suburbians, I being left to
my device.

Sat alone here in these halls, near unto the windows, their shutters
closed tight, the length of the room before me, and by my lamp read
Kierkegaard on Mozart's *Don Juan.*

And of a sudden I am struck by piercing cold, as if one sat in a room
warmed 'gainst winter and abruptly a window burst open upon the
frost. But it came not from behind where the windows are, but rather
falls upon me at my front. Starting up from my book, I gaze out into
the chamber, see that Sch. is apparently come back already, for I am no
more alone: Someone is there in the twilight, seated upon the horsehair
couch that stands with table and chairs nearer the door, toward the
room's middle, where we make our breakfast of a morning—sits in one
corner of the couch, his legs crossed, but it is not Sch., it is another,
smaller than he, not so comely by far, and no true gentleman whatsoever. But the cold continues to rush against me.

"Chi è costà!" is what I call from a throat in part constrained, prop-
ping my hands on the arms of the chair in such fashion that the book
falls from my knees to the floor. The steady, slow voice of the other answers, a schooled voice as it were, with pleasant resonance in the nose:

"Speak only German! Avail yourself of naught but good old-
fashioned German, no feignings, no presence. I understand it. Squarely
said, my favourite language. At times I understand only German. But
fetch your top-coat upon the by, and hat and rug as well. You'll feel
the cold. Your teeth will clatter, dear boy, though you will not take
an ague."

"Who speaks familiarly with me?" I ask, waxing angry.

"I do," he says. "I do, by your leave. Oh, you mean, do you, because you employ the familiar pronoun with no one—not even the waggish gentleman here—excepting your childhood playfellow, who faithfully calls you by your proper name, but not you him? It makes no matter. There is by now a relation twixt us for such familiarity. How now? Will you fetch yourself warmer attire?"

I stare into the twilight, fix him with an angry eye. Is a man of a more spindled figure, not near so tall as Sch., yet shorter than I—a sporting cap tugged at one ear, and on the other side reddish hair extending from the temple upward; reddish lashes round likewise reddened eyes, the face pale as a cheese, with the tip of the nose bent slightly askew; a stocking-knit shirt striped crosswise with sleeves too short and fat-fingered hands stuck out; trousers that sit untowardly tight, and yellow, overworn shoes ne'er to be clean again. A *strizzi*. A pimp-master. And with the voice, the enunciation of a player.

"How now?" he repeated.

"Foremostly I wish to know," I said, trembling to find command of myself, "who it is presumes to intrude upon me and seat himself here."

"Foremostly," he repeated. "Foremostly is not at all bad. But you are oversensible to any visit you deem unexpected and undesired. I do not come to fetch you into company, to flatter you to join some musical confrairy. But rather, to speak of business with you. Will you fetch your things? There can be no discoursing with teeth clattering."

Sat several seconds more without taking my eye from him. And the chill from off him rushes gainst me, so piercingly that in my light suit of apparel I am defenceless and naked before it. So I depart. Do indeed stand up and enter through the next door to my left, where my bed-chamber lies (the other being farther on the same side), take from the press my winter coat that I wear in Rome on days of tramontane and brought along perforce, for I knew not where to leave it elsewise; do on my hat as well, snatch up my plaid rug, and return thus furnished to my place. As before he still sits in his.

"You are yet here," I say, turning up the collar of my coat and winding the rug about my knees, "though I did depart and return again? That mazes me. For 'tis my strong conjecture you are not here."

"Not here?" he asked with resonance of the nose, as schooled. "Wherefore not?"

I: "Because it is most improbable that a man would seat himself here by evening, speaking German and giving forth cold, professedly to discuss with me matters of business whereof I know and wish to know naught. It is the more probable that I am taking some malady and in my dazed state transfer unto your person the chill of fever against which I have wrapped myself, and behold you merely but to see its source in you."

He (calm and with a player's persuasive laugh): "What nonsense! What intelligent nonsense you do speak! It is, as they say in good old-fashioned German, unfeigned folly. And so artificial! A clever artifice, as if pilfered from your opera. But let us make no music here, for the nonce. It is moreover pure hypochondry. Play no infirmities with me, please! Be but a little proud and do not pack off your five senses. You are not taking any malady, but are in the best of youthful health after that slight visitation. Beg pardon, I would not be rude, for indeed what is good health? But, dear boy, this is not the manner of your malady's eruption. You have not a trace of fever, and there is no need that you ever should have."

I: "Further, because your every other word lays bare your nothingness. You say only such things as are in me and come out of me, but not out of you. You counterfeit Kumpf in his turns of phrase and yet do not look ever to have been at a university or academe, or ever to have sat beside me upon the dunce's bench. You speak of the indigent gentleman and of him with whom I use the familiar pronoun, even of such as have used it with me and got no recompense. And speak of my opera, too, no less. Whence could you know all that?"

He (laughs again his practised laugh, shaking his head as at some precious childishness): "Whence could I know? But you see that I do know. And from that you would, to your own discredit, conclude that you do not see rightly? That would truly mean to stand all logic on its head, as one learns in academes. Rather than construe from my informed state that I am not present in the flesh, you would do better to conclude that I am not merely in the flesh, but am also he for whom you have taken me all this time."

I: "And for whom do I take you?"

He (with courteous reproach): "Pooh, you know well! Nor should you make false pretence, feigning you had not long since expected me. Know as well as I that our relation presses sometime for discussion. If I be—and I think you admit of that now—I can be but One. Do you mean by your who am I: How am I called? But sure you still have memory of all those scurrilous little nicknames from your academes, from your first course of study, when you had not yet shoved Holy Writ out the door or under the bench. You can tell them all by heart and take your pick thereof—I have 'most only such, 'most only nicknames, with which the people give my chin a chuck, so to speak—the which comes from my foremost German popularity. Indeed one willingly brooks it, this popularity, even when one has not sought it out and is persuaded in the main that 'tis grounded in a misconceiving. It is ever flattering, ever beneficial. Choose then for yourself, if you need name me, though you mostly do not call others by their names, not knowing them for lack of interest—choose one as you will from 'mongst those rustic blandishments! Only one I would not and will not hear, for it is a most certain spiteful slander and befits me not in the least. He who calls me Master *Dicis-et-non-facis* is on the slippery slope. 'Tis also meant as a chuck under the chin, but calumny it is. I do what I say, keep my promises to a tittle, indeed that is my very principle of business, much as Jews are the most reliable of merchants, and if fraud there was, well, it is proverbial that it was I, ever a believer in fidelity and probity, who was defrauded. . . ."

I: "*Dicis et non es.* You warrant truly to sit there on the couch before me and to speak to me from without in good Kumpfian scraps of old-fashioned German? Warrant to have searched me out here in alien Italy of all places, where you are quite out of your realm and enjoy not the least popularity? What an absurd want of fashion! In Kaisersaschern I would have suffered you. In Wittenberg or on the Wartburg, even in Leipzig I would have thought you credible. But surely not here, under a heathen Catholic sky!"

He (shaking his head and clicking his tongue in distress): "Tut tut tut, ever the skeptic, ever the same lack of self-regard. Had you but courage to say to yourself: 'Where I am, there is Kaisersaschern,' why then, of a sudden the matter would be in accord, and Master Aestheticus would no more need sigh the want of fashion. Cod's eyes! You would be right to speak thus, but lack courage or pretend its lack. You value yourself too low, my friend—and value me too low as well in limiting me so, wishing to make naught but a German provincial of me. German I am, German to the core, if you will, but then surely in an older, better sense, to wit: cosmopolitan at heart. You would disallow me here and make no account of the old German yearning and romantic itch to travel to Italy's fair shore! German I shall be, yet you, good sir, begrudge me that I should, in good Dürer fashion, freeze to pursue the sun—and do so even when, quite without regard to the sun, I have urgent business here with a fine creature well-created. . . ."

Here an unutterable loathing came over me, so that I shuddered violently. Yet there was no true distinction between the causes of my shudder; at one and the same time it might have been from the cold, for the chill off him had turned abruptly sharper, piercing my coat's cloth and me to the marrow. Angrily I ask:

"Can you not abate this nuisance, this icy breeze?"

He in reply: "Alas, no. I regret I cannot accommodate you there. Plainly, I am so cold. How else should I endure it and dwell at my ease where I dwell?"

I (instinctively): "You mean in hell's horrid hole?"

He (laughs as if tickled): "Excellent! A crude and German and roguish phrase! And has many a pretty name, besides, so eruditely solemn, all known to Master Ex-Theologus, as *carcer, exitium, confutatio, pernicies, condemnatio,* and so forth. But, there's no help for it, the homely and humorous German names always remain my favourites. But let us leave aside for now the place and its particularities. I read from your face that you are about to ask me concerning them. But that lies far afield and is no burning matter—forgive me the jest, that it is not burning!—there will be time, abundant, immeasurable time. Time is what is real, the best we give, and our gift is the hour-glass—indeed 'tis subtly narrow, that bottle neck through which the red sand runs, so hairlike its trickle that the eye beholds no diminishment in the upper chamber, and only at the very end does it appear to go fast and fast be gone. But that is yet so distant, what with the narrowness, that it deserves nor mention nor thought. Simply that the hour-glass has been turned, that the sand has begun to run—about that would I come to an understanding with you, dear boy."

I (duly mocking): "You love what is most extraordinarily Dürer-like, first your 'how I should freeze to pursue the sun' and now the hour-glass of *Melancolia.* Can the reckoning square of numbers be far behind? I am prepared for all and grow customed to all. Custom myself to your impudence that you use the familiar pronoun and call me 'dear boy,' to which I take special offence. For, to be sure, I do address myself familiarly—which most likely explains that you do so as well. You would maintain that I am conversing with Black Kesperlin—Kesperlin being Caspar, and thus Caspar and Samiel are one and the same."

He: "There you are at it again."

I: "Samiel. It could make a man laugh! Where is your C-minor *fortissimo* of string tremolos, woodwinds, and sackbuts, that ingenious bugbear for the Romantic audience, rising from the abyss of F minor as you from your crags? I am mazed not to hear it!"

He: "Let it be. We have many a laudable instrument, and hear them you shall. We shall indeed strike them up for you, but only when you are ripe for the hearing. It is all a matter of ripeness and sweet time. And for that reason would I speak with you. But Samiel—the term is foolish. I am considerate of what is popular, but Samiel is foolish, and was corrected by Johann Balhorn of Lübeck. The name is Sammael. And what does Sammael mean?"

I (keep mutinous silence).

He: "Mum, mum's the word. I am kindly disposed to the discretion you show in leaving the German rendering to me. It means 'Angel of Poison.'"

I (between teeth that would not rightly stay shut): "Yes, of a certainty, you look the part! Why, very like an angel, exactly so! Do you know how you look? Common is scarcely the word for it. Like churlish dross, a bawd, an utter pimp-master, is how you look, is the guise you thought to put on to visit me—but no angel!"

He (gazing down over himself with arms spread wide): "How then, how then? How do I look? No, it really is a good thing that you ask me if I know how I look, for in truth I do not know. Or I did not know, for you first call it to my attention. Be assured I have not the least regard to my appearance, leaving it to itself, so to speak. It is pure chance how I look, or rather, comes about thus, it stablishes itself as circumstance demands, without that I give it any heed. Conformation, mimicry, you know it well, the mumchance and conjuring of Mother Nature, who always keeps her tongue in her cheek. But surely, dear boy, you will not apply this conformation, of which I know as much and as little as the leaf butterfly, to yourself and take it ill of me. You must admit that on its other side it has it suitableness—on that side from which you came by it, and indeed forewarned, on the side of your pretty song with its alphabetical symbol—oh, truly wittily done and very near by inspiration:

> And so it was by giving
> Me cooling drink by night
> You poisoned life and living . . .

Excellent.

> And on the wound the serpent
> Now tightly clings and sucks . . .

'Tis truly a gift. And that is what we recognized betimes and why we have had an eye upon you from early on—we saw that your case was entirely worth our attention, that it was a case of favourable disposition, out of which, presupposing but a little enkindling, incitement, and inebriation, something lustrous might be made. Did not Bismarck observe that the German needs half a bottle of champagne to attain his natural elevation? Meseems he said much the like. And rightly so.

Gifted, but lame is the German—gifted enough to be vexed by his lameness and overcome it by illumination, and devil take the hindmost. You, dear boy, knew well enough what you lacked, and held true to your German nature when you made your journey and, *salva venia,* caught the French measles."

"Hold your tongue!"

"Hold my tongue? Look there, I call that advancement on your part. You grow warm. At last you cast courtesies aside and turn familiar, as is only proper between people who strike a compact and find agreement for time and eternity."

"I said, keep silence!"

"Silence? But we have kept silence soon these five years and must sometime converse with one another and deliberate the whole matter and the interesting circumstances in which you find yourself. And here silence is but natural, yet not twixt us nor over time—not when the hour-glass has been turned, not when the red sand has begun to run through that subtly subtle bottle neck. Oh, only just begun! What lies below is still as nothing in comparison with the quantity above—we give time, abundant, immeasurable time, the end of which one need not contemplate, not for a long while, nor even yet have cause to be fretted with that point in time when one might begin to think on the end, when '*Respice finem*' might pertain, inasmuch as it is an unsteady point in time, subject to vagaries and temper, and no man knows where it ought be set and at how far a distance from the end. It is a fine jest and splendid contrivance: how the very uncertainty and haphazard of the moment when it will be time to think on the end waggishly befogs the momentary view of one's appointed end."

"Triflings and trumpery!"

"Go to, there is no pleasing you. You treat even my psychology rudely—when you yourself upon your local Zion did once call psychology a nice, neutral middle point and psychologists lovers of the truth. I trifle not in the least, nor even at all, when I speak of time given and of an appointed end, but am speaking narrowly to our argument. Everywhere the hour-glass has been turned and time has been given, incomprehensible, but bounded time and an appointed end, there are we upon the field, there grows our sweet clover. Time is what we sell— twenty-four years, shall we say—can one forethink it? Is it a requisite sum? A man might live like a pig in the old Kaiser's sty and set the world in astonishment as a great nigromancer with much devilry; he might forget all lameness the more, the longer the years and transcend himself by high illumination, yet never become a stranger to himself, but be and remain himself, except lifted to his natural elevation by his half-bottle of champagne, and might in drunken indulgence taste every bliss of almost intolerable infusion, till he be convinced more or less rightly that there has not been such an infusion for thousands of years and till in certain wanton moments he may plainly and honestly deem himself a god. How would such a man ever come to be fretted by the point in time when it is time to think on the end! Except, the end is ours, in the end he is ours, that demands agreement, and not merely of the silent sort, however silent things may else proceed, but from man to man and expressly."

I: "So you would sell me time?"

He: "Time? Mere time? No, my good man, that is no Devil's ware. For that we would not earn the price of an end that belongs to us. What sort of time—there is the pith of the matter. Great time, mad time, most devilish time, in which to soar higher and higher still—and then again a bit miserable, to be sure, indeed deeply miserable, I not only admit of it, but also say it with proud emphasis, for that is but meet and fair, such being surely the way and nature of the artist. Which, as all men know, ever tends to extravagancy in both directions, is regularly a bit excessive. The pendule always swings widely to and fro twixt good cheer and melancholy, that is customary, and is, so to speak, still of the more civilly moderate, more Nurembergish sort, in comparison with what we purvey. For in this respect we purvey in extremes: We furnish upliftings and illuminations, experiences of release and unshackling, of liberty, security, facility, such states of power and triumph that our man trusts not his senses—incorporating, moreover, a colossal admiration of his own achievement, for which he could easily forgo that of any stranger and alien—the self-glorious shudder, yea the precious horror of himself, in which he seems to himself a mouthpiece well graced, a divine monster. And commensurably deep, venerably deep, is likewise his descent at intervals—not only into emptiness and waste and rich sorrow, but also into pain and nauseas—companions, by the by, who were always there, who are part of the propensity, yet now most worthily enhanced by illumination and sensible pot-valiance. They are pains that one gladly and proudly takes in the bargain with pleasures so enormous, pains such as one knows from a fairy tale, pains like slashing knives, like those the little mermaid felt in the beautiful human legs she had acquired for a tail. You know Andersen's little mermaid, do you not? What a darling that would be for you! Say but the word, and I shall lead her to your bed."

I: "If you could but keep silence, you jackanapes."

He: "Now, now, be not always so quick with insult. You would have naught but silence still. I am not of the family Schweigestill. And, by the way, Mother Else prattled with charitable discretion a great deal about her occasional guests. I am in no way come to you on this heathen shore for silence and stillness, but for express ratification between us two and firm covenant as to service and payment. I tell you, we have kept silence now for more than four years—and yet all is taking its finest, most exquisite, most promising course, and the bell is now half cast. Shall I tell you how it stands with you and what's afoot?"

I: "It seems I must indeed hear."

He: "Would moreover like to hear and are well-content that you can. I even believe you are more than a little in the mood of hearing, and would whine and grumble privately were I to keep it from you. And rightly. It is so snug and dear, this world wherein we are together, you and I—we both are very at home in it, pure Kaisersaschern, good old German air from *anno* fifteen hundred or so, shortly before the arrival of Dr. Martinus, who stood upon such stout and cordial terms with me and threw a hard roll, no, an inkpot, at me, long before the thirty-year festivities. Do but recall the lusty temper of the folk among you in Germany's midst, along the Rhine and everywhere, in the excitation of high spirits and yet constrained enough, full of foreboding and ill at ease—the hot yearning for pilgrimage to the Sacred Blood in Niklashausen in the valley of the Tauber, children's crusades, and bleeding hosts, famine, insurrection, war, and pest in Cologne, meteors, comets, and great signs, stigmatical nuns, crosses that appear upon men's garments, and now they hope to advance against the Turks 'neath the banner of a maiden's shift marked by a wondrous cross. Good times, devilish German times! Does your mind not take warm comfort in the thought? The proper planets met together in the house of the Scorpion, just as a most well-instructed Master Dürer drew it for his medicinal broadsheet, and there arrived in German lands the small delicate folk, living corkscrews, our dear guests from the Indies, the flagellants—you prick up your ears, do you not? As if I spoke of the vagabonding guild of penitents, scourging their backs for their own and all mankind's sins. But I mean the flagellates, the tiny imperceptible sort, which have flails, like our pale Venus—the *spirochaeta pallida,* that is the true sort. But right you are, it sounds so snugly like the high Middle Age and its *flagellum haereticorum fascinariorum.* Ah, yes, they may well prove to be *fascinarii,* our revellers—in better cases, such as yours. And are, by the way, long since properly mannered and domestical, and in old lands, where they are at home so many centuries of years now, their buffooneries are not so crude as before, with open boils and pestilences and noses rotted off. Neither does the painter Baptist Spengler look as if he ought to swing the warning rattle as he walks about and stands, his carcass mummied in haircloth."

I: "Is such the state of Spengler, then?"

He: "And why not? Should it be your state solely? I know you would have what is yours to yourself alone and are vexed by all comparison. Dear boy, one always has a host of fellows. But assuredly Spengler is an Esmeraldus. Not in vain does he wink so audaciously and craftly with his eyes, and not in vain does Inez Rodde call him an underhand sneak. So goes it—though Leo Zink, the *faunus ficarius,* has still scaped it yet, but the spruce and prudent Spengler was snatched right early. Yet be calm and spare yourself any envy. 'Tis a dull and humdrum case, without least consequence. That is no Python with which we shall do astounding feats. By its reception he may have grown a bit cannier, more given to the intellect and would mayhap not read so gladly the diary of Goncourt or his Abbé Galiani had he not the connexion to higher things, had he not his secret memorandum. Psychology, dear boy. Disease, and most specially opprobrious, suppressed, secret disease, creates a certain critical opposition to the world, to mediocre life, disposes a man to be obstinate and ironical toward civil order, so that he seeks refuge in free thought, in books, in study. But it goes no farther than that with Spengler. The time still given him to read, to quote, to drink red wine and idle about—we did not sell him that, it is naught but time made congenial. A man of the world, lightly singed and stale, of demi-interest, nothing more. He will cripple along with liver, kidneys, stomach, heart, and gut, and one day be all hoarse of voice or deaf and after a few years will perish inglorious, a skeptical jest upon his lips—but what else? There was nothing to it, there was never an illumination, enhancement, and excitation, for it was not of the brain, was not cerebrose, you see—our small folk had no concern for his noble, uppermost part, which parently had no allurement for them, it never came to a metastasis into the metaphysical, metavenereal, metainfectious . . ."

I (with rancour): "How long have I to sit and freeze and listen to your intolerable gibberish?"

He: "Gibberish? Have to listen? Now that is the most facetious of ballads for you to strike up. To my mind you listen most attentively and are merely impatient to know more and all. You made particular inquiry concerning your friend Spengler of Munich, and had I not cut you off, would have zealously interrogated me this whole time about hell's horrid hole. I beg you do not play the importuned! I, too, have my self-regard and know that I am no unbidden guest. In short and plain, metaspirochaetosis, that is the menengial process. And I do assure you that it is indeed as if some certain of these small folk may have a passion for the uppermost, a special estimation for the region of the head, the meninges, the dura mater, the tentorium, and the pia, which defend the tender parenchyma within, and would swarm ardently thither from the moment of that first general infection."

I: "It suits you, this mode of speech. The pander appears to have studied medicine."

He: "No more than you theology, which is to say by bits and starts and speciality. Would you deny that you have studied the finest arts and sciences only as a specialty and pastime? Your chief regard was— me. I am much obliged. And why should I, Esmeralda's friend and keeper, as which you see me here before you, not have a special regard for the material, personal, most immediate field of medicine and be specially at home in it? And indeed I follow with constant and greatest attentiveness the most recent consequences of investigation. Item, several *doctores* would claim and swear by all swearing's worth that among the small folk there must be brain specialists, whose pastime is the cerebral sphere, in short, a *virus nerveux*. But they are upon the old familiar slope. It is rather contrariwise. It is the brain that lusts after a visit and waits expectant for theirs, as you have for mine, that invites them to it, draws them to it, as if it could not bear the expectation. Do you still recall? The Philosopher, *De anima:* 'Actions by an actor are performed on one previously disposed to suffer them.' There you have it, the disposition, the readiness, the invitation is all. That some men are better endowed than others for the performance of witchery, and that we know well to distinguish them—the worthy authors of the *Malleus* were already familiar to that."

I: "Slanderer, I have no dealing with you. I did not invite you."

He: "Ah, ah, sweet innocence! The far-traveled client of my small folk was not warned, was he? And you likewise sought out your physicians on sure instinct."

I: I came upon them in the street directory. Whom should I have asked? And who could have told that they would leave me in the lurch? What did you do with my two physicians?"

He: "Dispatched, dispatched. Oh, in your interest to be sure, we dispatched those bunglers. And at the right moment, neither too early nor too late, once they had set matters on the right path with their quick- and quacksalvery, and had we left them, could only have botched so lovely a case. We permitted them their *provocatio*—and then *basta*, away with them! As soon as they had duly limited the first, specially cutaneous general infiltration and so had given a powerful upward stimulus to the metastasis, their business was done, they were to be disposed of. Those ninnies do not know, you see, and if they know cannot alter the case, that the uppermost metavenereal process is accelerated by such general treatment. It is, to be sure, likewise expedited often enough by not treating the fresh stages—in short, do what one will, 'tis false. In no case could we permit the *provocatio* by quick- and quacksalvery to continue. The reversal of the general pervasion could be left to itself, in order that the upward progression might continue at its pretty slow pace, that there might be reserved for you years, decades of lovely, nigromantic time, a whole hour-glass of devilish time, of genius time. Today, four years after you came by it, that uppermost place is narrow and small and finely circumscribed—but extant it is—the hearth, the workshop of the small folk, who have come there by the liquorous path, on a waterway so to speak, to the place of incipient illumination."

I: "Do I catch you, blockhead? You betray yourself and have told me the spot in my brain, the feverish hearth, that conjures you up, and without which you were not! You have betrayed to me that I see and hear you out of perturbation, but that you are a mere semblance before my eyes!"

He: "Ah sweet logic! Little fool, inside out 'twill make a shoe. I am not the production of your pial hearth up there, understood? But that hearth enables you to perceive me and without it, surely, you would see me not. Is my existence therefore governed by your incipient tipsiness? Do I therefore belong to your subjective mind? Many thanks! Have but patience. What may ensue and progress there will render you capable of quite other things, will pull down quite other obstacles and soar with you high above your lameness and hindrance. Wait until Good Friday, and 'twill be Easter soon! Wait one, ten, twelve years, until the illumination, that bright radiant annulment of all lame scruples and doubts, reaches its pitch, and you will know for what you pay and why you bequeath us body and soul. And osmotic growths will sprout *sine pudore* from apothecary seeds . . ."

I (flying into a rage): "Now hold your filthy tongue! I forbid you to speak of my father!"

He: "Oh, your father is not at all misplaced upon my tongue. He is sly, always wanting to speculate the elements. From him you also have that megrim in your head, the starting place for those knifing pains the

little mermaid knows. . . . I spoke quite rightly, by the way, since the
whole wizardry is osmosis, a diffusion of liquor, a proliferous process.
You have there the spinal sac, a pulsing column of liquor within, reaching to cerebral regions, to the meninx, in whose tissue the furtive vene-
real meningitis goes about its soft, silent work. But however much our
small folk be drawn to the inmost part, to the parenchyma, and however great the yearning to draw them thither, they could never enter—
without the diffusion of liquor, the osmosis with the pia's cellular fluid,
watering it, dissolving tissue, and clearing a path to the inmost part for
our flagellants. It is all a matter of osmosis, my friend, in whose
sportive products you early took such delight.

I: "Their misery made me laugh. I would that Schildknapp might re-
turn that I could laugh with him. I would tell him tales of a father, even
I. Would tell him of the tears in my father's eye when he would say:
'Even though they are dead!'"

He: "Zounds! You were right to laugh at his compassionate tears—
irrespecting that he who by nature has dealing with the Tempter always stands on contrary terms with others' feelings and is always
tempted to laugh when they weep, and to weep when they laugh. What
can 'dead' mean when such coloured and multiform flora flourishes
and grows rank—and what if it be heliotropic, too? What can 'dead'
mean when the drop manifests so healthy an appetite. One ought not,
my boy, leave to the suburbanite the final word as to what is sick and
what is healthy. Whether he understand rightly about life remains a
question. Many a time has life joyously taken up what has arisen by
paths of death and sickness, that it might let itself be led thereby farther
and higher still. Have you forgotten what you learned at your academe, that God can bring good out of evil, and that the occasion thereto
ought not be curbed? Item, one has always had to grow sick and mad,
that others need no longer do so. And where madness begins to be
malady no man can easily tell. If in a rapture a man write in his margin:
'Am in bliss. Am beside myself! I call this new and grand! Conception's seething delight! My cheeks glow as molten iron! In a frenzy am
I, and you will all grow frenzical when this comes to you! May God
help your poor souls then!'—is that still madding health, common
madness, or are the meninges infected? The townsman is the last to discern it; in any case he remarks nothing for a long while, for artists, says
he, be always lunatic. And should he cry the next day in recoil: 'Oh
foolish desolation! Oh dog's life, that one can complish nothing! Were
there but a war without, that something might be afoot. Could I but
perish in decent fashion! May hell have mercy, for I am a son of hell!'—

is that to be taken as real? Is it the literal truth, what he says there of hell, or is it but a metaphor for a bit of commonplace Dürer-like melancholy? In sum, we purvey merely that for which the classical poet, the most worthiest of all, so prettily thanked his gods:

> All they give, do the gods, do the unending gods,
> To their darlings, entire:
> All the joys, and all unending joys,
> All the pain, the pains unending, entire."

I: "Mocking liar! *Si Diabolus non esset mendax et homicida!* If I must hear you, then at least speak not to me of untainted greatness and native gold! I know that gold made by fire stead of by the sun is not genuine."

He: "Who says so? Has the sun better fire than the kitchen? And untainted greatness? The mere mention thereof! Do you believe in such a thing, in an *ingenium* that has nothing whatever to do with hell? *Non datur!* The artist is the brother of the felon and the madman. Do you esteem that a merry work has ever come about without that its maker had learned to practise the condition of the felon and the lunatic? How now, diseased and healthy! Without disease life would never have fared well its whole life long. How now, genuine and false! Are we mountebanks? Do we draw good things from the sleeve of nothing? Where nothing is, the Devil, too, has lost his right, and no pale Venus complishes anything of merit. We create nothing new—that is others' business. We merely deliver and set free. We let the lameness and shyness, the chaste scruples and doubts, go to the Devil. We stimulate and, with but a little tickle of hyperæmia, we sweep away weariness—be it small or large, private or that of the age. That's the thing—you are not thinking of time in its courses, you are not thinking historically when you complain that some one or another could have it entire, joys and pains unending, without that his hour-glass had been turned or that at the end his bill be presented him. What he could at best have without us in time's old classic courses, only we can offer now-a-days. We offer better still, we offer foremostly the right and true—a thing no longer even classic, dear boy, which we let be experienced, a thing archaic, primal, a thing that has long since ceased to be attempted. Who knows still today, who knew even in classic times, what inspiration, what genuine, ancient, primal enthusiasm is, enthusiasm ne'er sicklied o'er with criticism, lame prudence, and the deadly reins of reason—what holy rapture is? The Devil, I believe, is held to be the man of ravaging criticism? Slander—once again, my friend! God's bodykins! If there be something he hate, something most contrary in all the world, it is ravaging criticism. What he wishes and spends, that is verily the triumph over and beyond such, the shining want of thought!"

I: "Charlatan."

He: "Of a certain! When, more out of love of truth than of self, one sets right the rudest misconceivings about oneself, one is a vapourer. I shall not let my mouth be stopped by your ungracious shamefastness, for I know you do but suppress your affects and hearken to me with as much pleasure as does the maid to the whisperer in church. . . . Take for instance your 'fresh idea'—or what you call such, what you all have called such for one or two hundred years now—for that category did not exist in olden times, as little as musical copyright and all that. The fresh idea, then—a matter of three, four bars, no more, is it not? All the rest is elaboration, the grindstone. Is it not? Good, we, however, are sapient and know the literature and remark that the idea is not fresh at all, that it recalls all too much something that occurs in Rimsky-Korsakov or Brahms. What to do? One simply changes it. But a changed idea—is that still a fresh idea at all? Take Beethoven's sketch-books! Not one thematic conception remains as God gave it. He fashions it new and adds: '*Meilleur.*' Little trust in God's prompting, little respect of it is expressed in that scarcely exuberant '*Meilleur*'! A veritably gladding, ravishing, undoubtful, and believing inspiration, an inspiration for which there can be no choosing, no bettering, no mending, in which everything is received as blessed decree, which trips up and tumbles, ruffling sublime shudders from pate to tiptoe over him whom it visits and causing him to burst into streaming tears of happiness—that comes not from God, who leaves to reason all too much to do, but is possible solely with the Devil, the true Lord of Enthusiasm."

A little and a little during his last speech, something else had happened to the fellow before my eyes. When I looked at him direct, he seemed different to me from before: sits there no longer the pimp-master and bawd but rather, begging your pardon, a better gentleman, has a white collar and a bow-tie, spectacles rimmed in horn atop his hooked nose, behind which somewhat reddened eyes shine moist and dark; the face a mingling of sharpness and softness; the nose sharp, the lips sharp, but the chin soft, with a dimple in it, and yet another dimple in the cheek above; pale and vaulted the brow, from which the hair indeed retreats upward, whereas that to the sides stands thick, black, and woolly—an intellectualist, who writes of art, of music, for vulgar newspapers, a theorist and critic, who is himself a composer, in so far as thinking allows. Soft, lank hands as well, that company his speech with gestures of refined clumsiness, sometimes stroking gently over the thick hair at temples and nape. This was now the portrait of the visitor in the couch's corner. He had not grown larger; and above all the voice, nasal, distinct, schooled to please, had remained the same; it preserved identity for the transitory figure. And thus I hear him say and observe his broad mouth, crimped at the corners 'neath the poorly shaven upper lip, puckering to articulate:

"What is art today? A pilgrimage upon a road of peas. Takes more than a pair of red shoes to dance now-a-days, and you are not alone in being distressed by the Devil. Look at them, at your colleagues—I know well you do not look at them, you do not attend them, you nurse the illusion of solitude and want everything for yourself, all the curses of the age. But do console yourself with a look at them, at your coinaugurators of new music—I mean the honest, serious ones, who draw consequences from the situation! I speak not of those folklorists and seekers of neoclassical asylum, whose modernity consists in forbidding music to break open and who, with more or less dignity, wear the garb of a pre-individualistic age. Who convince themselves and others that what is tedious has grown interesting, because what is interesting has begun to grow tedious. . . ."

I had to laugh, for although the cold continued to press me, I was forced to admit that since his alteration I had grown more at ease in his company. He smiled with me, but only in that the closed corners of his mouth contracted more firmly and he shut his eyes a little.

"You, too, are impotent," he went on, "but I believe that you and I prefer the estimable impotence of those who disdain to conceal the general malady under a dignified mummery. The malady, however, is universal, and honest men observe the symptoms both in themselves and in those who compose back to the past. Is there not a threat that production will cease? What is of merit and still put to paper betrays effort and reluctance. External social causes? Lack of demand—so that, as in the preliberal era, the possibility of production greatly depends on the accident of a patron's favour? True, but that does not suffice as an explanation. Composition itself has grown too difficult, desperately difficult. Where work and sincerity no longer agree, how is one to work? But so it is, my friend—the masterpiece, the structure in equilibrium, belongs to traditional art, emancipated art disavows it. The matter has its beginnings in your having no right of command whatsoever over all former combinations of tones. The diminished seventh, an impossibility; certain chromatic passing notes, an impossibility. Every better composer bears within him a canon of what is forbidden, of what forbids itself, which by now embraces the very means of tonality, and thus all traditional music. What is false, what has become a vitiated cliché—the canon decides. Tonal sounds, triads in a composition with today's technical purview—they can outdo every dissonance. As such, they can be used if need be, but cautiously and only *in extremis*, for the shock is worse than was once the harshest discord. Everything depends on one's technical purview. The diminished seventh is right and eloquent at the opening of Opus 111. It corresponds to Beethoven's general technical niveau, does it not?—as the tension between the utmost dissonance and consonance possible to him. The principle of tonality and its dynamics lend the chord its specific weight. Which it has lost—through a historical process no one can reverse. Listen to that defunct chord—even isolated from the whole it stands for a general technical state that contradicts our reality. Every sound bears the whole within it, and the whole of history, too. But that is why the ear's judgment of what is right and false is directly and irrefutably tied to it, to this one chord that is not false in itself, quite apart from any abstract reference to the general technical niveau. What we have here is a claim to rightness that the figure places on the artist—a bit harshly, don't you think? Are his endeavours not quickly exhausted simply in executing what is contained within a work's objective requirements? In every bar he dares conceive, the general technical state presents itself to him as the problem, demands of him at every moment that he do justice to it as a whole and to the single right answer it permits him at each moment. The result is that his compositions are nothing more than such answers, nothing more than the solution to technical puzzles. Art becomes criticism—a very honourable thing, who would deny it! It involves a great deal of insubordination within strict obedience, much self-reliance, much courage. But the danger of being uncreative—what do you say? Is it truly still a danger, or already a fixed and settled fact?"

He paused. He gazed at me through his spectacles with moist, reddened eyes, raised his hand in a dainty motion and stroked his hair with two middle fingers. I said:

"What are you waiting for? Am I to admire your mockery? I have never doubted that you know to tell me what I know. Your method of presentation is quite deliberate. In all this, you mean to tell me that for my intents and work I would neither need nor have any one except the Devil. And yet you cannot exclude the theoretical possibility of spontaneous harmony between one's own needs and the moment, the 'rightness'—the possibility of a natural accord out of which one might create with neither constraint nor forethought."

He (laughing): "A very theoretical possibility indeed! Dear boy, the situation is too critical for an uncritical mind to be a match for it! I reject, moreover, the accusation of having cast matters in a tendential light. We no longer need indulge ourselves in dialectic extravagance for your sake. What I do not deny is a certain satisfaction allowed me by the state of the 'work' quite in general. I am against works on the whole. How should I not take some pleasure in the indisposition under which the idea of the musical work languishes. Do not cast the blame on social conditions! I know that it is your inclination and habit to say that such conditions present nothing that would carry sufficient obligation or sanction to assure the harmony of the self-sufficient work. True, but impertinent. The prohibitive difficulties of the work lie deep within the work itself. The historical movement of musical material has turned against the self-contained work. The material shrinks in time, it scorns extension in time, which is the space of the musical work, and leaves time standing vacant. Not out of impotence, not out of an inability to shape form. But rather, an implacable imperative of density—disallowing all superfluity, negating the phrase, shattering all ornament—stands averse to temporal expansion, the very life-form of the work. Work, time, and illusion are one, together falling victim to criticism. It no longer tolerates illusion and games, or the fiction, the self-glorious form, that censures passions and human suffering, assigning them their roles, transposing them into images. Only what is not fictitious, not a game, is still permissible—the unfeigned and untransfigured expression of suffering in its real moment. For suffering's impotence and affliction have swelled till illusion's games can no longer be endured."

I (very ironical): "Touching, touching. The Devil waxes pathetical. The woeful Devil moralizes. Human suffering goes to his heart. To his greater glory, he beshits his way into art. You would have done better not to mention your antipathy to works—not if you did not want me to discern your deductions to be but vain Devil's farts to abuse and injure the work."

He (without annoyance): "So far, so good. Surely you are in fundamental agreement with me that it can be termed neither sentimental nor malicious if one acknowledges the facts of one's world and time. Certain things are no longer possible. The illusion of emotions as a compositorial work of art, music's self-indulgent illusion, has itself become impossible and cannot be maintained—the which has long since consisted of inserting preexisting, formulaic, and dispirited elements as if they were the inviolable necessity of this single occurrence. Or put the other way round: The special occurrence assumes an air as if it were identical with the preexisting, familiar formula. For four hundred years all great music found contentment in pretending such unity was achieved without a breach, took pleasure in conventional universal legitimation, which it endeavours to confuse with its own concerns. My friend, it will work no more. Criticism of ornament, of convention, of abstract generality—they are all one and the same. What falls prey to criticism is the outward show of the bourgeois work of art, an illusion in which music takes part, though it produces no external image. To be sure, by producing no such image, music has the advantage of the other arts, but in the unwearying reconcilement of its specific concerns with the rule of convention, music has nevertheless taken part in this sublime chicanery with might and main. The subordination of expression to all-reconciling generality is the innermost principle of musical illusion. And that is over. The claim to presume the general as harmonically contained within the particular is a self-contradiction. It is all up with conventions once considered prerequisite and compulsory, the guarantors of the game's freedom."

I: "One could know all that and yet acknowledge freedom again beyond any criticism. One could raise the game to a yet higher power by playing with forms from which, as one knows, life has vanished."

He: "I know, I know. Parody. It might be merry if in its aristocratic nihilism it were not so very woebegone. Do you think such tricks promise you much happiness and greatness?"

I (repost angrily): "No."

He: "Short and peevish! But why peevish? Because I put to you friendly questions of conscience, just between us? Because I have shown you your desperate heart and with a savant's insight set before your eyes the downright insuperable difficulties of composing now-a-days? You might hold me in esteem as a savant at least. The Devil surely knows something of music. If I mistake not, you were reading just now in that book by the Christian enamoured of aesthetics? He knew what was what and made a point of my special relation to this fine art—the most Christian of arts, he deems it—posited in the negative, to be sure, employed and developed by Christendom, true, but repudiated and excluded as a demonic realm—and there you have it. A highly theological matter, music—just as is sin, just as am I. The passion of that Christian there for music is true passion, the which is indeed comprehension and addiction in one. True passion is found only in ambiguity and as irony. The highest passion is spent on what is absolutely suspect. . . . No, musical I am, depend on it. And I have played the mocking Judas because of the difficulties in which music, like everything today, finds itself. Should I not have done so? But, indeed, I did so merely to intimate that you should break through it, that you should raise yourself above it to the most dizzying heights of self-admiration and make such things that a holy horror of them should come over you."

I: "To wit: an annunciation. I am to grow osmotic vegetation."

He: "'Tis much of a muchness! Ice flowers or such as are made of starch, sugar, and cellulose—both are nature, and the only question is for which one ought to praise nature the more. Your inclination, my friend, to inquire after what is objective, the so-called truth, while suspecting nothing of value in the subjective, in pure experience, is truly philistine and worth your overcoming. You behold me: Therefore am I here for you. Does it pay to ask whether I really am? Is 'really' not what works, and truth not experience and feeling? What raises you up, what augments your sense of energy and power and mastery is the truth, damn it—and were it ten times a lie viewed from a virtuous angle. And I will assert that an untruth of the sort that enhances energy is a match for every unprofitably virtuous truth. Will assert as well that creative disease, genius-bestowing disease, which takes all hurdles on horseback, springing in drunken boldness from rock to rock, is a thousand times dearer to life than plodding health. Never have I heard anything more stupid than that only sick can come from sick. Life is not squeamish, and cares not a fig for morality. It grasps the bold product of disease, devours, digests it, and no sooner takes it to itself than it is health. Before the fact of life's efficacy, my good man, all distinction of disease and health is undone. A whole horde and generation of receptive lads, all healthy to the core, throw themselves upon the work of the diseased genius whom disease has made a genius, admire, praise, and exalt the work, carry it away with them, refashion it among themselves, bequeath it to the culture, which does not live by homebaked bread alone, but equally by donations and poisons from the apothecary of the Blessed Messengers. Thus saith the untransmogrified Sammael. He guarantees to you not only that toward the end of your hour-glass years the sense of power and mastery will more and more outweigh the pains of the little mermaid and finally mount to a most triumphant well-being, to an enthusiastic surge of health, to the life and manner of a god—that is but the subjective side of the matter, I know; it would not suffice for you, would seem unsolid to you. Then know this: We pledge to you the vital efficacy needed for what you will accomplish with our help. You will lead, you will set the march for the

future, lads will swear by your name, who thanks to your madness will
no longer need to be mad. In their health they will gnaw at your madness, and you will become healthy in them. Do you understand? It is
not merely that you will break through the laming difficulties of the
age—you will break through the age itself, the cultural epoch, which is
to say, the epoch of this culture and its cult, and dare a barbarism, a
double barbarism, because it comes after humanitarianism, after every
conceivable root-canal work and bourgeois refinement. Believe me,
barbarism has a better understanding even of theology than does a culture that has fallen off from the cult, which even in things religious saw
only culture, only humanitarianism, but not excess, not the paradox,
the mystical passion, the ordeal so utterly outside bourgeois experience. I truly hope you are not mazed that Old Clootie speaks of things
religious? 'Sblood! Who else, I would like to know, should speak to
you today of religion? Surely not the liberal theologian? I am by now
the only one who still preserves it! Whom would you credit with theological existence if not me? And who can lead a theological existence
without me? Religion is as assuredly my field, as it is not that of bourgeois culture. Since culture has fallen off from the cult and has made a
cult of itself, it is no longer anything but offal, and after a mere five
hundred years all the world is so weary and surfeited, as if, *salva venia,*
it were force-fed with iron cauldrons."

It was now—or even somewhat earlier, already during that mockage
he had delivered as a fluent lecture on himself as the preserver of religious life, on the Devil's theological existence—that I perceived it: Yet
again the look of the fellow on the couch was changed; he no longer
appeared as the bespectacled musical intellectualist as which he had
spoken to me the while, nor sat he any longer in his corner, but rather
rode *légèrement,* half-sitting upon the rounded arm of the couch, his
fingertips interlaced in his lap and both thumbs stuck out wide. A
small forked beard on his chin bobbed up and down as he spoke, and
above his open mouth, revealing little sharp teeth within, was a moustache ending in stiff twirled points.

And though mummied gainst the frost, could not but laugh at his
metamorphosis into something old and familiar.

"Your very humble servant," say I. "I ought to know you thus, and
I find it courteous of you to read me a private lecture here in my hall.
Given what mimicry has now made of you, I hope to find you ready to
quench my thirst to know and to provide fine proof of your independ-
ent presence, in that you will lecture to me not only on things which
I know of myself, but for once also on such as I would first like to

know. You have lectured to me much on the hour-glass time in which
you deal, and also on the payments in pain to be made now and again
for the lofty life, but not on the end, on that which comes after, the
eternal extinction. My curiosity is for that, and you have, as long as
you have been perched there, made no room for the question in your
discourse. Am I not to know the price in pence and farthings of our
dealing? Give account! What is life like in Old Scratch's house? What
awaits those who have taken you for liege in your horrid hole?"

He (laughs in a high titter): "You would have knowledge of the *pernicies,* of the *confutatio?* I call that pert, I call it the erudite courage of
youth! There is so much time for that yet, immeasurable time, and first
comes so much excitation that you will have other things to do than to
think on the end, or even simply to pay heed to the moment when it
might be time to think on the end. But I would not refuse you the intelligence and need not dress it prettily, for how can you be fretted seriously by a thing still so far off? Except, it is not easy to speak of it
actually—which is to say: Actually one cannot speak of it in any manner whatsoever, because the actuality is not congruous with the words;
one may use and fashion a great many words, yet all of them are but
representative, stand for names that do not exist, can make no claim to
designate that which can never ever be designated and denounced in
words. That is the secret delight and security of hell, that it cannot be
denounced, that it lies hidden from language, that it simply is, but cannot appear in a newspaper, be made public, be brought to critical notice
by words—which is why the words 'subterranean,' 'cellar,' 'thick
walls,' 'soundlessness,' 'oblivion,' 'hopelessness,' are but weak symbols. One must, my good man, be entirely content with *symbolis* when
one speaks of hell, for there all things cease—not only the signifying
word, but everything altogether—that is, indeed, its principal characteristic, and at the same time, just to say something of it very generally,
that is what the newcomer first experiences and what he at first cannot
grasp with his, so to speak, healthy senses and will not understand because reason, or whatever limitation of the understanding it may be,
prevents him from doing so, in short, because it is unbelievable, so unbelievable that it turns a man chalk-white, unbelievable, although in
the very greeting upon arrival it is revealed in a concise and most
forcible form that 'here all things cease,' every mercy, every grace,
every forbearance, every last trace of consideration for the beseeching,
unbelieving objection: 'You cannot, you really cannot do that with a
soul'—but it is done, it happens, and without a word of accountability,
in the sound-tight cellar, deep below God's hearing, and indeed for all

eternity. No, it is bootless to speak of it, for it lies apart from and outside of language, which has nothing to do with it, has no relation to it, and that is also why language never rightly knows which tense to apply to it and makes shift perforce with the future, for as it is said: 'There shall be wailing and gnashing of teeth.' Good, those are a few quoted words, chosen from a rather extreme sphere of language, but for all that, mere weak symbols and with no real connexion to what 'shall be'—unaccountable, in oblivion, between thick walls. It is right to say that it will be quite loud in a sound-tight hell, loud beyond measure, filling the ear to more than overflowing with bawling and squalling, yowling, moaning, bellowing, gurgling, screeching, wailing, croaking, pleading, and exuberant tortured cries, so that none will hear his own tune, for it is smothered in the general, tight, dense, hellish jubilee and abject trilling extracted by the eternal infliction of the unbelievable and unanswerable. Nor to forget the monstrous groaning of lust commingled therein, because an endless torment to which no limit is set—no faltering in its travail, no collapse, no impotence—degenerates instead into obscene pleasure, which is indeed why those with some intuitive knowledge also speak of the 'lusts of hell.' Thereto, however, is linked the element of mockage and extreme ignominy that is bound up in the torment; for this hellish bliss is much the same as a most pitiable taunting of the immeasurable suffering and is accompanied by fingers pointed in scorn and whinnying laughter—whence the doctrine that the damned must bear mockery and shame together with their agony, indeed, that hell is to be defined as a monstrous combination of derision and entirely unbearable sufferings that are nonetheless to be eternally endured. They shall devour their tongues at so great a pain, yet form no fellowship against it, but rather are full of scorn and mockery for one another, and midst trills and groans call out filthiest curses each to each, whereby those most refined and proud, who never let a foul word pass their lips, are forced to employ the filthiest. A portion of their anguish and obscene lust consists in having to muse upon whatever is utterly filthy."

I: "I beg you, this is the first word you have told me concerning the manner of suffering that the damned have to endure there. Pray note that you have actually lectured me only on the effects of hell, not, however, on what in point of fact and deed the damned have to expect there."

He: "Your curiosity is boyish and indiscreet. I note that first and foremost, but am very well aware, my good man, of what lies hid behind it. You undertake to interrogate me in order to be set affright, affright of hell. For thoughts of turning about and rescue, of so-called salvation and a retreat from your promise, lurk at the rear of your mind, and you endeavour to draw upon the *attritio cordis*—that is, the heart's anguish at conditions there—about which you may have heard that through it a man can achieve the state of so-called blessedness. Be informed that is a fully antiquated theology. The doctrine of attrition is scientifically obsolete. What has been proven necessary is *contritio*, the real and true Protestant remorse of sin, which means not merely the fearful penitence of churchly ritual, but inner, religious conversion—and whether you are capable of that, do but ask yourself, and your pride will hasten to answer. The longer, the less will you be able and willing to condescend to *contritio,* inasmuch as the extravagant existence that you will lead is a great pampering, from which willy-nilly one does not find a way back to wholesome mediocrity. Therefore, to your consolation, let it be said that hell will have nothing essentially new to offer you—only that to which you are more or less customed, proudly customed. In its fundament it is merely a continuation of your extravagant existence. To put it in but two words: Its essence, or if you will, its point is that it allows its denizens only the choice between extreme cold and fire that could bring granite to melt—between these two conditions they flee yowling to and fro, for within each the other ever appears a heavenly balm, but is at once, and in the most hellish sense of the word, unbearable. The extremes of it must please you."

I: "It pleases me. Meanwhile I would warn you not to feel all too sure of me. A certain shallowness in your theology could tempt you to it. You depend upon my pride's preventing me from the remorse necessary to salvation, yet do not make account of there being a prideful remorse—that of Cain, who was of the fast opinion that his sin was greater than could e'er be forgiven him. *Contritio* without hope and as utter unbelief in the possibility of grace and forgiveness, as the sinner's deep-rooted conviction that he has behaved too grossly and that even unending goodness will not suffice to forgive his sins—only that is the true remorse, and I would remember you that it is to redemption most proximate, to goodness most irresistible. You will admit that grace can have only a workaday concern for the workaday sinner. In his case the act of grace has little impulsion, is but a dull enterprise. Mediocrity leads no theological life whatsoever. A sinfulness so hopeless that it allows its man fundamentally to despair of hope is the true theological path to salvation."

He: "Sly cap! And where will the likes of you find the simpleness, the naive candour of despair that were the presumption for this hopeless path to salvation? Is it not clear to you that purposed speculation on the charm that great guilt exercises upon goodness renders the very act of its grace utterly impossible?"

I: "And yet it is only by means of this *non plus ultra* that one arrives at the highest enhancement of dramatically theological existence, which is to say: at the most reprobate guilt and, through it, at the last and irresistible provocation of infinite goodness."

He: "Not bad. Truly ingenious. And now I shall tell you that precisely minds of your sort constitute the population of hell. It is not so easy to enter into hell; we would long since suffer a want of space if every Tom and Tib were let in. But your theological type, such an arrant desperado who speculates upon speculation, because speculation is in his blood from his father's side—if he were not the Devil's, why 'twould surely be old craft."

As he says it, and indeed somewhat before, the fellow changes yet again, as clouds are wont to do, and yet by his own account knows it not: sits no longer on the arm of the great chair before me in the hall, but once again in its corner as the male bawd, the cheese-pale master-pimp in his cap, with reddened eyes. And says to me in his nasal, slow, player's voice:

"That we come to an end and conclusion is surely agreeable to you. I have devoted much time and tarrying to deliberate this thing with you—would hope you own as much. You are however an attractive case, I admit it freely. From early on we had an eye on you, on your nimble, haughty mind, on your excellent *ingenium* and *memoriam.* They induced you to study divine sciences, as in your conceit you had devised, but soon you wished no longer to call yourself a theologue, but shoved Holy Writ under the bench and thenceforth held entirely to the *figuris, characteribus,* and *incantationibus* of music, which pleased us not a little. For you, haughtiness's great longing was for things elemental, and you thought to achieve it in the form most conformable to you, there where as algebraic magic it is wed to concordant cunning and calculation and yet all the while is daringly aimed gainst reason and common sense. But did we not know even then that you are too prudent and cold and chaste for what is elemental, and did we not know that in your coy prudence you would find there only vexation and pitiable dullness? And so we were diligent that you should run into our arms, which is to say: the arms of my little one, of Esmeralda, and that you should come by it, by that illumination, the aphrodisiac of the brain, after which you so very desperately longed with body and soul and mind. In short, betwixt us there need be no four crossway in

the Spesser Forest and no circles. We are in league and in business—
with your blood you have certified it and promised yourself to us and
are baptized ours—this visit of mine is intended merely for confirmation. From us you have taken time, genius time, high-flying time, a full
twenty-four years *ab dato recessi,* which we set as your bound. And
when they are over and their course run, the which cannot be foreseen,
and such a time is likewise an eternity—you shall be fetched. In recompense of which we will meanwhile be subject and obedient to you
in all things, and hell shall profit you, if you but renounce all who live,
all the heavenly host and all men, for that must be."

I (blown hard by utter cold): "How? That is new. What would this
clause say?"

He: "It would say renounce. What else? Do you think jealousy is at
home only in the heights and not in the deeps as well? You, fine creature well-created, are promised and betrothed to us. You may not love."

I (must truly laugh): "Not love! Poor Devil! Would you attest to
your reputed stupidity and bell yourself as a cat, by wanting to found
your business and promise on so pliant, so captious a term as—'love'?
Does the Devil propose to prohibit lust? If not, then he must chance
sympathy and even *caritas,* else he is betrayed in consummate fashion.
That which I have come by, the very reason you allege that I am
promised to you—what is its source, pray tell, but love, though poisoned by you at God's leave? The league in which you claim we stand,
has itself to do with love, you ninny. You allege that I wanted it so and
went into the forest, to that four crossway, for the sake of the work.
But it is indeed said that the work itself has to do with love."

He (laughing through his nose): "Do, re, mi! Rest assured that your
psychological stratagems will not snare me any better than do your
theological! Psychology—merciful God, you still hold with that? It is
but a poor, bourgeois, nineteenth-century thing! The epoch is wretchedly sick of it, 'twill soon be a red flag to it, and he who would disrupt
life with psychology will simply earn a thwack on the head. We are entering an age, dear boy, that will not wish to be harried by psychology.... This but in passing. My proviso was clear and upright,
ordained by hell's legitimate zeal. Love is forbidden you insofar as it
warms. Your life shall be cold—hence you may love no human. What
can you be thinking? The illumination leaves your intellect's powers
unsullied to the last, indeed at times enhances them to dazzling rapture—what in the end should be its object but the sweet soul and the
precious life of the affections? A total chilling of your life and of your
relations to humans lies in the nature of things—indeed it already lies

in your nature, verily, we impose nothing new, the small folk make nothing new and strange of you, they do but deftly bolster and magnify all that you are. Is not coldness a precedence with you, just as is that paternal head ache, from which shall come the pains of the little mermaid? We want you cold, till scarcely the flames of production shall be hot enough for you to warm yourself in them. You shall flee into them from the coldness of your life. . . ."

I: "And out of the fire back into the ice. It is evidently an anticipated hell you prepare now for me on earth."

He: "It is extravagant existence, the only one that will suffice for a proud mind. Your arrogancy would truly never wish to exchange it for a lukewarm one. Do I have your hand on it? You shall enjoy it for the work-filled eternity of a human life. And should the hour-glass run out, I shall have good dominion to lead and to rule, after my fashion and at my pleasure to do and to deal with the fine creature well-created— with it all, being body, soul, flesh, blood and goods in all eternity. . . ."

There it was again, the incontinent loathing that had seized me once before, that shook me, together with an even mightier glacial wave of frost off the tight-trousered bawd pressing gainst me anew. I forgot myself in my wild disgust, it was like to a swooning. And then from the corner of the couch I heard Schildknapp's voice saying leisurely:

"You missed nothing, of course. *Giornali* and two games of billiards, a round of Marsala, and the doughty fellows hauled the *governo* over the coals."

I was indeed sitting in my summer suit, by my lamp, the Christian's book upon my knees! Can be naught else: in my indignation, must have chased the bawd away and borne my covers to the adjacent room before my companion arrived.

XXVI

I FIND IT COMFORTING to tell myself that the reader cannot blame me for the extraordinary size of the foregoing chapter, which considerably exceeds the disquieting number of pages in the one on Kretzschmar's lectures. The attendant demand made upon the reader lies outside my authorial responsibility and need not trouble me. Not even consideration for the public's taxable attention span could induce me to subject Adrian's manuscript to any sort of mitigatory editing, to break up the "dialogue" (please note the protesting quotation marks I have provided the word, though, to be sure, without concealing from myself that they can remove only a part of the horror inherent in it), to break up the conversation, then, into individually numbered sections. With painful reverence I had to reproduce a given, to transcribe it from Adrian's music paper to my manuscript; and I did so not only word for word, but also, I dare say, letter for letter—often laying my pen aside, interrupting myself in order to recover, to measure my study with pensive steps, or to throw myself on the sofa, hands clasped across my brow; so that in point of fact, as strange as it may sound, a chapter that I needed only to copy out did not proceed from my often trembling hand any more quickly than previous ones of my own composition.

Thoughtful, meaningful copying is indeed as intense and time-consuming an endeavor as putting one's own thoughts to paper (at least it is for me; but Monsignor Hinterpförtner likewise agrees with me on this); and just as at earlier points the reader may have underestimated the number of days and weeks that I have devoted to my late friend's life story, so, too, his notion of the point in time at which I am composing these present lines will fall short of the mark. He may smile at my pedantry, but I consider it proper to let him know that since I began this account almost a year has come and gone and April 1944 arrived during the writing of the latest chapters.

It goes without saying that by this date I mean the point marking my present activity—not the one to which my narrative has advanced, for that is the autumn of 1912, twenty-two months prior to the outbreak of the previous war, when Adrian returned to Munich from Palestrina with Rüdiger Schildknapp and for his part took temporary lodging in a small hotel (the Pension Gisella) in Schwabing. I do not know why this double-entry account of time intrigues me, and why I am compelled to call attention to it—to both its personal and objective forms, the time in which the narrator moves and that in which his narrative takes place. It is a peculiar intertwining of time's courses, which are ordained moreover to be bound up with yet a third—that is, with the time the reader will one day take for a receptive reading of what is told here, so that he will be dealing with a threefold ordering of time: his own, that of the chronicler, and that of history.

I will not lose myself any farther in these speculations, which in my own eyes bear the stamp of a certain agitated idleness, and will merely add that the word "history" applies with far more dire vehemence to the time in which, rather than to that about which, I write. In the last few days the battle for Odessa raged with heavy losses, but in the end that famous city on the Black Sea fell into the hands of the Russians—though, to be sure, without the enemy's having been able to disrupt our tactical regrouping. Nor will he be capable of doing so in Sevastopol, either, yet another of our pawns that the apparently superior foe now intends, it seems, to wrest from us. Meanwhile the terror of the almost daily air raids on our nicely encircled Fortress Europe increases to dimensions beyond conceiving. What good does it do that many of these monsters, raining destruction with ever-growing explosive power, fall victim to our heroic defenses? Thousands of them darken the skies of this brashly united continent, and more and more of our cities collapse in ruin. Leipzig, which plays such a significant role in Leverkühn's evolution, in the tragedy of his life, has recently borne the full impact: Its famous publishing district is, I sadly hear, only a heap of rubble and an immeasurable wealth of literary and educational material is now the spoil of destruction—a heavy loss not only for us Germans, but also for a whole world that cares about culture. That world, however, is apparently willing—whether blindly or correctly, I dare not decide—to take the loss into the bargain.

Yes, I fear it will be our ruin that a fatally inspired policy led us simultaneously into conflict with two powers: the first, greatest in manpower and filled, moreover, with revolutionary zeal; the second, mightiest in productive capacity—and it now appears that the American machinery of production did not even have to run at full throttle to spew an overwhelming profusion of implements of war. To learn that enfeebled democracies do indeed know how to use these dreadful tools is a startling, a sobering experience, disabusing us more and more each day of the fallacy that war is a German prerogative and that in the art of force others must surely prove to be dilettantes and bunglers. We have begun (and here Monsignor Hinterpförtner and I are no longer the exception) to expect truly anything and everything from Anglo-Saxon military technology, and tension rises with the fear of invasion. An attack on our European castello—or should I say our prison, or perhaps our madhouse?—is expected from all sides, with superior arms and millions of soldiers, and only the most impressive descriptions of our preparations against an enemy landing (preparations that look to be truly phenomenal and are meant to protect us and our continent from the loss of our current leaders) are able to provide a psychological counterbalance to the general dread of what is to come.

Certainly the time in which I write has disproportionately greater historical momentum than that about which I write: Adrian's time, which led him only to the threshold of our incredible epoch; and it seems to me as if one should call out to him, call out a "Lucky you!", a heartfelt "Rest in peace!" to him and all those who are no longer with us and were not with us as it began. Adrian is secure from our own times—that fact is dear to me, I value it, and in exchange for being permitted an awareness of it, I gladly accept the terror of the time in which I live on. It seems to me as if I am standing in his place and living in his stead, as if I bear the burden that has been spared his shoulders, in short, as if I were showing him my love by relieving him of the task of living; and this idea, illusory and foolish though it be, does me good, it flatters my constantly cherished wish to serve him, to help and defend him—the same desire that was granted such scant fulfillment during my friend's lifetime.

*

I STILL FIND IT remarkable that Adrian's stay at his pension in Schwabing lasted only a few days and that he made no attempt whatever to track down a better permanent residence in the city. While still in Italy, Schildknapp had written his former landlords on Amalien Strasse and secured his familiar quarters anew. Adrian had no intention of renting a room again from Frau Senator Rodde, or even of remaining in Munich. His silent resolve had apparently been fixed a long time before—so that he did not even make a preliminary journey to Pfeiffering near Waldshut to reconnoiter and come to some agreement, but substituted for it a simple telephone conversation, and a very brief one at that. He called the Schweigestills from the Pension Gisella—it was Mother Else herself who answered the phone—introduced himself as one of the two bicyclists who had once been permitted to inspect the house and farm, and inquired whether and at what price they would be willing to rent him a bedroom on the second floor, with use of the abbot's study on the ground floor during the day. Frau Schweigestill put aside for now the question of price, which turned out to be very moderate, including board and maid service; she first determined with which of her two visitors that day she was dealing, the writer or the musician, learned (while obviously mulling over her impressions from that day) that this was the musician, and then expressed her misgivings about his request, solely in his own interest and from his perspective— and this too put only in a way that suggested he ought to know what was best for him. They, the Schweigestills, she said, did not regularly let rooms out as a business, but only occasionally took in renters and boarders, on a case by case basis so to speak; the gentlemen could have concluded that right off from what she had told them that day, and whether he, the caller, represented such an instance, such a case, she would have to leave him to be the judge of that. He would find things awfully quiet and monotonous there with them—primitive, too, by the by, as far as comforts went: no bathroom, no toilet, just a standard farm outhouse, and she wondered why a gentleman who was, if she understood rightly, not yet thirty and pursued one of the fine arts would want to take quarters in the country, such a long way off from places where cultural things went on. Or rather, "wondered" was not the right word, it wasn't her or her husband's way to wonder about things, and so maybe, if it was exactly what he was looking for, because most people wonder far too much, really, why then he could come right ahead. But it was worth considering that especially Max, her husband, and she herself, too, were anxious that such an arrangement not be done just on a whim, with notice given after just a short try at it, but that it be seen as something long-term from the start, don't y' know? and so on.

He would be coming for good, Adrian replied, and the matter had

been under consideration for a long time now. The kind of life awaiting him had been carefully weighed, found good, and embraced. The
price of one hundred twenty marks a month was acceptable. He would
leave the choice of bedrooms upstairs to her and was looking forward
to using the abbot's study. In three days he would be moving in.

And that is what happened. Adrian used his brief stay in the city for
meetings with a copyist who had been suggested to him (by Kretzschmar, I think), a man named Griepenkerl, the first bassoonist with
the Zapfenstösser Orchestra, who earned a little extra money with this
sideline; Adrian left a part of the score of *Love's Labour's Lost* in his
hands. He had not quite completed work on it in Palestrina, was still
orchestrating the two last acts, and was not yet clear in his own mind
about the overture, which he had written in sonata form but whose
original conception had been drastically altered by the introduction of
that striking second theme—quite foreign to the opera itself and yet assuming such a brilliant role in the recapitulation and final allegro.
There was, moreover, the laborious task of entering tempi and performance markings, which he had neglected to note during the composition of extensive passages. It was clear to me as well that it was not by
chance that the completion of the work and the end of his sojourn in
Italy failed to coincide. Even had he consciously striven for such a co-
ordination, a subconscious plan prevented it. He was much too much
a man of the *semper idem* and of self-assertion against circumstance to
view as desirable a change in life's scenery that would be simultaneous
with the completion of a project pursued in the previous setting. For
the sake of inner continuity, he said to himself, it would be better to
bring a remnant of the project belonging to the old conditions along
into the new and to cast his inner eye on some new project only when
the new externals had become routine.

Sending two boxes of books and belongings by freight and carrying
his always rather light baggage (including a portfolio housing his score
and a rubber basin that had served him as a bathtub even in Italy), he
boarded a train at Starnberger station, one of the locals that stopped
not only in Waldshut, but also, ten minutes later, at his goal in Pfeiffering. It was late October, the weather was still dry, though already raw
and gloomy. Leaves were falling. The son of the Schweigestill household, Gereon, the same fellow who had been trying out the new
manure-spreader, a rather standoffish and abrupt young man, but a
farmer who knew his business it seemed, was waiting for him outside
the little station, seated on the box of a char-à-banc with a high frame
that rode hard, and while porters loaded the baggage, he let the lash of

his whip play across the backs of the team, two muscular bays. Only a few words were exchanged during the ride. From the train Adrian had already recognized the Rohmbühel with its wreath of trees and the gray mirror of Klammer Pool; now from close-by his eyes lingered on these features. The baroque cloister of the Schweigestill house soon came into view; in the open square of its courtyard, the vehicle pulled around the obstacle of the old elm, whose leaves for the most part now lay upon the bench encircling it.

Outside the gate with its religious coat-of-arms stood Frau Schweigestill and Clementina, her daughter, a brown-eyed country girl dressed in modest country garb. Their words of greeting were lost in the barking of the watchdog, who trampled his bowls in his excitement and almost tugged loose his house bedded with straw. It was to no avail that both mother and daughter, as well as the dairymaid (Waltpurgis), who with dungcaked feet helped unload the baggage, called to him with their "Kaschperl, now whist!" (a dialect form of the even more archaic "husht"). The dog continued to rage, and then Adrian, after watching and smiling at him for a time, walked over. "Suso, Suso," he said, without raising his voice, but in a certain surprised tone of admonishment, and behold: Presumably as a result of the soothing, buzzing sound, the animal calmed down almost immediately and let the wizard stretch out a hand and pat his old battle-scarred skull—and there was deep seriousness in those yellow eyes gazing up at him.

"My respects, you're a brave man," Frau Else said when Adrian returned to the gate. "Most people are afraid of the beast, and when it carries on like that you can't blame a body, either. The young teacher in the village who used to come tutor our kids—my, my, he wasn't no more than a puppy himself—would say every time: 'That dog of yours, Frau Schweigestill, scares me!'"

"Yes, yes," Adrian said with a laugh and a nod, walked into the house, into the pungent, tobacco-laden air, and went upstairs, where his landlady led him down the whitewashed, musty corridor to the bedroom assigned to him, with its brightly painted wardrobe and its bed piled high with fresh featherbeds. Someone had added the final touch of a green armchair, and at its feet, to cover the pine floor, lay a rag rug. Gereon and Waltpurgis set his bags down on it.

Both here and on the way back downstairs, they began to talk about arrangements for the guest's comfort and daily regimen, continuing and then settling the matter below in the abbot's study, that patriarchal room so rich in character, of which Adrian had long since taken emotional possession: a large jug of hot water in the morning, strong coffee in his bedroom, the hours for meals—Adrian was not to take them with the family, that had not been expected, they took them too early for him, besides; a place would be set just for him at half-past one and at eight, and the best spot, Frau Schweigestill suggested, would be the large room at the front (the rustic drawing room with its Winged Victory and square piano), which was always at his disposal in any case. And she promised a light diet: milk, eggs, toast, vegetable soups, a good rare beefsteak with spinach at midday, topped off with a modest omelet filled with apple jelly—in short, fare that both nourished and was agreeable to a delicate stomach like his.

"The stomach, my dear, is mostly not the stomach at all, it's the head, the delicate, overtaxed head, that has such powerful influence over the stomach, even when there's nothing wrong with it," as everyone knew from seasickness and migraine headaches. . . . Aha, so he had the migraine sometimes, and right nasty, too? She had thought so! She had indeed thought so just now up in the bedroom, when he had checked the shutters to see how dark he could get the room; for darkness, lying in the dark, night, black, with no light whatever in the eyes, that was just the thing, as long as the misery lasted, plus real strong tea, made real sour with lots of lemon. Frau Schweigestill was not unacquainted with the migraine—which was to say: She hadn't made its personal acquaintance, but early on her Max had suffered periodically from it; in time the pains had gone away. She wouldn't hear of her guest apologizing for his infirmity and that he had smuggled himself into her house as a patient with a recurrent fever, so to speak, and simply replied: "Oh go on with you!" A body would have had to think something of the sort, she said, since for a man to leave a place where culture went on and come out here to Pfeiffering, why, he would surely have his reasons, and apparently this was a case that had every claim to her understanding, "don't y' know, Herr Leverkühn?" And this was a place of understanding, if not of culture. Plus all the rest that the good woman had to say.

That day as they stood or walked about, she and Adrian made arrangements that, perhaps to the surprise of them both, would regulate his external life for eighteen years. The village carpenter was called in to measure the space next to the door of the abbot's study for shelves that could hold Adrian's books, but that were not to be any higher than the old wainscoting beneath the stamped leather; it was also agreed that the chandelier with its stubs of wax candles should be electrified. In time various other changes were made to the room, which was destined to witness the birth of so many masterpieces, all of them more or less still withheld today from public awareness and admiration. The worn planks were soon covered by a carpet that filled almost the entire floor and proved only too necessary in winter; and to the corner bench, which except for the Savonarola chair at the desk had provided the only place to sit, there was added only a few days later a very deep reading and lounging chair upholstered in gray velvet—but with nothing fussy about it, that was not Adrian's style—and purchased from Bernheimer in Munich: a commendable piece, which, when its matching footstool, a cushioned taboret, was shoved up against it, deserved to be called more a chaise longue than an ordinary divan and which served its owner well for almost two decades.

I mention these purchases (carpet and chair) from that palace of household furnishings on Maximilian Platz partly in order to make it clear that commuting into the city was made quite convenient by numerous trains, including several express trains that took less than an hour, and that by settling at Pfeiffering Adrian certainly had not—as one might conclude from Frau Schweigestill's way of putting things—buried himself in total isolation and cut himself off from "cultural life." Even when he would attend some evening affair, a concert at the Academy or one by the Zapfenstösser Orchestra, an opera performance, or a party (and that did occur as well), he could still catch an eleven o'clock train for the trip home that night. To be sure, he could not then count on being fetched at the station by the Schweigestill's vehicle; in such cases advance arrangements could be made with a livery service in Waldshut. But in fact on clear winter nights he loved to take the path beside the pond and make his way home to the slumbering Schweigestill farm on foot—but also knew to give the signal from some distance to keep Kaschperl or Suso, who was free of his chain at that hour, from setting up a racket. He did this with a metal whistle whose tone was adjustable by a screw and that could produce a frequency so high that the human ear barely perceived it even at close range, whereas its effect on the quite differently evolved eardrum of a dog was very powerful, even from astonishing distances, and Kaschperl would keep still as a mouse whenever the secret tone that no one else could hear pierced the night.

It was curiosity, but also the pull that my friend's personality—coolly aloof, indeed shy in its arrogance—had on so many people, that soon drew this or that visitor in the opposite direction, to leave the city and look in on his retreat. I will grant Schildknapp the precedence he had in reality—naturally he was the first who came out to see how Adrian was doing at the spot they had discovered together, and later on, especially in summertime, he often spent weekends with him in Pfeiffering. Zink and Spengler dropped by on their bikes, for while shopping in town Adrian had paid a call on Ramberg Strasse and the two painter friends had learned from the Rodde girls of his return and new residence. It must be presumed that the initiative for a visit in Pfeiffering had come from Spengler, since Zink, the more talented and enterprising of the two, but of much less refined humanity, had no sense whatever for Adrian's personality and had simply come along as the inseparable companion—with Austrian blandishments, with "I kiss your hand," with shammed "mercy-me" admiration for everything he was shown, with basic antipathy. In return, his clowning, the ludicrous uses to which he put his long nose and those close-set eyes that had such a ridiculously hypnotic effect on women, evoked no response from Adrian, who was usually so gratefully receptive to anything comic. But comedy is marred by vanity; Zink the faun, moreover, did indeed have a boring way of listening for any word in a conversation that might be read as a double-entendre he could then pick up on—a mania that, as Zink was well aware, did not exactly delight Adrian.

Spengler, blinking and with a dimple in his cheek, would laugh in hearty bleats at such incidents. Sexuality interested him in a literary sense; for him sex and intellect were closely linked—nor was he so very wrong about that. His refinement (as we well know), his sense for higher things, for esprit and critique, was based in the accident of his delicate relationship with the sexual realm, with a physical fixation on it, which was a bit of pure bad luck and not at all characteristic of his temperament or passion in that regard. In the fashion of that aesthetic epoch of culture, which seems now to have sunk into oblivion, he would smile and chatter on about artistic events, literary and bibliophilic publications, would pass along Munich gossip and drolly linger over a story about how the Grand Duke of Weimar and the dramatist Richard Voss had once been traveling together in the Abruzzi when they were waylaid by an authentic band of robbers—which had most certainly been arranged by Voss. He paid Adrian clever compliments on his Brentano Songs, which he had purchased and studied at his piano. On the same occasion he also remarked that to occupy oneself with these songs was to spoil oneself in a categorical and almost dangerous fashion—afterward, one would not be easily pleased by anything else in the genre. And said some other very fine things about being spoiled—which primarily concerned the artist, given his needs and wants, but could be dangerous for him. For with every completed work he only made his life more difficult and ultimately probably even impossible, since by spoiling himself with the extraordinary and ruining his taste for all else, he must in the end be driven to disintegration, to do what it was impossible to do or execute. The problem of the highly gifted person was how, despite being progressively spoiled, despite an ever-spreading nausea, he could still hold to the doable.

That is how clever Spengler was—though only on the basis of his specific fixation, as the blinking and bleating suggested. After him, Jeannette Scheurl and Rudi Schwerdtfeger came to tea, to see where and how Adrian was living.

Jeannette and Schwerdtfeger sometimes played music together, both for the guests of old Madame Scheurl and privately, and so they had arranged for a joint trip to Pfeiffering, with Rudolf in charge of telephoning their plans. Whether the suggestion was his or came from Jeannette cannot be determined. They even argued about it in Adrian's presence, each giving credit to the other for the attention paid him. Jeannette's droll impulsiveness speaks for her as the initiator; but, then again, the notion fits all too nicely with Rudi's amazingly confiding familiarity. He appeared to be of the opinion that he and Adrian had achieved the intimacy of familiar pronouns two years before, whereas that form of address had happened only very occasionally, at carnival, and then certainly only on a one-sided basis—on Rudi's, that is. But he now blithely started in with it again and backed off (without taking any offense, by the way) only after Adrian refused a second or third time to respond accordingly. Fräulein Scheurl's undisguised amusement at this defeat of attempted familiarity did not affect him at all. No trace of confusion was apparent in those blue eyes that could burrow with such urgent naiveté into the eyes of anyone who said something clever, cultured, or erudite. Even today, in thinking back on Schwerdtfeger, I ask myself to what extent he actually understood Adrian's loneliness and the neediness, the ease of seduction that such solitude brings with it, and so tried to use it to prove his own winning, or to put it crudely, fawning charms. Without doubt he was born to win and conquer; but I fear I would be unfair to view him from only that side. He was also a good fellow and an artist, and I prefer to regard the fact that later on he and Adrian did indeed address one another with familiar pronouns and first names not as some cheap triumph of Schwerdtfeger's coquetry, but rather as the result of his honest recognition of the value of this extraordinary man, of a genuine fondness for him, from which he drew the amazing imperturbability that finally won the victory over the coldness of melancholy—a calamitous victory, by the way. But I am falling into my old bad habits and getting ahead of myself.

In her big hat, from whose brim a delicate veil was pulled down over her nose, Jeannette Scheurl played Mozart on the square piano in the Schweigestill's rustic salon, and Rudi Schwerdtfeger whistled along with an artistry so enjoyable it was almost absurd. I myself later heard him do it at the Roddes' and Schlaginhaufens', and he told me how even as a very young boy, before he ever took violin lessons, he had begun to develop the skill, practicing just whistling along to a piece of music no matter where he happened to be, and had later continued to perfect his mastery of the art. It was brilliant—a proficiency that was fit for a cabaret performance, almost more impressive than his violin playing, and for which he must have innately been especially favored. The cantilena was utterly pleasant, its character more like that of a violin than a flute, the phrasing masterful, and the short notes, whether staccato or legato, almost never failed to be delightfully precise. In short, it was exquisite and was lent special merriment by the combination of serious artistry and the cobbler-lad's nonchalance that simply comes with the technique. One laughed and applauded automatically, and even Schwerdtfeger would laugh in his boyish way, easing his jacket into place with a shrug and giving that quick grimace with one corner of his mouth.

These, then, were Adrian's first guests in Pfeiffering. And soon thereafter I arrived myself and on Sundays would walk beside him around his pond and up the Rohmbühel. I spent only the one winter yet, after his return from Italy, apart from him; at Easter 1913 I obtained my position at the high school in Freising—the Catholic heritage of my family working to my advantage. I left Kaisersaschern and with my wife and child settled by the banks of the Isar, in this venerable town that has been a bishopric for many centuries, where, in easy communication with the capital and so, too, with my friend, I have spent my life (with the exception of a few months during the war) and have been a loving, unnerved witness to the tragedy of his.

XXVII

GRIEPENKERL THE BASSOONIST had done a very creditable piece of work in copying the score of *Love's Labour's Lost.* More or less the first words Adrian spoke to me when we met again concerned this almost perfectly flawless copy and what joy it gave him. He also showed me a letter that the man had written while still engaged in his punctilious task and in which he disclosed, in a most intelligent fashion, a kind of worried enthusiasm for the object of his painful endeavor. He could not express, he wrote its composer, how the work took his breath away in its boldness, its novelty. He could not admire enough the delicate subtlety of its workmanship, the versatility of rhythms, the technique of orchestration by which the complexity of interweaving voices was often kept perfectly lucid, and above all the compositional fantasy demonstrated by the way a given theme was transformed in manifold variations: for instance, the use of the lovely and yet semi-comic music associated with the character of Rosaline, or better, with Berowne's desperate feelings for her, in the middle section of the final act's three-part bourrée, itself a witty revival of an old French dance—he called it simply brilliant and deft in the very best sense. He then added: This bourrée was more than a little characteristic of the playfully archaic element of conventional restraint, which contrasted so charmingly, and yet challengingly with the "modern," with what was free and more than free, rebellious, as well as with passages that scorned every restraint of musical key; and so he had to fear that those sections of the score, with all their unfamiliarity and aggressive heresy, would be more inaccessible to an audience than would the orthodox and strict parts. For they often ended in a numbing speculation of notes, more intellectual than artistic, in a tonal mosaic that was no longer even effective as music, but seemed intended more to be read than heard, etc.

We laughed.

"All I need is to hear about hearing!" said Adrian. "In my opinion it suffices fully if it is heard just once—that is, when the composer conceives it."

After a while, he added, "As if people ever hear what he heard then. Composing means commissioning the Zapfenstösser Orchestra to perform an angelic chorus. And by the way, I consider choirs of angels to be highly speculative."

For my part I disagreed with Griepenkerl on his sharp distinction between the work's "archaic" and "modern" elements. They merged into each other, they interpenetrated, I said, and Adrian accepted that, but showed little inclination to discuss the completed product, and instead seemed to want to leave it behind as finished and no longer of any interest. He left it to me to consider what to do with it, where to send it, to whom to show it. That Wendell Kretzschmar should read the score—that was important to him. He sent it to him in Lübeck, where that stutterer was still in charge, and a year later, even though war had already broken out, the theater there did indeed produce the opera, in a German version in which I had some involvement—with the result that two-thirds of the audience left the theater in the middle of the performance, just as is said to have happened in Munich six years before at the premiere of Debussy's *Pelléas et Mélisande.* It was repeated only twice, and for the time being the work got no farther than the Hanseatic city on the Trave. And the local critics were almost unanimous in their agreement with the lay audience and sneered at the "decimating music" Herr Kretzschmar had taken on. Only in the *Lübeck Market Courier* did an old professor of music named Jimmerthal (doubtlessly long since deceased) speak of an error in judgment that time would set right, and in a quaint, old-fashioned style declared the opera to be a work full of profound music that contained the future within it, its composer certainly a mocker, but at the same time "a god-witted man." That touching phrase, which I had never heard or read before, nor ever ran across again, either, made a most peculiar impression on me; and just as I have never forgotten the astute, but queer bird who used it, so too, I think, he will be held in honor by the same posterity he called as witnesses against his flabby and obtuse fellow critics.

At the time when I moved to Freising, Adrian was busy composing several lieder and songs, both in German and in another language,

English, to be precise. He had first returned to William Blake and had set to music a very strange poem by this author he so loved: "Silent, silent night," with its four stanzas, each of three lines ending on one rhyme, the last of which reads, curiously enough:

> But an honest joy
> Does itself destroy
> For a harlot coy.

The composer had provided these elusively scandalous verses with very simple harmonies, which in comparison to the musical language of the whole seemed more ragged, more eerie and "false" than the most audacious dissonances, and which in fact allowed the triad to come to monstrous fruition. "Silent, silent night" is for piano and voice, whereas Adrian provided two hymns by Keats (the eight stanzas of "Ode to a Nightingale" and the shorter "Ode on Melancholy") with an accompaniment by string quartet—to be sure, leaving far behind, and below, any traditional meaning of the term "accompaniment." For in fact this consisted of an extremely ingenious form of variation, in which not a single note by the voice or the four instruments did not belong to the theme. Holding sway here, without interruption, is the tightest linkage of the voices, so that it is not a relationship between melody and accompaniment, but in the strictest sense between constantly alternating principal and secondary parts.

These are splendid pieces—and until now have been left almost mute, for which their native language is to blame. I had to smile at the odd depth of feeling with which the composer accedes to the yearning for the sweet life of the South awakened by the "immortal bird" in the soul of the poet of the "Nightingale"—since in Italy Adrian had never shown much enthusiastic gratitude for the consolations of a sunny world that lets man forget "the weariness, the fever, and the fret—here where men sit and hear each other groan." Without doubt, what is musically the most precious and artful moment comes with the melting and vanishing of the dream at the end, with the

> Adieu! the fancy cannot cheat so well
> As she is fam'd to do, deceiving elf.
> Adieu! adieu! thy plaintive anthem fades
>
> .   .   .
>
> Fled is that music:—Do I wake or sleep?

I can well understand how these odes presented a challenge to wreathe their vaselike beauty with music—not to make them more perfect, for they are perfect, but rather to give stronger articulation to their proud, sorrowful charm, to set it in relief, to lend fuller permanency to the precious moment of each detail than is ever granted to the soft breath of words: to such moments of compressed imagery as the declaration in the third stanza of "Melancholy" that "in the very temple of Delight veil'd Melancholy has her sovran shrine, though seen of none save him whose strenuous tongue can burst Joy's grape against his palate fine"— which is simply dazzling and scarcely leaves much for music to add. Perhaps it can merely avoid doing damage by speaking along *ritardando*. I have often heard it said that a poem should not be too good if it is to provide a good song. Music does much better when its task is to gild the mediocre—just as virtuoso acting shines most brightly in poor plays. But Adrian's relationship to art was too proud and critical for him to have wished to let his light shine in the darkness. He truly had to entertain the highest intellectual esteem if he was to feel himself called upon as a musician, and so the German poem to which he devoted his productive energies was likewise of highest rank, even if it lacked the intellectual distinction of Keats's lyric poetry. Literary pre-eminence found an advocate here in something more monumental, in the exalted and exuberant fervor of religious, hymnic praise, which in its invocations and descriptions of majesty and mildness ceded even more to music, and confronted it more guilelessly, than did the Greek nobleness of those British images.

It was Klopstock's ode "The Festival of Spring," the famous song about the "drop in the bucket" to which Leverkühn composed music, with only slight abridgments of the text, for baritone, organ, and string orchestra: a thrilling piece of work, performances of which, with the help of courageous conductors open to new music, were arranged at several centers of music in Germany, as well as in Switzerland, during the First German World War and for several years afterward—to the enthusiastic applause of a minority and, granted, to snickering philistine objections as well, of course—such performances contributing significantly, by the twenties at the latest, to the aura of esoteric fame that began to surround the name of my friend. But I wish to say the following: As deeply as I was moved (if not actually surprised) by this eruption of religious emotion, whose effect was all the more pure and devout in its refusal to employ cheap effects (no rippling harps, though the text truly almost demands them; no timpani to depict the thunder of the Lord); as much as certain beauties or grand truths of praise touched my heart, and did so without any banal tone-painting whatever—such as the oppressively slow transformation of the black cloud;

the thunder's twofold cry of "Jehovah!" while the "demolished woodland steams" (a powerful passage); or the chord, so new and transfigured, sounded by the high register of the organ and strings at the end,
when divinity is no longer in the weather, but approaches in hushed
rustlings, amidst which "spans the arching bow of peace"—nevertheless, at the time I did not understand the work in its true psychological
meaning, in its secret intent and anguish, in its fear that seeks grace in
praising. Did I at that time know the document my readers now know
as well, the written account of the "dialogue" in the stony hall? Before
knowing it, I could only conditionally have called myself "a partner in
your sorrow's mysteries," as the "Ode on Melancholy" puts it at one
point—my sole justification being a vague concern I had felt since boyhood for the health of Adrian's soul, rather than any true knowledge of
its state. Only later did I come to understand the composition of "Festival of Spring" to be the atoning sacrifice to God that it was: a work
of *attritio cordis,* created—as I now shudder to surmise—under the
threats of that visitor who insisted on his visibility.

But there was yet another sense in which at the time I did not understand the personal and intellectual background of this composition
based on Klopstock's poem. I should have seen its connection with
conversations that I had with him around that time, or better that he
had with me, when with great enthusiasm and urgency he would report to me about studies and researches that were quite remote from
my own curiosity and conception of science: exciting additions to his
knowledge of nature and the cosmos, which I found highly reminiscent of his father and that pensive mania to "speculate the elements."

Indeed, the composer of "Festival of Spring" did not concur with
the poet's statement that he would rather not "fling himself entire in
the ocean of the worlds," but wished only to hover adoring above the
earth, above the "drop in the bucket." Adrian most certainly did fling
himself into those immeasurable realms that astrophysical science attempts to measure—only to arrive at measurements, numbers, orders
of magnitude to which the human mind can no longer relate at all and
that lose themselves in theory and abstraction, in the domain of the
non-sensory, if not to say, nonsensical. But I also would not have it be
forgotten that it all began with his hovering about the "drop," a word
that indeed does not fit badly, since the earth consists primarily of water, of the water of its seas, which "did escape the Almighty's hand"
when the grand design was hurled into being—that is, I say, it all really
began with his inquiries into that drop and its dark hiding places; for
the wonders of the sea's deep, life's follies there below, where no ray of

sun can penetrate, were the first such things that Adrian told me about, and in a peculiar, whimsical way that both amused and perplexed me—that is, in a style as if he had personally seen and experienced it all.

Needless to say, he had only read about these things, had acquired the appropriate books and fed his imagination with them; but whether he was so committed to the subject and thus retained its images so clearly, or whether it was simply some whim or other, he pretended that he had made the descent himself—in the area of the Bermudas to be precise, several sea miles east of St. George, where the natural fantastic phenomena of the abyss had been shown him by a companion named Capercailzie, whom he described as an American scholar and with whom he claimed to have set a new record for depth.

I have very vivid memories of this conversation. It took place during a weekend I spent at Pfeiffering, after a simple supper that Clementina Schweigestill—austerely dressed as always—had served us in the large room with the piano. And then she had brought us each a pint mug of beer to the abbot's study, and there we sat, smoking cigars—good, light Zechbauers. It was the time of day when Suso the dog—or rather, Kaschperl—had already been set free to roam the courtyard.

And it was then that Adrian indulged himself in the joke of telling me in the most graphic detail how he and Mr. Capercailzie had climbed into a spherical diving bell, measuring only four feet in interior diameter and fitted out much like a stratospheric balloon, and together had been dropped from a crane on the convoy ship into seas that were of monstrous depth here. It had been more than simply exciting—at least for him, if not for his mentor or cicerone, whom he had induced to take him along, but who took the matter more coolly, since this was not his first descent. Their situation in the confines of the two-ton hollow ball was anything but comfortable, their compensation being the knowledge that their shelter was absolutely dependable: Built perfectly watertight, it was equal to the enormous pressures and came equipped with an ample supply of oxygen, a telephone, high-powered searchlights, and quartz windows for viewing on every side. All in all they had remained inside it beneath the ocean's surface for more than three hours, which passed in no time thanks to the views and glimpses afforded them onto a world whose silent, alien madness was justified—and explained, so to speak—by its inherent lack of contact with our own.

All the same, it had been a strange moment, one to make the heart falter a bit, when one morning at nine o'clock the four-hundred-pound armored door closed behind them and they glided down from the ship to be immersed in their element. At first they had been surrounded by crystal-clear water illumined by the sun. But this illumination by the greater light of the interior of our "drop in the bucket" extends only 187 feet; then everything ceases, or better: A new world, in which we are no longer at home and have no point of reference, begins—a world Adrian claimed to have penetrated and, together with his guide, to have spent there a good half-hour at nearly fourteen times that depth, at around 2,500 feet, conscious at almost every moment of the fact that 500,000 tons of pressure were being exerted on their shelter.

On the way down, the water had gradually taken on a gray hue, the color of darkness, and yet still mixed with some intrepid light, which did not easily give up forging ahead—its nature and will were to illuminate, and it did so to its utmost, lending, even as it fell behind, yet more color than before to the next stage of its exhaustion. Through their quartz windows the travelers now stared out into a blue-black difficult to describe but perhaps best compared to the duskiness along the horizon of a sky swept by föhn winds. Then, to be sure, long before the bathometer read 2,400, then 2,500 feet, all-around there reigned perfect blackness—the darkness of interstellar space unvisited for eternities by even the weakest ray of sun, the eternally silent and maiden night, which now had to endure being illumined by and examined under a brutal artificial beam, not of cosmic origins, but brought down from the world above.

Adrian spoke of the prickling sensation that came with realizing one was exposing to sight what had never been seen, was not to be seen, had never expected to be seen. The accompanying sense of indiscretion, indeed of sinfulness, could not be fully mitigated and neutralized by the exhilaration of science, which must be permitted to press onward as far as it is given wit to go. It was all too clear that the incredible oddities—some ghastly, some ludicrous—that nature and life had managed here, these forms and physiognomies that seemed to bear scarcely any kinship with those on earth above and to belong to some other planet, were the products of concealment, the flaunting of their having been hidden in eternal darkness. The arrival of a human spacecraft on Mars—or perhaps, better, on the side of Mercury eternally turned away from the sun—could not have caused a greater sensation among whatever residents may live on those "nearby" bodies than did the appearance here below of the Capercailzian diving bell. The demotic curiosity shown by these abstruse creatures of the abyss as they crowded around the house of their guests had been indescribable—and likewise indescribable, amid the blur of flitting forms scurrying past the gondola's windows, had been the mad grotesqueries, organic nature's secret faces: predatory mouths, shameless teeth, telescopic eyes; paper nautiluses, hatchetfish with goggles aimed upward, heteropods, and sea butterflies up to six feet long. Even things that drift passively in the current, tentacled monsters of slime—the Portuguese man-of-war, the octopus, and jellyfish—seemed caught up in some spasmodic, fidgety excitement.

It may well have been, by the way, that all these natives of the deep regarded the beaconed guest that had descended to them as an oversize subspecies of themselves, for most of them could do what it could do—that is, shed light all on their own. The visitors, Adrian explained, had only to douse their dynamo-driven light for another, even more peculiar spectacle to be revealed to them. For some distance, the darkness of the sea was illuminated by circling and darting will-o'-the-wisps, by the luminous energy with which many of the fish came equipped, so that the entire body of some was phosphorescent, while others were at least furnished with an organ for light, an electric lantern, which they presumably used not only to light their own path through the eternal night, but also to lure prey or signal for love. The beam of white light emitted by a few larger ones, in fact, was so intense that it blinded the eyes of their observers. The pipelike, protruding stalk-eyes of some of them, however, were apparently made to perceive from as far away as possible light's softest shimmers, as both warnings and lures.

The reporter regretted that there was no conceivable way to catch and bring to the surface some of these ogres of the deep—at least those that were totally unknown. For that, some apparatus would have been needed during the ascent to maintain the tremendous atmospheric pressure to which their bodies were accustomed and adapted—and which (and what a disconcerting thought it was!) thrust against the walls of the sphere. The creatures counteracted it by an equally powerful tension within their tissues and body chambers, so that with any decrease in exterior pressure, they would inevitably burst. Unfortunately, this happened to some of them merely by their coming in contact with this vehicle from on high—as was the case with an especially large, flesh-colored, and almost nobly formed merman they spotted, who shattered into a thousand pieces upon soft collision with their gondola.

This was how Adrian told it as he smoked his cigar, quite as if he had made the descent himself and had been shown it all—and with just half a smile he kept the joke going to the end, so that, although I laughed and marveled, I also could not help gazing at him with some astonishment. His smile probably likewise expressed teasing amusement at a certain resistance to his narrative on my part, which must have been noticeable, for he was well aware of my lack of interest, bordering on distaste, for the pranks and mysteries of natural phenomena, for "nature" in general, and of my devotion to the sphere of humane letters. Last but not least, it was apparently this awareness that tempted him to continue to badger me that evening with his investigations or, as he pretended, his experiences in regions monstrously above and beyond us humans, and to go right ahead now and "fling himself entire"—and me with him—"into the ocean of the worlds."

His previous descriptions made the transition easy. The deep sea's grotesquely alien life-forms, which did not seem to belong to our planet, provided one connection. A second was Klopstock's phrase about the "drop in the bucket," which in its rapt humility is only too justified by the quite subsidiary, remote location (and given the grand scale of things, the smallness of the object makes it almost impossible to locate) of not just the earth, but also of our entire planetary system, the sun and its seven satellites, within the spinning Milky Way, "our" Milky Way—to say nothing of the millions of others—to which it belongs. The word "our" lends a certain intimacy to the monstrosity to which it refers, enlarging, in an almost comical way, the idea of home to an expanse that loses all real meaning, but in which we are to regard ourselves as humble, but securely housed citizens. This sense of security, which places us profoundly inside the whole, is apparently an expression of nature's preference for spherical arrangements—and this was the third point of connection for Adrian's discussion of the cosmos: He had come to it in part by way of that strange experience of living inside a sphere, Capercailzie's deep-sea gondola, which he claimed to have shared with its owner for several hours. We all spent all our days inside a sphere, so he had learned, and as regards galactic space, in which we had been assigned a tiny, out-of-the-way spot, the details were as follows:

It was shaped more or less like a flat pocket-watch—that is, round and not nearly as thick as it was vast—a not immeasurable, but certainly monstrously large whirling disk of concentrated quantities of stars, star groups, star clusters, double stars (which revolved in elliptical orbits around one another); of nebulae, luminous nebulae, ring nebulae, star nebulae, and so forth. This disk, however, was merely like the circular section of an orange that had been sliced through the middle, for it was surrounded in all directions by a multi-stellared, vaporous mantle, which, once again, one could not term immeasurable but

whose exponential power had to be termed monstrous, and within its
expanses, primarily empty space, the given objects were so distributed
that the entire structure formed a globe. Deep inside this absurdly spacious sphere, then, and as part of this disk-like, condensed swarm of
worlds, there was located—in a quite subsidiary spot scarcely worth
mentioning and very hard to find—the fixed star around which, along
with its larger and smaller comrades, the earth and its little moon frol-
icked. "The sun" (which scarcely deserved the use of the definite article), a gas ball a mere nine hundred thousand miles in diameter and
with a surface temperature of ten thousand degrees Fahrenheit, was as
far from the center of the galactic inner plane as the latter was thick—
that is, thirty thousand light-years.

My general knowledge allowed me to link the term "light-year"
with some rough meaning. It is, of course, a spatial concept, and the
word denotes the distance that light travels in the course of one entire
earth year—at its own specific speed, of which I had only a vague notion, whereas Adrian had the exact figure in his head: 186,000 miles per
second. That meant that a light-year, nicely rounded off, equalled some
six trillion miles, and the eccentricity of our solar system came to thirty
thousand times that figure, while the diameter of our galactic sphere
totaled two hundred thousand light-years.

No, it was not immeasurable, yet this was how it had to be measured. And what should one say to such an attack on human reason? I
admit I am so fashioned that I have only a resigned, and somewhat
dismissive shrug for anything so super-impressive, so beyond all realization. Without doubt there is psychological pleasure in admiring
greatness, in being enthusiastic about it, indeed in being overwhelmed
by it, but that is only possible on a human and earthly scale that one
can comprehend. The pyramids are great, Mont Blanc and the interior
of St. Peter's are great—that is, if one prefers not to reserve that attribute for the moral and intellectual world, for the grandeur of the human heart and mind. The dates of the cosmos's creation are nothing
but a numbing bombardment of our intelligence with numbers that
come furnished with a comet tail of two dozen zeros and the pretense
that they still have something to do with measurement and reason. For
people like myself, there is nothing about this monster that could lay
claim to goodness, beauty, greatness; and I will never understand the
happy cries of "hosanna" that the so-called works of God—the
physics of the universe, that is—can evoke from certain temperaments.
And can a production ever be declared a work of God, if one's response to it can just as well be "so what" as "hosanna"? It seems to me

that the former is the better response to a dozen zeros after a one—or a seven, since that really makes no difference anyway—and I can see no reason for groveling in the dust to adore a quintillion.

It was also significant that Klopstock, the high-soaring poet, both in expressing and arousing enthusiastic reverence, had restricted himself to things of this earth, to the "drop in the bucket," and had disregarded the quintillions. As noted, the composer for his hymn, my friend Adrian, expatiated on them; but it would be unfair of me to leave the impression that he did so with any sort of deep feeling or emphasis. The way he spoke about the galaxies closest to our own, which, if I am not mistaken, lay at a distance of eight hundred thousand light-years from us, whereas a ray of light emitted by one of the farthest of these stellar assemblages visible to our optical instruments had to have begun its journey through space over one hundred million years ago, more or less, for it to stimulate the eye of an astronomer now scanning the expanses of the cosmos—the way he treated these insanities, then, was cold, casual, tinged with amusement at my undisguised aversion, and yet there was about it a certain initiate's familiarity with these matters as well, which is to say: He steadily maintained the fiction that he had won such knowledge not by reading on the sly, but by personal experience—that it was knowledge transmitted, taught, demonstrated by the likes of his aforementioned mentor, Professor Capercailzie, who, it turned out, had traveled with him not only down to the night of the deep, but also to the stars. . . . He halfway pretended he had learned from him—and indeed more or less by observation—that the physical universe (to use the word in its most comprehensive sense, including what is most distant) could not be called either infinite or finite, since both terms somehow connoted something static, whereas the true state of affairs was thoroughly dynamic and the cosmos had for a long time now at least (or more precisely: for 1,900 million years) been in a state of furious expansion—that is, of explosion. The shift in red light reaching us from countless Milky Ways, whose distance from us was definitely known, allowed for no doubt: The greater the change in the color of light at the red end of the spectrum, the greater the distance of these nebulae from us. Apparently they were drawing away from us, and the speed at which those complexes farthest away (some one hundred fifty million light-years) were moving was equal to that reached by alpha particles in radioactive substances, which achieved 15,600 miles per second—compared to which the speed of fragments from a bursting grenade move at a snail's pace. If, then, all galaxies were racing away from one another at the most exaggerated rates, the word "explosion" just barely, or perhaps already no longer, sufficed to describe the state of the universe and its mode of expansion. It might have been static at one time, its diameter measuring a mere billion light-years. But as things now stood, one could speak of expansion, but not of any sort of achieved expanded state, whether "finite" or "infinite." It appeared that the only thing Capercailzie had been able to assure his questioner was that the sum of all currently extant galaxies was on the order of a magnitude of one hundred billion, of which only a paltry million were visible through present-day telescopes.

The words of Adrian, as he smoked and smiled. I appealed to his conscience and demanded he concede this whole phantasm of numbers ending in nothingness could not possibly excite a feeling for God's splendor or instill any sense of moral elevation. Instead, it all looked more like a devilish prank.

"Admit it," I said to him. "The horridities of creation as defined by physics are in no way conducive to religion. What reverence, what tempering of the heart born of reverence, can come from such immeasurable mischief as the notion of an exploding universe? Absolutely none. Piety, reverence, decency of the soul—these are possible only in terms of man and through man, only when restricted to what is earthly and human. Their fruit should, can, and will be a humanism colored by religion and defined by a sense of man's transcendental mystery, by proud awareness that he is not merely a biological creature, but rather that a decisive part of his nature belongs to a spiritual and intellectual world; by awareness that the absolute has been given him—concepts of truth, of freedom, of justice—that he has been charged with the duty of approaching what is perfect. In this solemn attitude, in this duty, in this reverence of man for himself, there is God; I cannot find Him in hundreds of billions of Milky Ways."

"So you are against works," he replied, "and against physical nature, from which man comes and with him his intellect, something that ultimately can be found in other places of the cosmos, too. Physical creation, this world production you find so annoyingly monstrous, is indisputably the prerequisite for what is moral, which would have no soil without it, and perhaps one should call good the flower of evil—*une fleur du mal.* In the end—no, beg your pardon, not in the end, but before all else—your *homo Dei* is really a piece of gruesome nature with a not exactly generously allotted quantum of potential for spiritualization. It is amusing to note, by the way, how very much your humanism, and probably all humanism, tends toward medieval geocentrism—by necessity, evidently. It is popularly believed that humanism is friendly to science; but that cannot be, for one cannot regard the subjects of science as the Devil's work without regarding science in the same light. That is the Middle Ages. The Middle Ages were geocentric and anthropocentric. The Church, in which that view has survived, has chosen to do battle, in a humanistic spirit, with astronomical knowledge, has declared it the Devil's work, has forbidden it in honor of man, has insisted on ignorance out of humaneness. You see, your humanism is pure Middle Ages. Its concern is the parochial cosmology of Kaisersaschern, which leads to astrology, to observation of the positions of the planets, of their constellation and auspicious or ruinous forecasts—which is only natural and right, for what is patently clear is the intimate interdependence of bodies, their mutual neighborly bearing upon one another, within such a closely knit group in one little corner of the cosmos, like our solar system."

"We once spoke about astrological conjuncture," I broke in. "It was long ago, we were taking a walk around the Cattle Trough, and the conversation was about music. You defended constellation that day."

"I defend it today as well," he replied. "Astrological ages knew a great deal. They knew or surmised things that truly wide-ranging science is picking up on again now. That illness, plagues, epidemics have something to do with the position of the stars was an intuitive certainty in those days. And today we have come to a point where we debate whether the germs, bacteria, organisms that cause, let us say, an influenza epidemic on earth come from other planets, from Mars, Jupiter, or Venus."'

And now he told me about a scientist in California who claimed to have found living bacteria trapped in meteorites millions of years old. One could not easily prove to him that it was impossible, since it was certain that germs, living cells, could withstand temperatures approaching absolute zero—minus 460°F, the temperature of interplanetary space. Infectious disease, pestilences like the plague, the Black Death, were probably not from our own star, especially since it was almost certain that life itself, its very origin, was not of this earth, but had migrated here from outside. Helmholtz in his day had assumed that life had been brought to earth from other stars by meteorites, and doubt had grown ever since whether life's original home was the earth. He himself had it on the best authority that it came from neighboring planets enveloped in a much more favorable atmosphere containing lots of methane and ammonia—like Jupiter, Mars, or Venus. From them, or from one of them—he left the choice to me—life had come at some point, whether borne by cosmic missiles or simply by force of radiation, to our rather sterile and innocent planet. My humanistic *homo Dei,* this crown of life, along with his spiritual duty, was therefore presumably the product of marsh-gas fecundity on some neighboring star. . . .

"The flower of evil," I repeated with a nod.

"That mostly blossoms into evil," he added.

Thus he teased me—and not only with my benign worldview, but also by persisting in his whim of pretending to be especially, personally, directly informed about the affairs of heaven and earth. I did not know, though I should have realized, that all this was driving toward a new work—that is, toward cosmic music, with which he had become preoccupied, once the episode of new songs was over. It was the amazing symphony or orchestral fantasy in one movement that he labored over from the last months of 1913 into the early months of 1914 and that was given the title *Marvels of the Universe*—very much against my wishes and suggestion. For I was apprehensive about the frivolity of that title and suggested the name *Symphonica cosmologica.* But Adrian laughed and insisted on that other pseudopathetic, ironic designation, which to be sure better prepares cognoscenti for descriptions of monstrosity that are thoroughly farcical and grotesque in character—though grotesque in an often austerely solemn and mathematically ceremonious way. This music has nothing whatever in common with the spirit of the "Festival of Spring"—which, however, in a certain sense did prepare the way for it—that is, with its spirit of humble glorification; and were it not for certain personal hallmarks of the musical signature pointing to the same author, one might scarcely believe the same soul had produced them both. The nature and essence of this nearly thirty-minute orchestral portrait of the world is mockery—a mockery that confirms only too well the opinion I expressed in our conversation that the pursuit of what is immeasurably beyond man can provide piety no nourishment; a Luciferian travesty; a sardonic lampoon apparently aimed not only at the dreadful clockwork of the universe, but also at the medium in which it is painted, indeed repeated: at music, at the cosmos of tones. All of which contributed not a little to the reproach that my friend's artistry earned for displaying a virtuoso anti-artistic spirit, for blasphemy, for nihilistic sacrilege.

But enough of that. I intend to devote the next two chapters to several experiences in society that I shared with Adrian Leverkühn at the turn of the year, and epoch, from 1913 to 1914, during that last carnival in Munich before the outbreak of war.

XXVIII

I HAVE ALREADY NOTED that the Schweigestills' boarder did not bury himself entirely in monkish solitude watched over by Kaschperl-Suso, but in fact cultivated, though sporadically and discreetly, a certain social life in the city. Nonetheless, he seemed to find reassurance in always having to depart quite early, necessitated, as everyone knew, by his dependence on the eleven o'clock train. We would meet at the Roddes' on Ramberg Strasse, joining their circle—the Knöterichs, Dr. Kranich, Zink and Spengler, Schwerdtfeger, violinist and whistler—with all of whom I came to be on quite friendly terms; or it might be at the Schlaginhaufens', or maybe at the home of Schildknapp's publisher, Radbruch, on Fürsten Strasse, or in the elegant *bel étage* apartments of Bullinger, the paper manufacturer (originally from the Rhineland), to whom Rüdiger had likewise introduced us; and finally, during carnival, at artists' galas in Schwabing, where acquaintances from all these other meeting places, whose circles of friends also overlapped, would meet again in topsy-turvy confusion.

Both at the Roddes' and in the Schlaginhaufens' columned salon, people enjoyed listening to me play the viola d'amore, which to be sure was the chief social contribution that I, a simple scholar and schoolmaster and never a dashing conversationalist, could offer. It had been the asthmatic Dr. Kranich and Baptist Spengler who had in fact first urged me to do so on Ramberg Strasse—the one out of a numismatist's antiquarian interest (he enjoyed conversing with me in his precisely enunciated and well-ordered sentences about the historical forms of the viola family); the other out of general sympathy for anything out of the ordinary, for oddities. But in that household I had to be mindful of Konrad Knöterich's eagerness to be heard snorting away at his cello—and also of that little audience's quite justified preference for Schwerdt-feger's captivating violin. And so it flattered my vanity all the more (I don't deny it) that a very lively demand for me to perform—though I had always played purely as an amateur—came from the much larger and more elegant circle of people whom the ambitious Frau Dr. Schlaginhaufen, née von Plausig, knew how to assemble about her and her hard-of-hearing husband with his heavy Swabian accent, so that I was almost always obliged to bring my instrument along to Brienner Strasse, in order to treat the company to a chaconne or sarabande from the seventeenth century, a *plaisir d'amour* from the eighteenth, or to present them with a sonata by Handel's friend Ariosti or one of the pieces written by Haydn for the viola di bordone, but certainly play-able on the viola d'amore.

Such suggestions came as a rule not only from Jeannette Scheurl, but also from the general intendant, His Excellency von Riedesel, whose patronage of my old instrument and old music sprang, to be sure, not from learned, antiquarian interests as with Kranich, but rather from a purely conservative bias. That, needless to say, makes a great differ-ence. This courtier, a former cavalry colonel, who had been ordered to his present post solely because he was known to play the piano a little (how many centuries ago now, the days seem when one became a the-ater intendant because one was of noble birth and could play a bit of piano!)—Baron Riedesel, then, saw in whatever was old and historic a bulwark against all things modern and subversive, a kind of feudal polemic against them, and in that spirit he supported the old without in fact understanding anything about it. For just as little as one can un-derstand what is new and young without being at home in tradition, so, too, love for the old must remain inauthentic and sterile if one closes oneself off to the new, which arises from the old out of histori-cal necessity. And so Riedesel cherished and promoted the ballet—simply because it was "graceful." The word "graceful" was for him a conservative, polemical shibboleth against the subversively modern. He had not the vaguest about the artistic world of tradition found in Russian and French ballet, as represented, let us say, by Tchaikovsky, Ravel, and Stravinsky, and was not even remotely aware of ideas such as those that the latter-named Russian musician later expressed about classical ballet: As a triumph of measured plan over effusive emotion, of order over chance, as a pattern of consciously apollonian action, it was the paradigm of art itself. Rather, what Riedesel dimly had in mind was simply gossamer skirts, dancers tripping past on pointe, arms arched "gracefully" above their heads—before the eyes of court society in their loges, maintaining the "ideal" and tabooing anything ugly and problematical, while a bridled bourgeoisie sat in orchestra seats below.

To be sure, a great deal of Wagner was performed at the Schlaginhaufens' as well, especially since the dramatic soprano Tanya Orlanda, a stupendous woman, and the heldentenor Harald Kjoejelund, a quite rotund man with pince-nez and voice of brass, were frequent guests. Wagner's music, without which the Hoftheater could not have existed, had been more or less incorporated into the feudal realm of the "graceful" (though it was loud and violent) by Herr von Riedesel, who was all the more willing to hold it in esteem because there were newer works that went far beyond it, which as a conservative one could reject by playing them off against Wagner. It might even happen that His Excellency would himself accompany the singers on the piano, which they found flattering—although his artistry as a pianist was hardly a match for the piano reduction and more than once jeopardized their intended effects. I did not at all enjoy it when Kjoejelund the concert singer would blast Siegfried's endless and rather dull smithy songs, setting the salon's more sensitive pieces of decor, the vases and glass objets d'art, vibrating and humming excitedly along. But I admit that I find it hard to resist the thrill of a heroic female voice, such as Orlanda's was at the time. The force of personality, the power of the organ, the skilled use of dramatic accents, all lend the illusion of a regal female soul at the pitch of emotion; and at the end of her presentation of say, Isolde's "Know'st thou not the Lady Love?" ending in her ecstatic cry, "This torch, and though it be my life's own light, laughing now, I do not quail to quench" (whereby the singer emphasized the dramatic action with an energetic downward thrust of her arm), it would not have taken much for me to have knelt with tears in my eyes before this triumphantly smiling woman now showered with applause. It was, by the way, Adrian who on that occasion had consented to accompany her, and he, too, smiled as he stepped away from his piano bench and with a passing glance noted the agitation in my face and that I was on the verge of weeping.

In the wake of such impressions, it does one good to be able to contribute something to an evening's artistic entertainment, and so I was touched when afterward His Excellency von Riedesel—immediately seconded by the tall, elegant lady of the house—encouraged me in words spoken with the soft lilt of southern Germany, though sharpened by an officer's tone, to repeat the andante and minuet by Milandre (1770) with which I had only recently obliged them on my seven strings. How weak man is! I was grateful to him, completely forgot my dislike of his smooth, vacant aristocratic physiognomy—so imperturbably impudent as to be almost serene—with its twirled blond moustache beneath pudgy clean-shaven cheeks and sparkling monocle tucked in one eye beneath a whitish brow. For Adrian, as I well knew, this nobleman cut a figure beyond all pronouncement, so to speak, beyond hate and disdain, beyond laughter even; he found him hardly worth a shrug—and that was actually my response, too. But at such moments, when he would invite me to be an active participant, so that by means of something "graceful" the party could recover from the onslaught of that now established revolutionary, I could not help liking him.

It was, however, very strange—partly embarrassing, partly comic—when von Riedesel's conservatism came up against another kind of conservatism, one for which it was not only a matter of "still" but also of "once again," a post- and counterrevolutionary conservatism, an assault on bourgeois liberal values from the other side, not from before, but from after. By 1913 the Zeitgeist was supplying ample opportunity for these encounters, which the old, uncomplicated conservatism found both encouraging and perplexing, and thus in the salon of Frau Schlaginhaufen, who, being socially ambitious, composed her gatherings as colorfully as possible, such an opportunity was also provided: in the person, that is, of the independent scholar Dr. Chaim Breisacher, a very thoroughbred of the type, an advanced, indeed reckless intellect, and a man of fascinating ugliness—who here played the role, apparently with a certain malicious delight, of the foreign leaven in the bread. Our hostess valued his dialectical skill with words (spoken, by the way, with a Palatinate accent) and his love of paradox, which would leave the ladies clasping their hands above their heads in a kind of prim jubilation. As for himself, it was probably snobbishness that was the source of the pleasure he took in such society, along with the need to amaze elegant, simple minds with ideas that would presumably have been less of a sensation at a literary roundtable. I did not like him in the least, always saw him as an intellectual obstructionist, and it was my conviction that Adrian found him disagreeable as well, although for reasons unclear to me we never got around to any detailed exchange about Breisacher. But I have never denied his keen sensitivity for the intellectual commotion of the time, his nose for each new expression of its will, and I was confronted with some of all that for the very first time in his person and soiree conversations.

He was a polyhistor, who could talk about anything and everything, a philosopher of culture, whose opinions, however, were directed against culture insofar as he affected to see all of history as nothing but a process of decline. The most contemptuous word from his mouth was "progress"; he had a scathing way of saying it, and one indeed sensed that he understood the conservative scorn he devoted to progress to be his true passport into this society, the badge of his presentability. He showed wit, though not of a very sympathetic sort, when, for instance, he would jeer at painting's progress from flat two-dimensional representation to perspective. For someone to declare that pre-perspective art had spurned the optical illusion of perspective out of incompetence, fecklessness, or simple clumsy primitivism, and probably then to add a shrug of pity as well—that was what he called the height of foolish modern arrogance. To spurn, to forgo, to disparage—that was not incompetence or ignorance, not proof of intellectual poverty. As if illusion were not the basest principle of art, just what the rabble wanted; as if to wish to know nothing of it were not simply a token of noble taste! Not wishing to know about some things, that ability—so close to wisdom, or, better, part of it—had unfortunately been lost, and the most vulgar impudence called itself progress.

For some reason the denizens of the salon of a Frau née von Plausig felt right at home with such views, and, I believe, more likely had a sense that Breisacher was not quite the right man to represent those views, than that they might not be the right people to applaud them.

It was much the same, he said, with the transition of music from monody to singing in parts, to harmony, which people loved to regard as cultural progress, whereas, in fact, it had been an acquisition of barbarism.

"Did you say . . . beg pardon . . . of barbarism?" Herr von Riedesel crowed, who was indeed accustomed to seeing in barbarism a form—if a slightly compromised form—of the conservative principle.

"Most certainly, Your Excellency. The origins of music for several voices, that is, of singing concurrently in fifths or fourths, are very remote from the center of musical civilization, from Rome, which was the home of the beautiful voice and its cult; those origins lie in the raw-throated north and appear to have been a kind of compensation for such raw-throatedness. They lie in England and France, particularly in savage Britain, which was the first to accept the interval of the third into harmony. So-called higher development, musical complexity, progress—sometimes those are the achievement of barbarism. I leave it to you whether one should praise barbarism for it or not. . . ."

It was all too clear that he was making fun of His Excellency and the

whole gathering by playing up to them as a conservative. Apparently
he did not feel comfortable so long as anyone else still knew what he or
she was supposed to think. Needless to say, polyphonic vocal music,
that invention of progressive barbarism, had become the object of conservative protection as soon as the historical transition from it to the
principle of harmonic chords—and with it to the instrumental music
of the last two centuries—had taken place. But this had in fact marked
the decline—the decline, namely, from the grand and only true art of
counterpoint, that cool and sacred game of numbers, which thank God
had still had nothing to do with the prostitution of emotions or shameless dynamics; and in that decline, at its very center, had belonged the
great Bach of Eisenach, whom Goethe had quite rightly called a harmonist. One could not be the inventor of the tempered clavichord—
and that meant of the possibility to perceive each note ambiguously
and exchange it enharmonically—and thus of the romanticism of modern harmonic modulation, without deserving the harsh name that the
connoisseur of Weimar had given him. Harmonic counterpoint? There
was no such thing. That was neither fish nor flesh. The mitigation,
emasculation, and adulteration, the reinterpretation of what was old
and genuine by turning polyphony, once experienced as the interplay
of various voices, into a music of harmonic chords, had begun already
in the sixteenth century, and people like Palestrina, both Gabrielis,
and, on this very spot, our own doughty Orlando di Lasso had all
played a dishonorable part in it. These fine folk had wanted to bring us
"humanly" closer to the concept of vocal-polyphonic art, and, yes,
they had therefore seemed to us the greatest masters of the style. But
that was due simply to their having indulged themselves in purely
chordal composition, and their treatment of the polyphonic style had
already been quite wretchedly mitigated by considerations of harmonic concord, of the relation between consonance and dissonance.

And while the others all marveled and beamed and slapped their
knees, these annoying remarks made me seek out Adrian's eyes—but
he would not return my glance. As for von Riedesel, he had fallen prey
to utter confusion.

"Beg pardon," he said, "if you please . . . Bach, Palestrina . . ."

For him those names possessed the nimbus of conservative authority, and now they had been assigned to the realm of modernistic disintegration. He sympathized—but at the same time found this so eerily
disconcerting that he even removed his monocle from his eye, thereby
robbing his face of every trace of intelligence. Nor did he do any better when Breisacher's cultural-critical peroration moved on to matters

of the Old Testament, to the sphere of his personal origins, turned to the Jewish race or nation, and here, too, displayed a highly equivocal, indeed incredible, but nonetheless malicious conservatism. According to him, decline, stultification, and the loss of all feeling for what was old and genuine had begun early on and in a place so respectable that no one would ever have dreamt it. I can only say: The whole thing was insanely funny. For Breisacher, biblical personages revered by every Christian child (such as King David and King Solomon, as well as the prophets with their pious harangues about God in His heaven) were already decrepit representatives of a diluted late theology, which no longer had any notion of the old and genuinely Hebrew presence of Yahweh, the people's Elohim, and saw only "riddles of ancient days" in the rites by which this national god had once been worshiped, or better had been compelled to be physically present. He was especially hard on "wise" Solomon and treated him so roughly that the gentlemen whistled through their teeth and cheers of amazement could be heard from the ladies.

"Beg pardon!" von Riedesel said. "I am, to put it mildly . . . King Solomon in all his glory . . . Ought you not . . ."

"No, Your Excellency, I ought not," Breisacher replied. "The man was an aesthete enervated by erotic excess and a progressivist blockhead when it came to religion, was typical of the involution by which a cult built around the effective presence of a national god, that quintessence of a people's metaphysical power, becomes mere preaching of an abstract and generally humane God in heaven—the decline from a religion of the *volk* to a workaday religion. For proof of which we need only read the scandalous speech that he gave upon the completion of the first temple, and in which he asked 'But will God indeed dwell on the earth among men?'—as if Israel's whole and exclusive task did not consist in creating a dwelling, a tent, for God and employing any means to provide for His constant presence. Solomon, however, is impudent enough to declaim 'The heaven cannot contain Thee, how much less this house that I have builded!' That is drivel and the beginning of the end—that is, of the degenerate notion of God held by the psalmists, for whom God has already been banned entirely to the heavens and who constantly sing about God in heaven, whereas the Pentateuch knows nothing about heaven as the seat of the godhead. There Elohim goes before His people in a pillar of fire; there He wishes to dwell among His people, to walk among them, and to eat at His table of slaughter—to eschew the scrawny word 'altar' coined much later in human history. How is it even conceivable that a psalmist has

God ask 'Will I eat the flesh of bulls, or drink the blood of goats?' It is simply outrageous to put such words in God's mouth, a slap by impertinent enlightenment in the face of the Pentateuch, where the sacrifice is expressly called 'the bread'—that is, the actual food of Yahweh. It is only a step from such a question, as well as from the locutions of wise Solomon, to Maimonides, the ostensibly greatest rabbi of the Middle Ages, but in truth an assimilator of Aristotle, who manages to 'explain' sacrifices as God's concession to the heathen instincts of the people, ha, ha! Fine, the sacrifice of blood and fat, salted and seasoned with sweet odors, that once fed God, giving Him His body, is for the psalmist nothing but a 'symbol'" (and I can still hear the indescribable disdain with which Dr. Breisacher spoke that word); "one does not slaughter the animal, but—as incredible as it may sound—thanksgiving and humility. 'Whoso slaughtereth praise,' it now says, 'glorifieth me.' And at another point: 'The sacrifices of God are a contrite heart.' In short, it has long since ceased to be *volk* and blood and religious reality, and is only a humane watery gruel. . . ."

This merely as a sample of Breisacher's archconservative effusions. It was as amusing as it was repulsive. He could not get enough of describing the authentic rite, the cult of the real God of the *volk* (who was not at all abstractly universal, and thus not "omnipotent" or "omnipresent," either), as a magical technique, a physical manipulation of dynamic powers, which was not without the risk of bodily harm and could easily end in accidents, catastrophic short circuits resulting from mistakes and blunders. The sons of Aaron had died because they had offered "strange fire." That was a technical accident, the causal outcome of a mistake. A man named Uzzah had thoughtlessly touched the chest, the so-called ark of the covenant, when it threatened to slip off the cart on which it was being transported, and had immediately fallen over dead. That, too, was a discharge of transcendent dynamic power, caused by negligence—the negligence, namely, of David, the king who played his harp far too much and who, in fact, had likewise no longer had any understanding of things and had ordered the ark be conveyed Philistine-fashion, by cart, instead of having it borne on long poles. David was already no less stultified and alienated from his origins—if not to say, grown no less brutish—than Solomon. He had no longer known about the dynamic dangers of a census and by conducting one had brought on a severe biological smiting, an epidemic, a pestilence— a predictable reaction of the metaphysical powers within the people. For a genuine *volk* would simply not endure that kind of mechanized registration, the enumerated fragmentation of the dynamic whole into identical solitary units. . . .

Breisacher was only too glad when one woman interjected how she had had no idea that a census could be such a sin.

"Sin?" he replied, exaggerating the interrogatory rise in his voice. No, in the genuine religion of a genuine *volk* such flabby theological concepts as "sin" and "punishment" simply did not occur in the context of a causality reduced to the merely ethical. This was all about the causality of mistakes and on-the-job accidents. Religion and ethics were related only insofar as the latter was the former in decay. All morality was a "purely intellectual" misunderstanding of ritual. Could there be anything more godforsaken than the "purely intellectual"? He would leave it to world religions lacking all character to turn "prayer," *sit venia verbo,* into mere begging, into a plea for mercy, an "Oh, Lord" and "God, take pity," into a "help me" and "give me" and "be so good as to. . . ." So-called prayer . . .

"Beg pardon," von Riedesel said, with real emphasis this time. "All well and good, but the command always was: 'Helmet off for prayer!'"

"Prayer," Dr. Breisacher concluded implacably, "is a late form— vulgarized and watered down by rationalism—of what was once very energetic, active, and strong: the magical invocation, the coercion of God."

I truly felt sorry for the baron. It must have brought deep confusion to his soul for him to watch his cavalier's conservatism be trumped with the dreadfully clever card of atavism, with a radicalism of preservation that had about it nothing of the cavalier, but something more revolutionary and that sounded more destructive than any sort of liberalism, but all the same had, as if in mockery, a laudable conservative appeal—I could imagine the sleepless night it would probably give him, although that may have been taking my sympathy too far. And yet most certainly not everything in Breisacher's remarks was in order; one could easily have refuted him, pointing out to him, for example, that the spiritual disdain for animal sacrifice is first found not among the prophets, but in the Pentateuch itself, where Moses himself declares sacrifice to be patently secondary and puts all the emphasis on obedience to God, on keeping His commandments. But a man of tender sensitivities finds disruption unpleasant; he finds it unpleasant to break in on a well-constructed train of thought with his own logical or historical objections culled from memory, and even in the anti-intellectual he will honor and respect the intellect. Today we can see clearly enough that it was the mistake of our civilization to have been all too generous in exercising such forbearance and respect—since on the opposing side we were indeed dealing with naked insolence and the most determined intolerance.

I was reminded of all this when, at the very beginning of this account, I qualified my confession of pro-Jewish sympathies with the remark that quite annoying specimens of the race had crossed my path and the name of the independent scholar Breisacher slipped prematurely from my pen. Can one hold it against Jewish sagacity if its keen-eared sensitivity for what is new and yet to come, proves itself in aberrant situations as well, where the avant-garde and the reactionary coincide? It was on that evening at the Schlaginhaufens' and in the person of this man Breisacher that I, at any rate, had my first taste of the new world of anti-humanity, about which, in my naive good nature, I had known nothing at all.

XXIX

Munich's carnival of 1914—I still have vivid, or better, ominous memories of those lax weeks of fraternization and cheeks flushed with festivities celebrated between Epiphany and Ash Wednesday at all sorts of public and private affairs, in which I, still a youthful high-school professor from Freising, participated either on my own or in Adrian's company. It was after all the last carnival before the onset of the four-year war that, viewed historically, now merges with the horror of our own time into a single epoch—of the so-called First World War, which put an end forever to an aesthetic innocence of life in the city on the Isar, to its dionysian coziness, if I may put it that way. It was indeed also the period during which before my eyes fateful developments unfolded for certain individuals within our circle of acquaintance, developments scarcely noticed by the larger world, of course, but that would lead to catastrophes of which these pages will have to speak, because some of them closely touched the life and fate of my hero, Adrian Leverkühn—indeed, as I am profoundly aware, because in one of them he was actively involved in a mysteriously fatal way.

By that I do not mean what happened to Clarissa Rodde, that proud, wry blond woman with a bent for the macabre, who was still part of our circle at the time, still lived with her mother, and joined in the amusements of carnival, but was already preparing to leave the city to become the ingénue with a provincial theater company, an engagement arranged by her teacher, the Hoftheater's lead actor in heroic and fatherly roles. That would prove to be a disaster, and her theatrical mentor, Seiler by name and an experienced man, should be absolved of any responsibility. He had previously written a letter to Frau Senator Rodde, in which he explained that his student was indeed extraordinarily intelligent and full of enthusiasm for the theater, but that her natural talent was insufficient to guarantee a successful career on the stage; she lacked the primitive foundation for all dramatic art, the comedic instinct, what people call theater blood, and in all good conscience he would have to advise against her pursuing her present course. This led to a crisis, with Clarissa bursting into a tearful despair that touched her mother's heart, who then prevailed upon Seiler (who had, after all, covered himself by his letter) to terminate instruction and use his connections to find a beginner's position for the young woman.

Twenty-two years have now passed since Clarissa's pitiable destiny was fulfilled, and I shall report it in its chronological place. But here my eye is upon the fate of her gentle and sad sister Inez, who cultivated the past and sorrow—as well as upon poor Rudi Schwerdtfeger's fate, which I recalled in horror just now when I could not refrain from speaking ahead of time about solitary Adrian Leverkühn's involvement in these events. The reader is accustomed to such prematurity from me, and he should not interpret it as befuddlement or a lack of literary restraint on my part. It is simply that even from a distance I fix my eye with fear and uneasiness, indeed dread, on certain matters about which I must report from time to time and that I find oppressive long beforehand, but whose weight I seek to distribute by alluding in advance to them in words that, admittedly, only I understand. By letting them halfway out of the bag, I hope to make it easier for myself to share them later on, to remove the thorn of horror, to attenuate their uncanniness. All of which is my way of apologizing for a "faulty" narrative technique and explaining my difficulties. I scarcely need mention that the beginnings of the developments mentioned here were very remote from Adrian; he paid them hardly any notice and was directed toward them to some extent only by me, whose inherent social curiosity—or should I say, human sympathy—was greater than his. What happened is as follows.

As previously indicated, the two Rodde girls, both Clarissa and Inez, did not get along especially well with their mother, the Frau Senator, and not infrequently made it apparent that the tame, lightly lascivious demi-Bohemianism of her salon, her uprooted life furnished with remnants of a patrician, bourgeois past, got on their nerves. Both strove in different directions to get away from this hybrid state: proud Clarissa moving toward a decisively artistic life, for which, however, as her mentor had been forced to observe after a time, she lacked a true calling in her bones; and the delicately melancholy Inez, with her basic fear of life itself, moving back into the refuge, the psychological protection, of a secure middle-class life, the path to which was a respectable marriage, concluded if possible out of love—but otherwise even without love, for God's sake. With her mother's heartfelt sentimental approval, of course, Inez strode down that path—and came to grief, just as her sister did in following her road. The tragic outcome was first, this ideal did not actually suit her personally, and second, the epoch itself, which changed and undermined everything, no longer permitted it.

At the time she had been approached by a certain Dr. Helmut Institoris, an aesthetician and art historian, an instructor at the Technical Institute, where he would have photographs passed around the class while he lectured on the theory of the beautiful and the architecture of the Renaissance, but a man with good prospects of one day being called to the university, to a professorial chair, to membership in the Academy, etc., particularly if, being a bachelor from a well-to-do Würzburg family and with expectations of a significant inheritance, he were to enhance the worthiness of his existence by establishing a household as a gathering place for society. He went courting, and did not need to worry about the financial status of the young lady of his choice—on the contrary, he belonged in fact to those men who enter marriage wanting to keep the ledger in their own hands and to know that their wives are quite dependent on them.

That does not bespeak a sense of personal strength, and Institoris was in fact not a strong man—which was likewise evidenced by the aesthetic admiration he cultivated for all things strong and bursting with ruthless vitality. He was rather short, but quite elegant, and had a long, oval head, with smooth blond hair parted in the middle and lightly pomaded. A blond moustache projected slightly beyond his upper lip, and gazing out from behind gold spectacles, his blue eyes had a gentle, noble expression that made it hard to understand—or perhaps for that very reason one did understand—how he could revere brute force, though of course only if it was beautiful. He belonged to a type bred during those decades, the kind of man who, as Baptist Spengler once so aptly put it, "with cheekbones glowing from consumption, constantly shouts, 'How strong and beautiful life is!'"

Well, Institoris did not shout, but spoke instead in a low lisping voice, even when proclaiming the Italian Renaissance as an age "reeking of blood and beauty." Nor was he consumptive, or at most, like almost everyone else, had had a touch of tuberculosis in early youth. But he was delicate and nervous, suffering from weakness in the sympathetic nerves of the solar plexus, which is the source of so many anxieties and forebodings of early death, and he was a regular at a sanatorium for the wealthy in Meran. Certainly he promised himself—and his doctors promised him—invigorated health, too, from the routine of married life.

And so during the winter of 1913–14, he approached our Inez Rodde in a manner that led us to guess it would end in an engagement. To be sure we were kept waiting a good while, on into the early years of war—timidity and conscientiousness on both sides presumably enjoined a longer, more careful examination of whether they were truly born for one another. But when one saw this "couple" together in the Frau Senator's salon (once Institoris had arranged to be properly introduced there) or at public galas, where they often sat off to themselves chatting in a corner, this very question appeared to be under discussion between them, either directly or half in words; and the sympathetic observer, who saw a kind of trial engagement in the offing, automatically felt an urge to discuss the same issue with himself.

That Helmut had cast his eye on Inez of all people might set one to wonder, only to understand it all quite well in the end. A Renaissance female she was not—anything but, given her psychological fragility, her veiled gaze full of distinguished sadness, the neck thrust forward at a tilt, and a mouth pursed for gentle and precarious stabs at mischief. But this suitor would have had no idea how to cope with his aesthetic ideal; his manly superiority would have been very much the loser in that case—one needed only imagine him at the side of a resounding, robust personality like Tanya Orlanda to be amusingly convinced of that. And yet Inez was in no way lacking in feminine charm; it was quite understandable that a man looking about for a wife had fallen in love with her masses of hair, her small hands folded and cupped, her elegantly self-assured youthfulness. She may well have been what he needed. Her circumstances drew him to her—that is, her patrician heritage, which she stressed, but which in her present transplanted state had eroded and become slightly déclassé, so that she no longer posed a threat to his preponderance; rather, in making her his, he could have the feeling of raising her up, of rehabilitating her. A widowed mother who was semi-impoverished and slightly hedonistic, a sister who had joined the theater, a circle of more or less gypsy friends—those were matters that in the interests of his own dignity did not displease him, especially since by this connection he compromised nothing socially, did not endanger his career, and could be certain that Inez, whom her mother would fondly and correctly outfit with a dowry of linens, perhaps even silver, would provide him an impeccable wife and hostess.

That was how things seemed to me from Dr. Institoris's point of view. But if I tried to see him through the young lady's eyes, the affair lost its validity. Employing all the powers of my imagination, I could not credit this thoroughly fussy and self-absorbed man—whose frame, to be sure, was delicate and exquisite, but physically quite unimposing (he even had a mincing gait, by the way)—with any appeal for the opposite sex; whereas I felt that Inez, despite all her reserved virginal austerity, ultimately needed just such appeal. To this was added the contrast between their philosophical attitudes, their theoretical dispositions toward life—which one would have to call diametrical, and downright exemplarily so. It was, to put it in the briefest terms, the dichotomy between aesthetics and ethics, which to a great extent governed the cultural dialectics of the era and was more or less personified in these two young people—the contradiction between a scholarly glorification of "life" in its glittering thoughtlessness and a pessimistic veneration of suffering, with its depths and its wisdom. One can say that at its creative wellspring this dichotomy had formed a personal unity and only in this era had it rancorously fallen apart. Dr. Institoris was—and one really must add: good God!—every inch a man of the Renaissance, and Inez Rodde was incontestably a child of pessimistic moralism. She had not the least use for a world "reeking of blood and beauty," and as for "life," that was precisely what she sought protection from—in a strictly bourgeois, elegant, and economically well-cushioned marriage that would, if possible, withstand every shock. It was ironic that the man—or manikin—who appeared to want to offer her this refuge was such an enthusiast for beautiful ruthlessness and Italian poisonings.

I doubt that, when alone, these two indulged in disputes about worldviews. They probably spoke then about more immediate matters and simply tested how it would be if they were to become engaged. Discussion of philosophy was more a refined social entertainment, and I do indeed recall several occasions when—among a larger circle of friends, over wine at an alcove table in a ballroom—their attitudes collided in conversation, when Institoris, for instance, would assert that only people with strong, brutal instincts could create great works, and Inez would counter this, protesting that greatness in art had often proceeded from the most Christian people, those bent low by conscience, tempered by suffering, and taking a gloomy attitude toward life. It seemed to me that such antitheses were pointless, too tied to our own era, and did not do justice to reality—that is, to the always precarious balance between vitality and infirmity that is seldom achieved and yet apparently constitutes genius. But here for once, one party represented what she was—life's infirmity—and the other what he worshiped—strength; and so one had to let them be.

Once, I recall, we were sitting together (the Knöterichs, Zink and Spengler, Schildknapp, and his publisher Radbruch were also in the party) and the friendly dispute arose not between the two lovers, as we could surely begin to call them, but instead, almost comically, between Institoris and Rudi Schwerdtfeger, who happened to be sitting with us, very handsomely dressed as a young huntsman. I no longer really know what the topic was; at any rate, the difference of opinion had originated with a quite innocent remark of Schwerdtfeger's, one to which he had given little or no thought. It concerned "merit," that much I do recall—achievement realized by battle and struggle, by willpower and self-mastery; and Rudolf, who had just praised such occurrences with all his heart, calling them meritorious, could not understand where Institoris could possibly get the notion to contradict him and refuse to recognize merit in anything that required sweat. From the standpoint of beauty, Institoris said, will was not to be praised, but only talent and it alone was to be pronounced meritorious. Exertion was for the rabble; what came from instinct, automatically and with ease, that alone was elegant, and thus that alone was meritorious. Now good Rudi was no hero of self-mastery and had never done anything in his life that had not come easily to him—as for example, and above all, his excellent violin playing. But what the other man said went against his grain, and though he vaguely sensed that somehow there was something "higher" about it, something beyond his reach, he simply would not stand for this. With lips curled in outrage, he stared into Institoris's face, and his blue eyes bored by turns into the other man's, now left, now right.

"No, can't be, that's plain nonsense," he said, but in a rather low and subdued voice that indicated he was not so certain of his position. "Merit is merit, and talent simply isn't. You're always talking about beauty, doctor, but it really is very beautiful when someone prevails over himself and does a thing better than he has been gifted by nature to do. What do you say, Inez?" he said, turning to enlist her help, a question that once again revealed his total naiveté, for he had no idea just how fundamentally Inez's opinion in such matters was opposed to Helmut's.

"You're right," she replied, a delicate blush suffusing her face. "At any rate I think you're right. Talent is amusing, but by the word 'merit' we imply an admiration that in no way applies to talent or what is instinctive."

"There you have it!" Schwerdtfeger cried in triumph.

And Institoris laughed and rejoined, "But of course. You shopped in the right place."

There was, however, something strange happening here that no one could help notice, at least fleetingly, and that was confirmed by Inez's blush, which did not quickly vanish again. It was quite consistent with her viewpoint for her to say that her suitor was wrong about this and every similar question. But for her to say that our lad Rudolf was right, that was not consistent with it. He was, after all, quite unaware that there was such a thing as Immoralism, and one cannot very well say someone is right if he has no understanding of the counterthesis—at least not before one has explained it to him. Although Inez's verdict was quite logically natural and justified, there was nonetheless some-thing peculiar about it, and for me this was underscored by the burst of laughter with which Schwerdtfeger's unmerited victory was greeted by her sister Clarissa—by that proud woman with her receding chin, who certainly did not fail to notice when superiority compromised itself for reasons that had nothing to do with superiority, and yet was equally certain that it did not thereby compromise itself.

"And now," she cried, "Hop to, Rudolf! Say 'thank you,' stand up, my lad, and bow! Go fetch your rescuer some ice cream and ask her for the next waltz."

That was how she always did things. She very proudly made com-mon cause with her sister and always said "Hop to!" when Inez's dig-nity was at issue. And she also said "Hop to!" to Institoris, the suitor, whenever he proved somehow slow or obtuse in his gallantries. Out of pride, she made common cause with superiority in general, and she looked after it and displayed the greatest amazement if it was not given its due on the spot. "If someone wants something from you," she seemed to want to say, "you jump." I remember quite well how she once said "Hop to!" to Schwerdtfeger on Adrian's account, who had expressed some wish about a Zapfenstösser concert (it was a ticket for Jeannette Scheurl, I believe), to which Schwerdtfeger had offered an objection or two.

"All right, Rudolf! Hop to!" she cried. "For God's sake, what's the problem? Do you need a shove?"

"No, that won't be necessary," he replied. "I'm quite sure . . . but . . ."

"There won't be any 'buts'," she grandly proclaimed, half in fun and

half in earnest rebuke. And both Adrian and Schwerdtfeger laughed—
the latter with his shrug, his familiar boyish grimace with one corner of
his mouth, and a promise to arrange things.

It was as if Clarissa saw in Rudolf a kind of suitor, who had to
"jump"; and in fact he was forever trying to win Adrian's favor in the
most naive fashion, undauntable in his confiding familiarity. She often
tried to pump me for my opinion about the real suitor, the man wooing her sister—which, by the by, Inez herself likewise did, but in a fragile, shy way, almost as if at the same time she were flinching back and
both wanted to hear and yet did not want to hear or know it. Both sisters trusted me, which is to say: They appeared to value me as someone
justifiably capable of evaluating others, which, however, if the trust is
to be complete, also demands a certain standing-apart from the game,
an unruffled neutrality. The role of the confidant is always simultaneously flattering and painful, since one plays it really only under the
precondition that one is of no consequence oneself. But how much
better it is, I have often told myself, to instill trust in the world than to
arouse its passions. How much better to appear to it as "good" rather
than "beautiful"!

A "good person"—in Inez Rodde's eyes that was surely someone to
whom the world relates on a purely moral, not on some aesthetically
excited basis; hence her trust in me. I must say, however, that I treated
the sisters somewhat unequally and in small ways fitted out my opinion of Institoris the suitor according to the person who asked it. In
conversation with Clarissa I expanded far more fully, expressed myself
as a psychologist on the motive behind his hesitancy (though, to be
sure, the hesitancy was not one-sided) in choosing, and, with her permission, did not shrink from poking a little fun at this milksop who
idolized "brute instincts." Things were different when Inez herself
asked me. Then I would take into consideration those feelings that I
pro forma presumed to be hers, without actually believing in them—
show consideration, then, more for the reasonable basis on which she
would in all probability marry the man, and spoke with measured respect for his solid qualities, his knowledge, his humane integrity, his
splendid prospects. Lending my words the appropriate warmth—
though not too much of it—was a ticklish task; for it seemed my responsibility both to strengthen the young woman in her doubts,
making inhospitable the very shelter she longed for, and to persuade
her to take refuge there despite such doubts; yes, now and then, for one
particular reason, encouragement seemed to me more responsible than
dissuasion.

Usually, you see, she had soon heard enough of my opinion of Helmut Institoris and pushed her trust in me farther still, generalized it in a sense, by asking to hear my view about other people in our circle as well, about Zink and Spengler, for instance, or, to give another example, about Schwerdtfeger. She wanted to know what I thought of his violin playing, of his character; whether and to what extent I respected him, and what shades of seriousness or humor that respect exhibited. I replied with all due discretion and as fairly as possible (in just the same fashion as I have also spoken about Rudolf in these pages), and she listened attentively, so that she might then supplement my friendly commendation with remarks of her own, with which I, in turn, could only agree, though I was also struck by the pained urgency of some of them—which should not really have surprised me, given the young woman's character and the way she viewed life from under a veil of mistrust, and yet there was something disconcerting about that urgency when applied to this subject.

Nonetheless, it was ultimately no wonder that she—who had known this attractive young man so much longer than I and treated him, as did her sister, as a kind of brother—had observed him more closely than I and could speak confidentially about him in greater detail. He was a man without vices, she said (she did not use that word, but some milder one, yet it was clear that was what she meant), a pure man—which explained his confiding familiarity, for purity has a confiding quality about it. (A touching word in her mouth, for she herself never confided in others—though she did in me, by way of exception.) He did not drink—always just lightly sweetened tea with no cream, although that three times a day, to be sure—did not smoke, or at most only on rare occasions and, then, quite free from any force of habit. For all such manly stupefaction (I believe I recall that was how she put it), for such narcotics, he substituted flirtation, to which, however, he was completely addicted and for which he was born: not for love or friendship—given his nature, he turned those, on the sly so to speak, into flirtation. A social butterfly? Yes and no. Certainly not in the ordinary, banal sense. If you wanted to see the difference, you needed only to see him together with Bullinger, the manufacturer, who took such monstrous delight in his wealth and loved to warble songs like:

> A happy heart and health untold
> are better than your goods and gold—

just to taunt people and make them even more envious of his money. But Rudolf made it difficult for you to perceive his value and to keep it in mind because of his niceness, his coquetry, his playing the role of social dandy, his love of a social whirl that, in fact, had something frightening about it. Did I not find, she asked, that the whole debonair and dashing artistic scene here in the city—that precious Biedermeier party at the Cococello Club, for instance, that we had both attended recently—did it all not stand in agonizing contrast to the sadness and untrustworthiness of life? Did I not know the feeling as well, the horror at the intellectual vacuity and nothingness that reigned at the average "affair," in garish contrast to the attendant feverish excitement that came from wine, music, and the undercurrent of people interacting. Sometimes you could see with your own eyes how one person would be conversing with another, mechanically maintaining all the social niceties, while his mind was somewhere else entirely—that is, with someone he was watching. . . . And then the way the evening would slip toward ruin, the progressive disorder, the abandoned and squalid look of a salon at the end of an "affair." She admitted that after such parties she sometimes lay in her bed and wept for an hour. . . .

She went on to express more general worries and criticism, and seemed to have forgotten Rudolf. But when she came back to him, one had little doubt that he had ever left her mind for a moment. In saying he played the social dandy, she noted, she meant something quite harmless, something you could laugh at, but, then again, it did make you feel melancholy at times. He was always the last to arrive at a party, out of a need to keep people waiting—always wanting others to wait for him. And then he would accommodate the competition's social jealousies, by telling how he had been here and there yesterday, at the Langewiesches' and all the rest of them; at the Rollwagens', who had those two smashing daughters. ("I just have to hear the word 'smashing,' and I take alarm.") But he would mention it all apologetically, make light of it, as if to say: "I do have to show my face there, too, once in a while," whereby you could be quite sure that he had said the same thing there as here and wanted to leave everyone with the illusion that he most preferred to be with them—as if that simply had to be of greatest importance to each. But there was something infectious about his conviction that he brought joy to every heart. He would arrive at five o'clock for tea and say that he had promised to be somewhere else, at the Langewiesches' or the Rollwagens', between five-thirty and six— which was not at all true. Then he would stay until half-past six to show that he would rather be here, was your captive, that the others could wait—and was so certain that you would be delighted by it, that you might very well actually be delighted.

We laughed, though I did so with reticence, for I saw the knit of distress on her brow. And yet she spoke as if she thought it necessary (or did she in fact think it necessary?) for me not to set all too much store by Schwerdtfeger's charms—that is, to warn me against them. There was nothing to them. She had once been standing off at a little distance and heard, word for word, how he had demanded that someone who, she was certain, was of absolutely no consequence to him should stay at the party—with nice confiding familiarity and Bavarian turns of phrase like: "Now now, be a sweetheart, stick right here with me!" So that such persuasion on his part, which he had used with her, too, and might probably use with me as well, had been cheapened forever.

In short, she confessed a painful distrust of his seriousness, his professions of sympathy, his attentions—when you were sick, for instance, and he would come to see you. It was all done, as I would come to learn myself, only "to be nice" and because he thought it appropriate, socially advisable, but not out of any deeper feeling; you simply dared not make anything of it. You also had to overlook truly tasteless things—for example, that ghastly exclamation of his: "There are lots of unhappy women already!" She had heard him say it with her own ears. Someone had jokingly warned him not to make some girl—or it might have even been a married woman—unhappy, and he had actually had the impertinence to respond: "Oh, there are lots of unhappy women already!" You could only think to yourself, "Heaven help people like that! What absurd ignominy to be one of them!"

But she did not want to be too hard on him—which she had perhaps been with the word "ignominy." I should not misunderstand her: There could be no doubt that Rudolf's character had a certain more noble foundation. At some social affair, with just a subdued reply or one silent look askance, you could wrench him from his usual loud mood, win him over, so to speak, to a more serious frame of mind. Oh indeed, he sometimes truly seemed to be won over—given how extraordinarily easy it was to influence him. The Langewiesches and the Rollwagens, and all the rest, then became only shadows and phantoms to him. But, to be sure, all it took was for him to breathe some new air, to be exposed to other influences, for total estrangement, a hopeless remoteness, to take the place of trust and mutual understanding. He would sense it, for he was a sensitive man, and would contritely attempt to set things right. It was comically touching, but in order to restore the relationship, he would be sure to repeat some more or less fine phrase you had once spoken yourself, or words you once happened to quote from some book—as a token that he had not forgotten and was at home with loftier things. It could truly reduce a person to tears. And finally there was the way he would take his leave for the evening—always showing his ready contrition and desire to improve. He would come over and say goodbye with a few dialect witticisms that made you wince—perhaps in part a pained reaction from fatigue. Then after having shaken hands all round, he would return once more and say a simple, cordial adieu, which, of course, evoked a better reply. And so he had finished well—and he had to finish well. At the next two parties he still had to attend, he would presumably do much the same thing again. . . .

Is that enough? This is not a novel, in the composing of which an author presents scenes that indirectly reveal his characters' hearts to the reader. As a biographical narrator, I am certainly entitled to name things straight-out and simply state the psychological facts that influenced the life story I am to present. But given the singular statements that memory has just now dictated me to write, statements of what I might call a specific intensity, there can surely be no doubt about the fact to be communicated here. Inez Rodde loved young Schwerdtfeger, which led to only two questions: first, whether she knew it; and second, when, at what point in time, had what was originally a sociable brother-sister relationship with the violinist taken on this ardent and pained character?

The first question I answered with a yes. A young woman whose poetic eye was always on her own experience and who was as well-read, one might indeed say as psychologically trained as she, naturally had insight into the development of her feelings—however surprising, or incredible, that development may have appeared to her at first. The apparent naiveté with which she bared her heart to me did not prove any lack of knowledge; for what looked like innocence was in part an expression of a compulsion to speak out and in part a matter of trust in me—a strangely disguised trust, for she pretended to some extent that she thought me innocent enough to notice nothing (which, after all, would also have been a form of trust), and yet hoped and in reality knew that the truth would not escape me, because, to my credit, she regarded her secret well kept with me. Which it most definitely was. She could be certain of my humane and discreet sympathy, however difficult it is for a man constitutionally to enter into the soul and mind of a woman passionately in love with an individual of his own sex. Naturally it is much easier for us to follow the feelings of a man for a female—even if she means nothing whatever to us—than to enter into the emotions the other sex feels for someone of our own. Ultimately, one does not "understand" it, as a cultivated person one simply accepts it with objective respect for the law of nature. Indeed, a man tends to behave here with more generous tolerance than does a woman, who usually casts a very jealous eye at any member of her own sex from whom she learns that she has set a man's heart aflame, even when she herself feels only indifference for that heart.

Thus in terms of understanding I did not lack for friendly goodwill, though nature may have barred understanding in the sense of empathy. My God, little Schwerdtfeger! After all, his face had something puggish about it, his voice was guttural, and there was more of the boy than of the man about him—though I'll gladly grant the lovely blue of his eyes, his trim figure, and his captivating violin playing and whistling, not to mention his general niceness. And so Inez Rodde loved him, not blindly, but all the more deeply for that, and my own reaction was much like that of her wry sister Clarissa, with her quite arrogant attitude toward the opposite sex—I, too, wanted to tell him, "Hop to! Hop to, man! What can you be thinking? Jump, if you please!"

But that leap, even had Rudolf recognized it as his duty, was not all that easy. For there was Helmut Institoris, after all, the fiancé or fiancé *in spe,* Institoris the suitor—and with that I return to the question of when Inez's sisterly relationship to Rudolf had turned passionate. My human powers of intuition tell me: It had happened when Dr. Helmut had approached her, man to woman, and begun to court her. I was convinced then and still am now that Inez never would have fallen in love with Schwerdtfeger had not Institoris entered her life as a suitor. He courted her, but did so in some sense for another. For by his courtship and the train of thought it awakened, this bland man could indeed arouse the woman in her—that he could manage. But he could not arouse it for himself, though she was prepared to follow him out of the dictates of reason—that was beyond him. Rather, her awakened femininity immediately turned to another, for whom she had long been conscious of only serene, half-sisterly feelings, but for whom quite different emotions were now freed within her. That is not to say she would have thought him the right man, the worthy man. But, rather, her melancholy, which sought out misfortune, fixed on the man whom to her disgust she had heard say: "There are lots of unhappy women already!"

How strange, by the way! For she took something of the admiration that her unsatisfactory fiancé felt for unreflective, instinctual "life," but that was so contrary to her own views, and applied it to her infatuation with the other man—deceived Institoris with his own convictions, so to speak. For to her knowing, melancholy eyes, did not Rudolf represent the dearness of life itself?

Compared with Institoris, who merely instructed about beauty, Rudolf had on his side the advantage of art—which nourishes passion and transfigures all things human. The person of one's beloved is only enhanced, of course, and one's feelings for him understandably find ever new nourishment, when the perception one has of him is almost constantly bound up with intoxicating impressions of his art. Inez basically despised the lust for beauty felt by this city that reveled in the senses and to which her mother's curiosity about greater freedom in matters of morality had transplanted her; but for the sake of her bourgeois station she took part in the festivities of a society that was one grand art association—and that proved dangerous to the very peace she sought.

My memory retains pregnant and disquieting scenes from those days. I see us—the Roddes, the Knöterichs, perhaps, and myself as well—standing with the audience in one of the first rows of Zapfenstösser Hall and applauding an especially brilliant performance of a Tchaikovsky symphony. The conductor had motioned for the orchestra to rise so that along with him it could receive the audience's thanks for their beautiful work. Schwerdtfeger, not far to the left of the concertmaster (whose chair he would assume not long thereafter), stood turned toward the hall, his instrument under his arm; flushed and beaming, he nodded to us—with an intimacy that was not quite authorized—in personal greeting, while Inez (and I could not help stealing a glance her way), her head thrust forward on a tilt, her lips pursed with defiant roguishness, kept her eyes stubbornly trained on some other spot, on the conductor, or no, somewhere even farther off, on the harps. Or: I can see Rudolf himself, waxing enthusiastic over a performance of some standard piece by a guest artist, still standing at the front of a now almost empty hall, zealously clapping up at the podium, where the virtuoso is taking his tenth bow. Two steps away from him, between chairs pushed aside in disarray, stands Inez, who has had no more contact with him this evening than the rest of us, gazing at him and waiting for him to let it go at that, to turn, notice her, and greet her. He does not stop and does not notice her. Or better, out of one corner of his eye he does look her way—or, if that is saying too much, his blue eyes are not fixed quite steadfastly on his hero up there, but, without actually moving to one corner, are deflected slightly to the side where she stands waiting, yet without his ever interrupting his exuberant applause. Another few seconds—pale and with creases of anger between her brows—she turns on her heel and hurries away. At once he desists from calling the star out one more time, and follows her. He catches up with her at the door. She assumes an air that displays cold surprise at his presence here, at his very presence in the world, refuses to offer him a hand, a glance, a word—and hurries on her way.

I realize I ought not to have included these trifles and crumbs of observation here. They are out of place in my book and may seem rather silly in the eyes of the reader—who may well blame me for what seems irksome and unwarranted. He should at least credit me for suppressing a hundred others like them that were also swept up in my sympathetic awareness of my friends and that, thanks to the calamity to which they accrued, are never to be erased from my mind. Though, to be sure, this catastrophe played a very insignificant role in the general scheme of the world, I watched it grow over the years, but held my tongue with everyone about what I saw, about what troubled me. I spoke of it only once, at the very start, with Adrian in Pfeiffering—though on the whole I had little inclination, indeed was always somehow hesitant, to speak about social incidents of this sort with him, for he lived in monkish detachment from all love affairs. I did it nonetheless, told him in confidence that, from what I could see, even though Inez Rodde was about to become engaged to Institoris, she was helplessly, fatally in love with Rudi Schwerdtfeger.

We were sitting in the abbot's study, playing chess.

"That's news!" he said. "You probably want me to botch my move and lose my rook there, don't you?"

He smiled, shook his head, and added, "Poor heart!"

Then, still considering his move and with a pause between sentences, he said, "It's no fun for him, either, by the way. He needs to watch that he gets out in one piece himself."

XXX

THE FIRST BLAZING August days of 1914 found me changing from one overcrowded train to another in teeming railroad stations—their platforms filled with rows of abandoned baggage—on a headlong journey from Freising to Naumburg in Thuringia, where as a reserve staff sergeant I was immediately to join my regiment.

War had broken out. The destiny that had brooded over Europe for so long was unleashed, and, disguised as a disciplined implementation of all contingency plans and training, it raced through our cities, raging in all the minds and hearts of men as terror, exaltation, and frenzied urgency, as the thrill of fate, the sense of power, the readiness to sacrifice. It may well have been (I gladly believe it was) that in other places, in enemy and even allied lands, this short-circuiting of fate was experienced as a catastrophe and *"grand malheur"*—a phrase that, once in the field, we so often heard on the lips of French women, who, to be sure, had war on their own soil, in their parlors and kitchens: *"Ah monsieur, la guerre, quel grand malheur!"* But there is no denying that in our Germany its primary effect was elation and historical exuberance, the rapture of beginning anew and tossing the everyday aside, liberation from a global stagnation that could take us no farther, enthusiasm for the future, an appeal to duty and manliness—in short, a heroic festival. In Freising it meant that my senior students' faces were flushed, their eyes beaming. Youth's lust for action and adventure was united with the expedient fun of emergency final exams and hasty graduation. They stormed the recruiting stations, and I was happy not to have to play the role of the slacker.

And in general, I will not deny that I shared completely in the popular elation I have just attempted to characterize, even though such intoxication was foreign to my nature and being brushed by it felt a bit uncanny. My conscience—and I use the word here in a more-than-personal sense—was not quite pure. Such a "mobilization" for war, however stony its face and grim its call to universal duty, always feels something like the start of a wild holiday—like casting away real duties, playing hooky, allowing instincts that are not gladly bridled to bolt—has too much of all that for a staid man like myself to feel fully at ease; and bound up with such personal, temperamental resistance is the moral doubt as to whether one's nation has behaved so well until now that it should actually be permitted to be so blindly enraptured with itself. But here now, there enters the element of readiness to sacrifice, even unto death, which helps move one beyond so much and is, so to speak, the final word to which nothing more can be added. If war is felt to be, with more or less clarity, a universal ordeal, in which each individual—and each individual nation—must do what he must do and be ready to atone with his blood for the frailties and sins of the epoch, including his own, if war presents itself to the emotions as a sacrificial rite by which the old Adam is laid aside so that a new, higher life may be secured in unity, then quotidian morality is thereby superseded and falls silent before what is extraordinary. Nor would I forget that we marched off to war at the time with a comparatively pure heart and did not believe our previous behavior at home had been such that a bloody global catastrophe need be regarded as the inevitable logical consequence of our domestic conduct. That was true, God help us, five years ago, but not thirty. Justice and law, habeas corpus, freedom, and human dignity had been tolerably honored in Germany. Granted, cultivated people were embarrassed by the way that thoroughly unsoldierly playactor who sat on the imperial throne danced about brandishing his sword, although he was made for anything but war—and his attitude toward culture was that of a retarded idiot. His influence in that regard, however, had been exhausted in empty regulatory gestures. Culture had been free, had stood at an admirable pinnacle, and if it had long since grown accustomed to being totally irrelevant to the state, its younger representatives wished to regard the great national war that had now broken out as the means for breaking through to a new form of life in which state and culture would be one. Here there reigned, as always among us, a strange self-preoccupation, a fully naive egoism, for which it is of no importance (to which, indeed, it seems self-evident) that for the sake of the process of Germany's

growth (and we are always growing) a whole world—already farther
along and certainly not obsessed with the dynamics of catastrophe—
has to shed blood along with us. That is held against us, and not all that
unfairly; for from a moral standpoint, the means that a nation employs
to break through to a higher form of communal life—if those means
are to be bloody—should not be a war beyond its borders, but a civil
war. We, however, find that exceptionally abhorrent, whereas we
thought nothing of the fact—on the contrary, thought it splendid—
that our national unification (and then only a partial, compromised
unification) had cost three fierce wars. We had been a great power all
too long already; we were accustomed to the status, but it did not make
us as happy as expected. The feeling that it had not made us more appealing, that our relation to the world was rather worse than better,
brooded, whether we admitted it or not, deep in our hearts. A new
breakthrough seemed due, the breakthrough that would make us a
dominant world power—which, to be sure, could not be effected by
moral homework. War then, and if need be, against everyone, in order
to convince everyone, to win them over, that was the "destiny" (how
"German" the word *"Schicksal"* sounds—primal, pre-Christian, a
tragical-mythological motif from a music drama!) that had been assigned to us and for which we (and we alone) marched off enthusiastically—filled with the certainty that the hour of Germany's era had come,
that history was holding its hand over us, that after Spain, France, and
England it was now our turn to put our stamp upon the world and lead
it, that the twentieth century belonged to us, and that now that a bourgeois epoch had run its hundred-and-twenty-year course, the world
was to be renewed under the emblem of Germany, under the emblem
of a militaristic socialism yet to be completely defined.

    This notion, to avoid calling it an idea, dominated minds in harmo-
nious company with the notion that we had been forced into war, that
sacred necessity had called us to arms (well-stockpiled and well-drilled
arms, to be sure, whose superiority may have fed the constant, secret
temptation to put them to use), in company, that is, with the fear of being overrun on all sides, for which our sole defense was our own great
might—or better, our ability to carry war immediately onto other people's soil. Attack and defense were the same in our case; together they
formed the high emotion of our ordeal, of our calling, of the great moment, of sacred necessity. The nations out there might consider us dis-
turbers of peace and justice, intolerable enemies of life—we had the
means to bang the world over the head until it formed another opinion
of us, and not only admired us, but loved us as well.

Let no one think I am poking fun! There is no cause for it, none—above all, because I can in no way pretend I excluded myself from the general exaltation. I shared honestly in it, even though my natural staidness as a scholar may have kept me from joining in every noisy hurrah—yes, even though there may have been a mild, subconscious stirring of critical doubts, even though a slight uneasiness about thinking and feeling what everyone was thinking and feeling may at times have briefly overcome me. People like myself have doubts whether what every man thinks can be right. But still, for the superior individual it is a great pleasure just for once—and where might one find that once, if not here and now—to drown body and soul in the commonalty.

I remained in Munich for two days to say goodbye here and there and to supplement my gear with some minor items. The city was a ferment of solemn festivity, with added fits of panic and fearful rage—when, for instance, the wild rumor arose that the water supply was poisoned or someone thought he had detected a Serbian spy in the crowd. In order not to be taken for one and slain by mistake, Dr. Breisacher, whom I ran into on Ludwig Strasse, had pinned countless black, white, and red cockades and pennants on his chest. The state of war, for which the highest authority was transferred from civilians to the military, to a general who issued proclamations, was greeted with a cozy shudder. It was comforting to know that the members of the royal household, who as commanders were on their way to headquarters, would have competent chiefs of staff at their sides and so could work no real royal mischief. And thus exuberant popularity accompanied them. I saw regiments with bouquets on their rifle barrels march out of barrack gates under an escort of women holding handkerchiefs under their noses and to the cheers of a crowd of civilians who quickly gathered—to whom these farm lads promoted now to heroes responded with foolish, proud, and embarrassed smiles. I saw one very young officer in full marching gear standing on the rear platform of a streetcar, looking back, obviously preoccupied with thoughts of his young life, staring off into space and deep inside himself—and he abruptly pulled himself together and with a quick smile checked all around to see if anyone had been watching him.

To repeat, I felt happy to know that I was in the same situation as he, and not left to sit behind the men now guarding our nation. In point of fact I was, at first at least, the only person of our circle of acquaintances to go—after all, we were strong and populous enough that we could afford to be choosy, to consider cultural priorities, to declare a great many positions indispensable, and to rush to the front only those of our youth and manhood who were perfectly fit. Almost everyone in our circle proved to have some sort of health problem, about which one would scarcely have known anything, but which now resulted in their being exempted from service. Knöterich the Sugambrian was slightly tubercular. Zink the painter suffered from asthma attacks that sounded like whooping cough, so that he usually withdrew from society until they passed; and his friend Baptist Spengler was subject, as we know, to a host of afflictions by turns. Bullinger, the manufacturer, though young in years, was apparently indispensable as an industrialist on the home front; and the Zapfenstösser Orchestra was too important an element in the capital's artistic life for its members, including Rudi Schwerdtfeger, not to have been exempted from military service. In this connection, moreover, it came as a matter of fleeting surprise to learn that in his youth Rudi had been forced to undergo an operation that cost him one of his kidneys. He lived, we suddenly heard, with only one—quite competently, so it appeared, and the ladies soon forgot all about it.

I could go on to mention many instances of disinclination, protection, and lenient dispensation that occurred in the circles that frequented the Schlaginhaufens' and the home of the ladies Scheurl near the Botanical Gardens, circles in which, just as had been the case in the war previous, there was no lack of fundamental antipathy to this war—rooted in a nostalgia for the Rhine League, a fondness for France, Catholic aversion to Prussia, and similar sentiments. Jeannette Scheurl was profoundly unhappy and close to tears. She was in despair over this savage burst of antagonism between the two nations to which she belonged, France and Germany, and which she believed should complement one another, not brawl. *"J'en ai assez jusqu'à la fin de mes jours!"* she exclaimed with an angry sob. Despite my divergent sentiments, I could not refuse her a gentleman's sympathy.

In order to say goodbye to Adrian—whose personal indifference to the entire matter was perfectly self-evident to me—I went out to Pfeiffering and upon arrival found that the son of the house, Gereon, had only just left with several horses to report for induction. There I also found Rüdiger Schildknapp, who had not been called up as yet and was spending the weekend with our friend. He had previously served in the navy and was to be called up later, only to be discharged again within a few months. And was it all that much different with me? I shall say right out that I remained in the field for scarcely a year, until the Argonne campaign of 1915 and was then shipped home—decorated with a cross awarded merely for my having put up with discomforts and having come down with a case of typhoid.

Enough of what still lay ahead. Rüdiger's view of the war was conditioned by his admiration for England, just as Jeannette's was by her French blood. The British declaration of war had come as a total shock and left him extraordinarily peevish. In his opinion, they should never have been challenged by our marching into Belgium in contravention of treaty. France and Russia—fine, one might take them on if need be. But England—what dreadful folly! And so, being given to morose realism, he saw in the war nothing but mud, stench, gory amputation, sexual license, and lice, and bitterly mocked the sort of ideological journalism that glorified this lunacy as a grand enterprise. Adrian did not refute him, and I, though I partook of deeper sympathies, gladly admitted that his statements contained some words of truth.

We three ate together that evening in the large Winged-Victory room, and the quiet, cheerful comings and goings of Clementina Schweigestill, who served us our meal, put me in mind to ask Adrian how his sister Ursula was doing in Langensalza. Her marriage was a most happy one, and as for her health, she had recovered nicely from a weakness in the lung, a slight upper-lobe catarrh, that had followed the birth of three children in rapid succession, in 1911, 1912, and 1913. Those were the Schneidewein progeny who had come into the world by then: Rosa, Ezechiel, and Raimund. As we sat together that evening, it would be another nine years yet until the birth of the enchanting Nepomuk.

There was considerable discussion during the meal and afterward in the abbot's study about political and moral matters, about the mythic emergence of national character that occurs at such historical junctures and concerning which I spoke with some emotion in order to provide a little counterbalance to the drastically empirical view of war that Schildknapp saw as the only permissible one; we talked, that is, about Germany's role, about the violation of Belgium, so very reminiscent of Frederick the Great's incursion into formally neutral Saxony, about the world's shrill cry of outrage and about our philosophical chancellor's speech, with its brooding admission of guilt, its proverbial, and untranslatable, assertion that "Necessity knows no law," and its disregard—answerable solely before God—of an old legal document in face of our present life-threatening exigency. It fell to Rüdiger to set us laughing about it, although he did acknowledge my rather emotion-laden remarks; by parodying that ponderous thinker and his draping of a cloak of moral tropes over a long-standing strategy, he transformed all those brutal sentiments, solemn regrets, and respectable atrocities into something irresistibly comic—and made something even more comical of them than of the virtuous roar of a stunned world, which had in fact

long since known every dry expeditionary detail. And since I saw that
our host preferred this and was grateful for the chance to laugh, I
gladly joined in the mirth, not without remarking, however, that
tragedy and comedy sprout from the same branch and that a simple
change of lighting suffices to turn the one into the other.

Indeed, I did not let my understanding and feeling for Germany's
predicament, for its moral isolation and condemnation by the world,
which, it seemed to me, was merely an expression of a general fear of
our power and our lead in preparation for war (though I admitted that
those, the world's fear and our lead, gave but scant comfort amid our
ostracism)—indeed, I say, I did not let my patriotic sentiments, which
were so much more difficult to champion than those of the others, be
curtailed by humorous representations of our national traits; and as I
paced the room, I clad those sentiments in words, while Schildknapp
sat in the deep lounge chair smoking his shag pipe and Adrian, as
chance would have it, stood before the lectern that rested atop the old-
fashioned table with its sunken middle section and that he used for
both reading and writing. For remarkably enough, he also wrote on its
tilted surface, very like Erasmus in Holbein's portrait. On the table lay
a few books: a small volume of Kleist, with a bookmark inserted at the
essay on marionettes, plus the inevitable sonnets of Shakespeare, and
another volume of plays by the same poet—*Twelfth Night* was one,
Much Ado about Nothing, and if I am not mistaken, *Two Gentlemen of
Verona.* What he was working on at present, however, lay on the
lectern—loose sheets, rough drafts, beginnings, notations, sketches at
various stages of completion, often with just the top line of the violins
or woodwinds and way at the bottom the flow of the bass, and only a
white void in between; in other places, the harmonic connection and
the instrumental groupings had already been made clear by notation of
other orchestral voices as well. And with a cigarette between his lips,
he had stepped up to look it over, the way a chess player examines the
progress of a match on the checkered board—to which indeed musical
composition bears so much resemblance. We were so at ease in company together that, as if he were quite alone, he even picked up his pencil to enter a clarinet or horn figure where it seemed appropriate.

We knew few details about what was occupying him now that his
cosmic music had appeared with Schott & Sons in Mainz, the provi-
sions for its printing being the same as those for the Brentano Songs
before it. He was working on a suite of dramatic grotesques, whose
subjects, so we were told, were taken from an old book of anecdotes
and tales, the *Gesta Romanorum,* and was having a go at them without

rightly knowing yet whether this would amount to anything or if he would even stick with it. In any case, the characters were intended to be played by puppets rather than people. (Which explained the Kleist!) As for the *Marvels of the Universe,* that solemnly cheeky work had been scheduled for a foreign performance, but with the outbreak of war that had fallen through. We had spoken about it at supper. The Lübeck production of *Love's Labour's Lost,* as unsuccessful as it had been, together with the mere existence of the Brentano cycle, had had its own quiet effect and had begun to lend Adrian's name a certain esoteric, if rather tentative renown in the innermost circles of art—though even that was hardly the case in Germany and not at all in Munich, but only in other, more receptive places. A few weeks before, he had received a letter from Monsieur Monteux, the director of the Russian ballet in Paris and formerly of the Colonne Orchestra; in it the conductor, as a friend of experiment, had announced his intention to perform *Marvels of the Universe* along with some orchestral pieces in a straight concert version of *Love's Labour's Lost.* He was planning this concert for the Théâtre des Champs-Elysées and invited Adrian to come to Paris for it, perhaps even to rehearse and present his own works. We had not asked our friend if he might have accepted the invitation. In any case, circumstances were now such that his acceptance was no longer an issue.

I can still picture that wainscoted old room—with its oversize chandelier, its wardrobe with wrought-iron fittings, the flat leather cushions on the corner bench, the deep embrasure—and myself pacing the carpet and floorboards and declaiming about Germany, more for myself and perhaps for Schildknapp than for Adrian, whom I expected to pay me no attention. Accustomed to teaching and speaking, I am, presuming I have warmed to my topic, not a bad orator; I even rather enjoy listening to myself and take a certain pleasure in my command over words. Adding more than a few animated gestures, I left it to Rüdiger whether to consider my words part of the bellicose journalism that so annoyed him; but in my opinion one had to acknowledge as natural a certain psychological sympathy for a state of mind—itself not without some touching traits—that this one historical moment had shaped from an otherwise multiform German character, even if in the final analysis we were dealing simply with the psychology of a new breakthrough.

"For a nation such as ours," I declared, "the psychological element is always primary, the essential motivating factor; political action is of secondary importance, a reflex, an expression, an instrument. At the deepest level, what people mean by the breakthrough to world power to which destiny has called us is a breaking out into the world—from a loneliness of which we are painfully aware and that no vigorous involvement in the world economy has been able to shatter since the founding of the Reich. The bitter thing is that it must be the empirical phenomenon of war that appropriates what in truth is our yearning, our thirst for unification . . ."

"May God bless your *studia*," I heard Adrian say *sotto voce* and with a brief burst of laughter. He had not looked up from his musical notations.

I stopped and stared at him, though that did not matter to him.

"To which," I replied, "in your opinion, one must presumably add: 'Because you won't amount to much, hallelujah!'?"

"Or better perhaps: 'They won't amount to much,'" he riposted. "Forgive me for falling into student jargon, but your oration reminded me very much of our disputes in the straw back in the days of yore— what were those lads' names? I notice that old names are starting to get away from me." (He was twenty-nine as he lived and breathed.) "Deutschmeyer? Dungersleben?"

"You mean the strapping Deutschlin," I said, "and a fellow whose name was Dungersheim. There was also a Hubmeyer and a Teutleben, too. You've never paid much attention to names. They were good, serious-minded lads."

"Were they ever! Just think, there was a boy who answered to the name of Schappeler, and then there was a certain 'social' Arzt. What do you say to that? You weren't really one of them, weren't a theology major. But listening to you now, it's as if I'm listening to them. Straw to sleep on. By which I mean, once a student, always a student. The academic life keeps one young and frisky."

"You shared a major with them," I said, "but basically were more of an auditor than I. But of course, Adri. I was only a student, and you may well be right to say that I have remained one. But so much the better, then, if academic life keeps one young, which means: preserves a loyalty to the mind, to free thought, to higher interpretation of the crude event . . ."

"Is loyalty the issue here?" he asked. "I understood you to say that Kaisersaschern wants to become a world city. That's not very loyal."

"Go on," I shouted. "You didn't understand anything of the sort, but understood quite well what I meant by Germany's breaking out into the world."

"It wouldn't help much," he replied, "if I did understand, because for now at least the crude event will only make our being shut out and shut in absolute, no matter how far your troops swarm out over Europe. As you see—I cannot go to Paris. You all are going in my place. That's fine, too! Just between us—I wouldn't have gone anyway. You're saving me the embarrassment . . ."

"The war will be short," I said in a choked voice, for his words had pained me. "It can't possibly last long. We are paying for our swift breakthrough with the guilt of an admitted wrong, declaring that we shall make it good again. We must take that guilt upon ourselves . . ."

"And will know how to bear it with dignity," he interrupted. "Germany has broad shoulders. And who would deny that such a real breakthrough is worth what the meek world calls a crime! I hope you don't assume that I have a low opinion of the idea that you have decided to mull over there on your bed of straw. Ultimately there is only one problem in the world, and its name is: How does one break through? How does one reach free and open air? How does one burst the cocoon and become a butterfly? The whole situation is governed by that question. Here, too," he said, tugging at the red ribbon in the volume of Kleist lying on the table, "the issue of breakthrough is dealt with, in the splendid essay on marionettes, to be precise, where it is specifically called 'the last chapter of world history.' Although it speaks only about aesthetics, about charm, about the free grace that in actuality is reserved solely for the puppet and for God—that is, for the unconscious and for endless consciousness—whereas every reflection between zero and infinity kills such grace. Consciousness, so this writer suggests, must pass through an infinity in order for grace to reappear, and Adam must eat again of the Tree of Knowledge in order to fall back into the state of innocence."

"I am so glad," I cried, "that you have just read that! It is splendidly conceived, and you are right to incorporate it within the idea of the breakthrough. But don't say, 'speaks only about aesthetics,' don't say, 'only'! It is very wrong to see aesthetics as a narrow and separate segment of the human enterprise. It is much more than that; ultimately aesthetics is all things, whether their effect is engaging or off-putting, just as for the author the word 'grace' has the broadest possible meaning. Aesthetic deliverance or confinement, that is destiny, that is what determines one's happiness or unhappiness, whether one is comfortably at home on this earth or lives in hopeless, if proud isolation. And one need not be a philologist to know that what is ugly is despised. The longing to break through, to break free from confines, from being sealed inside what is ugly—you may go right ahead and tell me I am threshing straw, but I feel, have always felt, and will plead against all crude appearances that this is German *kat exochen*, deeply German, the very definition of Germanness, a psychological state threatened by the poison of loneliness, by eccentricity, provincial standoffishness, neurotic involution, unspoken Satanism . . ."

I broke off. He looked at me, and I believe the color had drained from his face. The look he directed at me was the look, that familiar look that made me unhappy—and it mattered little whether it was aimed at me or someone else—mute, veiled, so coldly aloof as to be almost offensive, and it was followed by the smile, with lips closed, nostrils twitching in scorn, and by his turning away. He moved away from the table, not toward Schildknapp's chair, but to the window nook, on whose wainscoted wall he straightened a picture of a saint. Rüdiger offered a few remarks—given my viewpoint, he said, I should be congratulated on being sent to the field right off, and on horseback no less. One ought, he said, to take the field of battle only on horseback, or not at all. And he patted the neck of his imaginary nag. We laughed, and our goodbye—for I had to make my train—was easy and cheerful. A good thing it was not sentimental, that would have been rather out of place. But I took Adrian's look with me into battle—perhaps it was that look, and only ostensibly typhoid fever carried by lice, that brought me home to his side again so soon.

XXXI

"YOU ALL ARE going in my place," Adrian had said. But we never got to Paris! Shall I admit that I, very privately and apart from any historical aspect, felt deeply, intimately, personally ashamed of the fact? Week after week we sent home terse, affectedly lapidary reports of victory, couching triumph as a cold matter of course. Liège had long since fallen; we had won the battle for Lorraine, had swung across the Meuse with five armies as dictated by our longstanding secret master plan, had taken Brussels and Namur, had gained the day at Charleroi and Longwy, had won a second string of battles at Sedan, Rethel, Saint-Quentin, and had occupied Reims. As it swept us along, our advance was swift and, just as we had dreamt, was borne as if upon pinions by the "yes" of destiny and the favor of the god of war. To remain steadfast while gazing upon the incendiary aspect inseparable from that advance was our manly duty, the chief demand placed upon our heroic courage. With remarkable ease and clarity I can still recall today the picture of a gaunt French woman standing on a hill around which our battery was moving and beneath which a bombarded village still smoldered. "I am the last!" she cried out to us with a tragic gesture no German woman would know how to make. *"Je suis la dernière!"* And with raised fists hurled her curse out over our heads, repeating it three times: *"Méchants! Méchants! Méchants!"*

We looked the other way. We had to win, and this was the hard business of winning. Sitting astride my bay, I took some comfort in the miserable torments of a cough and rheumatic pains that came with dank nights spent under canvas.

Borne upon pinions, we bombarded many more villages. Then came what was incomprehensible, seemingly absurd: the order to retreat. How were we to understand that? Our army, under Hausen, lay south of Châlons-sur-Marne and was poised for the march on Paris, as was Kluck's army at another position. We were unaware that elsewhere, after a five-day battle, the French had broken through Bülow's right flank—reason enough for an anxious, overcautious supreme commander (promoted to that post because of who his uncle was) to give it all back. We passed through the same villages we had left smoldering behind us—even the hill where the tragic woman had stood. She was no longer there.

The pinions had deceived us. It was not to be. This war was not to be won in one swift onslaught—and no more than people at home did we comprehend that fact. We did not understand the world's frenzied joy at the outcome of the Battle of the Marne, or that with it, the short war on which our salvation depended had become a long war we could not endure. Our defeat was merely a matter of time and of its cost to others—we could have laid down our weapons and forced our leaders to make an immediate peace, had we realized all this; but presumably only one or two of them even secretly allowed himself to think it. They had barely grasped the fact that the age of localized war was past and that any campaign into which we saw ourselves forced had to end in a global conflagration. In such a case, we had on our side the advantages of short supply lines, a fighting spirit, a high level of preparedness, and a firmly established state with a strong sense of authority—all of which contributed to our chances of a lightning-quick victory. But failing that chance (and it was written that we had to fail it), whatever we might accomplish in the years to come, our cause was lost, on principle and in advance—this time, next time, always.

We did not know this. Slowly, torturously the truth permeated us, and the war—despite occasional semivictories that kept a scant, deceptive hope flickering—became a war of rot, decay, misery. The war that I, too, had said could only be a short one, lasted four years. Should I here recall at length and in detail the slow, steady slide toward breakdown, the exhaustion of our armies and supplies, the shabbiness of a threadbare life, the increasing wretchedness of our food, the loss of morale that went with scarcity, the taste for thievery, and the crude ostentation of riffraff grown rich on war? I could then be rightly censured for recklessly overstepping the bounds of a task I have defined as personal and biographical. Everything to which I have alluded, from its beginning to its bitter end, I experienced at home, first on leave and then as a discharged soldier restored to his teaching post in Freising. For in the fields around Arras, during the period of the second battle for that stronghold, which lasted from early May until well into July 1915, the delousing measures were evidently inadequate: The infection put me in isolation barracks for weeks. Finally, after another month in a convalescent home for wounded soldiers in the Taunus, I did not resist the view that I had fulfilled my patriotic duty and could serve better by resuming my old post of maintaining the educational system.

Which I did—and was once again able to be a husband and father in the same modest home whose walls and familiar objects, though fated perhaps for destruction in a bombing attack, still serve me today as the framework for my secluded and emptied existence. Let it be noted once again, and certainly not in any boastful sense, but as a simple statement, that, although without exactly neglecting my life, I have always given it only half my attention, have led it with my left hand so to speak, as if it were merely coincidental; my true concern, anxiety, and regard have been dedicated to my childhood friend, and my being led back into proximity with him gave me such great joy—if the word "joy" applies to my painful awareness of his lack of response or to a soft, cool shudder of anguish that had its origins in his increasingly creative loneliness. "To keep an eye on him," to watch over his extraordinary and enigmatic life, always seemed to be the true and urgent task assigned to my own life; it formed its true content, and that is why I spoke of the emptiness of my present days.

He had been relatively fortunate in his choice of a home—and indeed it was his "home" in a special repetitive sense of which I somehow could never quite approve. Thank God the care he received from his farmers, the Schweigestills, was as adequate as one could hope for during those years of breakdown and gnawing, increasingly nasty shortages; and although he neither realized nor honored the fact, he remained almost untouched by the corrosive changes to which his blockaded and besieged nation was subjected despite its ongoing military offensives. He accepted all this as a matter of course, never mentioned it, as if its origins were within him, within his nature, whose power of inertia and fixation on the *semper idem* prevailed individually against all outward circumstance. The Schweigestill farm was fully able to satisfy his simple habits of diet. Moreover, upon my return from the field I found him being looked after by two females, who had approached him and, quite independently of one another, appointed themselves his devoted, caring friends.

These two ladies were Meta Nackedey and Kunigunde Rosenstiel—

the one a piano teacher, the other an active partner in a visceral enterprise, that is to say, in a firm that produced sausage casings. It is truly
remarkable: an esoteric early renown such as had begun to be associated with Leverkühn's name, although totally hidden from the broad
masses, has its focus in certain initiated spheres, in a response among
leading experts, of which the invitation to Paris had been a token; but
at the same time that renown may also be reflected in humbler, more
modest realms, in the needy emotions of poor souls whose lonely and
passionate sensibilities (cloaked as "higher aspirations") remove them
from the masses and who find happiness in a veneration they cherish
all the more for its very rarity. That such souls are ladies, indeed
maiden ladies, can come as no surprise; for human abstinence is surely
the source of prophetic intuition, which is no less valuable for its
stunted origins. There was no question but that personal issues played
a decisive role here, indeed outweighed intellectual considerations,
which in both cases could at most be understood and assessed only in
vague outline, in terms of feeling and intuition. But do I—as a man
who can speak of an early, significant infatuation of head and heart
with Adrian's cool and enigmatically self-contained existence—do I have
the least right to mock the fascination that his solitary, nonconforming
way of life had on these women?

Our Nackedey was a timorous creature in her thirties, who was forever blushing and perishing in instant embarrassment and, whether
speaking or listening, blinked her eyes in spasms of amiability behind
her perched pince-nez, all the while nodding her head and wrinkling
her nose—this woman, then, had found herself standing on the front
platform of a streetcar one day, right next to Adrian, who happened to
be in town, and upon discovering this had taken mindless, fluttering
flight through the crowded car to the one behind, where she collected
herself for a few moments, only to return and speak to him, address
him by name, divulge her own, add a few words, amid alternate blushes
and blanches, about her circumstances, and tell him that she considered
his music sacred, to all of which he responded with a word of thanks.
So began their acquaintance, but Meta had not initiated it in order to
leave things at that. She renewed it only a few days later with a visit to
Pfeiffering and a bouquet of homage, and from then on she constantly
nurtured this acquaintance—in open competition, spurred on by mutual
jealousy, with our Rosenstiel, who had commenced things differently.

She was a big-boned Jewish woman about the same age as Nackedey,
with unmanageable frizzy hair and eyes in whose brown depths was
written an ancient sadness that the daughter of Zion had been brought

down and her people were as lost sheep. An energetic woman in a crude business (for there is something crude about a sausage-casing factory), she nevertheless had the elegiac habit of beginning every sentence with a plaintive "ah!" "Ah, yes," "Ah, no," "Ah, believe me," "Ah, but then why not," "Ah, I'm going to Nuremberg tomorrow," she would say with a deep, doleful voice rough as desert winds, and even when one asked her, "How are you?" she would answer, "Ah, fine as always." Things were quite different, however, when she wrote—and she had an extraordinary love of writing. For not only was Kunigunde, like almost all Jews, very musical, but she also maintained, without having read widely, a much purer and more fastidious relationship to the German language than the average citizen, indeed than most men of letters, and had initiated her acquaintance with Adrian, which for her part she always called a "friendship" (and did it not over time truly become that?), with an excellent letter, a long, well-phrased letter of esteem—remarkable not for its content, but modeled stylistically on the example of an older humanistic Germany—which its recipient read with a certain astonishment and whose literary value he found impossible to pass over in silence. But, despite countless personal visits, she kept on writing frequent letters to him in Pfeiffering in this same fashion. Lengthy, not very concrete, not any more exciting in terms of substance, but in a language that was meticulous, tidy, and readable—though never in longhand, but on her office typewriter, with typed commercial ampersands—these missives declared a veneration she was either too modest or simply unable to justify or define more closely. It was simple veneration, an instinctual reverence and devotion, which she sustained loyally over the years and for which one truly had to hold this splendid woman, quite apart from her other abilities, in highest regard. I at least did so and endeavored to pay our timorous Nackedey the same tacit respect, although Adrian, given the complete inattentiveness of his nature, may have always merely tolerated his devotees' ovations and offerings. And, ultimately, was my lot all that different from theirs? I credit myself with having made it a point to treat them well (whereas, in the most primitive fashion, they could not stand one another and would measure each other with squinted eyes whenever they met); for in a certain sense, I was a member of their guild and would have had good reason to be annoyed by this debased and spinsterish duplication of my own relationship with Adrian.

During these hungry years, then, these two always arrived with their hands full, bringing to a man already well taken care of in regards to basic nourishment, everything conceivable, everything obtainable on the sly: sugar, tea, coffee, chocolate, baked goods, preserves, and shag tobacco for rolling cigarettes, which he then shared with me, Schild-knapp, and even Rudi Schwerdtfeger, whose confiding familiarity never wavered—and we often bestowed blessings on the names of those helpful women. As for tobacco, Adrian did without it only if co-erced—meaning, on days when his migraine overcame him like a sud-den and violent attack of seasickness and he kept to his bed in his darkened room, which happened two or three times a month; other-wise he could not do without that diverting stimulant, which had become a habit with him rather late in life, during his Leipzig years—least of all when he was working, for he swore he could not have kept at his work as long as he did without occasionally rolling and inhaling a cigarette. At the time I returned to civilian life, however, he was fiercely devoted to his work—in my view not so much because of its actual object, that is, the *Gesta* music, or not exclusively so at least, but because he was anxious to put it behind him and to ready himself for the new demands of genius that were announcing themselves. On the horizon, of this I am certain, there already stood, presumably even be-fore the outbreak of war—which for powers of divination such as his meant a deep rift, both a turning and a cutting-off point, an opening onto a new, tumultuous, and earthshaking period of history glutted with wild adventures and sufferings—on the horizon of his creative life, then, there already stood the *Apocalipsis cum figuris,* the work that was to give his life dizzying impetus, and until then (or so I see the process at least) he waited, passing the time with his imaginative pup-pet grotesques.

Schildknapp had introduced Adrian to the book, which is consid-ered the source for most of the romantic myths of the Middle Ages and is a translation from the Latin of the oldest collection of Christian fairy tales and legends—and I am happy to give credit here to Adrian's fa-vorite with the same-colored eyes. They had spent many an evening reading it together, and what came to the fore above all was Adrian's sense of the comic, his craving for laughter—indeed, his ability to laugh till he cried, which my rather dry personality never rightly knew how to nourish and was held back from encouraging by a kind of un-seemliness that my anxious mind saw in those outbursts of mirth from a personality for which I felt a strained and fearful love. Rüdiger of the same-colored eyes did not in the least share my apprehension—which I kept very much to myself, by the way, and which did not prevent my joining sincerely in these merry moods whenever they happened to oc-cur. It was patently obvious, however, that the Silesian took decided satisfaction in them, as if this was his mission, as if he had done his

duty whenever he succeeded in reducing Adrian to tears of laughter—
and with this book of anecdotes and tales he had undeniably succeeded
in a highly gratifying, fruitfully constructive fashion.

I would assert that the *Gesta*, with its historical illiteracy, pious
Christian didacticism, and moral naiveté, with its curious casuistry in
matters of patricide, adultery, and tangled incest, with its undocu-
mented Roman emperors and their daughters, kept under incredible
guard so that they may be sold off under the most ingenious conditions—it cannot be denied, I say, that all these fables of knights pil-
grimaging to the Promised Land, of wanton wives, sly bawds, and
clerics given to black magic, can have an extraordinarily humorous effect when told in pompous Latin or in an indescribably artless translation. There was every likelihood that they would excite Adrian's sense
of parody, and the idea of a musical dramatization of several of these
stories in condensed form for marionette theater occupied him from
the day he first made their acquaintance. There is, for instance, in anticipation of the *Decameron,* a basically immoral tale, "The Godless
Cunning of Old Wives," in which an abettor of forbidden passions,
dressed in a nun's holy habit, convinces even an uncommonly honest
wife, whose trusting husband is on a journey, that she should sinfully
comply with the wishes of a young man consumed with desire for her.
The crone, after starving her little bitch dog for two days, gives it bread
coated with mustard, bringing great tears to the animal's eyes. She then
takes the bitch with her to the strait-laced wife, who receives her with
reverence, since, like everyone else, she believes the crone to be a saint.
When the lady notices the dog's weeping and asks in amazement about
the cause of its condition, the old woman pretends she would rather
avoid the question, and only upon being pressed does she confess that
this little bitch was once her all-too-chaste daughter, who, by stubbornly refusing to oblige a young man burning with desire for her, had
driven him to his death and in punishment was changed into her present form and, of course, now must shed ceaseless tears of remorse over
her doggy existence. And as she tells her calculated lies, the bawd weeps
as well; the lady, however, is terrified at the thought of the similarity
between her own case and that of the punished girl and tells the old
woman of the young man aching for her, whereupon the crone somberly
paints for her the irreparable damage that would follow if she, too,
were changed into a bitch—and is indeed charged with fetching the
languishing lad, so that, in God's name, he may cool his lust, with the
result that the two of them celebrate sweetest adultery at the instigation
of godless mischief.

I still envy Rüdiger for having been the first to read this story to our friend there in the abbot's study, though I must admit that had I done so, it would not have been the same. In any case, his contribution to the future work was limited to this initial stimulus. When it came to re-working the fables for the puppet stage, their recasting as dialogue, he refused such an unreasonable demand upon his precious time (or upon his familiar obstinate sense of freedom), and Adrian, who did not hold it against him, made do in my absence with sketching out a loose sce-nario and approximate exchanges of speech, until later, then, in my spare time, I quickly shaped them into their final form, a mixture of prose and rhymed verse. In accordance with Adrian's wishes, the singers who lend their voices to the gesticulating puppets are assigned places among the instruments, in the orchestra (a rather sparse orches-tra, consisting of violin and double-bass, clarinet, oboe, trumpet, and trombone, together with a single percussionist, who also plays a set of bells), and included among them is a narrator, who, like the *testo* in an oratorio, summarizes the plot in recitative and narration.

This open form works best in the fifth tale, the suite's *pièce de résis-tance,* the story entitled "The Birth of Saint Gregory the Pope"—a birth whose sinful singularity by no means marks the end of the tale, since the many terrible vicissitudes of the hero's life are not only no impediment to his final elevation as Christ's vicar on earth, but rather make him appear to be especially called and predestined for that office by God's peculiar grace. The intricate chain of events is long, and it is surely unnecessary for me to recount here the story of two orphaned royal siblings, of whom the brother loves his sister immoderately, so much so that he loses his head, leaving her in more than a delicate con-dition and making her the mother of a boy of exceptional beauty. The entire story revolves around this boy, a child who, in the most awful sense, is his own best cousin. While his father attempts to do penance by joining a crusade to the Promised Land and dies there, the child drifts toward an uncertain fate. For the queen, determined not to be re-sponsible for baptizing a child so monstrously sired, orders him and his princely cradle to be carefully placed into a barrel—not without the addition of an explanatory legend, plus gold and silver for his educa-tion—and entrusted to the waves of the sea, which "on the sixth feast day" bear him to a cloister presided over by a pious abbot. He finds the boy, baptizes him with his own name, Gregory, and provides him with an education that, given the boy's exceptional physical and mental gifts, yields happiest results. Meanwhile the sinful mother, to the great regret of her subjects, pledges never to marry—quite evidently not only because she feels herself profaned and unworthy of Christian marriage, but also because she maintains an equivocal loyalty to her missing brother. When a powerful foreign duke seeks her hand in marriage, which she then refuses him, he becomes so enraged that he makes war upon her kingdom and conquers all but a single fortified city, into which she retreats. The lad Gregory, having learned of his origins, makes plans for a pilgrimage to the Holy Sepulcher, but is driven off course and finds himself in the city of his mother, where he learns of the monarch's misfortunes; he arranges to be brought before her and offers his services to her, who, so it says, "eyes him sharply," but does not recognize him. He then defeats the enraged duke, frees the land, and is now proposed by the liberated queen's advisers to be her spouse; and although she plays rather coy and stipulates that she be given a day—just one—to think it over, she then consents, counter to her own pledge, with the result that, amid great applause and jubilation by the whole nation, the wedding is performed and unsuspected horror is heaped upon horror when the son of sin climbs into the nuptial bed with his mother—but I shall not amplify on all that.

I would like to recall only the emotionally charged high points of the story, which in this puppet opera come into their own in a strangely wonderful way. When, for instance, at the beginning the brother asks his sister why she looks so pale and why "her eyes have lost their dark luster," she replies: "'Tis no wonder, for I am with child and full of remorse." Or when, upon receiving the news of the death of the man she knows to be a transgressor, she breaks into the remarkable lament: "Gone is my hope, gone is my strength, my only brother, my second self!" and then lavishes kisses upon the corpse from the sole of its feet to the crown of its head, so that her knights, disconcerted by such exaggerated sorrow, feel compelled to pull their mistress off the dead man. Or when, upon realizing with whom it is she lives in tenderest wedlock, she says to him: "Oh my sweet son, you are my only child, you are my husband and my lord, you are both my and my brother's son, oh my sweet child, and oh Thou my God, why didst Thou let me be born!" For upon finding the explanatory legend, which she herself wrote, in a secret compartment of her husband's, she learns with whom she shares her bed, though, thank God, without having borne him yet another brother or grandchild to her own brother. And now it is his turn once again to consider a penitential journey, which he begins at once barefoot. He comes to a fisherman who, "seeing the fineness of his limbs," realizes that he is not dealing with a common traveler and agrees with him that utter solitude is the only proper solution. The fisherman sails him sixteen miles out to sea, to a rock

washed by surging tides, and there, once fetters have been placed on
his feet and the key flung into the sea, Gregory spends seventeen years
of penitence, at the end of which there comes an overwhelming—
though he, it seems, finds it hardly surprising—elevation by grace. For
the Pope is dying in Rome, and no sooner is he dead than a voice de-
scends from heaven: "Seek out Gregorius, the man of God, and make
of him my vicar on earth!" Messengers scurry in all directions and pay
a visit as well to the fisherman, who recollects. He now catches a fish in
whose belly he finds the key once cast to the bottom of the ocean. He
transports the messengers out to the penitential rock, and they call up:
"O Gregorius, thou man of God, climb down from that rock, for it is
the will of God that thou shouldst be made His vicar upon earth!" And
what does he answer them? "If it please God," he says serenely, "may
His will be done." As he arrives in Rome, however, and the bells are to
be rung, they do not wait, but ring on their own—all the bells ring of
their own accord, announcing that there has never before been so pious and instructive a pope. And the fame of the blessed man reaches his
mother as well, and since she rightly concludes that she can entrust her
life to no one better than to this chosen one, she sets out for Rome to
confess to the Holy Father, who, upon hearing her confession, recognizes her and says: "Oh my sweet mother, sister, and wife. Oh my
friend. The Devil thought to lead us into hell, yet God's greater power
has prevented him." And he builds her a cloister where she may govern as abbess, but only for a brief while. For it is soon granted unto
both of them to surrender their souls back to God.

For this exuberantly sinful, simple, and grace-filled story, then,
Adrian had gathered all the wit and terror, all the childlike insistence,
fantasy, and solemnity of musical depiction, and one might well apply
to this piece, or particularly to this piece, that curious epithet of the old
professor from Lübeck, the term "god-witted." Memory prompts me
to do so, because the *Gesta* does in fact represent something of a re-
gression to the musical style of *Love's Labour's Lost,* whereas the tonal
language of *Marvels of the Universe* is more suggestive of the *Apocalypse,* or even that of *Faustus.* After all, such anticipations and overlap-
pings are common in the creative life; yet I can easily explain the
artistic stimulus that this material had provided my friend—it was its
intellectual charm, not without a hint of malice and unraveling travesty, for it had arisen out of a critical response to the swollen pathos of
an artistic era that was drawing to a close. Music drama had taken its
stuff from romantic sagas, from the world of medieval myth, and had
insinuated that only such subjects were worthy of music, compatible

with its nature. Such dicta appeared to have also been obeyed here, but in an utterly destructive fashion, inasmuch as bizarre whimsy, especially at moments of erotic farce, replaces sacerdotal morality, the whole inflated pomp of music drama's resources is cast aside, and the action transferred to what is, after all, the burlesque of a puppet stage. During the period he worked on the *Gesta* pieces, Leverkühn made a particular point of studying the specific possibilities of puppetry, and the Catholic-baroque theatrical tastes of the people among whom he led his hermit's life provided him many opportunities to do so. In nearby Waldshut lived a chemist who carved and costumed marionettes, and Adrian visited the man repeatedly. He also traveled to Mittenwald, the village of violin-makers at the upper end of the Isar valley, where an apothecary devoted to the same hobby lived and, with the help of his wife and talented sons, put on puppet shows in the style of Pocci and Christian Winter, attracting a large audience of both locals and outsiders. Leverkühn attended these shows and, as I noticed, also studied literature on the very ingenious hand puppets and shadow plays of the Javanese.

What festive, exciting evenings those were when we (that is, myself, Schildknapp, and perhaps Rudi Schwerdtfeger as well, who was determined to be present now and again) gathered in the Winged-Victory room with its deep window nooks, and Adrian sat at the old square piano and played newly composed music from this whimsical score, in which the most imperious harmonies and labyrinthine rhythms were applied to the simplest material—and, vice versa, the most extraordinary tales were set to the musical style of a child on a toy trumpet. The reunion of the queen with the now sainted husband whom she had once borne to her brother and had embraced as her spouse, evoked tears such as had never before moistened our eyes, a unique mingling of laughter and fanciful sentiment. And Schwerdtfeger, in a burst of familiarity, seized the license of the moment to exclaim, "What a splendid job you've done!" and pressed Adrian's head against his own in an embrace. I saw Rüdiger's normally bitter smile turn into a censorious grimace, and even I could not help muttering an "Enough!" and reaching out a hand as if to pull back this man who had abandoned all distance and inhibition.

He may have had some trouble, then, in following the conversation that took place after this intimate performance in the abbot's study. We spoke about the linking of the avant-garde with folk traditions, about the closing of the rift between art and accessibility, between high and low, achieved at one point to some extent by Romanticism, in both literature and music—after which the destiny of art proved to be an even deeper, more alienating rupture between what is good and easy, admirable and diverting, progressive and generally enjoyable. Was it sentimentality for music—which stood for all art—to demand, with growing awareness, that it step out of its worthy isolation and find a sense of the communal without becoming common, to speak a language that a man untutored in music could also understand, as he had once understood the "Wolf's Glen" scene, the "Bridal Wreath" scene, Wagner? In any case, sentimentality was not the means to this goal. Far more useful, rather, were irony, mockery, which cleared the air by opposing Romanticism, pathos, and prophecy, and joining literature and the intoxication of sound in a common front with what is objective and elemental—which is to say, with the rediscovery of music itself as organization of time. A very precarious start! For did not a false primitivism—which was, once again, Romanticism—lie close at hand? To hold to the heights of intellect; to dissolve the most select achievements of European musical development into something so self-evident that everyone could grasp its newness; to become its master by straightforwardly using it as freely available building material, while letting tradition be felt and yet restamped into the very opposite of epigonism; to make one's handiwork, however highly developed, totally inconspicuous, allowing all the arts of counterpoint and instrumentation to vanish and melt into an effect of simplicity far beyond anything simple, into an intellectually supple artlessness—that, it seemed, was the task, the desire of art.

It was Adrian who spoke for the most part, while we others seconded him only lightly. The excitement of his performance had left his cheeks red and eyes aglow, and he spoke slightly feverishly—though not in a torrent, but simply tossing his words away, and yet with such animation that it seemed to me I had never seen him thrust out of himself so eloquently before, be it in my or Rüdiger's presence. Schildknapp had expressed a disbelief in a de-Romanticizing of music. Music was too deeply, too essentially bound up with the Romantic ever to deny it without suffering severe natural losses. To which Adrian replied:

"I'll gladly admit you're right, if by Romantic you mean a warmth of feeling, which music, being in the service of a technical mentality, denies nowadays. It is really self-denial. But what we called the refining of the complicated into the simple is ultimately the same thing as regaining vitality and the power of feeling. Whoever might be able to achieve the—how would you put it?" he said, turning to me, and answered himself, "—the breakthrough, you'd say, whoever might achieve the breakthrough out of intellectual coldness into a risk-filled world of new feeling, that person would be called art's redeemer. Redemption," he continued with a nervous shrug, "a Romantic word; and a word that harmonists love, shoptalk for the bliss of harmonic music's resolved cadences. Funny, isn't it, how for a long time music saw itself as a means of redemption, and all the while, like all art, it needed redemption, that is, needed to be redeemed from a solemn isolation that was the fruit of culture's emancipation, of the elevation of culture to ersatz religion—needed to be redeemed from being left alone with a cultured elite, known as the 'audience,' which will soon no longer exist, which already no longer exists, so that art will soon be all alone, alone to fade away and die, unless, that is, it should find a way to the *volk*, or to put it un-Romantically, to human beings?"

He had said, and asked, all this as if in one breath, in a conversational *sotto voce*, but in a tone concealing a quiver that one only truly understood as he concluded:

"Art's entire mood and outlook on life will change, believe me— meaning, it will become both more cheerful and more modest. It is inevitable, a stroke of good fortune. A great deal of melancholic ambition will fall away from art, and a new innocence, yes, a harmlessness will become its portion. Art will hold the future within it, will again see itself as the servant of a community that is embraced by far more than 'education' and that does not acquire culture, but perhaps is culture. We have difficulty imagining it, yet it will come to pass and be quite natural—art without suffering, psychologically healthy, that confides without solemnity, that trusts without sorrow, an art that is on a first-name basis with humanity . . ."

He broke off, and we three sat silent and shaken. It is at once both painful and stirring to hear loneliness speak of community, unapproachability speak of trust. But moved as I was, I was also deeply dissatisfied with his statement, and truly dissatisfied with him. What he had said did not suit him, did not suit the pride, the arrogance, if you will, that I loved and to which art has every right. Art is intellect, mind and spirit, which has no need whatever to feel obligated to society, to the community—dare not do so, in my opinion, for the sake of its freedom, of its nobility. Art that "joins the *volk*," that makes the needs of the crowd, of the average man, of small minds, its own, will end in misery, and such needs will become a duty, for the sake of the state perhaps; to allow only the kind of art that the average man understands is the worst small-mindedness and the murder of mind and spirit. It is my conviction that the intellect can be certain that in doing what most disconcerts the crowd, in pursuing the most daring, unconventional advances and explorations, it will in some highly indirect fashion serve man—and in the long run, all men.

That was undoubtedly Adrian's natural opinion as well. But he was enjoying denying it, although I was very mistaken to regard it as a denial of his arrogance. Presumably it was more an attempt at affability—born of extreme arrogance. If only there had not been that quiver in his voice when he spoke of art's need of redemption, of its being on a first-name basis with humanity—it was an agitation that tempted me, despite everything, to press his hand clandestinely. I refrained, however, and instead kept a worried eye on Rudi Schwerdtfeger, for fear he might actually embrace him again.

XXXII

THE MARRIAGE of Inez Rodde to Professor Dr. Helmut Institoris took place in the spring of 1915 (at the start of the war, when my country's condition was still good, fortified by hope, and I was still in the field) and was executed with all the proper bourgeois trimmings: a civil and a church ceremony, a wedding dinner at the Hotel Vier Jahreszeiten, and the subsequent departure of the young couple for a trip to Dresden and Saxon Switzerland—the culmination of a long mutual testing, which had evidently led to the conclusion that they were surely suited to one another. The reader will sense the irony intended, though truly without any malice, by my "evidently," since there was in fact no evidence for such a conclusion—unless, that is, it had been present from the very beginning and the relationship between the two had undergone no development whatever since Helmut first approached the senator's daughter. What had spoken for the union on both sides at the outset was the same, no more and no less, as spoke for it on the occasions of their engagement and marriage—nothing new had been added. But the classic admonition, "Pay heed before you wed for aye," had been tendered sufficient formal observation, and the period of testing seemed by its very length to demand a positive solution at last, added to which there was a certain urgency for union stemming from the war itself—which had indeed already brought to swift maturity many an unsettled relationship. Another very weighty incentive for Inez to give her consent (which she had long been more or less prepared to give for psychological—or should I say, material, or perhaps better still, common-sense—reasons) was the fact that Clarissa had left

Munich toward the end of the previous year and had accepted her first acting engagement at Celle on the Aller, leaving her sister alone now with a mother whose Bohemian tendencies, tame as they were, she disparaged.

The Frau Senator, moreover, was moved and pleased by her child's settling into bourgeois arrangements, which after all had also been her maternal goal in entertaining socially at home and maintaining a salon. She herself had been repaid in the process by being able to cater to her relaxed, "southern German" lust for life, in the hope of making up what she had missed, all the while allowing the men she invited—Knöterich, Kranich, Zink, and Spengler, those young acting students, etc.—to pay court to her declining beauty. Yes, I am not going too far, indeed am finally going just far enough, when I say that her rapport with Rudi Schwerdtfeger was also a jocular, teasing travesty of a mother-son relationship, and that when she conversed with him the dainty, cooing laugh that we all knew well was heard particularly often. After everything I previously indicated, indeed explicitly stated about Inez's emotional life, I shall leave it to the reader to imagine the tangled resentments, the embarrassment and shame she felt when observing such dalliances. I was present at one such episode when she left her mother's salon, her face all flushed, and retreated to her room—on the door of which, just as she had perhaps hoped and expected, Rudolf came knocking fifteen minutes later to inquire about the reason for her disappearance (though he surely knew it, even if, of course, it could never be uttered), to tell her how very much she was missed across the way, and by employing every tone, including that of brotherly tenderness, to coax her to return. He would not budge until she had promised to rejoin the party—not with him, no that was unnecessary, but within a little while.

I may be pardoned for including, long after its occurrence, an episode that stamped itself on my memory, but had been tenderly banished from Frau Senator Rodde's now that Inez's engagement and marriage were accomplished facts. It was not simply that she had arranged for the wedding to be conducted with all due form and that, in the absence of a significant monetary dowry, she had made sure that there was a considerable trousseau of linens and silver, but she had also divested herself of many a piece of furniture from the old days, some carved chests, one or two gilt lattice-back chairs, as her contribution to the décor of the elegant apartment the young couple had rented on Prinzregenten Strasse—two flights up, the front rooms with a view to the English Garden. Indeed, as if to prove to herself and others that her enjoyment of society, those festive evenings in her salon, had truly served but one purpose, the future prospects and security of her daughters, she now made clear her explicit desire to go into retirement, to withdraw from the world; she no longer entertained and within a year after Inez's marriage she broke up her household on Ramberg Strasse in order to place her widow's life on another, totally different footing—out in the country. She moved to Pfeiffering, where, almost without Adrian's even noticing, she took up residence in the low building that stood behind the chestnut trees, in the open space across from the Schweigestill's courtyard—formerly the lodgings of the artist who painted those melancholy landscapes of the Waldshuter Moor.

This modest yet tasteful corner of the world held a strange attraction for every sort of nobler resignation or bruised humanity. The explanation most probably lies in the character of the owners, especially of that robust farm wife, Else Schweigestill, and her gift for "understanding," which she demonstrated with amazing clearsightedness in her occasional talks with Adrian, particularly when telling him that the Frau Senator was thinking of moving in across the way. "It's very simple," she said, eliding her vowels and consonants in the Bavarian fashion, "very simple and understandable, Herr Leverkühn, I saw it right off. She's had her fill of town and people and society, of ladies and gents, 'cause she's getting skittish in her old age. Course there's differences, too, there are them that it makes no nevermind and they get used to it, and do right nicely, too. They just get downright grand and scampish as time goes on, with pretty white curls at their ears, don't y' know, and so on, and the things they used to do, they let those peek through their new dignity, hinting that it was pretty racy—that charms the gentlemen far more often than you'd think. But for some, that just don't work and it's not their way, and when the cheeks get wrinkly and the neck gets scrawny and there's not much in the way of teeth when they laugh, they feel shamed and fretful when they look in the mirror and avoid other people's eyes and get the urge to hide, like some sick kitten. And if it ain't the neck and the teeth, then its the hair that embarrasses them and makes them miserable. And with the Frau Senator, it's the hair, I saw it right off. Otherwise she'd still have it all nicely together, but the hair, y' see, it's falling out at her brow, till the hairline's all futsch and even with a curlin' iron she can't do much of anything with it up front, driving her to despair, 'cause it's a great sadness, believe you me! and so she's putting the world behind her and moving out to the Schweigestills, it's very simple."

The words of the matron—with her lightly silvered hair pulled back tight, revealing the part's white stripe of skin. Adrian, as noted, was less affected by the arrival of the new renter across the way, who, on her very first visit to the farm had her landlady take her to him for a brief courtesy call, but then—knowing his need for peace and quiet to work and donning an aloofness to match his own—only once and very early on did she invite him to tea in her ground-floor lodgings behind the chestnut trees, two rooms with low ceilings and simple whitewashed walls filled, to curious enough effect, with the rest of her elegantly bourgeois household furnishings: candelabra, upholstered armchairs, the "Golden Horn" in its heavy frame, the grand piano covered by a brocade cloth. From then on, if they chanced to meet in the village or on country lanes, they merely exchanged a friendly greeting or just stood for a few minutes conversing about their nation's sad state or the growing lack of food in the cities, which was so little a problem here— and which indeed lent the Frau Senator's seclusion a practical justification, the appearance of a deliberate precaution that allowed her to supply her daughters, even former friends of her house like the Knöterichs, with goods from Pfeiffering: eggs, butter, sausages, and flour. Packing and mailing these items became her very profession during the sparest years.

Inez Rodde—now rich, socially secure, and cushioned against life— had adopted the Knöterichs from the little clique of her mother's former salon guests and made them part of her and her husband's own social circle, along with, for instance, Dr. Kranich the numismatist, Schildknapp, Rudi Schwerdtfeger, and myself—though not Zink and Spengler or the theatrical, artistic crowd who had been Clarissa's fellow students—supplementing them with academic types, older and younger docents and their wives from both universities. She was even on friendly, indeed intimate footing with Frau Knöterich, Natalia of the exotically Spanish look, despite the fact that it was reputed (and probably rightly so) that this quite charming woman was addicted to morphine—a rumor confirmed by personal observation of her engaging, bright-eyed volubility at the beginning of a party and occasional disappearances to refresh her gradually waning high spirits. That a woman as concerned with conservative dignity and patrician respectability as Inez—who had, after all, entered into marriage in order to gratify those aspirations—preferred Natalia's company to that of the stolid spouses of her husband's colleagues (typical German professors' wives all), visited her privately, and spent time alone with her, revealed to me quite clearly the conflict in Inez's personality and how ultimately dubious was the legitimacy and relevance of her homesickness for a bourgeois world.

I never doubted that she did not love her husband—that scholar of beauty, narrowly concerned with indulging his own ambitions of aesthetic power. What she gave him was a studied, decorous love, and this much is true: She fulfilled her supportive role with perfect distinction, further refining it with her singular delicate and intricate roguishness of expression. The punctiliousness with which she ran his household and prepared his receptions might well be termed an agonizing pedantry—and under economic conditions that made maintaining bourgeois correctness more difficult from year to year. To assist her in keeping this expensive and lovely apartment with its Persian carpets spread over shiny parquet floors, she employed two well-mannered maids, dressed *comme il faut* in caps and aprons with starched bows—one of whom, the chambermaid, served as her abagail. She loved to ring for her Sophie. She did it constantly for the pleasure of being elegantly served and as a way of assuring herself of the care and protection she had bought with her marriage. Sophie was also the one who had to pack the countless trunks and boxes that Inez took with her when accompanying Institoris on trips to the country, to Tergernsee or Berchtesgaden, even if only for a few days. These mountains of luggage with which she encumbered even the briefest outings from her fastidious nest were for me likewise a symbol of her need to be protected, of her fear of life.

I have yet to describe the apartment on Prinzregenten Strasse, eight rooms safeguarded from every particle of dust. With its two salons, of which the one was more intimately furnished and served as the family living room, a spacious dining room in carved oak, a gentlemen's smoking room done in comfortable leather, a conjugal bedroom with hints of canopies floating above the pair of polished, yellow pearwood beds and a lady's dressing table with rows of gleaming bottles and silver implements arranged precisely by size—it was, I say, a model home of German bourgeois culture, a model that would endure for a few years, even as it fell apart, a model not least because of the "good books" that one found displayed everywhere, in the living, reception, and smoking rooms, but in whose acquisition anything provocative or seditious had been avoided, partly out of social, partly out of tender psychological considerations: worthy educational books, history by Leopold von Ranke, the works of Gregorovius, volumes of art history, German and French classics—in short, a solid basic collection for preserving things as they were. Over the years, the apartment grew more beautiful still, or at least more crowded and colorful, for Dr. Institoris was a friend of several of those Munich artists associated with the more sober Glass Palace school (his artistic taste being rather tame despite his theoretical advocacy of glittering violence), in particular of a certain Nottebohm—a native of Hamburg, a married man, gaunt-cheeked, goateed, and droll, with an amusing talent for imitating actors, animals, musical instruments, and professors; a pillar of those carnival balls that now, to be sure, were on the wane; a man adept at the social technique of ensnaring his subjects and, I may say, an inferior, all-too-smooth painter. Institoris, accustomed to associating with masterpieces on a scientific basis, either did not distinguish between these and a skilled mediocrity or believed commissions to be incumbent on good friendship and in fact desired for his own walls nothing that was not politely inoffensive and elegantly soothing, in which he doubtless found solid support from his wife, if not on the basis of taste, then on that of shared opinions. For which reason they asked Nottebohm to paint very expensive, very similar and inexpressive likenesses, one of each individually, and one of them together—and later, once children arrived, the jester was commissioned to produce a life-size family portrait of the Institorises, an insipid representation, over whose considerable expanse a great quantity of highly varnished oils was squandered, and which, set in a costly frame and provided with its own electric illumination from above and below, adorned the reception room.

When children arrived, I said. For children did arrive, and with what propriety, with what resolute, one would almost like to say, heroic denial of circumstances that were increasingly less favorable to bourgeois luxury, they were tended and reared—for a world, so to speak, as it had been, not as it would become. Before the end of 1915 Inez presented her husband with a little daughter, christened Lucrezia, who had been sired in the yellow polished bed under a curtailed canopy, next to the silver items arrayed in symmetric rows on the glass-topped dressing table; and Inez at once declared that she intended to make of her a perfectly well-educated young girl, *une jeune fille accomplie,* as she put it in her Karlsruhe French. Two years later a set of twins followed, girls again, Ännchen and Riekchen, who were likewise baptized at home from a bowl wreathed with flowers, in a proper ceremony with chocolate, port wine, and confects. Like very fair shade plants, each tenderly pampered, all three were lisping creatures of luxury, who, evidently under the pressure of their mother's obsession with spotless perfection, were very concerned about their bowed frocks and vain in a sad sort of way; they spent their early years in precious little bassinets with silk curtains and appeared under the linden trees of Prinzregenten

Strasse in a low-slung, rubber-wheeled pram of the most elegant construction, pushed along by their wet-nurse (for Inez did not nurse
them herself; her physician had advised against it), a simple woman all
gussied up in bourgeois finery. Later a governess, a trained kinder-
garten teacher, looked after them. The bright room in which they grew
up, where their little beds were placed and where Inez visited them as
soon as her housekeeping duties and her own careful grooming permitted, was a perfect model of a domestic children's paradise, with an
encircling frieze of fairy tales, furniture fit for fairy-tale dwarves, colorful linoleum flooring, and a world of toys carefully arranged on
built-in shelves—teddy bears, woolly lambs, jumping jacks, Käthe
Kruse dolls, and trains.

Must I now say or repeat that something was definitely not correct
about all this correctness, that it was based in mere futile willing, if not
to say in a lie, and was not only challenged more and more from without, but also to the sharper eye, to the eye sharpened by sympathy, was
crumbling from within, bestowing no happiness, no belief at the
depths of the soul, and in truth was merely willed? To me all this happy
correctness had always been a conscious denial and whitewashing of
the problem; it stood in strange contradiction to Inez's cult of suffering, and in my opinion the woman was too clever not to see that this
ideal bourgeois nest into which she had primly transfigured her children's existence was the expression and overcorrection of the fact that
she did not love them, but viewed them merely as fruits of a union that
as a woman she had entered upon in bad conscience and in which she
lived despite physical repulsion.

Good God, it was obviously no intoxicating bliss for a woman to
sleep with Helmut Institoris! Even I understand that much about
women's dreams and needs, and I was always forced to imagine that
Inez had conceived her children by him purely out of an acquiescent
sense of duty, looking the other way, so to speak. For they were his, the
resemblance of all three to him allows no doubt of it, since it far outweighed their resemblance to their mother—perhaps her own participation had been so slight at their conception. And in general I would
not in any way wish to offend that little gentleman's natural sense of
honor. He was certainly a whole man, though in manikin form, and
through him Inez learned about desire—a luckless desire, on whose
meager soil her passion could grow wild.

I did, in fact, note that when Institoris began courting the virginal
Inez, he did so in another man's place. And so now, too, as a husband
he was merely awakening errant desires and a partial, but essentially

frustrating sense of happiness that demanded fulfillment, confirmation, satisfaction and that allowed the pain Inez had suffered on Rudi Schwerdtfeger's account, which had revealed itself so curiously in my conversation with her, to burst into the flame of passion. It is quite clear: When she was an object of courtship, her thoughts turned to him in sorrow; as an experienced wife, she fell in love with him, fully aware of what that meant and with all her feelings and desires for him intact. Neither can there be any doubt that the young man could not help responding to an emotion pressed upon him out of such torment and intellectual superiority. I almost said it would have been "lovelier still" had he not responded, and ringing in my ears are those sisterly words, "Hop to, man! What can you be thinking? Jump, if you please!" To repeat, I am not writing a novel and make no pretense of omniscient authorial insight into the dramatic phases of an intimate process removed from the eyes of the world. But this much is certain: Rudolf, once driven into a corner, quite instinctively replied, "What can I do?"—and obeyed the proud command. But I can easily imagine how his love of flirtation, his initial harmless enjoyment of an exciting, incendiary situation lured him ever farther into an adventure, which, had he not had a penchant for playing with fire, he might also have avoided.

In other words, under the cover and protection of bourgeois respectability, for which she had felt homesick for so long, Inez Institoris lived in adultery with a man who, in terms of both psychological makeup and behavior, was still a boyish ladykiller and who became a source of doubt and woe, the way a fickle woman is usually a source of doubt and woe to any man seriously in love—and in his arms her senses, awakened by a loveless marriage, found satisfaction. She lived that way for years, from a point in time, if I see things rightly, that can only have been a few months after her marriage, until toward the end of the decade; and if she no longer continued to live that way it was because he, to whom she tried to hold on with all her strength, extricated himself from her. It was she who directed, manipulated, and covered up their affair, and all the while she played the model housewife and mother, juggling a double life each day, which naturally wore on her nerves and, to her great consternation, threatened the precarious charms of her appearance—deepening, for example, the two creases above her nose between her blond eyebrows, and lending her an almost maniacal look. And yet, despite all the caution, cunning, and virtuoso discretion devoted to hiding from society these strayings from the path, the will to conceal is never completely clear and unbroken for either party—not for the man, who, after all, must feel flattered if people at least guess at his good luck, or for the woman, whose sexual pride has as its secret, but real goal the recognition that she need not be content with a husband's caresses that no one could value very highly. Therefore I am hardly mistaken in assuming that an awareness of Inez Institoris's indiscretion was rather widespread in her Munich social circle—though I never exchanged a word with anyone about it, other than with Adrian Leverkühn. Yes, I would go so far as to consider the possibility that even Helmut himself knew the truth. His display of a certain mixture of cultivated kindness, pitying forbearance, and a head-shaking peaceableness speaks for that assumption; nor is it all that rare for society to believe the husband to be the only blind man, even while he is of the opinion that no one knows except him. These the remarks of an old man who has seen something of life.

It was not my impression that Inez particularly cared about other people's knowing. She did her best to deter it, but that was chiefly maintaining decorum—if people really wanted to know what was what, let them, as long as they left her alone. Passion is too conceited to imagine anyone might seriously oppose it. At least that is true in love affairs where feeling lays claim to every right in the world and, however forbidden and scandalous, quite automatically expects under-standing. How else, if Inez had considered herself quite unobserved, could she have presumed as a matter of course that I was in the know? For she was as good as reckless about it—without ever directly men-tioning a certain name—in a conversation that we had one evening (in the fall of 1916, I believe) and that she obviously had very much wanted to have. Unlike Adrian, who always stuck to his eleven o'clock train home to Pfeiffering after spending an evening in Munich, I had rented a room in Schwabing, on Hohenzollern Strasse, not far beyond the Victory Gate, in order to be independent and have a roof over my head in the capital as occasion required. And so having been invited for dinner as a good friend of the Institorises, I was happy to comply when Inez, seconded by her husband, asked me during the meal to keep her company afterward, once Helmut had left, as planned, to play cards at the Allotria Club. He departed shortly after nine o'clock, wishing us a pleasant chat. There we sat, the lady of the house and her guest, in the family living room, with its cushioned wicker furniture and a bust of Inez, done in alabaster by a sculptor friend and set atop a columned pedestal—a very good resemblance, very piquant, considerably smaller than life-size, but extraordinarily like her, with her thick hair, veiled eyes, gently tilted, extended neck, and lips pursed in unruly roguishness.

And I was her confidant once again, the "good" man who awakened no emotions in her, as opposed to the world of excitement that Inez apparently found embodied in the young man about whom she felt compelled to speak with me. She said it herself: Things, events, experiences, good fortune, love, and pain were not being given their due if they remained mute and were merely enjoyed or endured. It was not enough for them to linger in night and silence. The more secret they were the more one needed a third party, a confidant, a good man, to whom, with whom one could talk about them—and I was that man. I understood that and accepted my role.

After Helmut's departure we spent a little time—as if he were still within earshot, so to speak—talking about unimportant matters. Suddenly, almost as if to catch me off guard, she said, "Serenus, do you blame me, despise me, condemn me?"

It would have been pointless to pretend I did not understand.

"Not at all, Inez," I replied. "God forbid! I've always heard it said that 'Vengeance is the Lord's, He will repay.' I know that He implants the punishment in the sin, letting sin soak its fill, until the one cannot be distinguished from the other, until happiness and punishment are the same. You must be suffering a great deal. Would I be sitting here if I had made myself a judge of morals? I do not deny that I am afraid for you. But I would have kept that to myself as well, had you not asked me if I blame you."

"What is suffering, what are fear and mortifying danger," she said, "in comparison with that sweet, indispensable triumph without which one would not wish to live—the triumph of compelling someone frivolous, evasive, worldly, who torments one's soul with irresponsible niceness, but who also has true human worth, the triumph of compelling that someone to hold fast to his own serious worth, of moving his foppish heart to be serious, of being able to possess someone so elusive, and finally, finally (and not just once, for one can never be reassured enough, have it confirmed enough), of seeing him in the state that matches his worth, in a state of devotion, of deeply sighing passion."

I am not saying that the woman used precisely these words, but she expressed herself in very much this fashion. She was indeed well-read and was not accustomed to leading a mute interior life, but to articulating it, and even as a young girl had attempted to write poetry. Her words had a refined precision and something of the boldness that always arises when language strives earnestly to match feelings and life, to let them germinate within it, to let them truly come to life for the first time. This is not an everyday aspiration, but rather a product of emotion, and to that extent emotion and intellect are related—but, then, to that extent the intellect can also move the emotions. As she continued to speak, only occasionally listening with half an ear to my interjections, her words—and I shall be frank—were drenched in a sensual bliss that makes me hesitate to repeat them verbatim. Sympathy, discretion, humane regard prevent me from doing so—and also, perhaps, a philistine reluctance to impose embarrassment upon the reader. She repeated herself several times—out of an eagerness to give more suitable expression to what she had said, out of a sense that it had not yet been given its due. But it all centered around the curious equation of worth and sensual passion, around the fixed and strangely euphoric notion that inner worth could only be fulfilled, could only be realized in desire, which evidently was equal in seriousness to "worth"—and that the highest and simultaneously most indispensable happiness was to make it do so. I find it absolutely impossible to describe the tone of ardor and melancholy, but also of uneasy satisfaction that this mixing of the concepts of worth and desire took on when coming from her mouth, or to describe the way desire formed the essential element inside worth's envelope of lovableness, which had to be taken away, ripped away, so that worth might be had all alone, utterly alone, alone in the ultimate sense of the word. Disciplining lovableness to become love—it all revolved around that; but at the same time around something more abstract, or around something in which thought and sensuality melted eerily into one: around the idea that the contradiction between the frivolity of, say, a festive party and the sad untrustworthiness of life was reconciled by embracing it—an embrace that carried with it the sweetest revenge for the pain.

As for my interjections, I can hardly recall a single one, except for a question whose purpose was indeed to suggest that she was placing too high an erotic value on the object of her love and to inquire how that was possible. I remember I carefully hinted that the object to which passion clung in this case was not exactly the most vitally splendid, perfect, or highly desirable, since a review of its fitness for military service had revealed a defect in physiological function, a surgically removed organ. Her answer was to the effect that this limitation only brought his lovableness closer to her suffering spirit, that without it her spirit would have had no hope, that it had made his fickleness receptive to her own cry of pain. What was more, significantly enough, for someone who desired to possess the object, any shortening of life that might result from it was more consoling, soothing, reassuring,

than it was depressing. . . . Moreover, all the strangely anguished details of the conversation in which she had first revealed her infatuation
to me were repeated, but were dissolved now in almost malicious satisfaction. A placating remark to the effect that he had had to show his
face again at the Langewiesches' or the Rollwagens' (people one did
not even know) might well betray that he had said much the same thing
there, had remarked that he had to show his face to her again, too—but
there was triumph in the thought. The fact that the Rollwagens'
daughters were "smashing" no longer caused pain and fear, not when
her mouth was pressed to his, and the venom had even been taken from
those cajoling pleas not to leave just yet made to people of no consequence to him. That ghastly "There are lots of unhappy women already!"—it carried a sigh that removed the thorn of ignominy. This
woman was obviously consumed by the thought that although she did
indeed belong to the world of knowledge and suffering, she was also a
female and in her femininity possessed the means to snatch life and
happiness for herself, to force impertinence to succumb to her heart.
At one time it had taken, if need be, a glance, a serious word, to cause
foolishness to stop and think, to be won over for a moment; one had
been able to make foolishness return after some first flippant word of
goodbye and set things right with a quiet and earnest farewell. But
now those ephemeral victories had been buttressed by possession,
by union—insofar as possession and union were possible in duality,
insofar as a shadow-clad femininity could secure them. Which was
exactly what Inez doubted, for she revealed her distrust of her
beloved's faithfulness. "Serenus," she said, "it is inevitable, I know
it. He will leave me." And I noticed the creases between her brows
deepen willfully. "But then woe to him! Woe to me!" she added in
a toneless voice, and I could not help recalling Adrian's words when
I first told him of the affair: "He needs to watch that he gets out in
one piece!"

The conversation was a true sacrifice on my part. It lasted two
hours, and it required a great deal of self-denial, human sympathy, and
friendly goodwill for me to stay with it. Inez appeared to realize as
much, but I must say that, remarkably enough, her gratitude for the
patience, time, and nervous strain devoted to her was quite unmistakably complicated by a certain malicious satisfaction, almost a schaden-
freude that betrayed itself in an occasional enigmatic smile and that I
cannot recall even today without wondering how I put up with it for
so long. Indeed we sat there until Institoris returned from the Allotria,
where he had been playing tarok with some other gentlemen. When he

saw us still together, an embarrassed look of conjecture passed over his face. He thanked me for being kind enough to take his place, and I did not sit down again after greeting him this second time. I kissed his wife's hand and walked home to my lodgings through the deserted streets—very much unnerved, half-angry, half-shaken with sympathy.

XXXIII

FOR US GERMANS, the period *about* which I am writing was an era of governmental collapse, capitulation, revolts born of exhaustion, and helpless surrender into the hands of strangers. The period *in* which I write, and which must serve to help me here in my silent seclusion to put these memories to paper, bears within its horribly swollen belly a national catastrophe compared with which our former defeat now looks like a mild mishap, a sensible liquidation of a failed enterprise. An ignominious ending will always be more normal, something quite other than the divine judgment that hangs over us at present, just as it once descended upon Sodom and Gomorrah—a judgment that we did not, after all, call down upon ourselves that first time.

It is drawing near, there has been no holding it back for some time now—I cannot believe anyone can still have the slightest doubt of it. Monsignor Hinterpförtner and I certainly can no longer be alone in this dreadful and at the same time—God help us!—secretly uplifting realization. That it remains wrapped in silence is an eerie fact all its own. For although there is something uncanny if those few who do know have to live with lips sealed amid a great throng of the dazzled and blind, the horror grows absolute, or so it seems to me, when in fact everyone knows, but they all stand in spellbound silence together, while each man reads the truth in the furtive or anxious stare of his fellows.

While day after day, in a constant state of silent agitation, I have faithfully attempted to do justice to my biographical task, to give worthy form to intimate and personal matters, I have simply let happen those outside events that are part of the age in which I write. The Allied invasion of France, long known to be a possibility, has since taken place—a technical and military feat of first, or simply of totally new rank, which was accomplished after perfect and careful preparation and which we were all the more at a loss to prevent because we did not dare assemble our defensive forces at any one landing point out of uncertainty whether it might not be just one among many, with further attacks to be expected at points beyond our guessing. Our apprehension was both in vain and ruinous. For this was it—and soon more troops, tanks, artillery, and every other kind of equipment had been put ashore than we were able to cast back into the sea. Cherbourg, whose harbor we were assured the prowess of German engineering had rendered totally unusable, capitulated after both the commanding general and an admiral had sent their heroic radiograms to the Führer; and for several days now a battle has been raging for the city of Caen in Normandy—a struggle that, if our worries are correct, has in fact as its goal the opening of the way to the French capital, to Paris, which in the New Order was assigned the role of a European amusement park and bordello, and where resistance is already boldly raising its head, barely held in check by the united forces of our secret police and their French collaborators.

Yes, what all has happened to affect my own solitary task without my ever having bothered to notice! It was not four days after the astounding landing in Normandy that our new retaliatory weapon, to which the Führer frequently alluded in advance with genuine elation, made its appearance in the western theater of war: the robot bomb, such an admirable piece of ordnance that only sacred necessity can have inspired the genius who invented it. Countless numbers of these unmanned, winged messengers of destruction were fired from the coast of France and fell exploding over southern England and, if we are not totally deceived, will soon have proved to be a veritable calamity for our foes. Will this weapon be able to avert substantial losses? Fate did not permit the necessary installations to be completed in time for these flying missiles to disrupt and forestall the invasion. Meanwhile we read that Perugia has been taken, which (just between us, of course) lies halfway between Rome and Florence; there are even rumors of a strategic plan to withdraw entirely from the Apennine peninsula— perhaps to free up troops for the flagging defensive war in the east, to which our soldiers do not wish to be sent at any price. A Russian wave of attack is moving at full force, has taken Vitebsk and is now threatening Minsk, the capital of Belorussia, after whose fall, so the whisperers allege, there can be no stopping the foe in the east, either.

No stopping them! Oh my soul, do not think it through to the end! Do not venture to measure what it would mean if in our extreme, singularly awful situation the dams were to break—as they are about to do—and there were no stopping the immeasurable hatred that we were adept at fanning up against us in the nations roundabout. Granted, the destruction of our cities from the air has long since turned Germany into an arena of war; and yet we find it inconceivable, impermissible, to think that Germany could ever become such an arena in the true sense, and our propaganda has a curious way of warning the foe against incursion upon our soil, our sacred German soil, as if that would be some grisly atrocity. . . . Our sacred German soil! As if anything were still sacred about it, as if it had not long ago been desecrated again and again by the immensity of our rape of justice and did not lie naked, both morally and in fact, before the power of divine judgment. Let it come! There is nothing else to hope for, to want, to wish. The call for peace with the Anglo-Saxons, the offer to continue the battle alone against the Sarmatian flood, the demand that the call for unconditional surrender be modified somewhat—which means negotiation, but with whom?—is pure, preposterous nonsense. It is the demand of a regime that does not wish to grasp, that apparently does not understand even now, that it has been condemned, that it must vanish, laden with the curse of having made itself intolerable to the world—no, of having made us, Germany, the Reich, let me go farther and say, Germanness, everything German, intolerable to the world.

Such is the background of my biographical effort at the present moment. I believe I owed the reader yet another such synopsis. As for the background of my actual narrative at the point in time to which I have advanced it, I did in fact characterize that period at the opening of this chapter with the phrase "into the hands of strangers." "It is a terrible thing to fall into the hands of strangers"—how often during those days of collapse and capitulation did I think and suffer through the bitter truth of that statement; for as a German man—despite the universalist hue that Catholic tradition casts over my relation to the world—I cherish a lively sense of peculiar national identity, of the unique life that defines my country, of the idea, so to speak, of how one refracted ray of humanity asserts itself against other such variations (which, without doubt, deserve equal rights), but can do so only if it enjoys a certain external prestige under the protection of an intact, upright state. The novel and dreadful thing about a decisive military defeat is the overturning of this idea, its physical refutation by a foreign ideology bound up, above all, with a foreign language—the total submission to something from which, precisely because it is foreign, nothing of benefit to one's own nature can apparently come. The defeated French tasted this same awful experience in the previous war, when their negotiators, in an attempt to soften the conditions set down by the victors, considered the entry of our troops into Paris as exacting a very high price in renown, in *la gloire*, and the German statesman replied that the word *gloire*, or any equivalent thereof, was not to be found in our vocabulary. And so in 1870, the French lower house spoke in terrified, hushed tones, anxiously attempting to comprehend what it means to be totally at the mercy of an adversary whose understanding of the world does not include *la gloire*.

I often thought of this when the virtuous Jacobin-Puritan jargon that had opposed the war propaganda of those "in agreement" became the orthodox language of victory. And I also found proof that it is not far from capitulation to pure abdication and the offer to let the victor go right ahead and govern the affairs of the fallen nation just as he pleases, since for its part that nation no longer knows up from down. France had felt such impulses forty-eight years before, and they were not foreign to us now. They were, however, rejected. The fallen nation is left to fend for itself somehow, and the only purpose of outside tutelage is to make sure that the revolution that fills the vacuum caused by the death of the old authority does not become extreme and thereby also endanger the bourgeois order of the victors. And so in 1918, even after laying down their arms, the Western powers maintained their blockade in order to control the German revolution, to keep it on a bourgeois, democratic track, and to prevent its deteriorating into something Russian and proletarian. And so bourgeois imperialism, accustomed now to victory, could not warn enough against "anarchy," could not be forceful enough in its rejection of any dealings with workers' and soldiers' councils or similar such bodies, could not remonstrate enough that peace could be concluded only with a stable Germany, that only such a Germany would be fed. What little government we had followed this paternal lead, joined with the National Assembly against a proletarian dictatorship, and obediently declined all Soviet overtures, even offers to deliver grain. Not to my total satisfaction, I might add. As a temperate, cultivated man, I entertain, to be sure, a natural horror of radical revolution and a dictatorship of the lower classes, which by my very nature I can envisage in scarcely anything but images of anarchy and mob rule, in short, of the destruction of culture. But when I recall the grotesque anecdote of how those two saviors of European civilization, the German and the Italian (and both in the pay of capitalists) strode together through the Uffizi in Florence, where they truly did not belong, and the one assured the other that all these "splendid treasures" would have ended up being destroyed by Bolshevism had heaven not prevented it by raising up the both of them—then my notions of mob rule are refocused in a new light, and the rule of the lower classes begins to seem to me, a middle-class German, an ideal state in comparison (for the comparison is now possible) with the rule of scum. To my knowledge Bolshevism has never destroyed works of art. That has proved to be much more within the scope of activity of those who sought to protect us against it. Would it have taken much for the works of the hero of these pages, of Adrian Leverkühn, also to have fallen victim to their lust for trampling under the things of the mind—a lust quite foreign to so-called mob rule? Would not their victory and its historical mandate to shape the world according to their vile ambition have slain his work and robbed it of immortality?

Twenty-six years ago, it was my disgust at the self-righteous cant of that rhetorical bourgeois who called himself a "son of revolution" that proved stronger in my heart than any fear of disorder and made me want precisely what he did not: for my defeated country to seek protection from its brother in suffering, from Russia—and I was even prepared to accept in the bargain, indeed to applaud, the social upheaval that would result from such a comradeship. The Russian Revolution thrilled me, and in my eyes there was no doubt that its principles were historically superior to those of the powers who had set their feet upon our necks.

Since then, history has taught me to regard with a different eye our conquerors from that period—who soon, in alliance with the revolution from the east, will be our conquerors again. It is true that certain strata of bourgeois democracy appeared then, and still appear now, ripe for what I called the rule of scum—are willing to ally themselves with it in order to eke out a privileged life. And yet leaders have risen up within democracy who, no different from myself, a son of humanism, saw in that rule the last thing that could or should be imposed upon humanity and moved their world to life-and-death struggle against it. These men cannot be thanked enough, and they are proof that the democracy of the West—however outdated its institutions may prove over time, however obstinately its notion of freedom resists what is new and necessary—is nonetheless essentially on the side of human progress, of the goodwill to perfect society, and is by its very nature capable of renewal, improvement, rejuvenation, of proceeding toward conditions that provide greater justice in life.

All this in passing. What I wish to recall here in terms of biography is the loss of the authority of a monarchical military state that had for so long been the shape and habit of our lives—a loss already far advanced as defeat approached, that became total upon its arrival; with collapse and abdication came constant want and an ever-worsening depreciation of the currency, resulting in conditions of discursive laxity and loose speculation that empowered the bourgeoisie to exercise a kind of pitiful and undeserved independence and dissolved the framework of a state long bound together by discipline into debating camps of underlings who had lost their master. A very gratifying sight it is not, and the reader should subtract nothing from the word "painful," when I use it to characterize my impressions as a purely passive observer attending the assemblies of certain "Councils of Intellectual Workers," etc., that had come to life in the ballrooms of Munich's hotels. If I were a novelist, I would describe for the reader one such meeting, during which, for instance, a belletrist spoke, not without charm, indeed with dimpled sybaritic fuzziness, on the topic of "Revolution and Brotherly Love," thereby unleashing a free (all-too-free), diffuse, and confused discussion among those outlandish sorts who emerge into the light for a brief moment only on such occasions: buffoons, maniacs, specters, nasty obstructionists, and petty daydreamers—I would, I say, gather my tortured memories to describe in graphic fashion one such helpless, hopeless council meeting. There were speeches for and against brotherly love, for and against the military, for and against the people. A little girl recited a poem; a man in field gray was prevented only with difficulty from reading a manuscript that had begun with the greeting, "my dear citizens and citizenesses," and doubtless would have lasted all night; an angry graduate student ruthlessly took to task every single speaker who had preceded him, but he never once deigned to offer those assembled a single positive opinion of his own—and so on. The manners of the audience, who were given to crude, shouted interruptions, were turbulent, childish, and coarse, those in charge inept; the air was dreadful, the result less than zero. Looking about, you repeatedly asked yourself if you alone were suffering, and in the end were happy to gain the street, where trolley service had been halted hours before and several presumably meaningless gunshots echoed through the winter night.

Leverkühn, to whom I reported these same impressions, was extraordinarily ill at the time—suffering from something like the degrading tortures, the pinching agonies of red-hot tongs; yet there was no need to fear directly for his life, though it seemed to have reached a low point, so low that he merely eked out his existence, barely dragging himself from one day to the next. He had come down with an intestinal condition that even the strictest diet could not relieve; every few days it would return, beginning with a violent headache, followed by hours, sometimes days of vomiting, even on an empty stomach—the sheerest misery, undignified, devious, and degrading, each attack ending in complete exhaustion and persistent sensitivity to light. There was no question of his illness having psychological causes or being traceable to current distressing events, to the defeat of his country and its ugly attendant circumstances. In his monastic, rural isolation far from the city, he was scarcely touched by such things, even though he was kept posted about them—not by newspapers, which he did not read, but by Frau Else Schweigestill, who continued to tend him with imperturbable sympathy. These events, which for the insightful person came not as an abrupt shock, but as the fulfillment of something long expected, barely elicited a shrug from him, and his responses to my attempts to win from the disaster some good that might be hidden within it were no different from his replies to similar pronouncements in which I had indulged at the start of the war—and here I am thinking back to his chilly, skeptical answer of "May God bless your *studia!*"

And yet! As impossible as it was to find an emotional correlation between his deteriorating health and our national calamity, my inclination to see some objective connection or symbolic parallel between the two, an inclination that may well have been based merely on their contemporaneity, was not vanquished by his remoteness from outside events—though I carefully kept that thought to myself and took pains not even to hint at it in conversation with him.

Adrian had not asked for a doctor because he wanted to see his illness as something basically familiar, merely an acute aggravation of his inherited migraine. It was Frau Schweigestill who finally insisted on consulting Dr. Kürbis, the local physician for the Waldshut district, the same man who had once helped the young lady from Bayreuth give birth. The good man would not hear of migraine, since the often extreme headache was not confined to one side, as is the case with migraine, but was felt as a gnawing torment in and above both the eyes—and in any case was regarded by the physician as only a secondary symptom. His diagnosis, with some reservations, was a stomach ulcer or the like, and while warning his patient of some occasional bleeding, which never occurred, he prescribed a lunar caustic solution to be taken internally. When that did not help, he switched to a strong dose of quinine to be drunk twice daily, which did in fact provide temporary relief. At two-week intervals, however, and for two days at a time, severe attacks very similar to seasickness returned, and Kürbis's diagnosis quickly began to waver, or rather was reinforced in a different sense—he was now certain in his belief that my friend's ailment should be treated as a chronic gastric catarrh with a significant dilation of the stomach on the right side, accompanied by hyperemia, which impaired the flow of blood to the brain. He now prescribed Karlsbad salts and a diet aimed at the smallest possible volume of intake, with a menu that consisted almost exclusively of tender meats and that banned liquids and soups, as well as vegetables, flour, and bread. This was also meant to counter a dreadfully acute build-up of acidity from which Adrian suffered and that Kürbis was inclined to ascribe, at least in part, to nervous causes, that is, to a central agency, meaning the brain, which now for the first time began to play a role in his diagnostic speculations. Once the dilation of the stomach had been cured without any alleviation of the headaches and severe attacks of nausea, he began to assign more and more of the ailment's symptoms to the brain—bolstered in this view by his patient's desperate need to be kept out of the light. Even when he was not in bed, he spent half the day in the closely curtained shadows of his room, for a sunny morning sufficed to exhaust his nerves to the point where he thirsted for darkness, basked in it like some beneficial element. I myself have spent many daylight hours chatting with him in the abbot's study, when it was kept so dark that only after long adjustment could my eyes distinguish the outlines of the furniture and a pale luster to the walls.

During this period, ice-packs and cold dousings of the head were prescribed morning therapies, and they proved more useful than those that had preceded them, although only as palliatives whose mild effect did not justify any talk of recovery. The strange condition was not remedied, the attacks recurred intermittently, and the stricken patient declared that he was prepared to put up with them, if only it weren't for one ongoing problem, the constant pain and pressure in his head and behind his eyes, a feeling of total paralysis that was difficult to describe and went from the crown of the head to the tip of the toes; it also seemed to impede the organs of speech, so that the ailing man's words, whether he was aware of it or not, at times had something halting about them, were imperfectly enunciated by sluggish lips. I am rather disposed to think that he paid it no attention, since he did not let it hinder him from speaking; on the other hand, I sometimes had the impression that he intentionally used the impediment and fell into it in order to say things that seemed suitable for this method of communication, to speak in a not quite articulate fashion that was meant to be only half-understood, as if spoken out of a dream. This was how he spoke to me about the little mermaid in Andersen's fairy tale, for which he felt extraordinary love and admiration, not least because of its truly remarkable description of the horrible realm of the sea witch, an octopus forest that lies behind all-devouring whirlpools and into which the child ventures, yearning to replace her fishy tail with human legs and even perhaps, through the love of the black-eyed prince (she herself had eyes "as blue as the deepest sea"), to gain an immortal soul like the one human beings had. He played with the comparison between the knife-sharp pains that the mute beauty was willing to suffer with every step of her white walking-pins and those that he constantly had to endure, called her his sister in sorrow and presented a kind of intimate and humorously objective critique of her conduct, her willfulness, her sentimental longing for the two-legged world of human beings.

"It all starts with the adoration of the marble statue of a boy—evidently by Thorvaldsen—that has found its way to the ocean floor," he said, "and that, against all prohibitions, she finds far too much to her liking. Her grandmother should have taken the thing away from her, instead of letting the little mermaid plant a pink weeping willow beside it in the blue sand. She was allowed to get away with too much early on, so that later her longing for a hysterically overrated upper world and an 'immortal soul' can no longer be held in check. An immortal soul—to what end? A totally absurd wish! It is much more comforting to know that after death one will become foam on the sea, the way nature intended for her. A proper nixie would have seduced this hollow-headed prince (who has no sense at all of her worth and marries another girl before her very eyes) there on the marble steps of his castle, dragged him into the water, and gently drowned him, instead of making her fate depend on his stupidity the way she does. His love would presumably have been much more passionate had she had the fish tail she was born with, rather than those painful human legs. . . ."

And with an objectivity that was necessarily facetious, and yet with knit brows and lips moving reluctantly, leaving the words only partially clear, he spoke of the aesthetic advantages of the nixie's form over that of bifurcated humans, about the charming line where the hips of the female body melted into a smooth-scaled, strong, and supple fish tail, made for easy steering while darting about. He denied there was anything monstrous about it, even if that was normally the case with mythological combinations of human and animal, and pretended not to admit that the concept of mythological fiction was even applicable here. Mermaids had a most engaging organic reality, were perfectly beautiful and necessary, as became quite evident when one considered the pitifully stunted and deficient condition of the little mermaid after she had purchased legs, for which no one would ever thank her. Mermaids were an indubitable piece of nature that nature owed to us—that is, if she still owed it to us, which he did not believe, indeed, which he knew was not the case, and so forth.

I can still hear him speaking, or muttering, with a dark facetiousness, to which I offered facetious replies—my heart filled, as usual, with some anxiety, together with silent admiration for the whimsy he could wrest from the burden obviously weighing upon him. It was this mood that allowed me to endorse his rejection of suggestions Dr. Kürbis felt duty-bound to make at the time: He recommended, or at least offered for consideration, a consultation with higher medical authority; but Adrian dodged the idea, would have none of it. First off, he said, he had total confidence in Kürbis, and he was convinced, moreover, that he would have to deal with the malady more or less on his own, rely on his own strength and constitution. That accorded with my own feelings. I would have been more inclined to try a change of air, a stay at a spa, something the doctor likewise suggested, without—as could have been predicted—being able to talk his patient into it. Adrian was far too fond of the accustomed sphere of existence he had so explicitly chosen, too fond of house and farm, steeple, pond, and hill, of his old-fashioned study, his velvet chair, ever to have consented to the idea of exchanging it all for even four weeks of the horrors of spa life, with its table d'hôte, promenade, and band concerts. Above all he pleaded that consideration be shown Frau Schweigestill, whom he did not want to offend by choosing the commonplace care of strangers over her own—particularly since, in fact, he felt himself in the best of hands here under the imperturbable, maternal eye of a woman who knew human need and understood it. One could truly ask where he could have things better than here with her, since, following latest medical advice, she now brought him something to eat every four hours: an egg, cocoa, and zwieback at eight; a small beefsteak or cutlet at noon; soup, meat, and a vegetable at four; cold roast and tea at eight. The regimen did him good. It impeded the fever that came with digesting larger meals.

Our Nackedey and Kunigunde Rosenstiel took turns calling at Pfeiffering. They brought flowers, preserves, peppermint lozenges—whatever the latest shortages allowed. They were not always ushered in to see Adrian, actually only rarely, which did not bother either of them. Kunigunde's compensation for a refusal was an especially well-turned letter, composed in the purest and most dignified German. Our Nackedey, to be sure, lacked this solace.

I was always glad when Rüdiger Schildknapp, he of the same-colored eyes, visited our friend. His presence had such a calming, cheering effect on Adrian—if only it had been granted him more often. But Adrian's illness was one of those serious cases that tended to immobilize Rüdiger's charm—indeed we know that any sense of his being urgently needed resulted in his being perversely sparing of himself. He had no lack of excuses (which is to say, rationalizations) for this peculiar psychological trait—he was yoked to his literary daily bread, to those miserable translations, couldn't possibly get away, and besides, his own health was compromised by poor nutrition and he suffered frequent bouts of intestinal catarrh. When he did appear in Pfeiffering, for he came by now and again all the same, he would wear a flannel body wrap, and sometimes even a moist throat compress wrapped in gutta-percha—a source of bitter comedy and Anglo-Saxon jokes for him and of amusement for Adrian, who could rise above his physical torments to find liberation in jests and laughter with no one else so well as with Rüdiger.

From time to time, Frau Senator Rodde stopped by as well, of course, leaving her refuge overstuffed with bourgeois furniture to come across and inquire of Frau Schweigestill how Adrian was doing, even if she could not see him herself. When he did receive her, or if they happened to meet outdoors, she would tell him about her daughters, making sure to keep her lips closed over a gap in her front teeth when she laughed; for this, too, and not just her hairline, was now a source of worry to make her flee the company of others. Clarissa, she reported, truly loved her artistic profession and was not allowing the joy she took in it to be diminished by a certain coldness of the audience, the nit-picking of critics, or the cheeky cruelty of various directors who attempted to spoil her mood by shouting "Pick it up! Pick it up!" to her from the wings whenever she was about to savor a solo scene. Her initial engagement in Celle had come to an end, and the next one had not exactly led her farther up the ladder: She was now playing ingénue roles in the remote East Prussian town of Elbing, but had prospects for a contract in the western part of the Empire, in Pforzheim to be precise, which ultimately was just a short hop to the stages of Karlsruhe or Stuttgart. The main thing in such a career was not to get stuck in the provinces, but to get a foothold early on at a large state theater or at a commercial stage of intellectual significance in a major city. Clarissa was hoping to make her way. But from her letters, at least those to her sister, it was evident that the nature of her successes was more personal, or better, more erotic than artistic. She was beleaguered by countless advances and exhausted a portion of her energies simply in countering them with chilly scorn. She had informed Inez, although not her mother directly, that a rich department store owner, a well-preserved gray-haired man, had offered to make her his mistress, promising her a luxurious apartment, a car, and clothes—which would surely have shut up that impudent director with his "Pick it up! Pick it up!" and might have turned the critics around as well. But she was too proud to build her life on such a foundation. Her chief concern was her personality, not her person; the major retailer had been turned down, and Clarissa had gone off to new battles in Elbing.

The Frau Senator spoke less engagingly about her daughter Frau Institoris in Munich. Her life appeared less exciting and daring, more normal, more secure—when viewed superficially, and Frau Rodde evidently wished to view it superficially, which is to say, she described Inez's marriage as happy, and indeed that required a strong dose of cozy superficiality. At that time, the twins had just come into the world, and the Frau Senator spoke with simple, tender emotion about the event—about those three pampered bunnies, those three little Snow Whites, whom she visited from time to time in their ideal nursery. She was proud and energetic in her praise of her elder daughter and the resilience with which she maintained an impeccable household despite adverse circumstances. It could not be determined if she was truly unaware of what was the talk of the town—the affair with Schwerdtfeger—or only pretended to be. Adrian, as the reader knows, knew all about the matter through me. One day he even listened to Rudolf confess it—and what a singular event that was.

During our friend's acute illness, the violinist proved very attentive, loyal, and devoted, indeed it appeared as if he wanted to use this opportunity to prove just how much Adrian's favor and goodwill meant to him—what is more, I had the impression that he felt he ought to take advantage of Adrian's ailing, reduced, and (so he probably presumed) rather helpless condition by displaying all his indestructibly ingratiating ways and considerable personal charms in order to overcome a brittle shyness, a coolness, an ironic rejection that vexed him for more or less serious reasons, or hurt his vanity, or wounded his true feelings—God only knows how things really stood! And if one speaks—as one must—of Rudolf as a flirt, one easily risks saying one word too many. But neither should one say one word too few; and for my part, his character, the manifestations of his character, always appeared in an absolutely naive, childish, impish, indeed a demonic light, the reflection of which I sometimes thought I could see in those very pretty blue eyes of his.

Enough. As I said, Schwerdtfeger took an active interest in Adrian's illness. He frequently called Frau Schweigestill on the telephone to inquire about how he was doing and offered to pay a visit as soon as Adrian could tolerate it as a welcome diversion. And soon then, during a period of improvement, he was allowed to come; he displayed the most beguiling delight in their reunion and twice addressed Adrian with familiar pronouns at the beginning of his visit, only to correct himself the third time (for Adrian had not once returned this familiarity) and let the matter rest with the formal pronoun and a first name. More or less in consolation and by way of experiment, Adrian now and then called him by his first name as well, though not by the abbreviated nickname that people generally used with Schwerdtfeger, but in the full form of Rudolf—but he soon dropped that as well. Adrian congratulated him, moreover, on the great success he had recently enjoyed as a violinist. He had given a concert in Nuremberg and his rendition of the Partita in E Major by Bach (for solo violin) had created quite a sensation both with the audience and the press. This had resulted in his appearing as a soloist at one of the concerts of the Munich Academy at the Odeon, where his clean, sweet, and technically perfect interpretation of Tartini had been especially well-received. People were willing to accept his small tone, for in return he offered musical (and personal) compensations. His promotion to concertmaster of the Zapfenstösser Orchestra (the gentleman previously holding that post having retired to devote himself exclusively to private instruction) was, despite his youth—and he still looked considerably younger than he was, indeed, remarkably enough, even younger than when I had first made his acquaintance—his promotion, I say, was now a foregone conclusion.

All the same, Rudi seemed depressed by certain circumstances of his private life—by a liaison with Inez Institoris, about which he spoke at length and in confidentiality as he sat face to face with Adrian. The term "face to face" is, however, not quite accurate, or at least inadequate, since the conversation took place in a darkened room and the two could not see each other's faces at all, or at best only as shadows— no doubt to Schwerdtfeger's relief, emboldening him to make his confession. It was in fact an exceptionally bright, sunny day, with snow glistening under a blue January sky in the year 1919; and immediately after greeting Rudolf upon his arrival outside, Adrian had come down with such an awful headache that he asked his guest to share the proven comfort of darkness with him for at least a little while. They had then exchanged the Winged-Victory room, to which they had first moved, for the abbot's study and had banned every bit of light with shutters and curtains, until it was just as I knew it: At first night shrouded the eyes completely, but then they learned to make out the approximate placement of the furniture and could perceive the faint shimmer of daylight seeping into the room and lending a pale luster to its walls. Adrian, in his velvet chair, repeatedly apologized into the darkness for the inconvenience, but Schwerdtfeger, who had taken the Savonarola chair at the desk, had no objection whatever. If darkness helped—and he could indeed imagine that it must do some good—then he liked it best that way, too. They spoke in muted, indeed low tones, partly because Adrian's condition encouraged it, partly because the voice automatically drops in darkness, which even has a certain tendency to create pauses in conversation, bring it to a halt. Schwerdtfeger's Dresden urbanity and social training, however, permitted no pauses, and he chatted away, smoothly patching over dead spots, defying the uncertainty one feels about someone's reaction when it is hidden under the cloak of night. They touched on the volatile political situation, the fighting in the nation's capital, moved on to the topic of the latest music, and Rudolf whistled with great purity something from Falla's "Nights in the Gardens of Spain," and Debussy's Sonata for flute, violin, and harp. He also whistled the bourrée from *Love's Labour's Lost*, in its proper key no less, and followed it up with the comical theme of the weeping bitch from the marionette piece, "The Godless Cunning"—all without his being able to tell for sure if this amused Adrian or not.

Finally he sighed and said that he wasn't at all in the mood for whistling, but that his heart was really quite heavy, or, if not heavy, at least vexed, fretful, impatient, and indeed perplexed and worried, too, and so in fact heavy. Why? It was of course not easy to give an answer and not even permissible really, or at best only between friends, where the rules of discretion were not of such consequence, rules that applied to a cavalier for keeping his affairs with women to himself, rules he was indeed accustomed to obeying, for he was not a telltale. But he was not simply a cavalier, either, it would be a great mistake to take him for such—for a superficial man about town, a lady's man, he shuddered at the thought. He was a human being and an artist, and he cared not a whit—or a whistle, either, for that matter—about a cavalier's discretion, not when the man he was talking to surely knew as well as everyone else what was going on. In short, this was all about Inez Rodde, or better, Institoris and his relationship with her, which he simply couldn't help. "I simply can't help it, Adrian, believe me, you must believe me! I did not seduce her, she seduced me, and little Institoris's horns, to use a stupid expression, are purely her work, not mine. What do you do if a woman clings to you as if she were drowning and is determined to make you her lover? Do you leave your garment in her hand and flee?" No, men no longer did that, because there were other rules for a cavalier to obey in that case, rules one did not resist, assuming that the lady was pretty, if in a somewhat disagreeable and anguished way. But he was disagreeable and anguished himself, an intense and often worried artist; he was not some happy-go-lucky sunshine boy, or whatever it was people imagined about him. Inez imagined all sorts of things about him, the wrong things, and that created a skewed relationship, as if such a relationship was not already skewed enough on its own, given the foolish situations that were constantly cropping up and the caution it demanded in more ways than one. Inez negotiated it all much more easily, for the simple reason that she was passionately in love—and he was all the more prepared to call it that, because her love was based on her false imaginings. He was at a disadvantage; he was not in love. "I have never loved her, I frankly admit it. My feelings for her have always been those of a brother, a comrade, and my becoming intimate with her and letting this stupid relationship that she clings to simply drag on—it has, on my part, all been merely a matter of my doing my duty as a cavalier." Confidentially, he also had to add, it was somehow awkward, indeed degrading when passion, and a desperate passion at that, was felt by the woman and the man was only fulfilling his cavalier's duty. It reversed the proprietary relationship somehow and led to the woman's unpleasant domination of the love affair, so much so that he had to say Inez dealt with his person, with his body, the way a man should in fact and by rights deal with a woman—added to which her abnormal and agitated (and by the way, quite unjustified) jealousy amounted to an exclusive possession of his person; quite unjustified, as he had said, since she was quite enough for him, indeed he had had quite enough of her and her clinging, and given such circumstances, his invisible vis-à-vis could hardly imagine what a balm it was just to be near a highly distinguished man of whom he himself thought so highly, to enter into the sphere of such a man, to converse with him. People usually judged him wrongly—he would much rather have a serious, elevating, and beneficial conversation with a man like that than to be lying next to some woman. Indeed, if he were to characterize himself, he believed, after much careful self-examination, that he would do best to call his a platonic personality.

And suddenly, as if by way of illustration of what he had just said, Rudi began to speak of the violin concerto that he so very much wanted Adrian to write for him, to write so that it would fit like a glove, giving him, if possible, exclusive performance rights—that was his dream! "I need you, Adrian, for my elevation, for my improvement, my betterment, even, in a certain sense, my purification from all these other matters. I give you my word, it's true, I have never been more serious about anything, about something I need. And the concerto I would like you to write is only the most compacted, or might I say, the symbolic expression of that need. You would do a wonderful job, much better than Delius or Prokofiev, with an incredibly simple and singable first theme in the exposition that reemerges after the cadenza—that's always the finest moment in a classical violin concerto, when the first theme is restated after the solo acrobatics. But you don't have to do it that way, you don't even have to write a cadenza, that's old hat. You can throw all the conventions overboard, even the division into movements—it doesn't need to have movements, for all I care the *allegro molto* can be in the middle, a downright devilish trill where you juggle the rhythm the way only you can do it, and the adagio could come at the end, like a transfiguration—the whole thing could not be unconventional enough, and in any case I'd milk it until tears welled up in people's eyes. I'd make it part of me, so I could play it in my sleep, and cherish and coddle every note like a mother, because I'd be it's mother, and you would be the father—it would be like a child between us, a platonic child—yes, our concerto, that would truly be the fulfillment of everything the word 'platonic' means to me."

The words of Schwerdtfeger that day. I have argued in his favor several times in these pages, and even today as I let all this pass in review again, I tend to regard him indulgently, prompted to some extent by his tragic end. But the reader can now better understand certain terms I applied to him, like the "impish naiveté" or even the "childish, demonic light" that I indicated were pertinent to his nature. In Adrian's place—though, to be sure, it is absurd for me to put myself in his place—I would not have tolerated some of what Rudolf said. It was definitely an abuse of the darkness. Not only was he repeatedly far too candid about his relationship with Inez, but he also went too far in a different direction, culpably and impishly far—seduced by the darkness might I say, if the term "seduction" may seem properly employed here and it were not better to speak of a cheeky plot of confiding familiarity against lonely solitude.

That is indeed the term for Rudi Schwerdtfeger's relation to Adrian Leverkühn. The plot was years in the planning, and one could not deny it a certain sad success—over time, solitude's defenselessness against such wooing became evident, although it proved the ruin of the wooer.

XXXIV

DURING THE PERIOD when his health was at its nadir, Leverkühn compared his torment with something else besides the knifelike pains of the "little mermaid"; in conversation he also applied to it another, remarkably precise and vivid image that I recalled a few months later, in the spring of 1919, when the burden of illness was removed from him as if by a miracle and his mind soared phoenix-like to the most sublime freedom and astounding power in a period of unrestrained, if not to say, uninhibited, or at least unstoppable and onrushing, almost breathless productivity—and it was that very image that revealed to me how those two states, of depression and of elation, were not sharply set off from one another, did not break apart without any connection, but rather that the latter had been preparing itself in the former and to some extent was already contained within it—just as, vice versa, the period of health and creativity was anything but a time of ease, but likewise in its own way a time of obsession, of painful urgency and distress. . . . Oh, how badly I'm writing! My eagerness to say everything at once allows my sentences to rise like a flood, propelling them away from the thought they intend to set down, until riding waves of words they seem to lose sight of it. It is a good idea to steal the march on my reader's criticism. My ideas tumble topsy-turvy and go astray because of the excitement that comes with recalling the period I am describing, the period after the collapse of the German authoritarian state, which brought with it that radical loosening of discourse that also dragged my thoughts into its vortex and stormed my staid worldview with new ideas it did not find easy to digest. The feeling that an epoch was coming to an end, an epoch that embraced not just the nineteenth century, but also reached back to the end of the Middle Ages, to the shattering of scholastic ties, to the emancipation of the individual and the birth of freedom, an epoch that I quite rightly had to view as that of my extended intellectual home, in short, the epoch of bourgeois humanism—the feeling, I say, that its last hour had come, that a mutation of life was about to happen, that the world was trying to enter into a new, still unnamed sign of the zodiac—this feeling, then, which demanded one pay it closest heed, had first arisen not with the end of the war, but with its outbreak, fourteen years after the turn of the century and had formed the basis of the shock, the sense of being seized by destiny, that people like myself felt at the time. No wonder, then, that the disintegration that came with defeat brought this feeling to its peak, and no wonder, either, that in an overthrown nation like Germany it occupied people's minds more than it did those of the victors, whose average emotional state was, as the result of victory, far more conservative. They in no way felt the war to be the deep and severing rift in history that it appeared to be to us, and instead saw in it a disruption that had now come to a happy conclusion, after which life would be returned to the track out of which it had been shunted. I envied them that. In particular I envied France the justification and confirmation that, to all appearances, victory had granted to its abiding bourgeois state of mind, envied the sense of being secure within classic rationalism that France was able to draw from its victory. In those days I would most assuredly have felt more at ease, more at home on the far side of the Rhine than here with us, where, as I said, many new, disruptive, and worrisome ideas (with which for reasons of conscience I had to grapple) had been thrust upon my worldview. And here I am reminded of confused discussions that took place of an evening in the Schwabing apartment of one Sixtus Kridwiss, whose acquaintance I had made at the Schlaginhaufens' and to whom I shall return soon enough, remarking for the present only that the gatherings and intellectual deliberations that occurred at his home, in which I frequently took part out of pure conscientiousness, caused me no little distress—while at the very same time, as a close friend and with my whole, excited, and often terrified soul, I was witnessing the birth of a work that did not lack certain bold and prophetic connections to those discussions, that confirmed and realized them on a higher, more creative plane. . . . And if I were to add that amidst all this I had to attend to my teaching position and to avoid any dereliction of my duties as a head of household, it may be easy to understand that the overtaxing strain, along with an inadequate diet, resulted in my losing not a few pounds.

And I say this only by way of characterizing those rash, dangerous times and certainly not in order to direct the reader's sympathy to my inconsequential person, which deserves only a place in the background of these memoirs. I have already expressed my regret that my hurried eagerness must here and there leave the impression of thoughts in headlong flight. But that is a false impression, for I am indeed in firm control of my train of thought and have not forgotten that I wished to introduce a second powerful and telling comparison, besides that of the little mermaid, that Adrian used during the period of his most agonizing suffering.

"How do I feel?" he said to me at the time. "About like John the Martyr in his cauldron of oil. You have to imagine it almost exactly like that. I sit here like a pious wretch in his tub, a wood fire crackling merrily beneath him, while a fine conscientious lad fans the flame with a hand-bellows; and before the eyes of His Imperial Majesty, who has come for a first-hand look (it is Nero, you should know, a splendid sultan with Italian brocade on his back), the hangman's assistant, dressed in a flowing cloak and codpiece, dips a long-handled ladle into the simmering oil in which I'm devoutly sitting and pours some down the back of my neck. I'm being basted as artfully as a roast, a devil of a roast, it is worth watching, and you are invited to join the genuinely interested spectators behind the barrier, the municipal officials, the invited guests, some in turbans and some in good old-fashioned German cowls topped off with hats. Worthy townsfolk—and their contemplative mood enjoys the protection of halberdiers. One of them shows another what being a devil of a roast is like. They put two fingers to one cheek and two under the nose. A portly fellow raises his hand, as if to say: 'God save us, every one!' Homely edification on the faces of the women. Do you see? We're all squeezed close together, the scene is scrupulously filled with figures. The little dog of Master Nero has come along as well, so that not a spot is left empty. It has a fierce little pinscher face. In the background you can see the steeples, peak-roofed oriels, and gables of Kaisersaschern. . . ."

Of course he should have said: of Nuremberg. For what he was describing, with the same intimate vividness with which he had described the mingling of a mermaid's body with her fish tail (so well that I recognized it long before his description had come to an end) was the first sheet in Dürer's series of woodcuts on the Apocalypse. How could I not have been reminded later, then, of this comparison—which at the time seemed so strangely far-fetched and yet immediately wakened certain premonitions—when Adrian's intentions slowly revealed themselves as a work that he mastered by letting it master him and for which his energies had been gathering even as they lay in torment? Was I not correct in saying that the artist's states of depression and productive elation, his illness and health, were not sharply separated from one another, but rather that in his illness and under its aegis, so to speak, elements of health were at work, while those elements of illness that contribute to genius were being transferred to health? It is beyond dispute, and I thank a friendship that brought me great sorrow and dismay, but always filled me with pride, for the insight: Genius is a form of the life force that is deeply versed in illness, that both draws creatively from it and creates through it.

The conception of the apocalyptic oratorio, his secret preoccupation with it, reaches therefore far back into a period when Adrian's life forces seemed totally exhausted; and the vehemence and speed with which, afterward, it was put to paper within the space of a few months, always prompted me to imagine his state of misery to be a kind of refuge and hiding-place into which his nature had retreated, where, with no one listening or suspecting, safely disengaged, painfully isolated from our healthy life, he could tend and develop conceptions for which common good health cannot provide the audacious courage and that, as if stolen from the depths, are brought up from below and borne into the light of day. I already noted that whatever he was planning was revealed to me only step by step, visit by visit. He was writing, sketching, collecting, studying, combining—that could not remain hidden from me, and I watched it all with genuine satisfaction. For weeks, my groping inquiries were countered with a half-playful silence, an annoyed, half-timid defensiveness that guarded some uncanny secret, with a smile and raised brows, with phrases like: "Mind your business and keep your soul clean!" or, "You'll find out soon enough as always, my good man!" or, more to the point and somewhat closer to an admission, "Yes, holy horrors are abrewing. One cannot, it would seem, get the theological virus out of one's blood so easily. Out of nowhere comes a stormy relapse."

That hint confirmed suspicions that had arisen from observing his reading habits. I discovered an exotic old tome on his desk, a thirteenth-century French rendition in verse of the *Vision of St. Paul,* the Greek text of which goes back to the fourth century. In reply to my question of where it came from, he said:

"Our Rosenstiel got it for me. Not the first curio she has dug up for me. An enterprising female. It has not escaped her that I have a soft spot for people who have 'made the descent.' I mean the descent into hell. That creates a bond of familiarity between such totally disparate figures as Paul and Virgil's Aeneas. Do you remember how Dante refers to them as brothers, as two who have been down below?"

I did remember. "Unfortunately," I said, "your *filia hospitalis* cannot read it to you

"No," he said with a laugh, "I have to use my own eyes for Old French."

During the period when he had not been able to use his eyes, you see, when the painful pressure above and deep within them made reading impossible, Clementina Schweigestill had often had to read to him—and from texts that sounded strange enough, or then again not all that incongruous, from the lips of this amiable country girl. I myself had stumbled upon the good child in the abbot's study with Adrian, as he lay resting in his chair purchased from Bernheimer's while she sat very straight-backed in the Savonarola chair at the desk and in the touchingly awkward tones of her stilted grammar-school High German read to him from a foxed volume in boards, which had probably entered the house via our resourceful Rosenstiel and dealt with the ecstatic experiences of Mechthild of Magdeburg. I sat down quietly on the bench in the corner and listened in amazement for a good while to this piously murky and clumsily eccentric presentation.

And then I learned that this was often the case. In her chaste country garb—a habit of olive-green wool that was a testimony to clerical stricture, with a bodice that was studded with two closely set rows of metal buttons, closed high at the neck, flattened her youthful bosom, and fell to a tapered point over the wide full-length gathered skirt, its only ornament a chain of old silver coins worn under the ruche at her throat—the brown-eyed maiden sat beside the invalid and like a schoolgirl intoning a litany, read to him from texts to which the parish priest would certainly have had no objection: early Christian and medieval visionary literature and speculations about the world beyond. Now and then Mother Schweigestill would stick her head in at the door to check on her daughter, whom she may well have needed in the house, but would then give the pair a nod of friendly approval and withdraw again. Or she might sit down on a chair beside the door and listen for ten minutes, only to vanish again without a sound. And if it was not the transports of Mechthild that Clementina recounted, it was those of Hildegard of Bingen. And if not that, then it was the German version of the *Historia Ecclesiastica gentis Anglorum* by that learned monk, the Venerable Bede, a work in which a goodly portion of Celtic fantasies about the next world and the visionary experiences from the early years of Irish and Anglo-Saxon Christianity have been handed down. All these ecstatic writings, proclaiming Judgment, pedagogically fanning the fears of eternal punishment, and arising out of pre-Christian and early Christian eschatologies (of which the Revelation of John of Patmos is but one example rich in parallels), from the testaments from the north of Europe to Italian documents of the same sort, like the dialogues of Gregory the papal choirmaster or the vision of Alberich the monk of Monte Cassino, both of whom clearly influenced Dante—this literature, I say, forms a quite dense sphere of tradition, which is filled with recurrent motifs and in which Adrian immersed himself as a way of readying himself for a work that gathered all such elements into a single focus, compressing them into a menacing latter-day artistic synthesis and, as if under an implacable injunction, holding the mirror of revelation up to humanity's eyes, so that it may see what is approaching and near at hand.

"An end is come, the end is come, it watcheth for thee; behold it is come. The morning is come unto thee, O thou that dwellest in the land." These words, which Leverkühn has his *testo*, his witness and narrator, proclaim in a ghostly melody moving in steps of pure fourths and diminished fifths and resting atop stationary unrelated harmonies, words that then form the text of the daringly archaic responsory repeated in unforgettable fashion by two four-part choirs moving against one another—these words do not belong to the Apocalypse of John at all; they come from a different layer, from the prophecy of Babylonian exile, the stories and lamentations of Ezekiel, to which, moreover, that mysterious epistle from Patmos, written in the days of Nero, stands in very curiously dependent relation. For instance, the "eating of the book," which Albrecht Dürer boldly uses as the subject of one of his woodcuts, is taken almost verbatim from Ezekiel, except for the one detail that in Ezekiel's case the "roll" wherein was written lamentation and mourning and woe, tastes as sweet as honey in the mouth of him who obediently eats it. So, too, the great whore, the woman who sits upon the beast (for whose depiction the artist from Nuremberg blithely helped himself to the portrait of a courtesan, a study he had brought back with him from Venice) is largely prefigured in the very similar terminology of Ezekiel. And indeed there is a traditional apocalyptic culture that provides ecstatics with a set of, to some extent, fixed visions and experiences—however psychologically remarkable it may seem for one man's delirium to imitate his predecessor's delirium and for one man's raptures to be ancillary borrowings modeled on the raptures of another. Such are, nonetheless, the facts of the matter, and I refer to them in connection with the observation that in preparing the text for his incommensurable choral work, Leverkühn in no way confined himself exclusively to the Johannine apocalypse, but also, as it were, incorporated the entire visionary tradition I just mentioned, so that his creation is tantamount to a new apocalypse of his own, a résumé in some sense of all previous proclamations of the end. The title, *Apocalipsis cum figuris,* pays homage to Dürer and is surely intended to emphasize the visual objectivization—including the graphically realized minutia and the density of a space filled with fantastically precise detail—shared by both works. But it is far from the case that Adrian's monstrous fresco programmatically follows those fifteen illustrations by the man from Nuremberg. To be sure, it underlays its dreadfully ingenious sounds with a great many words from the mysterious document that also inspired Dürer; but it has expanded the scope of musical possibilities in choruses, recitatives, and ariosos by incorporating into their texts many of the more doleful verses from the Psalms (the piercing cry, for instance, of "For my soul is full of troubles, and my life draweth nigh unto the Pit"), as well as the most vivid denunciations and images of terror from the Apocrypha, plus certain fragments of Jeremiah's Lamentations (which seem utterly offensive nowadays), and other even more remote texts, all of which can only contribute to creating the general impression of the next world opening up before us, of the final reckoning rushing at us—of a descent into hell, into which visionary power has worked the images of the beyond from both earlier, shamanistic levels and those of antiquity and Christendom, on up to Dante. Leverkühn's sonorous painting draws on Dante's vision to a great extent, but even more on that overpopulated wall swarming with bodies, where here angels blast the trumpets of doom, there Charon's barque unloads its cargo, where the dead arise, the saints adore, demonic figures await the signal of Minos, who is girded with serpents, and one damned fleshy voluptuary, surrounded, carried, dragged by the grinning sons of the pit, takes his ghastly departure, a hand covering one eye, the other staring in horror at eternal damnation, while not far away grace snatches the souls of two other plummeting sinners and lifts them toward salvation—in short, from the structured episodes and groupings of the *Last Judgment.*

When trying to speak about a work so terrifyingly close to him, an educated man—such as I happen to be—may be forgiven for comparing it with specific and familiar monuments of culture. Doing so pro-

vides me with the same reassurance I still need today in speaking about
it that I needed in those days, when I attended its birth, with horror,
amazement, apprehension, and pride—an experience that was surely
inherent in my loving devotion to its creator, but actually beyond my
psychological capacities, to the point where it made me tremble. After
initial tokens of concealment and defensiveness, Adrian very soon offered his childhood friend access to his accomplishments and endeavors, so that with each visit to Pfeiffering (and of course I came by as
often as I could, almost every Saturday and Sunday) I was allowed to
partake of new sections of the work being born—drafts that grew at
times to incredible size from one visit to the next, so that, especially
when one took into account a compositional style subject to the
strictest laws of intellectual and technical complexity, a person accustomed to a work's progressing at a stolid, proper bourgeois pace might
readily turn pale with horror. Yes, I admit that what contributed to almost all of my (some might say simple, I shall call it human) fear of the
work was the absolutely uncanny rapidity with which it came into being—the bulk of it in four and a half months, the same time one might
have estimated to be required for the mechanical process of simply
copying it out.

Evidently and by his own admission, the man was living at the time
in a state of high tension, in which invention definitely did not simply
cheer, but also harried and enthralled him, in which the flash of a problem as it posed itself—that is, the compositional task as he had pursued
it from the start—was as one with the illumination of its solution,
barely leaving him time to put his quill, his pen to a rush of ideas that
gave him no rest, made him their slave. Still in very fragile health, he
worked ten hours a day or more, interrupted only by a short pause at
noon and now and then by a walk in the open air, around Klammer
Pool, up Mount Zion, hasty excursions that were more like attempted
flight than recreation and, judging from his now headlong, now halting
gait, were merely another form of restlessness. On many a Saturday
evening I spent in his company, I indeed observed how little he was
master of himself, how incapable he was of pursuing with me some
conversation that dealt with everyday or even indifferent things and
that he had deliberately sought by way of relaxation. I can see him suddenly sit up from his reclining position, see his gaze grow rigid and attentive, his lips separate, his cheeks take on a flush I did not welcome,
betokening some kind of attack. What was this? Was it one of those
melodic illuminations to which he was subject, I might almost say at
risk in those days, and by means of which powers that I wish to know

nothing about kept their word? Was this the rising up within his mind
of one of those powerfully graphic themes of which there was such an
abundance in this apocalyptic work, but which were always immediately subjected to chilling mastery, reined in, as it were, recast into
rows, treated as mere building blocks of composition? I can see him
murmuring his, "Go on! Go on with what you were saying!" as he
steps over to his desk, tears open his folder of orchestral sketches, actually ripping one page at the bottom as he violently flips it over, and
with a grimace whose mixture of emotions I will not try to name, but
that in my eyes always disfigured the clever and proud beauty of his
face, casts it a glance—perhaps at the spot where he had sketched out
the terrified chorus of humanity as it flees and staggers before the four
horsemen, only to stumble and be overridden; at the notes of "The
Bird's Cry of Woe," that gruesome call assigned to the mocking, bleating bassoon; or perhaps at the inserted exchange of song, much like an
antiphon, that so deeply stirred my heart at the very first hearing—the
strict choral fugue set to the words of Jeremiah:

> Wherefore doth a living man complain,
> A man for the punishment of his sins?
> Let us search and try our ways,
> And turn again to the Lord!
>
> . . .
>
> We, we have transgressed
> And have rebelled;
> Thou hast not pardoned;
> Thou hast covered with anger and persecuted us;
> Thou hast slain, thou has not pitied.
>
> . . .
>
> Thou hast made us as the offscouring
> And refuse in the midst of the people.

I call the piece a fugue, and it has a fugal feeling, although the theme
is never faithfully repeated, but rather is itself developed along with the
development of the whole, so that a style, to which the artist apparently wished to subject himself, is dismantled and carried, so speak, to
absurdity—and all of this accomplished not without reference to the
archaic fugue forms of certain canzoni and ricercari of the period before Bach, in which the fugue's theme is not always clearly defined and
adhered to.

He would gaze at some passage or another, reach for his pen, toss it
aside again, muttering, "That will do, till tomorrow," and then return

to me with his brow still flushed. But I knew or feared that his "till to-morrow" would not hold, but that after my departure he would set to work again and finish what had come over him all unbidden during our conversation—and follow it up with two luminol tablets that would have to give his slumber some depth to compensate for its brevity, only to begin anew at dawn. He quoted:

> Awake, psaltery and harp!
> I myself will awake early.

For he lived in fear that this state of illumination with which he was blessed, or afflicted, would be withdrawn from him prematurely, and in fact, shortly before bringing the work to its end, to the dreadful con-clusion that demanded all his courage and, far removed from any Ro-mantic music of redemption, ruthlessly confirmed the theologically negative and merciless character of the whole—in fact, I say, just before composing that onrushing welter of brass in an inordinate host of voices at the extremes of their range, giving the impression of an abyss that will engulf everything in its hopeless maw, he suffered a three-week relapse into his previous condition of pain and nausea, a state during which, in his own words, the very memory of what it meant to compose music and how it was done, vanished. This passed, and he was working again by early August 1919, and before that month of a great many very hot, sunny days had ended, the oratorio was com-pleted. The four and a half months I attributed to the work describes the period from its beginning to the interval of exhaustion. If one adds the weeks of both that pause and the final labors, it took him, amazingly enough, six months to put the finished draft of the *Apoca-lypse* to paper.

XXXIV

continued

AND IS THAT now everything I have to say in the biography of
my late friend about this work, which is hated by thousands who
have regarded it with disgust, and yet is already loved and celebrated
by hundreds as well? Not really. Many things still weigh on my mind
about it, but I had intended first to characterize those qualities and
traits by which it depressed and terrified me (while, need I say, also
evoking my admiration), or better, awakened my anxious concern—I
had intended, I say, first to characterize all that in connection with certain abstract propositions to which I had been exposed during those
discussions in the apartment of Herr Sixtus Kridwiss of which brief
mention was previously made. After all, it was the novel conclusions
reached during those evenings, together with my participation in
Adrian's lonely work, that produced the mental strain under which I
lived at the time, and that indeed caused me to lose a good fourteen
pounds.

Kridwiss was a graphic artist, an ornamenter of books, and a collec-
tor of East Asian color woodcuts and ceramics, an interest that resulted in invitations from one cultural organization or another for him
to give expert and astute lectures in various cities of the Reich and even
abroad; he was a small, ageless, rather gnomelike gentleman with a
strong Rhine-Hessian accent and uncommon intellectual enthusiasms,
who, although without any definable system of beliefs, kept a curious
ear cocked for the stirrings of the age and now and then termed what
he happened to hear, "rilly 'norm'sly 'mportant." He made a point of
turning his apartment on Martius Strasse in Schwabing, whose recep-

tion room was decorated with charming Chinese works in ink and watercolor (from the Sung dynasty!), into a meeting place for whatever number of leading minds—or at least of insiders with an interest in intellectual matters—the good city of Munich might shelter within its walls, and he organized evenings of discussion for gentlemen, intimate round-table sessions of never more than eight to ten personages, for which one dropped by after dinner, around nine o'clock, and which, without costing the host much by way of entertainment, were intended purely for informal sociability and the exchange of ideas. The conversation, by the way, was not kept at a constant level of intellectual high tension; it often drifted off into cozy everyday chitchat, if only because, thanks to Kridwiss's social tastes and obligations, the intellectual niveau of the participants was indeed somewhat uneven. And so these sessions might well include two members of the reigning house of the grand duchy of Hessen-Nassau who happened to be studying in Munich, amiable young fellows, whom our host, with some gusto, called the "handsome princes" and for whose presence, if only because they were so very much younger than the rest of us, we had to make some allowances in our conversation. I would not say they disrupted it. A high-flown conversation often passed right over their heads without their much caring—they would pretend to listen in smiling modesty or earnest astonishment. Personally, I was more annoyed by the presence of Dr. Chaim Breisacher, that lover of paradoxes with whom the reader is already acquainted and whom, as I admitted some time ago, I could not stand, even if his subtlety and keen receptivity seemed indispensable on such occasions. It also irritated me that Bullinger, the manufacturer, was among those invited—authorized solely on the basis of his high income-tax bracket loudly to blow off steam about the weightiest cultural issues.

I wish to go even farther and admit that I could take no great liking to or place unequivocal trust in anyone at this roundtable, with the possible exception of Helmut Institoris, who also sometimes attended these discussions and with whom I felt a bond of friendship through my relation with his wife—although, to be sure, his presence awakened anxious worries of another sort. There is, moreover, the question of what I could possibly have against Dr. Unruhe, Egon Unruhe, a philosophical paleozoologist, whose writings linked in a most ingenious fashion the study of fossils and geological strata with a vindication and scientific confirmation of materials found in ancient sagas, so that by his theory—a sublimated Darwinism, if you will—all the things that an advanced humanity had long since ceased to believe became true and real again. Yes, what *was* the source of my distrust of

this learned man engaged in such serious intellectual endeavors? Or of
the distrust I felt for Professor Georg Vogler, the literary historian,
who had written a widely regarded history of German literature from
the perspective of tribal membership, whereby each writer was treated
and valued not as a writer *per se*, not as a universally trained mind, but
as the genuine, blood-and-soil product of a real, concrete, specific corner of the world, out of which he was born and to which he bore witness? It was really all very respectable, manly, solid, and deserving of
critical thanks. Yet another guest, the art historian and Dürer scholar,
Professor Gilgen Holzschuher, made me feel uneasy for similar reasons that I find it hard to justify; and that was doubly true for the poet
Daniel Zur Höhe, who was also often in attendance—a gaunt thirty-
year-old clad in clerical black up to his tight collar, with the profile of
a bird of prey and a hammering way of speaking that went something
like: "Indeed, indeed, not bad, no doubt at all, one can well say
that!"—while he nervously and urgently tapped the floor with the ball
of his foot. He loved to cross his arms over his chest or to hide one
Napoleonic hand in his bosom, and his poetic dreams told of a world
that bloody crusades had made subject to pure Spirit and that was kept
in fear by that Spirit's sublime discipline—just as he had described it all
in his (I believe, only) work, *Proclamations,* published before the war
on hand-made paper, a lyrico-rhetorical outburst of voluptuous ter-
rorism, to which one had to concede considerable verbal power. The
signature beneath these proclamations was that of an entity named
Christus Imperator Maximus, an Energy who enlisted and commanded troops prepared to die in the cause of subjugating the globe,
who issued bulletins much like orders of the day, reveled in laying
down implacable stipulations, proclaimed poverty and chastity, and
could not get enough of unquestioned, unbounded obedience to his
fist-pounding demands. "Soldiers!" the poem concluded, "I entrust to
you the plundering—of the world!"

   It was all "beautiful" and had a very strong sense of its own "beauty";
it was "beautiful" in a cruel and utterly beauty-bound way, in that un-
conscionably detached, jesting, irresponsible spirit that poets in fact allow themselves—and the sheerest aesthetic mischief I have ever
encountered. Helmut Institoris, of course, was quite partial to it, but
the author and his work enjoyed the serious esteem of others as well;
my antipathy for both, however, was not so totally sure of itself, for I
knew that it was conditioned by my general irritation with Kridwiss's
circle and its presumptuous assertions of cultural criticism, which a
certain sense of intellectual duty demanded I take note of nonetheless.

   I shall attempt to provide as concise an outline as possible of the es-

sential conclusions reached, which our host quite rightly found "rilly
'norm'sly 'mportant" and which Daniel Zur Höhe punctuated with his
stereotypical, "Oh no doubt at all, not bad, indeed, indeed, one can
well say that!"—even if those conclusions did not lead directly to the
plundering of the world by soldiers sworn forever to the cause of
Christus Imperator Maximus. That was, needless to say, merely symbolic poesy, whereas our deliberations were devoted to surveying
sociological reality, to determining what was and what was yet to
come—which to be sure had things in common here and there with the
ascetically beautiful terrors of Daniel's fantasies. I previously noted of
my own accord that there was a lively sense that the war had disrupted
and destroyed what had seemed to be life's fixed values—particularly
in the defeated nations, which in that sense had something like an intellectual head start over the others. It was an emotion deeply felt and
objectively confirmed in the monstrous loss of self-worth that each individual had suffered through the events of the war, in the disregard
with which life strode right over every single person nowadays, and in
a general indifference to each man's suffering and perishing that had
found its way into people's hearts. This disregard, this indifference toward the fate of the individual might well have seemed to have been
sired by our recent four-year bloody circus; but one ought not to be
misled—for here, as in many other regards, the war had only completed, clarified, and forged as a common drastic experience something
that had long been developing and establishing itself as the basis of a
new sense of life. But since this was not a matter of praise or censure,
but simply a factual observation and determination, and since there is
always some approbation in every dispassionate recognition of reality,
stemming simply from the joy of recognizing it, how could such views
not be linked to a multifaceted, indeed comprehensive critique of the
bourgeois tradition—by which I mean values like culture, enlightenment, humanity, and dreams like the improvement of nations through
scientific civilization? That those who offered this critique—offered it
jauntily and frequently accompanied by smug, intellectually amused
laughter—were men of culture, education, and science, lent the matter
its especially prickly and disconcerting or slightly perverse charm; and
it is probably superfluous to say that the form of government assigned
us Germans by defeat, the very freedom that had fallen into our laps,
in a word, our democratic republic was not accepted for a single moment as a serious framework for the new situation they had in mind,
but was unanimously shrugged off as self-evidently ephemeral, as predestined to meaninglessness in the present situation, indeed as a bad
joke.

They quoted Alexis de Tocqueville, who had said that two streams flow from the wellspring of revolution—one allowing men to build free institutions, the other leading to absolute power. Of the gentlemen conversing at Kridwiss's not a one believed any longer in "free institutions," particularly since freedom was a self-contradictory notion, insofar as in order to maintain itself freedom is forced to limit the freedom of its opponents, that is, to negate itself. This was its fate—that is, if one did not simply toss all that emotional stuff about human rights overboard from the start, which these times appeared much more inclined to do, rather than embark upon a dialectical process that eventually turned freedom into the dictatorship of its own cause. Everything ended in dictatorship, in violence, in any case; for with the demolition of traditional forms of government and society by the French Revolution, an age had dawned that—consciously or not, admittedly or not—was moving toward despotic tyranny over atomized, disconnected masses leveled to a common denominator and as powerless as the individual.

"Quite right! Quite right! No doubt at all, one can well say that!" Zur Höhe declared with an insistent tap of his foot. Of course one could say it, but since this was ultimately the description of the advent of barbarism, one should have said it, or so it seems to me, with somewhat more fear and trembling and not with such blithe satisfaction—which at best one might still barely hope was bound up with the realization of these things and not with the things themselves. I would like to provide a vivid illustration of the jauntiness that so depressed me. No one will be amazed to learn that a book by Sorel entitled *Réflexions sur la violence,* which had appeared seven years before the war, played a significant role in the discussions of this cultural avant-garde. Sorel's unrelenting prediction of war and anarchy, his characterization of Europe as the soil of armed cataclysms, his theory that the nations of this continent have always been able to unite around only one idea, that of engaging in war—all that entitled this to be called the book of the age. And what justified the term even more was his insight and declaration that in the era of the masses, parliamentary discussion would necessarily prove utterly inadequate as a means of shaping political will; that in the future what was needed in its place were mythic fictions, which would be fed to the masses as the primitive battle cries necessary for unleashing and activating political energies. This was in fact the book's crude and intriguing prophecy: that henceforth popular myths, or better, myths trimmed for the masses, would be the vehicle of political action—fables, chimeras, phantasms that needed to have nothing whatever to do with truth, reason, or science in order to be productive nonetheless, to determine life and history, and thereby to prove themselves dynamic realities. It is easy to see that the book did not bear its menacing title in vain, for it dealt with violence as the triumphant counterpart of truth. It made it possible to understand that truth's fate was closely related to that of the individual, indeed identical with it—and that fate was devaluation. The book opened a sardonic rift between truth and power, truth and life, truth and community. Its implicit message was that community deserved far greater precedence, that truth's goal was community, and that whoever wished to be part of the community must be prepared to jettison major portions of truth and science, to make the *sacrificium intellectus*.

And now one must picture (to return to the "vivid illustration" I promised) how these gentlemen—Vogler, Unruhe, Holzschuher, Institoris, and Breisacher, too—themselves scientists, scholars, academics, reveled in a state of affairs that held so many terrors for me, but that they regarded either as having already been achieved or as necessary and inevitable. They shared the fun of imagining a court of law in which one of those mass myths that functioned as a political impulse and undermined bourgeois social order was under debate and where its protagonists had to defend themselves against the charge of "lies" and "fraud," and where, then, the two parties, plaintiff and defendant, not only assailed one another, but also talked right past one another, each hilariously missing the other's point. The grotesque part was the vast machinery of scientific witnesses brought in to prove the humbug to be a humbug, a scandalous insult to truth—yet from that angle there was in fact no arguing with a dynamically and historically productive fiction, with a so-called fraud, with, that is, a community-building belief; and the look on its advocates' faces grew all the more sardonically arrogant the more diligently one attempted to refute them on a basis that for them was totally alien and irrelevant, on the basis of science, of respectable, objective truth. Good God!—science, truth! That exclamation echoed the predominant tone and spirit of these small-talker's dramatic fantasies. They found no end of amusement in the desperate assault of critical reason against an invulnerable belief that reason could not even touch, and they joined forces to place science in the light of an impotence so comical that even the "handsome princes" could enjoy themselves splendidly, in their childish sort of way. The delighted roundtable did not hesitate to ascribe the same self-abnegation that they themselves practiced to the court of justice, which had to speak the final word and pronounce judgment. A jurisprudence that wished to base itself in popular sentiment and not isolate itself from the community, dared not allow itself to adopt as its own view that of theoretical, counter-communal, so-called truth; it had to prove itself to be both modern and patriotic—patriotic in the most modern sense— by respecting the fertile falsehood, acquitting its apostles, and showing a defeated science the door.

Oh no doubt, no doubt, yes indeed, one can well say that. Tap, tap.

Although I felt queasy in the pit of my stomach, I did not dare play the spoilsport and allow my revulsion to show, but had to join in the general merriment as best I could—particularly since it did not imply agreement as such, but only, for the present at least, a smiling, intellectually amused recognition of what was now or was yet to be. I did indeed once suggest, "if we wanted to be serious for a moment," that we consider whether or not a thinker, to whom the needs of the community might matter a great deal, would not perhaps do better to set truth rather than community as his goal, since indirectly and over time community is better served by truth, even by bitter truth, than by a mode of thinking that claims to serve it at the expense of truth, but in reality, by the very denial of the basis of genuine community, works from within in a most sinister fashion for its destruction. But never in my life have I made a remark that fell so utterly flat, that evoked so little response as that one. I even admit that it was tactless, since it did not match the intellectual mood and was inspired by an idealism that was of course familiar, all too familiar—to the point of being banal—and that only disrupted their new ideas. It was far better for me to observe and explore those new ideas with the rest of the guests and, instead of presenting my sterile and actually quite boring opposition to them, to shape my own ideas to conform to the flow of the discussion and use its framework to envision for myself the world that was coming, that was already covertly in the making—whatever the state of affairs in the pit of my stomach.

It was an old-new, revolutionarily atavistic world, in which values linked to the idea of the individual (such as, let us say, truth, freedom, justice, reason) were sapped of every strength and cast aside, or, by having been wrenched free of pale theory, had at least taken on a very different meaning from that given them over the last centuries and, now relativized and red-blooded, were made applicable at the much higher level of violence, authority, the dictatorship of belief—not in some reactionary way that looked back to yesterday or the day before, but in a way that was tantamount to humanity's being transferred, along with all these new ideas, back into the theocratic situations and conditions of the Middle Ages. That was no more reactionary than the path around a sphere—which, of course, leads around or back around it—can be termed regressive. There you had it: regress and progress, the old and the new, past and present—all became one, and the political right coalesced more and more with the left. Unbiased research and free thought, far from representing progress, belonged instead to the boring world of those being left behind. Freedom had been given to thought in order to justify force, just as seven hundred years ago reason had been free to discuss faith and prove dogma; that had been its purpose, and that was the purpose of thought today, or would be tomorrow. Research, to be sure, had its premises—indeed it did! And those were the force, the authority of the community—premises so axiomatic that it never entered science's head that it might not be free. They were thoroughly subjective—within an objective restraint so natural and ingrained that it was in no way felt to be a shackle. In order to see clearly what lay before us, to ban every foolish fear of it, one need only recall that the unconditionality of specific premises had never been an impediment to the imagination and to individual boldness of thought. On the contrary, precisely because the intellectual uniformity and closed world provided by the Church had seemed absolutely self-evident to medieval man, he had been far more a man of imagination than any citizen of the individualistic age, had been able to surrender himself individually to the powers of his own imagination with that much less worry, that much more security.

Oh yes, force gave one firm footing, it was anti-abstract, and in concert with Kridwiss's friends, I found it easy to imagine how these old-new ideas would systematically change life in one arena or another. The pedagogue, for example, knew that even today the tendency in elementary education was to move away from the initial learning of letters by sounding them out and to turn instead to the whole-word method, to link writing to the concrete look of things. This meant, so to speak, a retreat from an abstractly universal alphabet bound to no particular language, and a return, as it were, to the ideographs of primitives. And I secretly thought: Why words at all, why writing, why language? Radical objectivity had to embrace things, nothing else. And I recalled a satire by Swift, where reform-minded professors, in order to spare the lungs and encourage brevity, abolish words and speech entirely and converse solely by displaying the things themselves—although for discourse to take place, one therefore had to carry about as many such things as possible on one's back. The passage is very funny, especially since it is the women, the vulgar, and the illiterate who rebel against this invention and insist that they be allowed to speak with their tongues. Now, my interlocutors did not go so far with their own suggestions as had Swift's professors. They assumed more the air of detached observers, and contemplated as "'norm'sly 'mportant" the general and already clearly apparent readiness to drop all such so-called cultural advances for the sake of necessary, timely simplification, which, if one wished, might be termed a deliberate rebarbarization. Could I trust my ears? I had to laugh and literally winced when in this same connection the gentlemen suddenly turned to dentistry, and quite concretely, to Adrian's and my symbol of musical criticism, the "dead tooth"! I am quite certain that my face turned red with laughter, when to our intellectual amusement, the topic addressed was the growing tendency of dentists summarily to rip out teeth if the nerves were dead, since they had now decided to regard them as infected foreign bodies—this, after the nineteenth century's long, hard labor to develop highly refined techniques of root-canal work. Mind you (and it was Dr. Breisacher who made this subtle point, greeted with general approval) the hygienic view should be seen more or less as a rationalization of the primary, pre-existent tendency to drop, forgo, desist, simplify—for when it came to hygienic arguments, one must always suspect ideology to be at work. No doubt there would also be hygienic arguments for maintaining the nation and race, when one day they would proceed to leave the sick unattended on a large scale and kill the feeble-minded and those incapable of survival, whereas in reality (it was not to be denied, on the contrary, it must be emphasized) it would be a matter of far more profound decisions, of the renunciation of all humane pampering and emasculation, which had been the work of the bourgeois epoch—a matter of mankind's instinctively getting into shape for hard and dark times that would scoff at humanity, for an age of great wars and sweeping revolution, presumably leading far back beyond the Christian civilization of the Middle Ages and restoring instead the Dark Ages that preceded its birth and had followed the collapse of the culture of antiquity. . . .

XXXIV

conclusion

WILL THE READER find it credible that a man can lose fourteen pounds digesting such novelties? Certainly I would not have lost them had I not believed the conclusions drawn at these meetings at Kridwiss's, had I been convinced that these gentlemen were babbling nonsense. But I was most definitely not of that opinion. Indeed, I could not, even for one moment, conceal from myself the fact that they had laid their fingers with remarkable sensitivity on the pulse of the age and were foretelling truth by its beat. I would nonetheless have been infinitely grateful—I must repeat myself here—and presumably would not have lost fourteen, but perhaps only seven pounds, if they themselves had been somewhat shocked by their findings and had countered them with a little moral criticism. They might have said: "Unfortunately, it does indeed look as if things are about to take this or that course. Consequently one must step in, warn against what is coming, and do one's best to prevent it." What they said, however, was more or less: "It's coming, it's coming, and once it's here it will find us at the crest of the moment. It is interesting, it is even good—simply because it is what is coming, and to recognize that fact is both achievement and enjoyment enough. It is not up to us to take measures against it as well." The covert words of these learned men. Their joy of recognition, however, was a sham. They sympathized with what they recognized, and without that sympathy would probably have not recognized it at all. That was the issue. That was the cause of my anger and agitation, and of my loss of weight.

And yet everything I just said is not correct, either. My dutiful participation in Kridwiss's gatherings and the taxing ideas to which I deliberately exposed myself there, would not of themselves have caused my weight loss, not fourteen pounds, not half that many. I would never have taken their bombast so much to heart as I did, had it not provided frosty intellectual commentary to a scalding experience of art and friendship—by which I mean, the birth of a work of art near to my heart (near to me because of my friendship with its creator, not because of itself—that I dare not say, for to my mind there was something far too off-putting and frightening about it), of a work that was taking shape with feverish speed there in that lonely, all-too-homey rural retreat and that strangely corresponded to and stood in intellectual congruence with what I had heard at Kridwiss's.

Had not a main point on the agenda at our roundtable been a critique of tradition, a critique that had resulted from the destruction of human values long considered inviolable, and had not someone (I am not sure I know who—Breisacher? Unruhe? Holzschuher?) explicitly remarked that this critique must necessarily turn against traditional forms and genres of art—for instance, against the aesthetic kind of theater that had been part of the bourgeois circle of life, an occasion for its refinement? And now before my eyes the dramatic form was being superseded by the epic, music drama being transformed into oratorio, opera drama into opera cantata, all in a spirit and out of a fundamental attitude that was in perfect agreement with the dismissive judgments of my interlocutors on Martius Strasse about the state of the individual and, indeed, of all individualism in the world—out of an attitude, I mean, which, being no longer interested in things psychological, insisted on being objective, on a language that expressed something absolute, binding, and obligatory, and that therefore preferred to put on the gentle chains of pre-classical strict forms. How often, while anxiously watching Adrian at work, was I forced to recall the impressions stamped upon us boys so early on by that loquacious stutterer who had been his teacher: the opposition of "harmonic subjectivity" and "polyphonic detachment." The path around the sphere, which had been the subject of tortuously clever conversation at Kridwiss's, that path, by which regress and progress, the old and the new, past and future become one—I saw it realized here in a return that was rich in novelty and moved well beyond the already harmonic art of Bach and Handel, back into the deeper past of genuine polyphony.

I have kept a letter that Adrian sent to me in Freising from Pfeiffering at the time—during his work, that is, on the hymn of praise by the "great multitude, which no man could number, of all nations, and kin-

dreds, and people, and tongues, who stood before the throne and before the lamb" (see Dürer's seventh woodcut), a letter in which he
urged me to visit him and that he signed with "Perotinus Magnus." A
telling joke and a playful, self-mocking way of identifying himself, for
this Perotinus was the director of music for Notre Dame in the twelfth
century and a choirmaster whose precepts of composition led to further development in the young art of polyphony. This jocular signature reminded me of a similar instance, when, while working on
Parsifal, Richard Wagner added the title "Member of the High Consistory" beneath his name on a letter. For the non-artist it is a very intriguing question how serious an artist is about what should be and
appears to be a matter of particular seriousness—how seriously he
takes himself and how much playfulness, masquerade, and higher
mirth are involved. If the question were unwarranted, how could that
grand master of the music drama have given himself such a nickname
while laboring over that work of solemn consecration? I felt much the
same way about Adrian's signature; indeed, my questions, cares, fears
went well beyond it and, in the silence of my heart, were directed at the
very legitimacy of his activity, at his temporal claim to the sphere in
which he had immersed himself and whose re-creation he pursued
with most highly developed, the uttermost, means. In short, out of
both love and fear, I suspected it of an aestheticism that cast the most
tormenting doubts on my friend's statement that the antithesis that
would replace bourgeois culture was not barbarism, but community.

No one can follow my argument here who has not experienced as I
have how close aestheticism and barbarism are to each other, or who
has not felt how aestheticism prepares the way for barbarism in one's
own soul—though, granted, I have known this danger not of my own
accord, but with the help of my friendship for a dear artist and imperiled spirit. The renewal of cultic music out of a profane age has its dangers. Cultic music served the purposes of the Church, did it not? But
before that, it served the less civilized purposes of the medicine man
and the magician, during eras, that is, when, as the agent of the super-
natural, the priest was also a shaman and sorcerer. Can it be denied that
this was a pre-cultural, a barbaric state of the cult? And is it not understandable, then, that the later cultural renewal of things cultic, in its
ambition to create community out of atomization, seizes upon means
that belong not only to an ecclesiastical stage of civilization, but to one
that is primitive as well? The incredible difficulties that Leverkühn's
Apocalypse presents in rehearsal and performance are directly connected with all this. There are ensembles that begin as speaking cho-

ruses and only by stages, by way of the oddest transitions, arrive at the richest vocal music; choruses, that is, that move through all the shades of graduated whispering, antiphonal speech, and quasi-chant on up to the most polyphonic song—accompanied by sounds that begin as simple noise, as magical, fanatical African drums and booming gongs, only to attain the highest music. How often has this forbidding work—with its urgent need to let music reveal the most hidden things, from the beast in man to his most sublime emotions—incurred reproaches both of bloody barbarism and bloodless intellectuality. Incurred both, I say—for its attempt to subsume within it, as it were, the life-history of music, from its premusical, elemental, magically rhythmic stages on up to its most complicated perfection, exposes the work to the latter reproach not just in part, perhaps, but indeed as a whole.

By way of example I shall present something that has always especially stirred my humane anxieties and been an object of mockery and hate among hostile critics. For this I must step back a bit. We all know that the first concern, indeed the earliest achievement of the art of music was to separate sound from nature, to wrest from chaos a system of tones, and to assign individual notes to song—which originally among primitive humans must have been a howl that glided over several pitches. It is surely self-evident: A norming of sound into ordered units was a precondition and the first self-manifestation of what we understand as music. Frozen within it, as a naturalistic atavism, so to speak, a barbaric rudiment of premusical days, is the sliding tone, the glissando—a musical device that, for profoundly cultural reasons, is to be employed with utmost caution and in which I have always tended to hear something anticultural, indeed anti-human, even demonic. What I have in mind is Leverkühn's (and since of course one ought not call it a preference for, then let us say) extraordinarily frequent use of the sliding tone, at least in this work, in the *Apocalypse*, whose images of terror certainly supply the most enticing and, at the same, legitimate reasons for employing this wild device. In the passage where the four voices from the altar order the four avenging angels to be let loose to slay horses and riders, emperor and pope, and a third part of mankind, trombone glissandi represent the theme—and the devastating slide across the instrument's seven positions is used to terrifying effect! The howl as a theme—how ghastly! And what acoustic panic flows from the repeated instrumentation for timpani glissandi, a musical or sound effect achieved here by adjusting the pedal mechanism of the timpani to various pitches even as the hands are performing the drum roll. The effect is extremely eerie. But the most bone-chilling sound is the appli-

cation of the glissando to the human voice (which as the first object of
tonal ordering had, after all, been liberated from its primal howl across
a range of pitches), the return, that is, to a primal stage, as it is horrifyingly reproduced by the chorus of the *Apocalypse* when it assumes the
role of screaming humanity upon the opening of the seventh seal,
when the sun grows black, the moon is turned to blood, and all ships
founder.

I really must beg to be permitted to insert a word about the treatment of the chorus in my friend's work, this never previously attempted dispersal of vocal forces into disjointed and interwoven
antiphonal groupings, into dramatic dialogues and isolated cries,
which, to be sure, take as their distant classical model the shouted answer of "Barabbas!" from the *St. Matthew Passion.* The *Apocalypse*
abandons orchestral interludes, with the result that at more than one
point the chorus takes on an amazingly explicit orchestral character—
as in the choral variations that represent the hymn of the 144,000 redeemed who fill the heavens, where the nature of the chorale is
preserved simply by having all four voices moving constantly to the
same rhythm, while the orchestra accompanies or opposes them in the
most richly contrasted rhythms. The extreme polyphonic harshness of
this work (and not just this work) has been the cause of much scorn
and hatred. But that is how it is, one must accept it; I at least accept it
with ungrudging amazement, for the entire work is governed by the
paradox (if it is a paradox) that its dissonance is the expression of
everything that is lofty, serious, devout, and spiritual, while the harmonic and tonal elements are restricted to the world of hell or, in this
context, to a world of banality and platitudes.

But I wanted to say something else. I wanted to point to the strange
exchange of sounds that often occurs between the vocal and instrumental parts of the *Apocalypse.* The choral and the orchestral do not
stand in clear juxtaposition as human and material, but each merges
into the other, the chorus is instrumentalized, the orchestra vocal-
ized—to such an extent that the boundary between men and things
seems to have been purposely moved, which certainly enhances the
artistic unity, but which nevertheless (at least to my mind) also has
something oppressive, dangerous, malevolent about it. A few details
by way of illustration: The voice of the whore of Babylon, the woman
upon the beast, with whom the kings of the earth have fornicated, is assigned, surprisingly enough, to the most graceful coloratura soprano,
and her virtuoso runs are at times so completely like a flute that they
melt into the orchestra. On the other hand, variously muted trumpets

imitate the most grotesque vox humana—as does the saxophone as well, which plays a role in several of the small splinter orchestras that accompany the devils' tunes, those vile catches sung by the sons of the Pit. Adrian's powers of sardonic imitation, deeply rooted in the melancholy of his own nature, become productive here in parodies of the diverse musical styles in which hell's insipid excess indulges: burlesqued French impressionism, bourgeois drawing-room music, Tchaikovsky, music hall songs, the syncopations and rhythmic somersaults of jazz—it all whirls round like a brightly glittering tilting match, yet always sustained by the main orchestra, speaking its serious, dark, difficult language and asserting with radical rigor the work's intellectual status.

But onward! There is still so much in my heart to say about my friend's scarcely explored legacy, and yet it would seem best if from here on I would present my remarks in the light of a reproach, for which I admit there are explanations, though I would rather bite off my tongue than admit they are justified—the reproach of barbarism. This charge was leveled against the fusion of oldest and newest elements that is so characteristic of the work, but is in no way arbitrary, since it lies, rather, in the nature of things—by which I mean, that it is based on the curvature of the world, which allows the earliest things to come round again in what is most recent. The ancient musical arts did not know rhythm the way music later understood it. The meter of a song was set by the rules of speech, it did not move in bars, in a periodically divided measurement of time, but rather obeyed the spirit of free recitation. And what is the status of rhythm in our most recent music? Has it not also moved closer to the accents of speech? Been broken up by a varied, drastic flexibility? Even in Beethoven there are movements whose rhythmic freedom hints at what is to come. With Leverkühn, all that is missing is for the bars not even to be marked. They are—ironically, conservatively—present. But the rhythm, lacking all consideration of symmetry and purely adapted to the accents of speech, changes in fact from bar to bar. I spoke of impressions stamped upon us. There are those that—without, it would seem, reason's ever being aware—continue to work in the soul, exercising a subconsciously determinative influence. So, too, the character and the dogmatically naive musical enterprises of that odd duck from across the sea, about whom we learned in our youth from yet another odd duck, from Adrian's teacher, and about whom my companion had spoken with such arrogant approval as we wandered home—so too, then, the story of Johann Conrad Beissel had made just such an impression. Why should I pretend as if I have not for some time now been reminded repeatedly of that rigorous schoolmaster and renewer of the art of singing, hard at work there in Ephrata across the sea? A whole world lies between his naively plucky pedagogy and the work that Leverkühn pushed to the very limits of erudition, technique, and intellectuality. And yet, as a knowledgeable friend, I find that work haunted by the ghost of the inventor of "master and servant tones" and of the musical recitation of hymns.

Does the inclusion of this personal remark help explain the reproach that so pains me and that I am trying to explain without making the least concession to it: the reproach of barbarism? Surely that charge has more to do with a decided trace of what feels like the icy touch of mass modernity in a work of religious vision, a work that perceives the theological element almost exclusively in terms of judgment and terror—a trace of something "streamlined," to risk an insulting term. Take, for instance, the *testo,* the witness and narrator of these awful events, the "I, John," who describes the beasts of the abyss with the faces of a lion, a calf, a man, and an eagle—this role, traditionally given to a tenor, is also written here for a male voice, but one almost in the range of a castrato, whose cold, reporterlike, matter-of-fact crowings stand in horrible contrast to the contents of his catastrophic message. When in 1926—at the festival of the International Society for New Music held in Frankfurt am Main—the *Apocalypse* was given its first and thus far last performance (under Klemperer), this extremely difficult role was sung in masterly fashion by a eunuchoid tenor named Erbe, whose piercing announcements did indeed sound like "the latest news from doomsday." This was very much in the spirit of the work, the singer had grasped that spirit with great intelligence. Or, to take another example of technology at ease with horror, consider the loudspeakers (in an oratorio!) whose use the composer specified at various points to produce directional and acoustic gradations that had never been achieved before—so that with their help, some things could be given prominence and others pushed into the background, like a distant choir or distant orchestra. One need only recall, moreover, the, admittedly very infrequent, introduction of jazz sounds for purely infernal purposes—and I may then perhaps be pardoned my ironic use of the term "streamlined" for a work that, in its basic intellectual and psychological mood, has more to do with "Kaisersaschern" than with a modern sleekness of attitude and whose nature I would prefer to call (to use a daring term) explosive antiquarianism.

Soullessness!—I know very well that is what people mean when they attach the word "barbarism" to Adrian's creation. Have they ever, if only with the reading eye, listened to certain lyrical passages (or dare I only say, moments?) in the *Apocalypse*—pieces of song, accompanied by a chamber orchestra, which, like a fervent plea for a soul, could bring tears to the eyes of a harder man than I? I may be forgiven for a more or less randomly directed polemic, but I regard it as barbarism, as inhumanity, to term as soullessness such longings for a soul—the longings of the little mermaid!

I am deeply moved as I write this in its defense—and am seized with yet another emotion: the recollection of the pandemonium of laughter, of infernal laughter, that forms the brief, but ghastly conclusion of the first part of the *Apocalypse*. I hate, I love, I fear it; for (and may I be forgiven that all too personal "for"!) I have always feared Adrian's penchant for laughter, which, unlike Rüdiger Schildknapp, I was always poor at encouraging—and I feel that same fear, that same timid and anxious helplessness when listening to this sardonic *gaudium* of Gehenna as it sweeps across fifty bars, beginning with the giggle of a single voice, only to spread rapidly and seize choir and orchestra, then, amid rhythmic upheavals and counterblows and jettisons, to swell to a horrible *fortissimo tutti*, to a dreadful mayhem of yowls, yelps, screeches, bleats, bellows, howls, and whinnies, to the mocking, triumphant laughter of hell. So greatly do I loathe this episode in and of itself—this passage whose very position emphasizes it over all else, this whirlwind of infernal fits of laughter—that I would scarcely have been able to bring myself to speak of it, if it had not revealed to me in precisely this context and in a way that makes my heart falter, the deepest mystery of music, which is a mystery of identity.

For this hellish laughter at the end of part one has its counterpart in the totally strange and wonderful children's chorus, accompanied by a small orchestra, that immediately thereafter opens part two—a piece of cosmic music of the spheres, icy, clear, transparent as glass, austerely dissonant, to be sure, but whose sound is so sweet, might I say, so inaccessibly alien and superterrestrial that it fills the heart with hopeless longing. And in its musical substance, this piece—which has won, touched, enraptured even reluctant hearers—is, for him who has ears to hear and eyes to see, a reprise of the Devil's laughter. At every turn, Adrian Leverkühn is great at making unlike what is in essence alike. He is well known for his method of rhythmically modifying a fugue theme in the very first answer, in such a way that, although the thematic is strictly maintained, it can no longer be recognized as a repetition. The same thing happens here—and nowhere so deeply, mysteriously, grandly as here. Every word that suggests the idea of "moving beyond," of alteration in a mystical sense, of mutation—that is, of transformation, transfiguration—is to be understood here literally. The horrors that have just been heard are now transported, with fully different instrumentation and restructured rhythms, into a totally different register by this indescribable children's chorus. But there is not a note in these searing, susurrant tones of the spheres and angels that did not appear with strictest correspondence in the laughter of hell.

That is Adrian Leverkühn in his entirety. It is the music that he represents in its entirety; and correspondence is, in its profundity, calculation elevated to mystery. That is how a friendship marked by pain taught me to see music, although, given my own simple nature, I would perhaps have gladly seen something else in it.

XXXV

A NEW NUMBER stands at the head of a section that will report a death in my friend's immediate circle, a human catastrophe—but, my God, what sentence, what word, that I have written here is not caught up in catastrophe, which has become the very air of life for us all? What word has not been secretly shaken, often along with the hand that wrote it, by the vibrations of the catastrophe toward which my narrative toils and, simultaneously, of the calamity under whose sign the world—or at least the humane, bourgeois world—now stands?

We are dealing here with an intimately human catastrophe that the outside world scarcely noticed, but that was the fruition of many contributing factors: male villainy, female weakness, female pride, and professional failure. Twenty-three years have now passed since the actress Clarissa Rodde, whose sister Inez was obviously just as imperiled as she, perished almost before my eyes. After the end of the winter season of 1921–22, she returned in May to her mother's home in Pfeiffering, where—with little consideration for her mother's feelings—she hastily, but resolutely took her life with the poison she had long kept at the ready for the moment when her pride could no longer endure life.

I wish to be brief in recounting both the events that led to that terrible deed—which shocked us all, but for which we ultimately could not blame her—and the circumstances under which it was committed. It has already been hinted that the concerns and warnings of her teacher in Munich had proved only too valid and that over the years Clarissa's artistic career did not seem to want to rise from provincial lowlands to more respectable and worthy heights. From Elbing in East Prussia she returned to Pforzheim in Baden—meaning she had made no, or very little, progress. The nation's larger theaters were not interested in her; she was unsuccessful or had no real success, for the simple reason—however hard it may be for the person involved to grasp it—that her natural talent did not match her ambition. She lacked the theater blood that would have let her turn hopes and knowledge into reality and helped her to win the minds and hearts of a recalcitrant public. She lacked some primitive instincts that are determinative in all art, but most definitely in the actor's art—be that to the credit or discredit of art, and to the world of the stage in particular.

Something else contributed to the confusion of Clarissa's life. As I had long since observed to my regret, she was not good at keeping the stage and her own life separate; she was an actress, and perhaps because she was not a true one, she accentuated that fact in her life outside the theater as well; the physical and personal nature of her art led her to wear heavy makeup, coiffures padded with switches, and extravagant hats, even in civilian life—a fully unnecessary and easily misconstrued self-dramatization, whose effect was to embarrass her friends, scandalize the average citizen, and, quite unintentionally and mistakenly, encourage men to lust after her. For Clarissa was the most mockingly aloof, cool, chaste, noble creature—though this armor of ironic haughtiness may well have been a defense mechanism against those female desires that made her a true sister to Inez Institoris, the lover, or cidevant lover of Rudi Schwerdtfeger.

In any case, in the wake of that well-preserved man in his sixties who had wanted to make her his mistress, many another swell with less solid prospects had likewise found himself ingloriously snubbed, including one or two whose critical opinion might have proved useful to her, but who, of course, revenged their defeat in scornful disparagement of her work. But at last destiny overtook her and brought all her sneering to a woeful end; "woeful" I said, because the man who conquered her virginity was in no way worthy of his victory, was not regarded worthy of it even by Clarissa herself: a skirt-chaser with a pseudo-demonic goatee, a backstage Johnny and provincial roué, a criminal defense lawyer from Pforzheim, who came equipped for his conquest with nothing but a cheap, cynical gift of gab, fine linens, and a great deal of black hair on his hands. One evening after a performance, presumably tipsy from wine, this prickly and brittle, but basically inexperienced and defenseless woman succumbed to his practiced routine—to her own great anger and furious self-contempt; for, to be sure, her seducer had known how to captivate her senses for a moment, but she felt nothing for him but the hate that his triumph aroused in her—though her succumbing also included a certain amazement of her heart that he had known how to entrap her, Clarissa Rodde. Afterward, she had most assuredly and with added scorn, refused his advances—but always in constant fear that the man might spread the rumor that he had been her lover, something he had already threatened as a way of pressuring her.

Meanwhile, decent, bourgeois prospects had opened up to rescue this tormented, disappointed, humiliated woman. The man who offered them to her was a young Alsatian industrialist whom business brought to Pforzheim from Strasbourg on occasion and who, upon making her acquaintance within a large circle of friends, had fallen desperately in love with this mocking, shapely blond. That Clarissa had been engaged at all that second year by the Pforzheim Theater—though with no permanent contract and only for minor, rather thankless roles—was due to the sympathy and intercession of an older dramaturge, who also probably did not believe in her calling for the stage, but who, as a man of literary ambition, knew to prize her for her general intellectual and human qualities, which considerably, and often disruptively, exceeded those common among a troupe of strolling players. Perhaps, who knows, he even loved her and was too much a man of disillusion and renunciation to summon the courage for his unspoken attachment.

At the start of the new season, then, Clarissa met this young man, who promised to rescue her from her failed career and in its place offered, as her husband, a peacefully secure, indeed well-situated existence in a world that was, granted, foreign to her, but not unlike that of her bourgeois origins. In letters filled with obvious joy, hope, gratitude, and indeed tenderness (which was a fruit of gratitude), she told her sister, and even her mother, about Henri's courtship and about the resistance with which his wishes were meeting at home, at least for now. Approximately the same age as the woman he had chosen, the oldest son (or better, perhaps, sonny boy) of the family, his mother's darling, his father's partner in business—he pled his cause with ardor and certainly with resolution at home, although perhaps something more might have been necessary swiftly to overcome the biases of his bourgeois clan against this actress, this vagabond, and a *boche* at that. Henri understood quite well his family's concern for its quality and purity, its fear that he might be selling himself short. It was not so easy to make clear to them that by making Clarissa his bride he would be doing nothing of the sort. The best thing would be to introduce her personally to his family, to present her to his loving parents, jealous brothers and sisters, and judgmental aunts for their inspection, and for weeks now he had been working on the arrangements and attempting to gain their approval for such an *entrevue*—and reported to his sweetheart about his progress both in a series of notes and repeated trips to Pforzheim.

Clarissa was confident of victory. Her equal social rank, clouded only by a profession that she was willing to abandon, would be obvious to Henri's anxious clan once they had met her personally. In her letters and in conversations during a visit to Munich, she presupposed her official engagement and the future to which she was looking forward. It looked very different from anything this uprooted patrician child with her intellectual, artistic ambitions had ever dreamt, but it was her safe harbor, her happiness—a bourgeois happiness that evidently appeared more acceptable because of the charm of its foreignness, the novelty of a different nation as the framework for the life into which she would be transferred. She could picture her future children prattling in French.

And then the ghost of her past, a stupid, inconsequential, contemptible ghost, but brazen and unmerciful for all that, rose up against her hopes and cynically knocked them to pieces, driving the poor creature into a corner and to her death. That juridical scoundrel, to whom she had given herself in a weak moment, blackmailed her with his one and only victory. Henri's family, Henri himself would learn of his relationship with her if she did not bend to his will once again. From everything we were able to learn later, there must have been desperate scenes between this murderer and his victim. At first the woman pleaded with him in vain—on her knees toward the end—to spare her, to release her, not to force her to pay for peace of mind by betraying the man who loved her and whom she loved in return. But that very confession only roused the monster to cruelty. He let it be plainly understood that by surrendering to him now, she would be gaining her peace only for a moment, only for now, would be buying a trip to Strasbourg, an engagement. But he would never release her, would force her again and again, whenever he chose, to show her appreciation to him for his silence, which he would break the instant she refused him such appreciation. She would have to live in adultery—that would be just punishment for her philistinism, for what the man called her cowardly slinking into bourgeois security.

But if she could not go on, or if even without this cad's assistance her

fiancé were to find her out, she always had the stuff that could put
everything to rights and that she had kept for ages inside her objet
d'art, inside the book with the skull. It would not be for nothing that
she had felt superior to life, mocked it with her macabre joke, with the
proud possession of her Hippocratic medicine—a joke that suited her
better than the bourgeois peace treaty with life that she had been willing to conclude.

In my opinion the blackguard was intent not just on extorting pleasure, but also on her death. His heinous vanity demanded a female
corpse across his path; he craved to have a human being die and perish,
if not exactly for him, then at least on his account. Ah, that Clarissa had
to do him the favor! As things stood, she probably did have to, I realize that, we all had to realize it. She gave in to him once more in order
to win a stopgap peace, and in doing so was more at his mercy than
ever. She probably assumed that once she had been accepted by the
family, once she was married to Henri (and safe on foreign soil), she
would find means and a way to defy her extortionist. It never came to
that. Apparently her tormentor had decided not even to allow the marriage to take place. An anonymous letter, which spoke of Clarissa's
lover in the third person, did its work with the family in Strasbourg,
and with Henri himself. He sent her the text—for her to refute if she
could. His accompanying letter did not exactly reveal the strong, un-
shakeable faithfulness of the love he felt for her.

Clarissa received the registered letter in Pfeiffering, where, for a few
weeks since the closing of the theater season in Pforzheim, she had
been a guest at her mother's little house behind the chestnut trees. It
was early afternoon. The Frau Senator saw her child returning in hot
haste from a walk she had undertaken on her own after lunch. Brush-
ing past her mother with a dull, cursory, confused smile, Clarissa hurried across the little porch and into her room, where the key in the lock
turned quickly and energetically behind her. A while later, from her
own adjoining bedroom, the old woman heard her daughter gargling
with water at the washstand—we now know this was to cool the horrible burning of the acid in her throat. Then came silence—and it continued eerily when, about twenty minutes later, the Frau Senator
knocked on Clarissa's door and called her name. But however urgently
she repeated it, no answer came. Frightened now—and despite her
unmanageable hairline and the gap in her front teeth—she ran across
to the main house and in a few choked words informed Frau
Schweigestill. That experienced soul followed her back, bringing along
a farm hand, who, after repeated calls and knocks by the women,

forced the lock. Clarissa lay with open eyes on the settee at the foot of the bed (a piece of furniture from the seventies or eighties, that had a low back and arms and that I knew from Ramberg Strasse), where she had hastily thrown herself when death swept over her as she gargled.

"There's precious little we can do now, my dear Frau Senator," said Frau Schweigestill, laying a finger to her cheek and shaking her head as she gazed at the half-seated, half-recumbent figure. I, too, beheld this only too compelling sight later that evening, when, upon receiving a telephone call from the landlady and having hurried over from Freising, I stood there, an old family friend, holding the whimpering mother in my consoling arms and—together with her, Else Schweigestill, and Adrian, who had come across with us—gazed with deep emotion at the body. Dark blue smudges of congested blood on Clarissa's beautiful hands and face suggested a rapid death by suffocation, the abrupt paralysis of the breathing mechanism by a dose of cyanide that could easily have killed a company of soldiers. On the table lay the bronze container, empty now, its underside unscrewed— the book that bore the name of Hippocrates in Greek letters, the skull resting atop it. Beside it, a note for her fiancé, hastily written in pencil. It read:

"*Je t'aime. Une fois je t'ai trompé, mais je t'aime.*"

The young man attended the funeral, the arrangements for which it fell to me to make. He was inconsolable, or rather *désolé*, which, quite erroneously, sounds rather more like a figure of speech and not quite so serious. I had no reason to doubt the pain with which he cried out, "Ah, monsieur, I loved her enough to forgive her. Everything could have turned out all right. *Et maintenant—comme ça!*"

Yes, *comme ça!* Everything could truly have turned out differently, had he not been such a lame sonny boy and Clarissa had found in him a more dependable support.

That night, while the Frau Senator sat in profound grief beside the rigid remains of her child, we three—Adrian, Frau Schweigestill, and I—composed a public announcement of death that needed to be both unambiguous and discreet, since Clarissa's closest family would have to sign it. We agreed upon a formulation that said the deceased had departed this life, having suffered a grave, incurable affliction of the heart. The dean of the church in Munich, whom I called upon in order to obtain the church funeral that the Frau Senator so fervently wished, read the text. I began, not all too diplomatically, but with trusting naiveté, by admitting straight out that Clarissa had preferred death to a life of dishonor, but the clergyman, a robust man of God of the best

Lutheran stamp, would have none of it. I admit that it took a while before I realized that although on the one hand the Church did not wish
to be seen as uninvolved, neither was it ready to bless an avowed suicide, however honorable—in short, that what this sturdy gentleman
really wanted was for me to lie. And so I relented with almost ridiculous abruptness, pronounced the entire affair to be quite inexplicable,
admitted the possibility, indeed probability of an accident, a mix-up of
bottles, and by letting the thick-headed fellow feel flattered by the importance attached to the participation of his sacred firm, managed to
get him to consent to perform the funeral service.

This took place at the Waldfriedhof cemetery in Munich and was
attended by everyone in the Rodde's circle of friends. Even Rudi
Schwerdtfeger, even Zink and Spengler, even Schildknapp did not fail
to show. Their grief was sincere, for they all had been fond of poor,
saucy, proud Clarissa. Bundled in black, Inez Institoris stood in for her
mother, who did not appear, and accepted condolences with gentle dignity, slender neck extended, head tilted. I could not help seeing the
tragic outcome of her sister's struggle with life as a bad omen for her
own fate. In conversation with her, by the way, I rather had the impression that she envied Clarissa more than she mourned her. Her husband's circumstances were growing increasingly worse as a result of
the massive inflation that had been desired and engineered by certain
circles. The bulwark of luxury, the frightened woman's defense against
life, was threatening to crumble, and she was already questioning
whether they would be able to keep their elegant apartment on the
English Garden. As for Rudi Schwerdtfeger, as a good comrade he had
indeed paid his last respects to Clarissa, but had then left the cemetery
as quickly as possible—after having first stopped to express to her
most immediate relative his condolences, the formal brevity of which I
pointed out to Adrian.

It was probably the first time that Inez had seen her lover since he
had severed their relationship—with considerable brutality, I fear, for
it was hardly possible to do so "in a nice way," given the desperate
tenacity with which she clung to him. As she stood there at her sister's
grave beside her dainty husband, she was an abandoned woman and,
one had to presume, terribly unhappy. As a kind of comforting substitute, however, there had formed around her a little band of women,
some of whom also attended the funeral, though more for her sake
than in Clarissa's honor. Included in this small but steadfast group, this
cooperative or collective or club of friends, or however I should put it,
was Inez's closest confidante, the exotic Natalia Knöterich; there was

also a divorced Romanian authoress from Transylvania, who had written several comedies and maintained a Bohemian salon in Schwabing; plus Rosa Zwitscher, an actress from the Hoftheater, whose performances often had a grand nervous intensity—and one or two other female figures who need not be characterized, particularly since I am not certain in every case of their active membership in the club.

The glue that held it together was—the reader has in fact been prepared for this—morphine, a very strong adhesive; for not only did the club members, as part of their peculiar partnership, supply one another with this exhilarating and pernicious drug, but also in a moral sense there is a sad, if tender mutual respect and solidarity among slaves to the same addiction and weakness. In our case the sinners were likewise bound together by a definite philosophy or maxim that had originated with Inez Institoris, and to which all five or six friends subscribed as their justification. Inez, you see, espoused the view—I have heard it from her lips on occasion—that pain is something beneath man's dignity, a disgrace not to be suffered. Moreover, quite apart from the concrete and specific debasement of physical pain or afflictions of the heart, life itself, in and of itself, mere existence, animal survival, is an unworthy and ponderous chain, a vile encumbrance, and anything but noble and proud; it is an exercise of our human rights and a legitimate spiritual act to thrust aside this burden, so to speak, to be rid of it, and to gain freedom, lightness, bodiless well-being, as it were, by supplying one's physical nature with this blessed stuff, which grants the body emancipation from suffering.

That such a philosophy was willing to risk the morally and physically ruinous consequences of this self-indulgent habit was apparently part of its elegant nobility, and presumably it was the awareness of a shared early ruin that disposed these sorority members to such tenderness, indeed to a loving adoration of one another. Not without some distaste did I observe the lustrous rapture of their glances, their emotional embraces and kisses when in company together. Yes, I confess my own inner intolerance of this free self-expression—confess it with some surprise, since I normally do not take any delight whatever in the role of moral paragon and faultfinder. Perhaps what instills such an insurmountable aversion in me is a certain mawkish dishonesty to which the vice lends itself, or that is peculiar to it from the start. I also blamed Inez for the reckless indifference she showed toward her own children in abandoning herself to this mischief—thereby revealing her coddling of those pale creatures of luxury to be a lie. In short, I was disgusted to my very soul with this woman once I knew and saw what license she allowed herself. And she was well aware that I had released her from my heart, underscoring that awareness with a smile that in its crabbed and roguish malice reminded me of the smile she had displayed for two whole hours while pocketing my genuine sympathy for the pains and passions of her love.

Oh, she had little reason for her amusement—because the way she debased herself was purest misery. It was apparent that she took overdoses that did not create a sense of animated well-being, but rather put her in such a state that she dare not be seen. The Zwitscher woman's acting showed some genius when she was under the drug's influence, and it enhanced Natalia Knöterich's social charms. But on repeated occasions poor Inez appeared for dinner in a state of semiconsciousness, and with glassy eyes and a nodding head would sit down to join her eldest daughter and her fussily chagrined husband at the still elegantly laid table with its sparkling crystal. I will admit one thing more as well: A couple of years later Inez committed a capital crime that provoked general revulsion and put an end to her bourgeois existence. But however much the deed made me shudder, as an old friend I was nevertheless almost proud, no, was decidedly proud that despite her sunken state she had found the strength, the fierce energy to commit it.

XXXVI

OH GERMANY, YOU are perishing, and I remember your hopes! I mean the hopes that you aroused (without perhaps sharing them); the hopes that the world wanted to place in you after your first, comparatively gentle collapse, after the abdication of the Kaiser's empire; the hopes that for a few years—despite your rowdy behavior, despite the totally mad, fiercely desperate, wildly demonstrative "bloating" of your misery, that inflation of currency scrambling drunkenly skyward—you seemed to justify to some extent.

It is true that those times, which sneered at the world in the hope of shocking it, already contained a great deal of the fantastic naughtiness that had never been thought possible before—shared the monstrous untrustworthiness, eccentricity, and virulent sans-culottism of our deportment since 1933 and especially since 1939. But that billionaire's spree, that bombastic misery, finally came to an end one day; an expression of reason returned to the grimacing countenance of our economic life; and we Germans had some inkling, it seemed, of an age of psychological recovery, of social progress in peace and freedom, of mature and forward-looking cultural endeavor, of a well-intentioned accommodation of our emotions and thoughts to what the world considers normal. Without doubt, despite all its inherent weakness and its own antipathy toward itself, that was the purpose, the hope of the German republic—and here again, I mean the hope that it awakened in other nations. It was an attempt, a not totally unpromising attempt (the second after Bismarck's abortive scheme of unification) to normalize Germany—in the sense of Europeanizing or even "democratizing" it—to incorporate it intellectually in the social life of nations. Who will deny that a great deal of honest faith in the possibility of that process was alive in other nations? And who will dispute that hopeful progress in that direction was indeed discernible among us—everywhere throughout Germany, that is, with the exception of one or two obstinate spots, of which our good city of Munich was an exemplary model?

I am speaking of the century's decade of the twenties and especially, of course, of its second half, which quite frankly brought with it a shift of cultural focus from France to Germany—as is most tellingly evident in the fact that, as previously noted, it was during those years that the premiere, or more precisely, the first complete production of Adrian Leverkühn's apocalyptic oratorio took place. Even though it was performed in Frankfurt, a city whose spirit was one of the most easygoing and open in the Reich, it goes without saying that this did not happen without angry protests and loud, embittered claims that art was being mocked, a musical crime perpetrated, without charges of nihilism and (to employ the most common term of abuse at the time) "cultural Bolshevism." But the work and the bold venture of its presentation also found intelligent, eloquent defenders; and already during the first half of the decade, that same good courage—so open to the world, so at ease with freedom—which reached its height around 1927 and formed the counterpart to nationalistic, Wagnerian, Romantic forces of reaction (such as those at home in Munich, in particular), most definitely constituted an element in our public life as well. And here I am thinking of cultural events such as the Festival of Composers in Weimar in 1920 and the first music festival at Donaueschingen the following year. On both occasions, along with other pieces representative of this new intellectual music, works by Leverkühn—unfortunately in the absence of the composer—were performed before an audience that was by no means unreceptive, I might say, an audience whose artistic views were "republican." In Weimar, it was the *Cosmic Symphony,* under the direction of Bruno Walter, who is especially dependable in matters of rhythm; at the festival in Baden, in connection with Hans Platner's famous marionette theater, all five sections of the *Gesta Romanorum* were performed—an unprecedented experience, in which one's emotions were tossed back and forth between pious sentiment and laughter.

I also wish to mention the role that German artists and friends of the arts played in the founding of the International Society for Contemporary Music in 1922 and the performances that this organization

arranged two years later in Prague of choral and instrumental fragments of Adrian's *Apocalipsis cum figuris,* which were heard by an audience that included a great many famous guests from throughout the
musical world. The work had already appeared in print by then—
though not published by Schott in Mainz, as Leverkühn's previous
works had been, but set within the framework of the "Universal
Edition" in Vienna, whose director, Dr. Edelmann—a youthful man
barely in his thirties, yet who already played an influential role in the
musical life of Central Europe—had unexpectedly appeared in Pfeiffering one day even before the *Apocalypse* was complete (it was during
those weeks when work had been interrupted by Adrian's relapse) to
offer his publishing services to the Schweigestill's lodger. His visit was
expressly connected with an article devoted to Adrian's work that had
recently appeared in the *Anbruch,* a radically progressive Viennese
music periodical, and that had come from the pen of one Desiderius
Fehér, a Hungarian musicologist and cultural philosopher. Fehér had
written about the high intellectual level and religious content, the pride
and the despair, the sinful cleverness of a music driven toward pure inspiration, which he wanted here and now to call to the attention of the
cultural world, had expressed himself with a fervor that was intensified
by his admitted embarrassment that he, the writer, had not discovered
this most intriguing and thrilling music on his own, had not chanced
upon it at the behest of a bidding from within, but rather had had to be
guided to it from outside, or, as he said, from above, from a sphere
higher than academia, from the sphere of love and faith, in a word, by
the eternal feminine. In short, this essay, mixing analytical and lyrical
elements not inappropriate to its topic, revealed as its true inspiration,
though in very vague outlines, the figure of a sensitive, knowledgeable
woman actively engaged in the cause of her knowledge. And since Dr.
Edelmann's visit proved to have been inspired by this Viennese publication, one could say his visit, too, was indirectly a contrivance of that
same tender energy and love, which preferred to remain hidden.

Only indirectly? I am not quite sure. I consider it possible that direct
suggestions, hints, instructions were provided the young musical busi-
nessman from that same "sphere," and I am strengthened in this conjecture by the fact that he knew more than what the article, in its
somewhat cagey fashion, had condescended to provide: He knew the
woman's name and mentioned it—not right off, not straightaway, but
in the course of the conversation, toward its end. Although he had almost been rebuffed at first, he had managed to obtain an interview,
during which he begged Leverkühn to share something about his work
in progress and heard, then, about the oratorio (for the first time? I

doubt it!) and even persuaded Adrian, despite his being so ill that he was close to collapse, to play several longer sections from the manuscript for him there in the Winged-Victory room—and on the spot Edelmann acquired the work for his "Edition." (The contract arrived the very next day from the Hotel Bayerischer Hof in Munich.) Before departing, however, Edelmann had asked Adrian, using a form of address that the Viennese had adapted from the French:

"*Meister,* do you know,"—indeed, I think he said: "Does the *meister* know"—"Madame de Tolna?"

I am about to introduce into my narrative a figure such as a novelist would never dare present to his readers, since invisibility stands in apparent contradiction to the essentials of artistic endeavor, and so, too, of the novel. Madame de Tolna, however, is an invisible figure. I cannot set her before my reader's eyes, can provide no indication whatever as to her appearance, for I have never seen her or obtained a description of her, since no one of my acquaintance has ever seen her, either. I shall leave as an open question whether Dr. Edelmann, or perhaps only just that contributor to the *Anbruch,* who happened to be her compatriot, could boast of her acquaintance. As for Adrian, he replied in the negative to the question of the Viennese. He did not know the lady, he said—and inasmuch as he did not inquire who she might be, Dr. Edelmann, then, refrained from offering any explanation, and simply responded, "In any case, you have"—or, "the *meister* has"—"no more fervent an admirer."

Evidently he took that "not knowing" as truth veiled in discretion, as the conditional reply that it was. Adrian could answer as he did because his relationship with this aristocratic Hungarian woman had been free of any personal contact, and—let me add—would, by silent, mutual agreement, remain so forever. It was quite another matter that he had been exchanging letters with her for some time now—a correspondence in which she proved to be both a very wise and rigorous authority on and admirer of his work and a caring friend and adviser, a woman who served him unconditionally; and in which he, for his part, went as far in sharing and trusting as lonely solitude is capable of doing. I have spoken of those two needy female souls who by selfless adoration have gained modest mention in the biography of a man who will surely prove immortal. Here is a third, of a very different stamp, who not only matches the unselfishness of those simpler souls, but outstrips them in it—by an ascetic renunciation of every direct contact, by an inviolable observance of secrecy, by a reticence that never troubles and remains forever invisible, but that surely could not have been the result of some awkward shyness, for she was a woman of the

world, who also truly represented the world to the hermit of Pfeiffering: the world as he loved, needed, tolerated it, the world at a distance,
the world that wisely, considerately held itself at some remove.

I can only say what I know about this strange creature. Madame de
Tolna was a rich widow, whose husband, a dissipated nobleman—he
had, however, not succumbed to his vices but had died in a horseracing
accident—had left her childless and the owner of a palace in Pest and a
huge estate several hours south of the capital, near Székesfehérvár, between the Danube and Lake Balaton, as well as a castlelike villa overlooking that same lake. The estate, with a splendid, comfortably
renovated manor house from the eighteenth century, comprised both
vast fields of wheat and a sugar-beet plantation, whose harvests could
be processed in the estate's own refinery located on the property. The
owner of these residences—townhouse, estate, summer villa—used
none of them for any long period of time. For the most part—one
might say, almost always—she traveled, leaving her homes, of which
she apparently was not fond and from which restlessness or painful
memories drove her, to the care of managers and major-domos. She
lived in Paris, Naples, Egypt, the Engadine, and was accompanied
from place to place by a lady's maid, a male employee who functioned
as something between a courier and a quartermaster, and a physician
whose services were reserved solely for her, which would suggest she
was in delicate health.

Her mobility did not appear to suffer because of it, and together
with an enthusiasm based on instinct, intuition, sensitive knowledge—
on God knows what! on mysterious empathy, kinship of soul—this
could result in her showing up at surprising places. It turned out that
this woman, mixing inconspicuously with the audience, had always
been on hand wherever someone risked a performance of a piece of
Adrian's music: in Lübeck (at the scorned premiere of his opera), in
Zurich, in Weimar, in Prague. How often she was in Munich—and thus
very close to her own residence—without calling attention to herself, I
cannot say. But she also knew Pfeiffering—for occasionally it would
come to light that she had been quietly learning about Adrian's landscape, his immediate surroundings, and, if I am not mistaken, had actually stood at the window of the abbot's study and left without being
observed. That is startling enough, but to me even more strangely
moving and suggestive of a pilgrimage or a quest, is the fact that (as it
slowly became apparent, more or less by chance) she had also traveled
to Kaisersaschern, knew all about the village of Oberweiler and even
Buchel Farm, and so was familiar with the parallelism—that I had al-

ways found rather oppressive—between the arena of Adrian's childhood and the framework of his later life.

I forgot to mention that she had not left out Palestrina, the town in
the Sabine mountains, had spent a few weeks in the Manardi household and, so it seemed, had quickly struck up a cordial friendship with
Signora Manardi. Whenever she referred to that landlady in her letters,
written half in German, half in French, she called her "Mother Manardi," "Mére Manardi." She favored Frau Schweigestill with the same
title, having seen her, as it was clear from what she said, without having been seen—or even noticed. And herself? Was it her idea to attach
herself to these mother figures and call them sisters? What name best
suited her—in her relationship with Adrian Leverkühn? What title did
she wish, did she claim? That of a tutelary goddess, an Egeria, a phan-
tom lover? The first letter she wrote to him (from Brussels) was accompanied by a gift sent in homage, a ring unlike any I have ever
seen—which, however, does not mean all that much, since this writer
is truly not well-versed in the treasures of this world. It was—in my
eye—a jewel of immeasurable value and of greatest beauty. The enchased ring itself was old, a Renaissance piece; the gem, a large-faceted
emerald, a splendid pale green stone from the Urals, was a marvel to
behold. One could imagine that the ring had once adorned the hand of
a prince of the Church—the pagan inscription it bore scarcely spoke
against the notion. The hard surface of the central facet of this noblest
of beryls, you see, had been engraved with two verses in the most delicate Greek script, which when translated read something like:

> What a trembling now seized Apollo's sacred laurel tree!
> Trembling in all of its beams! Unholy one, flee and escape it!

I did not find it difficult to identify these lines as the opening words of
a hymn to Apollo by Callimachus. With holy terror they describe the
tokens of an epiphany of the god at his shrine. Despite its tininess, the
inscription was preserved with perfect clarity. Beneath it, somewhat
more blurred, was an engraved vignette-like emblem, which one could
make out (though best under a magnifying glass) as a winged, serpent-
like monster whose darting tongue was in the shape of an arrow. This
mythological phantasm reminded me of the arrow wound or bite suffered by Philoctetes of Chryse, likewise of the term Aeschylus once
used to describe the arrow, "hissing winged serpent," and also of the connection made between the arrows of Phoebus and the rays of the sun.

I can attest that Adrian took childish delight in this exceptional gift
that had come to him from a distant, sympathetic stranger, accepted it

without a second thought, and, though he never wore it for others to see, made a habit, or should I say, ritual of putting it on during the hours of work—I know that all the while he was composing the *Apocalypse,* he wore this jewel on his left hand.

Did he ever think that a ring is the symbol of a bond, indeed, a shackle of bondage? He evidently gave the matter no thought, but regarded this precious link in an invisible chain, which he placed on his finger when composing, as nothing more than the connection between his solitude and the "world"—which for him seemed faceless, with scarcely any personal definition, and concerning whose individual traits he apparently had far fewer questions than I. Was there, I asked myself, something in the external appearance of this woman that would explain the basic principle of her relationship with Adrian: the invisibility, the avoidance, the refusal to meet? She might have been ugly, crippled, hunchbacked, disfigured by skin disease. I do not assume so; rather, I believe that if there was some defect, it was psychological, disposing her to show forbearance and consideration wherever it was required. Nor did her partner ever attempt to undermine this law, but silently complied with the idea that the relationship should be kept strictly on a purely intellectual basis.

I do not like to use that banal phrase, "purely intellectual basis." It has something so colorless and feeble about it, something that fits poorly with a certain practical vigor that was peculiar to this distant, veiled devotion and concern. The letters exchanged during the period of preparation for and composition of the apocalyptic work were informed by the general European and solid musical education she had received in her native land, lending her words a quite objective backbone. She was able to assist my friend with suggestions for the textual structure of the work, to provide him with materials that were all but impossible to obtain—and, of course, it turned out that the Old French rendition in verse of the *Vision of St. Paul* had come to him from the "world" outside. The "world" served him energetically, if by way of detours and intermediaries. It was the "world" that had produced that spirited article in the *Anbruch*—to be sure, the only place at the time where Leverkühn's music might have been spoken of with admiration. That the "Universal Edition" had secured the oratorio before its completion was to be credited to the promptings of the "world." In 1921, although the source of the grant was never clear, it was the "world" that covertly placed considerable funds at the disposal of Platner's marionette theater for the expensive and musically flawless production of the *Gesta* in Donaueschingen.

I wish to insist on the term "at the disposal of" and on the expansive gesture that went with it. Adrian could have no doubt whatever that in his solitude he had at his disposal what his worldly admirer had to offer—her riches, which as one clearly sensed, were a burden to her for reasons of conscience, though she had never known, presumably could not have led, a life without them. It was her desire, she did not deny it, to sacrifice on the altar of genius as much of them as she possibly dared offer; and if Adrian had wished it, he could have changed his entire mode of life from one day to the next, patterning it after that jewel—which, when it adorned his hand, was seen only by the four walls of the abbot's study. He knew that as well as I. Surely I need not say that he never gave the possibility a moment's serious thought. Unlike myself—for whom there was always something intoxicating about the notion of a vast fortune that lay at his feet and for which he needed only to grasp in order to enjoy a princely existence—he had never come close to even entertaining the idea. And yet on the one exceptional occasion when he left his Pfeiffering behind for a real trip, he did take a few trial sips of an almost royal style of life that I could not help secretly wishing might be permanently his.

That was twenty years ago now, and it came about because he accepted Madame de Tolna's irrevocable standing invitation to take up residence for as long as he wished at any of her homes whenever she was not there herself. In the spring of 1924, he went to Vienna, where at Ehrbar Hall, as part of one of the so-called *Anbruch* evenings, Rudi Schwerdtfeger at last gave his first performance of the violin concerto written for him—and with great success, in particular for him. By saying "in particular" what I mean is "above all," for a certain concentration of interest on the art of its interpreter is definitely intended by the piece, which despite its unmistakable musical signature is not one of Leverkühn's loftiest and proudest works, but rather, at least in certain sections, has something obliging, condescending, or better, patronizing about it, something that reminded me of a prediction made previously by lips that have since fallen silent forever. When the concerto ended, Adrian also refused to appear before the enthusiastically applauding audience and had already left the hall by the time we went looking for him. We—that is the producer, beaming Rudi, and I—met him later in the restaurant of the little hotel on Herren Gasse where he had put up, whereas Schwerdtfeger had felt he owed it to himself to take rooms in a hotel on the Ring.

Our celebration was brief, since Adrian had a headache. I can well understand, however, that, given this momentary relaxation in the pat-

terns of his life, he decided the next day not to return at once to the
Schweigestill farm, but to gratify his worldly friend by paying a visit
to her Hungarian estate. The condition that she be absent was already met, since she was presently staying—invisibly—in Vienna. A telegram announcing his imminent arrival was sent directly to the estate,
whereupon, or so I assume, hastily agreed-upon arrangements flew
back and forth between there and some hotel in Vienna. He departed,
and his traveling companion unfortunately was not I, who had barely
been able to get away from official duties for the concert; nor this time
was it Rüdiger Schildknapp, he of the same-colored eyes, who had not
even bothered to come to Vienna and had probably lacked the funds to
do so. But it was, quite understandably, Rudi Schwerdtfeger, who was
already at hand and available for an excursion, with whom there had
just been a successful artistic collaboration, and whose unflagging confiding familiarity was in fact crowned at this period with success in
general—a fateful success.

In his company, then, Adrian spent twelve days of domesticity in the
magnificent splendor of Tolna Castle, and, after being received like a
lord returning home from his journeys, enjoyed its *dixhuitième* salons
and chambers, as well as drives through the principality-sized estate
and to the sunny shores of Lake Balaton, was attended by a retinue of
humble servants, some of them Turks, and benefited from a library of
books in five languages, two splendid grand pianos on the dais in the
music hall, a house organ, and every other sort of luxury. He told me
that they had visited the village attached to the estate and found it in a
state of profoundest poverty, at a thoroughly archaic and pre-revolu-
tionary stage of development. Their guide, the estate administrator
himself, had told them, with many a sympathetic shake of his head, as
if these were facts worth knowing, that the inhabitants ate meat only
once a year at Christmas and did not even have tallow candles to burn,
but literally went to bed with the chickens. Any change in these shameful conditions, to which custom and ignorance had rendered these people insensible—the indescribable filth of the village street, for instance,
or the total lack of hygiene in their hovels—would surely have been a
revolutionary act that no single person, least of all a woman, would
dare undertake. But one can presume that the sight of the village was
among those things that ruined stays on her estate for Adrian's hidden friend.

For the rest, I am not the man to provide more than a sketch of this
slightly extravagant episode in my friend's austere life. I was not and
could not have been the man at his side, even had he asked me. That
was Schwerdtfeger; he could tell about it. But he is dead.

XXXVII

A s with earlier sections, I would do better not to give this
one its own number, but to identify it as properly belonging to
the previous chapter, as its continuation. The right thing would be to
forge ahead without any deep caesura, for this is still the chapter entitled "The World," the chapter about my late friend's relationship or
lack of relationship with the world—which here, to be sure, abandons
all its mysterious discretion and is no longer embodied in a heavily
veiled tutelary goddess proffering precious symbols, but in a naively
officious, airily engaging, and for me, despite everything, even attractive sort of fellow undaunted by lonely solitude, in a gentleman named
Saul Fitelberg, an international music agent and concert producer, who
made a call at Pfeiffering one lovely late summer afternoon, a Saturday,
when I just happened to be present (my intention being to return home
Sunday morning, as it was my wife's birthday), and entertained Adrian
and me absurdly well for a good hour, and then, having accomplished
nothing (to the extent, that is, that there was anything, any business, to
accomplish), departed without the least irritation.

It was in 1923—one cannot say that the man had roused himself especially early. All the same, he had not waited for the concerts in
Prague and Frankfurt, those still lay in the not too distant future. But
there had been Weimar, there had been Donaueschingen—quite apart
from the Swiss performances of Leverkühn's youthful works—and it
no longer required an amazingly prophetic intuition to guess that here
was something of value worth promoting. The *Apocalypse* had likewise already appeared in print, and I consider it perfectly possible that
Monsieur Saul had been in a position to study the work. Be that as it

may, the man had picked up the scent, he wanted to get involved, to build up a reputation, to pull a genius into the spotlight, and as its manager to introduce that genius to the curiosity of the fashionable society in which he himself moved. It was in order to initiate all this that he paid his visit and unabashedly intruded on a refuge of creative suffering. It happened as follows:

I had arrived in Pfeiffering early that afternoon, and as Adrian and I were returning from the country walk we had undertaken after tea, at a little after four, then, we were amazed to see an automobile parked under the elm in the courtyard—not an ordinary taxi, but more like a private car, the kind one hires with a chauffeur by the hour or day from a livery concern. The chauffeur, his uniform likewise betraying hints of elegance, was standing beside the car smoking and, as we passed, doffed his cap to us with a broad grin—recalling, presumably, the banter of the peculiar guest he had brought us. Frau Schweigestill met us at the door and, calling card in hand, began to speak in a low, terrified voice. A "man of the world" was there, she explained—and the term, especially as the whispered, rapid summing-up of a man she had only just let into her house, sounded to me somehow eerie and sibylline. This portentous term is perhaps explained in part by the fact that Frau Else at once pronounced the man waiting for us to be a "crazy hoot-owl." He had called her "cher Madame," and then "petite Maman," and had given Clementina's cheek a pinch. She had locked the girl in her room for now, until this man of the world was gone. She hadn't been able to send him packing because he had come in a car from Munich. He was waiting in the big living room.

With doubt written on our faces, we passed between us the calling card that provided all the information we might wish to know about its bearer: "Saul Fitelberg. *Arrangements musicaux. Représentant de nombreux artistes prominents.*" I was glad to be on hand to provide Adrian protection. I did not like to think of him left alone to the mercies of this "representative." We proceeded to the Winged-Victory room.

Fitelberg was standing near the door, and although Adrian let me enter first, the man's attention was immediately and totally directed toward him. After a fleeting glance at me through his horn-rimmed glasses, he even turned his stout body to one side to peer behind me at the man for whom he had gone to the expense of a two-hour car ride. It is, of course, no great feat to distinguish between someone marked by genius and a simple high-school professor; nevertheless, there was something impressive about the man's powers of swift orientation, about the dispatch with which he recognized my unimportance, despite my having entered first, and attached himself to the right man.

"*Cher Maître,*" he began with a smile, chatting away with a heavy accent, but uncommon fluency, "*comme je suis heureux, comme je suis ému de vous trouver! Même pour un homme gâté, endurci comme moi, c'est toujours une expérience touchante de rencontrer un grand homme.—Enchanté, Monsieur le professeur,*" he added in passing and, since Adrian had introduced me, casually offered me his hand, only to turn immediately back to the proper party.

"*Vous maudirez l'intrus, cher Monsieur Leverkühn,*" he said, accenting the third syllable as if the name were written "Le Vercune." "*Mais pour moi, étant une fois à Munich, c'était tout à fait impossible de manquer* . . . Oh, I do speak German, too" he said, interrupting himself with the same, hard, but really quite pleasant articulation. "Not well, not exemplarily, but well enough to be understood. *Du reste, je suis convaincu* that you speak French perfectly. Your settings of Verlaine's poems are the best proof of it. *Mais après tout,* we are on German soil—indeed, how German, how homey and cozy, how full of character! I am enchanted by the idyllic world with which you have been wise enough to surround yourself, *Maître. . . . Mais oui, certainement,* do let us sit down, *merci, mille fois merci!*"

He was probably forty years old, a fat man, not pot-bellied, but with fat, soft limbs and white, well-padded hands; he had a clean-shaven, round face with a double chin, strongly defined, arched eyebrows, and, behind those horn-rimmed glasses, almond-shaped eyes full of melting Mediterranean merriment. Though his hair was sparse, he had good, white teeth that always showed because he was always smiling. He was dressed with summer elegance in a blue-striped flannel suit tucked at the waist and set off by shoes of canvas and yellow leather. The term that Mother Schweigestill had applied to him was jauntily justified, however, by the easy carelessness of his manners, by a refreshingly light touch, which was inherent both in his rapid, slightly blurred, rather high speaking voice, breaking at times into the treble, and in his whole demeanor, and which stood somewhat in contradiction to the stoutness of his figure and yet again, was in harmony with it. I call this light touch refreshing, because it was so much a part of his life-blood that, in fact, it instilled in one the amusingly comforting sense that one unnecessarily took life all too seriously. It constantly seemed to imply: "But then why not? Is that all? It doesn't matter. Let's enjoy ourselves!" And automatically one set to work to join him in this attitude.

What I intend to record of his conversation, which even today I still recall quite vividly, will make it clear beyond a doubt that he was anything but stupid. The best thing would be for me simply to let him speak for himself, since what Adrian—or I, at any rate—replied and interjected played hardly any role. We took our seats at one end of the massive long table that was the rustic room's main piece of furniture—Adrian and I side by side, our guest across from us. He did not beat around the bush for very long about his plans and wishes, but came to the point without much ado.

"*Maître,*" he said, "I understand perfectly how attached you must be to the stylish seclusion of the place you have chosen to reside—oh, I have seen it all, the hill, the pond, the village with its little church, *et puis, cette maison pleine de dignité avec son hôtesse maternelle et vigoureuse. Madame Schweigestill! Mais ça veut dire: 'Je sais me taire. Silence, silence!' Comme c'est charmant!* How long have you lived here? Ten years? Without interruption? Or hardly any? *C'est étonnant!* Oh, very understandable! And yet, *figurez-vous,* I have come to abduct you, to tempt you to be unfaithful for a time, to carry you off through the air on my cloak and show you the kingdoms of the world and their glory, and what is more, to lay them at your feet. . . . Forgive me for putting it so pompously! It is truly *ridiculement exagérée,* especially when it comes to 'glory.' It is not nearly so grand and distant, this glory, not nearly so thrilling—and I tell you this, even though I am the child of simple people, come from a very humble, if not to say wretched background, from Lublin, you see, in the middle of Poland, of truly very simple Jewish parents. I am a Jew, you should know—Fitelberg, that is a downright wretched little Polish-German-Jewish name; except that I have made it the name of a respected champion of avant-garde culture and, I may say, of a friend of great artists. *C'est la vérité pure, simple et irréfutable.* The reason is that, from childhood on, I have striven for higher things, for what is intellectual and amusing—and above all for what is new, what is still scandalous, and yet a scandal with honor and a future, a scandal that come tomorrow will be highly paid, the latest fashion—that will be art. *A qui le dis-je? Au commencement était le scandale.*

"Thank God, that wretched Lublin lies far behind me! For more than twenty years now I have lived in Paris—would you believe, I once even attended lectures in philosophy at the Sorbonne for a whole year. But *à la longue* it bored me. Not that philosophy cannot be scandalous as well. Oh, indeed it can. But it is too abstract for me. And then I have the vague feeling that one would do better to study metaphysics in Germany. Perhaps my honored *vis-à-vis,* the Herr Professor, will agree with me there. . . . Next, I directed a little, exclusive playhouse, *un creux, une petite caverne* that held a hundred people, *nommé Théâtre des fourberies gracieuses.* Is that not a bewitching name? But what is one to do—it was not economically profitable. Tickets for those few seats had to be so expensive that we were forced to give them all away. We were offensive enough, *je vous assure,* but also too highbrow, as the English say. But one cannot survive with just James Joyce, Picasso, Ezra Pound, and the Duchess de Clermont-Tonnère in the audience. *En un mot,* the *Fourberies gracieuses* had to be closed again after a very short season, but the experiment had not proved unfruitful for me, either, since it had brought me into contact with the elite of Parisian artistic life, with painters, musicians, poets, and in Paris today—as I may surely note even here in this spot—there beats the pulse of the living world. It also opened doors for me, in my role as director, to several aristocratic salons frequented by those same artists. . . .

"You are surprised perhaps. You will say perhaps, 'How did he do it? How did the little Jewish boy from the Polish provinces manage to move in such exclusive circles among the *crème de la crème?*' Ah, gentlemen, nothing could be easier! How quickly one learns to tie one's white tie, to enter a salon with perfect nonchalance, even if there are a few steps down, to banish every thought of worrying about what to do with one's hands. And after that, one simply says *'madame'* over and over. *'Ah, madame, oh, madame, que pensez-vous, madame, on me dit, madame, que vous êtes fanatique de musique?'* That's almost all there is to it. People on the outside vastly overrate such things.

"*Enfin,* the connections I owed to the *Fourberies* came in handy for me and even multiplied when I then opened my office for arranging performances of contemporary music. The best part was that I found myself, for as you see me here now, I am an impresario, it is in my blood, it is a necessity—it is my joy and my pride, *j'y trouve ma satisfaction et mes délices* in highlighting talent, genius, some interesting personality. I love to beat the drums and arouse society's enthusiasm— or if not its enthusiasm, its excitement, for that is all that it demands, *et nous nous rencontrons dans ce désir.* Society wants to be excited, provoked, blasted apart into pro and con, and is grateful for nothing so much as an amusing fracas, *qui fournit le sujet* for caricatures in the papers and for endless chatter. In Paris, the road to fame leads through notoriety. At a real premiere, everyone must leap up from their seats at several points during the evening, and while the majority roars, *'Insulte! Impudence! Bouffonnerie ignominieuse!'* six or seven initiates—Erik Satie, a few surrealists, Virgil Thomson—shout from their loges: *'Quelle précision! Quel esprit! C'est divin! C'est suprême! Bravo! Bravo!'*

"I fear I am shocking you, *messieurs*—if not *Maître Le Vercune,* then perhaps the Herr Professor. But first let me hasten to add that such a concert evening has never actually had to be halted and cut short—for that is ultimately not the object of even the most outraged, on the contrary, they wish to be outraged repeatedly, that is the very pleasure such an evening offers them; moreover, it is remarkable how the experts, though few in number, maintain a surpassing authority. And second, this is definitely not to say that the things I have described must go on at every performance of a progressive nature. With adequate publicity and preparation, with sufficient intimidation of the stupid in advance, one can guarantee a quite dignified evening, and today especially, if one presents a citizen of the former enemy nation, a German, one can count on the audience's behaving with perfect politeness.

"That same sound speculation, in fact, forms the basis of my suggestion, my invitation. A German, *un boche qui par son génie appartient au monde et qui marche à la tête du progrès musical!* That is nowadays an extremely piquant means of provoking curiosity, of challenging the audience's good manners, its open-mindedness, its *snobisme*—all the more piquant the less the artist denies the stamp of his nationality, his Germanness, the more he provides occasion for the cry, '*Ah, ça c'est bien allemand, par exemple!*' For you do that, *cher Maître, pourquoi pas le dire?* You give them occasion to do so at every step—not so much at the beginning, in the days of *cette 'Phosphorescence de la mer'* and your comic opera, but later on, more and more with every work. You are sure to be thinking that what I have in mind is your fierce discipline, *et que vous enchaînez votre art dans un système de règles inexorables et néoclassiques,* that you force your art to move in those iron chains—if not with grace, then with intelligence and boldness. But if that is the sort of thing I mean when speaking of your *qualité d'Allemand,* at the same time I mean more than that. I mean—how shall I put it?—a certain squareness, rhythmic ponderousness, immobility, *grossièreté,* that are venerably German—*en effet, entre nous,* one finds them in Bach as well. Will you take offense at my critique? *Non, j'en suis sûr!* You are too great for that. Your themes—they almost always consist of even values, of half, quarter, eighth notes; they are syncopated and tied, to be sure, but nonetheless persevere in what is often a machinelike, stamping, hammering inflexibility and inelegance. *C'est 'boche' dans un degré fascinant.* Do not think I am finding fault with it! It is simply *énormément caractéristique,* and that same note is indispensable for the series of concerts of international music that I am arranging.

"You see, I am spreading my magic cloak. I want to take you to

Paris, Antwerp, Venice, Copenhagen. You will be received with the most intense interest. I shall place the finest orchestras and soloists at your disposal. You will conduct the *Phosphorescence,* selections from *Love's Labour's Lost,* your *Symphonie Cosmologique.* You will play the piano accompaniment for your settings of French and English poets, and all the world will be enchanted to find that a German, yesterday's enemy, reveals such wide-heartedness in the choice of his texts—*ce cosmopolitisme généreux et versatile!* My friend, Madame Maja de Strozzi-Pečič Croatian with perhaps the most beautiful soprano voice in both hemispheres today, will consider it an honor to sing these pieces. For the instrumental accompaniment to the hymns by Keats, I shall engage the Flonzaley Quartet from Geneva or the Pro Arte Quartet from Brussels. The best of the best—are you satisfied?

"What's this I hear? You don't conduct? You won't do it? And you don't want to be a pianist, either? You refuse to accompany your own songs? I understand. *Cher Maître, je vous comprends à demi mot!* It is not your habit to linger over something already completed. For you the composition of a work is its performance, it is finished once it is written down. You will not play it, you will not conduct it, for then you would immediately change it, break it up into variants and variations, develop it farther, and perhaps destroy it. How well I understand! *Mais c'est dommage, pourtant.* The concerts will suffer a definite loss of personal appeal. Ah, pah—we'll manage in any case! We shall search for an interpreter among world-famous conductors—and we won't have to search for long! The permanent accompanist of Madame de Strozzi-Pečič will take over the songs, and if you, *Maître,* will simply come along, simply be there to show yourself to the public, nothing will be lost and everything gained.

"That is, of course, the condition—*ah, non!* you dare not hand your works over to me for performance *in absentia!* Your personal appearance is imperative, *particulièrement à Paris,* where one's musical fame is made in three or four salons. What does it cost to say a few times, '*Tout le monde sait, madame, que votre jugement musical est infaillible*'? It costs you nothing, and you will even find considerable amusement in it. As social events, my concerts rank second only to the premieres of Monsieur Diaghilev's Ballets Russes—if they do rank second. You will be invited out every evening. Nothing is more difficult, generally speaking, than breaking into Parisian high society. For an artist, however, nothing is easier—even if he is only in the initial stages of fame, the scandalous subject of a great deal of talk. Curiosity lowers every *barrière,* it puts to rout every sort of exclusivity.

"But here I am going on about high society and its curiosity! I can see I have not ignited your curiosity with that, *cher Maître*. And how could I? I wasn't even making a serious attempt at it. What does high society matter to you? *Entre nous*—what does it matter to me? In terms of business—this or that. But personally? Not so much. This milieu, this Pfeiffering, and my being here together with you, *Maître*, contribute not a little to making me aware of my indifference, of the low opinion in which I hold that world of frivolity and superficiality. *Dites-moi donc*—do you not come from Kaisersaschern on the Saale? What a serious, worthy hometown! As for me, I call Lublin my place of birth—yet another worthy town gray with age, from which one carries a wealth of *séverité* into life, *un état d'âme solennel et un peu gauche.* . . . Ah, I am the last person to want to praise high society to you. But Paris will give you an opportunity to make the most interesting, stimulating acquaintances among your brothers in Apollo, your peers and fellow strivers—artists, writers, stars of the ballet, above all musicians. The elite of European tradition and artistic experiment, they are all my friends, and are ready to be yours, too: Jean Cocteau, the poet, Massine, the choreographer, Manuel de Falla, the composer, Les Six, those six greats of contemporary music—that entire lofty and amusing sphere of daring and outrage is waiting just for you. You are part of it the moment you wish to be. . . .

"Is it possible that I read in your expression some resistance to this as well? But, *cher Maître*, any timidity, any *embarras* is truly out of place here—whatever may be the reasons for such a desire to isolate oneself. Far be it from me to inquire about those reasons—a respectful and, may I say, cultivated awareness of their existence quite suffices for me. This Pfeiffering, *ce refuge étrange et érémitique*, has its own interesting, psychological significance—this Pfeiffering does. I shall not ask, but shall calculate the possibilities, give frank consideration to them all, even the most extraordinary. *Eh bien*, what then? Is there any reason for *embarras* when encountering a sphere that knows no limit to its open-mindedness—an open-mindedness that has its own good reasons as well? *Oh, la, la!* Such a circle of fashionable authorities on art and geniuses who are arbiters of taste usually consists of nothing but *demi-fous excentriques,* of jaded souls and hardened debilitated sinners. An impresario is a kind of nurse, *une espèce d'infirmier, voilà!*

"But look how poorly I am advancing my own cause, *dans quelle manière tout à fait maladroite!* That I notice the fact is the only thing that speaks in my favor. In hope of encouraging you, I have angered your pride and can see with my own eyes that I am working against

myself. For naturally I tell myself that someone like you—but I should
not speak of someone like you, but of only you—that you regard your
existence, your *destin* as something too unique and holy to be lumped
together with other anyone else's. You don't want to know anything
about other *destinées,* but only about your own, as something singular—I know, I understand. You abhor all degrading generalizations,
rankings, subsumptions. You insist on the incomparability of the individual case. You espouse a personal loftiness of isolation that may indeed be necessary. 'Does one live if others live?' I read that question
somewhere, I'm not sure where, certainly in some prominent place.
Whether explicitly or silently, you all ask that same question and acknowledge one another purely out of courtesy and for appearance'
sake—if you acknowledge one another at all. Wolf, Brahms, and
Bruckner lived for years in the same city, in Vienna, and the entire time
each avoided the others and none of them, as far as I know, ever met
the others. It would indeed have been *pénible,* given their opinions of
one another. Those were not opinions of critical collegiality, but of
outright dismissal, of *anéantissement*—each wanted to be the only one.
Brahms thought as little as possible of Bruckner's symphonies; he
called them formless giant serpents. In return, Bruckner had an extremely low opinion of Brahms. He found the first theme in the D minor concerto to be quite good, but was convinced that Brahms never
came close to finding one equal to it. All of you want nothing to do
with one another. For Wolf, Brahms was *le dernier ennui.* And have
you ever read his review of the Bruckner Seventh in the Vienna *Salon-
blatt*? There you'll find his opinion of the man's general significance.
He accused him of a 'lack of intelligence'—*avec quelque raison,* for
Bruckner was indeed a simple, childlike soul lost in his own majestic,
figured-bass music and a complete idiot in all other matters of European culture. But then one reads Wolf's letters and happens upon statements about Dostoevsky, *qui sont simplement stupéfiants,* and one can
only ask oneself how his own mind was shaped. He called the libretto
to his unfinished opera *Manuel Venegas,* produced by one Dr. Hörnes,
a marvel, Shakespearian, the peak of poesy, and turned tastelessly vi-
cious when friends expressed their doubts. Moreover, not satisfied
with just composing a hymn entitled "To the Fatherland" for male
chorus, he even wanted to dedicate it to the German Kaiser. What do
you say to that? His petition was refused! *Tout cela est un peu embar-
rassant, n'est-ce pas? Une confusion tragique.*

"*Tragique, messieurs.* I call it that, because in my opinion the world's
misfortune is founded in the disunity of the intellect, in stupidity, in a

lack of comprehension that separates the mind's spheres from one another. Wagner reviled the impressionist paintings of his day as daubings—being strictly conservative in that field. Even though his own harmonic effects have a great deal to do with impressionism, lead directly to it, and as dissonances often move beyond it. He pits Titian against these Parisian daubers—he was the true painter. *A la bonne heure.* But in reality, his taste in art was probably more like something between Piloty and Makart, the inventor of the decorator bouquet, whereas Titian was more to Lenbach's taste, who for his part had such a great understanding of Wagner that he called *Parsifal* music-hall stuff—and to the master's face no less. *Ah, ah, comme c'est mélancolique, tout ça!*

"Gentlemen, I have strayed terribly from my path. By which I also mean—I have given up my objective. Take my volubility as an expression of the fact that I have abandoned the plan that brought me here! I am now convinced that it cannot be carried out. You, *Maître*, will not board my magic cloak. I shall not lead you into the world as your manager. You refuse, and that ought to be a greater disappointment to me than it actually is. *Sincèrement*, I ask myself if it is a disappointment at all. One comes to Pfeiffering perhaps for some practical purpose—but that is always and by necessity of secondary importance. One comes, even if one is an impresario, first and foremost *pour saluer un grand homme.* No practical set-back can diminish that pleasure, particularly not if a good portion of one's positive satisfaction has its basis in disappointment. And that is the case, *cher Maître,* your inaccessibility gives me, among other things, satisfaction as well, and does so by virtue of the understanding, the sympathy with which I instinctively greet it. I do so against my own interest, but I do it—as a human being, I might say, if that were not too broad a category. I should express myself more precisely.

"You probably do not realize, *Maître*, how German your *répugnance* is—for, if you will permit me to speak *en psychologue*, it is characteristically composed of feelings of arrogance and inferiority, of disdain and fear, and is, I might say, the resentment that seriousness feels for the salon of the world. Now, I am a Jew, you should know—Fitelberg, that is a patently Jewish name. I have the Old Testament in my bones, and that is no less a serious matter than Germanness—it basically leaves little predisposition for the sphere of the *valse brillante.* To be sure, it is a German superstition that there is nothing but *valse brillante* in the world outside, and seriousness only in Germany. And yet, as a Jew one is basically skeptical of the world and inclined toward Germanness, though, of course, such an inclination brings with it the risk of a kick in the pants. German, that means above all else: popular, national, *volkstümlich*—and who would believe that of a Jew? Not only is he not believed—they bang him over the head a few times if he insists on trying it. We Jews have everything to fear from the German character, *qui est essentiellement anti-sémitique*—reason enough for us, of course, to hold with the world, for which we arrange amusements and sensations, without its implying, however, that we are windbags and dim-witted. We are quite aware of the difference between Gounod's and Goethe's *Faust,* even if we do speak French, even then. . . .

"Gentlemen, I say all of this only out of resignation. We have no more business to discuss, really, I am as good as on my way, have the doorknob in hand—we have been on our feet for a while now, and still I prattle on merely *pour prendre congé.* Gounod's *Faust,* gentlemen, who would turn up his nose at it? Not I and not you, as I see to my delight. A pearl—*une marguerite*—full of the most ravishing musical invention. *Laisse-moi, laisse-moi contempler*—bewitching! Even Massenet is bewitching, *lui aussi.* He must have been especially charming as a pedagogue, as a professor at the Conservatoire—there are anecdotes about him. From the very start, his composition students were to be encouraged to write works of their own, whether or not their technical ability was sufficient for an impeccable movement. Humane, is it not? German it isn't, but humane. A young man came to him with a freshly composed song—a fresh idea, revealing some talent. '*Tiens!*' Massenet said. 'That is really quite nice. Now listen—you have a little sweetheart, I'm sure. Play it for her, it is certain to please her, and the rest will take care of itself.' It is unclear just what he meant by 'the rest'—presumably everything possible, both in love and in art. Do you have students, *Maître*? They would certainly not have it so good. But, then, you have none. Bruckner had students. From very early on he himself had wrestled with music and its sacred rigors, like Jacob with the angel, and he demanded the same of his students. They had to practice the sacred craft, the fundamentals of harmony and the strict style, for years before he allowed them to sing a song, and his musical pedagogy had not the least connection with little sweethearts. One is a simple, childish soul, but music is a mysterious revelation of the highest knowledge, divine worship, and the profession of the musical teacher is a priestly office. . . .

"*Comme c'est respectable! Pas précisément humain, mais extrêmement respectable.* Should we Jews—since we are a priestly people, even if we do mince about in Parisian salons—not feel ourselves drawn to Germanness and not allow that to dispose us to irony over against the world, over against art for little sweethearts. Popular nationalism on our part would an impertinence that would provoke a pogrom. We are international—but we are pro-German, like no one else in the world, if only because we cannot help seeing the similarity of the roles German-ness and Jewishness play in the world. *Une analogie frappante!* They are both equally hated, despised, feared, envied, are both equally re-sented and resentful. One speaks of the age of nationalism. But in re-ality there are only two nationalisms, the German and the Jewish, and all the rest is child's play—just as the ramrod Frenchness of an Anatole France is purest cosmopolitanism in comparison to German solitude—and to Jewish conceit as the chosen race. . . . 'France'—a nationalistic *nom de guerre.* A German writer could not very well call himself 'Ger-many,' one christens a battleship with that at best. He would have to be content with 'German,' with 'Deutsch'—and would be giving himself a Jewish name, *oh, la, la!*

"Gentlemen, this is now truly the doorknob, I am already outside. I have only this to say yet. The Germans should leave it to us Jews to be pro-German. The Germans, with their nationalism, their arrogance, their fondness for their own incomparability, their hatred of being second or even placed on a par, their refusal to be introduced to the world and to join its society—the Germans will bring about their own misfortune, a truly Jewish misfortune, *je vous le jure.* The Germans should allow the Jew to play the *médiateur* between them and society, to be the manager, the impresario, the agent of Germanness—the Jew is definitely the man for the job, he should not be sent packing, he is international, and he is pro-German. . . . *Mais c'est en vain. Et c'est très dommage!* But why am I still talking? I am long gone. *Cher Maître, j'etais enchanté. J'ai manqué ma mission,* but I am enchanted. *Mes respects, Monsieur le professeur. Vous m'avez assisté trop peu, mais je ne vous en veux pas. Mille choses à Madame Schwei-ge-still. Adieu, adieu . . .*"

XXXVIII

M Y READERS HAVE been informed that Adrian had complied with the wish that Rudi Schwerdtfeger had insistently nurtured and frequently expressed over the years, had written him a violin concerto all his own, personally dedicating to him that brilliant piece so extraordinarily suited to the instrument, and had even accompanied him to Vienna for its premiere. In its proper place I will also speak of the fact that a few months later—that is, toward the end of 1924—he was present for repeat performances in Bern and Zurich. But first, in a most serious context, I would like to return to my perhaps flippant (perhaps for me, even unbecoming) previous characterization of this composition, to the effect that in its musical attitude, in a certain obliging concession to concert virtuosity, the piece lies somewhat outside the framework of Leverkühn's relentlessly radical and uncompromising oeuvre. I cannot help believing that posterity will agree with my "judgment"—my God, how I hate that word!—and that what I am doing here is merely providing posterity a psychological explanation for a phenomenon to which it would otherwise lack the key.

There is something peculiar about the piece. Written in three movements, it has no key signature, even though, if I may put it this way, three tonalities are built into it: B minor, C minor, and D minor—of which the musician can see that the D minor forms a kind of dominant of the second degree, the B minor a subdominant, and with the C minor exactly in between. The work ingeniously plays with these keys, in such a way that for most of the time none of them clearly takes over, but rather each is only hinted at by proportions established among the notes. Over long complex passages, all three are superimposed, until finally, and indeed in a triumphant fashion that electrifies every concert audience, the C minor declares itself openly. In the first movement, which is designated *andante amoroso* and whose sweetness and tenderness constantly verge on mockery, there is a dominant chord that to my ears has something French about it: C–G–E–B-flat–D–F-sharp–A, a chord that, along with the violin's high F above it, contains, as one can see, the tonic triad of each of the three main keys. One has in it the soul of the work, so to speak, but one also has in it the soul of the main theme of the movement, which is then taken up again as a series of colorful variations in the third movement. It is, in its own way, a marvelous melodic find, a swelling cantilena that numbs the mind as one is carried away on its wide sweeping arc and that has something decidedly showy, boastful about it, but also a melancholy that is not without its charm if the violinist is so inclined. What makes this invention so particularly ravishing is that the melodic line, having arrived at its highpoint, unexpectedly surmounts itself and with delicate accentuation moves one pitch higher, from where it then flows back again and—in always perfect taste, perhaps all-too-perfect taste—sings itself out. In its physical effect, in the way it grabs one by the head and shoulders, it is one of those manifestations of beauty that border on the "heavenly" and of which only music and no other art is capable. In the last part of the variation movement, this same theme undergoes a *tutti* glorification that brings with it the eruption into undisguised C minor. This effect is preceded by a kind of bold running start in a dramatic *parlando*—an obvious reminiscence of the first violin's recitative in the last movement of Beethoven's A Major Quartet—except that the grand phrase there is followed by something quite different from a festival of melody in which the parody of being carried away becomes passion of such serious intent that one feels somehow embarrassed.

I know that before composing the piece, Leverkühn made a careful study of the treatment of the violin by Bériot, Vieuxtemps, and Wieniawski, and applied all this in a style that was half-respectful, half-caricaturing—and which, by the way, made such technical demands on the soloist (especially in the extremely rollicking and virtuoso second movement, a scherzo, where there is a quote from Tartini's "Devil's Trill" Sonata) that our good Rudi had to summon his utmost skill to do them justice. Each time he performed the task, sweat beaded up underneath his unruly blond curls and the whites of his pretty cornflower-blue eyes were netted with red veins. Yet what great compensation, to be sure, what a grand opportunity for "flirting" in the higher sense of the word, was granted him by a work that I had called "the apotheosis of drawing-room music" to the *meister*'s face—in the certainty that he would not be offended by my characterization, but would accept it with a smile.

I cannot think of this hybrid creation without recalling a conversation whose setting was the residence of Bullinger the industrialist—the *bel étage* of the splendid apartment house that he had built on Widenmayer Strasse in Munich and beneath whose windows the Isar's unspoiled mountain water rushed past in its well-regulated bed. This wealthy man's table was set for about fifteen people for dinner at seven; with its well-trained staff, supervised by a housekeeper with affected manners and the hope of marrying one day, his was a hospitable house, and it was usually people from the world of finance and business whose company he kept. But we know, of course, that he loved to blow off steam in intellectual circles, and so there were also evenings when artistic and academic elements gathered in his comfortable residence—and no one, myself included, I must admit, saw any reason to scorn the culinary delights of his table or the elegant ambiance his salons offered for stimulating conversation.

This time the guests were Jeannette Scheurl, Herr and Frau Knöterich, Schildknapp, Rudi Schwerdtfeger, Zink and Spengler, Kranich the numismatist, Radbruch the publisher and his wife, Zwitscher the actress, the woman from Bukovina who wrote comedies and whose name was Binder-Majoresku, plus myself and my dear wife—and Adrian had come as well, after much persuasion exerted not only by me, but also by Schildknapp and Schwerdtfeger. I will not pursue whose request had tipped the scale, and certainly do not flatter myself that it was mine. Since at dinner he sat next to Jeannette, whose presence always did him good, and since he was also surrounded by other familiar faces, he seemed not to regret having given in, but to be quite at ease during the three hours he spent there—and all the while I once again observed to my silent amusement the instinctive courtesy (which for only a few had any basis in real knowledge of his work) and more or less shy deference with which society treated a man only just turned thirty-eight. The phenomenon, as I said, amused me—and then again, it weighed more anxiously on my heart, since the reason behind people's behavior was in fact the atmosphere of indescribable aloofness and solitude that increasingly surrounded him, a distancing that during these years was becoming ever more noticeable and could indeed make one feel as if Adrian came from some land where no one else dwells.

On that evening, as I said, he seemed to be quite at ease and talkative,

credit for which must be given to Bullinger's champagne cocktails with
a splash of bitters and his marvelous Pfälzer wine. Adrian talked with
Spengler, who was doing very poorly (his illness had now affected his
heart), and laughed, as we all did, at Leo Zink's clowning, who had
leaned back at the table, pulled his giant damask napkin like a bed sheet
up to his grotesque nose, and peacefully folded his hands over it. He
was even more amused by this jokester's adroitness when Bullinger,
who was an amateur painter in oils, showed us a still life, and in order
to duck any critical response and to spare us others having to make any
as well, Zink regarded the well-intentioned painting from all sides,
even turned it upside down once, and greeted it with a thousand cries
of "Jesus"—which might mean any number of things. Such gushing in
cries of absolutely noncommittal amazement was, by the way, also the
technique this basically unpleasant man employed in any conversation
that went beyond his own horizons as an artist and carnivalist, and he
even used it for a while during the exchange I have in mind, which
touched on issues of aesthetics and morality.

It unfolded at the conclusion of some mechanically produced music
with which our host entertained us after coffee, while people went on
smoking and sipping their liqueurs. At the time, the quality of gramo-
phone records was making great progress, and Bullinger let several enjoyable works resound from his expensive cabinet player: first, as I
recall, a fine performance of the waltz from Gounod's *Faust,* to which
Baptist Spengler now objected that he found the melody definitely too
elegant, too much like drawing-room music, for a folk dance on the
meadow. It was agreed that this style worked much better in the case of
the charming ball music in Berlioz's *Symphonie fantastique,* which was
then requested. There was no recording of it. Instead, Schwerdtfeger
whistled the melody with his infallible lips, a pure, excellent rendition
in the timbre of a violin, and laughed at the applause, adding his typical shrug inside his jacket and tugging a corner of his mouth down in a
grimace. By way of comparison with the French, someone requested
the Viennese style, waltzes by Lanner and Johann Strauss the younger,
and our host readily spent of his largess, until one lady—I recall quite
well that it was Frau Radbruch, the publisher's wife—wondered
whether all this frivolous stuff might not be boring the great composer
present in our midst. She was met with anxious agreement, which
Adrian noticed now with some surprise, since he had not heard the
original question. When it was repeated, he protested vigorously. For
God's sake, no, that was a misunderstanding. No one could take more
delight than he in such things—which in their own way were masterly.

"You underestimate my musical education," he said. "In my tender youth I had a teacher"—and he glanced my way with his beautiful, delicate, and profound smile—"an enthusiast stuffed full to overflowing with all the sounds the world can produce, who was too much in love with every, and I do mean every sort of organized noise, for me ever to learn from him to be stuck-up, to think myself too good for certain music. A man who definitely knew his stuff when it came to things lofty and strict. But for him music was music, if that was what it was, and his objection to Goethe's statement that 'art is concerned with the serious and the good,' was that something light can be serious, too, if it is good, which it can be just as easily as something serious can. Some of that has stuck with me; I got it from him. Indeed, I have always taken him to mean that one must have a very firm grasp of the serious and good to be able to handle what is light."

Silence fell over the room. In essence, he had said that he alone had the right to enjoy the pleasantries that had been offered. People tried not to take it that way, but suspected that was what he had meant. Schildknapp and I looked at one another. Dr. Kranich went, "Hmm." Jeannette said softly, *"Magnifique!"* Leo Zink could be heard to utter his stupefied, but in reality sardonic "Jesus!" "Genuine Adrian Leverkühn!" cried Schwerdtfeger, red in the face from countless glasses of Vielle Cure, but not just from them. I knew that secretly he was offended.

"You don't by chance," Adrian went on, "have Delilah's aria in D-flat major from Saint-Saëns' *Samson* in your collection, do you?"

The question was addressed to Bullinger, who took great satisfaction in being able to respond, "Me? Not have the aria? My dear man, what do you take me for! Here it is—and not 'by chance,' that I can assure you."

To which Adrian said, "Ah, good. It comes to mind because Kretzschmar—that was my teacher, an organist, a man of the fugue, you should know—had an oddly passionate regard for the piece, a true weakness. He could laugh about it as well, to be sure, but that in no way detracted from his admiration, which was intended, perhaps, only for the exemplary nature of the thing. *Silentium.*"

The needle was placed in the groove. Bullinger let the heavy lid down. From the latticed speaker came a proud mezzo-soprano rather unconcerned about good enunciation—one understood the *"mon coeur s'ouvre à ta voix"* and then hardly anything more. But her singing, accompanied unfortunately by a somewhat whiny orchestra, was marvelous in its warmth and tenderness, in its dark lament for happiness—as was the melody itself, whose two stanzas are constructed alike, with the passage of fullest beauty beginning first toward the middle before reaching its stunning conclusion, especially the second time, when the violin, now quite sonorous, joins in, basking in the voluptuous melodic line, and repeats its final figure in a plaintively tender postlude.

Everyone was deeply moved. A lady dabbed her eye with an embroidered fancy handkerchief. "Idiotically beautiful!" Bullinger said, employing one of the standard phrases that for some time now had been a favorite of aesthetes and connoisseurs as a way of crudely tempering the awestruck "beautiful." But one might well say that here the term was exact and literally appropriate, and that may be what amused Adrian.

"Well now!" he shouted with a laugh. "Now you understand how a serious man can be capable of worshiping such a number. It's beauty is not intellectual, but exemplarily sensual. But ultimately, one ought not fear or be embarrassed by what is sensual."

"Perhaps one ought," Dr. Kranich, the director of the coin museum, was heard to remark. He spoke, as always, extraordinarily distinctly, firmly, with clear, reasonable articulation, even though his voice whistled with asthma all the while. "In art, perhaps one ought. Surely in that realm one ought indeed fear and be embarrassed by what is exclusively sensual, for, as the poet said, it is something vulgar. 'Vulgar is all that does not speak to the mind and rouses naught but sensual interest.'"

"A noble thought," Adrian replied. "One should let it echo for a while before raising the least objection to it."

"And what would be your objection?" the scholar wanted to know.

Adrian first shrugged and pursed his lips as if more or less to say, "I can't help the facts," before remarking, "Idealism overlooks the fact that the mind, the human spirit, is by no means addressed only by things intellectual, but rather can be profoundly moved by the animal sadness of sensual beauty. The mind has paid its homage even to frivolity. Philine is ultimately just a little harlot, but Wilhelm Meister, who is not all that distant from his author, pays her a respect that openly denies any vulgarity in sensual innocence."

"Indulgence and forbearance in the face of ambiguity," the numismatist replied, "have never been the most commendable traits in the character of our Olympian. And in any case, one can surely see a danger to culture if the mind closes one eye to what is vulgarly sensual, or even winks at it."

"We are apparently of different opinions about that danger."

"Why don't you call me a coward straight-out!"

"God forbid! A knight who defends fear and reproach is not a coward, but simply a knight. The only thing for which I am taking up the cudgel is a certain broad-mindedness in matters of artistic morality. It seems to me one grants it, both to oneself and others, more readily in the other arts than in music. That may do music considerable honor, but it dangerously restricts its arena of life. What is left of the whole ding-dong-ding, if one measures it by the most rigorous intellectual and moral standards? A few pure spectra of Bach. Perhaps nothing audible whatever is left."

A servant arrived with whisky, beer, and soda water on a large tea tray.

"And who would want to be a spoilsport," was Kranich's parting shot, to which Bullinger added a resounding "Bravo!" and a clap on the shoulder. For me, and surely for one or two other guests, this exchange had been a quickly erupting duel between rigorous mediocrity and an intellect pained by the depth of experience. I have included this scene, however, not only because I detect such a strong relation between it and the concerto on which Adrian was working at the time, but also because it pressed upon me his relation to the person of the young man at whose stubborn insistence that work had been written and for whom it meant success in more than one sense.

Presumably it is my fate that I can speak only in stiff, dry, introspective, and general terms about a phenomenon that Adrian had once described for me as an amazing and always somewhat unnatural alteration of the relation between the self and the non-self—the phenomenon of love. The basic inhibitions of reverence before a mystery, as well as those of one's personal reverence, likewise contribute to my sealed lips or at least to my taciturnity when speaking of the demonically enveloped transformation undergone here by this phenomenon—which in and of itself is a semi-miracle contradicting the isolation of the individual. All the same, I hope it is evident that it was the specific sharpness of wit gained from classical philology—an aptitude, that is, which usually tends to dull the mind in its dealings with life—that put me in a position to see and comprehend anything at all here.

There can be no doubt—and it must be reported with all due composure—that tireless, absolutely undaunted confiding familiarity finally gained its victory over the most brittle lonely solitude, a victory that, given the polarity (and let me emphasize the word "polarity") of difference, the intellectual distance between the two partners, could have only one specific character—the same character that, in an impish way, had always been striven for. It is perfectly clear to me that for a flirtatious nature like Schwerdtfeger's, familiarity's triumph over lone-liness had from the start, whether consciously or not, had that special meaning and coloring—which is not to say that it lacked other nobler motives as well. On the contrary, the suitor was very much in earnest when he remarked how necessary Adrian's friendship was for the ful-fillment of his own nature, how it benefited, lifted, bettered him; ex-cept that to gain friendship, he was illogical enough to put his inborn flirtatiousness into play—and then feel offended when the melancholy affection that he aroused betrayed marks of erotic irony.

For me the most remarkable and touching thing about all this was observing with my own eyes how the vanquished man did not see that he had been bewitched, but credited himself with an initiative that be-longed entirely to the other party, how he seemed to be full of fantas-tic wonderment at plainly forward ingratiation and obligingness, which was more deserving of the name seduction. Yes, he spoke of the miracle of an imperturbability that no melancholy or emotion could confound, and I have little doubt that his "astonishment" went as far back as that long-ago evening when Schwerdtfeger had appeared in his room to beg him to return to a party that was so boring without him. And yet within this so-called miracle, there truly was that nobleness, artistic openness, and decency that also marked poor Rudi's character and that I have repeatedly praised. A letter exists that Adrian wrote to Schwerdtfeger around the time of the discussion held that evening at Bullinger's and that, needless to say, Rudi should have destroyed, but that he preserved—partly out of sentiment, but also, to be sure, as a trophy. I refuse to quote from it, but wish to describe it simply as a hu-man document whose effect is like the baring of a wound and whose painfully undisguised candor its writer probably even saw as a great risk. It was not. But the really beautiful thing is how it proved not to be. At once, posthaste, without any tormented hesitation, the letter's addressee arrived in Pfeiffering for a visit, a discussion, an assurance of his deepest gratitude—and what revealed itself was a simple, bold, and sincerely tender demeanor zealously intent on preventing any em-barrassment. . . . I must praise it, I cannot help doing so. And I sus-pect—with a certain sense of approval—that on this occasion the composition and dedication of the violin concerto were decided upon.

It took Adrian to Vienna. And afterward, it took him along with Rudi Schwerdtfeger to that castle on a Hungarian estate. Upon their return, Rudolf enjoyed the prerogative that until then had been exclu-sively mine because of a shared childhood—he and Adrian addressed each other by the familiar "you."

XXXIX

Poor Rudi! The triumph of your childish demonry was brief, for it became tangled in the field of power of a profounder and fatefully stronger demonry that swiftly broke, devoured, and annihilated it. Luckless "you"! Neither did that familiar "you" befit the blue-eyed inconsequentiality that had won it for itself, nor could he who deigned to grant it help avenging the abasement—however happy it may have made him—that came with it. The revenge was automatic, prompt, cold-eyed, mysterious. I shall tell it, tell it all.

In the final days of 1923, repeat performances of the successful violin concerto took place in Bern and Zurich, as part of the program of two concerts by the Swiss Chamber Orchestra, whose conductor, Herr Paul Sacher, had invited Schwerdtfeger as soloist, extending very favorable terms and expressly stating his wish that the composer lend the occasion special prestige by his presence. Adrian demurred; but Rudolf knew how to beg, and at the time their familiar "you" was still new and powerful enough to pave the way for what was to come.

Thanks to the totally devoted exertions of the soloist, the concerto, as the centerpiece of a program that included classical German and contemporary Russian works, once again demonstrated its intellectual and audience-captivating qualities in both cities—in the hall of the Bern Conservatory and in the Zurich Tonhalle. The critics remarked on a certain lack of unity in its style, indeed in its niveau of composition, and the audiences likewise responded with somewhat more reserve than in Vienna, but nonetheless not only gave the performers lively ovations, but also, on both evenings, insisted on the appearance

of the composer, who did his interpreter the favor of repeatedly standing hand in hand with him to thank the audience for its applause. I was
not in attendance for this doubly unique event of solitude's personal
surrender to the crowd. I had been excluded from it. But there was
someone who was present the second time who told me about it—
Jeannette Scheurl happened to be in Zurich at the time and even encountered Adrian in the private home where he and Schwerdtfeger
were guest lodgers.

This was at a house on Mythen Strasse, near the lake, the home of
Herr and Frau Reiff, a wealthy, childless couple well along in years,
lovers of the arts who had always enjoyed entertaining prominent
touring artists and offering them a tasteful refuge. The husband was a
former silk manufacturer retired now from business, a Swiss citizen of
sterling old democratic stamp; he had a glass eye that gave his bearded
face a certain rigidity—a deceptive impression, for he was fond of liberal good cheer and loved nothing more than a dalliance in his salon
with ladies of the theater, heroines or soubrettes. At his receptions he
would also sometimes play the cello—and not badly, either—accompanied by his wife, who came from Germany and had once studied
voice. She lacked his humor, but was the personification of the energetically hospitable housewife and was of one accord with her husband
about the pleasures of sheltering fame in her home and allowing the
carefree spirit of virtuosity to reign within its walls. In her boudoir was
a whole table covered with photographs signed by European celebri-
ties and acknowledging a debt of gratitude for the Reiffs' hospitality.

The couple had invited Schwerdtfeger even before his name appeared in the papers, for as an openhanded patron the old industrialist
was informed of upcoming musical events before the rest of the world;
and they had promptly enlarged the invitation to include Adrian as
soon as they were informed of his coming. Their spacious home had
ample room for guests, and indeed as the two men arrived from Bern
they found Jeannette Scheurl already ensconced there as a friend of the
family, on her annual visit of a few weeks. But it was not she next to
whom Adrian was seated at the little supper given for a small circle of
initiates in the Reiffs' dining room after the concert.

The host sat at the head of the table, drinking heartily of a non-
alcoholic beverage from an exquisitely cut glass and—face rigid as always—joked with the municipal theater's dramatic soprano beside
him, a powerful woman who in the course of the evening thumped her
bosom a great deal with a balled fist. There was another member of the
local opera present, its heroic baritone, a tall man from the Baltic who

said intelligent things in a booming voice. Plus, of course, Kapellmeis-
ter Sacher, who had organized the evening's concert, Dr. Andreae, the
Tonhalle's permanent conductor, and Dr. Schuh, the excellent music
critic for the *Neue Zürcher Zeitung*—all of them with their wives. At
the other end of the table spry Frau Reiff sat between Adrian and
Schwerdtfeger, who had as neighbors to their left and right a young, or
still young professional woman, Mademoiselle Godeau, and her aunt,
a thoroughly good-hearted, almost Russian-looking old lady with a
moustache, whom Marie (that was Mlle. Godeau's first name), being
French Swiss, called *"ma tante"* or "Tante Isabeau" and who by all
appearances lived with her niece as a companion, housekeeper, and
lady-in-waiting.

I am surely qualified to offer a picture of the niece, since a short
while later I kept my eyes on her for some time, earnestly examining
her for good reason. If ever the word *sympathique* was indispensable
for describing a person, then that was the case with this young woman,
who from head to foot, in every feature, with every word, every smile,
every expression of her being, fulfilled the calmly unextravagant, aesthetically moral sense of the word. She had the most beautiful black
eyes in the world, and with them I begin—black as jet, as tar, as ripe
blackberries, eyes not all that large, but with an open gaze, clear and
pure in its very darkness, beneath brows whose fine, regular line had as
little to do with cosmetics as did the subtly robust red of her gentle
lips. Her looks had nothing artificial about them—no accenting, no
shading, no coloring. There was something objectively natural and
agreeable in the way, for instance, that her dark brown hair, heavy at
the nape, was left free at the ears and drawn back from the brow and
delicate temples—and that was true of her hands as well, sensibly
beautiful hands, not dainty at all, but slender and small-boned, the
wrists encircled by the simple cuffs of a white silk blouse. In the same
way, her neck was set in the circle of a flat collar and rose up out of it
like a round, indeed chiseled, column and was crowned by the charmingly tapered oval of her ivory-toned face with its delicate and well-
shaped nose, remarkable for the animated flair of its nostrils. Her
smile, which was rather seldom, and her laughter, which was even rarer
and always accompanied by a certain touching tension at her almost
transparent temples, revealed the enamel of even and close-set teeth.

It is understandable that I put much effort and love into my attempt
to summon up the figure of the woman whom Adrian briefly thought
of marrying. I, too, first saw Marie in that same white silk formal
blouse, which, it is true, was probably intended to emphasize her dark

eyes and hair to some extent, but most especially I saw her later in one of her even more becoming, simple, everyday traveling suits of dark plaid, with a patent leather belt and mother-of-pearl buttons—and, to be sure, in a knee-length smock that she wore over it when working at her drawing board with lead-pencil and colored crayons. For she was an artist (as Adrian had been informed beforehand by Frau Reiff), a designer for smaller opera and operetta stages in Paris, for the Gaîté Lyrique and the old Théâtre du Trianon, who created and sketched the costumes and sets that served as models for tailors, carpenters, and painters. A native of Nyon on Lake Geneva, she now pursued her career in Paris, living with her Aunt Isabeau in the tiny rooms of an apartment on the Île de Paris. Her competence and creativity, her expertise in costume history and her impeccable taste, all contributed to her growing fame, and there were professional reasons not only for her stay in Zurich, but as she told her tablemate on her right, within a few weeks she would also be going to Munich, where the Schauspielhaus had commissioned her to design the costumes for a modern comedy.

Adrian divided his attention between her and their hostess, while across from him the tired, but happy Rudi bantered with *"ma tante,"* who easily shed good-hearted tears when she laughed and frequently nodded to her niece in order to repeat—her face damp, her voice wobbling—one of her neighbor's humorous comments that in her opinion she simply had to share. Marie would then nod amiably back at her, evidently glad that her aunt was amusing herself so well, and her eyes rested with a certain grateful acknowledgement on the man dispensing this mirth, who apparently was making it his business to tickle the old woman's urge to pass on one joke after another. Mlle. Godeau chatted with Adrian, responding to his inquiries about her career in Paris, about recent works of French ballet and opera, with only some of which he was familiar—the creations of Poulenc, Auric, Rieti. Their discussion warmed up as they spoke about Ravel's *Daphnis et Chloé* and the *Jeux* by Debussy, about Scarlatti's music for Goldoni's *Donne di buon umore*, Cimarosa's *Il matrimonio segreto,* and *Une Education manquée* by Chabrier. Marie had designed a new production of one or another of these works and now demonstrated her solutions for several scenes with a few lines sketched in pencil on her place card. She knew Saul Fitelberg well—but of course! And it was at this point that the enamel of her teeth sparkled and a cordial laugh sweetly strained her temples. Her German was effortless, with a slight, charming accent; her voice had a warm, winning timbre, a voice meant for singing, vocal "material" without a doubt—to be specific, it did not merely resemble Elsbeth Leverkühn's voice in both range and color, but when listening to it, one sometimes truly believed one heard the voice of Adrian's mother.

A dinner party of some fifteen persons like this one generally breaks up into different groups after the meal, as people seek to vary their contacts. After supper Adrian exchanged hardly another word with Marie Godeau. Messrs. Sacher, Andreae, and Schuh, along with Jeannette Scheurl, kept him engaged for a good while in a conversation about musical matters in Zurich and Munich, while the ladies from Paris, along with the opera singers, the host couple, and Schwerdtfeger, sat at the table with the costly Sèvres service and watched in amazement as old Herr Reiff downed one cup of strong coffee after another—which, as he explained in weighty Swiss words, he was willing to do on medical advice that it would strengthen his heart and make it easier to fall asleep. As soon as the other guests departed, the three lodgers almost immediately withdrew to their rooms. Mlle. Godeau was staying on for several days yet with her aunt at the Hotel Eden au Lac. In saying goodbye to the ladies, Schwerdtfeger, who intended to leave the next morning with Adrian for Munich, was quick to express the hope that he would see the ladies again there; Marie waited a moment until Adrian repeated the wish and then added her friendly endorsement.

THE FIRST WEEKS of 1925 had already passed when I read in the paper that my friend's charming tablemate in Zurich had arrived in our local capital and had taken lodgings with her aunt in the same little hotel where Adrian had lived for a few days upon his return from Italy, the Pension Gisella—and not by accident, for Adrian had told me that he had recommended it to her. In the hope of increasing public interest in its forthcoming premiere, the Schauspielhaus had floated this bit of news, and it was promptly confirmed by an invitation from the Schlaginhaufens to spend the next Saturday evening with them and the renowned stage designer.

I cannot describe the suspense with which I looked forward to that gathering. Anticipation, curiosity, joy, and apprehension all merged in my mind to become a profound excitement. Why? Not—or not only—because upon his return from the tour of Switzerland, Adrian had told me, together with other things, about his meeting with Marie and had given me a description of her person that included, as a casual observation, the resemblance of her voice to his mother's—along with other remarks that likewise made me prick up my ears at once. It was certainly no enthusiastic portrait that he provided me; on the contrary, his voice was low and casual, his expression impassive, his glance directed elsewhere in the room. That the acquaintance had made an impression, however, was evident from the fact that he recalled both the first and last names of the girl (and as I've said, at any larger gathering, he seldom knew the name of the person to whom he was talking) and that his account went decidedly beyond simple mention of her.

But there was something else as well that made my heart beat so strangely with joy and doubt, for on my next visit to Pfeiffering Adrian let drop some remarks to the effect that he had perhaps lived here for too long a time, that changes in the externals of his life were possibly at hand, that if need be his loner's solitude might quickly come to an end, that he was toying with a plan to make an end of it, etc.—in short, remarks whose only possible explanation was that he intended to marry. I found the courage to ask whether his hints had some connection with a chance social meeting that had occurred during his stay in Zurich, to which he replied:

"Who can keep you from making your conjectures? Anyway, this narrow chamber is not the proper setting. If I am not mistaken, it was on Mount Zion at home that you once tendered me kindred disclosures. We should have climbed the Rohmbühel for our conversation."

One can imagine my amazement!

"My dear fellow," I said, "that is sensational, thrilling news!"

He advised me to contain my excitement. In the end, he suggested, being forty years old was admonition enough for him not to let the moment pass. I should not ask any more questions and would see for myself. I could not hide from myself my joy that his intentions would mean release from his elfin bond to Schwerdtfeger, and indeed I was inclined to see them as a conscious means to accomplish that. How, on his part, that fiddler and whistler would react was a secondary issue that I hardly found unsettling, since his boyish ambition had achieved its goal, his concerto. After that triumph, I thought, he would be ready to resume a more reasonable place in Adrian Leverkühn's life. The only thing that kept running through my mind was the peculiar way in which Adrian spoke of his plan, as if its realization depended solely on his will and as if one need not worry at all about the girl's consent. I was more than ready to endorse a self-confidence that believed it had only to choose, only to declare its choice! And yet my heart quailed at the naiveté of that belief, which I was inclined to see as an expression of the loneliness and detachment that formed the aura around him and that led me reluctantly to doubt whether this man was made to attract the love of a woman. And if I was totally candid with myself, I even doubted whether ultimately he believed in this possibility himself, and I had to fight back the feeling that he quite purposely pretended that success was a matter of course. It remained unclear for now whether the woman he had chosen had even an inkling of the thoughts and plans he attached to her person.

It was still unclear to me after the evening of the party on Brienner Strasse, where I became acquainted with Marie Godeau. How pleased I was with her can be seen in my previous description of her. I was won over to her not only by the gentle night of her gaze (to which I knew just how susceptible Adrian was), by her charming smile, her musical voice, but also by her friendly and intelligent reserve, by the businesslike assurance, indeed standoffishness of an independent professional woman who disdained any sort of cooing femininity. It delighted me to think of her as Adrian's partner in life, and I could indeed understand the feelings she instilled in him. Did not the "world" from which in his solitude he shied away—including what in artistic and musical terms one might call the "world" outside Germany—did it not come to him in her, in a most serious and friendly guise that awakened trust, promised complementary fulfillment, encouraged union? Did he not love her from out of his world of oratorios, with its musical theology and mathematics of magic numbers? It filled me with hopeful excitement to see these two people enclosed within the same space, though from what I saw their personal contact was only fleeting. When by chance at one point in the social ebb and flow, a group formed of Marie, Adrian, myself, and a fourth party, I moved off at once in the hope that the fourth would have enough sense to go his own way as well.

The evening at the Schlaginhaufens' was not a dinner, but a nine o'clock reception, with a buffet laid out in the dining room adjoining the columned salon. The social scene had changed considerably since the war. There was no Baron Riedesel to advocate things "graceful"; the piano-playing cavalryman had vanished through history's trapdoor. Even Schiller's great-grandson, Herr von Gleichen-Russwurm, was no more—for he had been convicted of an abortive attempt at fraud, a silly and ingenious scheme that had banished him from the world and held him under semi-voluntary house arrest on his estate in Lower Bavaria. The affair was almost beyond belief. The baron had allegedly carefully packaged a necklace, insured for far above its value, and sent it to a distant jeweler for resetting—who, upon receiving the package, found nothing inside but a dead mouse. The mouse had proved inept at fulfilling the task its sender had assigned to it. The idea had apparently been for the rodent to bite through the package and escape, creating the illusion that the necklace had fallen through a hole of God knew what origin and was now lost, a loss for which the insurance company would have to make good. Instead, the animal had perished without creating the exit that would have explained the disappearance of jewelry that had never been included—and the instigator of this bit of roguery found himself ridiculously exposed. Quite possibly he had run across the idea in some book of cultural history and was a victim of his own reading. Perhaps, however, the general moral confusion of the day was solely to blame for his crazy notion.

In any case, our hostess, née von Plausig, had been forced to dispense with many things and to abandon almost entirely her ideal of uniting noble birth and artistry. The old days were called to mind by the presence of some erstwhile ladies of the court, who spoke French with Jeannette Scheurl. But otherwise, along with stars of the theater, one saw various politicians of the Catholic People's Party, even a noted Social Democratic parliamentarian, and a few high and not so high functionaries of the new state, among whom there were still people of good family, like Herr von Stengel, a fundamentally jovial man who would try anything once—but also certain elements who were energetically ill-disposed toward the "liberalistic" republic and on whose brow was boldly written their intent to avenge Germany's disgrace and their awareness of representing a coming world.

So there it is—an observer would have seen me sharing the company of Marie Godeau and her good aunt more than did Adrian, who had doubtless come for her sake (why else would he have come at all?) and who had also greeted her with obvious delight, only then to spend the great bulk of his time conversing with his dear Jeannette and the Social Democratic member of parliament, who was a serious and knowledgeable admirer of Bach. The concentration of my attentions, quite apart from the agreeableness of their object, should be understandable given what Adrian had confided to me. Rudi Schwerdtfeger was also with us. Tante Isabeau was enchanted to see him again. As in Zurich, he often made her laugh—and Marie smile—but in no way hampered a sober discussion that concerned artistic developments in Paris and Munich and even touched on European politics and German-French relations—a discussion in which, at the very end as he stood to take his leave, Adrian joined for a few moments. He always had to catch his eleven o'clock train to Waldshut, and his participation in the soiree had lasted barely an hour and a half. We others stayed a little longer.

This was, as I said, on a Saturday evening. On the following Thursday, I heard from him by telephone.

XL

H E RANG ME up in Freising, to ask a favor, as he put it. (His voice was subdued and somewhat monotone, which suggested a headache.) He had the feeling, he said, one ought to do the ladies at the Pension Gisella the honors of Munich in some small way. The plan was to offer them an excursion into the outlying area, since the beautiful winter weather was indeed inviting. He laid no claim to authorship of this idea, it had originated with Schwerdtfeger. But he had taken it up and given it some thought. One possibility was Füssen, with nearby Neuschwanstein. But even better perhaps was Oberammergau and a sleigh ride from there to the monastery at Ettal, a personal favorite of his, by way of Linderhof Castle, a curiosity worth a visit in its own right. What did I think?

I pronounced the idea of an excursion a good one and Ettal a fine, appropriate choice as a goal.

"Of course you must come along," he said, "you and your wife. We'll do it on a Saturday—as far as I know you have no classes on Saturday this semester. Shall we say a week from the day after tomorrow, that is, if we don't get a bad thaw. I've already told Schildknapp what's up, too. He's simply mad about this sort of thing and wants to tie a rope to the sleigh and ski behind us."

I said I thought the whole idea excellent.

But there was something else he wanted me to know, he went on. The plan had, as noted, originally come from Schwerdtfeger, but I would surely understand his, Adrian's, wish that this not be the impression given at the Pension Gisella. He didn't want Rudolf to make the proposal, but attached some importance to doing it himself—although not all too directly. Would I be so kind as to manage the scheme—that is, pay a call on the ladies in town on my way to Pfeiffering next time, in other words, on that coming Saturday, and extend the invitation more or less as his messenger, if only by inference.

"By performing this friendly service, you would be doing me much good," he concluded with peculiar stiffness.

I started to respond with questions, but suppressed them and promised simply to act in accordance with his wishes, assuring him that I was happy for him and that we were all looking forward to the trip. And I truly was. I had been seriously asking myself how the plans he had confided to me were to be promoted, how things were to be set into motion. It seemed hardly advisable to leave further opportunities for meeting the lady of his choice to simple luck. Circumstances did not exactly offer luck excessive latitude. Some helpful preparation, some initiative was necessary, and here it was. Had Schwerdtfeger really initiated things, or had Adrian merely attributed that to him out of embarrassment at playing the role of a lover suddenly devising outings and sleigh rides—something quite counter to his own nature and mood? For in fact it all did seem so beneath his dignity that I wished he had told the truth when making the violinist responsible for the idea—although once again I could not quite suppress the question of whether that elfin platonist might not have had some interest of his own in the enterprise.

Questions? Actually I had only one: Why in fact, if Adrian wished to let Marie know that he was interested in seeing her, did he not approach her directly, call her up, even travel to Munich, pay the ladies a visit, present his suggestion to them? At the time I did not know that there was a tendency at work here, an idea, a kind of rehearsal for something yet to come—a preference for sending someone else to his beloved (for so I must call her), for having someone else speak to her on his behalf.

But for now, it was I who had been entrusted with a message and I gladly carried out my assignment. It was on this occasion that I saw Marie in the white smock that she wore over her collarless plaid blouse and that suited her so well. I found her at her drawing board, a thick slanted piece of wood to which an electric lamp was screwed and from which she stood up to greet me. We sat together for about twenty minutes in the little living room of the ladies' rented suite. Both of them appeared decidedly receptive to the attention paid them and eagerly greeted the plan for an excursion, about which I merely said that I had not come up with it—after having first casually mentioned that I was on my way to see my friend Leverkühn. They noted that without such chivalrous guides they might never have seen anything of Munich's famous environs, Bavaria's alpine countryside. The day and hour of gathering for departure were arranged. I was able to bring Adrian a satisfactory report, recounting all the details and weaving into it my praise of how flattering the smock had looked on Marie. He thanked me by saying without irony—as far as I could tell:

"So you see, it is a good thing to have reliable friends after all."

The railroad line to the village of the Passion Play—which for the most part is the same as that to Garmisch-Partenkirchen, splitting off from it only at the very end—passes through Waldshut and Pfeiffering. Adrian lived halfway to our goal, and so it was only we others— Schwerdtfeger, Schildknapp, our Parisian guests, my wife, and I—who gathered at the train in Munich's central station, shortly before ten on the agreed-upon day. Without my friend for now, we passed the first hour of the trip moving across the still flat and frozen land. The time was shortened by a breakfast of sandwiches and Tyrolean red wine that my Helene had prepared, and as we ate we laughed heartily at Schildknapp's humorous display of exaggerated anxiety not to be slighted. "Don't short Knappi," he said (which was the Anglicized name he had given himself and that others generally used as well), "don't short Knappi on the knapsack!" His natural, undisguised, and comically accentuated enjoyment of the meal was irresistibly funny. "Ah, do you taste splendid!" he groaned, his eyes sparkling as he chewed a tongue sandwich. And his jokes were unmistakably meant primarily for Mlle. Godeau, who of course pleased him as much as she pleased us all. She looked her very best in a becoming olive winter suit trimmed with narrow bands of brown fur, and more or less obeying my emotions— simply because I knew what was coming—I delighted over and over in looking at her black eyes, at that merry sheen of pitch and coal beneath the shade of her lashes.

When Adrian climbed aboard in Waldshut and was greeted by our band with the high spirits of people on an outing, I was struck by something strangely frightening—if that is the word for what I felt. In any case there was an element of fright in it. Only now, you see, did I become aware of the fact that as we sat there crowded into the compartment we had claimed for ourselves (not a closed one, however, but merely one section in an open second-class car), the black, the blue, and the same-colored eyes—eyes of attraction and indifference, excitement and calmness—were gathered together under Adrian's eye, would remain together for the rest of our excursion that day, which more or less stood under the sign of this constellation, perhaps had been meant to stand under it, so that the initiated might recognize in it the true idea behind the day.

It was only natural and right that once Adrian had joined us the landscape outside began to gain significance, to rise and reveal, though still at a distance, a world of snow-clad mountains. Schildknapp distinguished himself by knowing the names of this or that wall of peaks that could be made out. The Bavarian Alps boast no giants of exalted rank among their summits, but all the same we found ourselves riding into a winter splendor clad in a pure garb of snow and mounting boldly, austerely from a changing vista of wooded ravines and wide plains. The day, however, was cloudy, with more chilly snow likely, and was to clear only toward evening. Nonetheless our attention was directed mostly to scenes outside, despite Marie's having steered the conversation to shared experiences in Zurich, to the evening in the Tonhalle and the violin concerto. I watched Adrian as he conversed with her. She was sitting between Schildknapp and Schwerdtfeger, and he had taken the seat across from her, while the aunt engaged Helene and me in good-hearted chitchat. I could clearly see how he had to guard against indiscretion when gazing at her face, her eyes. With his blue eyes, Rudolf observed Adrian's preoccupation, saw how he checked himself and turned away. Was there not some consolation and compensation in the way Adrian praised the violinist so energetically to the girl? Since she refrained from offering any opinion about the music itself, only the performance was discussed, and Adrian declared with emphasis that the presence of the soloist ought not to prevent him from calling his playing masterly, perfect, simply unsurpassable, and concluded with several warm, indeed laudatory words about Rudi's artistic development in general and the great future undoubtedly before him.

The lionized man apparently would have none of it, cried, "Now, now!" and "You can cut that out!" assuring her that the *meister* had exaggerated terribly, but blushing with pleasure. He doubtlessly liked being extolled in front of Marie, but his joy in the fact that the praise came from those lips was likewise unmistakable, and he showed his gratitude by expressing admiration for the way Adrian put things. Mlle. Godeau had heard and read about the performance of fragments of the *Apocalypse* in Prague and inquired about the work. Adrian cut her off.

"Let us not speak," he said, "of those pious sins!"

Rudi was thrilled by this.

"Pious sins!" he repeated triumphantly. "Did you hear that? The way he talks, the way he uses words! He is simply phenomenal, our *meister* is."

And with that he squeezed Adrian's knee—a habit of his. He was one of those people who always have to grab, feel, touch, an arm, an elbow, a shoulder. He did it even with me, even with women, who usually did not dislike it.

In Oberammergau our little party strolled up and down through the tidy town of perfect peasant houses with richly ornamented carvings on their roof-ridges and balconies—the homes of disciples, of the Savior and the Mother of God. While my friends went to climb the nearby Mount Calvary, I briefly broke away to find a livery service I knew of and order a sleigh. I found the other six again having their midday meal at a local inn, which had a glass dance floor that could be lit from below and was surrounded by little tables, so that during the season, and definitely for the Passion Play, this must have been an overcrowded tourist spot. But now, more to our liking, it was almost empty, with only two parties besides our own dining at distant tables near the dance floor: At one was a sickly-looking gentleman with his nurse in deaconess habit, at the other a group here for winter sports. Seated on a raised platform, a small five-man orchestra was playing drawing-room music for the guests, and no one regretted the long pauses the artists took between pieces. The music they offered was silly, and they offered it lamely and badly besides, so that after finishing his roast chicken, Rudi Schwerdtfeger could no longer stand it and decided to let his star shine in first-class form. He took the violinist's instrument from him, and having first turned it around in his hands to establish its origin, he improvised quite grandly on it, even inserting, just to make us laugh, a few bars of the cadenza from "his" violin concerto. The musicians' mouths hung open. He then asked the pianist, a weary-eyed young fellow who had surely dreamt of higher things than his present employment, whether he knew the accompaniment to Dvořák's "Humoresque," and even on this mediocre fiddle he played that delightful piece with all its numerous grace notes, charming slides, and smart double stops so jauntily and brilliantly that he won loud applause from everyone in the inn—from us, from the nearby tables and dumbfounded musicians, even from the two waiters.

It was basically just a trite joke, as a jealous Schildknapp muttered to me, but a dramatic and beguiling one all the same—in short, "nice" and Rudi Schwerdtfeger all over. We stayed longer than planned and were finally quite alone as we sat over coffee and gentian schnapps, and there was even some dancing on the glass floor—Schildknapp and Schwerdtfeger took turns gliding Mlle. Godeau and my good Helene, too, about the floor, moving to God knows what step under the benevolent gaze of the three who abstained. Our roomy sleigh, well-supplied with fur blankets and pulled by two horses, was already waiting outside. Since I took the seat next to the driver and Schildknapp carried out his intention of being pulled behind us on skis (the driver had brought a pair along), the other five could fit comfortably inside the sleigh. It was the most successfully planned part of our program that day, if one disregards the fact that Rüdiger's manly notion had some nasty repercussions. From standing in the icy wind of our wake and being dragged over a bumpy road that dusted him with snow, he came down with a cold that settled in his gut, one of his debilitating intestinal catarrhs that kept him in bed for days. But that was a mishap that revealed itself only later. Just as I have a personal fondness for bundling up warm and gliding along through the pure, bracing frosty air to the sound of muffled bells—the others, too, seemed to enjoy the occasion. Knowing that at my back Adrian was sitting eye-to-eye with Marie made my heart pound excitedly with curiosity, joy, worry, and fervent hopes.

Linderhof, Ludwig II's little rococo castle, lies in a secluded mountain woodland of magnificent beauty. Royal unsociability could not have found a more fairy-tale-like refuge. To be sure, whatever elevated mood the magic of the setting may create, the taste in which this escapist's restless rage to build (itself a demonstration of a longing to glorify his kingdom) expressed itself is truly an embarrassment. We stopped, and guided by a steward we toured the suite of small, overladen, ostentatious chambers that form this fantasy castle's "living quarters," where the melancholic man spent his days, filling them with nothing but the idea of his own majesty, letting von Bülow play the piano for him, and listening to Kainz's enchanting voice. The largest room in a prince's castle is usually the throne room. There is none here. Instead there is the bedroom of immense dimensions in comparison with the smaller day rooms and with a solemnly raised canopied bed that looks short because of its exaggerated width and is flanked by gold candelabra like a bier.

With proper interest and, to be sure, some private head shaking, we took it all in and as the sky cleared continued on our way to Ettal, which due to its Benedictine abbey, including a Baroque church, enjoys solid architectural renown. I remember that both during the trip there and while we sat at dinner in the neatly kept hotel cater-corner from those godly edifices, our conversation revolved around the person of this, as he is called, "unhappy" (why unhappy, really?) king, with the sphere of whose eccentric life we had just had some contact. The discussion was interrupted only by our visit to the church and was essentially a dispute between Rudi Schwerdtfeger and myself about Ludwig's so-called madness, his incompetence to govern, and his being removed from the throne and placed under a guardian—which to Rudi's great astonishment I declared an unjustified and brutal act of philistinism, as well as a political maneuver to secure the succession.

He stood entirely by the popular view, which is likewise the bourgeois official version, that the king was "booming mad" as he put it, and that for the nation's sake it had been absolutely necessary to hand him over to psychiatrists and keepers and to install a mentally healthy regency—and could not comprehend how there could be any disputing that. As was his habit in such cases—that is, when a point of view was all too new to him—all the while I was speaking, he pouted his lips in outrage and bored his blue eyes into mine by turns, now right, now left. I must say that—somewhat to my surprise—the subject moved me to eloquence, although it had hardly been of concern to me before. I found, however, that I had privately formed a decided opinion about it. Madness, I argued, was a very shaky concept, which the average man wielded all too haphazardly and on the basis of doubtful criteria. Such a person was very quick to set limits to reasonable behavior that were very close to those he set for himself and his averageness, and whatever went beyond it, was deemed crazy. The monarchical form of life, however—sovereign, enveloped by devotion, far removed from criticism and accountability, and licensed by its dignity to displays of style denied even the wealthiest private citizen—allowed its representatives such a latitude of fantastical proclivities, nervous urges and revulsions, odd passions and lusts, that the proud and absolute exploitation of them very easily took on the aspect of madness. What mortal, far beneath such lofty heights, would be at liberty to create golden solitudes in choice spots of scenic splendor, the way Ludwig had done! These castles were monuments of royal unsociability, to be sure. But since, given the standard character traits of our species, it was scarcely permissible to declare the retreat from one's fellows to be in general a symptom of madness—why should it then be permissible when that aversion expressed itself in royal forms?

But six learned and competent alienists had officially determined the king's total madness and declared it necessary that he be confined! Those compliant specialists had done so because they were called upon to do so, and they would have done it without ever having seen Ludwig, without ever having "examined" him according to their methods, without ever having spoken a word with him. To be sure, a conversation with him about music and poetry would have convinced those philistines of his madness. On the basis of their finding, however, a man who doubtless deviated from the norm, but who for all that certainly was not crazy, was denied the right to dispose of his person, degraded to the status of a psychiatric patient, and locked in a lake-bound castle with windows barred and door handles unscrewed. That he had not endured it, but had sought either freedom or death, dragging his medical jailer with him into death, spoke for his sense of dignity and not for the diagnosis of madness. Nor did the behavior of his entourage speak for it, who in their devotion would have taken up arms for him, nor did the country folks' fanatical love for their *Kini*, their little king. And if they had beheld him all alone at night, bundled in furs, riding through his mountains in his golden sleigh, lit by torch light and escorted by outriders, those peasants would not have seen in him a madman, but a king after their own rude, but dream-stricken hearts, and if he had succeeded in swimming across the lake, as had evidently been his intention, the farmers on the far shore would have defended him with pitchforks and flails against doctors and politicians.

But his compulsive extravagance had been downright pathological and no longer tolerable, and his incompetence at governing had been the simple result of his unwillingness to govern—in the end he had only dreamed of kingship but had refused to exercise it according to any reasonable norms, and a state could not live with that.

Pooh, nonsense, Rudolf. A normally constructed prime minister was capable of governing a modern federated state, even if its king was too sensitive to put up with his and his colleagues' faces. Bavaria would not have gone to rack and ruin, even if it had continued to grant Ludwig his lonely hobbies, and a king's compulsive extravagance didn't mean a thing—that was merely a phrase, a fraud, a pretext. The money had stayed in the country, and stonemasons and gilders had got fat on his fairy-tale castles. Besides which, they had long since been paid for several times over by entrance fees that the romantic curiosity of two hemispheres were charged for a visit. We ourselves today had contributed to turning craziness into good business. . . .

"I don't understand, Rudolf," I cried. "You puff out your cheeks in amazement at my apologia, but I'm the one who has every right to be astonished and not to understand how you in particular . . . I mean as an artist and so, in short, how you . . ." I searched for words to explain why I should be astonished at him, but there were none. And I also got tangled up in my own oratory because the whole time I had the feeling that it was inappropriate for me to hold forth like that in Adrian's presence. He should have spoken—and yet it was better that I did, for I was tormented by the fear that he was perfectly capable of agreeing with Schwerdtfeger. And I had to prevent that by speaking in his stead, in his behalf, in his true spirit; and it also seemed to me that Marie Godeau understood my advocacy in that sense and regarded me, whom he had sent to her for the sake of today's outing, as his mouthpiece. For all the while I had warmed to my topic, she had been looking across more at him than at me, exactly as if she were listening to him and not to me—though, to be sure, his expression constantly mocked my excitement with an enigmatic smile that was certainly a long way from confirming me as his representative.

"What is truth," he said finally. And Rüdiger Schildknapp quickly chimed in, remarking that truth had various aspects, and that in a case like this the medical and naturalistic aspect was perhaps not the most superior, but still could not be dismissed as totally invalid. It was remarkable, he added, how in the naturalistic view of truth the banal was joined with the melancholic—which was not intended as an attack on "our Rudolf," who most certainly was not a melancholic, but it could stand as the hallmark of an entire epoch, of the nineteenth century, which had had a singular propensity for banal gloominess. Adrian burst into laughter—not, of course, out of surprise. In his presence one always had the feeling that all the ideas and viewpoints spoken aloud around him were already united within him, and that he, listening with an ironic ear, left it to individual human dispositions to express and represent them. The hope was voiced that the youthful twentieth century might develop a more elevated and intellectually cheerful frame of mind. The conversation broke apart and exhausted itself in a disjointed discussion of the question of whether there were any signs of that or not. Exhaustion asserted itself generally after so many vigorous hours spent in the wintry mountain air. The timetable had a word to say as well; our driver was fetched and under a sky now brilliantly strewn with stars, the sleigh brought us back to the little station, where we waited on the platform for the train to Munich.

The trip home was rather quiet, if only out of consideration for the old aunt, who had dozed off. Schildknapp conversed now and then with her niece in a low voice; I spoke with Schwerdtfeger to make sure he had not taken any offense, and Adrian asked Helene about everyday matters. Contrary to all expectation—and to my silent, touched, and almost joyful delight—he did not take his leave from us in Wald-shut, but insisted on escorting our guests, the Parisian ladies, back to their home in Munich. At the central station we others said goodbye to them and him and went our way, while he brought both aunt and niece back to their hotel in Schwabing in a hansom cab—an act of chivalry that to my mind suggested that he spent the last hours of the day in the sole company of black eyes.

It was not until his usual eleven o'clock train that he returned to his modest solitude, where, still at a good distance off, he used his little high-pitched whistle to inform the vigilantly prowling Kaschperl-Suso of his arrival.

XLI

M Y SYMPATHETIC READERS and friends—I shall proceed. Ruin masses above Germany, rats grown fat on corpses inhabit the rubble of our cities, the thunder of Russian cannons rolls on toward Berlin, for the Anglo-Saxons the crossing of the Rhine was child's play and was made that, it seems, by the uniting of our own will with that of the enemy. An end is come, the end is come, it watcheth for thee and is come unto thee, O thou that dwellest in the land—but I shall proceed. To what happened between Adrian and Rudolf Schwerdtfeger two days after our memorable excursion, to what happened and how it happened—I know all about it, though the objection may be raised tenfold that I could not know, that I was "not there." No, I was not there. But it is a psychological fact today that I was there, because for anyone who has experienced an event, lived through it again and again as I have this one, a dreadful intimacy makes him an eye- and ear-witness of even its hidden phases.

Adrian telephoned his former Hungarian traveling companion to join him in Pfeiffering. He was to come as soon as possible, he said, the matter he wanted to discuss with him was urgent. Rudolf always came at once. The call had been at ten o'clock in the morning—during Adrian's working hours, a peculiar thing in and of itself—and by four that afternoon the violinist was on the spot. Moreover, he had to play for a subscriber's concert of the Zapfenstösser Orchestra that same evening, something to which Adrian had not even given a thought.

"Orders are orders. What's up?" Rudolf asked.

"Oh, in a moment," Adrian replied. "You're here, that's the main thing for now. I'm glad to see you, even more than usual. Keep that in mind!"

"It will lend a golden background to everything you have to say to me," Rudolf replied with a surprisingly pretty turn of phrase.

Adrian suggested a stroll, it was easier to talk when walking. Schwerdtfeger was happy to agree, and his only regret was that he did not have much time, since he would have to be back at the station for the six o'clock train if he was not to miss the concert. Adrian clapped a hand to his brow and apologized for his thoughtlessness. Perhaps Rudi would find it more understandable once he had heard him out.

A thaw had set in. Wherever the snow had been shoveled, it was melting in drips and trickles, and the paths were beginning to get slushy. The friends both wore galoshes. Rudolf had not even taken off his short fur jacket, Adrian donned his belted camel's-hair coat. They walked in the direction of Klammer Pool and then along its banks. Adrian asked about the evening's program. Brahms' First again, as the pièce de résistance? That "Tenth" Symphony again? "Well, just be glad you have flattering things to say in the adagio." Then he told about how when playing the piano as a lad, long before he knew anything about Brahms, he had come up with a motif that was almost identical with the highly Romantic horn theme in the final movement, without, to be sure, the rhythmic trick of the dotted eighth following the sixteenth, but melodically in exactly the same spirit.

"Interesting," Schwerdtfeger said.

Well, and how about the outing on Saturday? Had he amused himself? Did he think the other members of the party had?

"Could not have been nicer," Rudolf declared. He was certain that they would all have delightful memories of the day, except for Schildknapp perhaps, who had overtaxed himself and was sick in bed. "He's always too ambitious in the company of ladies." Moreover, he, Rudolf, had no reason to feel any sympathy, since Rüdiger had been rather impertinent to him.

"He knows you can take a joke."

"And I can. But he didn't have to tease me, not after Serenus had bombarded me with his loyalty to the king."

"That's a teacher for you. You have to let him lecture and correct."

"With red ink, yes indeed. I could care less about them both at the moment—now that I am here and you have something to tell me."

"Quite right. And since we're speaking of the outing, we've already arrived at the matter—a matter in which you would be doing me much good."

"Do you good? Yes?"

"Tell me, what do you think of Marie Godeau?"

"Mlle. Godeau? She's a person everyone has to like! Surely you like her too, don't you?"

" 'Like' is not quite the right word. I will admit to you I have been so seriously preoccupied with her ever since Zurich that it is difficult for me to regard that meeting as a mere episode, that the thought that she will be leaving soon, that I may perhaps never see her again, is hard to bear. I feel as if I should like to—as if I *must* see her always, have her near me always."

Schwerdtfeger stopped and stared at the man who had spoken these words, first into one eye, then the other.

"Really?" he said, walking on again and lowering his head.

"It's true," Adrian confirmed. "I'm sure you're not angry with me for putting my trust in you. That is the basis of my trust, that I do feel sure of it."

"You can be sure of it!" Rudolf murmured.

And Adrian went on, "Look at it all from a human point of view. I am getting on in years, already forty. As a friend, do you want me to spend the rest of my life in this hermit's cell? I mean, think of me as a human being who suddenly might realize that he has a certain fear of missing out, of being too late, that he has need of a warmer home, of a congenial companion in the fullest sense of the word, in short, that his life requires a milder, more human atmosphere—not simply for the sake of comfort, of a softer bed to lie in, but also and above all because he hopes that it will mean good and great things for his energy and desire to work, for the human content of his future work."

Schwerdtfeger was silent as he took a few more steps. Then he said in a dejected voice, "You've spoken the word 'human' or 'human being' four times now. I counted. Candor demands candor—something wrenches inside me when you use that word, when you use it in relation to yourself. It seems so incredibly inappropriate and—yes, humiliating from your lips. Pardon me for saying it. Was your music inhuman up till now? Then ultimately it owes its greatness to its inhumanity. Forgive me such a simple remark. I wouldn't want to hear a humanly inspired work of yours."

"No? You wouldn't want to, absolutely not? Even though you've played one three times for people already? Had it dedicated to you? I know you aren't intentionally saying cruel things to me. But don't you find it cruel to inform me that I am what I am only out of inhumanity and that humanness doesn't suit me? Cruel and thoughtless—just as cruelty always stems from thoughtlessness? I have nothing to do, dare have nothing to do with humanness—and that from someone who with amazing patience won me over to humanness and persuaded me to use a familiar 'you,' someone with whom I found human warmth for the first time in my life."

"It appears to have been a temporary stopgap."

"And what if it were? What if it were a way of practicing humanness, a preliminary stage that would lose nothing by being just that? There was someone in my life whose stout-hearted perseverance overcame death, one can almost say, who freed the humanity within me, who taught me happiness. It may perhaps never be known, never recorded in any biography. But would that detract from the services rendered, diminish the honor secretly due him?"

"You know how to turn things around very flatteringly for me."

"I'm not turning things around, I'm stating them as they are!"

"In fact we're not talking about me, but about Marie Godeau. In order to see her always, have her near you always, you want to make her your wife."

"That is my wish, my hope."

"Oh! Does she know of your plans?"

"I'm afraid not. I'm afraid I don't have at my command the means to express, to drive home my feelings and wishes—particularly not in the company of others, before whom I really am somewhat embarrassed to play the lady's man and cavalier."

"Why not pay her a call?"

"Because I find it distasteful to catch her off guard with confessions and proposals that, thanks to my awkwardness, she presumably does not in the least expect. In her eyes I am still simply an interesting loner. I'm afraid of her bewilderment and of the—perhaps overhasty—rebuff that could result from it."

"Why not write her?"

"Because presumably I would embarrass her even more by that. She would have to reply, and I don't know whether she is good at written words. What an effort it would be for her to spare me if she had to say no. And how painful for me her labors to spare me would be. I'm also afraid of the abstract quality of such an exchange of letters—it could, it seems to me, endanger my prospects. I do not like to think of Marie, all alone, by herself, uninfluenced by personal impressions—I might almost say, personal pressure—responding in writing to my letter. You see, I want to avoid a direct attack, but I also want to avoid approaching her by mail."

"And so what approach do you envision?"

"I already told you that you could be of help to me in this difficult matter. I would like to send you to her."

"Me?"

"You, Rudi. Would it seem so absurd to you if you were to crown the honor you do me—I am tempted to say, for my salvation—through services of which posterity will perhaps know nothing, or again, perhaps it will, by acting as my mediator, as the interpreter between me and life, as my intercessor with fortune? It is my own notion, a fresh idea like those that come to me when composing. One must always assume from the start that an idea is not totally new. When it comes to notes, what is ever absolutely new! But here, in this case, in this connection and under this light, it may indeed turn out that what has existed before is new after all, new to life so to speak, original and unique."

"Newness is the least of my worries. What you're saying is new enough to astound me. If I understand you rightly, I am to woo Marie for you, to propose to her for you?"

"You have understood me rightly—and could hardly have misread my words. The ease with which you understand me speaks for the naturalness of the matter."

"Do you think so? Why don't you send your Serenus?"

"You probably want to make fun of my Serenus. Evidently you are amused at the idea of my Serenus as a messenger of love. We were just speaking of those personal impressions that should not be totally lacking for the girl to make her decision. You needn't be amazed that I can imagine she would be more inclined to attend to your words than to a nuncio of more grave aspect."

"I'm not at all in the mood for jokes, Adri, if only because the role you ascribe to me in your life—and even for posterity—touches my heart and makes me feel solemn somehow. I asked about Zeitblom because he's been your friend for so much longer—"

"Yes, longer."

"Fine, simply longer, then. But don't you think that this 'simply' might make him more suitable, make his task that much easier for him?"

"Listen, how would it be if we leave him entirely out of it? In my eyes, he really has nothing to do with matters of love. You are the man, not he, in whom I have confided, who knows everything, to whom, as they used to say, the most secret pages in the book of my heart have been opened. And when you set out to see her, let her read from it, tell her about me, speak well of me, carefully divulge the feelings I have for her, the wishes for life that are bound up with them. Test her gently and genially, in that nice way of yours, to see if—yes, well, if she could love me! Will you do it? You don't have to bring me her final consent, God forbid. A little hope will be quite sufficient as the outcome of your mission. If you bring me back just enough to say that she does not find the idea of sharing my life with me totally repulsive, something monstrous—then my hour will come, then I will speak with her and her aunt myself."

They had left the Rohmbühel behind on their left and were now walking through a little piney woods beyond, where the boughs were dripping. Then at the edge of the village they took the path that would lead them back. The occasional crofter or farmer they met greeted the Schweigestills' guest of many years by name. Rudolf, after a period of silence, began again:

"You surely know that it will be easy for me to speak well of you there. All the easier, Adri, because you spoke so well of me to her. I want to be quite candid with you, however, as you have been with me. When you asked what I thought of Marie Godeau, I was quick to answer that everyone has to like her. I must confess that there was more to my answer than might immediately seem evident. I would never have confessed it to you if, as you put it in that old-fashioned poetic way, you had not opened the book of your heart to me."

"As you see, I'm truly impatient to hear your confession."

"Actually you've heard it already. I am not indifferent to the lass—but you don't like that word—to the girl, then, to Marie. And when I say, not indifferent, that's not the right way of putting it exactly. The lass is, I think, the nicest and loveliest bit of femininity I've ever chanced upon. Even in Zurich—after I had played, had played you and was feeling warm and impressionable—she fascinated me. And here then, you know I suggested our outing and—what you don't know—have been seeing her now and then, have had tea with her and Tante Isabeau at the Pension Gisella, and what an awfully nice time we had. . . . I repeat, Adri, it's only because of our conversation today, only for the sake of our mutual candor, that I even speak of it."

Leverkühn waited a bit. Then he said in an oddly faltering, equivocal voice, "No, I didn't know about that. Not about your feelings and not about tea. I seem to have been foolish enough to forget that you, too, are made of flesh and blood and not wrapped in asbestos against the charms of what is sweet and beautiful. So you love her, or, let us say, you are in love with her. But let me ask you one question. Is it the case that our intentions are at cross purposes, that you wanted to ask her to be your wife?"

Schwerdtfeger seemed to ponder this. He said, "No, I've not thought of that yet."

"No? Were you thinking perhaps merely of seducing her?"

"The way you put it, Adrian! Don't talk like that! No, I have no thought of that, either."

"Well, then let me tell you that your confession, your candid and commendable confession, is such that it inclines me more to stick firmly by my request, than that it could induce me to desist from it."

"How do you mean?"

"I mean it in several ways. I chose you for this mission of love because you are far more in your element there than, let us say, Serenus Zeitblom. Because you exude something that he lacks and that I regard as propitious for my wishes and hopes. That much, in any case. But now I learn that you even share my feelings to a certain extent, without however, as you assure me, sharing my intentions. You will speak from your own feelings—for me and my intentions. I cannot possibly imagine a more qualified, desirable suitor."

"If you see it in that light—"

"Don't think I see it in only that one! I see it as well in the light of a sacrifice, and you can truly demand that I regard it as such. Go ahead and demand it! Demand it with all due gravity! For that means that in recognizing the sacrifice as a sacrifice, you still want to make it. You make it in the spirit of the role that you play in my life, in the fulfillment of the honor that you have earned for the sake of my humanity, and that will perhaps remain a secret to the world, or perhaps not. Will you agree to do it?"

Rudolf replied, "Yes, I will go and, to the best of my ability, plead your cause."

"You shall have my hand on it," Adrian said, "when we say goodbye."

They had now circled back to the house, and Schwerdtfeger still had time to share a little snack with his friend in the Winged-Victory room. Gereon Schweigestill had harnessed the team for him; and Adrian, despite Rudolf's plea that he not go to the trouble, took a seat beside him on the hard-riding wagon to accompany him to the station.

"No, it's only proper. And this time it's especially proper," he declared.

The train, one slow enough to stop at Pfeiffering, pulled in, and they shook hands through the lowered window.

"Not another word," Adrian said. "Be good. Be nice!"

He raised his arm before turning to go. He never again saw the man who was now gliding slowly away. He only received a letter from him, one that he refused to answer.

XLII

THE NEXT TIME I was with him, some ten or eleven days later, he already had this letter in hand and informed me of his firm resolve to offer no reply. He looked pale and left the impression of a man who has taken a heavy blow—especially because there was particular evidence of a tendency to walk with his head and upper body tilted to one side (which, granted, I had observed for some time now). And yet he was, or pretended to be, completely calm, even cold, and almost appeared to want to apologize for his composure, for the way he haughtily shrugged off the act of betrayal committed against him.

"I don't suppose," he said, "you were expecting me to burst into moral indignation and fits of rage. A faithless friend. What else? I cannot summon much outrage against the way of the world. It is bitter, true, and one asks oneself who should be trusted, when one's own right hand is perjured to the bosom. But what would you? For such a friend is now. What is left to me is shame—and the realization that I deserve to be thrashed."

I wanted to know what he had to be ashamed of.

"Of conduct," he replied, "so foolish that it reminds me of a schoolboy who being overjoyed when finding a bird's nest, shows it to his companion—and he steals it."

What else could I say but, "It is no sin or shame to be trusting—surely those are the portion of the thief."

If only I could have met his self-reproaches with more conviction! Whereas in my heart I had to admit that his behavior, the whole arrangement—with Rudolf, of all people, as the intercessor and wooer—

seemed affected, artificial, culpable, and I needed only imagine having sent some attractive friend to Helene instead of having used my own tongue for disclosing my heart to her, to realize the whole puzzling absurdity of his course of action. But why feed his remorse—if remorse it was that spoke in his words, in his demeanor? He had at once lost both friend and beloved, and, one had to say, was himself at fault—if one, if I, could only have been quite certain that it was a fault in the sense of an unconscious blunder, a dreadfully imprudent act! If only the suspicion had not constantly crept into my broodings that he had more or less foreseen what would happen, and that it had happened just as he had wanted it! Could one even seriously credit him with believing that what Rudolf "exuded," that the man's undeniable erotic attraction, would work and woo for him? Could one believe that he had counted on him? At times the apprehension rose up within me that the man who had alleged he was demanding a sacrifice of another, had himself chosen the greatest sacrifice—that he had intentionally wanted to join what by its very lovableness belonged together, in order to retreat into his own self-abandoning loneliness. But that idea suited me better than him. It would have fit so nicely into my reverence for him if so soft, so painfully benign a motive had been the basis for his apparent mistake, for that so-called act of stupidity that he claimed to have committed! Events were to bring me face to face with a truth that was harder, colder, more cruel, a truth with which my good-heartedness could not cope without freezing in icy horror, a truth that was unproved, mute, recognizable only in its frozen stare—and may it remain mute, for I am not the man to give it words.

I am certain that as far as Schwerdtfeger himself knew, he had gone to Marie Godeau with the best, the most correct intentions. It is equally certain, however, that from the start those intentions were not founded on the firmest footing, but were endangered from within, were ready and waiting to relax, to collapse, to be reshaped. As a superior interpreter of such things, Adrian had impressed upon Schwerdtfeger the significance that his person had for his friend's life and humanity; this was not without its flattering and inciting effect on Rudolf's vanity, and he had accepted the idea that his present mission grew out of that significance. But working against these influences was the jealous insult he felt as a result of his conquest's change of mind, so that he was now only good enough to be a tool, a means to an end; and I do believe that secretly he felt free—that is, felt no obligation to return such demanding unfaithfulness with faithfulness. That much is rather clear to me. And it is also clear to me that to wander the paths of love for someone else is to take a seductive stroll—particularly for a fanatic flirt, whose morality must surely find something emancipating in the mere awareness that a flirtation, or an enterprise somehow related to flirtation, is involved.

Can anyone doubt that I could recount what took place between Rudolf and Marie Godeau in the same verbatim fashion as the conversation in Pfeiffering? Does anyone doubt that I "was there"? I think not. But I also think that no one could any longer find an exact, detailed account of the event essential or even useful. Its fateful outcome, however promising it first appeared—not to me, but to the others— was not, as one must needs assume, the fruit of a single conversation. A second proved necessary as well, given the way that Marie said goodbye to Rudolf after the first.

It was Tante Isabeau whom he encountered as he entered the little vestibule of the hotel apartment. He inquired about her niece, asked if he might exchange a few words with her alone, in the interest of a third party. The old woman showed him into the combination living room and studio—with a smile whose slyness betrayed disbelief in his talk of a third party. He stepped over to Marie, who greeted him with equal surprise and amiability and was about to tell her aunt something that, to her growing amazement, or at least obvious good cheer, he declared superfluous. Her aunt, he said, knew that he was here and would join them after he had spoken with her about a very important, very serious, and lovely matter. How did she reply? In a jocular, everyday sort of way, surely—with "I'm certainly curious to hear about it" or something of the sort. And would the gentleman please make himself comfortable to speak his piece.

He sat down in an armchair that he pulled over to her drawing board. No one can say that he broke his promise. He kept it, carried it out honestly. He spoke to her about Adrian, about his significance, his greatness, which the public would slowly come to realize, about his, Rudolf's, admiration and devotion to this extraordinary man. He spoke to her about Zurich, about the meeting at the Schlaginhaufens', about the day in the mountains. He confessed to her that his friend loved her—how does one do that? How does one tell a woman about another's love? Does one lean toward her? Gaze into her eyes? Does one make one's plea by taking the hand that one declares one would gladly lay in the hand of a third? I do not know. I had only to deliver the invitation to an excursion, not propose marriage. All I know is that she hastily withdrew her hand, whether from the clasp of his or simply from her lap where it had been lying, that a fleeting blush tinged the

southern paleness of her cheeks, and that the laughter vanished from
the darkness of her eyes. She did not understand, was truly not sure she
understood. She asked whether she was correct in assuming that
Rudolf was proposing to her for Dr. Leverkühn? Yes, he said, he was
doing so out of a sense of duty, out of friendship. Adrian, out of his
own sense of delicacy, had asked him to do it, and he felt he could not
refuse. Her obviously cool, obviously mocking reply—that that was
very kind of him—was not the sort that could ease his embarrassment.
Only now did he become fully aware of the exceptional nature of his
situation and role, mingled with the fear that she might find something
insulting about it. Her reaction, her totally surprised reaction, both
frightened and secretly delighted him at the same time. He stammered
on for a while in an attempt to plead his cause. She did not know how
difficult it was to refuse something to a man like that. He had also felt
more or less responsible for the turn that Adrian's life had taken on the
basis of this emotion, because he, Rudolf, had been the one who had
persuaded him to take the trip to Switzerland and so had brought
about the meeting with Marie. Remarkably enough, the violin concerto was dedicated to him, but ultimately it had been the means by
which the composer had first laid eyes on her. He begged her to understand that this same sense of responsibility had strongly contributed to his willingness to carry out Adrian's wish.

Here there was another brief retraction of the hand that he had tried
to clasp while making his plea. She answered as follows. She requested
that he not continue his attempt, that it was not a matter of her understanding the role he had accepted. She was sorry to have to disappoint
his hopes as a friend, but even though she naturally was not unim-
pressed by the personality of the man who had sent him, the respect
she felt for him had nothing to do with feelings that could supply the
basis for the union that had been so eloquently suggested to her. Her
acquaintance with Dr. Leverkühn was both an honor and a pleasure,
but unfortunately the reply that she must now give him would probably preclude any further meeting as too embarrassing. She sincerely
regretted having to think that this change in the situation would also
affect the messenger and advocate of hopes that could never be realized. After what had happened, it would doubtless be better and easier
not to see one another. And with that she had to bid a friendly
farewell—*"Adieu, monsieur!"*

"Marie!" he implored her. But she merely expressed her amazement
at his use of her first name and repeated her farewell—in a voice whose
tone I can hear so clearly: *"Adieu, monsieur!"*

He left—to look at him, abashed and defeated, but in his heart de-

lighted to the point of elation. Adrian's notion of marriage had proved
to be the nonsense that it was, and she had taken great offense that he
had allowed himself to be its presenter—how enchantingly sensitive
she had been about that. He did not hurry to provide Adrian a report
of the outcome of his visit—and how happy he was now that he had secured his position with him by an honest admission that he himself
was not unreceptive to the girl's charms. What he did was to sit down
and compose a missive to Mlle. Godeau, in which he said that he could
neither live nor die with her *"adieu, monsieur,"* and that it was a matter of life and death that he see her again, in order to put to her a question, the same question that he asked here and now with all his soul:
Whether she did not understand how a man could sacrifice and disregard his own feelings, make himself an unselfish advocate of another
man's wishes, out of admiration for him? And whether she could not
further understand how suppressed and faithfully restrained emotions
might burst forth to free, indeed exuberant expression the moment it
became apparent that the other man had not the least prospect of being
heard? He begged her forgiveness for a betrayal he had committed
against no one but himself. He could not regret having done so, but he
was overjoyed that no one could now consider it an act of betrayal if
he told her that he—loved her.

In that tone. Not at all inept. It was written on the wings of flirtatious enthusiasm and, or so I believe, without any clear realization that
after having wooed for Adrian, his own declaration of love remained
tied to a proposal of marriage, a notion that would never have entered
his flirtatious head. When Marie refused to accept the letter, Tante Isabeau read it aloud to her. Rudolf received no answer. But two days
later, when he had the Pension Gisella's housemaid announce him to
the aunt, he was not turned away. Marie was in town. After his previous visit Marie had shed tears on her Tante Isabeau's bosom, the old
lady revealed to him in arch reproach—pure invention, in my opinion.
The aunt stressed her niece's pride. She was a deeply sensitive, but
proud girl. The aunt could not give him definite hopes of an opportunity for another interview. But he should know this much—that
she would not fail to make it clear to Marie just how honorable his
conduct was.

After two more days he was at the door again. Madame Ferblantier—
that was the aunt's name, she was a widow—went inside to speak with
her niece. She remained there a good while, but finally returned and
with an encouraging wink admitted him. Of course, he had brought
flowers.

What else should I say? I am too old and too sad to paint a scene whose details can be of interest to no one. Rudolf submitted Adrian's proposal of marriage—but this time for himself, although that fluttering fellow was no more fit for marriage than I to be a Don Juan. But it is useless to think of the future, about the prospects of a union that had no future, but would be quickly undone by a violent fate. Marie dared to love this heartbreaker, this violinist with the "small tone," of whose merits and assured career as an artist she had received such warm guarantees from a serious source. She felt confident that she could hold him, bind him, domesticate this wild creature. She gave him her hands, she accepted his kiss, and it was not twenty-four hours before our entire circle of acquaintance had heard the happy news that Rudi was caught, that Concertmaster Schwerdtfeger and Marie Godeau were engaged. It was said, moreover, that he planned to break his contract with the Zapfenstösser Orchestra, to marry in Paris, and to offer his services to the Orchestre Symphonique, a new musical organization that was only just forming.

He was no doubt welcome there, and there was equally no doubt that negotiations for his termination proceeded rather slowly in Munich, where they were reluctant to let him go. In any case his participation in the next Zapfenstösser concert (that is, the first after the one when he had returned from Pfeiffering at the very last moment) was regarded as a kind of farewell performance. Moreover, since the conductor, Dr. Edschmidt, had chosen for that evening a program of Berlioz and Wagner that was sure to fill the house, all Munich, as they say, was there. Countless familiar faces gazed up from the rows, and when I stood up I found many people I had to greet: the Schlaginhaufens and the habitués of their receptions, the Radbruchs along with Schildknapp, Jeannette Scheurl, Mmes. Zwitscher and Binder-Majoresku, and several others, for whom not the last reason for attending was, to be sure, to see the future bridegroom, Rudi Schwerdtfeger, at his music stand up front on the left. His fiancée was not in attendance, by the way—but had already returned to Paris, so one heard. I bowed to Inez Institoris. She was alone, or better, had come in company with the Knöterichs but without her husband, who was unmusical and wished to spend the evening at the Allotria. She was sitting toward the back of the hall, wearing a dress whose simplicity was not far removed from indigence—her neck extended forward at a tilt, her eyebrows raised, her small lips pursed in miserable roguishness; and as she returned my greeting, there was no avoiding the annoying impression that she was still smiling with malicious triumph at having so splendidly exploited my patience and sympathy during that long evening conversation in her living room.

As for Schwerdtfeger, being well aware of how many curious eyes would meet his, he scarcely glanced into the hall once during the entire evening. At moments when he might have done so, he tuned his instrument or paged through his music. The concert concluded with, yes indeed! the Overture to *Meistersinger*, played broadly and lustily, and the already loud thunder of applause increased noticeably when Ferdinand Edschmidt bade the orchestra to rise and extended a congratulatory hand to his concertmaster. As this was taking place, I was already at the top of the middle aisle, worried about my hat and coat, which I was able to retrieve from the checkroom before a crowd had formed. My intention was to walk at least part of the way home—to my rented room in Schwabing, that is. Outside the concert hall I ran into a gentleman from the Kridwiss circle, Professor Gilgen Holzschuher, the Dürer expert, who had been in the hall as well. He engaged me in a conversation that began with a criticism on his part of the evening's program: This combination of Berlioz and Wagner, of foreign virtuosity and true German mastery, was tasteless, and what was more, it poorly concealed a political tendency. It smacked all too much of German-French reconciliation and pacifism, especially since Edschmidt was known to be a republican and patriotically undependable. The thought had bothered him all evening. Unfortunately everything was political nowadays, there was no intellectual purity left. To restore it, there would have to be, above all, men of indisputably German views at the head of the great orchestras.

I did not tell him that it was in fact he who was politicizing things, and that nowadays the word "German" was in no way synonymous with intellectual purity, but a party slogan. I simply asserted that a good portion of virtuosity, whether foreign or not, played a role in Wagner's internationally quite popular art—and then charitably diverted him from the topic by mentioning an article on the problems of proportion in Gothic architecture that he had recently published in the magazine *Art and Artist*. The compliments I paid him on it made him quite happy, soft, unpolitical, serene, and I used his improved disposition to take my leave of him, turning off to the right, while he went left.

Taking the upper end of Türken Strasse, I quickly reached Ludwig Strasse and followed that quite monumental highway (to be sure, it has been paved with asphalt for years now) on the left side, in the direction of the Victory Gate. The evening was cloudy and very mild; my winter coat began to seem a little heavy after a time, and I halted at the Theresien Strasse trolley stop to wait for a car from one of the lines to Schwabing. I don't know why it took unusually long for one to come. Traffic jams and delays do happen. It was a number 10 car, one quite convenient for me, that finally approached. I can still see and hear it coming from the Feldherrn Halle. Munich streetcars, painted Bavarian blue, are heavily built and make considerable noise, whether because of their weight or some special quality of the subsoil. Sparks of electricity constantly flashed under the vehicle's wheels and even more violently at the top of the contact pole, where cold flames scattered in great hissing showers.

The car stopped, and I moved inside from the front platform where I had boarded. Right next to the sliding door, to the left of where I entered, I found an empty seat that someone had evidently only just vacated. The car was full, two gentlemen were even hanging on to straps and standing in the aisle by the rear door. Concertgoers on their way home probably made up the majority of the passengers. Among them, in the middle of the bench opposite me, sat Schwerdtfeger, his violin case propped between his knees. Certainly he had seen me board, but he avoided my glance. Under his coat he wore a white muffler that covered his formal tie, but as was his habit he wore no hat. His curly, unruly blond hair made him look handsome and young; the work just completed heightened the color in his face, so that in his respectable heated state his blue eyes seemed even a little swollen. But that suited him, just as did those slightly pouting lips with which he could whistle so masterfully. I am not quick to take in my surroundings; only gradually did I realize that there were other acquaintances in the car as well. I exchanged greetings with Dr. Kranich, who was sitting on Schwerdtfeger's side, but much farther back by the rear door. I happened to bend forward and to my surprise spotted Inez Institoris, who was sitting on the same side as I, several seats away, toward the middle and cater-corner from Schwerdtfeger. I say to my surprise, for this was not the way home for her. But since I also noticed, a few seats farther on, her friend Frau Binder-Majoresku, who lived well out in Schwabing, even beyond the Grossen Wirt, I assumed Inez was planning to have evening tea with her.

But I now understood why Schwerdtfeger kept his pretty head turned to the right for the most part, offering me only his somewhat too blunt profile. It was not just the man whom he may well have regarded as Adrian's alter ego that he was studiously ignoring—and indeed I silently reproached him for having had to take precisely this streetcar, an unjust reproach presumably, since there was no telling if he had boarded it at the same time with Inez. She could have got on after him, just as I had, or, if it was the other way around, he could not have bolted at the mere sight of her.

We were passing the university, and the conductor in his felt boots was standing right in front of me to take my ten pfennigs and had thrust a ticket into my hand, when something incredible and at first, like anything totally unexpected, quite incomprehensible happened. Shots erupted in the car—even, sharp, cracking detonations, one after the other, three, four, five, with wildly deafening rapidity, and across the way Schwerdtfeger, his violin case between his hands, sank first on the shoulder and then into the lap of the lady sitting to his right, who like the lady to his left, pulled away from him in dismay, while a general confusion, more flight and shrieking panic than any clearheaded action, filled the car, and up front, the driver—God knows why—kept stepping on the bell like mad, perhaps to summon a policeman. There was none within earshot, of course. Inside the car, which had come to a halt now, there developed an almost dangerous press of people, since many passengers were trying to get out, while others, out of curiosity or the desire to do something, pushed to get inside from the platforms. Together with me the two gentlemen who had been standing in the aisle hurled themselves at Inez—much too late of course. We did not have to "wrest" the revolver from her; she had dropped it, or rather thrown it away, in the direction of her victim. Her face was as white as a sheet of paper, with sharply edged bright red spots on her cheekbones. Her eyes were closed and her pursed lips formed a crazed smile.

They pinned her arms, and I rushed across to Rudolf, whom someone had stretched out on the now empty bench. The lady on whom he had fallen had fainted onto another bench and lay there bleeding, having been grazed, harmlessly as it turned out, on the arm. Several people stood around Rudolf, including Dr. Kranich, who was holding his hand.

"What a horrible, senseless, irrational act!" he said, his face turning pallid, but speaking in that clear, academically well-articulated, though asthmatic way of his and pronouncing the word "har-r-r-ible," as one often hears even actors do. He added that never had he more regretted not being a physician but a mere numismatist, and at that moment the study of coins truly seemed to me the most futile of sciences, even more useless than philology—an utterly unsustainable position. Indeed no doctor was at hand, not one among so many concertgoers—although doctors do tend to be musical, if only because there are so many who are Jewish. I bent down over Rudolf. He showed signs of life, but was hideously injured. There was a bleeding entrance wound below one eye. Other bullets, as it turned out, had pierced the neck, the lung, the coronary artery. He raised his head in an attempt to say something, but bloody foam quickly appeared at his lips, which in their soft thickness suddenly seemed touchingly beautiful to me. He rolled his eyes and his head fell back hard on the wood.

I cannot express the poignant, almost overwhelming pity for this man that went through me. I felt that in some way I had always loved him, and I must admit that my compassion for him was far more intense than for the unfortunate woman who, though pitiable in her sunken state, had been brought to this heinous act by suffering and the demoralizing vice that numbs it. I explained that I was a close acquaintance of them both and proposed we carry the severely wounded man across to the university, where the custodian could telephone for an ambulance and the police, and where I knew there was also a small first-aid station. I arranged for the perpetrator to be brought there as well.

All of which was done. A solicitous, bespectacled young man and I lifted poor Rudolf out of the car, behind which two or three other streetcars were now backed up. From one of them a doctor came hurrying over to us at last, carrying his bag of instruments and issuing, rather superfluous, directives on how to carry Rudolf. A newspaper reporter arrived as well and gathered information. I am tormented by the memory of how difficult it was to ring the custodian awake in his ground-floor apartment. The doctor, a younger man, who introduced himself to everyone, tried to offer first aid once we had laid the unconscious man on a sofa. The ambulance arrived surprisingly quickly. Rudolf died—which as the doctor told me immediately after his examination was likely to happen—on the way to the municipal hospital.

For my part, I stayed with the policemen, who arrived later, and with the woman they arrested, who was now sobbing convulsively, so that I might inform the inspector of her situation and recommend that she be taken to a psychiatric clinic. Approval for that, however, could no longer be obtained that night.

The church bells were tolling midnight when I left the police station and, keeping an eye out for an automobile, set out on the painful errand that still remained to be done—on Prinzregenten Strasse. I regarded it as my obligation to inform her little husband, as gently as I could, of what had happened. The opportunity of a ride offered itself only after it was no longer worth taking. I found the house door locked, but I rang until a light went on in the stairwell, and Institoris himself came downstairs—to find me rather than his wife at the door. He had a way of snapping his mouth open for air, while drawing his lower lip tightly against his teeth.

"Yes, what is it?" he stammered. "So it's you? What brings you . . . Is there something you . . ."

I said almost nothing on the stairs. Up in his living room, there where I had heard Inez's agonized confessions, I told him, after first preparing him with a few words, what I had witnessed. He had been standing and when I finished quickly sat down in one of the wicker armchairs, but then demonstrated the composure of a man who had lived for a long time in an oppressively menacing atmosphere.

"So," he said, "that's how it was meant to turn out." And one clearly understood that he had only been anxiously waiting for how it would turn out.

"I want to see her," he declared and stood up again. "I hope they'll let me speak with her there." (He meant the police jail.)

I could not give him much hope for tonight, but in a weak voice he asserted that it was his duty to try, threw on a coat, and hurried out of the apartment.

Alone in the room where Inez's bust gazed, distinguished and dis-agreeable, from its pedestal, my thoughts drifted to where, as one can well believe, they had already dwelt often and at length over the last few hours. I still had, it seemed to me, one more painful message to de-liver. But a singular stiffness that had taken control of my limbs, af-fecting even the muscles of my face, prevented me from picking up the telephone receiver and asking to be connected with Pfeiffering. That is not true—I did pick it up, but held it in my lowered hand and heard the muted, underwater voice of the operator on the line. But the thought, born of almost morbid exhaustion, that I was pointlessly about to alarm the Schweigestill house in the middle of the night, that it was un-necessary to tell Adrian what I had experienced, indeed, that I would in some way be making myself ridiculous, thwarted my intention, and I laid the receiver back on the hook.

XLIII

M Y TALE HASTENS toward its end—as does everything. Everything is pushing and plummeting toward the end, the world
stands in the sign of the end, at least it stands in it for us Germans,
whose thousand-year history—confounded, carried to absurdity, proven
by its outcome to have gone fatally amiss and demonstrably astray—
is rushing into the void, into despair, into unparalleled bankruptcy, is
descending into hell amid the dance of thundering flames. If it is true,
as the German proverb has it, that every path to a right goal is right
every step of the way, then one must admit that the path that led to this
doom—and I use the word in its strictest, most religious sense—was
doomed at every point, at every turn, however bitter love may find it
to endorse this logic. The ineluctable recognition of hopeless doom is
not synonymous with a denial of love. I, a simple German man and
scholar, have loved many things German, indeed, my life (insignificant,
but capable of fascination and devotion) has been dedicated to the love,
the often terrified, always fearful, but eternally faithful love of a significant German human being and artist, whose mysterious sinfulness
and horrible end have no power over this love—which perhaps, who
knows, is but a reflection of grace.

Awaiting our fate, beyond whose calamity no man can surmise, I
have withdrawn into my hermit's cell in Freising and avoid the sight of
our hideously battered Munich—the toppled statues, the façades that
gaze from vacant eye sockets to disguise the yawning void behind, and
yet seem inclined to reveal it, too, by supplying more of the rubble
already strewn over the cobblestones. My heart falters when I think

in pity of my foolish sons, who believed with the nation's masses, believed, exulted, sacrificed, and struggled with them, and for a good while now, like blankly staring millions of their kind, have tasted the disillusion that is certain to become final helplessness, all-embracing despair. For me, who could not believe their beliefs or share their joys, their anguish will not bring them any closer. And they will also lay that to my account—as if things might have been different had I dreamt their vile dreams with them. God help them. I am alone with my old Helene, who tends to my bodily needs, and to whom I sometimes read certain sections, which she in her simplicity can deal with, of what I have written here, toward whose completion all my thoughts are directed amidst the destruction.

The prophecy of the end, entitled *Apocalipsis cum figuris*, resounded fiercely and grandly at Frankfurt am Main in February 1926, approximately a year after the terrible events I have had to report, and it may be due to the depressed state in which they left him that Adrian could not bring himself to break through his customary reserve and attend the event, which despite a lot of angry shouts and insipid laughter, was a great sensation. He never heard the work, one of the two main hallmarks of his austere and proud life—which, given what he was in the habit of saying about "hearing," one perhaps need not lament too greatly. Except for myself (and I saw to it that I was free to make the trip), the only person from our circle of acquaintance who went to Frankfurt, despite her modest means, was dear Jeannette Scheurl, who both attended the performance and stopped in Pfeiffering to offer a very personal account of it in her mixed French-Bavarian dialect. At the time Adrian particularly enjoyed the company of this elegantly rustic woman and in fact benefited from her calming presence, her protective energy as it were; and I have in fact seen him sit hand in hand with her in a corner of the abbot's study, gazing at her, saying nothing, as if safe and secure. This hand-in-hand was not like him, was a change that touched me, that I saw with joy but not without some anxiety, too.

Also at that time, he loved more than ever having Rüdiger Schildknapp around—him of the same-colored eyes. Even though he was as sparing as always of his presence, whenever that threadbare gentleman did turn up, he was prepared to share in those long country walks that Adrian loved to take, especially when he could not work, and that Rüdiger seasoned for him with bitter and grotesque humor. Poor as a church mouse, he was having trouble at the time with his neglected and decaying teeth and talked of nothing but perfidious dentists who had pretended to treat him out of friendship, but then suddenly presented exorbitant bills; he rattled on about payment schedules and unmet due dates, which had then forced him to engage someone else's services, while fully aware that he would never be able or even wish to pay for them—and more of the same. To his great agony, someone had pressed a large piece of bridgework right down over exposed and painful roots that very quickly began to loosen under the weight, so that a macabre disintegration of the artificial construct was in the offing and would result in his contracting more new and unpayable debts. "It's—breaking—apart," he announced in horror; but not only did he have no objection to Adrian's laughing to the point of tears at all his misery, that also seemed in fact to have been his intent, for even he would buckle over with boyish laughter.

The gallows humor of his company was just the thing for the lonely man at the time, and I, having no talent for offering him comedy, did what I could to secure such company by encouraging the usually recalcitrant Rüdiger to pay visits to Pfeiffering. During that entire year, Adrian's life was in fact devoid of work. As was evident from his letters to me, he had been overcome by a stagnation of the intellect, by a dearth of ideas that tormented, humiliated, and alarmed him and was, or at least so he explained to me, a principal reason for his refusal to go to Frankfurt. It was impossible, he said, to concern oneself with something done, when one was now in a state of being incapable of doing anything better; the past was only bearable if one felt superior to it, instead of having to stare stupidly at it in the awareness of one's present impotence. In letters sent to me in Freising, he called his state one of "emptiness, virtual idiocy," "a dog's life," "an unbearably idyllic, vegetal existence lacking all memory" and wrote that cursing it was his sole, abject means of saving some honor; it was enough to make him want to wish for a new war, a revolution, or some other external tumult, if only so that it might wrench him out of his stupor. He literally no longer had the least notion of how to compose, not the vaguest memory of how one went about it, and confidently believed that he would never set another note to paper. "May hell have mercy on me!" and "Pray for my poor soul!"—these phrases appeared repeatedly in those documents, which, despite the great grief they caused me, nevertheless lifted my spirits again, for I told myself that for once only I, the playmate of his youth, and no one else in the world could have been the recipient of such confessions.

In my replies I sought to console him by suggesting how difficult it is for someone to think his way beyond his present condition, which, though against all reason, he emotionally always tends to see as his permanent fate, since he is incapable of peeking around the next corner, so to speak—which is perhaps even truer of bad situations than happy ones. His lassitude was only too understandable, given the cruel disappointments he had recently suffered. And I was weak and "poetic" enough to compare the fallowness of his mind with "earth in her winter rest," in whose womb life secretly continues its work in preparation for sprouting anew—an image that even I felt was impermissibly benign and poorly suited to the extremes of his existence, to the swings between unshackled creativity and penitential paralysis to which he was subject. With the stagnation of his creative powers, his health, too, was again at a low point, though that appeared more an accompanying symptom than a cause. Severe migraine attacks kept him in darkness; he was beset with alternating catarrhs of the stomach, bronchi, and throat throughout the winter of 1926, and they alone would have sufficed to prevent him from traveling to Frankfurt—just as they caused his doctor categorically to forbid a far more urgent journey, one that was indisputably and palpably necessary in human terms.

At the end of the year, you see, by curious coincidence on almost the same day, Max Schweigestill and Jonathan Leverkühn both passed away, both at the age of seventy-five—the family father who ran the Upper Bavarian farm where Adrian had been a guest of many years and his own father on Buchel Farm up north. His mother's telegram reporting the gentle passing of that "speculator" reached Adrian as he stood at the bier of the equally quiet and thoughtful pipe-smoker who spoke a different dialect and who had long ago taken to leaving more and more of the burden of the farm to his heir Gereon, just as Adrian's father had presumably done with his own Georg, before retiring now for good and all. Adrian could be certain that Elsbeth Leverkühn had taken this death with the same quiet composure, the same understanding acceptance of human mortality, as had Mother Schweigestill. Given his condition at the time, a trip to Saxon Thuringia for the burial was out of the question. But although he had a fever that Sunday and was feeling very weak, he insisted, in spite of his doctor's warnings, on attending his landlord's funeral service, which was held in the village church at Pfeiffering and drew a crowd of people from all over the district. I, too, paid my final respects to the deceased, with the sense that I was simultaneously honoring the other man as well. We walked back together to the Schweigestill house, where we were strangely touched by the truly scarcely remarkable fact that as before, despite the old man's departure, the atmosphere was heavy with the pungent aroma of pipe smoke issuing from the open living room, although it was surely also deeply impregnated in the walls of the hallway.

"That will hang on," Adrian said, "for a good while; maybe as long as the house stands. It will hang on in Buchel, too. The length of time we hang on afterward, a little shorter, a little longer, is what is called immortality."

That was after Christmas—both fathers, though already turning away and half-estranged from earthly things, had spent the holiday with their families. As light increased now early in the new year, Adrian's health improved visibly, the series of tormenting illnesses that had confined him to his bed now halted abruptly; psychologically he appeared to have overcome the foundering of his life's plans and the shocking damage that had gone with it; his spirit rose anew—he may even have had difficulty remaining cool and collected amid the storm of ideas bombarding him, and the year 1927 became the year that yielded a miracle harvest of finest chamber music. First came a work for an ensemble of three strings, three woodwinds, and piano—a rambling piece, if I may put it that way, with very long, extempore themes that undergo development and resolution in manifold ways, and yet never recur openly. How I love the stormy surge of yearning that is its essential character, the Romanticism of its tone—since, after all, it is handled with the strictest modern methods; a thematic work, to be sure, but with such strong transformations that there are no true "reprises." The first movement is explicitly titled Fantasia; the second is an adagio that rises toward a powerful climax; the third, a finale that begins lightly, almost playfully, but as its counterpoint grows increasingly complex, simultaneously assumes more and more the character of tragic seriousness, until it ends in the funereal march of a somber epilogue. The piano is never used to fill in harmonic gaps, but is a solo instrument as in a piano concerto—an aftereffect, perhaps, of the style of his violin concerto. Perhaps what I admired most profoundly is the mastery with which the problem of combining timbres is solved. The woodwinds never cover the strings, but always allow them their tonal space and alternate with them, and in only a few passages are strings and woodwinds united in a *tutti*. And if I were to summarize my impression, it is as if one were lured from a solid and familiar point of departure into ever more remote regions—everything turns out differently from what one expected. "I did not wish to write a sonata," Adrian said to me, "but a novel."

The tendency toward musical "prose" reaches its height in the String Quartet, perhaps Leverkühn's most esoteric work, which followed on the heels of the ensemble piece. Whereas chamber music usually offers a playground for the working out of thematic motifs, here that is avoided in outright provocation. There are no linkages, developments, variations, or even repetitions of motifs whatever; uninterruptedly, in an apparently fully disjointed fashion, one new idea follows another, connected only by a similarity of tone or timbre, or, almost more frequently, by a contrast. There is not a trace of traditional forms. It is as if the *meister* were using this seemingly anarchic piece to take a deep breath before his *Faust* cantata, his most rigorously formal work. In the Quartet he simply yielded to his ear, to the inner logic of invention. And yet all the while, polyphony is heightened to its utmost, and each voice is completely independent at every moment. Articulation is supplied to the whole by very clearly contrasting tempi, although the movements are to be played without interruption. The first, marked *moderato,* is like a deeply meditative, intellectually strenuous conversation and deliberation among the four instruments, an exchange that moves at a serious and quiet pace, with almost no change in dynamics. There follows a *presto,* whispered as if in delirium by all four muted instruments; then a slow movement, shorter in length, in which the viola is the principal voice, accompanied by interjections from the other instruments, making it reminiscent of a scene with singers. Finally, in the *allegro con fuoco* polyphony gratifies itself in great long lines. I know nothing more exciting than the ending, where it sounds as if flames are licking at one from all four sides, a combination of runs and trills that give the impression one is hearing an entire orchestra. And in truth, by exploiting the broad register and finest tonal possibilities of each instrument, a sonority is achieved that breaks the bounds of normal chamber music, and I do not doubt that the critics will generally object that the Quartet is an orchestral work in disguise. They will be wrong. Study of the score discloses that the subtlest knowledge of the string-quartet form has been put to good use. Granted, Adrian repeatedly expressed to me his view that the old boundaries between chamber music and the orchestral style were not tenable, and that with the emancipation of tonal color they merged into one another. The tendency to hybridize forms, to mix and switch them, such as had already evidenced itself in the treatment of voices and instruments in the *Apocalypse,* was now indeed growing. "In studying philosophy," he in fact said, "I learned that to set limits is to go beyond them. I've always held to that notion." What he meant was Hegel's critique of Kant, and the statement reveals how profoundly his creativity was shaped by his intellect—and by things put to memory early on.

This was completely true of the Trio for violin, viola, and cello, which, though barely playable—indeed to be mastered at best only technically by three virtuosi—is as astonishing for the constructive fury, the cerebral achievement that it represents, as it is for the unanticipated mixing of sounds that an incomparable fantasy for combination, that an ear eager to hear what has never been heard before has wrested from all three instruments. "Impossible, but rewarding," was how Adrian in a good mood once characterized the piece, which he had begun to write even while composing the Music for an Ensemble and which he had carried in his mind and developed while still burdened by the work on the Quartet—this by itself, one should have thought, would have had to consume one man's powers of organization totally for a long time. It was an exuberant interweaving of inventions, challenges, attainments, and summons from old tasks to the mastery of new ones, a tumult of problems that burst upon you together with their solutions—"A night," Adrian said, "that never grows dark for the lightning."

"A less than mild and rather twitching sort of illumination," he added. "What else—I twitch myself, for it has me cursedly by the collar and drags me 'long so that all my corpse does twitch. Fresh ideas, dear friend, are a fiendish pack, they have hot cheeks, and make your cheeks hot, too, in not so loving a fashion. Surely as the bosom friend of a humanist, one may ever neatly draw a difference twixt felicity and martyrdom. . . ." And he pretended that at times he did not know if the peaceable incapacity in which he had only recently lived had not perhaps been the more desirable state compared with his present torment.

I rebuked him for ingratitude. From week to week, with amazement, with tears of joy in my eyes but also in secret, loving alarm, I read and heard what he put to paper (in a neatly precise, indeed dainty notation that betrayed no trace of carelessness), read what "his spirit and capercaillie" (or "caperkally" as he spelled it) prompted and demanded that he write. In a single breath, or better, breathlessness he wrote out the three pieces, of which one would have sufficed to make the year of its composition remarkable, and in fact began sketching out the Trio the same day he finished the *lento,* the last of the Quartet's movements to be composed. "I feel," he wrote to me, when at one point I was unable to visit him for two weeks, "as had I studied in Cracow"—a turn of phrase I did not understand right off, not until I recalled that it was at the University of Cracow where magic had been publicly taught in the sixteenth century.

I can assure the reader that I listened very attentively to such stylized forms of expression, which he had indeed always loved, but that now appeared more frequently than ever—or should I say "oftener times"?—in his letters and even in his spoken German. It would soon become clear why. My first hint came one day when my eye happened to catch a note left on his desk, where in broad pen strokes he had written the words: "Sorowe did move Dr. Faustum that he made writ of his lamentacion."

He saw what I saw and snatched the note away, saying, "Good sir and brother, what vain pertness is this!" For a long while afterward he kept from me the plan he was nursing on his own and intended to carry out with no man's aid. But from that moment on, I knew what I knew. Beyond all doubt, 1927, the year of the chamber music, was also the year when *The Lamentation of Doctor Faustus* was conceived. As unbelievable as it may sound, amid his struggle with tasks so highly complex that one can imagine their being achieved only with the most intense and all-excluding concentration, his mind was simultaneously looking ahead, testing, making contact, under the sign of his second oratorio—that crushing work of lament, from the commencement of which he was first to be distracted by an episode in his life as sweet as it was heart-rending.

XLIV

HAVING BORNE HER first three children one after the other in 1911, 1912, and 1913, Ursula Schneidewein, Adrian's sister in Langensalza, had suffered from lung problems and was forced to spend a few months in a sanatorium in the Harz Mountains. The upper-lobe catarrh seemed healed, and over the next ten years, until the birth of her youngest, little Nepomuk, Ursula was a happy and busy wife and mother, even though the years of hunger during and after the war never allowed her the full flower of health, so that she was troubled by frequent colds, which began as mere sniffles and then typically settled in the bronchi, and her appearance remained, if not sickly, then at least delicate and pale—although her kindly, cheerful, prudent ways did much to mask it.

The pregnancy of 1923 appeared to increase her vitality rather than to impair it. To be sure, she recovered only slowly from the delivery, and those troublesome fevers that had led to a stay in the sanatorium ten years previous flared up again. There was even talk at the time of her interrupting her duties as a housewife once more to receive appropriate therapy, but her symptoms faded again under the influence (or so I presume with some confidence) of the psychological benefits of maternal happiness, of the joy she took in her little son, who was the most lovable, quietly cheerful, easily tended baby in the world, and the valiant woman kept herself in good health for some years—until May 1928, when at age five Nepomuk came down with the measles, a bad case that severely taxed her energies as she anxiously nursed this exceptionally beloved child day and night. She herself suffered an attack of the same illness, in whose wake came fluctuations in temperature and a cough that would not go away, so that the doctor treating her categorically insisted on a sanatorium stay, which without any false optimism he estimated would last six months.

This brought Nepomuk Schneidewein to Pfeiffering. His sister Rosa, you see, was seventeen and like her brother Ezechiel, who was a year younger, was already working in the optical shop (whereas fifteen-year-old Raimund was still in school), but now, in her mother's absence, naturally she likewise had to assume her role of housekeeper for her father, and would in all probability be too busy to care for her little brother as well. Ursula had informed Adrian of how things stood, had written how the doctor thought it would be a happy solution if the convalescing child could spend some time in the country air of Upper Bavaria, and she asked him to gain his landlady's support for the idea of playing the part of mother or grandmother to the lad for a short while. Under Clementina's added persuasion, Else Schweigestill had been happy to agree, and so in the middle of June that year, while Johannes Schneidewein escorted his wife to the Harz Mountains, to the same sanatorium near Suderode that had done her such good once before, Rosa traveled south with her little brother and brought him to the bosom of her uncle's second parental home.

I was not present for the arrival of brother and sister at the farm, but Adrian described the scene for me—how the whole household, mother, daughter, eldest son, dairymaids, and farm hands, had gathered round the little boy and laughed happily in pure delight and could not get their fill of so much winsomeness. The women in particular, of course, were quite beside themselves, the country maids most blatantly of all, wringing their hands, bending down to the little fellow, crouching beside him, and crying, "Holy Mary, Joseph, and Jesus!" at the sight of the beautiful boy—while his indulgent big sister looked on, obviously expecting nothing else, having grown accustomed to everyone's falling in love with the youngest of her family.

Nepomuk, or "Nepo" as has family called him, or "Echo," as, with a whimsical bungling of consonants, he had called himself when he first began to babble, was dressed in a very simple summer outfit, nothing one would call city clothes: a white cotton short-sleeved shirt, very brief linen shorts, and well-worn leather shoes on his bare feet. Nevertheless, to behold him was the same as if one were gazing at an elfin prince. The graceful perfection of his little figure with its slender, well-formed legs; the indescribable charm of his small head, which was long but sturdy and topped by an innocent tangle of blond hair; facial

features, which though childish, somehow seemed strikingly finished
and definitive; the inexpressibly sweet and pure, yet deep and quizzi-
cal glance of clearest blue eyes from under long lashes—not even all
that was what evoked the sense of fairy tales, of a visitor from some
tinier, daintier, finer world. For added to this, there was the child's
stance and demeanor amid this circle of big people who laughed, uttered soft jubilant cries, sighed with emotion; there was his smile,
which of course was not free of a certain coquetry and an awareness of
his own magic; and there were his answers and statements, which had
about them a sweet hint of the instructive pedagogue; there was the
silvery voice in his little throat and there was that voice's speech,
which, intermixed with childish errors like "int" for "isn't," had the
lilt inherited from his father's speech, the same slightly deliberate,
slightly solemn and imposing Swiss drawl that his mother had adopted
early on, with its trilled *r* and droll hesitations between syllables like
"mud-dy" and "stud-dy," all of which the little lad accompanied with
explanatory gestures unlike any I have ever seen a child make—a
vaguely expressive use of arms and playful hands, which although
utterly charming often tended to make his meaning seem obscure and
enigmatic.

This then, in passing, is a description of Nepo Schneidewein, of
"Echo," as everyone at once took to calling him, following his own example—or as much a description as clumsily approximate words can
provide someone who was not present. How many writers before me
have lamented language's inadequacy at making things visible, at calling forth a truly precise likeness of an individual. Words are made for
praise and tribute, they have been granted the power to admire, to
marvel, to bless, and to characterize a phenomenon by the emotion it
arouses, but not to conjure it up, not to reproduce it. Rather than attempting a portrait of my darling subject, I shall probably do more for
him by confessing that even today, a good seventeen years later, tears
well up in my eyes at the thought of him, and at the same time I am
filled with a fundamentally strange, ethereal, not quite earthly joy
and serenity.

The answers, accompanied by enchanting gestures, that he provided
to questions about his mother, his trip, his stopover in the big city of
Munich, had, as noted, a decided Swiss lilt, and a good many dialect
words were wrapped in the silvery timbre of his voice: "cot" instead of
"house," "passing good" for "very fine," and "a titch" for "a little bit."
A preference for "indeed" was also evident, in phrases like "it was
pretty indeed," and other such oddities. And several worthy archaisms

from an older language likewise appeared in his speech; for instance, when there was something he could not recall, he would say, "'tis out of memory," or when he at last declared, "More new titings"—for "tidings"—"I do not know." He obviously said it simply because he wanted to break up the circle, for the very next words from his honey-sweet lips were "Echo doesn't think it proper to stay out o' doors now. It's only right he should go into the cot and greet his uncle."

And with that he put his little hand out to his sister for her to lead him inside. At that same moment, however, Adrian, who had been resting and had now put himself to rights, came out into the courtyard to bid his niece welcome.

"And this," he said, after greeting the young woman and declaring how much she looked like her mother, "is our new housemate?"

He took Nepomuk's hand and was swiftly caught up in the sweet light of the azure smile in those eyes that gazed up at him.

"Well, well," was all he said with a slow nod to the boy's escort, before turning back again to gaze at this sight. No one could fail to notice his emotion—including the child.

Yet there was nothing brash, but rather something courteously protective and artlessly calming about it, when in his first words to his uncle, Echo simply declared, as if to put matters on a smooth, friendly basis, "So you are glad I've come, aren't you."

Everyone laughed, Adrian as well.

"I should say so!" he replied. "And I hope you're glad to meet all of us."

"'Tis a right pleasurable meeting indeed," was the little boy's quaint reply.

Those standing around him were about to break into laughter once more, but Adrian put a finger to his lips and shook his head at them.

"We ought not," he said softly, "to confuse the child with laughter. There is no reason to laugh. What do you say, Mother Schweigestill?" he asked, turning toward her.

"No reason at all," she replied in an exaggeratedly firm voice and dabbed her eye with a corner of her apron.

"So let us go inside," he declared and took Nepomuk's hand again to lead him. "I'm sure you've prepared a little refreshment for your guests."

That she had. In the Winged-Victory room, Rosa Schneidewein was served coffee, the lad milk and cake. His uncle sat with him at the table and watched as he ate his snack neatly and daintily. Adrian made some conversation with his niece of course, but barely listened to what she said, being quite caught up in gazing at this elf—and likewise in discreetly holding his emotions in check so as to not make things awkward, an unnecessary concern, by the way, since Echo had long ago ceased to pay attention to silent admiration and spellbound glances. And in any event, it would have been sinful not to notice those eyes looking up in sweet thanks for a piece of cake or the preserves passed to him.

Finally the little fellow said the syllable "'nuff." That, as his sister explained, had long been his way of saying that he was full. Abbreviated baby talk for "I have had enough," for explaining that he wanted nothing more, the word "'nuff!" had lasted into the present. "'Nuff!" he said; and when hospitable Mother Schweigestill tried to force more on him, he declared with a certain lofty reasonableness, "Echo would rather do without."

He rubbed his eyes with his little fists, signaling that he was sleepy. He was put to bed, and while he slumbered Adrian spoke with the boy's sister Rosa in his study. She stayed for only three days; her duties in Langensalza called her home. When she left, Nepomuk cried a little, but then promised always to be "good" until she came to fetch him again. My God, as if he would not have kept his word! As if he were even capable of not keeping it! He brought something close to bliss, a constant cheering and tender warming of the heart, not just to the farm, but to the village as well, even to the town of Waldshut—where he was taken by the Schweigestills, mother and daughter, who, eager to be seen with him and certain of finding the same enchantment everywhere, presented him to the druggist, the grocer, the cobbler, so that he could repeat his little verses, always with that beguiling play of gestures and the most expressive drawling lilt: rhymes about Paul-on-Fire from "Shock-headed Peter," or about Jochen, who came home from play so "mud-dy" that it astounded Mrs. Duck and Mr. Drake and even put the pig into a deep "stud-dy." He folded his hands—held up a little distance from his face—and recited a prayer for the pastor of Pfeiffering, a queer old prayer, that began with the words, "There be no aide gainst timeful death"; and the man was so moved that he could only say, "Ah, thou babe of God, thou blessed one!" and pat the boy's hair with a white priestly hand and give him a brightly colored picture of the Lamb. And the teacher, as he told it later, had felt himself "a different man" when talking to him. In the market place and on the street, every third person inquired of Miss Clementina or Mother Schweigestill what this was that had fallen from heaven. As if dazed, people would say, "Why, look at that! Just look at that!" or in words not unlike the pastor's, "Ah, you sweet tyke, you blessed thing!" And women showed a general tendency to kneel beside Nepomuk.

When I next visited the farm, already two weeks had passed since his arrival; he had settled in and was known throughout the neighborhood. I saw him first from a distance; standing at the corner of the house, Adrian pointed him out to me as he sat all alone on the ground in the garden out back, among beds of strawberries and vegetables, one leg stretched out, the other half pulled up, strands of hair parted over his brow, studying, with what looked like rather detached enjoyment, a picture book his uncle had given him. He held it on his knees, his right hand resting on the margin. He turned the pages, however, with his little left arm and hand, and unconsciously held in that motion, they hovered there in an unbelievably graceful gesture, the hand with open palm in midair to the left of the book, so that I felt as if I had never seen a child sitting so charmingly (even in dreams my own would never have offered me such a sight!), and it occurred to me that the cherubs on high must turn the pages of their psalters in just that fashion.

We walked over so that I might make the acquaintance of this wonder of a lad. Collecting my pedagogical self, I firmly resolved that it be done nice and proper and vowed that I at least would show nothing out of the ordinary and would not fawn over him. To that end I furrowed my brow sternly, adopted a very deep voice, and spoke to him in that familiar, rough, patronizing tone of "Well, my lad? Being a good boy, are we? What are we up to here?"—but even as I put on such airs, I found myself utterly ridiculous; and the thing was that he noticed as much, obviously shared the feeling flooding through me, and in his embarrassment for me lowered his little head and pulled down the corners of his mouth like someone trying to suppress a laugh, which so completely undid me that for a long while I said absolutely nothing more.

He was not yet of an age when a boy has to stand up for adults and make his little bow, and, if any creature ever did, he surely deserved those tender privileges, that indulgent consecration we grant to those new to this earth, to strangers unversed in its ways. He told us we should "find a seat" (the Swiss way of asking someone to "sit down"); and so we did, with the elf between us on the grass, and joined him in looking at his picture book, which among the stock of children's literature offered in the shop had surely been among the most acceptable, with illustrations in the English taste, in a kind of Kate Greenaway style, and not half-bad rhymed verses, almost all of which Nepomuk

(I always called him that and never "Echo," which I was idiot enough to see as a kind of poetic coddling) already knew by heart and "read" to us, tracing the lines with his finger on the wrong spot.

The remarkable thing is that even today I still know these "poems" by heart myself, and only because I once—or might it have been several times?—heard them recited in his little voice with its marvelous accents. How well I still recall the one about the three organ grinders, who all end up on the same street corner, each angry at the other two, but no one willing to budge from the spot. I could recount for any child—although not remotely so well as Echo could—how the whole neighborhood was forced to endure the lovely racket they set up. The mice, they all began to fast, the rats all moved away! And then the ending goes:

> A puppy dog and no one else,
> was left once silence fell,
> but when the puppy got back home,
> he was not feeling well.

You had to have seen how the little fellow worriedly shook his head and to have heard how he lowered his voice in sorrow when telling about the sick puppy. Or you had to have observed the elegant *grandezza* with which he told of two odd little gentlemen meeting at the beach:

> Good morrow Mr. Caraway!
> I fear the swimming's bad today.

This was so for several reasons: first, because the water was so very wet and only forty-five degrees, but also because there were, it seems, "three guests from Sweden here":

> A swordfish, saw-fish, and a shark—
> Who've swum in close just for a lark.

He delivered these confidential warnings so drolly and made such big-eyes when counting off the three undesirable guests and had such a cozily eerie way of sharing the news that they had "swum in close" that we both laughed out loud. He looked directly into our faces, observing our mirth with roguish curiosity—particularly at mine, it seemed, since he probably wanted to check whether, for my own good, my preposterous dull and stern pedagogy had thawed out.

Good Lord, had it ever! After that first stupid attempt, I never reverted to it, except that I always addressed this little ambassador from the realm of childhood and elves as "Nepomuk" in a firm voice, and called him "Echo" only when his uncle spoke of him, since, like the women, he had picked up on that name. One can understand, however, that the teacher and mentor in me felt somewhat concerned, uneasy, indeed embarrassed when confronted by charms that admittedly were adorable, and yet subject to time and fated to ripen and fall prey to things of this earth. In a very short time the smiling sky-blue of those eyes would forfeit that primal purity from another world; the cherub-like face with its singular and explicit childishness, with its slightly cleft chin and enchanting mouth that revealed shimmering milk teeth when it smiled, but grew fuller at rest, and at whose corners were two softly contoured lines descending from the delicate nostrils to separate lips and chin from the cheeks—that face would become that of a more or less ordinary boy, whom one would have to handle in sober and prosaic fashion and who would no longer have any reason to greet such treatment with the irony with which Nepo had observed my own pedagogic approach. And yet there was something here—and that elfin mockery seemed to express an awareness of it—that made one incapable of believing in time, in its vulgar work and its power over this gracious presence; and that something was that presence's strange self-containment, its authority as the very presence of the Child on earth, the sense that it instilled of its having come down to us, of its being— to repeat myself—an adorable envoy, a sense that cradled reason in dreams beyond logic and with a tinge of our Christian heritage. That presence could not deny the inevitability of growth, but it found refuge in a conceptual sphere that is mythic and timeless, where all things are simultaneous and abide in parallel, where the male figure of the man is no contradiction to the babe in its mother's arms—which he likewise is, always is, forever raising his little hand in the sign of the cross to adoring saints.

What wild fancies! people will say. But all I can do is describe my experience and admit the profound awkwardness that this boy's gently floating existence always caused me. I should have patterned my behavior—and I did try to do so—on that of Adrian, who was not a schoolmaster, but an artist, and accepted things as they were, giving evidently no thought to their transience. In other words, he imparted to ineluctable becoming the character of being; he believed in the image, a belief that gave him a certain imperturbability and serenity of mind (or so it appeared to me at least)—and being accustomed to images, was not to be disconcerted by even the most unearthly of them. Echo, the elfin prince, had come—very well, one must treat him according to his nature, with no further fuss. That, it seemed to me, was Adrian's stand-point. Of course he had not the least inclination to furrow his brow and utter banalities like, "Well, my boy, being good, are we?" On the other hand, he left the ecstasy of, "Ah, you blessed child!" to the sim-ple folk outside. His attitude toward the boy was one of thoughtfully smiling or earnest tenderness, but with no fawning, no blandishments, not even expressions of affection. And in fact I never saw him caress the child in any way, hardly even smooth his hair. But he did like to walk hand in hand with him across the fields—that is true.

His conduct, to be sure, never dissuaded me from my observation that from the very first day he dearly loved his little nephew, that the boy's arrival had brought a radiant daylight into his life. It was all too obvious how the child's sweet, light, elfin charm clad in solemn old words and yet floating by, as it were, almost without a trace, had be-come for Adrian a deep, fervent, happy preoccupation that filled his days, although he had the boy with him only for an occasional hour or so, since of course it fell to the women to care for the lad—and since mother and daughter often had other things to do, he was also often left to himself in some safe spot. The measles had left him with that same strong need for sleep that very small children have, and he fre-quently yielded to it wherever he might happen to be, even outside the hours set apart for an afternoon nap. Whenever slumber overcame him, he would say, "Night!" just as he was accustomed to say before going to bed of an evening; but that was also his general word of fare-well, substituted for "Adieu!" or "Goodbye!" and repeated what-ever the time of day if he or someone else was leaving, the pendant to the "'Nuff!" with which he brought some pleasure to an end. Before going to sleep, whether lying in the grass or curled up in a chair, he would also put out his hand to shake as he said, "Night!"; and I once found Adrian in the back garden, sitting on a very narrow bench of three planks nailed together and watching Echo asleep at his feet. "He gave me his hand first," he declared when he looked up and saw me. For he had been unaware of my approach.

Else and Clementina Schweigestill reported to me that Nepomuk was the most well-behaved and obedient, least irritable child they had ever run across—which matched the accounts of his first days there. True, I saw him cry if he happened to hurt himself, but never heard him whine, snivel, or bawl the way unruly children do. That sort of thing was quite unthinkable with him. If he was reprimanded or forbidden to visit the horses at a time inconvenient for the stable boy or to join Waltpurgis in the cow stall, he accepted it with ready compliance, adding some consoling remark like, "a titch later, 'morrow morning maybe," intended, it seemed, less to comfort himself than the person who, very reluctantly to be sure, had denied him his request. Yes, he would even give that obstructive person a pat, as if to say, "Don't take it to heart. Next time you won't have to keep your own wishes in check and will let me do it."

It was the same when he was not allowed into the abbot's study to visit his uncle. He was very drawn to him, and it was already clear by the time I got to know Nepo only two weeks after his arrival that he was exceptionally fond of Adrian and strove to be in his company— most certainly also because Adrian's company was special and interesting and that of the women who tended him merely ordinary. How could he not have noticed that this man, his mother's brother, was accorded a unique and honored position among the rural folk of Pfeiffering, indeed was regarded with apprehension. Other people's reserve may have been precisely what spurred his childish ambition to be with his uncle. One cannot say, however, that Adrian was unqualifiedly receptive to the little boy's wishes. He might not see him for days, would not let him in, appeared to avoid him, to deny himself a sight he doubtlessly cherished. Then again he would spend long hours together with him, would take him, as I said, by the hand for long walks, as long as Adrian could reasonably demand of his tender companion, would wander with him in congenial silence or occasional chitchat through the moist lushness of the season in which Echo had arrived, amid the fragrance of black alder and lilac and at times of jasmine growing alongside the road, or would let the lightfoot lad precede him down narrow lanes, between walls of grain already ripening yellow for harvest, the eared stalks grown as tall as Nepomuk himself and nodding high above the soil.

Or perhaps I should say, "above the mold," for that was how the boy had announced his satisfaction that the "mizzle" had "whicknend the mold."

"The mizzle, Echo?" his uncle asked, having decided to let "whicknen" pass as some kind of baby talk.

"Yes, last night's mizzle," his hiking companion confirmed in somewhat more detail, but did not want to pursue the matter.

"Just think, he says things like 'whicknend' and 'mizzle,' Adrian reported wide-eyed to me on my next visit. "Isn't that peculiar?"

I could inform my friend that in some dialects "mizzle" had been a standard word for "light rain" well into the eighteenth century, and that "whicknen" or "quicknen" had once been just as common as "quicken."

"Yes, he comes from a long way off," Adrian said, nodding with a certain dazed acceptance.

When he had to go into the city, Adrian brought back gifts for the boy, all sorts of animals, a jack-in-the-box, a train that flashed its light as it sped around its oval track, a chest of magic tricks in which the most prized item was a glass of red wine that did not run out when you tipped it over. Echo was truly pleased by these gifts, but nevertheless quickly said "'nuff," once he had played with them, and much preferred his uncle to show him the grown-up objects he used himself and explain their function—always the same items, over and over, for children's persistence and appetite for repetition are great in matters of amusement. A letter opener made from a polished elephant tusk; the globe that spun on its own tilted axis and showed ragged continents engulfed in vast bluish oceans, slashed deep by bays, and dotted with bizarrely shaped inland seas; the chiming table clock, with a little crank for winding its weights back up from the depths to which they had sunk—those were a few of the curiosities the fine, slender lad wanted to examine when he would enter their owner's room and ask in his special voice:

"Are you cross with me 'cause I've come?"

"No, Echo, not especially cross. But the weights on the clock are only halfway down."

In this case it might have been a music box that he longed to see. It was my contribution; I had brought it for him: a little brown box with a key underneath for winding up its works. Then the little roll covered with metal nubs would turn past the tuned tines of a comb and play, at first with hurried delicacy, then ever more slowly, wearily, three nicely harmonized little Biedermeier melodies, to which Echo always listened with the same spellbound fascination, his eyes revealing an unforgettable mixture of amusement, wonder, and deepest reverie.

And he liked to look at his uncle's manuscripts, too, at those runes, some hollow, some black, all strewn across systems of lines and adorned with pennants and feathers, bound together with crooks and slashes, and wanted to have explained to him what all those symbols might be about—and, just between us, they were about him, and I would truly love to know whether he even vaguely surmised that, whether one could have read in his eyes that he understood as much from the *meister*'s explanations. This child, before all the rest of us, was allowed to gain some "idea" of the draft score of Ariel's songs from the *Tempest*, on which Leverkühn was secretly working at the time, having combined the first, "Come unto these yellow sands," sung by voices of nature all spookily scattered about, with the sweet purity of the last, "Where the bee sucks, there suck I," in a setting for soprano, celesta, muted violin, oboe, muted trumpet, and the flageolet tones of the harp—and truly anyone hearing these "gently spiriting" sounds, even if only with his mind's ear by reading them, may well ask with Ferdinand in the play, "Where should this music be? I' th' air or th' earth?" For he who had framed it had captured in his whispering gossamer web not only the floating, childlike grace and bafflingly deft lightness of "my dainty Ariel," but also that whole world of elves of hills, brooks, and groves, those weak masters and demipuppets, as Prospero describes them, whose pastime by moonshine is to make midnight mushrooms and green sour ringlets whereof the ewe not bites.

Echo always asked to see the place in the score where the dog goes "bowwow" and the chanticleer cries "cock-a-diddle-dow." And Adrian told him about the damned witch Sycorax and her little servant, whom, because he was too delicate a spirit to act her earthy commands, she confined in a cloven pine, in which rift he remained imprisoned for a dozen painful years until the good magician came and freed him. Nepomuk wanted to know how old the little spirit was when he was trapped inside the tree, and how old he was when he was freed again after twelve years; but his uncle told him that the little spirit had no age, but was the same delicate child of the air both before and after his imprisonment—which seemed to satisfy Echo.

The master of the abbot's study told him other fairy tales, too, as well as he could remember them: about Rumpelstiltskin, about Fallada and Rapunzel, about the Lilting, Leaping Lark; and of course the boy always wanted to climb on his uncle's knee to listen, would sit there sideways, sometimes wrapping his little arm around Adrian's neck. "'Tis a wondrous ring it all has," Nepomuk might say when a story was ended, but would often fall asleep before then, his head nestled against the storyteller's chest—who would sit there for a long time, never stirring, his chin resting on the hair of the slumbering boy, until one of the women came to fetch Echo.

As I said, Adrian sometimes kept the boy at a distance for days, whether because he was busy or because a migraine forced him to seek out silence, and indeed darkness, or for whatever reason. But especially on days when he had not seen Echo, of an evening after the child had been put to bed, he liked to step softly, scarcely noticed into the child's room and listen to the boy's prayers, which he said lying on his back, with the palms of his hands pressed together before his chest and with one or both of his nurses, Frau Schweigestill and her daughter, standing by. These were curious blessings, which he recited most expressively, the heavenly blue of his eyes turned toward the ceiling; and he had quite a number of them at his disposal, so that he hardly ever said the same one two evenings in a row. It should be noted that he pronounced the word "God" like "Goad" and liked to place an initial *s* in front of "which," "when," and "while," so that he would say:

> For whoso heedeth Goad's command,
> He liveth well in Goad's good hand.
> Swhen I obey my Goad's behest,
> I help myself to Goad's good rest. Amen.

Or:

> So be man's wrong how ever great,
> The grace of Goad hath larger weight.
> At sin, swhich hath a narrow space,
> My Goad doth smile, so wide His grace. Amen.

Or this prayer, remarkable for its unmistakable coloring of predestination:

> No man be given leave to sin
> But that there be some good therein.
> No man's good deed will be forlorn,
> Save that to hell he hath been born.
> May those I love all-ready be
> Made blissful for eternity! Amen.

Or on occasion:

> The sun doth shine upon the Deil
> Yet after spends its purest weal.
> Keep Thou me pure on earth each day,
> Till death's great toll I sometime pay. Amen.

Or finally:

> Mark that another's prayer is fit
> To save the prayer's soul with it.
> Swhile Echo prayeth for mankind,
> In Goad's good arms is he entwined. Amen.

I myself was profoundly touched to hear him recite this last verse, although I do not believe he was aware of my presence.

"What do you think of that theological speculation?" Adrian asked me as we stepped outside. "He's praying for all creation expressly so that he may be included himself. Should a pious child really know that he serves himself by praying for others? Selflessness is surely negated the moment one realizes that it serves one's own purposes."

"You're right to that extent," I replied. "But then he turns it back into selflessness, since he may not pray just for himself without praying for us all."

"Yes, for us all," Adrian said softly.

"In any case," I continued, "we're speaking as if he had thought these ideas up himself. Have you ever asked him where he got them? From his father or someone else perhaps?"

His answer was: "Oh no, I'd rather let the matter rest and assume he couldn't tell me anyway."

It appeared that the Schweigestill women felt the same. To my knowledge, they never asked the child how he had come by his evening verses, either. Those that I did not hear from the door myself, I have from them. I had them recite them for me when the day came that Nepomuk Schneidewein was no longer with us.

XLV

H E WAS TAKEN from us, that creature of strange grace was taken from this earth—ah, my God, why do I seek gentle words for the most inconceivable cruelty that I have ever witnessed, that even today goads my heart to bitter complaint, indeed to revolt. With horrible savagery and fury he was seized and snatched away within days by an illness of which there had not been a single case in the region for a long time, although good Dr. Kürbis, who was utterly amazed at the violence of the disease's recurrence, said that children recovering from the measles or whooping cough were probably susceptible to it.

It all lasted barely two weeks, including early tokens of a change in his state of health, even the earliest of which prompted no one—I truly believe, no one—to have the least suspicion of the horror to come. It was the middle of August and harvest, which required the hiring of additional hands, was in full swing. For two months Nepomuk had been the joy of the house. Sniffles now dulled the sweet clarity of his eyes—and surely it was only this annoying infection that robbed him of his appetite, made him irritable, and increased the sleepiness to which he had tended for as long as we had known him. He said "'nuff" to everything he was offered, to food, to games, to looking at pictures, to listening to fairy tales. "'Nuff!" he said, wincing and turning away. Soon, then, there developed an intolerance of light and sound—more disquieting than his previous moodiness. He appeared to be excessively sensitive to the noise of wagons pulling into the farmyard, to the sound of voices. "Speak softly!" he begged in a whisper, as if to set an example. He did not even want to hear the daintily tinkling music box, was quick to speak his tormented "'nuff, 'nuff!" and stopping it with his own hand, would break into bitter tears. And so he would flee the summer sunshine of farmyard and garden, seek out his room, sit there bent over, rubbing his eyes. It was hard to watch as he would search for relief, going from one person who loved him to another, give a hug, and then, having found no comfort, quickly move on. He clung to Mother Schweigestill, to Clementina, to Waltpurgis the dairymaid, and the same impulse brought him to his uncle on several occasions. He pressed against Adrian's breast, looking up at him, listening to the gentle, soothing words, even smiling weakly perhaps; but then, letting his little head drop deeper and deeper bit by bit, he would murmur "Night!"—and sliding to his feet, softly stumble from the room.

The doctor came to look at him. He gave him nose drops and prescribed a tonic, but did not conceal his conjecture that a more serious illness might be in the offing. He also expressed this concern in the abbot's study, to his patient of many years.

"Do you think so?" Adrian asked, turning pale.

"There's something about it that's not quite right," the doctor said.

"Not quite right?"

The phrase was repeated in such a terrified and almost terrifying tone that Kürbis asked himself if he might not have gone a bit too far.

"Well yes, in the sense I meant it," he responded. "You could be looking better yourself, my good sir. Awfully fond of the little tyke, aren't you?"

"Indeed I am," came the answer. "It is a responsibility, doctor. The child was entrusted to our keeping here in the country for his health. . . ."

"The symptoms of illness, if one can even put it that way," the physician replied, "offer no basis for a distressing diagnosis. I'll come back tomorrow."

He did and could now provide a diagnosis of the case with only all too great a certainty. Nepomuk had had an abrupt eruption of vomiting, and along with a moderately high fever came headaches that inside of a few hours had grown obviously unbearable. When the doctor arrived, the child had already been put to bed and was holding his little head between his hands and emitting cries that often lasted until his breath gave out—a torture for anyone who heard them, and one heard them all through the house. Between cries he would reach out his little hands to those around him and wail, "Help! Help! Oh head ache! Head ache!" Then a new savage vomiting spell would rend him, until he sank back again twitching violently.

Kürbis examined the child's eyes, whose pupils had become very small and displayed a tendency to squint. The pulse was rapid. Muscle contractions and the onset of stiffness in the neck were evident. It was brain fever, cerebrospinal meningitis—and wretchedly drawing his head to one shoulder, the good man spoke the words, presumably in hopes his audience would be unaware that his science was forced to admit almost total helplessness in the face of this dreadful infection. A hint of that lay in his suggestion that they might perhaps inform the child's parents by telegram. The presence of the mother would probably have a calming effect on their little patient. Moreover he demanded an internist be brought in from the capital, with whom he wished to share responsibility for this unfortunately rather critical case. "I am a simple man," he said. "It is wise to summon a higher authority." I believe there was sad irony in his words. He did, however, trust himself to perform an immediate spinal puncture, which was necessary to confirm the diagnosis and also the only means by which to provide the sick child some relief. Frau Schweigestill, pale but energetic and loyal as always to her humane principles, held the whimpering child as he lay crouched in bed, his chin and knees almost touching, and Kürbis inserted his needle between separated vertebrae, driving it into the spinal canal, from which liquid emerged drop by drop. Almost immediately the maddening headache abated. If it should return, the doctor said—and he knew that it had to return within a few hours, since the easing of pressure brought about by tapping cerebral fluid would last only that long—they should apply the obligatory ice pack and give the chloral that he would prescribe and that was fetched from the county seat.

Roused by renewed vomiting, by convulsions that seized his little body and pain that split his skull, Nepomuk awoke from the sleep of exhaustion into which he had fallen after the spinal tap and again took up his heart-rending laments and shrill cries—the typical "hydrocephalic cry," against which only a doctor's heart is tolerably armed, precisely because he sees it as typical. We react coolly to what is typical and are beside ourselves only when we recognize the individual case. That is the calmness of science. It did not deter its rural disciple from moving very quickly from the initial prescribed doses of bromide and chloral to morphine, with somewhat better results. He may have decided to do so as much for the sake of those who lived in the house— and I have one person in particular in mind—as out of pity for the tormented child. The tapping of fluid could be repeated only once every twenty-four hours, and the relief lasted only two. Twenty-two hours of the screaming, writhing torture of a child—of this child, who folds his trembling little hands and stammers, "Echo will be good, Echo will be good!" Let me say in addition that for those who saw Nepomuk, perhaps the most terrible thing was a secondary symptom—the way his heavenly eyes dimmed, squinting tighter and tighter, the result of a paralysis of the eye muscles associated with the stiffening of the neck. This, however, caused that sweet face to look strangely, horribly deformed; and especially when accompanied by fits of teeth-gnashing that were soon part of the affliction, the impression created was that of a child possessed.

The next afternoon the consulting authority, Professor von Rothenbuch, arrived from Munich, having been fetched from Waldshut by Gereon Schweigestill. Adrian had selected him, on the basis of reputation, from among those suggested by Kürbis. He was a tall, urbane man, whom the erstwhile king had personally raised to the nobility, whose expensive services were much in demand, and who had one eye that was half-closed, as if always engaged in examination. He objected to the morphine because it could simulate a coma, which had "not ensued as yet," and permitted only codeine. Apparently he was concerned above all with the case's progressing clearly through each of its distinctive stages. As for the rest, upon concluding his examination, he confirmed the directives his bowing and scraping rural colleague had given: The room was to be darkened, the head kept raised and cool, and utmost care taken when touching the little patient; alcohol rubs for the skin, a diet of concentrated nourishment, which it would probably become necessary to administer through a tube inserted up the nose. Presumably because he was not in the home of the child's parents, his consolations were of the candid and explicit sort. It would not be long before consciousness clouded—legitimately, and not prematurely as the result of morphine—and the coma quickly deepened. The child would then suffer less and ultimately not at all. One ought not, therefore, be all too distressed even by gross symptoms. After being good enough to perform the second spinal tap himself, he took his dignified leave and did not return.

Although kept informed of these sad events by daily telephone calls from Mother Schweigestill, I for my part did not arrive in Pfeiffering until Saturday, the fourth day after the disease's full eruption, when, amid raging seizures that tortured the little body as if upon the rack and caused the child's eyes to roll back in his head, the coma had already set in; the cries had fallen silent, only the teeth-gnashing continued. Frau Schweigestill, her face weary from lack of sleep, her eyes swollen from tears, received me at the gate and urgently suggested I go at once to Adrian. The poor child—and by the way, his parents had been with him since last night—well, I would see him soon enough. But the Herr Doctor was in sore need of my support, he wasn't doing well, and just between us, it seemed to her at times as if he were talking crazy.

Alarmed, I went to him. He was sitting at his desk and as I entered looked up with only a fleeting and, as it were, disparaging glance. Frightfully pale, he had the same reddened eyes of everyone in the house, and although his mouth was closed, his tongue flicked back and forth mechanically against his lower lip.

"You, good man," he said after I had walked over to him and laid a hand on his shoulder, "what do you want here? This is no place for you. At least make your sign of the cross, from brow to shoulders, the way you learned to do as a child for your protection."

And when I spoke a few words of comfort and hope, he interrupted me gruffly and said, "Spare yourself your humanist humbug! He is taking him. If only He would be quick about it. Perhaps He can be no quicker, given His wretched means."

And he jumped up, leaned against the wall, and pressed the back of his head against the wainscoting.

"Take him, monster!" he called out in a voice that chilled me to the marrow. "Take him, filthy blackguard, but make haste if You will not concede even this, scoundrel. I had thought," he said in a suddenly low and confidential voice, turning to me, stepping forward, and staring at me with a forlorn look I shall never forget, "that He would permit it, might allow this after all. But no, where should He, being far from grace, find grace, and in His beastly rage He surely had to crush this above all else. Take him, scum!" he shouted, stepping back from me again, as if upon a cross. "Take his body, over which You have dominion. But You will have to be content to leave his sweet soul to me—and that is Your impotence and Your absurdity, for which I shall laugh You to scorn for eons. And may eternities be rolled twixt my place and his, I will yet know that he is in the place from whence You, foul filth, were cast out. And that will be cooling water upon my tongue and a hosanna to mock You in my foulest curse!"

He covered his face with his hands, turned away, and pressed his brow against the wood.

What could I say? Or do? How was I to respond to such words? "Dear friend, for heaven's sake calm down, you're beside yourself, pain has you imagining crazy things," is what one says, more or less, and out of concern for psychological needs, especially in the case of such a man, one doesn't even think of physical calmatives and sedatives, of the bromides that were in the house.

But in response to my consoling pleas, he simply said, "Spare yourself, spare yourself and make the sign of the cross! Things are happening up there. Make it not only for yourself, but for me, too, and for my guilt! What guilt, what a sin, what a crime"—and he was sitting at his desk again, pressing his fists to his temples—"that we let him come, that I let him get near me, that I let my eyes feast on him! Surely you know that children are made of delicate stuff, are all too receptive to poisonous influences. . . ."

And now in point of fact it was I who shouted and in my outrage forbade such talk.

"Adrian, no!" I cried. "What are you doing to yourself, torturing yourself with absurd self-incriminations for a blind stroke of fate that could have overtaken that sweet child—for this world perhaps all too sweet a child—wherever he might be. It may rend our hearts, but it should not rob us of our reason. You have shown him nothing but love and kindness. . . ."

He just waved me aside. I sat with him for perhaps an hour, spoke softly to him now and again, but could barely understand his muttered answers. Then I said that I wanted to visit our patient.

"Do that," he replied, and added hardheartedly, "but don't talk to him the way you did that day with your 'Well, my boy, being good, are we' and so on. First because he cannot hear you, and second, because it's surely an offense against good humanist taste in general."

I made to leave, but he held me back, calling after me by my last name, "Zeitblom!"—which likewise sounded very hard.

And as I turned around he said, "I have discovered that it ought not be."

"What ought not be, Adrian?"

"The good and the noble," he replied, "what people call human, even though it is good and noble. What people have fought for, have stormed citadels for, and what people filled to overflowing have announced with jubilation—it ought not be. It will be taken back. I shall take it back."

"I don't quite understand, my dear fellow. What do you want to take back?"

"The Ninth Symphony," he replied. And then came nothing more, even though I waited.

Bewildered and grief-stricken, I proceeded to the fateful room. The atmosphere of a sickroom, close and heavy with medicine, sterile but stale, predominated despite open windows. The shutters had been closed to a mere crack. Nepomuk's bed was surrounded by several people, with whom I shook hands, all the while directing my eyes toward the dying child. He lay on his side, doubled up, elbows and knees tucked tight. His cheeks flushed, he would take a deep breath—and then there was a long wait until the next breath. The eyes were not completely shut, but between the lashes nothing of the blue of the iris could be seen, only the black of the pupils, which had grown larger and larger, though each to a different size, until they had almost swallowed up the flash of color. Yet it was good still to see some reflective blackness. For at times it would turn white inside the slit, and then the little arms would press more tightly to the child's flanks and a grinding spasm, horrid to behold, but perhaps no longer painful, would wrench the little limbs.

His mother sobbed. I had pressed her hand and did so again now. Yes, she was there, Ursel, the brown-eyed daughter of Buchel Farm, Adrian's sister, and I was touched by how much the woebegone features of her now thirty-eight-year-old face reminded me more than ever of the old-fashioned German features of Jonathan Leverkühn's face. With her was her husband, to whom the telegram had been sent and who had fetched her from Suderode: Johannes Schneidewein, a tall, handsome, simple man with a blond beard, Nepomuk's blue eyes, and the homely imposing manner of speech that Ursula had adopted from him early on and whose rhythm we had known in the sound of an elfin voice, Echo's voice.

Also in the room, besides Frau Schweigestill who was constantly moving to and fro, was frizzy-haired Kunigunde Rosenstiel, who, on one of the visits allowed her, had made the boy's acquaintance and passionately taken him to her melancholy heart. At that time she had written Adrian a long letter describing her impressions in impeccable German and typed, with commercial ampersands, on her crude firm's stationery. Having chased our Nackedey from the field, she had managed to gain the right to relieve the Schweigestills and, finally, Ursel Schneidewein as a nurse for the child—changing his ice pack, bathing him with alcohol, attempting to administer medicines and juices—and did not gladly, indeed seldom, let anyone take her place at his bedside at night.

Exchanging few words, we—the Schweigestills, Adrian, his relatives, Kunigunde, and I—sat together in the Winged-Victory room to eat our supper, during which one of the women frequently got up to check on the patient. Hard as it was to do so, I had to leave Pfeiffering on Sunday afternoon. I still had a whole stack of Latin tests to correct for Monday. With gentle wishes on my lips, I said goodbye to Adrian, and I preferred the way he took his leave then to the way he had received me the day before.

With a sort of smile he said, in English, "Then to the elements. Be free, and fare thou well!"

Then he abruptly turned away from me.

Nepomuk Schneidewein, Echo, the child, Adrian's last love, passed away twelve hours later. His parents took the little coffin back home with them.

XLVI

For almost four weeks now I have added nothing to this account, having been stayed first by a kind of psychological exhaustion that followed in the wake of the foregoing memories, and at the same by current events whose headlong, logical progression was predictable, in some sense even yearned for, but that nonetheless arouse incredulous dismay—events that our unhappy nation, sapped by misery and dread, is incapable of grasping and endures with apathetic fatalism, events before which even my heart, weary with old sadness, old horror, has proved helpless.

Since the end of March now—and the date today is 25 April in this year of destiny 1945—our nation's defenses in the west have plainly been in total disarray. Newspapers, already half-unshackled, record the truth; rumor, fed by the enemy's radio broadcasts and by the stories of those who have fled, knows no censorship and has carried the particulars of this rapidly expanding catastrophe to regions of the Reich that have not yet been swallowed up in it, not yet liberated by it—even to my refuge here. There is no stopping it: surrender on all sides, everyone scattering. Our shattered and devastated cities fall like ripe plums. Darmstadt, Würzburg, Frankfurt have succumbed. Mannheim and Kassel, even Münster, Leipzig—they all obey strangers now. One day, there the English stood in Bremen, the Americans in Hof in Upper Franconia. Nuremberg—the city of state ceremonials for the uplifting of unwise hearts—surrendered. Among the regime's great men, who wallowed in power, riches, and injustice, suicide rages, passing its sentence.

Russian troops, a million-man army free to force the Oder line once it had taken Königsberg and Vienna, advanced against the Reich's capital city (lying in rubble, abandoned by all government officials), and having completed with heavy artillery a judgment long since executed from the air, they are presently nearing the core of the city. That hideous man who was the target last year of a plot laid by desperate patriots attempting to salvage some last bit of national fortune, some future, but who escaped with his life—to be sure, now only an insanely flickering, fluttering life—ordered his soldiers to drown the attack on Berlin in a sea of blood and to shoot any officer who talks of surrender. The order has been obeyed many times over. Simultaneously, strange radio reports (broadcast in German, but likewise no longer of quite sound mind) ramble about the ether—both those that commend the populace (even the "much-maligned" agents of the Gestapo) to the magnanimity of the victors and those that offer reports of a "freedom movement" christened with the name "Werwolf," a unit of berserk boys who, by hiding in the forests to burst forth at night, have already rendered the fatherland meritorious service by doughtily murdering many an intruder. Oh what wretched grotesquery! And so, to the bitter end, the crudest fairy tale, that grim substratum of saga deep in the soul of the nation, is still invoked—not without finding a familiar echo.

Meanwhile a transatlantic general has the inhabitants of Weimar file past the crematoria of their local concentration camp and declares (should one say, unjustly?) that they, citizens who went about their business in seeming honesty and tried to know nothing, though at times the wind blew the stench of burned human flesh up their noses— declares that they share in the guilt for these horrors that are now laid bare and to which he forces them to direct their eyes. Let them look— I shall look with them, in my mind's eye I let myself be jostled along in those same apathetic, or perhaps shuddering, lines. Our thick-walled torture chamber, into which Germany was transformed by a vile regime of conspirators sworn to nihilism from the very start, has been burst open, and our ignominy lies naked before the eyes of the world, of foreign commissions, to whom these incredible scenes are displayed on all sides now and who report home that the hideousness of what they have seen exceeds anything the human imagination can conceive. I repeat, our ignominy. For is it mere hypochondria to tell oneself that all that is German—even German intellect, German thought, the German word—shares in the disgrace of these revelations and is plunged into profoundest doubt? Is it morbid contrition to ask oneself the question: How can "Germany," whichever of its forms it may be allowed to take in the future, so much as open its mouth again to speak of mankind's concerns?

One can call what came to light here the dark possibilities within human nature in general—but it was in fact tens of thousands, hundreds of thousands of Germans who committed the acts before which humanity shudders, and whatever lived as German stands now as an abomination and the epitome of evil. What will it be like to belong to a nation whose history bore this gruesome fiasco within it, a nation that has driven itself mad, gone psychologically bankrupt, that admittedly despairs of governing itself and thinks it best that it become a colony of foreign powers, a nation that will have to live in isolated confinement, like the Jews of the ghetto, because the dreadfully swollen hatred all around it will not permit it to step outside its borders—a nation that cannot show its face?

Damn, damn those corruptors who taught their lessons in evil to an originally honest, law-abiding, but all too docile people, a people all too happy to live by a theory! How good that curse feels, how good it would feel if it arose freely and unqualifiedly from the heart! A patriotism, however, that would boldly proclaim that the bloody state whose gasping agonies we are now experiencing, that "saddled itself" (to use Luther's expression) with untold crimes, a state whose bellowing proclamations and announcements canceling human rights swept the masses up into enraptured frenzy, and under whose garish banners our youth marched with flashing eyes, brazenly proud and firm in their faith—a patriotism that would proclaim that such a state was forced upon us as something without roots in our nature as a people, something totally alien to us, such a patriotism would, so it seems to me, be more high-minded than conscientious. Was not this regime, both in word and deed, merely the distorted, vulgarized, debased realization of a mindset and worldview to which one must attribute a characteristic authenticity and which, not without alarm, a Christianly humane person finds revealed in the traits of our great men, in the figures of the most imposing embodiments of Germanness? I ask—and am I asking too much? Ah, it is probably more than a mere question that for that very reason this defeated nation now stands wild-eyed before the abyss, because its final and most extreme attempt to find its own political form is perishing in such ghastly failure.

*

HOW SINGULARLY THE years in which I write now close ranks with those that frame this biography! Because the last years of my hero's intellectual life, the two years 1929 and 1930—following the collapse of his marriage plans, the loss of his friend, and his having had that marvelous child who had come to him snatched from him—belong in fact to the ascent and spread of that usurping power now perishing in blood and flames.

For Adrian Leverkühn these were years of highly excited and enormous—one is tempted to say, monstrous—creative activity, a kind of tumult that swept even sympathetic bystanders before it, and one could not avoid the impression that it was intended as payment, as compensation for his having been deprived of happiness in life, for having been denied permission to love. I speak of years, but that is incorrect—only a fraction of them, only the second half of one and a few months of the next, sufficed for the ripening of the work, his last and indeed in a historical sense somehow final and ultimate work: the symphonic cantata, *The Lamentation of Dr. Faustus*, the plan for which, as I have already revealed, preceded Nepomuk Schneidewein's stay in Pfeiffering. And to it I now devote the poor power of my words.

But first I dare not neglect to shed some light on the personal state of its creator, age forty-four at the time, on his appearance and way of life as it presented itself to my ever anxious observation. And what immediately comes to mind and paper is the fact that, as I noted by way of preparation quite early on in these pages, his face, which had so openly displayed his resemblance to his mother as long as it was smooth-shaven, had recently been altered by the growth of a dark beard sprinkled with gray, a kind of imperial that had a narrow drooping moustache above and that, although it did not leave the cheeks bare, was thicker at the chin—yet not like a goatee, since it was heavier at the sides than in the middle. This partial covering of his facial features was off-putting, and yet one accepted it, because together with a growing tendency to carry his head tilted to one shoulder, the beard lent his countenance a kind of spiritualized suffering, indeed, something Christlike. I could not help loving that expression, and I believed it all the more deserving of my sympathy because it plainly did not indicate weakness, but rather coincided with both an extremely energetic will and a state of good health so unexceptionable that my friend could not praise it enough to me. He did so in that somewhat sluggish, at times halting, at times slightly monotone manner of speech that I had noticed with him of late and that I gladly interpreted as a token of productive sobriety, of self-control in the midst of an overpowering whirl-

wind of creative ideas. The physical harassment whose victim he had
been for so long—the gastric catarrhs, the throat infections, the agonizing migraine attacks—had vanished. He could be certain of each
day, of the freedom to work, and he himself declared his health to be
perfection, a triumph; the visionary energy with which he rose each
day to his labors could be read—and it filled me with pride and yet
again gave me cause to fear relapses—in his eyes, which previously had
usually been half-veiled by the lids, but which now were open wider,
almost exaggeratedly so, allowing one to see a band of white above the
iris. This could appear somehow menacing, all the more so, since such
a wide-eyed gaze had a kind of rigidity about it, or should I say, one
noticed a kind of standstill, over whose nature I puzzled for a long
while, until I realized that it was caused by the pupils, which were not
perfectly round, but somewhat irregularly lengthened, and always
stayed the same size, as if they were not subject to the influence of any
change in light.

I am speaking here of a more or less secret and interior immobility,
which could be perceived only by a very careful observer. This was
contradicted by another, far more noticeable and external phenomenon—even dear Jeannette Scheurl noticed it during a visit with Adrian
and, quite unnecessarily, called it to my attention afterward. This was a
recently acquired habit of moving the eyes rapidly back and forth
(more or less equally to either side), to "roll" his eyes, as people say, at
certain moments, when pondering something, for instance—which
one could imagine might well alarm many people. And that is why,
even though I found it rather easy (and I seem to recall that I did find
it easy) to ascribe such, admittedly eccentric, peculiarities to his work
and the enormous strain it put him under, I was nevertheless secretly
relieved that hardly anyone beside myself ever saw him—precisely because I feared he might alarm people. In reality, all social visits to the
city had ceased for him. Invitations were declined on the telephone by
his faithful landlady, or were simply left unanswered. Even hasty practical trips to Munich for shopping and such had come to an end, and
those undertaken for buying toys for the dead child may well have
been the last. Garments previously worn in public, when he attended
dinner parties or other social affairs, now hung unused in his
wardrobe, and his clothes were of the simplest homely sort—not so
much as a dressing gown, which he had never liked to wear, not even
of a morning, and only threw on when he got up in the night to spend
an hour or two in his chair. A loose woolen jacket, a kind of peacoat
that buttoned high and thus required no cravat, worn with any old pair

of equally loose and unironed, small-checked trousers—that was his constant attire in those days, including for his customary, indeed requisite, lung-expanding walks. One might even have spoken of a neglect of his appearance, had such an impression not been curbed by the natural distinction that came with his intellect.

And for whom should he have gone to any trouble? He saw Jeannette Scheurl, with whom he worked through certain seventeenth-century scores she had brought him (I recall a chaconne by Jacopo Melani that literally anticipates a passage in *Tristan*); from time to time he saw Rüdiger Schildknapp, he of the same-color eyes, with whom he could laugh—though I cannot refrain from the mournfully bleak observation that only the same-colored eyes remained now, the black and the blue had vanished. . . . And, finally, he saw me whenever I spent a weekend with him—and that was all. Moreover, it was only for a few short hours that he had any use whatever for company, for he worked eight hours a day, even on Sunday (which he had never "kept holy"); and since his day also included an afternoon rest in the dark, I was left very much to myself during my visits to Pfeiffering. As if I had any regrets! I was near him and near the creation of a work loved despite pain and shudders, a work that has lain there for a decade and a half, a dead, banned, concealed treasure, whose revival may at last be brought about by the destructive liberation we now endure. There were years when we children of the dungeon dreamt of a song of joy—*Fidelio*, the Ninth Symphony—with which to celebrate Germany's liberation, its liberation of itself. But now only this work can be of any use, and it will be sung from our soul: the lamentation of the son of hell, the most awful lament of man and God ever intoned on this earth, which begins with its central character, but steadily expanding, encompasses, as it were, the cosmos.

A lament, a wailing! A *de profundis* that with fond fervor I can say has no parallel. But from a creative viewpoint, from the viewpoint both of music history and personal fulfillment, is there not something jubilant, some high triumph in this terrible gift for redress and compensation? Does it not imply the kind of "breakthrough," which, whenever we contemplated and discussed the destiny of art, its state and crisis, had so often been a topic for us, as a problem, as a paradoxical possibility? Does it not imply the recovery, or, though I would rather not use the word, for the sake of precision I shall, the reconstruction of expression, of emotion's highest and deepest response to a level of intellectuality and formal rigor that must first be achieved in order for such an event—the reversal, that is, of calculated coldness into an expres-

sive cry of the soul, into the heartfelt unbosoming of the creature—
to occur?

I clothe in questions what is nothing more than the description of a
state of affairs whose explanation is found in both objective reality and
formal artistry. The lament, you see—and we are dealing here with a
constant, inexhaustibly heightened lament, accompanied by the most
painful *Ecce homo* gestures—the lament is expression *per se*, one might
boldly say that all expression is in fact lament, just as at the beginning
of its modern history, at the very moment it understands itself as expression, music becomes a lament, a *"Lasciatemi morire,"* the lament
of Ariadne, softly echoed in the plaintive song of the nymphs. It is not
without good reason that the *Faustus* cantata is stylistically linked so
strongly and unmistakably to Monteverdi and the seventeenth century,
whose music—again not without good reason—favored echo effects,
at times to the point of mannerism. The echo, the sound of the human
voice returned as a sound of nature, revealed as a sound of nature, is in
essence a lament, nature's melancholy "Ah, yes!" to man, her attempt
to proclaim his solitude, just as vice versa, the nymphs' lament is, for
its part, related to the echo. In Leverkühn's final and loftiest creation,
however, echo, that favorite device of the baroque, is frequently employed to unutterably mournful effect.

A monumental work of lamentation like this one is, I say, by necessity an expressive work, a work of expression, and as such is a work of
liberation in much the same way as the early music to which it is linked
across the centuries sought to express liberation. Except that at the developmental level that this work occupies, the dialectic process by
which strictest constraint is reversed into the free language of emotion,
by which freedom is born out of constraint, appears infinitely more
complicated, infinitely more perplexing and marvelous in its logic than
was the case in the days of the madrigalists. I wish here to direct the
reader back to a conversation I had with Adrian during a stroll beside
the Cattle Trough on a day now long past, the day of his sister's marriage at Buchel, when under the pressure of a headache he elaborated
for me his notion of "strict style," deriving it from the manner in
which both the melody and harmony of the song "O sweet maiden,
how bad you are," were determined by a permutation of its basic motif of five notes, the symbolic letters H–E–A–E–Es. He allowed me to
perceive the "magic square" of a style or technique that develops the
utmost variety out of materials that are always identical, a style in
which there is nothing that is not thematic, nothing that could not
qualify as a variation of something forever the same. This style, this

technique, as it was called, permitted no note, not one, that did not fulfill its thematic function within the overarching structure—free notes
would no longer exist.

Now, in my attempt to present some idea of Leverkühn's apocalyptic oratorio, did I not refer to the substantial identity of what is most
blessed and most heinous, to the inner sameness of its children's angelic chorus and hell's laughter? To the mystic horror of those who can
hear it, what is realized there is a formal utopia of terrifying ingenuity,
which now becomes universal in the *Faust* cantata, taking possession
of the entire work and allowing it, if I may put it that way, to be totally
consumed by its thematic element. This gigantic *lamento* (lasting approximately an hour and a quarter) is, properly speaking, undynamic,
lacking development and without drama, in much the same way as
when a stone is cast into water the concentric circles that spread farther
and farther, one around the other, are without drama and always the
same. A single immense variation on lamentation (and as such, nega-
tively related to the finale of the Ninth Symphony with its variations
on jubilation), it expands in rings, each inexorably drawing the others
after it: movements, grand variations, which correspond to textual
units or chapters in the book and yet in and of themselves are once
again nothing but sequences of variations. All of them refer back, as if
to the theme, to a highly plastic basic figure of notes inspired by a particular passage of the text.

It will be recalled that in the old chapbook, which tells of the life and
death of the grand magician and which, with a few resolute modifica-
tions of its chapters, Leverkühn arranged as the basis for the movements of his work, Dr. Faustus, his hour-glass running out, invites his
friends and trusted associates, "magisters, baccalaurs, and other students" to the village of Rimlich near Wittenberg, entertains them liber-
ally there by day, and by night as well, drinking with them a "St. John's
farewell," and then, in a contrite but dignified speech makes known his
fate and announces its imminent fulfillment. In this *oratio Fausti ad
studiosus,* he begs them, upon finding him strangled and dead, to inter
his body mercifully in the earth; for he dies, he says, as both a wicked
and good Christian—good by virtue of his repentance, and because in
his heart he always hoped for grace for his soul; wicked, insofar as he
knows that he is now to meet a horrid end and the Devil will and must
have his body. The words, "For I die as both a wicked and good Christian," provide the general theme for this work of variations. If one
counts syllables, one finds twelve in all, and the theme is set to all
twelve tones of the chromatic scale, and is thereby related to all possi-

ble intervals. Musically, it is compellingly present long before the text is presented by a small choir, which functions as the soloist (there are no solos in *Faustus*), their song rising toward the middle and then sinking again, following the spirit and inflection of Monteverdi's *"Lamento."* The theme lies at the basis of every sound heard, or better, it lies, almost like a musical key, behind everything and builds the single identity of the most varied forms—the same identity that reigns between the crystal chorus of angels and the howls of hell in the *Apocalypse* and that has now become all-embracing, has become a formal arrangement of ultimate rigor that knows nothing that is unthematic, in which the ordering of the material is total, and within which the idea of a fugue, for instance, becomes meaningless, precisely because free notes no longer exist. Nevertheless, it serves a higher purpose, for—ah, what a miracle, what a profoundly demonic jest!—as a result of the absoluteness of the form, music is liberated as language. In a certain cruder sense, in terms of tonal material, the work as such is finished before its composition even begins and thus can now unfold outside all restraints—that is to say, abandon itself to expression, which, being beyond the constructive form, or inside its perfect strictness, has now been reclaimed. Working uninhibitedly within preorganized material and unconcerned about its preexistent construction, the creator of the *Lamentation of Dr. Faustus* can abandon himself to subjectivity. Therefore, this, his strictest work, a work of utmost calculation, is simultaneously purely expressive. The return to Monteverdi and the style of his era is precisely what I called the "reconstruction of expression"—of expression in its first and primal manifestation, the expression of lament.

And here are marshaled every means of expression from that emancipatory epoch, of which I have already mentioned the echo-effect—it being especially appropriate for a work that is nothing but variations, and thus in some sense static, and in which every transformation is itself an echo of what preceded it. There is no lack of reverberatory continuations, where a final phrase of a given theme is perpetuated by being repeated at a higher pitch. In the episode where Faust calls up Helen, who will then bear him a son, there is a gentle reminiscence of the accents of Orphic lament, thus making Faust and Orpheus brothers in their invoking the world of shades. There are a hundred allusions to the sound and spirit of the madrigal, and a whole movement—the consoling of friends at dinner on his last night—is written in correct madrigal form.

But here are also marshaled, precisely as if in résumé, all the elements of music conceivable as bearers of expression—needless to say, not in mechanical imitation, not as a retreat, but rather like an exercise of deliberate mastery over all the expressive characters ever precipitated in musical history, which here, then, by a kind of process of alchemistic distillation, are refined and crystallized to basic forms of emotional meaning. Thus one finds the deeply drawn sigh at such words as, "Ah, Faustus, thou desperate and unworthy heart, ah, ah, reason, mischief, presumption, and free will . . ."; one finds frequent use of suspension, if only as a rhythmic device, melodic chromaticism, fearful collective silence at the start of a phrase, repetitions like those in the *"Lasciatemi,"* the drawing-out of syllables, falling intervals, fading declamation—amid enormous contrast effects like the tragic entrance of the choir, *a cappella* and at full voice, that immediately follows Faust's descent into hell (itself an orchestral piece of grand ballet music, a galop of fantastic rhythmic variety) and is an overwhelming eruption of lamentation after an orgy of infernal gaiety.

This wild notion of setting Faust's being pulled into the depths to a *furioso* dance is most reminiscent of the spirit of the *Apocalipsis cum figuris,* as is likewise, perhaps, the gruesome—I do not hesitate to say, cynical—choral scherzo in which "the Evil Spirit besets the aggrieved Faust with curious, mocking jests and bywords"—with its dreadful "It is too late, be mum, refrain from telling others of thy pain, of God despair, thy prayers are vain, thy ill luck runneth now amain." But in general Leverkühn's late work has little in common with that written in his thirties. Its style is purer, darker in tone on the whole and without any parody; in its looking back, it is not more conservative, but milder, more melodic, more counterpoint than polyphony—by which I mean that the secondary voices, though independent, are more considerate of the principal voice, which often moves in long melodic arcs and whose core is that same phrase from which everything is developed, the twelve tones of "For I die as both a wicked and good Christian." It was long ago noted in these pages that the alphabetical symbol H–E–A–E–Es, that figure of the *Hetaera esmeralda,* which I was the first to perceive, also frequently governs the melody and harmony of *Faustus,* wherever, that is, mention is made of the pledge and bond, of the bloody pact.

Above all, the *Faust* cantata differs from the *Apocalypse* in its large orchestral interludes, which at times merely hint generally at the relation of the work to its subject by uttering a "So be it!", but which at times, as in the ghastly ballet music for the descent into hell, also assume a function in the story. The instrumentation for this dance of horrors consists only of wind instruments and an insistent accompanying ensemble made up of two harps, cembalo, piano, celesta, glockenspiel, and percussion—a kind of continuo that constantly reappears throughout the work. Some of the choral pieces are accompanied only by it. For some others wind instruments are added, in a few cases, strings; still others use full orchestral accompaniment. The conclusion is purely orchestral: a symphonic adagio movement that gradually develops out of the powerful burst of choral lamentation following the hellish galop—taking, so to speak, the opposite path of the "Ode to Joy," negating by its genius that transition from symphony to vocal jubilation. It is its revocation.

My poor, great friend! And when perusing this work from his musical remains, from his own downfall, which prophetically anticipates the downfall and ruin of so much else, how often have I thought of the painful words he spoke to me at the death of the child, of his statement that it ought not be, that goodness, joy, hope, ought not be, that it should be taken back, that one must take it back! "Ah, it ought not be!"—how those words stand almost like an instruction, a musical direction, set above the choral and instrumental movements of *The Lamentation of Dr. Faustus* and contained within every measure and cadence of this "Ode to Sorrow"! There is no doubt that he wrote it with an eye to Beethoven's Ninth, as its counterpart in the most melancholy sense of the word. But it is not merely that more than once it performs a formal negation of the Ninth, takes it back into the negative, but in so doing it is also a negation of the religious—by which I cannot mean, its denial. A work dealing with the Tempter, with apostasy, with damnation—how can it be anything but a religious work! What I mean is an inversion, an austere and proud upending of meaning, such as I at least find, for example, in the "friendly appeal" by Dr. Faustus to the companions of his final hour that they should go to bed, sleep in peace, and be not troubled. Given the framework of the cantata, one can scarcely help viewing this as the conscious and deliberate reversal of the "Watch with me!" of Gethsemane. And again, his last drink with his friends, the "St. John's farewell," has all the marks of ritual, is presented as another Last Supper. Linked with this, however, is the reversal of the notion of temptation, in that Faust refuses the idea of salvation as itself a temptation—not only out of formal loyalty to the pact and because it is "too late," but also because with all his soul he despises the positive optimism of the world to which he is to be saved, the lie of its godliness. This becomes even clearer and is still more forcefully elaborated in the scene with the good old "physician

and gossip" who invites Faust to him in a pious attempt at conversion
and whose role is quite purposefully drawn as that of a tempter. This is
an unmistakable reference to Jesus' temptation by Satan, just as an
"*Apage!*" is unmistakably found in the proudly despairing "No!" spoken against false and flabby bourgeois piety.

But yet another final, truly final reversal of meaning must be recalled
here, must be pondered with the heart, a reversal that comes at the end
of this work of endless lament and that, surpassing all reason, softly
touches the emotions with that spoken unspokenness given to music
alone. I mean the cantata's last orchestral movement, in which the chorus loses itself and which sounds like the lament of God for the lost
state of His world, like the Creator's sorrowful "I did not will this."
Here, toward the end, I find that the uttermost accents of sorrow are
achieved, that final despair is given expression, and—but I shall not say
it, for it would mean a violation of the work's refusal to make any concessions, of its pain, which is beyond all remedy, were one to say that,
to its very last note, it offers any other sort of consolation than what
lies in expression itself, in utterance—that is to say, in the fact that the
creature has been given a voice for its pain. No, to the very end, this
dark tone poem permits no consolation, reconciliation, transfiguration. But what if the artistic paradox, which says that expression, the
expression of lament, is born out of the construct as a whole, corresponds to the religious paradox, which says that out of the profoundest irredeemable despair, if only as the softest of questions, hope may
germinate? This would be hope beyond hopelessness, the transcen-
dence of despair—not its betrayal, but the miracle that goes beyond
faith. Just listen to the ending, listen with me: One instrumental group
after the other steps back, and what remains as the work fades away is
the high G of a cello, the final word, the final sound, floating off,
slowly vanishing in a *pianissimo fermata.* Then nothing more. Silence
and night. But the tone, which is no more, for which, as it hangs there
vibrating in the silence, only the soul still listens, and which was the
dying note of sorrow—is no longer that, its meaning changes, it stands
as a light in the night.

XLVII

"WATCH WITH ME!" Adrian may have turned those words of human and divine need into something lonely, more manly, and proud, into the "Sleep in peace and be not troubled!" of his Faust—there remains, however, the human, the instinctive desire, if not for assistance, then at least for the company of one's fellow human beings, the plea: "Forsake me not! Be about me in my hour!"

And so, with the year 1930 almost half over, in the month of May, by various means Leverkühn invited a group of people to Pfeiffering, all his friends and acquaintances, even some he hardly knew or did not know at all, a large crowd, about thirty people—some by written notes, some through me, with those invited being requested to pass the invitation on, and still others who had simply invited themselves out of basic curiosity, which is to say, had begged me or some other member of the closer circle to have themselves included. For Adrian had let it be known in his notes that he wished to give a favorably disposed gathering of friends an idea of his new, recently completed choral and symphonic work by playing some characteristic passages from it on the piano. There were in fact many who were interested whom he had not intended to invite, as for example the dramatic soprano Tanya Orlanda and the tenor Herr Kjoejelund, who got themselves included via the Schlaginhaufens, or Radbruch the publisher who, along with his wife, had Schildknapp front for him. The written invitations, by the way, had also included Baptist Spengler, although, as Adrian surely had to know, he had not been among the living for a good six weeks. Still only in his mid-forties, that witty man had unfortunately succumbed to his heart trouble.

I admit the whole affair left me somewhat uneasy. It is hard to say why. This summoning of a large number of people, most of whom were strangers, both inwardly and outwardly, to join him here in his place of retreat for the purpose of introducing them to his most lonely, private work—it did not fit Adrian at all; it made me uncomfortable not only in and of itself, but also because it seemed to me behavior quite alien to him—though I likewise found it distasteful in and of itself. But whatever my reasons, and I believe I did hint at them to him, in my heart I would have preferred to know that he was alone in his asylum, seen only by his landlady and her family, whose humane attachment was one of respect and devotion, and by us few others—Schildknapp, dear Jeannette, the adoring ladies Rosenstiel and Nackedey, and myself—rather than to have the eyes of a mixed crowd of people unaccustomed to him focused on him, a man disaccustomed to the world. Yet what else could I do but lend a hand to a project for which he had already made considerable preparations and follow his instructions and do my telephoning? There were no declined invitations—on the contrary, as I said, there were only additional requests for permission to participate.

It was not merely that I did not look forward to the event—I will enlarge on my confession and record that I was even tempted to absent myself. This, however, was countered by an anxious sense of duty, by the feeling that, gladly or no, I definitely had to be present and watch over things. And so on that Saturday afternoon I proceeded with Helene to Munich, where we boarded the local train for Waldshut-Garmisch. We shared our compartment with Schildknapp, Jeannette Scheurl, and Kunigunde Rosenstiel. The rest of the party was dispersed through several other cars, except for the Schlaginhaufens—the old retired scholar with the Swabian accent and his wife, née von Plausig, together with their singer friends, made the trip in their car. Having arrived in Pfeiffering before us, this vehicle was now put to good use traveling back and forth between the little station and the Schweigestill farm, transporting small groups of those guests who preferred not to walk—and the weather held, although there was a thunderstorm growling softly on the horizon. For no plans had been made for bringing people from the station to the farm—and Frau Schweigestill, whom Helene and I looked for in the kitchen and found along with Clementina very hastily fixing a snack of coffee, finger sandwiches, and cooled cider for all these people, explained with no little dismay that Adrian had not said a word to prepare her for this invasion.

Outside meanwhile, old Suso, or Kaschperl, kept leaping around in front of his doghouse, rattling his chain, barking angrily and incessantly, and calmed down only when no more new guests arrived and everyone had gathered in the Winged-Victory room, where the seating had been augmented by chairs that a maid and a farm hand had dragged in from the family living room and even from the bedrooms upstairs. In addition to persons already mentioned, I shall make a hit-or-miss attempt to recall from memory the names of those present: the wealthy Bullinger; Leo Zink, the painter, whom neither Adrian nor I actually liked, but whom he had probably invited along with the deceased Spengler; Helmut Institoris, who was a kind of widower now; the always clearly enunciating Dr. Kranich; Frau Binder-Majoresku; the Knöterichs; Nottebohm, the hollow-cheeked and jovial portraitist, who, together with his wife, had come with Institoris. In addition, there were Sixtus Kridwiss and the members of his discussion roundtable: Dr. Unruhe, who studied the earth's strata; Professors Vogler and Holzschuher; the poet Daniel Zur Höhe in his black high-buttoned cassock; and, to my annoyance, even the captious Chaim Breisacher. The music profession was represented not only by the opera singers, but also by Ferdinand Edschmidt, the conductor of the Zapfenstösser Orchestra. And to my complete surprise—and not just to mine—someone else had turned up: Baron Gleichen-Russwurm, who together with his plump, but elegant Austrian wife was making (at least as far as I was aware) his very first social appearance since the affair with the mouse. It turned out that Adrian had sent him an invitation a week beforehand, and Schiller's distant relative, having compromised himself in so strange a fashion, had evidently been very happy to seize this unique opportunity to rejoin society.

All of these people, some thirty of them as I said, are now standing in the rustic salon, waiting expectantly, introducing themselves, sharing their curiosity with one another. I can see Rüdiger Schildknapp in his perennial threadbare sporty outfit, surrounded by ladies, of whom there was indeed a considerable number. I hear the euphonious, dominant voices of the dramatic singers, Dr. Kranich's asthmatic but clear articulation, Bullinger's blowing-off of steam, Kridwiss's assurances that this gathering and what it promised was "rilly 'norm'sly 'mportant," followed by Zur Höhe's fanatic concurrence, accented by the tapping of the ball of his foot: "Indeed, indeed, one can well say that!" Baroness Gleichen moved about the room, seeking sympathy for the abstruse misfortune that had befallen her and her spouse. "You do know, of course, about this *ennui* we have had," she said here and there. From the start I observed that a great many of them did not even notice that Adrian had long since entered the room and went on speaking as if they were still expecting him—simply because they did not recognize him. Dressed as always now, he was sitting with his back to the window, in the middle of the room at the heavy oval table where we had once sat with Saul Fitelberg. But several of the guests asked me who that gentleman there was and to my initially surprised response were heard to utter a "Yes, of course!" of sudden illumination—and then hurried over to greet their host. How much he must have changed under my very eyes for that to have been the case! To be sure, the beard made a great difference, and I said that, too, to those who could not get over the fact that it was he. For some time now, our frizzy-haired Rosenstiel had been standing erect, like a sentinel, beside his chair, which explained why Meta Nackedey was keeping as far away as possible, hiding in one corner of the room. Kunigunde showed her loyalty, however, by leaving her post after a while, whereupon the other adoring soul immediately took it over. On the music desk of the square piano against the wall, lay the opened score of *The Lamentation of Dr. Faustus.*

Since I kept one eye on my friend even while conversing with one or another of the guests, I did not miss the signal he gave with his head and eyebrows to tell me I should ask those gathered here to take their seats. I did so at once by making the suggestion to those nearest me and beckoning to those somewhat farther off, and even brought myself to clap my hands to ask for silence for my announcement that Dr. Leverkühn wished to begin his lecture. A person can feel his own face turning pale, a certain distraught chill of the facial features warns him of it, and even the drops of sweat that may then bead up on his brow have that same chill. My hands, which I clapped together only softly and with some reserve, were trembling, just as they now tremble as I set about to commit the horrible memory to writing.

The audience obeyed fairly promptly. Silence and order were quickly established. It turned out that seated together with Adrian at the table were the old Schlaginhaufens, plus Jeannette Scheurl, Schildknapp, my wife, and I. The others were dispersed on various pieces of furniture—painted wooden chairs, horsehair easy chairs, the sofa—placed in irregular patterns at both ends of the room, and several gentlemen were leaning against the walls. Adrian had as yet given no indication that he was about to gratify general expectation, including my own, by moving to the piano to play. He sat with his hands folded, his head tilted to one side, his eyes raised only slightly and directed straight ahead, and in the now perfect hush he began (in that slightly monotone, and somewhat halting, fashion of his, which I knew well) to address the gathering—in words of greeting, or so it seemed to me at the start; and at first that is what they were. Though it pains me, I must add that he often misspoke himself and in the attempt to correct one such lapse (at which in my torment I dug my fingernails into my palms) made yet another, until in time he no longer paid any attention to such mistakes and simply passed over them. I should not, by the way, have let myself be so aggrieved by all kinds of irregularities in how he expressed himself, since to some extent, just as he had always liked to do when writing, he used a kind of antiquated German, which, given its defects and incomplete sentences, had always had something dubious and careless about it—and indeed, how long has it been since our tongue outgrew its barbaric stage and has to some extent obeyed both grammatical and orthographical rules.

He began very softly, in a murmur, so that only a few could understand what he said or make much sense of it, or else took it as some droll joke, since what he said was something like:

"Esteemable, peculiarly beloved brethren and sisters."

After which he was silent for a while, as if pondering, his cheek against a hand propped up on an elbow. What followed was likewise received as a droll introduction of humorous intent, and although the immobility of his face, the weariness of his glance, and his pallor spoke against this, the response that greeted him around the room was first one of laughter—soft snorts through the nose or titters from the ladies.

"Firstmost," he said, "I wish to extend my thanks for the goodwill and friendship, though both be undeserved, such as you would show by your having come hither, whether afoot or by conveyance, inasmuch as from the solitude of this hiding place I wrote and called unto you, and also let you be called and invited by the instrument of my exceeding faithful famulus and especial friend, the which still knows to remember me of our schooling from early youth on, for we studied together in Halle—but of that, and of how conceit and horror had their commencement in those studies, more hereafter in my sermon."

At this point many people grinned my way, although I was so touched that I could not smile, since it was not at all like my dear friend to mention me with such gentle words of remembrance. But most of them were amused precisely because they saw tears in my eyes; and I recall with disgust how Leo Zink blew his large nose—of which he made so much fun—loudly into his handkerchief in a conspicuous caricature of emotion, thereby garnering several giggles as well. Adrian appeared not to notice.

"But must afore all else," he continued, "also excurse"—he corrected himself and said, "excuse," but then repeated, "excurse"—"myself to you and beg you to take no offense that our hound Praestigiar, though he be called Suso, yet of a truth is named Praestigiar, did rise up and assail your ears with such hellish yelping and bawling, insomuch as you have ventured such trouble and burthen for my sake. We ought to have presented each of you a whistle of rare pitch, audible only to dogs, so that he had understood even from afar that only good and summoned friends are come eagerly to hear what I have complished upon his watch and how I have quitted myself these many years."

From here and there again came some polite laughter about the whistle, though with some embarrassment. He, however, went on, saying:

"Now would I make cordial Christian request of you that you not take and judge my discourse to the worse, but that it be understood to the best, for verily I have a longing to make full and fellowly confession to you, who are good and unharmful and, if not unsinful, sinful but in such common and tolerable wise that I do heartily detest, yet fervently envy you, for the hour-glass stands before my eyes so that I must needs behold when the last grain has run through the bottle neck and He will fetch me to whom I have pacted myself so dearly with my own blood that I shall eternally belong to Him body and soul and fall into His hand and dominion when the glass has run out and time, being His ware, is come to its end."

Here once again there were scattered snorts of laughter, but there were also several people who clicked their tongues, and shook their heads, too, as if at some tactless indiscretion, and some eyes took on a darkly probing look.

"Know it then," the man at the table said, "you good and pious souls, who with your middling sin rest in Goad's"—again he corrected himself and said, "God's," but then returned to the other form—"who rest in Goad's grace and forbearance, for I have smothered it within me so long, yet will keep it pent no longer that I have already since my twenty-first year been wed with Satan, and in full knowledge of the peril and with duly considered valour, pride, and presumption, I did, out of a wish to find fame in this world, make a bond and league with Him, in such wise that what I would complish within the term of four and twenty years and what men would rightly regard with distrust, would come to pass solely by His help and is Devil's work, poured out by the Angel of Poison. For I did consider well that you must set pins if you would bowl, and now-a-days you must pay your addresses to the Devil, in that you can use and have no one but Him for great enterprises and work."

An embarrassed, tense silence now reigned in the room. A few people were still listening comfortably, but one also saw a good many raised eyebrows and faces in which one read the question: What is he getting at, what is this all about? If just once he had smiled or winked by way of marking his words as artistic mystification, it would have set things halfway right again. But he did not, and instead sat there in ashen earnest. A few guests cast glances my way that asked how all this was intended and how I could justify it; and perhaps I should have intervened and broken up the gathering—but on what grounds? There were only those that meant disgrace and betrayal, and I felt I had to let things take their course, in hopes that he would soon begin to play from his work and offer notes instead of words. Never had I more strongly felt the advantage that music, which says nothing and everything, has over words, which lack ambiguity—indeed that art, safeguarded by being noncommittal, has in general over the compromising crudity of unmediated confession. Yet to interrupt this confession not only went against my sense of reverence, but also with all my soul I longed to hear it—even if among those hearing with me there might be only a very few who were worthy. Just hold out and listen, I said in my heart to the others, since after all he did invite you as his fellow human beings!

After pausing to reflect, my friend began anew:

"Do not believe, beloved brethren and sisters, that for the promission and establishment of the pact I had required a crossway in the wood and many circles and gross conjuration, for indeed St. Thomas already teaches that for apostasy there be no need of words by which to complish invocation, but rather any deed suffices, e'en without express obeisance. For it was a mere butterfly, a gaudy thing, *Hetaera esmeralda*, that charmed me by her touch, the milk-witch, and followed after her into the dusky leafy shade, the which her transparent nakedness loves, and where I snatched her, who in flight is like unto a wind-blown petal, snatched her and dandled with her, spite of her warning, and so was it happened. For as she charmed me, so did she work her charm and yielded to me in love—and I was initiate and the promise sealed."

I flinched, for at this point a voice from the audience interrupted—that of the poet Daniel Zur Höhe in his clerical garb, who struck a blow with his foot and pronounced his hammering judgment, "It is beautiful. It has beauty. Indeed, indeed, one can say that!"

A few people shushed him, and I, too, turned disapprovingly toward the speaker, even if secretly I was grateful to him for his words. For although silly enough, they placed what we had heard under a soothing and accepted aspect, the aesthetic, which, however inappropriate, however annoying I found it, nevertheless provided even me some respite. For I felt as if a relieved "Ah, yes!" passed through the assembly, and one lady, the wife of Radbruch the publisher, felt encouraged by Zur Höhe's words to say, "One feels one is listening to poetry."

Ah, but despite the comfort it offered, his tasteful interpretation was untenable; one did not believe it for long. For this had nothing to do with Zur Höhe's bizarre poetical mischief about obedience, violence, blood, and the plundering of the world, but was offered in dead and pallid earnest, was confession and truth, which a man in the last anguish of his soul had called his fellow men together to hear—an act of absurd trust, to be sure, for one's fellow men are not made or of a mind to greet such truth with anything but cold horror and the unanimous judgment that, once it very quickly proved impossible to regard this as poetry, they pronounced against it.

It did not appear as if any such objections had found their way to our host. His musings, whenever he paused, evidently made him insensible to them.

"Do but mark," he resumed, "peculiarly esteemable, beloved friends, that you deal here with a God-forsaken and desperate man, whose corpse does not belong in a place consecrate for pious deceased Christians, but upon a shambles for the carcasses of dead beasts. Upon its bier, so I prophesy, you will find it ever lying upon its face, and though you wend it five times, it will yet lie perverse. For long before I dandled with that poisonous moth, my soul, in its conceit and pride, was upon the road to Satan, and my *datum* was fixed that I should strive after Him from my youth on, for as you must know, man is made and predestined for bliss or for hell, and I was born for hell. Therefore I fed my haughtiness with sugar in that I studied theology at the academe in Halle, yet not for God's sake, but for the sake of that Other, and my divine study was secretly already the beginning of the bond and not covert progress to God, but to Him, the great *religiosus*. And he who will have the Devil can not be frustrated, nor can he defend gainst Him, and it was but a little step from the divine faculty over to Leipzig and to music, such that I did devote myself solely and entirely to *figuris, characteribus, formis coniurationum,* and whatsoever other names such evocation and magic be named.

"Item, my desperate heart did trifle it. Had indeed a good fleet brain and gifts graciously granted me from on high, which I could have used in all honesty and modesty, but felt only too well: It is an age when no work is to be done in pious, sober fashion and by proper means, and art has grown impossible sans the Devil's aid and hellish fire beneath

the kettle. . . . Yes, ah yes, beloved fellows, that art is stuck fast and
grown too difficult and mocks its very self, that all has grown too difficult and God's poor man in his distress no longer knows up from
down, that is surely the guilt of the age. But should a man make the
Devil his guest in order thereby to go beyond and break through, he
indicts his soul and hangs the guilt of the age round his own neck, so
that he be damned. For it is said: Be sober, be vigilent! But that is not
the business of some, and rather than wisely to attend to what is need-
ful on earth, that it might there be better, and prudently to act that
among men such order be stablished that may again prepare lively soil
and honest accommodation for the beautiful work, man would prefer
to play the truant and break out into hellish drunkenness, thus giving
his soul to it and ending upon the shambles.

"And so, kindly beloved brethren and sisters, did I deport myself
and let all my concern and desire become *nigromantia, carmina, incan-
tatio, veneficium,* and whatsoever other names may be named. And
soon did parley with Him, that killjoy, that bawd, in an Italian chamber, had intercourse with Him, Who had much to convey to me of
hell's quality, fundament, and substance. And also sold me time, four
and twenty immeasurable years, pledging great things and much fire
under the kettle, and promised and warranted me for such time that I
would be capable of the work, notwithstanding that it be grown too
difficult and my head too clever and disdainful. Except, to be sure, I
was in recompense to suffer knifelike pains within that time, much like
those the little mermaid suffered in her legs, who was my sister and
sweet bride, Hyphialta by name. For He led her to my bed as my con-
cubine, so that I commenced to woo her and grew in my love for her,
whether she came with her fishy tail or with legs. Though oftener times
she came in her tail, because the very pains she suffered like knives in
her legs outweighed her lust, and I had much liking for the pleasant
mingling of her dainty body into the scaly tail. I took still higher delight, however, in her purely human shape, and so for my part my lust
was greater when she visited me with legs."

At these words there was a stir in the audience and someone made to
leave. The old Schlaginhaufens in fact rose from our table, and glanc-
ing neither to the right or left, the husband took his wife by the elbow
and threaded his way softly among the chairs and out the door. Not
two minutes later, we heard the loud rattling noise of their car starting
out in the courtyard and realized that they were driving off.

This was very disturbing for some, since it meant the loss of the vehicle by which many of them had hoped to be transported back to the
train station.

But the other guests showed no discernible inclination to follow this example. They sat as if spellbound, and when the sounds of departure had died away outside, Zur Höhe was once again heard to utter his peremptory, "Beautiful! No doubt whatever, it is beautiful!"

And I was just about to open my mouth as well and beg my friend to put an end to his introduction and play now for us from his work, when, unaffected by the incident, he went on with his address.

"Whereupon Hyphialta grew great with child and rendered unto me a little son, to whom I clung with all my soul, a hallowed young boy, of a grace exceeding all common and as if come hither from some remote and ancient stock. But as the child was of flesh and blood and it being conditional that I might love no human creature, so did He slay it without mercy and to that end did use my own eyes. For you should know that if a soul be violently moved to wickedness, its gaze is poisonous and venomed, most specially for children. And so this small son full of sweet words was lost to me in the moon of August, though I had directly thought such fondness was permitted me. Had truly likewise thought, formerly, that I, being the Devil's own monk might love in flesh and blood that which was not female, who, however, with boundless familiarity wooed me for my 'thou' till I did grant it to him. Therefore I must needs kill him, and sent him to his death upon coercion and instruction. For the *magisterulus* had marked that I thought to marry my self, and great was His rage, for He saw in wedlock an apostasy from Him and a stratagem for expiation. Thus did He force me to employ that very same intent, that I coldly murder my familiar friend, and I will have confessed here today and before you all that I sit before you also as a murderer."

At this point another group of guests left the room: little Helmut Institoris, who, pale and with his lower lip drawn tightly against his teeth, got up in silent protest; plus his friends, Nottebohm the smooth portraitist and his wife, a buxom woman of marked bourgeois manners whom we used to call "the maternal breast." They departed without a word. But apparently they had not held their tongues outside, for a few moments after they left Frau Schweigestill entered quietly—still in her apron, her gray hair tightly pulled back—and folding her hands, remained standing near the door. She listened as Adrian said:

"But whatever a sinner I was, my friends, a murderer, an enemy to man, a votary of Devilish concupiscence, yet notwithstanding did diligently and steadfastly apply myself as a worker, never roistering"— once again he seemed to stop and consider and corrected the word to "resting," but then stayed with "roistering"—"nor sleeping, but gave myself to drudgery and complished what was difficult, according to the word of the Apostle, 'He who seeketh hard things shall have it hard.' For as God does no great things without our melting grease, neither does the Other. Only the shame and mockery of the intellect and what in the age was contrary to the work, those He did keep apart from me, the remainder I had to do myself, though only after strange infusions. For there often rose up in me a sweet instrument, of an organ or a positive, then the harp, lutes, fiddles, sackbuts, fifes, cromornes, and flutes, each with four voices, so that I had well believed myself to be in heaven had I not known otherwise. Of which I wrote much down. Often there were also certain children with me in the room, boys and girls, who sang me a motet from pages of notes, smiling right craftly the while and interchanging glances. And pretty children they were indeed. Sometimes their hair would rise as if upon hot air, and they smoothed it again with their pretty hands, on which were dimples and ruby stones. Sometimes little yellow worms wriggled from out their nostrils, crawled down their breasts, and vanished—"

These words were once again the signal for several listeners to leave the room—this time, the scholars Unruhe, Vogler, and Holzschuher, one of whom I saw pressing both wrists to his temples as he departed. Sixtus Kridwiss, however, at whose home they held their disputations, remained in his seat, but with a very agitated look—along with some twenty others who still remained after these departures, though many of them were standing now, evidently ready to flee. Leo Zink held his eyebrows raised in malicious expectation, repeating his "Jesus!" the way he used to do when passing judgment on someone's painting. As if to protect him, a few women had collected around Leverkühn: Kunigunde Rosenstiel, Meta Nackedey, and Jeannette Scheurl, those three. Else Schweigestill kept her distance.

And we heard:

"Thus the Evil One sustained his word in fidelity through four and twenty years, and all is finished but for the very last, midst murder and lewdness have I completed it, and perchance what is fashioned in wickedness can yet be good by grace, I do not know. Perchance God sees, too, that I sought out what was hard and gave myself to drudgery, perchance, perchance it will be reckoned to me and put to my account that I have been so diligent and complished all with pertinacity—I cannot say and have not the courage to set my hope therein. My sin is larger than that it can be forgiven me, and I have driven it to its heights in that my brain speculated that a contrite unbelief in the possibility of grace and forgiveness may be the greatest provocation for eternal goodness, even as I recognize that such brazen calculation renders mercy wholly impossible. Upon which basis, then, I went farther still in speculating and reckoned that such final reprobation must be the utter incitement for goodness to prove its infinitude. And so ever forth, that I engaged in villainous rivalry with the goodness on high as to which were more inexhaustible, it or my speculating—there you see that I am damned, and there is no mercy for me, because I destroy any such aforehand through speculation.

"But since the time I once purchased for my soul has now run out, I have summoned you to me before my end is come, kindly beloved brethren and sisters, and will not conceal from you my ghostly decease. And beseech you therefore that you would keep me in good remembrance, and also convey brotherly greetings to others whom I have forgotten to invite, and think moreover nothing ill of me. All this said and confessed, I will in farewell play for you some few things from the structure that I heard from Satan's sweet instrument, and which in part the craftly children sang for me."

He stood up, pale as death.

"This man," we heard the clearly articulated, if asthmatic voice of Dr. Kranich say in the silence, "this man is mad. Of that there can no longer be any doubt, and it is regrettable that no one representing psychiatric science is part of our circle. I, as a numismatist, consider myself completely incompetent here."

And with that he left.

Leverkühn, surrounded by the three women, but also by Schild-knapp, Helene, and me, had sat down at the brown square piano and began to smooth the pages of the score with his right hand. We saw tears trickle down his cheeks and fall on the keys, which, though wet, were now struck in a strongly dissonant chord. At the same time he opened his mouth as if to sing, but from between his lips there emerged only a wail that still rings in my ears. Bending over the instrument, he spread his arms wide as if to embrace it and suddenly, as if pushed, fell sideways from his chair to the floor.

Frau Schweigestill, who was in fact farther away, was beside him more quickly than we who were closer, since, though I don't know why, we hesitated for a second to assist him. She lifted the unconscious man's head and held his upper body in her motherly arms, calling out across the room to those still standing there gawking, "Clear out, all of you! You haven't the least understanding, you city folk, and there's need of understanding here. He talked a lot about eternal grace, the poor man, and I don't know if it reaches that far. But real human understanding, believe me, that reaches far enough for all!"

IT IS DONE. An old man, bent, almost broken by the horrors of the time in which he wrote and by those that are the subject of what he has written, gazes with wavering satisfaction at the large pile of enlivened paper that is the work of his diligence, the product of years thronged with both memories and current events. A task has been accomplished for which I am by nature not the right man, to which I was not born, but have been called by love, loyalty, and my role as an eyewitness. What those can achieve, what devotion can do, that has been done—I must be content with that.

As I sat down to write these memoirs, this biography of Adrian Leverkühn, there existed in regards to its author—but also in regards to the artistry of its hero—not the least prospect of their ever being made public. But now that the monster state that at that time held this continent, and more besides, in its tentacles has celebrated its last orgies, now that its matadors have had themselves poisoned by their doctors, then drenched in gasoline and set on fire so that nothing whatever might remain of them—now, I say, it might be possible to think of the publication of my mediatorial work. But just as those miscreants willed it, Germany has been so razed to the ground that one does not even dare hope that Germany will be able anytime soon to engage in any sort of cultural activity, in the printing of a book; and indeed I have now and then considered ways and means for having these pages reach America, so that for now at least they could be presented to people there in English translation. It seems to me as if this would not be all that contrary to the wishes of my late friend. Granted, the thought that in terms of content my book would surely arouse puzzlement in that cultural sphere is coupled with an anxious concern that its translation into English, at least in certain of its all too radically German passages, would prove an impossibility.

What I also foresee is some sense of emptiness that is sure to be mine once I have added a few words accounting for the close of this great composer's life and have put the final stroke of the pen to my manuscript. As upsetting and exhausting as these labors were, I shall miss them, for as a duty to be fulfilled they helped to keep me busy during years that would have been even harder to bear had I been totally idle, and for now I look in vain for some activity that might take the place of this work in the future. True, the reasons that compelled me to retire from my teaching position eleven years ago have fallen away under the thunder of history. Germany is free, insofar as one can call a devastated nation deprived of its sovereignty free, and it may be that nothing now stands in the way of my returning to my profession. Monsignor Hinterpförtner has already suggested it on occasion. Shall I once again urge upon senior students of the humanities the cultural ideal that defines piety as the merging of reverence for the divinities of the deep with the ethical cult of Olympian reason and clarity? But ah, I fear that over this savage decade a generation has grown up that will no more understand my language than I shall its; I fear the youth of my country have become too alien to me for me to be their teacher—and more: Germany itself, this unhappy land, is alien to me, utterly alien, precisely because I, certain of its ghastly end, held myself apart from its sins, hid from them in my solitude. Must I not ask if I was right in doing so? And again: Did I actually do so? I have clung to one man, one painfully important man, unto death and have described his life, which never ceased to fill me with loving fear. It is as if this loyalty may well have made up for my having fled in horror from my country's guilt.

*

REVERENCE FORBIDS ME from describing in detail Adrian's condition when he came to after the twelve hours of unconsciousness into which his paralytic stroke at the piano had plunged him. He did not come to himself, but rather to an alien self that was only the burned-out shell of his personality and that basically had nothing to do with the man called Adrian Leverkühn. Originally, the word "dementia" simply meant this deviation from one's own ego, this alienation from oneself.

I shall only say this much: He could not remain in Pfeiffering. Rüdiger Schildknapp and I assumed the heavy responsibility of transporting the patient, whom Dr. Kürbis had readied for the trip with sedatives, to Munich and a private mental clinic run by Dr. von Hösslin in Nymphenburg, where Adrian spent three months. This experienced specialist's immediate prognosis had stated without reservation that his was a mental illness that could only grow worse over time. As it progressed, however, its crassest symptoms would probably taper off and, with appropriate therapy, be replaced by quieter, if not any more hopeful phases. It was in fact this information that caused Schildknapp and myself, after some deliberation, to postpone for a time our notifying Adrian's mother, Elsbeth Leverkühn, at Buchel Farm. It was quite certain that upon hearing of a catastrophe in her son's life she would hasten to join him, and if some calming was to be expected, it seemed only humane to spare her the shocking, indeed unbearable sight of her child's condition, as yet unimproved by institutional care.

Her child! For that, and nothing more, was what Adrian Leverkühn once again was when the old woman appeared in Pfeiffering one day as the year was advancing into autumn, in order to take him back with her to his home in Thuringia, to those scenes of his childhood that the external framework of his life had for so long and so strangely paralleled—a helpless, infantile child who no longer retained any memory of the proud flight of his manhood, or only a very dark memory hidden and buried deep inside; who clung to her apron strings and whom, just as in times past, she now was forced, or better, permitted to tend, regiment, call, and reprimand for being "naughty." One cannot imagine anything more horribly touching and pitiful than when a spirit that has boldly and defiantly emancipated itself from its origins, that has traced a dizzying arc above the world, returns broken to its mother's care. It is my conviction, however, based on unequivocal evidence, that, despite all sorrow, maternal feelings take some gratification, some satisfaction in such a tragic return home. For a mother, the Icarus-flight of her hero son, the adventurous, steep, and manly ascent of the lad who has outgrown her, is in essence an equally sinful and incomprehensible error, in which with secret resentment she hears the estranged and austere words: "Woman, what have I to do with thee?" And when the "poor, dear child" tumbles to his ruin, she takes him back to her bosom, forgiving him everything and with no other thought than that he would have done better never to have left.

I have reason to believe that within the depths of Adrian's darkened mind, there still lived, as a remnant of his pride, a dread of this gentle humiliation, which he instinctively resisted before at last acceding and finding glum enjoyment in the ease that an exhausted soul presumably also derives from mental abdication. What speaks, at least in part, for this spontaneous revolt and urge to flee from his mother, is his suicide attempt upon our informing him that Elsbeth Leverkühn had been notified of his illness and was on her way to him. This is what happened:

After three months of treatment at the Hösslin clinic, where I was allowed to see my friend only seldom and always for just a few minutes, he had calmed down—I do not say improved, but calmed down—to a degree that enabled the doctor to consent to private care in the quiet of Pfeiffering. Financial reasons spoke for this as well. And so the patient was again received by familiar surroundings. At first he had to put up with being supervised by the attendant who brought him back. His behavior, however, appeared to justify the removal of such surveillance, and his care again lay completely in the hands of the people at the farm, especially in those of Frau Schweigestill, who, ever since Gereon had brought a sturdy daughter-in-law into the house (whereas Clementina had become the wife of the stationmaster in Waldshut), was more or less retired and had time to devote her humane understanding to her lodger of many years, who had long since become something like a special son to her. He trusted her as he trusted no one else. He was obviously most content just sitting hand in hand with her, in the abbot's study or in the garden behind the house. I found him like that the first time I visited Pfeiffering again. The gaze he directed to me as I approached had something vehement and distraught about it and then, to my sorrow, quickly veiled itself in gloomy animosity. He may well have recognized in me the companion of an alert existence of which he refused to be reminded. And since—in response to the old woman's cautious urgings that he say a kind word to me in reply—his look only darkened the more, indeed grew menacing, I had no choice but to withdraw in sadness.

The moment had come, however, for writing the letter that would gently acquaint his mother with recent events. To postpone it any longer would have meant encroaching upon her rights, and we did not have long to wait for the telegram announcing her imminent arrival. Adrian, as I said, was informed of her coming, though, by the way, without any certainty on our part that he had grasped the news. An hour later, however, when he was presumed to be asleep, he escaped from the house without anyone's noticing, and Gereon and a farm hand caught up with him at Klammer Pool only after he had already removed his outer clothing and stood submerged up to his neck in waters that deepened abruptly. He was about to vanish beneath them when the farm hand plunged in after him and brought him to shore. As they led him back to the farm, he went on and on about how cold the pond was and added that it was very hard to drown oneself in a pond in which one has often bathed and swum. Yet he had never swum in Klammer Pool, but only in its counterpart at home, in the Cattle Trough, as a boy.

It is my suspicion, almost approaching certainty, that behind this frustrated attempt at flight there also lay a mystical notion of salvation very familiar to an older theology, especially to early Protestantism: the supposition, that is, that he who invokes the Devil can save his soul only by "consigning the body." Presumably Adrian acted on the basis of this notion, among others, and God only knows whether it was right not to let him carry it out. Not everything done in madness should therefore be prevented at all cost, and the obligation to preserve life was discharged here in hardly anyone's interest except that of the mother—who doubtless prefers to find an infantile son rather than a dead one.

She came, Jonathan Leverkühn's brown-eyed widow, her white hair pulled back tight, determined to fetch her lost child back to his childhood. At their first meeting, Adrian lay trembling for a long while on the breast of this woman, whom he called mother—and addressed with the familiar pronoun, whereas he had always retained the formal pronoun with the other woman present, who kept her distance; and Elsbeth Leverkühn spoke to him in that voice that was still as melodic as always, but that all her life she had refused to raise in song. About halfway into Adrian's trip north to central Germany, however, on which, fortunately, they were accompanied by the attendant he knew from Munich, for no apparent reason the son erupted into anger against his mother—a totally unexpected fit of rage that forced Frau Leverkühn to leave the patient alone with his attendant and spend the rest of the journey in another compartment.

This was an isolated event. Nothing of the sort was ever repeated. When she approached him again upon their arrival in Weissenfels, he readily joined her with demonstrations of love and joy, dogged her every step once they were home, and was the most docile of children, whom she tended with that total dedication of which only a mother is capable. In the house at Buchel, where a daughter-in-law had likewise been in charge for years now and there were already two growing grandchildren, he lived in the same room upstairs that as a boy he had shared with his older brother; and it was once again the old linden tree, and not the elm, whose branches stirred beneath his window and to whose wonderful fragrance when it bloomed, in the same season as his own birth, he seemed to show some response. And there he would sit in its shade—the people at the farm soon found they could leave him to his vacant dozings—on the same circular bench where bawling barnyard Hanne had once practiced rounds with us children. His mother saw to it that he got exercise, putting her arm in his and taking him for walks across the silent landscape. To anyone they met he would—and she made no attempt to restrain him—extend a hand, while the person thus greeted and Frau Leverkühn exchanged indulgent nods.

For my part, I saw the dear man again in 1935, when, already an emeritus, I traveled to Buchel Farm to offer my sad congratulations on his fiftieth birthday. The linden tree was in bloom, I sat beneath it. I admit, my knees were shaking as with bouquet in hand I stepped toward him, there at his mother's side. It seemed to me he had grown smaller, which may have been due to his hunched posture, and there looking up at me was a shrunken face, an *Ecce homo* countenance, that despite a healthy country tan revealed a mouth opened in pain and unseeing eyes. If he had not wanted to recognize me that last time in Pfeiffering, there was no doubt now that, despite some reminders by the old woman, he associated no memories whatever with my appearance. Of what I said to him about the significance of the day, the point of my coming, he obviously understood nothing. Only the flowers seemed to awaken his interest for a moment—and then they, too, lay there unnoticed.

I saw him one more time, in 1939, after the conquest of Poland, a year before his death, which his mother, at eighty, lived to see. That day she led me upstairs to his room, into which she stepped, encouraging me, saying, "Come on in, he won't notice you," while I stood there in the door, overcome by a profound reticence. At the back of the room, on a chaise longue whose foot was turned toward me, so that I could look directly into his face, there lay, under a light woolen blanket, the man who had once been Adrian Leverkühn, and whose immortal part now bears that name. The pale hands, whose sensitive shape I had always loved, lay crossed on the chest, like those of a figure on a medieval gravestone. The now predominantly gray beard made the narrow face look even longer, so that it bore a striking resemblance to that of a nobleman by El Greco. What a sardonic trick of nature, one might well say, that she is able to create the image of highest spirituality where the spirit has departed! The eyes lay deep in their sockets, the brows had grown bushier, and from under them the specter directed at me an unutterably earnest, almost menacingly probing glance that made me shudder, but that within a second seemed to collapse, the eyeballs turning upward and vanishing half under the lids, to wander there restlessly back and forth. I declined to obey his mother's repeated invitations to come closer, and turned away in tears.

On 25 August 1940 news reached me here in Freising of the dying of what flames had remained of a life that—in love, anxiety, fear, and pride—had given my own life its essential content. At the open grave in the little cemetery at Oberweiler, there stood with me, besides the immediate family, Jeannette Scheurl, Rüdiger Schildknapp, Kunigunde Rosenstiel, and Meta Nackedey—plus a muffled, unrecognizable stranger, who had vanished again as the first clods fell on the lowered coffin.

In those days Germany, a hectic flush on its cheeks, was reeling at the height of its savage triumphs, about to win the world on the strength of the one pact that it intended to keep and had signed with its blood. Today, in the embrace of demons, a hand over one eye, the other staring into the horror, it plummets from despair to despair. When will it reach the bottom of the abyss? When, out of this final hopelessness, will a miracle that goes beyond faith bear the light of hope? A lonely man folds his hands and says, "May God have mercy on your poor soul, my friend, my fatherland."

THE END

✻   ✻

✻

Author's Note

It does not seem superfluous to inform the reader that the method of composition presented in Chapter XXII, known as the twelve-tone or row technique, is in truth the intellectual property of a contemporary composer and theoretician, Arnold Schoenberg, and that I have transferred it within a certain imaginary context to the person of an entirely fictitious musician, the tragic hero of my novel. And in general, those parts of this book dealing with music theory are indebted in many details to Schoenberg's *Theory of Harmony*.

Thomas Mann

A NOTE ON THE TYPE

This book was set in Stempel Garamond, a typeface based on a design by the famous Parisian type cutter Claude Garamond (1480–1561). This version of Garamond was modeled on a 1592 specimen sheet from the Egenolff-Berner foundry, which was produced from types thought to have been brought to Frankfurt by Jacques Sabon (d. 1580).

Claude Garamond is one of the most famous type designers in printing history. His distinguished romans and italics first appeared in *Opera Ciceronis* in 1543–44. While delightfully unconventional in design, the Garamond types are clear and open, yet maintain an elegance and precision of line that mark them as French.

Composed by NK Graphics,
Keene, New Hampshire

Printed and bound by Quebecor Printing,
Fairfield, Pennsylvania